"You make it sound as if you kidnapped him."

Frank Conley's voice was slightly uneasy.

Lexi paused and stroked her palm along the fringe at the base of a lampshade. "I don't like to think of it that way, Dad. Jake just wouldn't listen to reason. He didn't leave me any other choice. I just waited until the doctor shot him full of painkillers.

"Anyway, everyone agreed it was for the best. He's too banged-up to work at the rodeo again for two, maybe three, months. That's long enough for you to get back on your feet."

"You kidnapped Jake Thorn?" Frank asked with hollow disbelief. "If that don't beat all!" He grinned. "Well, at least he's here." The grin grew into a chuckle. "Oh, boy, Jake's gonna be madder than a hornet when he comes to in the morning...."

ABOUT THE AUTHOR

Popular author Ada Steward has been writing since she was twelve. Her ninth book, *The Cowboy's Lover*, marks a powerful Superromance debut.

A rodeo fan, Ada once witnessed a bull rider get caught in the bull's rigging. "Two bullfighters risked their lives to free this man," she says. "Without them, he wouldn't have survived. I wanted to pay this tribute to the unsung heroes of the rodeo, who go through as much as the bull riders ever do."

Ada lives in Tulsa with her husband, Randy, an eleven-pound Pekingese and a one-hundred-and-forty-pound rottweiler.

Ada Steward
The Cowboy's Lover

Harlequin Books

TORONTO • NEW YORK • LONDON
AMSTERDAM • PARIS • SYDNEY • HAMBURG
STOCKHOLM • ATHENS • TOKYO • MILAN
MADRID • WARSAW • BUDAPEST • AUCKLAND

ISBN 0-373-70619-7

THE COWBOY'S LOVER

The Cowboy's Lover

CHAPTER ONE

ALEXANDRA CONLEY OPENED the heavy front door of
the ranch house and stepped outside into the shade of the
portal. Her gaze skimmed the adobe wall of the courtyard, then traveled along the rutted dirt road that wound
past the barn and bunkhouse of the Lazy C, then through
miles of open pasture before reaching the county road.

Tense with expectation, she strained to see the plume
of dust in the distance that would signal her father's return, yet half hoped she would see nothing at all. Lexi
sighed with impatience.

She should have been with him instead of being stuck
here at the ranch, enduring endless hours of waiting and
worrying. But he wouldn't allow it. He'd said it would be
better if she stayed at home, better if she was there to fix
supper when Jamie came back from school. But what her
father really meant was that he didn't want her there to
hear the doctor's report. He didn't want to see her worry
or to hear her beg him to do what the doctors wanted.

Maybe this time will be different, Lexi thought. Maybe
this time they had made him stay. Even now he could be
lying in a hospital bed waiting for surgery in the morning. Lord, how she hoped it was so.

Squinting one last time into the dying sun, Lexi unclenched her fists and shrugged off the frustration of not
knowing. Then she turned and went back into the house.

"Jamie hon, supper's ready," Lexi called, walking a few feet deeper into the foyer. "There's no use waiting for your grandpa any longer. We might as well eat without him. Jamie?"

She listened for the sound of footsteps overhead. Instead, she heard only the eerie stillness that was becoming too much a part of her life since her father's illness. Lexi hurried down the hall toward the back of the house, but her steps slowed when she reached the closed door of what had once been a study and was now a bedroom for her ailing father. Frank Conley had always been the rock in her life, solid and eternal as Gibraltar. Now he was too weak to climb the stairs to his old room.

Before his heart began to fail she had never stopped to think that someday he would be gone. Lately, she seemed to think of little else. In less than a year, the broad shoulders that had once seemed able to hold the weight of the world had become stooped. The booming voice once capable of commanding and comforting with equal ease now grew breathless with the slightest exertion.

Her father was failing inch by inch, and his own stubbornness was killing him faster than anything else could. Grief turned to resentment, then anger, and the toe of her boot connected with the doorjamb in a swift, hard kick.

"Damn you, Frank Conley." Lexi's voice was a hoarse whisper, forced past the lump in her throat. "What about us? What are we supposed to do without you? Have you thought about that?"

Almost immediately, the anger went out of her again. Looking down at the cluster of recent scuff marks on the doorjamb, all made by the toe of her boot, Lexi shook her head and sighed.

"Why can't I say that to you when you're here?" she asked aloud. Her fingertips stroked the closed door, then she turned and continued slowly to the foot of the staircase.

Her hand on the banister, she looked up to the second-floor landing and called, "Jamie? Supper's ready, hon."

The faint squeak of rusty bedsprings caught her attention a second before a muffled voice answered, "I'm down here, Mom."

She closed her eyes and stifled a groan. Then, turning her back to the staircase, Lexi faced another closed door. The guest room, or Jake's room, as it was most often called, had over the years become more of a walk-in closet than a real bedroom, a catchall for the faded memories and once cherished mementos of a past too poignant to look at and too precious to discard.

Jake. Even now, Lexi could never enter the room without enduring a swift, stomach-wrenching spasm of loss. Stiffening her spine, she turned the knob and entered the room anyway. Inside, her ten-year-old son lay sprawled on his stomach across the old twin bed, his cowboy boots crisscrossing in the air as he leafed through the much-handled pages of an old scrapbook.

"Hi, babe," she said softly. A smile dimpled her cheeks as just the sight of him lifted her spirits. "Whatcha doing?"

Jamie looked up, his hazel eyes intense. His thick brown hair was cut in a burr except for one off-center sprig that extended from the nape of his neck down to his shoulder blades. A thoughtful frown crinkled his brow as he turned the scrapbook to where she could see it.

"Jake was really something, wasn't he?" Jamie's hand smoothed the yellowed newspaper article with reverence.

"He sure was." Pride, old and familiar, nudged at her. "When Jake was in his prime, he was one of the best."

The scrapbooks were hers, created in the fierce throes of hero worship when she was no older than Jamie.

"Think he'll ever come back, Mom?" Jamie rolled over and scooted to the edge of the bed. His feet hit the floor with a thump. "I'd sure love to meet him. You think he likes kids?"

The enthusiasm on her son's face brought an automatic smile to Lexi's as she slid into a straight-back chair. "Yeah, I think he likes kids."

"He liked you when you were a kid, didn't he?" Jamie asked encouragingly, giving Lexi her cue.

She and Jamie had had similar conversations a dozen times, and Jamie always found new ways to ask the questions, new ways to pull just a little more information from her reluctant memory.

"Yeah, I think he did. I was about two, I guess, when Jake's dad came to work as our foreman and his mom worked as our cook."

"Like Twyla does now," Jamie inserted, enjoying the story even though he already knew most of it.

Lexi nodded and smiled again, wondering what Jake would think if he knew he had become a legend in the Conley household. "That's right. Jake was about thirteen, I guess, when they first moved here. He used to baby-sit me sometimes after school.

"When I was in the first grade, it was Jake who taught me how to ride a bicycle without training wheels. I was just crazy about him." Lexi broke off with a sigh. "Anyway, then Mom and Dad got divorced and I spent a year in California with Mom. By the time I moved back to stay with Dad, Jake had hit the rodeo circuit and we didn't see him for long stretches at a time."

"How long before Jake won his first championship?" Jamie prodded. "How old were you then?"

"I was just a little older than you. Not too long after his first all-around championship, he was injured and came back here for a while to mend."

"And that's when he married Aunt Dolores, right?"

Lexi's heart gave an unsteady lurch and a knot began to form in the pit of her stomach. "No, that was after he'd bought the old Johnson place next door, hoping his parents would retire and live there. The next year, Jake was on his way to a fourth title when—"

She ran out of steam suddenly, not wanting to relive the awful moment when Jake almost died.

"When that bull stomped all over him?" Jamie supplied with a child's enthusiasm for the ghoulish.

Lexi cast a reproving glance at her son. "Jamie, really."

"That's what happened, isn't it?"

"Yes." She frowned to keep from laughing. "But you needn't sound so pleased."

"I'm not pleased," he said defensively. "But that *is* what happened. And *that's* when Jake married Aunt Dolores?"

Lexi nodded and plunged ahead. "When he got out of the hospital, Jake came back here to recuperate. Then Dolores came out from California for my sixteenth birthday, and three months later she and Jake were married. I guess she must have grown up a lot since the last time he'd seen her."

Hearing the sour note that had crept into her voice, Lexi sighed. "Anyway, about a month after the marriage, Jake's dad retired and Jake's mom and dad moved to Florida."

"'Cause they couldn't stand Aunt Dolores, huh?" Jamie added.

Obviously there were parts of the story he remembered all too well, Lexi thought wryly.

"Well, basically, yes." The unflattering words were hardly out of her mouth before she began to feel guilty. "But I think maybe Jake's parents just wanted to give Dolores and him a chance to be alone," Lexi amended in a sincere effort to be generous. "All newlyweds need a period to adjust. Your aunt Dolores really tried hard in the beginning. But she'd never learned to cook, and she'd never had to keep house, and after a while she began to miss the excitement of making movies in California."

"I *like* it here."

The little boy's scowl brought another smile to his mother's face. "I know you do, sweetheart, and so do I. And your aunt Dolores seemed to when she was younger, but once she grew up, she preferred the big city. That's why we hardly ever see her."

Trying hard not to show the emotion that was tugging at her heart, Lexi added, "That doesn't mean she doesn't love us. I know she cares for us all very much. She just gets really busy sometimes."

He shrugged. "I don't care. We don't need her, anyway. And I'm *never* goin' to the big city," he said with a curt nod to emphasize his point. "I'm gonna be a rodeo cowboy, just like Jake."

Ordinarily Lexi would have jumped in to defend her half sister, but she was too surprised by Jamie's last statement. Other than a brief ambition to become a fireman, being a rancher like his grandpa was the only thing he had ever talked about. She didn't know why his latest announcement should upset her so, except that it somehow seemed like a betrayal of her father at a time when he was most vulnerable.

"You want to be a rodeo cowboy?" she asked in a deliberately soft voice. "When did you decide that?"

Jamie rubbed the toes of his boots together and stared at the floor. "I don't know. I just decided."

"Today?" Lexi prodded. "Yesterday?"

Jamie shrugged. "Maybe."

Realizing she was overreacting in a big way, Lexi took a deep breath and forced herself to sit back. "You know," she said with studied calm, "Jake worked on this very ranch from the time he was a teenager. And when his dad retired, Jake took over as foreman here and ran the Lazy C right along with his own ranch. He and your grandpa worked side by side for the whole three years Jake and Dolores were married."

Jamie nodded, thrust out his chin and fixed her with an oblique, sideways stare that clearly said "So what?"

Faced with the challenge in his eyes, Lexi really didn't know "so what." She wasn't used to defiance from her son. And she didn't want him to switch his allegiance from his grandfather to Jake—not now.

Then, from some deep well of mother's intuition, she remembered her own toe scuffs on the doorjamb of her father's bedroom. She remembered the hurt, frustration and betrayal she felt when she thought of her father dying and leaving her alone with a ranch and a little boy. And she thought of the long hours Jamie had spent in Jake's room recently, poring over the old scrapbooks with a new intensity. "Are you scared?" she asked in the same soft, calm voice she would have used to soothe a skittish colt.

"'Bout what?" His sullen answer clearly said that he sensed a trap.

"About your grandpa."

Jamie shrugged one shoulder and refused to meet her gaze. "I don't know. Maybe."

Leaning forward in her chair, Lexi continued to speak just above a whisper. "I wish I could tell you there was nothing to be afraid of. I wish I could promise you he was going to be just fine, but I can't, because I don't know."

"What's *wrong* with him?" the boy demanded with a worried frown.

"It's his heart. I don't know much more than that. Maybe we'll know something when he gets back from the doctor." She glanced over her shoulder, through the open door of the bedroom to the heavy wooden door at the other end of the hallway as if it might open and reveal the answer.

Still watching the door, she went on, speaking almost to herself. "If he just wasn't so stubborn. He won't go into the hospital, and there's not much the doctors can do until he does."

"Is he going to die?"

She turned back then and caught the look of naked fear in her son's eyes. "I hope not," she said, fighting to keep her own despair in check. "But he's not doing what the doctors suggest, and he'll have to if he wants to get well."

"If Jake would come back and be foreman like he used to, then Grandpa could go into the hospital and he'd be okay."

"Jamie, where would you get an idea like that? We've got a foreman."

"But Grandpa said—" Jamie broke off suddenly and a grimace of guilt replaced the anxiety that had been so clear on his face.

"Grandpa said what?" Lexi demanded. When Jamie didn't answer immediately, she assumed her "I'm not kidding" tone and said, "Answer me, young man. What did your grandfather say to you?"

"Nothing." He hesitated only a second before rushing ahead. "I heard him talking on the phone to somebody. He was asking if they could help him find Jake. He said he needed him real bad."

"Was that all he said?"

"I don't know," Jamie mumbled, ducking his head. "You called me, and I had to quit listening."

"Shame on you, James Franklin Conley. I've told you never to eavesdrop on other people's conversations. Now you have the mistaken impression that Jake Thorn is going to come riding in here and save the day, and that's just not going to happen."

Jamie's head lifted and hope flamed in his hazel eyes. "It might. If Grandpa finds him, Jake would come."

"Oh, Jamie hon, don't count on Jake. This ranch is the last place on earth he wants to be. He left here eleven years ago, and he hasn't looked back since. I have no idea where he is, and neither does your grandpa, and it's hard to find a man who doesn't want to be found."

"'Cause of Aunt Dolores?"

"I guess your Aunt Dolores was part of it," Lexi admitted. "But Jake's world fell apart, hon. There are too many memories here, too many reminders."

"I'd sure like to meet him," Jamie said wistfully.

"Just don't count on it, okay?" Pushing herself to her feet, Lexi said, "Supper's getting cold. Why don't you put these things away and meet me in the kitchen?"

"Yes, ma'am." Rising, Jamie began to gather up the scrapbooks. His head bowed, he was the very picture of dejection.

Lexi's heart broke a little, knowing she had caused his pain. Relenting, she allowed a hint of encouragement to creep into her voice. "Of course, Jake *does* still own the Circle T. He might come back someday, even if it's only for a visit."

Eagerness shone again in Jamie's eyes. "You really think so?"

"It could be. You never know."

"I bet if anybody could find Jake, Grandpa could."

As much as she hated to think about it, she had to agree. "Yeah. You're probably right about that."

Smiling openly, Jamie set about his cleanup work, and Lexi went to the kitchen to reheat supper. She only hoped she hadn't done the wrong thing by allowing Jamie to go on hoping.

As for herself, she didn't know how she would feel if Jake came back. It was something she hadn't let herself think about for a long time. As a little girl, she had worshiped him; as a woman, she had loved him; and the day after he'd made all her dreams come true, Jake had turned around and walked away without a word.

She had spent years getting over him, years accepting that she would never see him again, and when her heart had finally healed, she had packed away her memories and closed the door. Wherever Jake was, whatever he was doing, she wished him well, but he was out of her life, and that's the way things were going to stay.

LEXI CLEARED the kitchen table and sent Jamie up to do his homework while she did the dishes and tried not to scream at the silence. She had just checked the phone for the third time to make sure it was still working when she heard the front door open. She flew from the kitchen in time to see her father and the ranch hand who had driven him enter the front parlor.

"Hi," Lexi said cheerily, practically skidding to a halt under the arched doorway leading from the foyer. "Have you eaten?"

"Yep," her father grunted. Leaning heavily on the arm of Manuel Ortega, Frank Conley headed for the comfortable armchair by the window where he spent most of his waking hours these days.

"*Sí*," Manuel answered, throwing Lexi an apologetic smile over the top of her father's bowed head. "Señor Frank, he was hungry, so we stopped before we left town."

"You can fix me a drink if you want," her dad said in the breathless, gravelly voice that signaled near exhaustion.

Lexi ignored him. The doctor had strictly forbidden the rye whiskey and cigars that had been her father's nightly ritual. Her dad only asked for them now to annoy her.

"You think maybe while Manuel's still here, we should just get you on into bed?" she asked.

"Nope." Frank Conley settled himself into the deep chair, leaned his head against the high back and expelled a sigh. Staring hard at his daughter, he said, "We've got to talk." He turned to Manuel and said, "Thanks, Manuel. You can go now."

"*Sí*, Señor Frank. You will call if you need me later?" he asked Lexi before leaving.

"Yes, Manuel. And thank you."

Despite her father's gruff manner, the men who worked for him were fiercely loyal, and Lexi was grateful to know that their loyalty extended to her, as well.

"Better take a seat," Frank said once he and his daughter were alone.

She felt her legs tremble as she lowered herself into the chair across from him. The urge to burst into tears was almost overwhelming. She wanted him well and whole and as powerful as he'd once been, and she knew the doctor's news today hadn't been good. She'd known it the minute she'd seen her father's stooped shoulders and the defensive jut of his jaw.

"Shoot," she said in the brave voice she knew he was counting on.

"You're not going to like it."

"Dad, don't drag this out. I can't take that."

"I'm not dying, girl. At least not yet."

Lexi released the breath she'd been holding and closed her eyes in a moment of silent thanksgiving. He was going to live. He was apparently going to be grumpy as all get-out, but he was going to live.

"So, what's the problem?" she asked when the first intense wave of relief had passed.

"Well, I've got two choices. I can sit here like a damned invalid and go on living until I finally keel over and die of boredom."

He gestured to the adobe wall that surrounded the front courtyard. His face was ashen with dark circles under his eyes. The ordinary age lines had been replaced by deep grooves carved from worry and pain.

"Will you get better if you do that?" Lexi asked, hoping that rest could work a miracle.

"Nope. Fact is, I'll probably get worse until finally, someday down the road, my heart just gives up."

"Well, that's no solution."

"My other option is an operation. With surgery, I can probably go back to being as good as new. Most people survive. Chances are I would, too. 'Course, I might not.

Even with simple surgery, they don't give no guarantees. Decision's mine, the doc says."

Lexi swallowed. She didn't know why he was hesitating. The Frank Conley she'd always known wouldn't have lived another minute as an invalid if there was an alternative, even if it meant taking a risk. The fact that her father wasn't in the hospital right now awaiting surgery meant there was something she still didn't know about.

"The problem is," Frank said slowly, "who's going to run the ranch while I'm off having this surgery? I'd be flat on my back for a couple of weeks before they'd even let me come home. And then it'd still be weeks before I could do much of anything. Doc says I might be fuzzy-headed for a while after something like this."

"Well, Dad, that's no problem. You've got a foreman who's been here for three years. And you know I can do the books and the paperwork," Lexi said. With any luck they could have him on his way to the hospital tomorrow.

"For how long, darlin'?"

"For a month?" she asked with a shrug. "Six weeks? How long could it take?"

"That's just it," Frank said softly.

The gentle sadness in his eyes and the patience in his voice were beginning to worry her.

"Lexi, there's always a chance of complications while I'm on the operating table. It's not a big chance, but it's there. There could be other complications—or I might not make it at all. Even if I survive, my recovery could be slow. We've got to go into this prepared for anything, and I've got to make sure this ranch is going to be okay. For your future, and for Jamie's future, I've got to be sure, Lexi. Do you understand?"

Lexi started to nod her agreement and then realized she would be lying. She had no idea what he was talking about. One minute he sounded as if he meant to have the operation, and the next he was listing all the reasons that he couldn't go through with it.

"I'm sorry, Dad, but no, I don't. I don't understand what the problem is at all. I can run the ranch."

"Lexi, it's not a question of your ability."

"Then what's it a question of? Because to tell you the truth, I'm confused. I don't know why you're balking at this. You can have your surgery, and I'll run the ranch. When you're better, you can take over again. It doesn't seem that complicated to me."

"Lexi," Frank said in a no-nonsense tone. "I'm gonna get Jake back here."

"You're what?" She shook her head, unable to believe what she was hearing.

"Jake's coming back to run the ranch while I'm in the hospital."

The simple statement rocked her. Jake wouldn't come back. In eleven years he hadn't sent so much as a Christmas card. "Why? Why would you even think of doing that?" she demanded. What her father was saying just didn't make sense.

"I have my reasons."

"Well, I want to know what they are."

"I'm a sick old man. Humor me."

"Oh, Dad." She knew he didn't mean it, but the fight went out of her, and she sank into the chair opposite him. "You've talked to Jake? He agreed?"

"No." Frank shook his head, meeting her gaze. "But I know where he is. At least, I know where he's gonna be tomorrow night."

"But what good does that do? You can't go."

He looked straight into her skeptical brown eyes as if he were searching her soul. Then he said very softly, "But you can."

"No!" Lexi shot to her feet, knocking her chair against the wall in the process. "Absolutely not! I wouldn't think of it."

"You've got to," her father insisted.

"No, I don't." Turning, Lexi started from the room. She took two steps before she saw Jamie standing in the foyer just outside the parlor door, listening.

"Why not, Mom?" Excitement danced in the little boy's eyes as he hurried into the room. "He'd come. If it'd help Grandpa, you know Jake would come."

"He might," Frank urged from behind her.

Feeling trapped, Lexi whirled to face him. Her hands were knotted into fists at her sides. "No, he wouldn't."

Her eyes pleaded with her father. Jamie was just a little boy. He didn't know what he was asking. Frank Conley did.

Her father shook his head slowly and stared back at her with flinty resolve in his eyes. "He'll come. Jake's been wanting to come home for a long time. He just doesn't know it."

"Dad," Lexi begged. "He knew what he was doing when he left. If he'd wanted to come back, he'd have found an excuse before now."

"I won't have the operation unless Jake's here to take over the ranch, Alexandra. I'll sit right here in this chair, and I'll die waiting if I have to. So you can go ask him to come back and run the ranch now or you can invite him to my funeral later. The choice is yours."

His voice allowed no hope for compromise, and Lexi was filled with the hollow echo of despair.

"You mean that, don't you?" she asked, knowing she was defeated even before he answered.

"I've never lied to you, girl."

"Can I go with you, Mom?" Jamie asked, jostling her in his excitement. "Huh? Please."

"No." She put her arm around the narrow shoulders of her son and gathered him against her side. "No, Jamie. This is something I have to do alone."

CHAPTER TWO

THE SWEAT OF MEN and beasts hung heavy in the evening air, bonding with the dust raised by restless hooves. The impatient bawling of cattle vied with the shrill whinnies of impatient horses. In the familiar surroundings Lexi knew she should have felt at home, but she didn't. She felt like an outsider, an intruder.

"Just relax," she muttered to herself. "What's the worst that could happen? All he can do is say no."

She rubbed sweaty palms against her denim split skirt. Her heart raced, and she gave up pretending that it was rejection she was afraid of. Seeing Jake again was what she feared.

Wondering what he would think of her, what she would think of him, what they would say to each other—it was all driving her crazy. Would she be able to look at him, talk to him, and not feel anything?

Shaking the maddening thoughts from her head, Lexi spotted a cluster of cowboys and started toward them, mustering her courage as she went. All around her were the sights, sounds and smells of her everyday life on the Lazy C. It didn't matter that here she was a foreigner, unwanted and out of place in the staging area of the rodeo arena. She was here to find Jake Thorn, and she had to start somewhere.

Arriving at the group of cowboys, who hadn't so much as glanced in her direction, she sucked in a deep breath for courage and tapped the shoulder of the man nearest her.

"Excuse me." Her voice emerged deeper than usual, with a husky throb.

The men turned toward her in unison, their faces reflecting surprised pleasure at the unexpected interruption, and Lexi finally began to relax. She even managed the beginnings of a smile, just enough to bring her dimples into play.

The cowboy whose shoulder she had tapped, a stocky youth with a bruise on his cheek and fancy turquoise chaps and shirt, swept off his hat and returned her smile with enthusiasm. "Yes, ma'am. Is there something I can help you with?"

"Yes." She paused to take another deep breath and continued, exhaling as she spoke. "At least I hope so." Anxiety returned to flutter through the pit of her stomach. She swallowed hard. "I'm looking for Jake Thorn. Somebody told me he'd be here tonight."

The smile on the young man's face slipped just the slightest bit, and Lexi could almost feel his companions pull back with sudden caution.

"Well, yes," the cowboy answered slowly, choosing his words carefully, "I believe he *is* here tonight, somewhere. In fact, I think I saw him go by just a little while ago. How about you fellows?" he said, turning to the others for help. "Any of you see which way ol' Jake was headed?"

Shrugs, head shakes and downcast eyes greeted his question, and Lexi knew better than to push for more. Jake was one of their own, and she was a stranger asking questions. Whatever these men knew, they weren't about to tell her without getting an okay from Jake first.

If Jake didn't want to be found, they would continue to be courteous because she was a woman. But whichever way they pointed, she could almost be certain Jake would be found in the opposite direction.

"Maybe you could try over on the other side," one of the older men said, hooking a thumb toward the other end of the arena, where calves were being loaded into the chutes for the roping and hazing events that would follow the opening parade.

With a sinking heart, Lexi turned away from the group of men who had so politely closed ranks against her. Her hand balled into a fist. Then, one by one, she forced her fingers to uncurl.

The last place on earth she wanted to be was here, and the last thing in the world she wanted to do was find Jake Thorn, but find him she would, with or without anyone's help. With her chin up and her shoulders straight, she started in the direction they had suggested. It was almost certainly a wild-goose chase, but she might as well circle around to the other side of the arena anyway, just in case.

"Uh, miss, could we tell Jake who's looking for him, just in case we happen to see him again?" one of the cowboys called after her.

Knowing that if Jake saw her first, she might never get near him, Lexi turned and forced a smile over her shoulder. "That won't be necessary. But I do thank you for offering." The syrupy purr of her voice camouflaged her frustrated anger. "I'll just wander around here until I find him."

She paused long enough to watch the curious expectation on their faces wilt, then she turned and continued on her way. As she went, she kept her gaze alert for a long legged, narrow-hipped, broad-shouldered cowboy with the smooth grace of a jungle cat and a head of wavy chestnut hair.

And while she scanned each lanky, blue-jean clad male she passed, Lexi told herself that she was only here because she had to be, not because her heart thudded with the expectation of seeing Jake again. At the back of the arena, Lexi greeted a pretty blond cowgirl who looked far too young to remember the glory days of Jake Thorn. After all, he had been at the height of his rodeo fame when this teenager was learning to walk. But maybe she had at least heard of Jake.

Offering a friendly smile, Lexi came to a full halt when the blonde smiled in return. "That's a nice-looking horse you've got there," Lexi said in all sincerity. "Is he a Thoroughbred?"

"Why, thank you. Yes, he is." Beaming, the young cowgirl drew her horse closer and rubbed the silken length of his nose with obvious pride. "I picked him up in a claiming race last year and started training him for the barrels."

Lexi's natural interest in horses made it easy for her to forget her own quest, if only for a moment. "How's he coming along?"

"Oh, Jackpot's a natural. We've got a good chance to win tonight."

The Thoroughbred snorted and shook out his mane with a toss of his head, as if he knew all eyes were on him. Lexi couldn't help laughing. "Well, I wish you luck. What's your name? I'll watch for you tonight."

"Susie Picket." Stroking the horse's neck idly, she turned her gaze back to Lexi. "Say, I haven't seen you around before, have I? Are you entered tonight?"

"No." The girl's question reminded Lexi of what she was supposed to be doing. "I'm here looking for an old friend. Maybe you know him. Jake Thorn?"

"Jake? Oh, sure."

"Have you seen him around tonight?"

"Yeah, he's around here someplace. You might try out by the trailers." The girl opened her mouth to say more, then closed it with an abrupt snap while a rosy blush crept over her cheeks. "Did you say you, um, know Jake really well?" she asked hesitantly.

With very little encouragement, Lexi would have gladly given in to her less-than-ladylike urge to curse. The young barrel racer's blush and the sudden silence told her clearly what the men's hesitancy had only hinted at earlier. Wherever Jake was, he was with a woman.

"I might have known," Lexi muttered under her breath. As if this night weren't going to be bad enough without having to drag Jake out of some woman's bed just to talk to him.

"Don't worry," she said tiredly while she fought back a sudden, sharp pang of jealousy she had no right or reason to feel. "I'm not an old girlfriend of his, or a new girlfriend of his, or any kind of a girlfriend of his. I'm just a friend. Period."

"Oh, good." With an audible sigh of relief, Susie Picket brightened and became a flowing fountain of information. "Well, in that case, you might find him over in Louanne Byers's trailer. They've been sort of, uh, friendly, if you know what I mean, for the past few days. You can't miss it. She's got her name painted on the side in these big purple letters. Real pretty."

A stiff smile firmly in place, Lexi took an automatic step in retreat, this time in possession of more knowledge than she really wanted. "Thank you very much.

You've been a big help." She couldn't help wondering if it was the lettering or Louanne herself that was "real pretty."

"You're going the wrong way," the girl called out, pointing toward the parking lot and the trailers beyond.

Lexi extended her arm toward the other end of the arena, toward the calves, and searched through her mind for any feeble excuse that would take her in the opposite direction of Louanne Byers's trailer. Then she dropped her hand to her side and nodded. "You're right. I am."

With her stomach churning in revolt, she set off toward the trailers. A muffled flurry of conversation floated in her wake as she passed the knot of cowboys a second time without glancing their way. Outside the arena she dodged cowboys on horseback and swirling lariats as she crossed the dusty blacktop of the parking lot to a rutted field that held a dizzying array of trucks, horse vans and travel trailers.

Now that she had escaped from the choking dust and compressed tension of the arena, the evening air was soft, cool and relaxing. Lexi sighed and rubbed her damp palms against the denim of her skirt as her steps faltered. Her father had sent her to find Jake, not drag him from another woman's arms.

Halting in midstride, she changed her mind yet again. She whirled blindly, started off in the opposite direction and almost immediately slammed full tilt into the solid body of a very large cowboy.

As Lexi bounced off him like a rag doll, he grabbed her by the shoulders and held her upright.

"Whoa, little lady. Are you okay?"

Breathless from the impact, she nodded and gasped for air. Through eyelashes that fluttered unsteadily, she caught a glimpse of a face that was vaguely familiar atop a body that was too big for any rodeo event but steer wrestling.

"Say...." The big cowboy leaned toward her. "Haven't I seen you someplace before?"

Still trying to catch her breath, Lexi nodded again and disengaged herself from his grasp. Aaron, she thought, casting back through clouded memories. That was his name, and he had come to their ranch one weekend with Jake. He was Aaron somebody, and he owned a place of his own in Oklahoma.

Holding out her hand in greeting, she said in a voice that still sounded breathless, "I'm Frank Conley's daughter, Lexi. You came to our ranch for Sunday dinner once with Jake Thorn."

"And stayed till Tuesday," Aaron said with a belly laugh that rumbled through his words. "I remember that. But you were just a baby then."

"I was fourteen," she corrected him, stiffening at the sting of his words.

At fourteen she had been wildly in love with Jake and aching to become a woman overnight. That same year she had made the mistake of telling him how she felt. Jake's embarrassed attempt to let her down easily was a memory that could still make her recoil in pain.

"Well, you're all grown up now," Aaron said. "Are you here with your dad?"

"No." Eager to put the past behind her again, Lexi turned back to the matter at hand. "Dad couldn't come, but he asked me to look up Jake for him."

"Oh." Lexi saw the flicker of uncertainty in his eyes. "Have you, uh, seen Jake yet?"

"I was on my way to find him when I bumped into you." She took a deep breath and plunged ahead, deciding there was no point in trying to run away now. "I was told I could find him at Louanne Byers's trailer. You wouldn't happen to know where she's parked, would you?"

Aaron's friendly grin grew mischievous, and he rubbed his hands in anticipation. "Boy, is old Jake gonna be one surprised cowpoke. Come on along with me, little darlin'." He hooked his arm through hers and turned her around. "I can take you right to it."

After several silent minutes while they wound their way deeper into the tangle of vehicles and trailers, her companion asked, "How long's it been since you've seen Jake?"

Lexi winced at the question, but she wasn't about to repay Aaron's kindness with a snub. "Eleven years."

"Ah," he said with a nod, "since the divorce."

"Yes." She wondered how much Jake had told Aaron.

"That was your older sister, wasn't it? What was her name?" Before Lexi could speak, he supplied the answer himself. "Dolores?"

"That's right."

"I hear she's an actress now. She uses the name Conley or Thorn?"

"Neither. She uses her father's name—Davies."

"Then you don't have the same dad?" He seemed surprised.

"No. Dolores is my half sister. Our mother was married previously," Lexi said, keeping it simple. A thorough revelation of their family history could rival the worst soap opera.

"Dolores Davies," Aaron said thoughtfully. "Yeah, I think I've heard of her. She's a blonde, right? Had a part in a TV series a few years back? She wore a bikini in almost every show."

"That's Dolores," Lexi agreed, relaxing with the big man on whom subtlety would have been wasted.

"So that's Jake's ex, huh? Sure is a small world, isn't it? Whose life is she making miserable now?"

"At the moment, she's married to a producer named Harvey Maxwell."

"I'll be doggoned." Stopping, Aaron released the arm he had kept tightly entwined in his and announced, "Well, here we are."

Raising a big fist without hesitation, he pounded on the door of the white travel trailer emblazoned with fuchsia lettering. After a moment, the door swung open to reveal a young woman with elaborately curled brown hair and a sparkling white shirt-and-pants set that was spandex tight and dripping with fringe.

"Oh, hi there, Aaron. You looking for Jake?"

"Hiya, Louanne. Is he around?"

She turned away toward the interior. "Jake, Aaron's here."

Lexi closed her eyes and counted to ten while her knees began to shake and her heart thudded uncontrollably.

"Come on in, buddy," came a familiar gravelly rasp that could make the simplest statement sound like an invitation to sin.

"Well, it's not me that's looking for you," Aaron replied. He wrapped his meaty hands around Lexi's shoulders and guided her into the doorway. "It's this little lady right here."

"Who the—" His voice faded away and his face registered disbelief. "Lexi?"

"Jake?" Her eyes were locked with his, and her heart told her it was Jake, but the man she was looking at could have been anyone.

He was dressed in the baggy, ragged clothes of a ro-deo clown, his face hidden behind white greasepaint, and only the eyes and voice told her she was indeed in the presence of James Jackson Thorn.

"Hadn't you better be getting on over to the arena, Louanne?" Aaron hinted with the delicacy of a sledge-hammer.

Planting her fists on her hips, Louanne stood her ground. "Who the hell is *she,* Jake?" she demanded shrilly.

"It's okay, Louanne." With a wave of his hand, Jake shooed her away. "Go on."

His gaze never left Lexi.

"Who *is* she?" Louanne demanded again.

"My name is Alexandra Conley," Lexi said. Climbing the three steps into the trailer, she calmly extended her hand. "My father, Frank Conley, owns the ranch that borders Jake's spread."

Louanne's hand automatically encased Lexi's in a quick, limp shake. "Why are you here?"

"I think that's between Lexi and me," Jake said, rising from the bar stool where he had been sitting with jars of greasepaint spread on the counter in front of him.

"But, Jake—" Louanne twisted toward him and ran out of words as he shook his head.

"Run along," he said in a kind voice that didn't invite argument. "You're going to be late, and this has noth-ing to do with you. I'll lock the door when I leave."

With a final, venomous look at Jake and Lexi, Louanne swept past and out of the trailer.

"Hope you don't mind my showing Lexi the way." Standing outside, Aaron shifted his weight from one big boot to the other. "Somebody'd already told her where you were."

Close enough now to see the green sparks in Jake's eyes, Lexi stepped out of the line of fire as he answered, "I'll deal with you later, old buddy."

Grinning irrepressibly, Aaron winked at Lexi. "I sure hope this visit was important to you. It sort of slipped my mind how much Jake dislikes surprises." With a nod to his friend, Aaron took a step back. "You go easy on her now, Jake. I'm kind of partial to this little lady."

"Goodbye, Aaron," Jake said with no attempt at good humor. He stared steely eyed at the open door until it closed. Only when they were alone did he turn back to Lexi. "Do you mind if I finish getting ready? I have to be at work pretty soon."

"No. Fine." Feeling behind her, Lexi lowered herself primly into an armchair and watched him, awestruck by the speed of events that had led her here.

"Did you just happen to be in the neighborhood?" Jake asked as he drew a heavy line of black paint across each brow.

"No."

"Then you're not here just to reminisce?"

"No."

"Well, I wish I had the time to really talk to you," he said while he selected another small jar of greasepaint and a fatter brush. "But unfortunately I don't. You caught me on a busy night."

Having no intention of being dismissed easily or quickly, Lexi said, "Oh, that's okay. I'll be around for a while. I hope I didn't, um, create any difficulties for you by showing up like this."

"You mean Louanne?" Jake chuckled softly, and his eyes sought Lexi's reflection in the mirror. "She's just a friend."

"Have you mentioned that to her?"

With a quick shake of his head, he returned his attention to what he was doing. "It never seemed necessary. When we work the same rodeo, we get together." He shrugged and began to store away the assortment of makeup and brushes. "I've never seen her act like that before." He spun around on the bar stool to face Lexi. "So, what do you think?" He spread his arms to indicate his appearance.

Silencing the dozen questions she longed to ask, Lexi shook her head in wonderment. "That's quite a getup."

"I'll bet you'd never have recognized me." His painted smile split to reveal even, pearl white teeth.

"I don't know. Some things don't change." She looked into his unforgettable eyes, the same fresh, crisp green as the first tender blades of spring grass.

His smile softened and tilted to one side. "*You* have. You're all grown up now."

Lexi's heart did a quick tap dance at the unexpected warmth in his wickedly sexy voice. She had prepared herself to face the anger and resentment she knew her request would bring. She hadn't prepared herself to face the possibility that other emotions might be aroused, as well, in both of them.

"Does it bother you that I noticed?" he asked in the soft rasp that could still turn her knees to water.

"No." The breathless waver in her voice was anything but convincing, and as if the swirling undercurrents were suddenly too dangerous, Jake abruptly shoved himself to his feet.

"It's about time for me to head on over to the arena," he said.

"I'll wait for you outside." Lexi launched herself out of her chair and through the trailer doorway without any further encouragement.

Alone in the faded evening light, she took a deep breath of the cool, tangy air and tried to slow down the gallop of her heartbeat. No man had a right to be that sexy—especially in that getup.

Inside, alone but far from peaceful, Jake laced up the spiked running shoes he wore to work in. *Damn!* He raked the fingers of one hand through his springy hair while he rubbed the palm of his other hand over the knot forming in the pit of his stomach. He couldn't believe she was actually here.

Lexi Conley. She had been a tender, trembling nineteen the last time he'd seen her, and so sweet and temptingly beautiful it almost broke his heart just to look at her. All coltish angles and freckled innocence, she'd offered salvation to his starving soul, and he'd run from her as if the hounds of hell were pursuing him. He could hear them even now, their hot breath just behind him.

He scooped up the makeup box and shoved it into his equipment bag, then zipped the bag and slung it over his shoulder. Flipping off the overhead light, he stood in the shadowed interior and looked out at her, standing in the soft light of dusk. The coltish angles were gone, replaced by sculpted curves and sloping hollows, but something of the freckled innocence remained.

Her black hair, long and straight, glistened with stardust highlights. Her eyes, a warm and spicy brown, stared into the distance, as if she were lost in thought—about what, he didn't dare contemplate. And her lower lip... No, he couldn't think about her lips. They had been his undoing the last time.

Slamming and locking the trailer door behind him, Jake pulled his hat low over his eyes. "Well, I hope you enjoy the rodeo," he said as he paused beside Lexi.

"Think you can find your way back around to the stands okay?"

"Well, yes, but—"

"Sorry, darlin', I'm a working man." Jake took a side step away from her toward the arena. "And I'm running late."

Lexi doggedly trailed behind him. "I'm willing to wait until you're through."

He shook his head and walked faster. "I leave for the next town as soon as the bull riding's over."

"I'll follow you if I have to," she said, steely resolve creeping into her voice.

Realizing she wasn't going to give up, Jake came to an exasperated halt. "What's so all-fired important, Lexi?"

"It's Dad. He's sick."

The simple statement hit Jake like a blow to the gut. Frank Conley was as tough and ornery as a Texas longhorn. He wasn't the kind of man to admit illness easily.

"Well, I'm sorry to hear that, Lexi," Jake said carefully, not wanting to admit even to himself how shaken he was. "You tell Frank he'll be in my prayers."

When Jake would have moved on, Lexi caught him by the arm and pulled him back with a show of surprising determination. "He wants more than that, Jake."

In her cinnamon eyes he saw fear, the same fear he himself felt at the thought of a world without Frank Conley in it. "I'm sorry, Lexi," Jake repeated softly. "I'm real sorry, but I don't have any more than that to offer."

"I'm not giving up that easily," she warned.

"You're wasting your breath, darlin'. You know that. You knew that before you even got here."

"Damn you, Jake Thorn." Lexi's fists twisted in the front of his shirt as she blocked his path with her body. "My daddy's not going to die because of you."

The fierce anger in her voice was startling, but it was the tear that slid from the corner of her eye that was almost Jake's undoing. "Ah, Lexi," he said with a sigh as his thumb smeared a wet streak across the petal softness of her cheek. "Don't do this, sweetheart. You know I love that old man."

"Then help him," she begged. "All he's asking is for you to run the ranch for a few months while he has his surgery."

"He doesn't need me, Lexi." Guilt warred with resentment inside Jake. "There are other men who can do it."

"Of course there are, but you know what Dad's like," she insisted, desperation naked in her voice as her fingers twisted deeper into the fabric of Jake's shirt. "He won't let anybody else do it. He wants *you*, Jake."

"I swore I'd never go back there."

"You mean you'd let Dad die before you'd go back on some stupid oath that nobody but you cares about?" Angry flames burned in the depths of her eyes, and scorn dripped from her words. "You're worse than he is."

"There's more to it than that, and you know it. Frank'll have his surgery, and he'll be just fine." Feeling himself weaken, Jake jerked away from her, popping a button off his shirt in the process. "And I won't be there," he called over his shoulder as he walked away before he could change his mind.

"I'm not through with you, Jake Thorn."

Passion rang in her voice, and he whirled back to face her. "Fine," he shouted. "But for right now, get your fanny up in those stands. They're going to be running livestock through here for the rest of the evening, and you're going to get yourself trampled if you don't get out of the way.''

With that, he turned and stalked off without a backward glance.

DAMN HIM! A half hour later Lexi still fumed, almost as angry with herself as she was with him. She hadn't expected Jake to be any more receptive than he had been, but he didn't have to be so darn stubborn. If he'd just been more reasonable, she would never have lost her temper and got dragged into a screaming match.

Mortified at the memory, she covered her face with her hands and wished she could take back everything that had happened in the past hour. She never should have gone to that trailer. That's when everything went wrong. She should have waited until Jake was alone, approached him reasonably and appealed to—

Appealed to *what?* she asked herself scornfully. His better nature? His tender sensibilities? She should be *grateful* he didn't want to come back with her. Except for one stubborn old man who refused to let sleeping dogs lie, no one wanted Jake back on the Lazy C anyway.

"Damn him," Lexi said again, no longer meaning Jake. She shoved herself to her feet as she saw two rodeo clowns in a barricaded area beside the chutes. Hoping one of them was Jake, she started down from the stands to make one more, less emotional, plea.

As she descended, she studied the group of men behind the barriers, two of them in greasepaint and tattered clothes and the others in chaps and cowboy boots. Like any athletes before an event, they began the ritual of stretching, limbering up and jogging in place, and Lexi allowed herself a fleeting moment of wonder that Jake, a rider who wore a champion's buckle, had now become a rodeo clown.

Pushing the thought aside, she wished she had paid more attention when she had seen him earlier. Both men wore identical makeup and she couldn't be certain which one was Jake.

Pausing at the base of the stairs, Lexi looked at the men more closely. Jake's long legs, his fluid movements and his broad shoulders were a dead giveaway.

Over the years his slender, lanky frame had filled out with muscle, but no amount of time could disguise his distinctive, catlike grace—just as no amount of time seemed to dampen the breathless rush of joy that swept over Lexi each time she saw him, or lessen the sudden anguish that followed. She couldn't still care that deeply about him. It just wasn't possible.

Minutes stood still while she fought to control the rush of memories and the chaos of her own traitorous emotions. Drawing in a deep breath, Lexi took another step closer. Her legs felt like rubber as she made her way through the milling crowd toward the barriers that plainly said "off limits."

A few yards away, she glanced up to see Jake watching her approach. He looked no more pleased with the prospect of a second meeting than she was but appeared just as determined not to run from it. Lexi wasn't sure her voice would work once she reached him, but she was going to say what she had come to say, even if she had to use sign language to do it. Sternly she forced her mind back to the job at hand as she reached the edge of the barricade and Jake left the others to join her.

"Have you got a few minutes?" she asked, her voice so whispery she could barely hear her own words over the thunder of her heartbeat. "I'd like to talk to you."

Jake shook his head. "Lexi—"

"I'm sorry," she rushed on. "I was just so mad I said some things I shouldn't have, and I didn't say any of the things I meant to."

Refusing to meet her gaze, Jake said again, "No, Lexi—"

"Please." She came around the end of the barrier and stood in front of him, looking up and trying not to feel overwhelmed. Jake had always been her hero. He had meant more to her than any other man, except her father.

"Please," Lexi said again, remembering that her father was the only reason she was here.

"Okay," Jake said, giving in reluctantly. "What?"

Lexi glanced behind him and encountered the quickly averted stares that she knew would be there. In the background, cowboys hastily busied themselves with their gear. "In private?" she whispered.

"I'll have to be ready for the first go-round in a few minutes." His green eyes grazed hers, then darted away again. "How about later?"

She forced herself to keep her feet still and stifled the groan that rose in her throat. She had to do this now while she still had the courage. Jake wasn't going to make it any easier for her later. "Just go with me somewhere where everybody isn't watching," she pleaded.

His heavy black brows lowered in a frown, and his lips twisted in a grimace. "Come on."

Jake hooked his hand around her arm more gently than she had expected and guided Lexi through the maze of fencing, equipment and cowboys until they wound their way behind the chutes and into the open area of the parking lot. Then he released her and turned around to lean against the side of a horse trailer, facing her.

"Is this good enough?" he asked abruptly.

"Yes." She tried not to be intimidated by the sharpness of his tone.

"So, talk," he ordered.

"You could be a little friendlier, you know."

Jake sighed and stared straight up at the white lights blinking against the black sky. "That wouldn't make this any easier for us, Lexi."

"I don't know why this is so hard," she said, as frustrated with herself as she was with him. "We were friends once."

"We were a lot *more* than friends once, too."

The sudden softness of Jake's voice stirred a cauldron of boiling emotions in the pit of her stomach. Everything she had wanted to avoid was rushing at her, and yet she couldn't turn aside. She couldn't even try.

"Just once," she said softly. "I wasn't sure you'd even remember."

"Oh, I remember all right. It comes back to me, bits and pieces of that night." As he spoke, his fingers curled around a lock of her hair, drawing it across his palm. "Here and there." The backs of his fingers brushed across the swell of her breast and continued down the length of her hair to where it ended just above her waist. "At all the wrong times and in all the wrong places," he said quietly. "Like now." His voice dropped to a whisper as his hand rose again, catching the underside of her chin and tilting her face toward his. "Funny, the tricks your mind plays on you."

Mesmerized and jelly-kneed, Lexi kept herself from swooning into his arms only with great effort. "Jake."

"But that's not what you came here to talk about, is it?"

"No."

Releasing them both from the spell he had cast, Jake tucked his hands behind him and leaned against the trailer once again. "What *did* you come here to talk about?"

Lexi drew in a deep, shaky breath. "Dad."

"We've already talked about him," Jake snapped, once again as prickly as a porcupine.

"You never asked what was wrong with him."

"Okay, what's wrong with him?"

Feeling as if she were beating her head against a wall, Lexi pressed on. "He needs a heart operation."

"I'm sorry to hear that."

"He needs you, Jake!" she cried, unable to believe the coldness she heard in his voice.

"Are you sure *he's* the one who needs me, Lexi?" Jake asked. The glittering light in his green eyes was anything but cold.

"Wha—what?" she gasped. "What do you mean?"

"I'm sorry. I thought that was pretty plain." Jake brought his hands from behind him and hooked his thumbs around the suspenders that held up his oversize pants. "What I meant was, if it's Frank who needs me so desperately, why'd he send you? Or did he send you?"

Jake's insolent tone did nothing to soothe the anger blossoming inside Lexi. "Look, if you're suggesting that I came here for myself—"

"I'm suggesting that it's possible." His voice changed from infuriatingly calm to downright seductive. "Just like it's possible that I'm not the only one who thinks about that night from time to time. Maybe you think about it, too. Maybe—"

Lexi knocked aside the hand that brushed her cheek. "Look, Jake, I asked you out here so I could apologize for losing my temper earlier. But if you touch me—" she backed away a step and stabbed a finger in the air between them ''—I'm not about to apologize for what I do next.''

The husky rasp of Jake's laugh reached out to her, igniting a flame in her already riotous insides; it also jarred her like a hard slap in the face.

''Whoa there, sweetheart,'' he said, amusement still rippling through his voice. ''I was just speculating. And apparently I was wrong.''

Lexi huffed, at a loss for words. Caught between fury and misplaced disappointment, she didn't know what to say or do next.

''I guess maybe your dad was just too sick to come all this way,'' Jake suggested gently in what was the closest thing to an apology she was likely to get.

''He can hardly get around by himself anymore,'' Lexi agreed, belatedly remembering why she had come—to convince Jake to do her father's bidding, by hook or by crook. The sadness in her voice was genuine. ''He tried to walk down to the barn this morning, and a couple of the hands found him sitting on the side of the road, about to pass out. They carried him back to the house.''

Try as she might, she couldn't stop the quiver in her voice when she said, ''I'm so scared he's going to die, Jake. I don't know what I'd do.''

She didn't want to sound weak. She hadn't come here to beg, but that's what she seemed to be doing—over and over again.

When Jake's strong arms engulfed her, she went stiff with guilt. ''I'm sorry,'' she mumbled, refusing to let her head rest against the tempting warmth of his chest.

''Lord, girl, but you do bring back memories.'' His fingers coiled through her hair, stroking, soothing. The hand at her back held her tighter than it should have.

"When you were just a little thing, your daddy used to call you a bundle of fire and grit with a big helping of cotton candy mixed in. I guess it was that cotton candy that got to me in the end."

Jake's voice trailed off and he released her, stepping back abruptly. "I'm sorry, Lexi. I'd do anything for Frank if I could, but I just can't do what you're asking. I can't go back there."

Allowing no time for her reply, Jake turned and headed back toward the arena. His long strides ate up the ground, while the click of his cleats against the blacktop grew fainter with each step that carried him farther and farther away from her.

Lexi watched him go, the sadness welling up inside her reminding her that she and Jake had once been the best of friends and that she had been the one to change that. But he was wrong about one thing. She didn't think about that night. She had held the memory at bay for years, and now he'd brought it all back, every unforgettable moment of it.

CHAPTER THREE

"DARLIN', WHAT'RE YOU doing out here all alone?" Aaron's big voice boomed from behind Lexi.

With a startled shriek, she jumped halfway out of her skin before clapping a hand to her throat and turning to face him. Her pulse danced against the palm of her hand while she struggled to regain her breath along with her composure.

"Aaron, you startled me."

He grinned. "No foolin'."

Lexi caught herself smiling along with him. "You could at least *try* to seem contrite."

"It'd be useless," he said with a shake of his head. "Everybody knows me too well. You making any headway with that damned fool?"

"What?"

"Well, you *are* trying to get Jake to go back with you to your ranch, aren't you?"

Stunned, Lexi almost glanced over her shoulder to see who else might have been listening. "How do you know that?"

"Rodeo's a small community with big ears."

"And a big mouth apparently."

"Big heart, too. Jake's got a lot of friends here."

"I'm not asking him to do anything that's going to hurt him," she said, coming to her own defense.

"Oh, I agree. And if he gave a flip about my opinion, I'd gladly encourage him to go with you."

"Really?"

"Sure. I mean, it's not like Dolores lives there anymore. I don't know what his problem is, really."

"Well, I suppose he would have to take time off from his work," Lexi said, suddenly finding herself in the position of defending Jake. "Maybe he just doesn't want to do that."

"But the doctors have been trying to talk him into doing just that for the past month."

"They have?"

"Yeah. He's got a shoulder separation that isn't getting any better. They keep telling him he's going to be looking at surgery pretty soon if he doesn't give it a chance to heal."

"Then why won't he stop?"

"Damned if I know." Aaron shrugged his massive shoulders. "Money's the only thing I can figure, but Jake won't talk about it. If I so much as mention the subject, he just swells up like a thundercloud and stalks off."

Resigned to getting into her car and driving away only minutes earlier, Lexi knew now that she couldn't leave, not yet. Jake needed the deal her father was offering almost as much as her father needed Jake to accept it.

"Aaron, can you get me through to where Jake is?"

"I can get you close, but by now he's in the middle of the first bull riding go-round."

"He is?" Worry made her frown, and tension stretched her already overwrought emotions tighter still. "Right now?" In the distance, she heard the excited roar of the crowd.

"Now, don't you fret," Aaron hastily reassured her. "Jake's an old hand. He knows what he's doing."

"I know." She nodded, not at all reassured.

She had been around rodeos enough to know that only one clown was actually there to be funny—the one who stayed in the barrel when the bull was in the ring. The other two were the ones who put themselves between the bull and the rider once the cowboy was down.

To the rodeo cowboy, those two clowns were saints, and they weren't called bullfighters for nothing. They were the difference between a safe ride and a crippling injury, sometimes even between life and death.

"Can we go now?" she asked, eager to be there, to see Jake safe with her own eyes.

"Sure." Tucking her arm into his, Aaron guided her quickly through the congestion behind the scenes until they reached the barricades at the side of the arena where the cowboys gathered in safety to watch the action in the ring.

Her heart in her throat, Lexi ignored the surprised stares all around as Aaron lifted her onto a platform and hoisted his bulk up beside her. Just below, and so close she could hear the creaking of the leather, a rider hunched forward on the back of a ghostly pale Brahma bull.

Readying himself for an eight-second ride that could last an eternity, the cowboy adjusted his hold on the braided bull rope that circled under the girth of the animal and crisscrossed just behind the shoulders. His grip on the rope and the strength of his legs were the only things holding the rider on the bull.

The Brahma shifted in the chute. His back arched as his strong hind legs gathered under him. Quick as lightning, the cowboy leapt from the bull's back onto the top rail of the chute, scrambling out of harm's way before the ornery beast could crush him against the side wall or worse.

With the rider gone, the bull settled down peacefully, and once again the cowboy was helped onto the animal's enormous back. The ends of the bull rope were pulled tight across the bull's back, and the cowboy slid his hand underneath, the rope's double thickness gripped in his palm. Taking one loose end of the rope, he wrapped it twice more around his gloved hand and held it firmly enough to withstand the battering to come.

Her heart pounding, Lexi looked quickly to the other side of the ring and saw Jake, his gaze riveted on the door of the chute. Feet spread wide, knees flexed, weight balanced, he was a warrior poised to spring, and pride swelled inside her, joining the anxiety that already pounded through her.

In the next instant, the cowboy's head jerked down in a nod, signaling that he was ready. The gate swung open, and he came rocketing out atop a snorting, spinning, one-ton chunk of muscle and temper. For the first time in her life, Lexi found herself holding her breath not for the cowboy hanging on for dear life but for the man in the greasepaint who was there to risk his own neck for the rider's safety.

She hardly noticed when the cowboy flew headfirst through the air and landed in a heap on the dirt floor of the arena. The bull continued bucking in a wide circle, trampling first the bull rope that had fallen free, then the cowboy's hat. The cowboy was on his feet and running toward the wall of the ring as the Brahma prepared to charge.

As the bull's head lowered and one long, curving horn aimed at the cowboy's back, a hat came arcing through the air and into the bull's face, turning him just in time for the cowboy to scramble unharmed onto the wall and over to safety.

Hatless, with the overhead lights glittering off the golden streaks interwoven in his thick chestnut hair, Jake bounded into the Brahma's path, drawing the charging bull toward the center of the arena. Before the animal could reach Jake, the second clown grabbed the dummy that stood in the center of the arena and threw it into the bull's line of vision.

Catching the dummy on his horns, the bull tossed it into the air, then circled smoothly around to the open gate that waited to close behind him. The audience applauded while the clowns took a bow and straightened the dummy and the barrel containing a third clown into their proper places.

Meanwhile, another rider readied himself, tightening and wrapping the bull rope around his heavy leather glove, testing the grip of his knees on the bull's sides. He nodded, and the gate of the next chute swung open with a bang. From it, a black-and-gray-mottled bull, bigger than the one before, launched himself straight into the air and came down with a jarring, stiff-legged thump.

Before the rider could adjust his grip, the bull kicked straight out with his hind legs and tucked himself into a tight, fast spin. Anticipating a quick end to the ride, Jake and his partner moved closer, staying just out of range of the whirling bull and his tempest-tossed rider.

Lexi held her breath, her gaze fixed on Jake. She didn't even know her hand had tightened in a viselike grip on Aaron's until he patted her shoulder with his free hand and whispered, "It'll be all right, darlin'. He does this every night and he— Oh, no!"

"What?" Lexi cried.

Seeing that Jake was in no danger, she sought the source of Aaron's concern. Then she almost echoed the scream that came from behind her in the stands.

No longer seated on the bull's back, the cowboy hung by one arm from the rope that was still securely wrapped around his hand. His feet dragged in the dirt of the arena floor and his head bounced against the bull's shoulder. His free arm flailed in the air as he tried without success to reach the hand that was entangled in the rope.

"Why isn't it releasing?" Lexi almost screamed as the scene in front of her unfolded like a newsreel in slow motion.

"It's tangled." Aaron's voice was tense enough to belie his outward calm.

"I know *that,*" she said, staring at the nightmare in the arena. "But why?"

Beside her the big man shrugged impatiently. "He wrapped it too tight. He wrapped it the wrong way. He wrapped it too many times. Who knows?" Aaron patted her arm. "It'll let go in a minute."

She could tell Aaron's last words were wishful thinking. "What happens if it doesn't?"

"Don't ask."

While the bull whirled, first one clown and then the other hurled himself at the side opposite the dangling cowboy. Reaching across the bull's broad back, they grabbed for the thick rope, hoping to pull it free of the cowboy's glove while he still had the strength to get away safely.

Each attempt failed, and the bull continued to spin in an endless circle, going faster and faster in his struggle to rid himself of the maddening burden of the man. The cowboy found his feet and ran for a few steps, still struggling futilely to jerk the end of the rope free.

But the bull's spin was faster than any man could run, and the cowboy slipped again, the weight of his body hanging by the increasingly fragile tether of his arm. As his boots dragged through the dirt, his legs slid under the belly of the bull, directly in the path of the animal's pounding hooves.

While Lexi held her breath, what seemed like endless minutes of terror ticked by. Tossed like a rag doll against the side of the enraged bull, the cowboy seemed weaker by the second, the clowns still unable to free him. With each grab at the rope, the bullfighter had only a second to work before he was slung aside by the force and speed of the bull's spin.

Almost afraid to look, Lexi forced her eyes from the desperate cowboy to the two men battling to free him. Jake stepped back, legs spread, ready to spring. He launched himself into the air as the bull's head whirled in front of him.

Lexi screamed as his body landed squarely in the narrow valley between the bull's long horns. In an unbroken motion, his strong arms wrapped over the top of their deadly curves. While he pulled down with all his weight, his cleated shoes dug heel-first into the dirt to slow the speed of the enraged animal.

In the same instant, the second clown threw himself at the side of the bull, reaching over to tug at the tangled knot of rope. Lexi barely had time to blink before both clowns were flung to the dirt, their bodies rolling from the force of the blow. Immediately they sprang to their feet and crouched for another try as the bull's head passed by again.

Jake leapt higher the second time, wrapping his arms tighter around the horns while he once again used his body as a brake to slow the bull. With a resilience that was heartening, the cowboy staggered to his feet just long enough to reach with his free arm to work at the bull rope along with the second clown.

Lexi prayed that this time would be the one. Then the cowboy stumbled and his legs slid under the bull's belly again.

The crowd gasped as he scrambled to pull his lower body from under the bull's powerful hooves and the second clown went flying as a horn raked the air a fraction of an inch from his back. At the same time, Jake hit the ground with a thud and lay there for the space of a heartbeat before he shoved himself to his feet barely a second before the bull's head passed by once more.

Lexi could almost hear the crack of Jake's ribs as his body slammed into the narrow space between the bull's horns yet again. Digging in his heels, he clung there with what was left of his waning strength.

This time the cowboy managed to get his feet under him for two long, running steps. Without the cowboy's full weight tugging at the rope, the second clown gave one hard, frantic tug. The bull rope dropped into the dirt, and the cowboy hit the ground beside it in a motionless heap.

Then, with the survival instinct that had kept more than one rider alive, he gathered his strength and rolled twice, then a third time, until he was safe from the immediate danger of trampling. The crowd burst into wild applause, and a half dozen cowboys poured over the wall and into the ring to help him to safety.

Lexi barely noticed them. She was too busy watching Jake. Releasing the bull's horns, he landed on his feet and sprang back, ready for action. Until the cowboy was behind the wall and the bull on his way back to his pen, the bullfighters' job wasn't over, and this bull still wanted someone to battle.

Skidding to a halt, he lowered his horns and pawed the dirt. His heavy head swung from one clown to the other, uncertain which to charge first. Glancing toward Jake, who looked none too steady on his feet, the second clown drew a red kerchief from his back pocket, wiggling his hips and yelling "Toro!" as he unfurled the kerchief in the bull's direction.

The animal took a step back. Looking more uncertain than ever, he pawed the earth again and snorted loudly. Sensing that the bull's first dangerous flush of anger was cooling and that the crowd needed a distraction from the scare it had just had, Jake withdrew a red kerchief from his own pocket and joined his partner in waving the tiny matador capes.

Issuing a final, shuddering snort of disgust, the suddenly docile bull whirled and trotted through the open gate behind him while the crowd rose to its feet and wild applause became a thunderous ovation. Jake and his fellow clown pocketed their kerchiefs and took a bow, Jake's very stiff and slight.

While the crowd still applauded, a badly listing Jake slowly made his way toward his battered hat. With a long sweep of his arm, he leaned forward to scoop the hat from the arena floor but collapsed instead, sinking with lazy grace, face-first into the dirt.

"HE'LL BE ALL RIGHT," Aaron said as he hustled Lexi through the crowd toward the doctor's trailer. "It's probably just that shoulder of his."

"Are you sure they'll let me in to see him?" Lexi asked, breathless in her effort to keep up.

"Oh, sure. I'll just tell them you're his sister."

"Oh, Aaron." Lexi groaned, reliving the terror of what had just happened. "He could have been killed."

"And if it weren't for Jake and Pete, he probably would have been. But that's what the clowns are there for, darlin', to keep the rider safe." When Lexi didn't answer, Aaron glanced down in time to see her guilty wince. "Oh," he said with a chuckle. "You weren't talking about poor old Billy, were you?"

"No." Lexi couldn't even look at him, she felt so ashamed. That poor boy could have been killed, or at least maimed, and she hadn't given him a second thought. "How is Billy? Do you know?"

"He looked a little shook-up, but not too much the worse for wear. Cowboys are tough. He'll probably be riding again in a day or two."

"How can you do it?" Lexi demanded, shuddering as she hurtled through the night in Aaron's wake, not even pausing to apologize when her shoulders collided with someone in passing. "Why would you want to?"

"Want to do *what*, darlin'?"

"This!" She flung her arms wide, encompassing the rodeo and everything surrounding it. "There's no money in it. The average accountant makes more money than one of these men will ever make. There's no fame in it. Even if you're a three-time, all-around champion like Jake was, nobody outside the rodeo circuit knows who you are. And the glamour," she said, her voice rising indignantly. "Don't even get me started on the glamour of it. Horse dung and sawdust are all I've ever seen."

"Well, even if all that's true, and mind you, I'm not saying it isn't," Aaron said softly, "Jake loves it and you love him."

"I do not!" Lexi protested.

"Oh, yes you do." He lifted her hand and patted it with his other one. "Why do you suppose I remember you so well all these years after I first met you, huh? How

come you think I took you to Jake, no questions asked?"
Aaron stopped his headlong race to the doctor's trailer
and faced Lexi, still holding her hand in his. "Because,
Lexi darlin', the first time I ever saw you look at Jake, I
told myself that if anyone ever looked at me with that
kind of love in her eyes, I'd die a happy man."

"That was a long time ago," Lexi said, refusing to
meet his gaze.

"Yeah, it was. That's why it's all the more heart-
warming to see that love still there."

"No!" She jerked her hand from his and took a stag-
gering step back from him. "I care for Jake, but I don't
love him. There's a big difference."

"Oh, darlin', wait." Aaron reached out to halt her
flight. "I didn't mean to upset you."

"That's okay," she said, eluding him. "I just— I
need—"

Air, she thought desperately. She needed air. And
space, lots of space. She needed to be away from this
place with all of its macho cowboys and the women who
loved them. She needed to draw one deep breath that
wasn't scented with testosterone.

Behind her a door was flung open and a flurry of
blazing voices followed.

"You can just go to hell for all I care," a woman
shouted.

"Fine. Great. Thank you. Ow! Damn it, Doc! Watch
it!"

The door slammed shut again and boots hurried across
the gravel. Lexi smelled the heavy perfume before she
turned and saw Louanne Byers fly past her, a flash of
long curly hair atop a fringed white outfit that sparkled
in the moonlight.

"Louanne, honey, how's Jake?" Aaron asked.

Without slowing her pace, Louanne snapped, "Mean as a rattlesnake. I hope he bites himself. I should have my head examined for even caring if he's dead or alive. I swear, I've never seen anybody with such a rotten temper." Her words faded as she disappeared quickly into the distance. She never looked back.

"Sounds like he's doing just fine," Aaron said, drawing even with Lexi.

"Lucky us." Uncharitably, Lexi almost wished Jake were still unconscious.

"I think I'll just wait out here until you've had a chance to talk to him," Aaron offered.

"Coward."

"Well, I'll tell you, hon. Jake Thorn in pain is a lot like a bear that's just been shot in the foot—crazy mean and lookin' to take a swing at anything that moves."

"Okay," she said, taking hold of the door handle. "Now that you've cheered me up, I guess I'll just go on inside."

"Allow me." Aaron put his hand over hers and pulled the door open, then gave her a gentle shove to propel her inside.

Lexi found herself facing a glaring Jake and a surprised doctor as the door closed behind her. "Uh, excuse me," she said, choosing the doctor to focus on. "I was just wondering how he was doing."

"And you are...?" the doctor asked, poised with a filled hypodermic needle.

"I'm—I'm an old friend," she stammered. "Of—of the family. I'm almost one of the family, actually. I—I'm his sister-in-law. Well, I *was,* anyway," she finished in a subdued mumble. An embarrassed flush heated Lexi's face when the senseless tumble of words finally ground to a halt. There was nothing simple about her relationship with Jake. Everything she had said was true, and yet—

The doctor turned his gaze to Jake. "Do you know this woman?"

A twitch of amusement tugged at the painted smile on Jake's face, now obscured by a fine powdering of brown dirt. "Vaguely."

"Do you want her to stay?"

Jake's grass-green eyes looked at Lexi coolly. "I don't mind. For the moment."

"Very well. I'll be right back. I have to check on those X rays." Laying the syringe in a metal tray on the counter behind him, the doctor turned to Lexi. "By the way, is there someone who can help him out of here when I'm through?"

"He has a friend waiting outside."

"Good." The doctor pointed to Jake. "Meanwhile, don't you move." With that, the doctor exited through a curtained doorway at the back of the room, leaving them alone.

Lexi stood there, awkward and out of place, wishing she had never come. She wanted to tell Jake how impressed she was by what he had done. In all his years as a rider, she'd never seen him do anything quite so brave— or terrifying.

"I guess I sounded pretty stupid a minute ago," she said instead.

"Nah." He shook his head and even the dirt-smeared makeup on his face couldn't hide the wince of pain. "One of the things I've always admired about you is that you don't lie worth a damn."

"I wasn't lying."

"No, but you wished you could."

In his pain-glazed eyes, she could see the faintest twinkle of amusement. "Well, yes," Lexi admitted. "Until I heard you yelling at Louanne, I was hoping you'd still be passed out. I was planning to tell the doctor I was your sister so he'd let me stay." She could feel herself blushing all over again. "But, unfortunately, you were awake. And looking at me. And I realized too late that I hadn't planned for that."

"Why are you here, Lexi?" Jake asked softly, his breathing slow and shallow.

She stopped inspecting the linoleum on the floor and looked at him again. His suspenders dangled in loops on either side of the examining table. His shirt lay in a heap on the floor, and his baggy pants were unfastened and drooping low on his hips, exposing a faint purpling across his hipbone. Lexi winced, imagining what the bruise would look like in a day or two.

"I wanted to see how you were," she answered slowly. Her gaze flickered over the broad band of white tape that encircled his ribs and the blue sling that supported his right arm.

"What's your opinion?" Only his hands moved, but that was enough for Lexi to see the raw scrapes across his palms.

"You look pretty banged up," she said. There were old scars, as well, pale against the tan of his skin. She couldn't help wondering how much was hurt that she couldn't see.

"I *feel* pretty banged up." His black brow lifted in an exaggerated arch. "Got any more cheerful observations?"

Goaded by his challenge, and irritated by her own awareness of the hard, masculine body beneath the bruises and abrasions, Lexi looked down to where an angry red bruise the size of an open hand showed through the soft furring of brown curls on his chest. An abundance of chestnut curls continued into the tape around his ribs, then emerged again as a narrow line ending just above his belly button.

She pointed to the band of white and the hair trapped beneath it. "That's going to hurt when they take the tape off."

"I hadn't thought that far ahead." He looked down and nodded. "But you're probably right." He lifted his head again, pinning her with a hard stare. "Anything else?"

She wished she'd just kept her mouth shut, and she certainly wasn't going to dig the hole any deeper. She'd seen Jake hurt before, and she knew better than to offer sympathy or give him a clear target for his anger.

"No."

"Well, Mr. Thorn," the doctor announced, returning without warning. "It seems you're a very lucky man." He held a set of X rays aloft. "Only a few cracked ribs. The rest are just badly bruised. Your sternum is bruised, but it will be healed before your ribs. And much less painful, I might add. Other than that, your right shoulder is an even worse mess than it was, but if you're very careful, you might still get by without surgery on it."

"That's lucky?" Lexi asked quietly.

"Great," Jake said in a heartier version of his normal rasp. "When do I go back to work?"

"Oh, I'd say two months minimum. Maybe three."

"Wha—" Midtwist and midshout, Jake froze. *"Ah-h-h."* The air seeped out of him in a long, painful sigh. Fingers splayed, head thrown back in a silent cry, he couldn't straighten, collapse or even twitch.

Calmly the doctor laid aside the X rays and retrieved the syringe he had filled. He looked at Lexi. "Is that friend of his very big?"

"Huge."

The doctor smiled. "Good." He swabbed a spot on Jake's left biceps. "I wouldn't make any sudden movements if I were you for, say, oh, two to three weeks at least. Those ribs are going to be very unforgiving at first." He stabbed the needle in without warning, then continued in a calm, soothing voice. "You'll feel better in just a little bit. You want to try to lie down until this takes effect?"

"I couldn't move if I had to," Jake gasped.

Lexi had to force herself to stay where she was. She couldn't help. He was battered and bruised in so many places there was nowhere she could touch without making his pain worse. But it wasn't easy to just stand and watch, the way she'd had to with her father for months now.

"We could help you lie down if you wanted," the doctor said. "Though I have to warn you, getting back up won't be any picnic even with the painkiller."

"Damn it, Doc," Jake growled between clenched teeth. "I can't stay off for two months."

"You've got no choice, son. You're lucky I'm not hospitalizing you. But I'm guessing you wouldn't stay there even if I had you admitted."

"You've got *that* right." Jake glowered ominously.

Smiling at him, not in the least intimidated, the doctor touched Jake's shoulder gently, then turned back to the counter and lifted a tablet.

"I'm going to write you a couple of prescriptions that you'll need to have filled right away. Take them both according to directions until they're gone. And as soon as you're settled someplace, I want you to see another doctor, next week at the latest. You're going to need to have someone monitoring your progress."

"Damn it, Doc!" Careful not to jar himself again, Jake fired off with all the fury he could muster. "What the hell am I supposed to do?"

"Smell the roses, son. Read a book, watch the grass grow, and heal. How about you, young lady? You have any influence with him?"

"None that I've noticed." Lexi took a step closer, her mind working as she carefully maintained her distance from Jake. "Would he be able to do the paperwork involved in overseeing a ranch? You know, act as manager so long as there was a foreman to see that the orders were carried out?"

"I don't see why not." The doctor tore off the prescriptions and handed them to Lexi. "See that he follows my directions. And I don't want him on horseback for at least six weeks." His gaze slid toward Jake. "Not even for a Sunday stroll on the gentlest horse alive."

"I'm not going with her." Jake held out his left hand to Lexi. "Give me those prescriptions."

"No." Lexi slipped the papers into her pocket. "And you are going with me. It's the perfect solution for everyone. You can fill in for Dad while you both recuperate. You'll have a home, a salary and people to look after you until you're feeling better."

"Over my dead body. I'm not going back there." His arm and his voice drooped simultaneously. "What's wrong with me?" He ran his tongue over his lips. "I don't feel so good."

Concerned, Lexi looked at the doctor, who shook his head.

"It's just the shot. He should sleep peacefully all night."

Jake squinted in the doctor's direction. "You mean you knocked me out?" he asked in a weak wheeze.

Afraid Jake would pass out before he could be moved, Lexi hurried to the door and threw it open. "Aaron?" She breathed a sigh of relief when Aaron stepped out of the shadows with two other cowboys close behind. "Can you carry Jake to my car for me?"

"Sure." Aaron bounded up the steps and into the trailer. "I can't believe you got him to agree."

Jake turned a wobbly head toward the door. Resentment blazed in his eyes. "I'm bein' hijacked," he mumbled in a slurred, sleepy voice that sounded too tired to care much anymore.

"What?" Aaron asked, carefully scooping Jake into his arms.

"He's being hijacked," Lexi repeated. "Do you know where the rest of Jake's things are?" She glanced at the shirt on the floor and decided to leave it. It was no more than a rag now anyway.

"They're in my truck. We were traveling together," Aaron said, following her down the stairs, the other cowboys at Jake's feet.

"Good. I'll pick them up after we get him into my car." She started across the parking lot. "I'm parked over this way. It's not too far, thank goodness."

"What all's wrong with him?"

"Ribs, sternum and shoulder. Cracked, bruised and separated even worse than before but maybe not requiring surgery. Plus multiple bruises and lacerations the doctor didn't even go into."

"Banged up pretty good, huh? How long's he got to be out?"

"Two to three months."

"Oh, man. I bet Jake howled."

"He tried, but it hurt too much."

She reached her car, unlocked the passenger door and reclined the bucket seat as far back as it would go. Aaron and the other cowboys settled Jake gently into the seat and buckled him in. Jake moaned but didn't wake up as Lexi closed the door and walked around to the driver's side.

Aaron followed her. "So, Jake didn't ever agree to go with you, did he?"

"No." Lexi opened her door and glanced inside at the sleeping man. "But he's going."

"He'll be one ornery critter when he wakes up in the morning."

"I'll take good care of him, Aaron."

"I know you will. If I didn't think this was the best thing for him, I wouldn't be helping you. Whatever happened on that ranch all those years ago, whatever he's been running away from ever since, he needs to go back and face it."

"I just need him to look after things for a while," Lexi answered, no more eager to stir up the past than Jake was.

"I just hope we don't live to regret forcing him into this. Well, I'll meet you back at my truck. It's that banged-up old black one parked right over there."

Lexi started her car and drove slowly over to where Aaron waited beside his truck. The whole way she was acutely conscious of the half-naked man reclining beside her and of the long drive through the night that was ahead of her, with no one but the sleeping Jake and her reawakened memories to keep her company.

While Aaron stowed Jake's gear in the trunk, Lexi told herself she should never have gone looking for him, and when he refused her request, she should never have persisted. For eleven years she had told herself that he would never come back to the Lazy C, that she didn't want him to. Her life was set. She was happy. And regardless of what her father thought, the last thing in the world they needed was Jake's presence stirring up the waters.

Now she was bringing him back by force, drugged and kidnapped. She'd be lucky if Jake didn't have her arrested tomorrow. She'd be doubly lucky if her life wasn't in tatters by the day after.

When Aaron finished, he waved goodbye and walked away. Alone in the shadowed privacy of her car, Lexi leaned toward Jake and took a long breath, drawing in the blend of scents that made it so hard to ignore his presence.

A faintly spicy cologne mingled with the not unpleasant aroma of sweat, earth and body heat to create a scent that was powerful and uniquely Jake. With the flat of her hand, she stroked the velvety warmth of his arm, feeling the strength of the muscles beneath her touch.

Unable to resist, she moved on to caress the hard contours and hair-roughened surface of his chest. Beneath her hand she could feel the strong, steady beating of his heart, a heart that would resent her with a fiery passion come the dawn.

She had loved him once, and for a moment she allowed herself to remember those long-ago days when he had been everything to her. Her lips brushed his shoulder, tasting the salty sheen of sweat in spite of the cool night, and bitter tears of regret stung her eyes.

"Jake, I'm so sorry," she whispered. "This should never have happened. I should never have done this to either of us. But I couldn't help it."

Realizing she was talking to herself, Lexi straightened and took a deep breath. She was through apologizing. Jake wasn't exactly a saint himself, and besides, he owed her. He owed her for eleven years of wondering. He owed her for the "morning after" she'd never got. And this time, he wasn't leaving until he paid up.

CHAPTER FOUR

"BE CAREFUL WITH HIM," Lexi cautioned as she led the way into the ranch house. "Especially his ribs and shoulders."

In the lighted entryway, she glanced back to where the three ranch hands gingerly carried Jake's sleeping form across the stone portal.

"Yes, ma'am," the cowboy in the lead grunted. "Which bedroom?" he asked as they shuffled their way into the foyer.

"Down here." Frank Conley stood in the doorway of the empty bedroom that had always been Jake's room. "I've turned down the covers." When they reached him, he stepped inside and let out a low whistle. "Lord have mercy, girl, was he *that* hard to convince?"

"Dad." The warning in her voice said she had had a long, hard day and was in no mood to be teased.

"Seriously, honey," Frank insisted. "Is he going to be all right? What in the world happened to him?"

Watching the men carefully settle Jake into the bed, Lexi rubbed a hand across the dull ache just above her eyes. "Oh, a rider got tangled in his bull rope. Jake was—" She searched for a word to replace the first one that came to mind, then gave up. "Wonderful," she finished, hoping she didn't blush.

To cover her confusion, she advanced into the room, motioning the cowhands back before they could withdraw. "We probably need to get some of these clothes off while he's still unconscious. You think you could ease those pants down? They're loose, so it shouldn't be too hard."

While the men slid the ragged pants over Jake's dirt-stained long johns, Lexi untied his cleated running shoes and slipped them from his feet as gently as if he were a sleeping child.

"My car keys are still in the ignition, Tonio," she said over her shoulder. "On your way out, could you get Jake's things out of the trunk and put them in the hall for me?"

"Yes, ma'am, Miss Lexi," the oldest of the hands muttered as he handed the oversize pants to her.

"Thank you," Lexi whispered. She studied the pants, stained with blood, dirt and goodness knew what else, before she folded them and dropped them on top of the shoes. Then, hoping for nothing more than to close the door and put Jake from her mind until morning, she joined her father in the doorway.

"What's he got?" Frank asked. "Cracked ribs?"

She nodded. "Cracked, bruised and a host of other things."

With her hand on the doorknob, she looked up to find Jamie peering down from the top of the staircase, his face alight with the eagerness of a child on Christmas morning.

"Is that him?" the ten-year-old asked in a stage whisper.

"Yes," Lexi whispered back. She lifted her finger to her lips. "Shh. Don't wake him, *please*. It wouldn't be pretty."

"A host of other things like what?" her father asked beside her.

"Oh, let me see, what else?" She rolled her eyes while her son hurtled down the staircase, oblivious of the noise. "Bruised sternum. Badly separated shoulder. The one with the sling. And, uh, what else is there? Basically just lots of bruises and scrapes, I guess."

"Is he going to be able to do anything?"

Jamie arrived, eagerly wedging himself between them. "Let me see him."

"No," Lexi said, answering her father as she absently hooked a restraining arm over her son's shoulder. "But then, Jake doesn't really have to do anything except sit at a desk, make decisions and give orders."

Dismay replaced the excitement in Jamie's voice. "That's Jake? What *is* that?" he demanded, pointing indignantly to the dirt-smeared paint on the sleeping man's face.

Lexi combed her fingers through her son's hair, sweeping it back from his forehead and out of his eyes while her father stifled a grunt of laughter. "That's his makeup," she explained in a whisper, hoping Jamie wouldn't be disappointed in his hero. "Jake's a clown now, sweetheart."

"A clown?"

She heard the shock in Jamie's voice, but she merely nodded. "You know, a rodeo clown. There wasn't time to take off his makeup before we left tonight."

"Damn," Jamie said with feeling.

"Jamie!"

Jerking his shoulder free of her hand, he twisted angrily away from her and stalked into the bedroom. "Jake can't be a clown. He was a champion!"

"Lower your voice," Lexi demanded in a whisper. She followed him into the room and took him by the arm, turning him around to face her. "Now you listen to me, young man," she whispered firmly. "Jake saved a cowboy's life tonight in the arena. He did a very brave thing, and he could have been killed doing it."

For the first time since he'd been put into the bed, she allowed herself to look at him, trying to be objective, trying to see him through the eyes of a child eager to measure a legend against reality. On Jake's chest and arms bruises had begun to form beneath raw red scrapes.

"You've been to the rodeo enough times to know that the clowns work as hard as anyone there," she said, her voice softening as she turned an unresisting Jamie around to look at Jake. "They risk their lives night after night for no glory and very little money. Jake's proud of what he does, and you should be, too."

"What happened to his pants?" Jamie asked, curiosity pushing aside his disappointment as he pointed to the thin layer of long, dirty red underwear that covered Jake from just below his waist to his ankles.

"We took them off so he'd be more comfortable."

"Is he real hurt?"

"He's not going to be very active for a while," Lexi answered, staring at the man in the bed.

"Can I touch him?" Jamie asked, already moving toward the bed.

"No!" Lost in thought, Lexi gave a guilty start. Taking a deep breath, she pulled Jamie back. "Not tonight, sweetheart. We'd better wait until tomorrow for that. We wouldn't want to wake him any sooner than we have to."

"I take it Jake isn't exactly happy about being back here," Frank said quietly as Lexi ushered Jamie through the doorway and into the hall.

"Uh, not exactly."

Grateful for the interruption, Lexi released Jamie and hurried toward the front door as the men entered with the luggage. "Just put it here," she said, pointing to the side of the hallway nearest the staircase.

"Oh, and, Tonio..." Pulling the prescriptions the doctor had given her from her pocket, Lexi extended her hand. "Could you be at the drugstore as soon as it opens in the morning and have these filled? For everyone's sake, I think Jake should have them as soon as he wakes up."

Smiling as he took the slips of paper, Tonio tucked them into his shirt. "Yes, ma'am, Miss Alexandra. And don't you worry. I remember Jake's temper like it was yesterday." Tonio patted his shirt pocket with a wink. "I'll take care of this first thing in the morning, for sure. You need us any more tonight?"

"Oh, no. And thank you." She smiled at the other two men, as well. "Thank you all so much. I'm sorry I had to get you up in the middle of the night."

"It was nothing," said one with a wave of dismissal while the other reached to tip a hat that had been left behind in his rush to dress.

With a sheepish grin, the man lowered his hand. "It'll be good to have Jake back again for a while," he said. Then, nodding at Frank, who had joined Lexi, the trio turned and left on tiptoe.

"Alexandra," Frank Conley said in the tone of a father about to give a lecture.

"Yes?" She felt nothing but fatigue as the events of the difficult day and the early morning hour combined to take their toll.

"We need to talk."

"Now?" Looking behind him, she saw an empty hallway with Jake's closed door at the end. "Where's Jamie?" she asked as confusion began to cloud her tired mind.

"I sent him up to bed. And yes, now."

"Oh, Dad." Almost too exhausted to think straight, she looked into her father's eyes and knew that he was even more tired than she was. His face was pale gray, and dark circles rimmed his eyes. "It's so late," she coaxed gently, knowing that her concern would only anger him. "Shouldn't you go back to bed now? We can talk in the morning."

"What did you mean by 'not exactly'?" Frank asked as if she hadn't spoken. Looping his arm through hers, he turned her toward the cozily cluttered Victorian front parlor.

"Gee, I don't know." She ran her fingertips over her brow and hoped against hope that the inquisition would be brief. "I'm so tired I'm dizzy. When did I say it?"

"I asked if Jake was happy about coming here, and you said 'not exactly.' What exactly does 'not exactly' mean?"

"It just means that Jake wasn't too thrilled about coming back here." This wasn't something she wanted to get into tonight. Earlier in the evening her actions had made perfect sense, but at the moment she had no idea how she could justify what she had done.

Frank released her arm and walked to the fireplace before he turned to face her. "Why *did* he agree to come back with you?" he asked, one arm braced against the smooth dark wood of the mantel.

"Well, gosh, Dad, look at him. I mean, he's injured. He can't work and he has no place else to go." Lexi slipped into an ornately carved rocking chair before her trembling legs gave way under her. Even after so many years of practice, deception still didn't come easily to her.

"Do you think he'll be happy once he gets settled?" Frank left the fireplace and began to pace. "I want him to be happy. I want him to stay."

Watching her father pace, Lexi felt herself growing more snappish by the second. "Well, I don't think you've got any say about that, Dad. Jake's just not very happy right now, period. Not here. Not anywhere. And there's nothing we can do to change that."

"But at least he agreed to come." With a sigh, Frank ceased his pacing and settled into a chair, leaning forward as he talked. "You know, I really wasn't sure you could get him to."

"Oh, that part wasn't so hard. The doctor shot him up with a painkiller." Unable to face her father at the moment, Lexi pushed herself to her feet and began to prowl the same path he had trod. "Jake passed out, and I got someone to load him into the car. The hard part is going to be keeping him here once he comes to."

"You make it sound like you kidnapped him," Frank said with an uneasy laugh.

Lexi paused and fingered the fringe at the base of a lamp shade. "I don't like to think of it that way."

In a flash, her father's expression went from hopeful amusement to shock. "Lexi!"

"Dad, don't fuss at me." She turned away from the lamp and stalked back toward the rocker. "I'm exhausted, and Jake just wouldn't listen to reason. He didn't leave me any other choice. Anyway, he can't work again for at least two, maybe three months." Dropping into the chair, she faced her father. "That's long enough for you to get back on your feet."

"You kidnapped him?" Frank asked with hollow disbelief.

"I had help. Everyone agreed it was for his own good."

"Boy, if that don't beat all." He shook his head in wonder. "When you set out to do something, you sure don't go halfway, do you?"

"I'm your daughter, remember? You're not exactly a model of moderation yourself." Gripping the arms of the rocker, she sank all the way back into it. "Besides, I didn't do it on purpose. It just sort of happened."

Frank grinned while a youthful gleam of mischief danced in his eyes. "Well, at least he's here." The grin grew into a chuckle. "Oh boy, Jake's gonna be madder than a hornet when he comes to in the morning."

Too tired to find any humor in the thought, Lexi nodded. "I expect so. You just let me deal with him, okay? I got myself into this, and I'll get myself out."

"Whatever you say." Rising, Frank kissed her lightly on the cheek and gave her shoulder a squeeze before he started toward the door. "I guess we've done all the damage we can do for tonight. See you in the morning, sugar."

"Dad?" When he stopped to look at her, Lexi asked quietly, "Why didn't you warn me?"

His eyes narrowed. "Warn you? About what?"

"About Jake. You told me where to find him, but you didn't bother to tell me what he was doing these days."

"And what was I supposed to tell you—'Jake's not the man he used to be, but don't let your pity show when you see him'?" Frank shrugged. "Some things are better left unsaid. I figured you'd find out soon enough."

"I *don't* feel sorry for him," she argued.

"But you would have. If you'd known, it would have been right there on your face, ready and waiting. You couldn't have hidden it, and Jake deserves better than that."

"Do you know what happened?" she persisted. "Why he stopped riding and became a—" She stumbled over the word *clown* and chose the alternative. "A bullfighter?"

With a shrug of dismissal, Frank said, "He got too old, I guess. Too many injuries. But the rodeo's all he knows. It's all he's got."

"No, it's not. He's got a ranch just a few miles away. It wouldn't take all that much money for him to take it over and run it himself again."

"I don't know." Frank massaged his forehead, then the bridge of his nose in a gesture of mounting fatigue. "Don't ask me, girl. Ask him." Her father jerked his head toward the bedroom at the end of the hall. "He's the one with the answers, not me."

Frank turned and left. Lexi listened to his footsteps moving slowly down the hall until he reached his makeshift bedroom and closed the door behind him.

"Good night, Dad," Lexi whispered, feeling very alone.

Ordinarily she could talk freely with her father, but on this issue he seemed resistant. He saw Jake's presence on the ranch as a simple, straightforward solution to a problem, while she saw Jake's arrival as one huge headache. But for the moment, whatever her dad wanted he got, with no arguments. And until he was back from the hospital, mended and good as new, that's the way things would be.

Frank Conley always had been and always would be a stubborn, bullheaded and infuriatingly willful man, but he was also generous, loving and honorable, and Lexi wasn't the only person who would do anything in the world for him. Jake Thorn had once felt the same way.

Shaking herself out of her reverie, Lexi started to her room. At Jake's door, she paused. She didn't want to wake him; there was nothing more she could do for him. But still her fingers tightened on the knob, slowly twisting as she silently nudged the door open.

Inside, he lay almost motionless. Above the tight binding of his ribs, his broad chest rose and fell in the heavy rhythm of a deep, drugged sleep. One sock-clad foot poked out from under the edge of a blanket she didn't remember spreading over him. Lexi eased through the door and walked lightly across the bare wood floor until she stood beside the bed.

Her fingers traced the air above his arm while his name echoed through her mind. James Jackson Thorn. Even with his face hidden, his body battered and his spirit bruised, he was still the most magnificent man she had ever known. Memories too tender to dwell on flickered through her mind. The first night they kissed. The night they—

Breathless, she closed her eyes and drew back from the thought and from him. Stumbling blindly against the chair tucked into the corner, she collided with something soft. She turned, and a booted foot hit the side of her knee.

"Ow," Jamie's sleepy voice complained.

Lexi stared down at the little boy slumped in the big armchair. With the back of his hand, he rubbed one eye.

"Mom?" he bleated as he gazed up at her through the other, half-opened eye.

"Shh, sweetheart," she whispered as she guided him to his feet. Gathering him to her, she started toward the door, supporting his weight as best she could and wishing for the days when she could have simply scooped him into her arms and carried him up the stairs. "I'm sorry. Did I hurt you?"

"Hmm," he mumbled grumpily.

By the time they reached the top of the staircase, Lexi's arms were aching from keeping him upright and her feet were bruised from being stumbled over by the cowboy boots he wore with his pajamas. Grateful to reach his bed at last, she pulled off his boots and tucked his sleeping form snugly under the covers. Then, unable to leave him, she stretched out beside her son and gathered him to her with the fierceness of a lioness protecting her cub.

What had he been doing in Jake's room? Lexi cuddled against Jamie's back, worried that his excitement would turn to disappointment when an angry Jake awoke with all the friendliness of a wounded grizzly. She hugged him tighter as she drew in a deep breath filled with the fresh-scrubbed little-boy smells of her son, who for ten years had been her main reason for living.

Nothing was going to hurt him. Nothing and no one. He was her life.

"Mom!" Jamie's voice squeaked.

"Yes, sweetheart?"

"You're squashing me."

With a fierce grunt, he twisted away as Lexi loosened her grasp. "Sorry, sweetheart."

"I love you, Mom," he whispered, his words of forgiveness slurred with sleep.

"I love you, too, Jamie."

Careful not to hold him too tightly, she nestled closer again and fell asleep.

"LEXI!" Jake's voice thundered.

Startled in the act of making her son's bed, Lexi jerked upright, banging her head on the overhead bunk. "Ow!"

Backing away from the bed with the blanket still clutched in one hand, she hopped across the floor, rubbing the back of her head. "Oh, ow, oh."

"Lexi!" Jake shouted again, twice as loud as before.

"Hold your horses!" Looking down in dismay at the blanket still in one hand, she continued to rub the back of her smarting head with the other hand. "What are you doing up so early, anyway?" she grumbled under her breath.

"Lexi! Damn it, woman, where are you?"

"Like you're the only person alive." The pain in her head subsiding, Lexi walked back to the bunk bed, shook out the blanket and let it float into place over the sheet.

"Lexi!"

The sound of glass shattering against the wall downstairs sent her tearing from the room with the bed still half-done. "Jake!" she shouted from the top of the staircase. "Now you stop that this minute!"

Taking the steps two at a time, she flung open his door to find him sitting half in the bed and half out. One arm was braced behind him and one foot was on the floor; the other leg was tangled in the sheets from midthigh down.

Jake's pain-glazed eyes fastened on her accusingly. "Where have you been?"

"Upstairs. What's so all-fired important?"

"I have to get to the bathroom." His jaw was set and angry resentment flared in his eyes, but he looked straight at her.

Instantly contrite, Lexi pointed to the door three feet from his bed. "Do you need some help?"

"Think you could untangle this sheet?" he asked, still biting off each word as if he begrudged the effort it took to speak. "I don't seem to be able to manage it."

"Sure." Lexi approached him with caution, as she would a caged tiger. He wasn't snarling or spitting at the moment, but she hated to get within striking distance nevertheless.

Moving closer, she bent only inches from his bare chest and gingerly began to peel back the twisted sheet. With each brush of her fingers against the soft, thin fabric of his long johns, she could feel a subtle, responsive twitch of his leg. She was only too happy when, with a final jerk, she pulled the sheet free, taking his sock off in the process.

Jake grunted and swung his leg over the side of the bed. "Thanks. I think I can handle the rest of this by myself." With a heave, he shoved himself halfway to his feet, cried out and collapsed backward across the bed. Stiff with pain, he lay there moaning slightly with each gasp.

Lexi hovered near, feeling as impotent as she had the night before. "Nothing sudden, the doctor said," she reminded him gently.

"Would you leave, please?" he asked through gritted teeth while he stared at the ceiling.

"Aren't you going to need me?"

"If I do," he answered, "you'll know it."

Lexi took a step backward, toward the door. "I'll be just outside."

"Go away. I'll call you if I need you."

"But how are you going to—"

"I'll crawl if I have to," he snapped without lifting his head from the mattress. "Now get out."

"Fine. Whatever you say." Lexi turned and marched to the door. "But I don't think you're going to find that crawling's any easier than walking, and you're still going to have to get off of that bed before you can do either."

Without giving him another glance, she slammed the door behind her and stormed up the stairs. She had just finished making Jamie's bed when the phone rang. Hurrying to her room across the hall, Lexi snatched up the receiver.

"Hello?" she gasped none too gently.

"Lexi dear, is that you?"

"M-Mother?" Lexi sank onto the bed before her rubbery legs collapsed under her.

Cordelia Davies Conley Lorton Smith Ridley laughed the high, tinkling laugh she used to deal with anything remotely awkward. "Well, you needn't sound so shocked."

"I'm sorry, but you normally call once or twice a year," Lexi said, too surprised for tact. "This is the second time you've called this month. And it's nowhere *near* Christmas."

"Now, Lexi dear, you know I'm concerned about your father. How is he doing?"

Lexi briefly wondered if her mother still carried a life insurance policy on her ex-husband and was instantly ashamed of herself. "Things haven't changed much from the last time we talked. He needs surgery, and he's dragging his heels about having it."

"That sounds just like him. He's the most stubborn man I've ever known." Cordelia sighed. "How does he look? Is it taking a toll?"

"He's paler than usual. And he gets tired easily." Lexi chose her words carefully. Cordelia exaggerated everything in her own mind, so Lexi made a point of understating anything she told her mother.

"Is he still handsome? When I first met him, I thought Frank Conley was the most handsome man I'd ever seen. To this day I still think of him that way," Cordelia said with the flare for dramatics that she'd passed on to her older daughter, Dolores. "I don't think I'll ever love another man the way I loved your father."

In her whole life, Lexi had never heard her mother say so many kind things about her ex-husband at one time. Far from being moved by it, she was growing more suspicious by the second.

"Well, if you loved him so much," Lexi asked, finally giving voice to a question that had haunted her for years, "why did you leave him?"

"Lexi dear, I thought you knew," Cordelia said, sounding far more surprised than offended. "Frank had no *money*."

"You're serious, aren't you?" Lexi almost wished she had never answered the telephone. Conversations with her mother always left her feeling bewildered, exasperated and hollow. She just didn't understand the woman.

"Well, of course, dear. I have no reason to lie to you about *that*. By the way, Dolores sends her love to you all."

Lexi tensed as soon as she heard her half sister's name. "That's good. Does she know about Dad?"

"Of course she does, dear," Cordelia said sweetly. "And she's very concerned. But she just tested for a very big part, and she can't leave town right now."

"Leave town? Good heavens, no!" Lexi's heart leapt like a racehorse out of the starting gate. With Jake there, she didn't even want Dolores to phone, much less show up on their doorstep. "I mean, I wouldn't expect her to," Lexi amended in a calmer voice.

"Well, she would if she could."

"Oh, no. I understand perfectly, and it's just fine."

"But she said to tell you that she *is* going to phone Jamie the first chance she gets. She knows you're right about wanting him to get to know her better."

Lexi started to protest again, then realized it wouldn't be necessary. She'd heard that same promise from her half sister dozens of times, and it meant nothing more now than it had before.

If Dolores had ever cared about anyone but herself, she had hidden it very well, but the same could be said for Cordelia, the woman who had mothered them both. Cordelia and Dolores were so much alike—beautiful, vain, exciting and exasperating—and every once in a while, just enough to make them totally unpredictable, they could be very kind and generous.

"Thank you for calling, Mother," Lexi said, suddenly drained by the conversation and eager to escape. "It was nice of you to care."

"Don't thank me, Lexi," her mother answered quietly. "I still love him, you know. You take good care of your father for me, you hear? And you'll let me know if anything changes?"

"Sure."

Her brain reeling, Lexi hung up the phone and went to her dresser to yank a brush through her hair. It was hard to believe that such a short time ago she had been a nervous wreck thinking about an encounter with Jake. Now she was too confused to worry about anything.

No wonder Jake's marriage to Dolores hadn't lasted. How could any marriage work in a family where love seemed to count for nothing? Maybe the kindest thing Cordelia had ever done for her younger daughter was to return her to the custody of her father a year after the divorce. Maybe to Cordelia it had been an act of love, but it hadn't seemed that way to Lexi at the time.

Then, and for a long time afterward, she had felt abandoned. It was years before she realized that she was the lucky one, not Dolores, because she was the one who had Frank Conley for both father and mother. He wasn't always an easy man, but in his heart he was kind and decent and loving, and he had never lied to her. She only prayed she would do as well by Jamie.

Putting down her brush, Lexi raised her tired arms to secure her hair with an interlocking comb. Gathered from the crown of her head to the nape of her neck, the hair tumbled around the sides of the comb and flowed in a long dark stream down the center of her back.

"Lexi!" Jake's imperious shout was as loud as ever.

Almost tempted to ignore him, Lexi cast an irritated glance over her shoulder at the open door.

"Lexi!" he called again, sounding less demanding and more desperate.

Remembering the glass he had thrown before, which had yet to be cleaned up, she started toward the door. "I'm coming!"

On the staircase she looked down over the railing and saw that Jake's suitcase lay open in the hallway. The clothes inside were churned into an untidy pile that dribbled over the sides onto the floor.

Shirts, socks and bikini-cut briefs were scattered like a trail of crumbs down the length of the hall to the open door of his bedroom. At the foot of the stairs Lexi scooped up a pair of teal blue bikini underwear. Dangling them by the waistband from the end of her index finger, she stepped through the door of Jake's room.

"You bellowed?" she asked sweetly.

"Where's Frank?" Jake sat on the side of his bed. His hands held the sheet across his middle, covering him from his waist to below his knees. His grubby long johns lay in a heap on the floor.

"He had to go into town."

"Who else is here?"

"Twyla. She's our cook now."

"Where are the hands?"

"Out on the range, I suppose." She looked at him with a perplexed frown. "Except for Tonio. He's in town getting your prescriptions filled. And then there's Mark. He's driving Dad this morning. Why? Are we playing twenty questions for some reason?"

Jake refused to meet her gaze. He refused to bring his eyes anywhere near her, in fact. "I need some help."

Lexi twitched her finger and set the briefs to swinging. "Not with this, I hope."

"No, that part's taken care of."

"Was this just your imaginative way of unpacking, then?" She waved her hand toward the string of clothes along the hallway.

"Yes, as a matter of fact," he answered tartly. "They started falling, and when I bent down to get them, I was unpleasantly reminded that I can't bend."

She suppressed a wince, instantly ashamed at her own insensitivity. "I would have unpacked for you," she offered gently.

"I don't *want* to unpack," he snapped, shoving his fingers through the springy tangle of his hair. "I just want to get dressed and get the hell out of here. Is that okay with you?"

"Fine." Smarting from the sting of his reply, she snapped right back at him. "Get dressed. Get the hell out of here. See if I care. But don't expect any help from me."

"Well, don't throw a snit fit. I didn't ask to come here, you know."

"I know it!" Guilty, angry and frustrated, Lexi wadded up his underwear and threw it at him, then turned on her heel and stormed up the hallway, trampling his scattered clothes in the process.

"In fact," Jake shouted after her, "I specifically remember *refusing* to come with you. Yet *somehow* while I was unconscious—"

Unable to leave his tirade unanswered, she whirled once again, entangling her boot in one of his shirts as she did so, and charged back toward the bedroom.

"You managed to bring me here," he finished at full volume.

With the shirt dragging behind her, Lexi stomped through the doorway and into the room. "Well, have you got a better idea? Because if you do, I suggest you cough it up, mister."

"You could have left me right where I was!"

"Nobody there wanted you! Louanne said you could go to hell, and Aaron's the one who carried you to my car."

"He did?"

"Yes, he did."

"I'll kill him," Jake snarled.

"Not until you can at least dress yourself, you won't," she said, breathing hard as she glared back at him in a face-off.

"Why don't you unwrap that shirt from your boot and toss it to me?" His question was voiced in a gritty rasp unexpectedly devoid of anger.

"Wouldn't you prefer a clean one?" With her temper cooling as quickly as his had, Lexi involuntarily raked her eyes over the long, firm expanse of his body.

Everywhere she looked, tanned skin stretched taut over muscles that rippled and flexed with the slightest movement he made. Wondering why she suddenly felt so lightheaded, she tore her gaze away and untangled the shirt from her boot.

"That one will be just fine, thank you," he answered.

Pulling the wrinkled shirt free, Lexi tossed it to him, only to watch it float to the floor three feet short of the bed and Jake's outstretched arm. In silence they both stared at the shirt as if it were a snake, coiled and ready to strike.

"Damn," Lexi muttered softly.

"Think you could move a little closer and try that again?" Jake asked with an acid edge returning to his voice.

"You know, for a man who isn't even capable of dressing himself, you'd think you could be a little nicer." Marching over to the shirt, she scooped it up and held it in her clenched fist. "How are you planning to get this on over that right shoulder?"

"I can manage."

"And how about that makeup? Are you intending to wear it until Halloween?"

"I might. Have you got any better offers? You want to help me take it off?"

"I might, if you asked real nice."

"Well, then how about a sponge bath, Lexi? I could use one of those, too." His voice grew dangerously husky. "Would you give me one of those if I asked real nice?"

The last two words came out in a seductive rasp that left her breathless even though she knew he was only baiting her. "I might."

"You wouldn't," he said, daring her.

"Well, you're going to need one sooner or later, and you certainly can't do it for yourself. You can barely move."

"Lexi, I was kidding."

"Well I'm not," she said, warming to her subject. "You're already starting to smell a little ripe, you know, and it's only been one day."

"You are *not* going to give me a sponge bath."

"Would you rather Twyla did it? Or one of the ranch hands?"

"No!" he shouted indignantly. "I'm perfectly capable of taking a shower by myself."

"I don't think you should get those bandages around your ribs wet. Not until you've got another doctor who can redo them or who can show me how to."

His voice softened. "Lexi, you're dreaming. I'm not going to stay here. As soon as I'm dressed and packed, I'm leaving."

"Today?"

"Yes, today. This morning if I can manage it."

"Well, that's just great." She opened her hand and let the shirt fall to the floor at his feet. "Okay, have it your way." Turning her back on him, she started toward the door. "Get dressed. And after you've done that—" she stopped with her hand on the door frame and looked at him over her shoulder "—I'll be more than happy to drive you and your bags to the airport in Albuquerque."

No longer even remotely gentle, he glowered at her as he demanded, "Come back here!"

"Why?" Except for lifting one eyebrow, she didn't move.

"I can't reach my shirt."

"Oh," Lexi said sympathetically, "that's too bad, isn't it? How will you ever manage on your own?"

"You can't make me stay here." He slid his bare toes under his shirt and pulled it closer to his outstretched arm, but not close enough to reach the shirt without bending.

"No, I can't," she agreed in the same sweet tone. "But then I don't have to *help* you, either, do I? Why don't you just come and get me when you're ready to leave?" She waved her hand vaguely toward the front of the house. "I'll be in the kitchen helping Twyla."

CHAPTER FIVE

WITH A BENIGN parting smile Lexi left, stepping carefully over his strewn clothes as she made her way up the hall. Inside her a small, guilty voice chided her for deserting him when he was so helpless, but Lexi sternly ignored it. With a man as infuriatingly stubborn as Jake, she was justified. After all, what she was doing was for his own good.

"Lexi!" Like a mighty clap of thunder her name rolled over her, threatening to shake the walls and rattle the windowpanes. "Get back in here and bring me a pair of pants when you come!"

Putting aside her argument with herself, Lexi turned and stared at the open doorway of Jake's bedroom. "Have you got your shirt on yet?"

"Hell no!"

Hot on the heels of his shout, the man himself appeared in the doorway. The veins on the sides of his neck stood out with the force of his frustrated anger. Wearing nothing but a blue arm sling, bandages around his rib cage and a pair of low-cut, navy blue underwear, he was a showcase for bruises, scrapes and hard, sculpted muscles.

Unable to stop her roaming eyes, Lexi studied the length of his thighs, tapering to his knees—one perfect, the other with a slashing scar across it—and the sleek swell of his calves.

"Jake, you've had knee surgery," she said weakly as she stared at his narrow feet, which were so much paler than the rest of him.

"Yeah, and oddly enough I survived it without your help." He extended his good arm and pointed to the suitcase next to her. "If you're through gawking, would you kindly bring me a pair of jeans?"

Closing her eyes as she skimmed over the most temptingly forbidden part of him, she looked at his face. The bulging veins on his neck had returned to normal, but with the smeared, thinning greasepaint still blurring his features and the ground-in arena dirt becoming more and more patchy, Jake's face was beginning to resemble a bad imitation of Picasso at his most abstract.

"I don't suppose the word *please* is in your vocabulary?"

"Please," he obliged with acid clarity.

"Oh, that's a lot better," Lexi mumbled as she leaned over to retrieve a pair of his jeans. "We're making progress now."

Straightening with the pants in her hand, she looked at him.

"Do you think we could do something about your face?" she asked. "Talking to you with that makeup on is like talking to someone who's wearing sunglasses indoors."

Jake cocked a finger in the general direction of his luggage. "Get the blue bag." Then he turned and disappeared into his room, leaving only the lingering image of a trim backside and a beguiling set of dimples just above the low slung waistband of his underwear.

Lexi released her breath in a soft huff of appreciation before she realized what she was doing. Then, refocusing her anger, she saluted the empty doorway.

"Yes, sir. Right away, sir," she muttered under her breath while she bent to pull the blue canvas bag from under a clump of clothes. "You're lucky I'm a patient person, sir. Because you're *really* asking for it."

Bag in one hand and jeans in the other, Lexi reentered the bedroom in time to hear the toilet flush from behind the closed bathroom door. Almost immediately came the sound of running water.

"Where are the washcloths?" Jake called through the closed door.

"In the cabinet to the left of the sink," she shouted in reply. "What do I do with—"

He emerged from the bathroom, catching her off guard and causing what was left of her anger to fizzle.

"—these?" she finished, holding up the canvas bag and jeans.

Jake's scowling eyes raked over her, lingering on the jeans before returning to her face. "Well, hell, I guess there's no way around it. Modesty will just have to be damned."

"I think we've pretty much accomplished that," Lexi agreed weakly. "What's next?"

"I'll never get those jeans on by myself. You'll have to help me."

"Help you?"

Heat flamed in her cheeks, and she started to argue. Then she realized he was right. Jake would never get those pants on by himself. Thank goodness he was still wearing that stupid makeup. At least she wouldn't have to see his face while she pulled up his jeans for him. Consoling herself that it wouldn't be so bad if she just didn't think about it, Lexi set down the canvas bag and turned back to face him.

"Okay," she said with false serenity. "Should we start with socks?"

"I just want to get my pants on," Jake answered in a voice devoid of expression. His studied composure told Lexi he was no more comfortable than she was. Knowing that made her feel a little better. "Maybe you'd better sit down."

As he lowered himself onto the edge of the bed, Lexi knelt and spread the jeans at his feet. While he slipped his feet inside and she guided the pants up his legs, she couldn't help noticing the curved scar that ran from thigh to calf along the inside of his knee. The line was narrow and white—obviously several years old.

Jake's hand reached down to take one side of the jeans. His fingers brushed over hers, and she snatched her hand away as he stood and tugged the snug pants up over his thighs and onto his hips on the left side. Lexi caught the waistband on the right side and pulled until she found herself in a very uncomfortable position.

Suppressing a gasp, she released the pants and stepped back. Heat flooded her face, searing her as she rose hastily, only to find Jake regarding her with a look as stunned as her own must be.

"I think I can take it from here," he said in a voice that sounded strained.

"Sure thing." She dropped her gaze from his.

"Maybe, uh—" He cleared his throat. "Maybe you can get the cold cream out of that blue bag for me."

"Right."

Pivoting, she fastened her gaze on her goal and crossed to the blue bag at the foot of the bed. Unzipping it, she found a shaving kit.

"That's not it," Jake said.

He sounded pained, and Lexi turned automatically to see why. He stood with his left arm behind his back, tugging at the jeans, whose waistband seemed to be stuck halfway up his hips.

As she watched, Jake twisted slowly, reaching for a better grip with his fingertips while his lips peeled back from his teeth in a grimace. Lexi ached for him. She had never realized what a struggle it must be to pull on a pair of jeans without bending or twisting, especially a pair as snug as his were.

"Are you sure I can't help?" she offered hesitantly.

"Thanks, but I've almost got it."

He didn't sound like someone who almost had it. However, Lexi wasn't eager for another close encounter with Jake's private parts, so she turned back to the canvas bag and shuffled through the contents some more.

Shampoo. Styling gel. *Styling gel?* Lexi held up the tube and looked at it. Sure enough, that's what it was. Would wonders never cease? Dropping the gel back into the bag, she continued. Comb. Brush. Elastic knee brace. Elastic ankle brace. Another knee brace. Rubbing cream for aches and pains. Industrial-size bottle of aspirin.

Lexi glanced over her shoulder again and saw Jake attempting without much success to zip his jeans with one hand. Turning away, she hunched over the bag again, renewing her search for cold cream while trying to ignore her impulse to help.

"Sometimes it's easier if you lie down," she said without lifting her head.

"What?"

"Sometimes tight pants are easier to zip if you lie down." Her hand closed around a sweatband.

"Why?" Jake asked.

She laid the sweatband on the bed and went back to looking for the cold cream. "I don't know. It redistributes the weight or something." Cold cream in hand, she stepped back in triumph.

Jake lay flat on his back on the mattress, tugging helplessly on the zipper, which had barely moved an inch from the bottom of the placket. He turned his head toward her.

"Somehow I have a feeling that even when lying down a person still needs two hands to do the job. I don't suppose you—"

Lexi stared at the wedge of navy blue beginning just above his groin and ending just below his exposed belly button. "Not on your life," she said with conviction.

"Come on, damn it, Lexi. I can't do this by myself."

Her gaze crept from the helpless anger in his green eyes, past the band of tape across his ribs to the flat, hard stomach below. "Don't you have any sweatpants we could have put on you instead?" Lexi demanded.

"No."

"Well, I think we're going to get some."

"You're still assuming that I'm staying."

"You know, I think probably the only thing worse than not being able to zip your pants when you *want* to would be not being able to unzip your pants when you *need* to. Of course, I guess you could always wait until some other guy came into the men's room and ask him to help you."

"Not on your life," he said, tossing her words back at her.

"Oh well, that's your problem."

Irritated once again by his stubborn refusal to cooperate or even to listen to reason, Lexi no longer cared about the intimacy of the situation. She'd zip his pants for him if that's what he wanted. Then she'd let *him* worry about what he was going to do after that.

Moving over to stand between his knees, she leaned forward and grabbed the waistband of the jeans and pulled it together. Then, holding it closed, she took the zipper tab between her fingers and, ignoring the denim bulge below, tugged upward with a sharp snap.

At the same time, Jake sucked in his breath in a soft gasp and angled forward as much as his cracked ribs would let him. "Okay, thank you," he rasped, struggling to rise onto his elbow. "That's just fine."

"Don't you want me to button them?"

"No, thanks." He sat up and draped his arm across his lap. "I can do everything else by myself just fine. Thanks."

"I seriously doubt that." She picked up the sweatband again. "You ever try to get on one of these with one hand?"

Jake's eyes narrowed and his voice dropped to a growl. "You're really enjoying this, aren't you?"

Lexi shook her head. "I'm just trying to make a point, Jake. You're not helpless, but your abilities are limited. And they probably will be for the next week or two. If you'll just quit trying to pack your bags and run away, I'll—" She stopped and groped for a nice way to say what she'd been doing, but she couldn't think of one. "I'll stop trying to rub your nose in it."

"I would appreciate that no end."

"Are you in pain?"

"Yes."

"A lot?"

"Yes."

She hooked her thumb toward the hall. "I've got the pills the doctor prescribed for you. I'm sorry. I should have remembered them sooner."

Jake shook his head. "Maybe later. Right now I'll just take a couple of aspirin." He pointed to his bag and Lexi quickly retrieved the giant bottle she had seen earlier.

"Are you sure?" she asked, shaking out two of the 500 mg tablets. "The doctor wouldn't have prescribed them if—"

He shook his head again. "I don't like pills. Plain old aspirin and horse liniment get me through most everything."

She handed him the aspirin and brought a paper cup of water from the bathroom. "You sound just like Dad."

"I'll take that as a compliment." Jake handed her the paper cup and pointed to the cold cream. "I guess you're going to insist on helping me with that."

"Well, I could leave you on your own and come back around suppertime to see if you're through yet."

"Very funny."

Without waiting for his permission, Lexi took the sweatband, put it on him and pushed it into place to hold his hair away from his face. Then she smeared cold cream across his face. Tipping up his head, she ignored the defiant eyes that bored into her and began to massage the cream into his skin with her fingertips.

When the worst of the dirt and makeup was loosened, she took a tissue and began to wipe away the layer of cream and debris. Refusing to look at the face she had uncovered, she began to reapply a second coating of cream.

"What are you doing?" Jake asked, jerking his head away from her hand.

"Maybe you didn't take a good look at your face." She caught his chin in one hand and held his head steady while she smoothed a clean white layer over his face once more. "Now you just sit still a minute, because I'm not through yet."

She gathered up the tissues she had tossed onto the floor and dropped them into a wastebasket on her way to the bathroom. There she wet a washcloth in warm water and returned to drape the cloth over his face.

"Mmm," Jake sighed. "Nice."

Lexi didn't answer. Instead, she pressed the cloth against his skin, starting with his forehead and moving down to his chin. Massaging with her fingertips through the cloth, she thought of the changes time had wrought.

What had been a lean, hard body when Jake was younger had become more defined, more powerful and even more masculine with age. His face had been a healthy, youthful type of handsome, with good bones and a strong jaw. What had set him apart were those cat green eyes and lips that were slim, expressive and sensual.

Even under the makeup, Lexi had seen that his eyes and lips hadn't changed, although their impact seemed to have strengthened with maturity. As for the rest, she didn't even want to think about it. When she removed the cloth, she turned without ever taking a real look at the results.

In the bathroom, she dropped the washcloth into the sink and leaned against the counter. She was ashamed of herself, but if there had been a back way out, Lexi would have taken it. All morning Jake had been trying to leave, while she'd thrown up every roadblock she could think of to make him stay. Now here she was, hiding in the bathroom, afraid to go back out and take a good look at his face.

"You know," Jake said from what could only be the bathroom doorway, "it's hard to believe that after all we've been through together this morning, you can't look at me without my clown face on. It seems a little kinky to me, Alexandra, but if you really like me better that way, I can always put it on again."

Lexi turned to face him, but her gaze stopped at his chest. "I don't know what you're talking about."

"Look at me, Lexi."

Her eyes inched up to his collarbone and fixed on the hollow of his neck, where she could see a faint pulse beating.

"I've been looking at you since last night," Jake said in a quiet voice that made each word sound seductive. "Now look at *me*, damn it."

Defiance flashed in her cinnamon eyes, and she glared at him. "Okay. I'm looking."

"Good." His lips parted slowly in a soft invitation. "You don't want me here any more than I want to be here, do you?"

Trapped by the challenge in his narrowed eyes, Lexi tightened her grip on the counter behind her. Giving in finally, she inched her gaze away from his and found herself captured by the compelling portrait time had drawn.

"I can be out of here today," he offered.

"No."

If she had never seen him before, she would have found him unforgettable. Once merely handsome, his face was stronger, the planes sharper, the hollows deeper. Character was etched in every rugged, sensual line.

His mouth twisted into a mocking smile. "There *are* people who would take me in, Lexi. Louanne isn't the only woman I know."

Stiffening at the thought, Lexi was as instantly and irrationally jealous as she had been the previous night. "Even so, that wouldn't solve Dad's problem, now would it?"

"Do you honestly think this is going to work?"

"It doesn't have to work for long. As soon as Dad is sure you're staying, he'll have his surgery. And in a week or so, you should be able to get your own pants on and off without anybody else's help."

Jake shook his head and a genuine, if grudging, smile softened the hard lines of his face. "You sure have grown up, haven't you?"

"I think it would be best if we didn't get personal, don't you?" Lexi asked.

"Are we just going to pretend that nothing ever happened between us?"

"We were friends. Let's leave it at that."

His gaze raked over her with a frankness that made her skin tingle and her pulse quicken. "That'd be a whole lot easier if you were just a little less beautiful."

"Maybe you should just *think* things like that and not say them out loud," Lexi suggested in a cool tone that in no way reflected the tempest in her soul.

The longer she looked at him, the more she ached for him to touch her. The very thought of his kiss left her faint. And she could never, ever let him guess the yearning he was arousing in her. He had loved her and left her once already. She didn't think she could survive it a second time. She was an idiot for even thinking about it.

"So." She pushed away from the counter and marched across the bathroom, heading straight for the small space of the doorway he wasn't filling. "Is there anything else I can get for you before I get back to my chores?"

Jake stepped back and gave her room to pass.

"A shirt would be nice," he said. "I guess I'd better take a look at what I'm supposed to be doing around here."

"Dad should be home anytime now." Retrieving the shirt Jake had kicked across the room, she came back to stand in front of him.

Her eyes were level with his chest as she fixed her gaze on the sling that protected his right arm and shoulder. She had lied earlier. He didn't smell bad at all. He smelled like a man, all warm and strong and maybe just a little salty. At the moment it was a very attractive scent.

"How are we going to do this?" she asked, lifting the shirt toward the sling.

"I'm going to...very gently..." He sucked in his breath as he slipped his arm from the sling and instantly caught it to his body with his left hand. He let out his breath in a sigh, and tiny beads of sweat formed a dewy sheen across his shoulders and chest.

"Oh, yeah," Lexi said softly. "This is going very well."

"Just slip that sleeve up over this arm," Jake rasped. He held out his right hand while he continued to support the arm with his left hand.

As delicately as she could, she slid the shirtsleeve over his hand and onto his arm. Inching the sleeve upward, she looked into Jake's strained face, wishing there was a way to make this easier and knowing there wasn't. When the task was finally done, she pulled the two halves of the shirt together in front of him while Jake eased his arm back into the sling.

"Where'd you say those pain pills were?" he asked in a voice that was reed thin.

"Out in the hall. On a table."

"I might try just one."

She glanced at his face and wished she hadn't. Grooves etched by pain lined either side of his mouth. The tip of his tongue raked his bottom lip. But his eyes gazed down at her with an intensity that had nothing to do with pain, and Lexi's stomach plunged like a roller coaster dropping over a peak.

"I'll get it."

She turned quickly toward the door, but not quickly enough. Jake's hand closed over her arm, stopping her and pulling her back.

"Lexi."

No, no, no! her mind shouted. Having Jake back was worse than she had ever imagined. It was driving her crazy. And it shouldn't be. She was over him. She'd been over him for a long time.

"I'll get it myself," he said. "If you'll just help me with these buttons."

"Buttons?" Slowly she pulled back.

"I'm afraid I don't make a very good invalid. It's a little humiliating to have to keep asking for help with the smallest things."

"Like buttons."

"Yes." His mouth softened into what was not quite a smile. "Please."

Grateful he couldn't read her mind, Lexi moved closer. The hair on his chest brushed her knuckles as Jake drew in a slow breath as far as his bandages would allow. "I should be able to do this myself in just a few days, a week at the most."

Finishing her task, she stepped back with a sigh that was more audible than she intended. "I'll be in the kitchen if you need me." She turned and started toward the door before he could think of anything even more embarrassing for her to do.

"Actually, I'm getting pretty hungry." He followed her. "Is it too late for breakfast?"

"Well, Twyla's probably got lunch ready by now, but there should be something left over from this morning. I'm going that way if you want to come along."

"No." He stood in the doorway as if reluctant to step over the threshold. "I'll be there in a minute. You go ahead."

Lexi hesitated, then started down the hallway toward the front of the house. If Jake's presence rattled her, she knew that being back here again must have him twice as rattled. She didn't blame him for needing some time alone. None of this was going to be easy for anyone.

Jake watched her walk away. With his left hand, he rubbed the row of buttons down the front of his shirt, remembering the feel of her hands as they had brushed his skin. Thank God she'd stopped when she did. He'd been one button away from lift-off.

—

CHAPTER SIX

By THE TIME JAKE WANDERED into the kitchen, his body
had returned to a low simmer. A quick glance around
told him Lexi wasn't there, which should have been a relief. Instead he was gripped by an irrational spasm of ir-
ritation.

While he pondered his next move, the plump woman
at the kitchen counter pulled her fist from the swollen
mound of bread dough she had been kneading and
glanced over her shoulder.

"Well, hello there. I thought I heard someone come in.
Are you hungry?"

Her round face greeted him with a sunny smile that he
couldn't help returning as he nodded. "Very."

"Well then, we'll have to feed you." She spread a
checked cloth over the dough and moved the bowl to the
end of the counter next to the stove. "Why don't you sit
down and I'll make you something to eat? My name's
Twyla, by the way. Twyla Donaldson."

"Pleased to meet you." He eased himself into the
comfortable Windsor chair at the end of the old pine
harvest table. "I'm Jake Thorn."

"Oh, I know who you are," she said, pulling contain-
ers from the refrigerator. "Frank's been in a dither for
months waiting for you to get here."

"For months?" Jake asked blankly.

"Sure. But he had to wait for the right time to send Lexi after you. He knew she'd take as much convincing as you would."

As she talked, Twyla carved a sizable slab of roast to reheat and put it in a pan along with a generous ladling of broth. She slid the pan into the already hot oven.

"I know he'll be right relieved to have you here finally," she went on as she put two pots of vegetables atop the stove to heat. "I was starting to get a little worried myself for fear Frank was going to cut it too close and keel right over before he made it into the hospital."

Twyla paused to push a lock of graying hair from her forehead with the back of her wrist. "But you're here now, and I guess everything's going to be all right."

"I hope so." Jake could smell the roast heating up in the oven and his stomach knotted in hunger. "Though I'm still not sure I'm really needed."

"But of course you are." Twyla's round blue eyes pinned him with a look of uncompromising honesty. "Frank Conley thinks the world of you, and he'd trust this ranch to no one else. Why, I can't tell you the number of times he's sat right there—" she nodded toward a chair at the other end of the table "—and told me how much he regrets ever letting you leave. Don't you doubt it for a minute, Mr. Thorn. You're needed here."

A little overwhelmed, Jake watched in silence as she dished up the hot roast and vegetables. She smiled as she set the plate in front of him.

"But then, I'm an old woman, and maybe I talk too much."

"Oh no, not at all. I—I appreciate everything you've said."

"What'll you have to drink? We've got iced tea if you'd like."

"That would be fine." A dozen questions buzzed through his mind as she poured the tea. She wasn't such an elderly woman, in her late fifties at the most. "You and Frank seem to be very close," Jake said cautiously as he took the tea from her hand.

"Well, I've been widowed for almost ten years now, and I've been working here for most of that time. So I guess he and I have come to know each other pretty well."

She said no more on the subject, and Jake didn't press, though he did wonder just how close she and Frank were.

Retrieving a hefty bowl of green beans from the back porch, Twyla joined Jake at the table and began snapping the beans.

"So, Mr. Thorn, I understand that your father was the foreman here for quite a number of years."

Caught with a mouthful of roast, Jake chewed vigorously and swallowed hard before answering, "Yes, from the time I was about thirteen. When he retired, I took over the job for another three years."

"And your mother worked here as cook for a while, I understand?"

Jake nodded. "For about six years."

His parents had gone to work on the Lazy C as a couple. His dad was the foreman; his mother was the cook. Jake himself had worked summers and weekends as a ranch hand all through high school.

"Once I started making enough money on the rodeo circuit, I talked Mom into quitting. But Dad never would, even after I bought the Johnson place next door. He'd live there, but he kept working for the Lazy C, right up until his health forced him to retire."

Twyla nodded her understanding. "I bet he was right proud to have you take over as foreman after him."

"Yeah." Jake stabbed a chunk of potato and chewed vigorously. "But he didn't stick around long to watch. After I got married, my parents moved to Florida."

Her fingers snapping the beans with the smooth rhythm of long experience, Twyla said, "I was sorry to hear about their passing."

"Thank you."

It was all he said—all he could think to say. Even after five years, the feeling of loss was overwhelming. His parents had died only six months apart. They had been good people, and good friends, and Jake missed them dearly.

"I would love to have met your mother. Lexi talks of her often." Twyla stood and picked up her bowl. "Well, now I'll let you finish your meal in peace. I've got to go out and work in my garden for a bit while that dough finishes rising."

He roused himself from the melancholy mood that had gripped him. "Oh, speaking of Lexi, do you know where she is?"

"Gone down to the barn to fetch her father, I expect. It's time for his lunch."

"I guess it's later than I thought." Jake cast around for a clock but saw none. His watch was packed away with his makeup.

Twyla smiled as if reading his mind. "It's a little after noon. We thought it best to let you sleep this morning." She put the bowl on the kitchen counter. "Well, it's been a pleasure to meet you finally, Mr. Thorn."

He stood. "Call me Jake, please. And the pleasure's all mine. Your food is excellent. I think my mother and you would have been very good friends."

"Since that can't be, perhaps you and I will be friends instead." With a twinkle in her eye, Twyla Donaldson picked up her basket and clippers and headed for her garden.

Jake sat down again to finish his meal, at home in the comfortable kitchen where he had once sat at this very table watching his mother turn out food to feed an army of ranch hands. He had forgotten what it was like to feel at home somewhere.

He would never admit it to Lexi, but it was good to be back, if only for a while. It was like coming home again.

"HI, MOM!" JAMIE SHOUTED as the heavy front door slammed closed behind him.

Seated at the desk in the front parlor, Lexi jerked, and her pen zigzagged across the check she was writing. She drew in a slow, calming breath, then released it with a sigh before she turned to smile at her rumpled, wind-blown son.

"Hi, sweetheart. You're home early today."

Jamie entered the room and tossed his book bag into a Victorian lady's chair covered in cranberry velvet. "Where is everybody?"

"Your grandpa's in the kitchen with Jake, and Twyla's gone down to the bunkhouse to start supper for the hands." Lexi smiled and batted her eyelashes innocently. "But I guess it was Jake you were really asking about, wasn't it?"

"Yeah. When can I meet him?"

"I don't think I've gotten my after-school hug yet."

"Okay."

Grudgingly, Jamie edged closer. Two years ago he had outgrown kisses, blushing and squirming furiously if anyone gave him so much as a peck on the cheek. Recently, he had begun to shy away from hugs, as well. Afraid to push her luck, and grateful at least that he no longer insisted she call him James, Lexi gave him a quick squeeze and released him.

Jamie took a step back and pinned her with an intense stare. "When can I meet him?"

"Well, I think they're talking business right now." She hesitated, worried by Jamie's eagerness. She didn't want him to be disappointed or hurt by Jake's sometimes mercurial moods. "You do realize that Jake's going to be a little surprised when he meets you?"

"Why?"

"Well, he doesn't know I have a son."

An indignant scowl contorted Jamie's face. "You mean you haven't even mentioned me?"

"You have no idea what today has been like." She passed a hand over her brow, exhausted just by the memory. "We spent the entire morning arguing about whether or not he was even going to stay."

Still indignant, Jamie demanded, "Didn't you tell him how much we need him? And how much we want him here?"

"No, actually, I don't think I did. I guess maybe I should have let you stay home from school and take care of it for me."

"Yeah."

She wanted to hug him then, to gather him close and hold him to her heart. He was such a little man sometimes, so ready to take charge. But he was still just a boy, a tender, vulnerable little boy, though she would never tell him so. Jamie thought of himself as very grown-up.

Controlling her protective instincts, she tapped the end of his nose gently with her fingertip. "My little guy."

His face wrinkled in disgust. "Mom."

Lexi laughed. "You want to meet him?"

"Yes!" he answered, practically shouting in his excitement.

She rose from her chair. "Just remember, he's still kind of skittish. Don't do anything to spook him."

Jamie screwed up his face, clearly confused. "Like what?"

Realizing she had no simple answer, Lexi shrugged and shook her head. "Ignore me. I don't know what I was thinking."

She hooked her arm over his shoulder and led him to the kitchen, where Jake and her father sat talking across the old harvest table. The low mumble of their voices stopped as she and Jamie entered.

"Jamie, you're home early." Frank's face lighted up at the sight of him. He motioned Jamie closer. "Come give your grandpa a big hug."

A little jealously, Lexi watched her son go to his grandfather without hesitation. Maybe hugs were only embarrassing when they came from mothers. She was still smarting from the thought when she looked from Jamie's willing embrace of his grandfather to Jake, who was staring at her with nothing short of shock. She felt herself flush at the thought of the explanations to come.

Reluctantly Jake dragged his gaze away from her, managing to wipe the surprise from his face before his eyes met Jamie's. Nestled in the curve of his grandfather's arm, the little boy smiled shyly at the man who was his hero.

"Hi," Jamie said simply, all his bravado gone.

Maternal pride swelled in Lexi. "Jake, this is my son, Jamie. Jamie, this is Jake Thorn."

"Jamie." Jake said the name softly, looking the boy over from head to toe. "Pleased to meet you, son," he said, motioning to his sling with his left hand. "Sorry I can't shake."

"Aw, that's all right." Jamie still leaned against his grandfather. "You're gonna be here awhile, aren't you?"

Lexi cringed, and her father frowned as he looked at Jake sharply.

"Jake hasn't quite made up his mind about that, Jamie." Frank turned to his grandson and his face softened. "Why don't you and your mom give us a little more time alone to talk about it?"

"Sure," Lexi said, holding out her hand to Jamie. She carefully avoided meeting Jake's eyes. "I'll just need my kitchen back in time to fix supper."

"Why don't we have pizza tonight instead?" Frank asked. "You and Jamie can run into town and pick it up while Jake and I finish hashing things out."

"Yeah!" Jamie said, practically airborne with enthusiasm. "That's a great idea. How about it, Mom?"

The idea of a twenty-mile trip into Santa Fe just to pick up pizza didn't send Lexi into paroxysms of joy, but she knew her father must have a reason for the request. Maybe he wanted an hour alone with Jake and knew this was one sure way to get it. Or maybe Frank just wanted one last pizza binge before checking into the hospital. Either way, she didn't have much choice.

"How about you, Jake?" Frank asked. "Pizza okay with you?"

"Sure." Jake began a slow, painful attempt to rise. "Just let me get my wallet."

Lexi fought the urge to push him back into his seat. She couldn't think of any way to do it without hurting him. "Oh, good grief, Jake. Sit down. Meals come with the job."

"I haven't agreed to take the job," he snapped as he lowered himself carefully into the high-backed Windsor chair.

"We'll still feed you. It's the least we can do."

"Thank you very much," he said stiffly.

Lexi turned and left, dragging Jamie with her.

Frank frowned across the table at Jake. "I seem to remember the two of you getting along better than that at one time."

"Don't beat a dead horse, Frank," Jake said wearily. He couldn't seem to stop himself from being snappish around Lexi. Just being in the same room with her made him want to run for high ground. "Now, what were you saying just before they came in?"

"I was saying that there's a problem. I can't figure out what it is, but I know it's there. The economy's been tough on everybody lately, and the Lazy C's no exception, but it's more than that. The ranch has lost money the past two years, and it shouldn't have. There's something wrong somewhere."

"Frank, if you couldn't figure out where the problem is, how can I? It's your ranch."

"I don't know. Maybe I'm too close to it to see clearly. Maybe you can sift through things and catch something I overlooked."

"How about Lexi? Does she have any ideas?"

"No!" Frank practically shouted. "She doesn't know anything about it. And I don't want her to know anything."

Taken aback by the older man's vehemence, Jake watched him with a perplexed frown, noticing for the first time the unhealthy pallor of his old friend.

"Why?" Jake asked, wondering if he should be arguing with a man whose condition was so obviously unwell.

"She's got enough to worry about just taking care of the house and Jamie and a sick old man who can't take care of himself anymore. She doesn't need to be worrying about what's going to happen to her and Jamie if I lose this ranch."

"Oh, come on, Frank. You know what this place means to her. Don't you think she's got a right to know if it's in danger?"

"No. With your help, we can get this fixed," Frank argued stubbornly. "She never has to know."

"Well, just for the record, I think you're wrong. But I know better than to waste my breath arguing with a fence post. So how about your foreman, McCauley? Has he got any ideas?"

"Brad McCauley has worked here for more than three years. He's been a good foreman, and I've never had any reason to suspect him of wrongdoing, but—"

Frank paused, and as the pause lengthened, Jake prodded him. "But?"

With a sigh, Frank went on. "But you're the only other living soul I've talked to about this, and until we get to the bottom of it, that's the way I want to keep it."

"Is that why you were so insistent on getting me here?"

"I trust you, Jake. If you were my own flesh and blood, I couldn't trust you more. And I know if anything happens to me, you won't let Lexi lose this ranch."

"Lord have mercy, Frank. Don't you think that's kind of a tall order? Especially considering the way I've screwed up my own life?"

"You didn't screw up your life, Jake. We screwed up your life. Dolores screwed up your life, and I wasn't much help to you at the time. Neither was Lexi, I suspect."

Jake wouldn't meet his gaze, and Frank went on. "I've got no right to ask you for your help, but I'm asking you anyway. I've got no right to expect you to do it, but I'd be mighty beholden to you if you would. I need you, Jake. Help me, son. Please."

Jake held up his hand. "All right. Stop," he said, as much to ward off his own emotions as to stem the flow of words. "Just stop, okay?"

He heaved himself to his feet in an effort that left him woozy with pain. The day had been long and trying, and as much as he resented his own weakness, it was time for another pain pill if he was going to last through supper.

At the door Jake paused and swung back toward the table. "When do you go into the hospital?"

"I'm hoping to put it off until next week."

Jake took a long, hard look at the older man and noticed his pallor had increased since they had begun talking. "We'll get started in the morning. You can show me everything you've got then, and I'll see what I need to have explained."

"Thank you, Jake."

"Don't thank me. I wouldn't be much of a man if I didn't do what I could. I only hope I can help."

"I know you can."

Jake shook his head. "I wish I deserved your faith. It's been a lot of years, Frank. People change."

OUTSIDE THE KITCHEN window, twilight faded to dusk and then to night. Inside, Lexi hummed along with the radio while she put away the last of the dishes and set a pot of beans on the stove to simmer. When she turned to go, she caught her breath in surprise at the sight of Jake lounging in the kitchen doorway.

Straightening, he padded into the kitchen on bare feet. "I thought we were having pizza."

"That's for tomorrow," she said with a nod toward the stove. "I make supper while Twyla feeds the ranch hands. The pizza's in the fridge, though, so if you're ready to eat, I can heat it up for you."

"If you wouldn't mind. All this inactivity is giving me an appetite." He lowered himself gingerly into a chair. "Where is everybody?"

"Dad's lying down. Jamie's upstairs doing homework."

"I guess I missed the party."

"Jamie wanted to wake you, but I thought maybe you could use the rest. I know it hasn't been an easy day for you." She put what was left of the pizza into the microwave. "You want some beer to go with that?"

"Sure would."

"Kind of figured you might." Smiling at him over her shoulder, Lexi took a bottle from the refrigerator. "I don't suppose you want a glass."

With a shake of his head, Jake rejected the idea. "I'm afraid it wouldn't be the manly thing to do."

His green eyes danced with a teasing light that Lexi remembered well, and her stomach reacted with a disconcerting flip-flop.

"Your microwave is beeping," he said with a lazy grin that somehow lent intimacy to his words.

Blushing, Lexi turned away to retrieve the pizza. She had to get a grip on herself. He was going to be around for weeks, maybe even months. She couldn't go all weak-kneed every time he got near her. Maybe they should go back to the old way of communicating—snapping and arguing with every other breath.

"Well," she said, putting a plate of pizza in front of him. "Here's dinner." She glanced around for something else to do.

"Aren't you going to have any?"

"I ate earlier." She glanced over her shoulder at the stove, then at the sink, the empty dish drainer and the already scrubbed counter. They offered no convenient distractions.

"Why don't you sit down anyway?" Jake's quiet question sounded more like an order than a request.

Lexi whirled to face him. "What?"

"We need to talk."

"Why?"

"Would you just sit down? Please?"

For an instant she considered refusing, then realized she couldn't act as if she were seventeen just because he made her feel that way at times. With a sigh, she pulled out a chair and sat facing him across the table.

"If you hate having me here so much, why did you work so hard to make me stay?" he asked quietly.

"I was afraid of what Dad would do if you weren't here at least until after his surgery."

"Well, at any rate you're honest."

With a shrug, Jake lifted his beer and took a long drink. When he put down the bottle, Lexi watched while he fought to lift and eat a limp piece of pizza with one hand.

Remorse nudged at her. At best, his life for the next few weeks would be anything but easy. The least she could do was to worry less about her own discomfort and be more aware of his.

"Look, I'm sorry," she said. "I know this isn't something you wanted to do, and I'm grateful that you consented. I'll try not to make things any harder for you than they have to be. This situation is awkward for everyone."

Wagging the pizza crust in his hand, Jake shot her a crooked, exasperated grin. "No. Just for you and me. Your dad's pleased as punch."

"I guess maybe Dad has different memories." Lexi jumped up and headed for the microwave. "You want another piece?" she asked, fixing a slice of the hot pepperoni for herself, after all.

"Sure." He motioned to the refrigerator. "Might as well grab yourself a beer and let's chow down."

Lexi did as suggested, bringing him a second beer while she was at it, and for the moment at least, the awkwardness between them eased.

"Do you think you're up to going into town tomorrow?" Lexi asked between bites. "Or do you trust me to find some clothes you can get into and out of by yourself?"

"Would that include shoes?"

"Sure. Maybe something simple you could just slip into."

"And a couple of pairs of sweatpants with elastic waists?" He seemed to be gaining enthusiasm.

She nodded. "That, too." Glancing up from her pizza, Lexi found herself caught by Jake's suddenly sober gaze. His hand moved toward hers, then stopped.

"I seem to be getting deeper in your debt by the minute." The intensity of his quiet voice said much more than his words.

"It's no problem," Lexi answered as her heart went into overdrive. Subtle currents eddied around them. "Really."

Hoping to hide the rapid increase in her breathing, she smiled, then picked up her empty plate and carried it to the kitchen sink. Facing weeks of being thrown together with Jake day in and day out, she simply had to get over her schoolgirl reaction to him. She wasn't Jake's girl. She never had been and she never would be. Dolores had seen to that.

"Lexi, are you married?"

Heat flamed in her cheeks as she reluctantly faced him. "No. Why would you ask?"

"You have a son."

"Yes." She reached behind her with a hand to anchor herself against the sink.

A thoughtful frown tugged at Jake's brow, and he was silent for a long moment before asking, "He's ten?"

"Yes," she said again, waiting for the question she knew was coming.

With obvious effort, Jake said, "Lexi—" He swallowed hard and tried again. "Lexi." Her name was almost a whisper, and the next words were even softer. "Is he mine?"

She leaned against the counter, feeling limp inside. This shouldn't be so hard.

"Lexi," he asked again, "did you have my baby?"

"No." The bitter sting of regret burned inside her. There had been a time when she had wished so much for exactly that—a time when she would have given anything for Jamie to be truly hers, hers and Jake's.

The awful tension in Jake's face softened for an instant and then returned. "Then Jamie is another man's?"

She shook her head, finding the words with difficulty. "He's— I— Jamie's not mine. Not by birth. He's adopted."

Surprise, relief, then amusement swept over Jake's face in quick succession. Finally he laughed. "Adopted." He combed his fingers through his hair, shaking his head. "And here I was thinking I went off and left you pregnant and never even knew it."

Stung by his reaction, Lexi wanted to burst into tears, to shout at him, to throw something. The son of a bitch was relieved.

"Sorry to scare you," she said in a tight, angry voice. "I guess I should have said, 'Meet my son, Jamie, and don't worry, you're not the father.'"

Perplexed, Jake sagged against the back of his chair. "Good grief, now you sound upset because I *didn't* get you pregnant."

"No. The last thing I would want is a child with a man who doesn't want him."

Still quaking inside, she turned her back and looked out through the window into the black night, her emotions rioting, and she wasn't sure why. All she knew was that she wanted him to care more, and he didn't.

"Lexi," Jake said softly. "You're not making any sense. Are you telling me the truth? Is he really not yours, or is this adoption story just a cover-up?"

She heard him leave his chair and move toward her. She knew that if he touched her, her fragile control would shatter. She had to stop him.

"Jamie's really not mine," she said, moving away from the sink to put more distance between them. "He really is adopted. And I don't want to talk about it anymore."

"Fine." Taking the hint, Jake stopped where he was. "It's just that I don't understand you, Lexi. Why would you adopt a child when you could have married and had one of your own?"

Lexi whirled to face him. "How dare you ask me something like that? Jamie is the most important thing in my life, and I don't owe an explanation of my love for him to you or anyone else."

Jake held up a hand to fend off her angry attack. "Sorry. I was out of line. It's just that with his age... Well, I just thought..."

"I told you, he's not yours," she snapped. "So count your blessings and drop the subject. All right?"

"Excuse *me*. I'll never mention it again."

"Thank you."

For a long moment, they stood glaring at each other, bristling with old and unspoken hurt. Then the anger in Jake's eyes melted away and he shook his head sadly.

"Really, Lexi," he said, softening before her eyes. "I'm sorry. He seems like a great kid. I guess meeting him just threw me for a loop. It got me to thinking and, well, my mind took me down some roads I haven't traveled in a while."

Lexi nodded. "I know. I've been traveling down some of those roads myself."

"Truce?"

She smiled to ward off the sadness that was engulfing her. "Sure. At least until tomorrow."

"I guess that's really the best we can hope for, isn't it?" he asked with a laugh. "See you in the morning?"

"See you in the morning," she agreed, still smiling as he turned and left the room. Once he was safely gone, she walked out into the night, released her breath in a sob and let the sadness come.

CHAPTER SEVEN

THE NEXT MORNING Lexi reached the bottom of the staircase in time to hear a loud thud followed by a cry of pain and a string of curses from behind Jake's closed door. Shoving open the door, she hurried into the room.

"What in the world—"

Lexi's words died in her throat when she saw Jake lying motionless, faceup across his bed. His eyes were closed, his mouth frozen in a grimace. A pair of blue jeans pooled at his bare feet, and he wore only the teal blue underwear she had found on the floor the day before.

"What have you done?" Her voice softened as she went to pick up the jeans.

Jake drew in a ragged breath and opened his eyes to narrow slits. He looked at her without answering.

Not intimidated, she continued just as softly, "Why didn't you call me if you wanted to get dressed?"

The grimace on his face turned to a scowl and the arch in his back slowly relaxed until he was resting flat on the bed. "I wanted to do it myself." He ground out the words between gritted teeth.

"But you can't." She lifted the jeans in her hand. "Not with these."

His whole body went stiff, and he let out another string of curses vile enough to turn the air blue. Lexi's eyes went round, and she took a step backward.

"I *hate* having to ask for help," Jake concluded in a growl that seemed to come all the way from his toes.

Going to the bedroom door, Lexi slammed it shut, then stormed back to stand over him. "I'll thank you to remember that a child lives in this house. I don't care how you talk when you're around your rodeo buddies, but in this house, mister, you watch your tongue."

Slowly the anger left Jake's face until the edges of his mouth softened into what was almost a smile. "Yes, *ma'am.*" On the heels of amusement came genuine contrition. "I wasn't thinking. Did he hear me?"

She shook her head. "Luckily, he's gone to school already. Now then..." She held up the pants that were clenched in her fist. "Do you need help with these or don't you?"

"Yes, ma'am, I reckon I do." He closed his eyes and heaved a sigh. "But I feel like a damn baby."

Slipping the jeans over his feet, Lexi pulled them up to his knees, and Jake took over. While he tugged and snaked his way into the pants, she went to the closet.

"Which shirt do you want today?"

Jake groaned. "Maybe I'll just do without until you get back from town. Do you think you can find me something sleeveless I can pull on over this sling without having to move my arm too much?"

"You mean like a tank top or a muscle shirt?" she asked, closing the closet door again. "It's a little late in the season, but maybe I can find something on sale."

"Great. Anything to get me through the next couple of weeks until this thing starts to heal some." He massaged the muscles of his arm above the elbow, moving as close as he could get to the damaged shoulder.

"Are those pain pills helping any?"

"I haven't taken one today."

"Maybe you should."

He shook his head with infuriating stubbornness. "I don't want to depend on something like that."

"Jake, the only reason you're not in the hospital is that the doctor knew you wouldn't stay. For goodness' sake, take the pills."

"Don't nag me, woman!"

Thoroughly irritated, Lexi flung her hands into the air. "Suit yourself. It's your life."

Jake bowed ever so slightly from the waist. "Thank you. It's so nice of you to remember that."

Her eyes narrowed and her mouth tightened into a frown. He was purposely goading her and she knew it, but she couldn't help reacting anyway.

"When you're ready for breakfast, Twyla's in the kitchen."

With that, Lexi turned and started from the room. She had reached the doorway and was fighting the urge to glance over her shoulder for one last glimpse of him, when she heard Jake's voice.

"Lexi."

She stopped but didn't turn. "What?"

"I need you."

Her heart thudded in her chest, and she turned in a graceful, slow-motion pirouette. He stood watching her, his unfastened jeans slung low on his hips as he clenched and unclenched the fist at his side.

Breathless with anticipation that she seemed helpless to fight, Lexi asked again, softly, "What?"

He gestured to the wide vee at the front of his well-worn jeans. Following the movement of his hand, her gaze crept from the flat, hard muscles of his stomach to the erotically intimate area beneath, which was thankfully hidden from view by faded, thinning denim.

He lifted his eyebrows in an unspoken question, and her thundering heartbeat took off at a full gallop. "What?" she asked one last time, not even sure she had said the word aloud.

"I can't do this alone," he said, indicating the gaping zipper and his exposed midsection. "And I can't go around like this all day."

The zipper. Of course. Remembering the ordeal of the previous morning, Lexi closed her eyes and stifled a moan. He wanted her to zip his pants. Her eyes slowly fluttered open again, focusing on the wall just to the right of him.

"Do you want to lie down?" she asked.

"Not if I can help it. You have no idea how bad it hurts just to get up off that bed."

She took a deep breath and let it out quickly. "Okay."

It was true she had no idea how much the simplest movements hurt him, but she had seen the lines of suffering etched on his face as the pain of exertion mounted. She had watched the sheen of perspiration build until his bronzed skin glistened. She had seen Jake turn away to hide the suffering he couldn't control.

Moving to stand in front of him, she pulled the two sides of his fly together with her left hand and delved into the recesses of denim until she clutched the metal tab of the zipper in her right hand. Then, with a sharp tug, she pulled upward and scraped the end of her finger on a protruding stub of metal.

"Ouch!" She lifted her index finger to her mouth and sucked the smarting fingertip.

"What happened?" Concerned, Jake leaned toward her until his face was directly above hers.

She pulled her finger from her mouth and shook her hand. "It's stuck."

"What's stuck? Did you hurt yourself?"

She sucked in her breath and rubbed the tip of her finger against the pad of her thumb. "It just stings." She shook her hand again, finally lifting her gaze to his. "The zipper's stuck."

Jake took her hand and turned it palm up in his. A red line slanted across the end of her index finger, but the skin wasn't broken.

"It's feeling better," Lexi said quickly. "It practically doesn't hurt at all anymore."

The corner of Jake's mouth lifted in a budding smile. "Sure you don't want me to kiss it and make it well?" he asked in a sandpaper rasp that made the suggestion sound utterly carnal.

A squadron of butterflies took off in formation across the pit of her stomach. "Jake." She meant to issue a stern warning, but his name came out in a shaky whisper instead.

"I still need those pants zipped." His green eyes burned down on her with an intensity that dared her to resist him.

Ignoring the tremor in her hands, Lexi grasped the zipper again. As she tugged at it, the knuckles of her clenched hand brushed over a hard bulge under the soft denim.

Jake's muffled gasp did nothing to calm the wild pounding of her heart, and as her struggle with the zipper increased, so did the pressure her knuckles exerted on his steadily swelling lower extremity. Shifting uncomfortably, he tried to pull away, but Lexi only tightened her grip.

"Stand still," she ordered.

"Look, it's okay. You can—"

"Listen, mister, you wanted these pants zipped, and you're going to get these pants zipped." Refusing to give ground, she continued tugging. "Now stand still."

"Oh Lord, could you please just hurry?"

"This was your idea," she said, puffing with exertion. "I don't know why you couldn't have just borrowed a pair of pajamas and a robe from Dad until I got back from shopping."

"I didn't think of it."

She pulled with all her strength, and the zipper finally broke free just as Jake's fingers brushed the hair at the side of her head.

"Lexi." The sound of her name was softer than a whisper, barely more than a thought half-spoken. His fingers slid around her arm, urging her closer. "Lexi," he said again.

She stepped back, away from the hand that would have drawn her nearer. His eyes glazed, his arm outstretched, Jake followed her, advancing a step for every one she retreated until her back was against the wall. Turning her head toward the open door less than a yard away, she slid along the wall toward her avenue of escape.

He reached out and slammed the door shut, then pressed the flat of his palm against the wall next to her head. "We've got to talk."

She stared at his chest, refusing to meet his eyes. "About what?"

"About us."

"There is no us."

"Yeah, right." He moved closer, until his thigh brushed hers. "That's why I had to ask you if I was the father of your child." His thumb gently stroked the curve of her cheek. His voice was a soft caress. "Because there is no us."

"Okay, so *once* there was something between us." She turned her head to evade his touch.

He caught her chin in his hand and tilted her face toward his. "Look at me." When she stubbornly resisted, he forced her head higher. "Look at me, I said."

"Let go!" she demanded between clenched teeth, glaring up at him finally with flashing eyes.

"Are you dating anyone?"

"That is none of your business!"

"There's a whole lot about you that seems to be none of my business. You know all about me," he said calmly. "Surely I have the right to know at least something about you."

"I hardly think that finding you in Louanne Byers's trailer constitutes knowing all about you."

"At least you know I've been sleeping with other women. All I'm asking is, have you been sleeping with other men?"

"How dare you ask me such a thing!"

"I admit I have no right to ask, but somehow while you were fumbling around with the front of my pants, it became a burning question in my mind."

"Well, you can just keep on wondering." She shoved his arm away from her. "Now unhand me before I'm forced to take a poke at those cracked ribs of yours."

His hand dropped to his side and he stepped back. "You *are* sleeping with someone, aren't you?"

"Whether I am or whether I'm not, it will *never* be any concern of yours." Sidling toward the door, she reached out to grasp the doorknob.

"Is he here on the ranch?" Jake persisted.

"Why?" She turned the knob and pulled the door open a crack. "Why would you even care?"

"I don't know." He shrugged, looking puzzled by his own actions. "Maybe because I was the first."

"Well, forget it. Whatever it is, just forget it. I didn't bring you back here so we could pick up where we left off."

"I know that."

"Whatever happened between us was a long time ago. We're not the same people now."

"I know that, too. But sometimes, in the dead of night—" his voice dropped to a silken whisper "—when the moon's full and you're all alone, don't you ever think about that night? Don't you ever wonder what it would be like now? The two of us, just one more time?"

Lexi flung open the door, turned and ran. Even after she was in her car and headed down the rutted dirt road that wound through the ranch, she was still running. She didn't stop running until she was halfway to Santa Fe.

"AH, BRAD." Frank rose and gestured his foreman into the parlor with a sweep of his arm. "I'm glad you're here. I was telling Jake all about you last night, and I know I don't have to tell you who Jake Thorn is."

Brad McCauley's eyes shifted from Frank to Jake and back to Frank. "Jake?" He shook his head. "I don't believe I've—"

"Aw, now I know you've heard of Jake," Frank said. "His dad was foreman here for almost fifteen years. Fifteen *good* years." He rested a hand on Jake's shoulder. "Jake himself was foreman for a while. He's an old friend of mine and an ex-son-in-law to boot."

"Oh, yeah," Brad said, extending a hand until he noticed the sling on Jake's right arm. He slowly withdrew his hand and let it fall to his side. "I believe you used to own the Circle T, didn't you?"

"Still does," Frank said brusquely. "I had a ten-year lease on it. That's up now." He gazed at Jake. "I'm just paying rent till Jake decides to move back home."

"Then I, uh—" Brad looked from Frank to Jake. "I guess I'm living in your home, Mr. Thorn. I hadn't realized."

Jake shrugged. "Better to have someone living in it than to have it sitting empty. I've got no plans for it right now."

"Oh?" Brad asked as his smile became almost genuine. "Are you just visiting, then?"

"Not exactly," Frank answered. "Jake'll be managing the place while I'm in the hospital."

"Managing the Lazy C?" Brad asked blankly. "I—I hadn't heard."

Frank smiled, looking pleased with himself. "Things happen fast sometimes."

"But I thought Lexi would be looking after things while you were gone," Brad said, a frown warring with his forced smile.

"You and Lexi been making plans for me, have you?" Frank asked quietly.

"Oh, no! No, sir. We had just speculated." Brad lifted his hands in a gesture of innocence. "That's all. Just thinking out loud. I'm sure this will work out just fine. Much better. It would have been an awful lot for her to do, what with looking after the house and Jamie and all."

"But if it had come to that, I'm sure you would have done all you could to help her," Jake offered with icy politeness.

"Oh, yes," Brad agreed. "I think a lot of Lexi. I already told her I'd do all I could."

"Well, I'm glad to hear that, Brad." Frank stood. "I'm sure you'll bring that same spirit of cooperation to helping Jake while I'm away."

"Oh yes, of course." Brad nodded and edged toward the door, realizing he was being dismissed.

Jake moved closer to Frank. "I'm happy to have met you, Brad. In a couple of days we'll get together and have a good long talk."

Brad replaced his hat on his head. "I look forward to it. Good day now."

He turned and left. Jake stood watching the closed door, feeling his gut churn. "Is it just me or is that man an oily snake?"

"He does give that impression sometimes, doesn't he? But he seems efficient at his job."

Jake's glance moved from the door to Frank. "What was all that about Lexi? Is there something between the two of them?"

Frank lifted one shoulder in a dismissive gesture. "They've dated a few times, but nothing will come of it if I can help it."

"That would have been quite a cozy little setup for him, wouldn't it? You in the hospital. McCauley working side by side with Lexi for weeks on end, maybe even months." Jake's eyes narrowed menacingly. "I'll bet he's fit to be tied right now, having me step in and ruin it all for him."

Frank smiled, a slow, wicked smile that spoke volumes. "You know, sometimes, Jake, I could swear you read my mind."

INSPIRED BY THE THOUGHT of another encounter like the one that morning, Lexi had brought a missionary zeal to her task of selecting new clothes for Jake. Never again would she have to zip him into skin-tight jeans. Never again would she have to feel the soft brush of his chest hair against her fingers as she buttoned his shirt. Never again would she have to fight her own reaction to the forced intimacy.

Still shaken from the images that seemed to be permanently burned into her brain, she had paid for her purchases and carried the bulging shopping bags to her car. Inside the bags were a multicolored variety of sweatpants that were easily donned with one hand and sleeveless undershirts with deep armholes.

The undershirts wouldn't cover much flesh, but they would make it easier for Jake to dress himself. The last purchase had been a pair of moccasins for him to wear around the house. With these things, Lexi would regain her freedom and, with any luck, her peace of mind. With her father going into the hospital, she might even be able to avoid Jake altogether for days on end. In no time at all, his stay would be over and he would be out of her life again, this time for good.

Lexi had waited for the sense of joy that the knowledge should bring, but it hadn't come. Instead, there had been sadness at the thought that she would never again see the forest green of his eyes or hear the sandpaper rasp of his voice when he was sleepy or angry or taunting—or aroused.

On the drive home she had been caught in a maelstrom of emotions, with all of her energy focused on trying to get Jake out of her head. But like an incorrigible jack-in-the-box, he just kept popping up again. Memories from the morning had swirled in her mind. Jake—his face grave but determined as he demanded answers to questions he had no right to ask. Herself—angry that he would intrude on her privacy and yet exhilarated that he would care.

Of course she had had lovers since him. Not many and not often, and none serious or enduring enough to marry, but she *had* gone on with her life. That he could make love to her once and then ask eleven years later if there had been others since smacked of an arrogance so profound she wanted to spit in his eye and shout, "Yes! Yes, I have had lovers!"

But it wasn't any of his business, and the truth was, she didn't want to tell him about the others because then she might be tempted to let slip that there had never been another like him. There had never been another who filled her heart and her soul, who haunted her dreams or who left her with a longing that never ended. There had never been another who could take Jake's place. They had come and gone, leaving barely a ripple on the surface of her life, while the memory of Jake had lived on.

Eventually she had stopped looking for someone to fill the void. It had been years since she had had more than a casual date with anyone. That was the truth of her life, a truth she would never tell.

Relieved to be home and no longer alone with her thoughts, Lexi pulled up in front of the garage just as Brad McCauley emerged from the shadows of the portal into the courtyard. Seeing her, he waved and walked to join her as she sifted through the shopping bags in the trunk.

"What are you doing here, Brad?" Lexi asked, setting the biggest bundle on the ground at her feet. "Have you been meeting with Dad?"

"And my new boss, Jake Thorn," Brad said with the barest trace of acrimony. "What do you know about him?"

"Goodness, Brad, surely you've heard of Jake." She looked at him with surprise.

"Yeah, I've heard of him, even if I wouldn't admit it in front of him. He's a rodeo rider and he used to be married to somebody in your family, but I don't know why that makes him able to run a ranch better than I can."

"Oh, I don't think Dad meant that, Brad," Lexi said, soothing the injured pride she knew Brad had hidden from her father. "It's just that Jake goes back a long way with this ranch. His dad was our foreman when I was a little girl, and his mother was our cook. Even after Jake bought the old Johnson place and married my older sister, he worked as our foreman for a while after his dad retired."

Brad frowned. "That still must have been a long time ago. What's he been doing since?"

Lexi shrugged. "I have no idea." And even if she did, it was none of Brad's business. "But I know Dad's been trying to find some way to get him back here for a long time." She laid her hand on the foreman's arm. "Just ride it out," she advised. "Jake won't be around long. He doesn't like being here any more than you like having him here."

The angry lines of Brad's face relaxed. "It's that obvious, huh?" he asked with a chuckle.

Lexi grinned. "Well, you weren't exactly mincing words for a minute there."

Brad laughed. "I'll try to be more careful in the future." He readjusted his hat on his head and stared at the toe of his boot for a second. "You have a date to the harvest dance yet?"

"No, not yet." She shook her head and wondered at her own lack of enthusiasm. "But I'm not sure I'm going. It kind of depends on how Dad's doing."

"Well, it's several weeks away. Maybe we can talk about it again when it gets a little closer."

"That sounds like a nice idea." She smiled encouragingly, relieved that she didn't have to make a decision yet. She had dated Brad a couple of times, but she had deliberately kept their relationship casual.

He nodded toward the bundle at her feet. "You need any help carrying that inside?"

"Oh, no. It's not much. I won't have any problem."

"Well then." He tugged at his hat in a parting salute. "I'll be moving along, I guess. I've got work to do, and I wouldn't want to get off on the wrong foot with the new boss."

"Don't let it keep you awake nights."

"Oh, I don't think it'll do that. I was around here before he came, and I imagine I'll be around here after he's gone."

With that, Brad climbed into his pickup, swung it in a wide circle and headed back down the road toward the cluster of buildings that included the barn and the bunkhouse.

From the shadows of the portal Jake watched with narrowed eyes and a mouth tight with anger. His gaze followed the pickup down the road. Maybe they were no more than two old tomcats circling each other, readying for a fight, but he hadn't liked the looks of Brad McCauley from the minute the man had strutted into the parlor acting for all the world as if he owned the place.

McCauley had said and done all the right things, but that hadn't been enough to convince Jake that Frank Conley was anything more than a weak old man in

McCauley's eyes—possibly a dying man with a pretty daughter who was unmarried and ripe for the plucking. Nothing Jake had just seen convinced him any differently.

When Lexi had laid her hand on McCauley's arm and stared up at him with those big brown doe eyes of hers, Jake nearly came unglued. Only the certain knowledge that a five-year-old could whip him to his knees in his present condition kept Jake from storming across the courtyard and yanking Brad McCauley right out of his boots.

Closing the trunk, Lexi lifted a shopping bag in each hand and started through the courtyard toward the house. Jake watched her come, taking in every detail, from the collar of the plain white shirt that stretched across high, full breasts to the cinched waist of the soft, faded, form-fitting blue jeans that emphasized her rounded hips and long, slender legs.

Her boot heels crunched in the gravel of the path as she drew closer, and Jake's gaze left the black tooled leather of her boots to travel up the length of her legs once more, past the seductive sway of her hips. He lingered on the rounded breasts that shifted gently beneath the cotton of her shirt with each step she took, drawing a slow breath before moving on to her face and the soft, full, shell pink lips that had haunted his dreams for longer than he could remember.

Her heels left the gravel and struck the Mexican tile of the porch. She was almost to the door when Jake stepped forward from the shadows.

"Are those for me?"

Gasping with surprise, Lexi dropped the biggest bag and fell back a step as she clapped a hand over her heart.

"Lord have mercy, don't *do* that," she said, still trying to catch her breath.

Jake almost smiled but stopped himself in time. "I didn't mean to scare you."

"How long have you been lurking there?"

"If you mean did I see you making goo-goo eyes at the foreman, yes, I did."

"That's not what I meant at all. And I don't appreciate being spied on."

He shrugged. "Your dad went in to lie down, and I came outside for some fresh air. The rest was just a happy coincidence."

"Happy for you, maybe," she said sharply as she gathered up the bag she had dropped and prepared to go into the house.

"Jamie's come and gone already." Jake reached out and took her arm. "Frank's in his room. Sit with me for a while." He nodded toward the chairs behind her. "Twyla's going to bring out some iced tea when she gets it made."

Lexi allowed him to take the bags and set them next to the door. "Twyla's still here? She's usually gone by now."

"She decided to stay until you got back, just in case one of the invalids needed something."

"You're hardly an invalid."

"She knows that, but I think she's the mothering kind. And it's sort of nice to be waited on, just a little. I don't get that a whole lot as a general rule."

"You mean Louanne wasn't the mothering kind?"

"Would you quit pestering me about Louanne? We were just friends, nothing more. As soon as the rodeo was over she was heading in one direction and I was heading in the other."

"And I suppose there would have been another Louanne waiting for you at the next stop."

"Probably." The look she gave him didn't quite mask her shock, and it irritated him that he felt compelled to defend himself. "Well, you asked. Hell, Lexi, I'm single, I'm on the road damned near all year, and a man gets lonely."

"It doesn't sound like you did."

"Just because you've got a warm body in bed beside you doesn't mean you're not lonely. A bed can get mighty cold, even with company."

"Why are you telling me this?" she asked in a small voice that made him want to reach out and wrap her in his arms.

Instead, he clenched his fists and stared off into the distance. "You asked."

"How was I to know you'd tell me the truth?"

He looked at her and knew in an instant that it had been a mistake. His eyes focused on her mouth. Her soft pink lips slowly parted and her breath hissed out in a sigh. Her lower lip, full and pouting, glistened with dewy moistness. Her lips were made to be kissed, nibbled, sucked, caressed and devoured.

When his mouth closed over hers, his heart slammed against his chest with painful fury. His hand held her head from behind while his mouth crushed hers, tasting and teasing and aching for more. When he finally had to stop for air, the tip of his tongue continued to caress the soft edges of her delectable mouth.

Renewed, he captured her lower lip once again, nibbling at it, tugging it gently with his teeth. His hand still cupped the back of her head, holding her captive as his kiss deepened. She moaned deep in her throat. Her back arched, pressing her breasts against his chest in a sweet agony of pain that was far outweighed by the pleasure of her response.

Moving closer, he increased the pressure of her body on his, reveling in the ripeness of her breasts, hot and full against him, while he ignored the sharpening pain that shot out like arrows from the center of his chest.

Wild with the ache that filled him, Jake caught her lower lip once again and drew it into his mouth, sucking tenderly, then releasing it to cover her lips with his in ravenous hunger, burning with the fires she alone ignited inside him. The throb in his loins grew to a dull roar that pulsed through his whole body.

He gathered her closer, twisting as he pressed her body flush against his. Lexi wrapped her arms around his middle and gave herself to him with a willingness that only fed his desire. Then the steady pains that had been slowly mushrooming inside him went off like rockets on the Fourth of July.

Jake's arm straightened, his fingers curling with the agony. He gasped for air that wouldn't come while a giant vise squeezed his chest and a thousand razors slashed at his insides, cutting off his breath, his reason and all conscious thought.

Deaf, dumb and blind with pain, he didn't even realize he had screamed until Lexi was standing over him, her face as white as a sheet.

"Jake!" she cried. "My God, what have I done? Are you all right?" She clasped his one good shoulder and shook him gently. "Say something."

"Oh Lord, shoot me. Please," he croaked.

"What is it? What?" she begged, almost frantic with worry.

As quickly as it had come the white-hot agony started to recede, and he began to breathe again. "I hurt," he said.

She held his hand and stroked his sweat-drenched face. "What have I done?"

"Nothing. I'll be okay in a minute." He was still woozy, but already the first mindless intensity of the pain was nothing more than a bad memory.

"What happened?"

"My ribs." He blinked and the world stopped spinning. "I guess bear hugs aren't a good idea until they've healed a little more."

"Should we get you to the hospital? Do you need a doctor?"

He shook his head and his lips curved into a lopsided smile. She was incredibly sexy, all soft and sweet and kitten cuddly one minute, then wild as a firestorm the next.

"Why are you smiling?" she asked, still visibly upset.

"I don't suppose you want to get back to where we were before I so rudely interrupted us?"

"How can you even ask that?" She drew back in horror. "I thought I'd killed you."

"I'm sorry."

"Are you sure you're all right?"

"All better." He stood, just to prove it to her, ignoring the low-level throb in his midsection. "I didn't mean to scare you."

"This is terrible! I must have been out of my mind. What was I thinking?"

"I don't think either one of us was thinking very much of anything for a few minutes there," Jake said gently.

He could see that he had genuinely frightened her, and he knew there would be no going back to the passion that had carried them away. Lexi put her hand to her forehead, looking puzzled and incredibly cute.

"How did that all happen anyway?" she asked. "I can't even remember what we were talking about."

"Neither can I. It probably wasn't anything of great importance."

"I—I think I should go in now."

He nodded toward the shopping bags sitting by the door. "Are all those for me?"

Lexi turned her head and looked at the collection of bags as if she'd never seen them before. She blinked and refocused. "All of them. I hope you're happy with what I picked."

"Oh, I'm sure I will be, except—" he let the word drag out "—I was sort of beginning to enjoy having you dress me in the mornings."

"Jake," she said with a warning frown, "that's never going to happen again." She stood. "And neither is what happened a few minutes ago."

Jake smiled. He knew the difference between wishful thinking and fact. "Never is a long, long time, Lexi."

"No one knows that better than I do, but until my father is well and home from the hospital, I have no intention of doing anything I might regret."

She was totally serious and, more than that, she was right. Jake nodded his agreement. "I can live with that."

"You can?" she asked, unable to hide her surprise, and possibly just a little disappointment.

"Sure. I've got a big job to do here, and you've got Frank to worry about and Jamie to take care of. We're both going to have our hands full. Besides—" Jake couldn't help grinning "—as we just proved so graphically, I'm too hobbled up to do anything but wish anyway."

She laughed, her dimples showing even in the shadows. "I guess that's right, isn't it?"

"It certainly is." Jake opened the front door for her. "So maybe we'll discuss this some more in about two weeks."

Lexi arched her brow skeptically. "We'll see about that."

"We certainly will," Jake agreed, ushering her inside. "We certainly will."

CHAPTER EIGHT

DEAD TIRED, Lexi pulled her car into the driveway and shut off the engine. Almost too woozy to move, she rested her head against the steering wheel and closed her eyes. Through the open window, she heard the familiar sounds of the night—the lowing of the cattle in the distance, the soft nicker of a horse, the dry rustle of the wind.

She was glad to be home. After nearly a week of camping out in the waiting room of the hospital's cardiac care unit, she was giddy with delight at the thought of a home-cooked meal and a good night's sleep in her own bed.

She was equally giddy with the knowledge that her father was recovering quickly from his surgery and would be moved to a regular room any day. Just a little longer and her life would be back to normal. Just a little longer...

"Lexi? Lexi, are you all right?"

A hand shook her shoulder, and Lexi struggled up through the gray veils of exhaustion that enveloped her.

"What? I'm here! Has something—" Blinking, she shook herself awake and realized she wasn't at the hospital. She was sitting in the front seat of her car in the dark, gripping the steering wheel with numb fingers.

"What?" she asked again. She slowly turned her stiff neck toward the open window beside her. Her tired eyes focused on the droopy waistband of a loosely tied pair of sweatpants.

Above the bare, narrow waist was a broad, newly bandaged chest and an unmistakable sling cradling the right arm. "Jake, you've been to the doctor." Lexi felt an instant pang of guilt. She was supposed to have taken him, and she had forgotten even to call.

"I got a ride. It was no problem." He opened the door for her. "Were you asleep?"

"I guess so." With an effort, she slowly dragged herself out of the car. "What time is it?"

"A little after ten. How long have you been here?"

"About an hour." She reached back inside for the overnight bag she had been living out of for most of the week. Jake took it and turned her toward the house.

"You've been out here asleep all that time?" He closed the car door and followed her along the gravel path through the courtyard. "You must be exhausted. I thought you were coming home yesterday."

"I had wanted to, but I decided to stay one more day, just to be sure Dad would be all right on his own. I promised him I'd bring Jamie up to see him in a night or two."

"Frank ought to get a kick out of that, and I know Jamie's dying to see for himself that his grandpa's really okay. I might even go with you. That is, if I wouldn't be in the way," he added, as if he sensed the sudden swarming of butterflies inside Lexi's stomach.

"Oh, no," she said in a higher voice than normal. "That would be just fine. I'm sure Dad's wondering how things are going." She rushed on breathlessly as she reached the front door. "Just so long as you don't let him get excited or upset about anything. But then you know not to do that."

Jake set down the overnight bag and caught her wrist as she opened the door. "Lexi, could we talk for a minute? Before we go in?"

Exhaustion clouded her brain like a heavy fog. Her defenses were down, and her emotions were frayed from too many days of watching and waiting and worrying.

"I'm so tired, Jake." She looked up at him, intending to plead with her eyes. Instead she found herself lost in the sight of him. Impossibly handsome, he stood there outlined against the moon. Why did he have to be everything she remembered, and more?

"It won't take long." He still held her wrist in his hand. "Something happened today."

As if suddenly remembering that he was holding her, Jake released her arm and stepped back, a halo of moonlight deepening the shadows that hid his eyes. "It's no big deal, really. I just wanted to tell you that it's okay. I'm okay with it."

"Okay with what? What happened?" The days she had been gone seemed like an eternity. She hadn't read a newspaper or watched television since her father had gone into the hospital. The world could be at war for all she knew.

Jamie! The thought ricocheted through her mind with a terror that turned her blood to ice and her legs to rubber. *Oh, dear Lord, no.* "Jamie!" she practically shouted. "Is Jamie all right?"

Instantly Jake took her hand again as she staggered toward him. He gathered her closer. "No. No, it's nothing like that. Jamie's fine. Twyla spent the nights here, and the hands and I were always around. Jamie's just fine," he reiterated.

Lexi's head sagged against his chest, and she fought back a rush of relief so strong she wanted to sob. Jake's arm circled her back, and his hand stroked her arm soothingly.

He brushed his cheek against her hair while he whispered, "I'm sorry, sweetheart, I didn't mean to scare you."

She shook her head. "It's not your fault. It's me. I'm a nervous wreck. I haven't been apart from Jamie since he was born, and it's been so hard being away from him this past week."

Lexi raised her eyes to Jake's, searching for understanding even as she sniffed back the tears that still threatened. "But I needed to be with Dad. Just in case. Until I knew he was going to be all right."

Jake looked back at her with compassion and empathy, at a total loss for words. Finally mustering the only response he could think of, he gave her a supportive hug and an enthusiastic "Sure."

A slow smile curled Lexi's lips. His answer wasn't poetry, but it made her feel better, and that was all that really counted. "Thanks." She sniffed one last time, just to put it all behind her. "Now, what was it you wanted to tell me?"

"Dolores called today."

Lexi gasped, stepped back and clasped a hand to the base of her throat.

"I answered the phone," Jake said simply.

Her eyes widened, and she drew her breath in again in a second, softer gasp.

"She asked for you first. I told her you were at the hospital. So she asked for Jamie, and after I called him to the phone, I left."

"Did you— Did she—" Lexi stuttered to a halt and just stared up at him while her mind raced on with a dozen questions she couldn't get out.

"I recognized her voice, but I didn't say anything. I don't know if she recognized mine or not."

A faint hope flickered to life, and then Lexi remembered her own instant recognition of Jake's voice at Louanne Byers's trailer.

"She recognized you," Lexi said, dashing any hope Jake might have been clinging to. "Your voice is too distinctive for her to have missed it. And if she had any doubt at all, Dolores would have asked Jamie and he would have told her everything he knows."

"Yeah." Jake chuckled softly. "He would have, wouldn't he?"

Suspicion sharpened Lexi's voice. "What do you mean by that?"

All innocence, Jake shrugged. "Just agreeing with you."

She knew there was more behind his answer than he was admitting, but she also knew better than to push the issue. For the time she had been gone, she was quite certain Jamie had spent every spare moment with Jake, asking questions and filling in the blanks in Jake's scrapbooks, along with the blanks she had been unwilling to talk about.

At the same time, Jamie had probably been supplying information and conjecture to Jake about anything and anybody who came into their conversations. Lexi shivered at the thought.

"Are you cold?" Jake asked.

"Yes." Involuntarily, she shivered again. It was late. She was tired. And she'd had enough shocks for one day. "I don't suppose Jamie said what Dolores wanted?" Lexi asked as her mind meandered back to the phone call.

Jake shook his head. "I didn't ask, and for once, Jamie didn't offer."

"Maybe she told him not to."

"That has an ominous ring," Jake said, mimicking Lexi's shiver.

"Doesn't it?" She threw back her head and groaned. "I *knew* I should have come back sooner."

He put his hand on her shoulder. "What's done is done. Don't waste time thinking about it."

"But if I'd been here to answer the phone—" she began.

Jake shook his head. "So what? Maybe I should have just talked to her. Maybe I should have said, 'Hi, Dolores. It's me, Jake, and guess what? I'm over you. I'm not angry. I'm not hurt, and I haven't thought about you in years. So how's your life?'"

"But you don't mean that."

"Hell yes, I mean that. Any love I ever had for Dolores was gone long before she left. It took longer to get over the anger, because no man likes to have his ego trampled like that. But even that I got over a long time ago."

"Well, you've got me confused now. If you're not upset about Dolores anymore, then why were you so adamant about not coming back here?"

Jake moved a step closer to Lexi and caught her chin in his hand, tilting her face toward his. The pad of his thumb stroked the full curve of her lower lip.

"Dolores was the least of what happened to me here," he said softly.

Lexi opened her mouth to ask what he was talking about and then caught herself. The look in his eyes told her she was flirting with fire. He couldn't mean her. There were a dozen other things he could mean. He couldn't mean what her stupid stampeding heart hoped he meant.

In slow motion, he released her chin and dropped his hand to his side. "I'd better go inside now. See you in the morning?"

She nodded. She was so tired she could cry. And in that moment she wanted him so badly she was in danger of making a complete fool of herself if she moved an inch. It was impossible for her to still love him. It was simply impossible.

DAMN! Lexi hurled the dress, hanger and all, across the room. Clenching her hands into fists, she glowered at her reflection in the full-length mirror.

A plain, simple woman looked back—a respectable woman, dressed the way she dressed nearly every day of her life. Her long black hair was gathered into a ponytail that reached past her shoulders. Her plaid shirt was western style and hung loose over blue jeans that had shrunk and faded through the years to a soft, comfortable fit. Her cowboy boots were black tooled leather, old and scuffed, and hadn't been anything more than functional even when they were new.

She stared toward the dress, which looked like a puddle of crumpled flowers at the base of the wall. Through narrowed eyes she regarded the full-skirted floral garment as if it were a sleeping snake that might come to life at any moment and whisper words of temptation in her ear.

Wear me. Come on, Lexi, you know you look good when you do. Show Jake how good you can look. A few curlers in your hair, a little makeup, some high heels and me. He'll fall at your feet.

Lexi closed her eyes and clenched her fists tighter, drowning out the thought with a low, frustrated growl. She was *not* going to waste her time trying to impress

Jake just because she had an occasion to wear something other than jeans. She didn't *want* Jake falling at her feet.

Forcing her eyes open, she took another look at herself in the mirror and decided that she *could* dress up for her father, at least a little. There was no need to go to the hospital looking as if she'd just finished her chores and hadn't had time to change.

Satisfied with the compromise, she retrieved the dress and hung it back in the closet. Then she took down a gathered split skirt in hunter green corduroy, found a matching belt and boots in soft leather and selected a simple white blouse with a high neckline and cuffs of lace.

Dressing quickly, she unfastened her ponytail and shook out her hair, then applied a bare minimum of makeup. Leaving her thick, dark hair to hang free, she stepped back and surveyed the result. The look was simple, stylish and respectable. She wasn't overdressed or underdressed, and she definitely couldn't be considered seductive.

Lexi closed her eyes and took a deep breath while she tried to slow the pounding of her heart. She looked good and she knew it. Maybe not knockout good the way the floral dress would have been, but good. She smiled and left her room.

Her heart thudded gently inside her chest as she descended the stairs. Jake and Jamie waited side by side at the front door. Jamie saw her first, his eyes growing round as saucers.

"Wow, Mom!" he cried with unrestrained enthusiasm. "You look great!"

Lexi's smile grew, but she lowered her eyes, unable to look at Jake. Jamie's reaction was gratifying but a little

embarrassing nonetheless. Continuing down the hallway, she laughed and answered, "Maybe it's been a little
too long since I put on a skirt."

"It looks good on you," Jake said, quietly echoing
Jamie.

Daring a glance in Jake's direction, Lexi fought down
a blush at the admiration she saw there. "Thank you."

Jake opened the door and stood to the side. "Your
chariot awaits, my lady."

Jamie screwed up his face and rolled his eyes at Jake.
"Oh brother."

Suddenly glad to have her son as a chaperon, Lexi
laughed just as the phone began to ring. "Oh, you two go
on. I'll be there in a second."

Waving them out the front door, she turned and hurried across the parlor to answer the phone. Her heart
pounding, she snatched the receiver off the cradle on the
third ring and gasped, "Hello."

"How *dare* you!" an angry feminine voice said on the
other end of the line.

Relieved that it wasn't the hospital and certain that it
must be a wrong number, Lexi politely inquired, "What
number were you calling?"

"I was calling *you*, Alexandra. And I demand to know
what you think you're doing."

Lexi's knees almost buckled as she recognized the
overwrought voice of her half sister. Rubbing cold fingers over her suddenly pounding forehead, Lexi lowered
herself into the chair beside the desk. "Dolores?"

"I guess you think you're real smart, don't you?"

"I was just on my way to the hospital, Dolores. Do you
think this could wait until later?" Lexi took a deep breath
and forced herself to control the wave of panic that was
leeching all the warmth from her body.

"No, it can't. I had to wait all day for Harvey to leave so I could make this call. And you're going to stay right there and talk to me until I'm through, if you know what's good for you. Now, would you care to explain to me what in the hell Jake Thorn is doing there?"

Still holding her head in her hand, Lexi said, "Dad hired him. Jake will only be here for the few weeks it takes Dad to recover from his surgery. By the way, he's doing just fine."

"I know that," Dolores spat. "I called the hospital this morning. So there. Even though he's only my step-father, I *do* care."

The sudden image of her sister as a little girl, blond curls bobbing around a Kewpie-doll face, flashed through Lexi's mind. In an instant, the pretty face contorted into a parody of itself, and a tongue protruded. From the petulant tone of her sister's voice, Lexi knew the tongue had just been stuck out, in spirit if not in fact. Somehow the knowledge took some of the sting from the words.

"Relax, Dolores. It'll all be over soon, and everything will be back to normal. There's no reason to get upset."

"No! You promised. It was part of our agreement that Jake would never be around Jamie." Dolores's voice grew shrill. "I won't have it. Do you hear me, Lexi? I won't have it!"

"Don't tell me what you'll have and won't have," Lexi snapped back. "You relinquished your rights a long time ago. Good grief, Dolores, I practically have to beg just to get you to call Jamie and talk to him. He knows he's adopted. He's starting to ask questions. How do you think I feel?"

"My God, you haven't told him, have you?"

"No, I haven't told him. But I'd like to. Someday."

"You can't."

"Yes, I can. And someday I will. But not right now, not when it might hurt him. When he finds out who his birth mother is, I want him to—"

"Hey, Mom," Jamie called from just beyond the open front door. "Come on. We're waiting."

"I have to go," Lexi whispered into the phone.

"Get rid of Jake," Dolores insisted. "I don't care how you do it, just get rid of him."

Lexi turned her back to the door where Jamie hovered and lowered her voice to a hiss. "What are you so upset about? You told me Jake has nothing to do with this."

"I just don't want him getting any ideas, that's all."

"Why would Jake get any ideas? Is there something you haven't told me?"

"No!"

Lexi wanted to scream with frustration. Trying to get a straight answer out of Dolores was almost as hard as trying to hold on to a greased pig. "I don't have time to go into this now, but I'm not through with you. And Dolores...?"

"Yes?"

"Don't ever threaten me again. Jamie's mine, and I'll decide what happens with his life."

"Don't be so sure, little sis. You just may not know as much as you think you do."

With that final verbal thrust, Dolores hung up and Lexi found herself listening to a dial tone.

"Mom?" Jamie asked, hanging on to the door frame as he leaned into the house. "Are we going?"

"Sure, sweetheart, I'm sorry." She winced as she glanced at her watch. She'd wasted more time than she realized on that phone call, and now she would be irritable and distracted for most of the drive. What had Dolores hoped to gain from that call, anyway?

Checking to make sure the front door locked behind her, Lexi followed Jamie toward the car, where Jake waited. His legs crossed at the ankles, he leaned against the driver's door, staring across the courtyard to the western horizon.

Halfway to the car, Lexi turned and followed his gaze to the pink-and-purple-stained sky. A slash of deep rose marked the passage of the sun.

"Jake and I watched the sunset together," Jamie piped up. "He says he don't hardly get to see one anymore 'cause he's always working. So we been watching the sunset together every night since Grandpa went into the hospital. It was real pretty tonight. I hollered, but you didn't hear me."

Lexi's gaze left the horizon and fixed upon her son. She was surprised by the sudden pang of resentment that tore through her. She had always encouraged Jamie to spend time with his grandfather and the ranch hands. With no father to call his own, he needed male companionship, and she had never begrudged the time he spent tagging along behind Manuel or Tonio or any of the others. So there was no reason for her to be jealous of Jamie's strengthening attachment to Jake. There was no reason for her to feel threatened by it, either.

"Just remember, hon," she said softly. "Jake's only going to be here for a little while."

"I know." A frown creased the smooth skin of Jamie's brow, and he shrugged off the hand she laid on his shoulder.

"I just don't want you to be hurt when he leaves."

"I won't."

Knowing she shouldn't have said anything, Lexi watched him turn sullen and walk past her toward the car. He was only ten. He didn't know how to guard his heart to keep it from being broken. He didn't understand why anyone would need to. Jake's friendship was a gift, and Jamie's enjoyment of it was pure and simple, just as it should be.

"Jamie," Lexi called.

When he turned, she motioned him back to her. He obeyed, but the expression on his face was a mixture of boredom and disapproval. Whatever she had to say had better be good if she expected him to listen.

"I guess you think I'm a party pooper, don't you?" she asked quietly.

He rolled his eyes to the side while he contemplated his answer, and then he nodded.

Lexi smiled. Even when she and Jamie were at odds, she loved him so she could hardly stand it. One of the greatest challenges of motherhood had been to avoid spoiling him beyond redemption.

"Mothers worry," she said with a shrug. "I'm sorry, but it's a fact of life."

Jamie quit staring at the hole the toe of his boot was digging in the gravel path. "I'm not a little kid anymore, Mom. I'm not going to start crying when Jake leaves or anything stupid like that."

"You might. But then I might, too. Those things just happen sometimes." She caught his chin and turned his face back toward hers when he started to look away. "The point is that I know there are times when I try too hard to protect you. And this was one of those times when you were right and I was wrong. Okay?"

"Okay." He squirmed away from her hand and rolled his eyes again. "Geez, you didn't have to apologize, Mom. I would have gotten over it."

Lexi laughed. "I know, but I didn't want to wait that long. Are we square now?"

"Sure." Jamie slung his arm through hers and walked her the rest of the way to the car.

"Are we ready?" Jake asked in a throaty growl. "Finally?"

Dressed in the soft moccasins Lexi had bought him and a pair of navy blue sweatpants with a matching tank top and denim work shirt flapping loose in the night breeze, he looked deliciously handsome in a relaxed, rumpled sort of way.

"Everybody in." Lexi walked past him and opened the driver's door.

Jake stepped up beside her. "I thought I'd drive."

"It's my car, and you have only one good arm."

"I can drive with one arm."

"Is this a male-chauvinist thing?"

"No. It's an I-prefer-my-own-driving thing."

"Look, Jake." Lexi stepped closer, conscious that Jamie was standing nearby, hanging on their every word. "In the past half hour, I've had a fight with everyone I've spoken to. I'm tired. I'm tense. I'm irritable. And I'm driving," she said quietly. "Now would you please go around to your side of the car and get in?"

"I don't suppose there's anything I could say to change your mind?"

"Not right now, no."

Jake held up his good hand in a gesture of surrender. "All right, you win. But just try not to hit too many bumps, okay?"

"Oh, good grief, Jake. You're the one who taught me how to drive!"

"I know."

The two words hung in the air as he turned to walk around the front of the car to the passenger side. Simmering at the implication, Lexi remembered the hours spent sitting next to him in the cab of the old pickup he had used for her driving lessons. Hours spent driving over ranch roads and old country lanes with the windows rolled down, the radio blaring and dust whirling through the air behind them. Hours when she'd been too busy concentrating on him to pay much attention to her driving.

After they were all inside and Jamie had closed Jake's door for him, Lexi twisted in her seat to help Jake with the seat belt he had managed to pull across him but was having trouble fastening. Her hand closed over his and guided the buckle into the fastener she held steady in her other hand.

Lifting her eyes to his, she found herself face-to-face with him, almost close enough to kiss. "I've improved since I was fifteen," she said, referring to her driving skills.

His gaze flickered to her lips before returning to her eyes with an intimacy that was shattering. "I've noticed."

Lexi recoiled and fumbled for the ignition with a hand that trembled. Without warning, Jake's left hand reached across her and closed around her own untouched seat belt. The back of his arm raked her breasts as he drew the buckle across the front of her, guiding it toward the seat between them.

Her breasts tingled, their tips hardening at the memory of his touch. A rush of heat prickled over her skin, and Lexi turned toward him, instinctively following the movement of his hand until she found herself once again face-to-face with him.

"You forgot to buckle yourself in." His eyes met hers while he waited for her to guide his hand once again.

"I'm buckled up," Jamie announced from the back seat.

"Oh." Released from the spell that held her, Lexi wrapped her fingers over Jake's, ignoring the warm response of his hand beneath hers. Together they slid the buckle into the coupling to secure her seat belt.

"Thank you," she said, trying to pretend that everything was normal while his thumb stroked the back of her hand and her heart leapt wildly about inside her chest.

"Can I pick the music?" Jamie asked.

Lexi jerked her hand from Jake's and her mind from the dangerous musings it had begun. "I'll leave that up to you two," she said as she started the car and backed it out onto the two-lane ranch road that would take them to the highway. She had a long drive ahead of her and a long trip back to reality.

She had seen the desire in Jake's eyes and felt her own ready response. Whatever was happening between them had to stop. Their histories were too tangled and their futures too uncertain for anything lasting to develop. Besides, she had Jamie to think of, and Jake was a tumbleweed who wanted nothing more than to keep rolling where the wind blew him. He wasn't the kind of man a woman could hold on to, at least not for any length of time. And Lexi wasn't the kind of woman who could let go easily.

Unlike her son, she guarded her heart closely, because when she loved, she loved with everything she had. She'd only loved like that once, and when Jake left the first time, it had torn her world apart. She couldn't risk it again. She wasn't sure she had the strength to survive losing him a second time.

CHAPTER NINE

"SAY WHEN," LEXI SAID, dividing her attention between her father and the button she was pressing to raise the head of the hospital bed.

"There! Right there. Hold it." Sitting nearly upright, Frank waved his hand toward the foot of the bed. "Now you've got to raise that end a little or I'll slide right out of here."

Dutifully, Lexi pushed the other button until he was tucked and tilted to his satisfaction and ready for conversation. After taking a walk from his room to the visiting area and back again with his grandson, her father seemed more than content to do the rest of his visiting from his bed.

"So." He relaxed against the pillows at his back. "You sure look all gussied up tonight."

"Well, I thought it might be a nice change." Not sure if her father's observation was a compliment or not, Lexi shifted her weight uncomfortably from one high-heeled boot to the other. "After nearly a week of sleeping in a chair in the cardiac care waiting room, I was looking pretty ragged when I left here the other day."

"You must not have looked too bad," her father said, rolling his eyes. "That nice, redheaded doctor who comes around every afternoon asked me if you were married."

"Dad, he didn't," Lexi protested, flushed with embarrassment. She had never got used to her father's teasing attitude toward the men in her life. He treated every date she had as if she were back in junior high and suffering from her first real crush.

"He most certainly did," her dad insisted. "And he seemed very disappointed when you weren't here yesterday."

"You're not trying to fix me up with him, are you?"

"He'd be a better catch than Brad McCauley."

"Oh, good grief. I've gone out with Brad exactly three times."

"Well, he's okay as a foreman, but I wouldn't want him as a son-in-law."

"I've never even considered any such thing."

"Considered marrying who?" Jake asked, entering the room quietly.

"No one," Lexi said, glaring at her father.

"That damned, skulking foreman of mine, that's who," her father said, glaring right back at her.

"Brad McCauley? That little snake?"

She whirled to face Jake with her hands on her hips. "You don't even know the man. And you—" She turned back to her father and forced her voice to a whisper. "You are not supposed to be getting excited. Brad and I are just friends, period."

"Thank God for that," he said grumpily as Lexi leaned to kiss him on the forehead. He squeezed the hand she placed in his and winked at her as she straightened and smiled down at him.

"Now, you be good, and I'll see you tomorrow," she said, returning the wink.

"If you get a chance to talk to that nice redheaded doctor, ask him when I can get out of here."

With a shake of her head and a wave goodbye, Lexi left. Jake watched her go and then turned back to the man he'd come to see. "How are you doing?"

"Fair. It still feels better sitting than standing."

Jake smiled and pulled a chair closer. "I feel pretty much the same way myself." Careful not to disturb his healing ribs or bump his ailing arm, he lowered himself into the chair. "Were you just needling her, or do you really dislike McCauley?"

"Whatever else he may be, McCauley's not the man for Lexi, I know that for *damned* sure."

"How closely did you check his references when you hired him? How much do you know about his background?"

Frank's gaze sharpened. "Why? Are you onto something?"

Jake shook his head. "Nothing specific. There are some things I *haven't* found, like receipts for purchases he's supposed to have made. Prices that seem a little too high on some other things."

"Kickbacks? You think he's been gouging me and then getting kickbacks?"

Holding up his hand to ward off more questions, Jake said, "I don't think anything yet. I've got a long way to go before I form any opinions, and I could be totally off base at this point."

"But you *are* seeing what I've been seeing. Expenses are too high and revenues are too low."

"It could be nothing more than sloppy record keeping at this point. The guy could be a great foreman and just be a lousy paper shuffler."

"Or he could be a crook."

Jake nodded. "Or he could be a crook. Getting back to those references of McCauley's, how well did you check him out?"

"Not well at all. The foreman I had before him hired Brad as a wrangler. He had a good reputation with horses, and he'd worked as a foreman off and on at some ranches up in the northwest. So when the other foreman left without notice, Brad stepped in until I could hire somebody else. That was almost four years ago, and I just never got around to hiring anybody."

"So he could have done this before. That is, if he's done anything at all."

For a moment, Frank said nothing. He merely stared at the younger man with a look that grew more solemn by the second. "Jake," he said at length, "I appreciate what you're doing."

"Frank, it's nothing."

"Yes, it is." Frank turned to stare at the wall of his room. "We both know I couldn't have asked anyone else to do this for me."

"I haven't done anything yet."

"You will." Frank nodded. "And when you do, I trust you to be fair."

"No matter who it turns out to be?"

"It's not Manuel or Tonio. I'd stake my life on that. But some of these newer hands I hardly know at all."

"Jamie knows them all."

Frank smiled. "Yeah, he does, doesn't he? He told me he'd been helping you some. Telling you how the ranch was run and who does what around the place. He's a pretty sharp little fellow, isn't he?"

"He sure is. He goes straight from school out to ride circuit on the ranch every day. Seems he's worked with every man on the place, helping where he can and watching and learning the rest of the time. And I think Jamie sees a lot more than some of those hands think he sees."

"Jamie's planning on running the Lazy C one of these days," Frank said with a nod. "He may be just a kid, but he knows it's his ranch. You think he might actually know something that could help you?"

"I know he doesn't like Brad McCauley. And there's a guy named Pepper that Jamie thinks is kind of sneaky."

"Pepper." Frank mulled over the name, then said, "Oh, yeah. He's worked with McCauley before. He hired on last year. Keeps to himself mostly."

"No harm in that, I suppose." With a groan, Jake pushed himself to his feet and slowly straightened his stiff and aching body. "I guess I'd better get on out of here and let you get some rest."

"You'll keep me posted?"

"Lexi made me swear I wouldn't talk business with you," Jake said with a lopsided grin. "And here I've gone and done nothing else. Why don't you just let me tell you when I find out something definite? Meanwhile you can work on getting well enough to come home."

Worn out from the evening, Frank nodded, and Jake left. In the corridor outside the waiting room, Lexi stood talking to a solid-looking, redhaired doctor in a white coat. Her dimples flashed as she laughed at something the man said, and Jake found himself burning with a sudden urge to plant his one good fist smack in the middle of the doctor's freckled, all-American face.

Stepping into their conversation, Jake glanced at the doctor and then turned to Lexi. "Are you ready to go?"

"Just about." Eyes dancing, she flashed her dimpled smile at Jake. "Dr. Kiley was just telling me how well Dad's doing. Isn't that wonderful?"

"Yeah, that's really great." Slipping a proprietary arm around Lexi's shoulders, Jake looked at the doctor. "So Frank's gonna be okay, then?"

Dr. Kiley nodded and assumed a more professional air. "Mr. Conley's progress seems to be right on track. We're very pleased."

"I just can't thank you enough, Doctor," Lexi said. "It means so much to know that Dad's in good hands."

The doctor's smile was warm and personal. "If you have any questions or need to get hold of me, just leave a message at the nurses' station." He held out a hand in parting, and Lexi took it eagerly. "We'll talk again soon, and there'll be a conference with you and your father before he goes home."

"Thank you so much, Dr. Kiley," Lexi said again, still holding his hand.

"Mom, can we go now?" Jamie came strolling up with a pop can in one hand and a bag of peanuts in the other. "I think I need some pizza or something. I'm getting hungry."

"That sounds good," Jake answered for her. "We could stop off for some on the way home."

"And I can play video games." Jamie shook a small avalanche of peanuts into his mouth. "How about it, Mom?" he asked, crunching the nuts.

"Don't talk with your mouth full, Jamie. You could choke on those things," Lexi said as the doctor edged his way out of the scene.

Feeling suddenly generous, Jake smiled at him in parting. After all, he seemed to be a pretty good doctor, and he couldn't really be blamed for finding Lexi attractive. At least he'd had the sense to back off once Jake arrived to stake a prior claim.

"I guess you're feeling pretty proud of yourself right now," Lexi said, intruding on Jake's thoughts.

He looked down to find her gazing up at him, his arm still holding her close. Her big cinnamon eyes sparkled ominously, and his first instinct was to release her and step back.

"What do you mean?" he asked, standing his ground.

She pointed toward the arm that held her plastered against him. "I mean this caveman thing." With a twist of her shoulders, she eased out of his grip and stepped to the side. "Thanks to you, that nice doctor will probably never flirt with me again."

"If you really want him, I could still go chase him down for you."

"That won't be necessary. Dad'll be in here another week or two."

With Jamie leading the way, they started toward the elevators. Jake brought up the rear, close behind Lexi.

"And then what? I thought your heart belonged to Brad McCauley."

"I've heard about all I want to hear about Brad McCauley tonight. Good grief, I'm almost sorry I ever went out with the man."

"I thought you were going to the harvest dance with him."

"Where did you hear that?" she asked, turning to Jake in surprise.

"I told him," Jamie said.

"Where did *you* hear that?" Lexi demanded.

Jamie shrugged and stepped into the elevator. "Everybody knows about it. I guess Brad told 'em. Which button do I push, Mom?"

She walked in behind him and pointed to the button for the downstairs lobby. Jake joined them, and the elevator doors closed.

"I said I'd think about it," Lexi said, still irritated. "I didn't say I'd go. I told him we'd have to see what happened with Dad."

Jake kept his gaze carefully trained on the wall in front of him. "It's been my observation that the man takes too many liberties."

"What's that supposed to mean?" she demanded.

"He acts as if he runs the place." The elevator doors opened and they all stepped out. Quickly orienting himself, Jake pointed toward the front doors. "This way."

As Jamie hurried ahead, Jake continued in an undertone, "Besides, Lexi, I don't like the way the man looks at you."

"You don't seem to like the way *any* man looks at me," Lexi snapped back, pinning him with flashing eyes.

Jamie stopped at the hospital entrance and motioned them on, then started toward the parking lot. Lexi and Jake trailed closely behind him, allowing just enough distance to keep their bickering private.

"Well, maybe I just know a little bit more about men than you do," Jake said.

"You sound like my father." At the edge of the parking lot, she stopped and turned to glare indignantly into Jake's eyes. "I'm not Little Red Riding Hood, you know, and I don't need to be saved from the big bad wolf. I can take care of myself very well, thank you."

He caught her arm and guided her between two parked cars, where he pulled her to within inches of him. "I'm not trying to be your father, Lexi, or even your big brother. So if that's what you're thinking, get it out of your head."

"Well, what *are* you trying to do?"

"Maybe I'm just trying to keep you away from other men, damn it," he said in a deadly quiet voice that fairly crackled with tension. "Didn't *that* ever occur to you?"

"But why?"

"Do you really have to ask?"

The ground heaved beneath her feet, and Lexi's insides turned to warm syrup. Part of her wanted to run to him, and part of her wanted to run the other way. Hardly daring to breathe, she whispered, "I want to hear you say it."

"I want you for myself. Okay? I said it." His hand twitched at his side, but he didn't move. "So now what?"

"Hey, you guys," Jamie shouted across two rows of parked cars. "I'm hungry. Come on."

"Now I guess we get pizza," Lexi said, trying to slow the gallop of her heartbeat and bring her feet back down to solid ground.

Jake slipped his fingers through hers and they began to walk again. "Thank God it's dark," he murmured for her ears only.

"Why?"

"Because I've got a hard-on as big as Texas, and there's not much I can do to hide it."

"Jake!"

"You asked," he said, tightening his fingers on her hand. "And don't tell me you don't feel the same way."

"I didn't think you could, uh, you know—with your ribs and your shoulder and all." Heat flamed in her cheeks. Her steps slowed. "I mean, you can barely get dressed by yourself. How could—"

"I probably couldn't." He stopped, and his knee brushed her thigh as he turned to face her. "But that doesn't stop me from wanting to try."

"Oh, Jake, I don't know."

Lexi shook her head in confusion. Her heart was pounding, her body was throbbing, her head was spinning, and all she could think about was what it had been like that one night, that one long, hot night when Jake had taught her what the word *love* meant in its fullest, sweetest, most erotic sense. All she could think about was what she would give to be there again.

Gently slipping her arm behind her back, her hand still locked in his, Jake pulled her against him and looked down into her eyes. They stood just outside a pool of light cast by an overhead lamp.

"We've got a lot to talk about," he said.

She nodded. His lips were so close she could almost taste them. She drew in a deep breath and felt her breasts flatten against his ribs.

"Am I hurting you?" she asked.

"It doesn't matter."

With her free hand, she reached inside his loose shirt and ran her fingers lightly over the bandages beneath the soft knit of his tank top. "You just insist on living dangerously, don't you?"

"I guess I do."

"I want you to get well."

"I want to make love to you."

Lexi closed her eyes, dizzy from the rush of blood to the center of her body. "We can't even kiss without leaving you doubled over in pain."

"That was a long time ago. I'm a lot better now."

She smiled and opened her eyes to find him looking down at her with a grin twitching at his lips. "That was two weeks ago," she corrected gently.

"It seems like a year." Sobering again, he said, "I know you're right, but that doesn't stop me from wanting you. And not being able to do anything about it only makes it that much worse."

She moved her hand from his ribs to his cheek. Her thumb stroked the outer edge of his mouth. "We *do* need to talk."

"Just don't tell me that it's never going to happen."

"Hey!" Jamie yelled, walking toward them. "I'm hungry!"

Guiltily, Lexi and Jake moved apart, but not before Jamie cocked his head to the side with sudden interest.

"What are you two guys doing, anyway?"

"Your mother stumbled," Jake said quickly. "I caught her just before she fell."

Jamie looked at them, his eyes going from Jake to Lexi and back before his gaze settled on his mother with eloquent skepticism.

"Are we going to eat?" he asked finally, letting the other subject drop.

"Sure, hon." Lexi started toward the car, pulling Jake with her. "Come on, Jake, let's go get some pizza."

The ride to Antonio's Pizza Heaven in Santa Fe was quiet. Jake turned his face toward the window and seemed to fall asleep almost as soon as the car started. Jamie sat in the back seat, giving every indication of sulking. And Lexi spent a solitary drive wrapped in guilt and self-doubt.

Her father was still in the hospital recovering from heart surgery. Her son was dealing with too many changes in his world. Her sister was breathing down her neck about things Lexi had no control over. And Jake's sudden libidinous impulses had to be the result of boredom and isolation. She couldn't believe there was more to it than that.

Luckily it was all a moot point anyway. Regardless of what either of them wanted, Jake wasn't capable of anything more than wishful thinking. And by the time he was, he would be gone. The thought should have cheered her. Instead, she felt a stab of regret so sharp she couldn't even try to lie to herself.

She wanted him. Heaven help her, even it was only for a night, she would rather spend the rest of her life reliving that one night than wondering what it might have been like if she had only had the courage to say yes.

"Hey, Mom, there it is!" Jamie shouted from behind her. A second later his arm shot over the seat next to Lexi's head, scaring her into next week.

"Oh, Jamie, don't *do* that!" Breathless with fright, she laid her hand over her heart as she braked hard and, at the same time, leaned away from his pointing finger.

"What the hell is all the commotion about?" Jake said, bracing his hand against the dashboard.

"But you were going to miss it!" Jamie shouted, practically in her ear.

"I—" Lexi started to deny it, but her conscience wouldn't let her. She'd been a million miles away. "Well, maybe. But you didn't have to yell."

"I scared ya, huh?"

She could almost hear him grin as he withdrew his arm and settled back into his seat.

"Yes, you did." Easing off the brake, Lexi turned across the traffic lane into the parking lot of the pizza parlor. "And for future reference," she said quietly, "it's not wise to yell at sleepwalkers or daydreaming drivers."

"Or sleeping bears," Jake added in a rumbling undertone. He directed an ominous glance over his shoulder into the back seat, then turned away to stare at the building in front of them. "Antonio's, huh? Is it still the same inside?"

Lexi turned off the ignition. "Do you remember video games?"

"No."

"Well, at least they still have drip candles stuck in Chianti bottles on every table."

"I guess that'll have to do." He unbuckled his seat belt and reached across himself with slow deliberation to open his own door.

"You *are* getting better, aren't you?" Lexi asked, her mind racing ahead to future possibilities.

"These ribs will be sore into the next decade." Jake began to ease himself out of the car. "But they don't hurt like they did."

"How nice." Lexi waited until everyone was out to lock the car doors. Then they all went inside.

Jake headed for a quiet table in the back, where the lights were dimmest and the candlelight brightest as it flickered on the red-and-white-checkered tablecloths. Jamie headed for the video games in an alcove off the entrance. After making sure he would stay where she could see him, Lexi took a deep breath and followed Jake.

Alone in the moonlight, under an open sky, the things she had said hadn't seemed so bold. Now, inside a restaurant, surrounded by people, she was embarrassed by the memory. *We* do *need to talk.* How could she have said such a thing? How could he have agreed? They had nothing to talk about other than the fact that they wanted to make love and couldn't.

That wasn't exactly something she wanted to discuss in public, or even in private, for that matter, now that she'd had a chance to come to her senses.

"You're frowning," Jake said as Lexi sat down next to him.

"Am I?" She brushed a hand over her forehead to smooth the lines. Her frown only deepened. "Sorry."

"What's wrong?"

"Nothing. I think I'm just tired."

"I could drive the rest of the way home," he offered generously.

Lexi chuckled and her face relaxed. "If you're not careful, I may let you."

"So what are we having?"

"Jamie likes pepperoni. Just plain pepperoni."

"And you like green pepper and onions."

Lexi smiled. "You have quite a memory."

"You'd be surprised at the things I remember." His voice slid to sultry depths, and Lexi's smile slipped. The flutter of butterfly wings tickled inside her.

"Oh?" she said as heat crept up her neck and cheeks at the erotic memories that flashed across her mind.

"Half and half?"

The words penetrated the daydream and pulled Lexi back to earth with a thud. "What?"

"Half pepperoni and half deluxe," Jake said, looking at her curiously. "Would that be okay?"

"Uh, sure. What size?" The heat creeping over her now was of pure embarrassment. She was only grateful he couldn't read her mind.

"Considering that we've got a growing boy and a starving man to feed, I'd suggest a large."

"Sounds good to me."

Jake rose to place their order, and left alone, Lexi found her imagination threatening to spiral out of control once again. She closed her eyes and drew in a long, deep breath.

She had to stop this. She wasn't a teenager anymore, and Jake definitely wasn't the hero she'd made him out to be in her virginal fantasies. He was flesh and blood with faults and weaknesses, and he was more than capable of breaking her heart and ruining her life. He wouldn't mean to do it, but he'd do it just the same.

She was earth and he was fire. And she knew there was no way she could be close to him without being seared by his heat. She still bore the scars from the last time.

Jake took his seat across from her and covered her hand with his. "You seem thoughtful."

In spite of her resolve, Lexi felt her heart leap and her stomach somersault at his touch. He was dangerous, but her heart told her he was worth the risk.

"Maybe a little," she answered, letting her eyes dwell a moment too long on the cool, clear green of his.

Jake's strong, work-roughened fingers stroked the back of her hand. "We both have things we want to say. Who goes first?"

"I'm not sure this is the time or the place." Lexi started to withdraw her hand, but his fingers tightened around her wrist.

"Why not?" His fingertips drew lazy circles across the back of her wrist.

"I don't think Jamie is very comfortable with the idea of us—you and me—being anything more than friends."

"Jamie isn't here right now." Jake withdrew his hand. Restlessly, he twirled his fork on the bare table. "Look, Lexi, this isn't very easy for me, either. I've been treading water when it comes to you for a long, long time."

"How long?" she asked.

"Since the night you turned sixteen, to be exact."

Her heart began to beat a furious tattoo inside her chest. She would never forget that night. She remembered the indigo blue of the evening sky and the scent of pine in the air. She remembered every word Jake had said and every glance that had told her more than words ever could. She had felt like a woman that night, a woman in love, and Jake had made her feel that way.

He pushed aside the fork he had been toying with and rested his hand flat on the table. "If you'd been even a year older, everything might have been different. But a sixteen-year-old girl, no matter how tempting, is way too young for a twenty-seven-year-old man to think about."

"But you *did* think about me."

"Oh yeah, I thought about you. The night of your party, you were pretty hard to ignore with your hair hanging down in curls, and you batting those big brown eyes at every man there."

"I did not," she denied.

"Yes, you did," Jake insisted with a grin. "And you wore that pink party dress with the neckline so low your dad was following around behind you with a sweater he kept trying to get you to put on."

Lexi laughed, remembering that part of the evening for the first time in years. "Poor Dad."

"Poor Dad, indeed. His little girl was growing up right before his eyes. Right before everyone's eyes. And everyone was noticing," Jake said, his voice lowering to a gravelly rasp.

Sensual heat, slow and delicious, spread through her at the sound of his voice. He could always do that to her. "I didn't care about everyone. I only cared about you."

Her eyelids felt heavy as she looked straight into the green fire in his eyes.

"Is that why you followed me away from the party when I left?" he asked, sparks of passion flaring in his gaze.

"Yes."

As if it were happening again, she could see him turning at the sound of her voice, waiting for her to reach him. With no one else in sight, she had asked him for a birthday kiss. He hesitated, and she had reached up on tiptoe, barely touching her lips to his in a feather-light caress. When she reluctantly moved away, Jake's arms had tightened around her, holding her against him.

That was all, nothing more, but it was enough. Emboldened, she had once again brushed her lips over his, and this time he had responded, at first reluctantly, then with an intensity that had ended in full body contact, rampaging hearts and breathless gasps.

The last thing she remembered was Jake's horrified expression as he had gazed down at her and then turned and fled into the night. Until that moment, the kiss had been everything she had dreamed it would be.

"Why did you leave the way you did?" she asked, remembering the hurt, the ache that wouldn't go away.

"Because I scared myself." He touched her hand, stroking his fingertips lightly up her wrist, over the back of her hand and down her fingers. "You were way too young to know what you were doing, and I was a grown man seriously considering things that were probably illegal, possibly perverted and not a damned bit gentlemanly."

"People have done it before," she argued without knowing why she persisted.

"Believe me, Lexi, it was very tempting for the one or two minutes I was completely out of my mind. Then I managed to remember that even if you didn't look like one or kiss like one, you were still a little girl. And I got the hell out of there while I still could."

"I wanted you so much."

"The feeling was mutual, believe me, but your daddy would have shot me, Lexi. And then probably hanged me. And he would have been right. That would have been the stupidest thing either one of us ever did."

"Oh, really? It would have been more stupid than you marrying Dolores three months later?"

"That's another story."

"I'd like to hear it," she insisted, still smarting from the memory.

"Another time, maybe." His fingers interwove with hers. "It's not something I want to talk about tonight."

"And what *do* you want to talk about tonight?"

"How much I want to make love to you."

Suddenly faint from the effect of his words, Lexi pressed the back of her hand to her forehead as if that would stop the spinning inside her head. "Jake."

"I know. We just came from the hospital. Your whole life is in turmoil, and my timing has never been worse."

"That's not it."

"What is it, then?" he asked gently.

"The last time—no, only time—we made love, you left without even saying goodbye. My father was the one who told me you weren't coming back."

"You're angry."

"I don't know." She shook her head. "I do know I'm scared, scared you'll do it again if I give you the chance."

"I should never have made love to you that night."

Furious suddenly, she tried to pull her hand from his, but his fingers only tightened until she stopped struggling.

"Hear me out," he insisted. "I shouldn't have, but I would have done it again in a minute if I'd had the chance. The only way I could stop myself was to leave."

What about me? she wanted to shout. Instead, she leaned closer, whispering intently. "What about what *I* wanted? *I'm* the one who seduced *you* that night."

The ghost of a smile traveled over Jake's face. "I don't remember fighting very hard." His thumb stroked the smooth skin on the back of her hand, and he frowned. "The next morning I came back down to earth, Lexi. I had no money, no job and no future. I'd even leased my ranch for ten years just to come up with Dolores's divorce settlement."

"Well, that's very noble, but what makes now any different from eleven years ago?"

"You're not nineteen anymore. And I'm too old to be noble. I can't even sleep at night for thinking about you. About all the lost chances." Passion vibrated in his voice, and his fingers tightened on hers again. "About how good you feel in my arms."

Lexi's anger was gone along with her heartbreak. She knew he wasn't offering her forever, but he was offering her more than she had ever had with any other man. He was offering her another chance at the most wonderful night of her life.

"I've had a few thoughts like that myself." She swallowed hard. "Where do we go from here?"

He raised her hand to his lips. "I just wanted you to know, I'm going to seduce you the first instant I'm able."

"Well, thank you," Lexi said, light-headed at the thought. "A lady does like to have warning."

"The pleasure's mine, I assure you."

CHAPTER TEN

LEXI STOOD at the kitchen window overlooking the backyard, where Jake and Jamie tossed a softball back and forth in the crisp autumn air, their camaraderie apparently in full bloom once again. The strain that had developed after the trip to the hospital a week earlier was all but forgotten, largely due to Jake's efforts.

As she watched, Jamie tossed an overhand lob straight at Jake, who took two steps back and gathered in the ball with both hands just before it plowed into his midsection. Twisting to his left, he released the ball again in a wobbly, left-handed pitch that Jamie caught with ease.

Jake still wore the sling, and his ribs were still bandaged, but three weeks after the ordeal in the arena he was healing. At the thought, her heart leapt with anticipation. She caught her lower lip between her teeth to keep from smiling, but her mouth spread in a wide grin anyway. Soon he would have two arms to hold her and a chest strong enough to stand her weight pressed against it.

And then what? The sobering question echoed through her mind, scattering her joy like a puff of smoke in the wind. Would one night, or two, be enough to sustain her through the heartache that would follow? Because whether or not they made love, he would leave again once her father was well.

Jake had said he wanted her; he hadn't said he loved her. He had said he dreamed of her; he hadn't said he would stay with her. He would make love to her, and then he would leave. She had been there before, and for a while she had thought she would die from the misery of wanting what she could never have.

Lexi gripped the sink and drew in a deep, shuddering breath. When she looked up again, she saw him walking toward the house in pursuit of a pitch that had gone wide to the right. Even in his moccasins and baggy gray sweatpants, he still managed to make her stomach tighten in a sudden spasm of longing.

His face was relaxed and smiling. His green eyes danced with laughter as he scooped up the ball and straightened again. The slight grimace the action brought still didn't wipe away his smile. At forty-one, he was a weathered, matured and even handsomer version of the boy she had first adored and the man she had grown to love.

Jamie's laughter rang out as Jake turned and aimed a long, looping, underhand pitch at him. Lexi watched her son back up and get into position to make a barehanded catch. His happy face and dancing eyes were so similar to the ones she had just been studying that her hands tightened on the edge of the sink till her knuckles turned white.

Leaning toward the window with a gasp, she blinked hard, then shook her head to clear her vision and looked again. Over the years, the similarities she had noticed had been shrugged off as the product of an overactive imagination. Now, as she watched, the whispering of old suspicions grew louder. It couldn't be. It just couldn't. But what if it was?

Dolores had sworn she hadn't slept with Jake for months before she left him. But then, Dolores had been known to lie. If anyone would know, it would be their mother. After all, it had been Cordelia's idea to hide Dolores's pregnancy behind Lexi's identity.

Even after ten years, the memory still hurt. It had never been a secret that Dolores was their mother's favorite, but Lexi had never realized to what extent until the day she saw Jamie's birth certificate. Her world had collapsed when she had read her name, Alexandra Lorraine Conley, listed as the mother of James Franklin Conley, the name she had planned to give her own son when she had one. Where the father's name should have been was one word: Unknown.

After that, things had gone from bad to worse.

Putting the memory behind her, Lexi hurried from the kitchen to the telephone in the front parlor. Her hand trembled with emotions long buried as she dialed her mother's number. On the fifth ring, she breathed a sigh of relief and was about to hang up when the maid answered. While she went to call the *señora* to the phone, Lexi tried to slow her racing heart.

"Yes?" her mother inquired sweetly into the phone.

"Mother?" Lexi said in a voice that was breathless with nervousness.

"Dolores? Dear, are you all right?"

"No, Mother. It's me, Lexi."

She eased herself into the desk chair and tried to remember what she was supposed to say next.

"Lexi? Well, what on earth— You don't sound like yourself." Her tone sharpened with alarm. "Is it your father? Has something happened?"

"No." Lexi shook her head automatically. "No, he's fine. They'll be sending him home in a week or so."

Cordelia released an audible sigh of relief. "I'm so glad. Dolores told me she had talked to you."

"Um, yes. That's sort of why I'm calling."

"Well, spit it out, dear. I have guests coming for dinner, and the florist should be here anytime now. There are a million details still to be taken care of."

"Sounds like some shindig," Lexi said, stalling while she built her courage.

"Oh, it's a small affair, but Lloyd likes everything to be just so. He's very particular. Now, what is it, Lexi dearest? I really do have to run."

"Well, Mother—" Lexi took a deep, calming breath and let it out slowly while her gaze searched the wall above her for inspiration. Finding none, she plunged ahead. "Have you ever noticed anything about Jamie that was, well, familiar?"

"Lexi, whatever are you talking about? He's my grandson. Of course he's familiar."

"No," Lexi said, growing as impatient as her mother. "No, that's not what I mean. Does he remind you of anyone? In his pictures, have you noticed that he bears a resemblance to someone?"

Cordelia huffed. "Well, he doesn't look like Dolores at all."

"On his visits, have you ever noticed the way he moves, some of the things he does?"

"Well, yes, and I've been meaning to speak to you about that, Lexi. I know he lives on a ranch and is used to a lot of freedom, but that child is entirely too boisterous. Lloyd was thinking perhaps a military school might be a good idea."

"Oh, good grief!" Lexi snapped. "If Lloyd was any stiffer, you might as well have him stuffed and mounted. That's *not* what I called to talk to you about."

"Lloyd may be a trifle starchy, but he's rich as Croesus, dear, and I expect you to be nice to him," Cordelia retorted. "Besides, I've already told him you'd never agree. Oh my, the florist is here, darling. I really have to go."

"Mother! Wait!"

"What?"

"I know Dolores denies it, but—"

"Jake is *not* Jamie's father," Cordelia said as if she could read Lexi's mind across the miles.

"When I see them together, that's awfully hard to believe."

"I'm your mother, Alexandra. Are you doubting my word?"

Years of disappointment, deceit and rejection swirled through Lexi's mind with dizzying speed, and she rested her head in her hand until the images receded.

With a tired sigh, she said, "Mother, if I have learned anything in my lifetime, it's that you will stop at nothing to protect Dolores. I've been a handy sacrifice for you more than once."

"It hurts me to hear you say that, Lexi."

"I can ask Jake, Mother. If I find out that Dolores slept with him just before she left— If I find out she lied to me about that, then I'll know that Jake could be the father and probably *is* the father."

"And then what will you do? Will you tell him? Will you risk having him take Jamie away from you? Because he could, you know. Fathers have rights now. Is that what you want?"

It was her mother's tone even more than her words that hurt, but it was a pain Lexi knew well. She had long ago accepted that she was a stepchild in her own mother's eyes. Yet she'd also learned that she was the lucky one in the end.

"If Jake is the father," Lexi said calmly, "he has a right to know."

"You're a fool, Lexi. As far as the world knows, you're Jamie's mother. I took care of that for you. *Me*, your mother. *I* fixed it so that the doctor and the hospital thought that Dolores was Alexandra Conley. *I* fixed it so that you could leave California with Jamie as your own child and no one would ever know the difference. Now you're threatening to ruin the whole thing!"

"It's my decision to make, Mother. Maybe you've lived your life based on deceit, but I don't plan to live that way. Jamie's always known that he was adopted, and when he's old enough, I plan to tell him who his mother really is."

Cordelia's gasp rang through the phone lines. "You wouldn't dare!"

"Of course I would," Lexi said quietly. "And when I tell Jamie about his mother, don't you think he's going to want answers about his father? Jamie's ten, Mother. He's begun asking questions already. How much longer do you think I can go on stalling him?"

"You can't tell him!" Cordelia cried. "You were never supposed to tell him. You promised!"

"I wasn't even twenty years old. I was in shock when I found out what you'd done behind my back. I came out to California to help my sister through a traumatic divorce. I didn't even know she was pregnant until I saw her. And I never dreamed that the only reason you wanted me there was to set me up."

"That doesn't make any difference. You took the baby. You agreed to it."

"Sure I took him, after Dolores threatened to give him up for adoption if I didn't." Lexi gripped the phone so tightly her fingers were beginning to cramp. "After I'd already been taking care of him for weeks. After I'd already fallen in love with him."

Tears crept into her voice at the memory, and her heart broke all over again at the thought of that tiny, perfect baby being tossed aside by a mother who had never wanted him in the first place. Some people should never be mothers. Dolores was one of those people, and Cordelia was probably another.

Like Lexi herself, Jamie was lucky to have been rejected, lucky to have been gathered up in his new mother's arms and carried back to the ranch outside Santa Fe where he, like she, would know what it was like to grow up being truly loved.

"Don't get emotional, Alexandra," her mother ordered. "You know how I dislike tears."

Lexi took a deep breath and shook off the sadness. The past was far behind her. Jamie was hers, and there was nothing anyone could do to change that. When the time came, she would tell him as much as he needed to know and no more. There was no reason he should ever have to bear the ugliness of the whole truth.

"Don't worry, Mother. I won't do anything yet. There's been enough pain. I don't want anyone to be hurt by any of this ever again." With the storm of emotions quieting, Lexi felt almost at peace. "I realize this has to be Dolores's decision, too."

"She'll *never* agree."

"I think she will, in time. I think the day will come when she'll want him to know."

"You're out of your mind."

"We'll see." As usual, whenever she talked to her mother, Lexi was eager to be finished with the conversation so she could reclaim her peace of mind. "Isn't your florist waiting?"

"Yes, well, promise me you'll give this some thought, Alexandra. I think if you look at this realistically, you'll come to your senses."

"Have a nice evening, Mother." She was already removing the receiver from her ear.

"Give your father my love, dear."

Her mother's parting request, barely heard, brought a smile to Lexi's face as she replaced the receiver in the cradle. The last time she had passed on her mother's greetings, her father had made it clear that he didn't want to hear anything more about "that damned woman." To him, the past was a closed book.

Lexi wondered if she might not be better off if she had the same attitude. Maybe something of what her mother said was right. Would Jamie be happier knowing the truth? Or would he feel the way Lexi had felt when her mother kept Dolores and returned Lexi to her father?

It had taken her half a lifetime to realize that the fault wasn't in her, but in her mother. Lexi didn't want Jamie to go through that, and yet she didn't know how she could stop it once she told him the truth.

Her head was reeling from the unanswerable questions as she pushed herself to her feet. She would deal with her problems the same way she *had* been dealing with them. Like Scarlett O'Hara, she wouldn't think about them until tomorrow. She would take things one day at a time, and pray to heaven that she could find an answer before her tomorrows ran out.

LEXI PULLED into the driveway just before sunset. She and her father had spent the morning in meetings with his doctors, and she was floating on air at the thought that her dad would be coming home after the weekend. He would still need a lot of care for the first month, but with Twyla and Manuel available to help out, she had been able to assure the doctors that there would be no problem.

A smile lighted her face as she exited the car and entered the courtyard. Instead of going into the house, she sat on the wide stone rim of the fountain. From the top, where water once flowed, a mandevilla vine cascaded instead. Its delicate pink flowers dripped down to pool among miniature white roses and fuchsia dianthus growing from a cool green carpet of ivy.

Her fingertips traced the tiny petals of a rose, and Lexi breathed in a deep sigh of contentment. Her father would live. He would be home soon. The degree of her relief told her just how worried she had been. Maybe now he would slow down and take time to enjoy life a little more.

From the questions he had asked, she knew he was still hoping Jake would stay on. She had almost begun to hope the same thing herself. Jamie came straight home from school these days, spending his late afternoon hours with Jake rather than riding the rounds with Manuel or one of the other ranch hands. Even Twyla seemed more pink-cheeked than usual when Jake was around, and meals on the ranch had never tasted better.

The front door of the house swung open with a jerk and closed with a slam. Lexi looked up, expecting to see Jake. Instead, she saw Brad McCauley charging across the portal and into the courtyard, aiming straight for her.

"Brad?"

She tried to suppress the instant swell of regret, but it remained undiminished. At his best, Brad was an attractive and reasonably charming man, but he was no Jake Thorn.

"Lexi." Brad skidded to a halt in front of her and jammed his fists onto his hips. "Could you please tell me what that maniac is trying to do?"

Not terribly interested in Brad's latest squabble with Jake, Lexi gave the question only the briefest consideration before she shrugged and shook her head. "Probably not. Jake's pretty much in charge of running the ranch right now, and I've been gone all day."

"Well, you've got to stop him. How am I supposed to do my job if I'm running up here all the time to baby-sit him?"

"What do you mean?"

"He's going back over every transaction I've handled for the past two years. He's making me dig up receipts for cattle sales and bills for feed purchases that have been boxed up and stored away for a year and a half." Brad's arms flailed wildly and a flush of anger suffused his face. "I'd hate to have to bother Frank at the hospital with this, but I'm not going to take much more."

"No!" Alarmed, Lexi jumped to her feet. "Don't do that! I'll handle it. Whatever the problem is, I'll get it straightened out. But under no circumstances are you to call Dad. I don't want him to think, hear or dream about work for at least the next six weeks."

"Of course," Brad said, cooling off visibly. "I—I wouldn't do that, Lexi. I shouldn't have even said it. I was just upset."

He took off his hat with one hand and ran the fingers of the other through his hair as he stared up at the darkening sky and breathed a sigh of exasperation. "Damn!" he said with feeling.

His expression reminded her of a disgruntled little boy, and Lexi caught herself smiling. "What's the matter, Brad?"

"Something about that man just rubs me the wrong way."

With a final finger-combing of his hair, he set his hat back on his head at a slightly off-center tilt, then tugged the brim just a touch lower over his eyes.

"That's understandable," Lexi said sympathetically. "Right now Jake's doing a job you'd like to have. And you have the job he used to do. A certain amount of antagonism between the two of you is only natural."

"It's more than that." Brad's pale blue eyes roamed over her face. "I think he's jealous of a lot more than a job."

Her heart picked up its tempo, and nervous flutters wound their way through her core. "What do you mean?" she asked, knowing he meant her and afraid to believe it.

Brad shook his head and dropped his gaze. "Nothing." When he looked up again, he was more relaxed. "Have you decided about the dance this weekend? I'd still like to take you if you think you want to go."

Genuinely surprised, Lexi gasped. "Is that *this* weekend?"

"Sure is." He smiled. "It'd probably do you good to get out and kick up your heels a little. You must be worn to a frazzle after all the hours you've put in up at that hospital."

"I am." She sat on the edge of the fountain and stared at her hands in her lap. "Gee, you've caught me off guard here. I didn't know it was so soon."

"It's just two nights away." He lifted her hand in his. "I'll tell you what—you think about it tonight and give me your answer tomorrow. How's that?"

"Good." Lexi smiled and nodded as she drew her hand away. "That would be good."

She rubbed her palm against her skirt as she watched him walk away. She didn't need a night to know that she wouldn't be going to the dance with Brad. She needed the night to figure out how she would tell him that.

With her earlier mood of celebration gone and the soft shadows of dusk creeping over her, Lexi was reluctant to leave her floral oasis in the desert. She wasn't prepared to confront the reason that the touch of another man's hand had become so unappealing. She wasn't ready to go into the house where Jake was waiting.

As if on cue, the front door opened and a tall, dark silhouette stepped into the lemon rectangle of light from the foyer. Trapped, Lexi wondered what Jake had to say. She didn't have long to wait.

"Are you coming in?"

She couldn't see his face clearly through the shadows of the veranda and the yellow halo that surrounded him, but his voice didn't sound pleased.

"I just thought I'd sit out here for a minute and enjoy the fresh air," she answered so softly she wasn't sure he could hear her.

Jake pulled the door closed behind him and advanced to the edge of the portal. "I've been waiting for you to get home."

Lexi leaned forward, her back stiff with alarm. "Is there anything wrong? Is Jamie—"

"No, Jamie's just fine," Jake snapped. "He's up-stairs doing his homework."

"Oh." Placing her hand over her racing heart, she took a deep breath of relief and slowly relaxed. Her father was fine. Jamie was fine. And so long as they were okay, she could handle anything else. "Well then, what's wrong?"

Jake stepped to the edge of the courtyard and leaned back against one of the rough posts that supported the portal roof. "Did I say anything was wrong?"

"No, but you sound like it."

"Maybe I just don't like to see you holding hands with a thief like Brad McCauley."

"What are you talking about?" Lexi's temper was instantly ablaze. "And what were you doing? Watching from the window?"

"As a matter of fact, I was," Jake said quietly. "I don't trust McCauley, so I was watching him leave. And guess what I saw instead?"

"What you saw was him complaining about you. Did you know he was ready to call Dad at the hospital?"

At that, Jake peeled away from the post with a grace that belied the still-healing injuries to his body. "That wouldn't be a good idea." He stood taut as if poised for battle and stared down the road that led away from the house.

"That's what I told him. So I promised I'd get everything straightened out. Now, what seems to be the problem?"

"Is that why he was holding your hand? He was thanking you for coming to his rescue?"

"Not that it's any of your business, but he was asking me to go to the dance with him on Saturday."

"That son-of-a-bitch," Jake almost whispered. "That scheming, low life son-of-a—"

"What is *wrong* with you?" Lexi demanded, coming to her feet with her hands on her hips. "I know you were foreman here once, but face the facts, Jake. You walked out on the job, and Brad's the foreman now. So just get over it."

"Get over it?" Jake covered the distance between them in huge, ground-eating strides. "Get over it?" he shouted again, coming to a halt almost on top of her. "Is that what you said?"

"Yes, that's what I said." Lexi took a step backward and thrust her chin in the air. "You're making a fool of yourself with this vendetta."

"I'm making a fool of myself," he said softly. The anger in his eyes was so intense they glittered. "*I'm* the fool? I don't think so. *I'm* not the one letting a thieving con man sweet-talk me right out of my shoes and into his bed."

Livid with fury, Lexi went poker stiff and clenched her hands into fists at her sides. "You're lucky I don't slap you for that."

"Are you going with him?" he asked, ignoring her threat.

"I haven't made up my mind yet."

"What do you mean you haven't made up your mind yet? It's a simple decision. Yes or no?"

"I don't *know.*"

The wall of the fountain pressed against the backs of her legs. She could retreat no farther, but Jake kept coming. His thighs brushed hers. His fingers threaded through her hair at the nape of her neck.

"Yes or no?" he asked again.

His fist closed around her hair and pulled gently, tilting her head back until her face was exposed to the fading light.

"No," she whispered. At the flash of triumph in Jake's eyes she changed her answer in the space of a heartbeat. "Yes."

"Which?" he demanded in a harsh growl.

His breath fanned her cheeks while his lips hovered almost close enough to brush hers as he spoke. Lexi's heart pounded wildly, but she couldn't give in to him. She couldn't tell him he had won.

"Yes."

"Damn you."

His mouth ground against hers in a punishing and furiously passionate kiss. His thigh pushed between her legs, pressing intimately while his tongue slowly penetrated the soft interior of her mouth in a wicked, thrusting seduction that reached to the center of her being.

Throbbing with a heat that built with each brush against his hard body, Lexi clung to him, drinking in the kiss that was no longer angry but deep and wild as a rampaging river. Her breasts tingled against the crush of his chest, and she ached to feel the sweet, heavy weight of his body on hers.

She was dizzy with longing and burning with a desire that was hot enough to self-ignite. When Jake lifted his mouth from hers, she gasped for air, then gasped again as his hand cupped her hip from behind and held her tight against him while his thigh began a rhythmic thrust between her legs.

Lexi moaned and pressed her face to his neck.

"You're not going with him, are you?" Jake asked in a raspy whisper next to her ear.

She shook her head and moaned again, unable to speak, unable even to believe what was happening to her.

"You're going with me." Jake lowered his head and nuzzled her cheek. His lips found their way toward hers. "Aren't you?"

She nodded and whispered, "Yes." She lifted her face to him. Her lips brushed his, opening, offering body and soul what she could no longer deny. She was his. She had always been his. Jake's mouth closed over hers, taking what was offered and giving tenderness and passion in return. His kiss reached deep, drawing her into him, probing, promising and tantalizing. In a mirror dance with her body, he warmed her, seduced her and fulfilled her with his kiss until he held her shuddering in his arms.

"Oh, Jake," Lexi moaned. She buried her face against his shoulder as she clung to him to keep from collapsing in a puddle at his feet.

"I want you so bad my teeth hurt." His husky voice raked seductively over each word.

She could feel his arousal—a hard, hot ridge pulsing against her stomach—and she felt guilty. First, that she had found release while he had not, and second, that she had been so blinded by lust that she had allowed it to happen.

"I shouldn't have—"

"Hush." Jake pulled her tighter into the circle of his arm. "I know we're right out in the middle of the courtyard, but it's nearly dark, and we're alone. And I've been almost out of my mind from thinking about this."

"This?" she asked, wondering if he meant the ground swell of passion that had just rolled over them.

"This." He pressed himself against her stomach, leaving no doubt that he was still fully aroused. "And this." His kiss was swift and hard as his leg slipped between hers again. "And this."

Nerve endings that were still aching and throbbing went wild, setting off tiny explosions all through her only temporarily sated system. "Oh, Jake, not now. Not here. Not again," she begged, fighting against the pleasure-pain that was swelling inside her.

"I know." Reluctantly he released her from the intensely erotic embrace and stepped back far enough for air to move between them. "But soon." He lifted her chin and gazed deeply into her eyes. "And when it happens, it's gonna be a long, long night."

CHAPTER ELEVEN

"THAT'S IT!" Jake slammed down the phone and pushed his chair away from the desk. "I've got him!"

Entering the foyer from the dining room on her way upstairs, Lexi halted in midstride and stared as Jake rose from his chair and lifted a fist in triumph.

"What on earth are you talking about?" she asked, glad for any excuse to interrupt him. Since their meeting by the fountain the night before, they had hardly had a moment alone together.

"Lexi, good. I was just going to call you." He motioned to the couch by the fireplace. "Why don't we sit over there?"

Puzzled, she let him guide her to the sofa, where he sat beside her and pulled her into the circle of his good arm. His gaze raked over her face, lingering on her lips before returning to her eyes.

"I've missed you."

Lexi dimpled, pleased by the open hunger in his eyes. "I didn't know you'd even given me a thought. You've been elbow-deep in work every time I passed by here."

"Oh, I've thought about you." His fingers toyed with her hair and his lips covered hers in a soft, searching kiss that ended much too quickly. "I haven't done much else," he whispered, his lips still brushing hers.

"Me, too."

Jake smiled and kissed her once again. "I'm glad to hear that, because I want to talk with you, and I don't want you to be upset."

Lexi pulled back far enough to look into his eyes. "Upset? About what?"

"About some of the things I've found out since I've been here. Things your dad asked me to look into while he was in the hospital."

"Things? What kind of things? And why haven't I heard about it before now?"

"Oh, you know your dad. He didn't want to worry you."

"Yes, I know my dad. I'm a woman, so it wasn't anything I should be concerned with. He'll never change." Lexi shrugged and stopped herself before she went any further. "So what is it?"

"Well, someone, with the help of one or two associates, has been carefully skimming the ranch's profits for several years now. And as Frank got sicker, they seem to have got a lot more blatant. This past year, they were stealing you blind."

"How?" She sat bolt upright in alarm, scarcely able to believe what she was hearing. "Who? Did Dad know?"

"He suspected, but he didn't have anything concrete. He thought maybe with me being an outsider I might notice something he overlooked."

"And did you?" Poised on the edge of the couch now, she stared straight into Jake's eyes.

"Eventually. You might not believe it, but Jamie was a big help. All those hours he spent after school riding line with Manuel and learning how the ranch worked, he picked up a lot."

"Is that why you've had him in here helping you?"

"Yeah. Jamie's helped with the calving the past couple of springs. He's got a good head for numbers, and being a kid, he really liked those calves. He remembers exactly how many survived, to the head, for the past two years. And the numbers don't match with the ones Brad McCauley gave your dad."

"No." In the first place, she didn't see why Brad would lie, and in the second place, she didn't see why something so small would matter.

"Yes," Jake said firmly. "The count he gave Frank was short by ten calves last year and fifteen this year."

"Look, Jake, I love my son, but if you're going to accuse Brad of theft, you've got to have more than that. So he miscounted. Big deal."

"Oh, but I do, Lexi. I have much more than that. I have a box full of feed bills, cattle sales, veterinary bills and I don't know what all where he just changed the numbers a little bit and pocketed the difference. It's small stuff, all of it, but it adds up."

Lexi turned to look over her shoulder at the stack of boxes beside the desk. If she wanted evidence, there was a lot of it. Grateful she was already seated, she leaned back. "This is hard to believe," she said quietly. "Does Dad know?"

More than a little stunned herself, she was frightened of what her father's reaction might be. He might not have liked Brad McCauley all that much, but he had trusted him.

"We talked this morning," Jake said. "Frank thinks we've got all we need. I can fire McCauley whenever I'm ready."

"Hold on just a minute." Images of dusky passion floated through Lexi's mind, and she didn't much like what she was thinking. "You knew this last night?"

"Well, I didn't talk to your dad till this morning, but I knew all the rest of it."

"And you were going to let me go to the dance with that—that—that—" She sputtered to a stop. "That thief?"

"I was trying my damnedest to stop you," Jake said, with just a hint of a smile.

"You could have just *told* me!" she cried, not at all amused. Shoving herself to her feet, she began to pace.

"But every time I tried, you started yelling about how jealous and narrow-minded I was being," Jake reminded her.

The fact that he was right only irritated her further. "Well, now I feel like a fool. I *dated* that man. I *defended* him."

"Aw, sweetheart, you didn't know. Frank didn't even know it was Brad."

She stopped pacing and turned to face him from the middle of the room. "He didn't?"

Jake rose and joined her. "No, and if I hadn't been so flat-out jealous and narrow-minded about old Brad, I'm sure I wouldn't have zeroed in on him nearly so fast."

Lexi sighed and allowed herself to feel a little less of an idiot as Jake stroked the backs of his fingers over her jaw. After all, Brad must have been pretty good at what he was doing to have gotten away with it for so long.

"I still wish you'd told me," she said, unhappy with the idea of Jake withholding the knowledge while wooing her away from a cattle rustler. "Was anyone else on the ranch involved?"

He tilted her chin higher and drew his fingertip down the side of her neck. "A fellow named Pepper, I'm pretty sure. And probably a new hand by the name of Carver."

She let out the breath she'd been holding. At least the bad news didn't extend to anyone they'd really known or cared about. For that, they could all be grateful.

"McCauley was pretty careful about who he brought in on it," Jake said. "I found out this morning that this isn't the first time he's done something like this."

"And you're just going to fire him?" She drew back a step as anger came hard on the heels of her relief. "Didn't he break any laws?"

"Well, sure, probably, but we just want to get rid of him."

"But what about the next ranch he goes to? If he's done this twice, he'll do it again."

"Word gets around. It won't be as easy for him next time, and I doubt very seriously that he'll ever work as a foreman again."

Without warning, the front door banged open and Brad McCauley blew in like a desert dust storm. "What the hell do you want now, Thorn?" he shouted, then stopped when he noticed Lexi half-hidden behind Jake. "What's this about, Lexi? Did you talk to him like you said?"

"I'm afraid I didn't get a chance to, Brad," Lexi answered, struggling mightily to control her venom. "Jake talked to me first."

"Well, then maybe we can all sit down now." Brad swung the front door closed behind him and sauntered into the parlor. "It's about time we got a few things straightened out around here." He sprawled in the big chair next to the sofa and waited for them to join him.

Jake hooked his arm around Lexi's waist and dipped his head toward her. "Maybe you should leave us alone for a few minutes, Lexi. I think Brad would rather do this in private."

"No, not at all." Brad faced Jake confidently. "I want Lexi to hear every word you have to say."

"She already has, Brad." Jake's hand tightened on her waist. "Lexi and I had quite a talk last night and again this morning. And by the way, she won't be going to the dance with you. She's going with me instead."

"What?" Indignant, Brad half rose from his chair.

"And another thing," Jake said. "I think I'd like my house back. You think you could be out of there by sometime tomorrow? You could use the bunkhouse to store your things until you find another place."

On his feet and spitting fire, Brad shouted, "Now wait just a minute, that house is the foreman's quarters. Everybody knows that."

Jake shook his head slowly. "No, that house is mine. Frank's lease on the Circle T has expired, and I've decided I want my house back now. If you can be out by noon tomorrow, I'll send Twyla over to clean up tomorrow afternoon."

"Well, what the hell am I supposed to do then?"

"We're getting to that part, Brad, old buddy. You still want Lexi to hang around?"

"Lexi." Brad turned pleading eyes on her. "Can't you stop him? Can't you do something? You know this isn't right."

Lexi lifted her gaze to Jake's, wondering how long he was prepared to drag this thing out. From the cold gleam in his eyes, she knew he was in no hurry.

"Actually, Jake is well within his rights. If he wants his house back, there's nothing we can do." She placed her hand over the one that cupped her waist. "And as for the rest, Jake has my full approval."

"The rest?" Brad stiffened and took a half step back. "What rest?"

With a toss of his head, Jake indicated the boxes of paperwork that were stacked in front of the window next to the cluttered desk. "Well, for starters, how about those doctored receipts you've been digging up for me for the past two weeks?"

"I don't know what you're talking about."

"Sure you do, Brad. You can play innocent. You can play dumb. Hell, you can play deaf and blind for all I care, but you still know what you did. And so do I."

"You're setting me up. Lexi, don't listen to him!"

The eyes that sought her out this time had become desperate. If she wasn't convinced of his guilt, she would have almost felt sorry for him.

"Give it up, Brad," she said quietly. "Nobody's buying the act anymore. You stole from my dad, and you tried to use me. You're lucky all they're going to do is fire you. If I'd had my way, you'd be going to jail."

"As it is," Jake said, "Mr. Conley is generously offering you two weeks' severance if you'll leave quickly and quietly. You can pick up the check at noon tomorrow. Your duties as foreman are terminated, effective immediately."

"You've been itching for this since you got here." Brad's teeth were bared like a snarling animal's. "I bet you feel real good right now."

"If I were you, I'd leave before too much more was said," Jake answered in a voice that was clear and icy as a mountain stream. "I may not be completely healed, but I'll take you on anytime you want to try it."

Brad took a step closer, his chin jutting. "I'd love to!"

"I'll just bet you would!" Lexi pulled free of Jake's arm and thrust herself between the men. "You!" She jabbed Brad in the chest with her finger. "You belly-crawling, low-life snake, you get out of here and start packing. I don't want to see your face until you pick up your check tomorrow, and if I hear one more threat of any kind, I'll just call the sheriff out here and see what *he* thinks of that stack of evidence over there. Now, move it!''

With a final glare in Jake's direction, Brad scuttled past Lexi and out of the house before she even had a chance to catch her breath.

''What the hell was the meaning of that?'' Jake demanded. ''I don't need you to fight my battles for me.''

''I wasn't fighting your battle. I was fighting mine. What am I supposed to do if you go and get yourself all banged up again? After all, you just fired the only other man who asked me to the dance on Saturday night.''

Slowly the fire went out of Jake's eyes and a lazy grin lifted one corner of his mouth. ''What in the world was I thinking about?''

''I don't know, but I sure wanted to stop it before it went any further.''

Chuckling, he gathered her to him. ''Well, I thank you most sincerely.''

''My pleasure.''

He pulled her closer. ''I'm really looking forward to tomorrow night.''

Lexi smiled slowly, surprised by the sincerity in his voice. ''So am I.''

He kissed her, then released her with a reluctance that made her tingle all over. ''I guess we'd better get back to work now. I've got to talk to Manuel about filling in for McCauley until next week.''

''What happens next week?''

''I figure by then I should be able to take over most of the foreman's duties.''

"Oh." Realizing she had sounded disappointed, Lexi brightened. "Well, that would be good. Does that mean you'll be moving back into your old house?"

"I was thinking about it. Just in case."

"Just in case what?"

Jake winced. "I wasn't going to say anything about it, but your dad mentioned that Dolores called him yesterday. She was talking about coming for a visit when he gets home from the hospital."

"Oh, no." A month ago, Lexi had been hoping for just such a visit. Now the thought filled her with dread. "Maybe she was just trying to make him feel better."

"It didn't work. Frank's about as eager to put up with Dolores's theatrics as I am. But at least I have someplace where I can go hide."

"Maybe we're not being kind here. Dolores really is very fond of Dad. After all, he was a father to her for six very formative years, and I know he's the only one of her stepfathers she ever called Daddy."

"If she was all that concerned, you'd think she'd have gotten here sooner."

"Mother said she was waiting for a call back on some part she tried out for." The excuse sounded as weak to Lexi's ears now as it had when her mother had used it.

"Which means she's either coming here to gloat or to lick her wounds."

"Probably," Lexi agreed. "Anyway, I've been wanting her to spend more time with Jamie. After all, she's the only aunt he's got, and I sometimes worry that he feels neglected."

Answering that with a short, derisive bark of laughter, Jake said, "With all the attention that kid gets around this ranch, I don't think he feels neglected. Besides, it's not as if she's a blood relation."

"I don't like to make that distinction. Family is family," Lexi said tartly.

"Excuse me. I didn't mean to offend you."

"I'm not offended," she said, unable to conceal her annoyance. He had struck a nerve, however unintentionally.

"You're pretty defensive for someone who's not offended."

Lexi took a deep breath and forced herself to calm down. If only it wasn't such a rotten time for her sister to show up. Finally, she said, "You're right. I don't know what got into me."

"I think maybe I do." Jake took her wrist and pulled her to him. He slipped his hand along the nape of her neck and tilted her face toward his. "I wasn't married to Dolores a month before I realized how big a mistake I'd made. Just in case you're worried about it happening again, don't be. Okay?"

He'd guessed wrong about what was troubling her, but Lexi was immensely relieved nonetheless by the quietly somber tone of his words. She offered a tentative smile. "Okay."

His teeth caught at his lower lip for an instant before he said, "Someday soon, I'll tell you all about what *really* happened back then."

Mesmerized as surely as if he were a spider seducing her into its web, she leaned toward him. "Tell me now," she whispered.

Jake laughed softly and shook his head, his lips still tantalizingly close. "Later." He kissed her gently, then released her and stepped back. "I'd better get back to work now. Maybe we'll talk more about it after the dance tomorrow."

JAKE PUSHED OPEN the front door of his ranch house on the Circle T and waited for Lexi to enter. Just inside the door she stopped, feeling strangely as if she were walking through a dream. The light of a full moon crept in through the windows and cast a soft, warm glow over the empty room.

"It looks the same, doesn't it?" Jake asked. Taking her hand in his, he pulled her with him into the room.

She nodded, lost in a reverie so real she could almost reach out and touch it. Eleven years seemed to melt away. Once again she saw the moon of that night, shining big and bright in a cloudless desert sky, seeping with the shimmer of candlelight into the nearly empty living room of Jake's ranch house.

"I hope you didn't mind leaving the dance early." Jake's voice broke into her thoughts, pulling her back to the present.

"No." She shook her head. "I felt a little self-conscious anyway."

"Because of me?"

"No." Lexi motioned to her low-cut and ultrafeminine dress. "Because of this."

To illustrate, she gave the short, full skirt a swish, then let it fall back into place, several inches shy of her knees. Below this, her slender, shapely legs were encased in sheer black stockings, and on her feet were black satin slings with stiletto heels never meant for a barn dance.

"You look wonderful." His voice held nothing but approval.

"Thank you." With an embarrassed laugh, Lexi cast her eyes down. She had given in to temptation and worn the dress just for him. "That *is* the effect I was going for."

His fingertip touched her chin, traveling from one side to the other just below the curve of her lower lip. "You succeeded magnificently. So much so, I had to get you away from that dance so I could have you all to myself."

Jake dropped his hand and stepped back, clearing his throat. "I think I'd better get a fire going in the fireplace." He pointed to the wall next to the dining room. "There's a tape player in the corner. Why don't you find a tape you like?"

While he busied himself with the fireplace, Lexi combed through the small stack of tapes, holding each one up to catch a ray of moonlight until she found a tape that sounded suitably romantic. She put it in to play, and once again, memories of that long-ago night eddied around her, riding on currents of excitement and longing. The same emotions that had urged her on that night eleven years ago filled her now. The only thing missing this time was the hopelessly romantic notion that tonight would be the beginning of a new life for them both. She knew better than to plan for a future with Jake. It was enough that she was here now, and he was with her.

Jake stood and held out his hand to her. "May I have this dance?"

"I'd love to." Smiling, she walked into the circle of his arm.

While the music flowed over them, he hesitated, then stepped back and slipped the sling from his shoulder. "I think I can dispense with this thing for the rest of the evening."

"Do you think you should?"

"I'll put it back on later." Jake tossed the sling aside and scooped Lexi into his embrace once again. "The doctor said it'll probably be coming off this week anyway."

"Really?" Held solidly in two strong arms, her heart pounding against his, she felt unaccountably lighthearted.

"Really," he echoed. "But just because I'm getting better, don't think you're going to be getting rid of me. Your dad's still a long way from well, and I'm a long way from gone."

"Aw, shucks," Lexi said, laughing. She couldn't remember the last time she'd been so happy. Then, locked in Jake's arms, twirling slowly in the empty room to the soft strains of a love song, with only the flicker of the firelight competing with the pale glow of a full desert moon, she was transported back to that night long ago, the last night she had spent in Jake's arms....

THE ONLY LIGHT CAME from the dying embers of the fireplace and the moonlight slanting through the windows. Lexi hadn't visited the little ranch house since Dolores's departure, and the emptiness of the rooms was shocking. There was no furniture, no lamps or drapes, not even a picture on the wall.

"What happened?" Lexi asked over the sound of the country-and-western song drifting from the open door of the pickup parked in front of the house.

"You mean the furniture?" The whiskey bottle Jake clutched in his hand bumped against Lexi's back as he gathered her into his arms and whirled her in lazy circles around the room. "Dolores. She even took the light bulbs, damn her eyes. That was just plain spiteful."

Without releasing Lexi, he tilted back his head to take a long swig of the whiskey. In the dim light, she couldn't see the anger she knew was in his eyes. She couldn't see the hurt, either, but she knew it was there, too.

"That was over a month ago, Jake," she said gently. "Haven't you replaced the light bulbs, at least?"

He turned away and walked to the fireplace, setting the half-empty whiskey bottle on the mantel with a thunk. Lexi watched him from a distance as he stood unmoving, gazing into the dying embers of the fire.

"That's why you moved into the bunkhouse after Dolores left? I thought it was because you couldn't stand to be here without her."

Jake's laugh was a low grunt. "Not exactly."

"But you *are* upset," Lexi insisted, remembering the reason she was here, the reason she had followed Jake, first when he'd stormed off the ranch and again when he'd left the bar where he'd gone to drown his sorrows. She remembered the divorce papers that had arrived today and were now wadded into a ball on the floor of his pickup.

"Hell yes, I'm upset," he growled. "That spoiled little bitch is trying to take everything she couldn't cart off the first time. She's not content with half of what's left. She wants it all."

Distressed to see him hurt so much by her own half sister, Lexi went to him. "Jake, I'm so sorry."

"Don't be." He reached out and pulled her against him. "At least I'm rid of her."

Glorying in Jake's touch, Lexi pressed herself to him. For three years she had stood aside, pining for him while he belonged to someone else. For three years she had watched helplessly as Dolores abused what Lexi would have given anything to possess.

"God, you feel good," Jake whispered next to her ear. "How could I have made such a mistake? How could I have let it go on for so long?"

"It's over now." She could hear the ache of longing in her own voice. "You're free. We're both free."

"Ah, Lexi." His arms loosened, and he began to push her away. "Don't tempt me. You don't know how weak I am."

She pressed her lips to his throat and felt the wild beating of his pulse. He wanted her as much as she wanted him. She knew it, even if he tried to deny it. "I've waited for you, Jake."

"No. You're just a baby. I'm too old for you."

"I'm nineteen, Jake." She moved her hands up his arms to his shoulders, edging closer to him. "I'm not a baby anymore."

"You don't know what you're doing," Jake said, making one last, insincere attempt to dissuade her.

"You know that's not true." Lexi brushed her cheek against his shoulder. "Make love to me, Jake." She lifted passion-glazed eyes to his. "Please."

He buried his fingers in her hair. "I hope you don't regret this in the morning."

"You have my solemn word that I will never regret this as long as I live."

"Lexi." And with that, he gave up the fight.

LEXI TILTED BACK her head and moaned low in her throat, a soft, almost purring sound, as the memories of that long-ago night swept over her. There were so many questions unanswered, so many things she had never understood. But none of that mattered tonight. Tonight she wanted only to relive the magic she had known only once in her life.

Jake pulled her closer and trailed kisses down the side of her neck and across to the pulse point at the base of her throat. Lexi moaned again. Memories of yesterday and thoughts of tomorrow were gone, lost to the sensations of the here and now.

"Lord, I've missed you." He pressed his lips against the fullness rising from the neckline of her dress.

The words sent shivers of pleasure racing down her spine. Her breasts ached for his touch. Her body cried out for an end to the waiting. "Show me."

"I don't want to rush it."

"Please," she whispered in an agony of desire. "If you have any mercy in you, rush it."

"Are you sure?"

"Absolutely positive."

He crushed her to him. "I'd pick you up and carry you to the bed if I could."

"Bed?" Her eyes fluttered open and she stared up at him in a momentary return to reality. "You have a bed?"

"I had it delivered this afternoon. I came over after Twyla left and made it up myself." He smiled, and even in the flickering light of the fire, she could see the mischief in his eyes. "Did you think I was planning to seduce you on the living room floor?"

"I was hoping you might have a bearskin rug stashed someplace."

His smile grew. "Maybe next time."

Taking her hand, he led her from the living room and down the hall to his bedroom. Here, too, moonlight cast its glow through the two long windows flanking a tall four-poster bed, complete with ruffled pillows and comforter.

For the first time, a glimmer of real hope sprang to life in Lexi's heart. This was not the bed of a rolling stone. This was not even a bed Jake would have chosen for himself. He had done this for her, and her alone.

Releasing her hand, he unbuttoned his shirt without effort and let it drop to the floor. The bronzed, hard-muscled breadth of his chest and shoulders was even more impressive in the moonlight, despite the strip of white bandages that still protected his ribs.

Seeing the object of her gaze, he stroked his fingers lightly over the bandages. "I wish I could take these off, too. But I guess I shouldn't push it."

With a smile that showcased her dimples, Lexi echoed his earlier words. "Maybe next time."

He slipped his arms around her waist and pulled her snug against him. "Maybe not. Next time's going to come awfully soon if I have anything to say about it."

Once more, hope surfaced. And once more Lexi pushed it down again, almost superstitiously afraid to give in to it. With Jake she would take things one day at a time—one night at a time. To wish for more would be asking for heartache.

His hand slid up her back, caressing the slender muscles that ran the length of her spine. When he reached the top of her dress, his fingers caught the tab of the zipper and pulled it down.

Lexi caught her breath as cool air brushed her bare skin.

"It's only fair," Jake whispered. "You once helped me undress. Now I can do the same for you."

He moved back and slid his fingers under the shoulders of her dress, pulling it away from her and down, then releasing it to let it fall around her feet. He held her hand to steady her as she stepped from the pool of flowers.

Letting out his breath in a sigh, Jake looked her slowly up and down and back again. Then tenderly, almost reverently, he cupped her silk-clad breasts in his hands.

Cradling the ripe weight in his palms, he smoothed his thumbs upward over the rounded curve to peaks that were visibly erect and waiting for his touch.

When he reached for the clasp between her breasts, Lexi caught his hand in hers and shook her head. "You first." She dropped her gaze to the jeans that still covered him.

One side of his mouth slid upward in a lazy smile as he flicked open the metal button at his waist and pulled down the zipper. Pausing, he sat on the foot of the bed and offered her his booted foot. "Maybe you'd better help me off with these first." His crooked smile widened.

Turning her back to him, Lexi tugged the extended boot free and let it fall to the floor with a thud. "I don't suppose moccasins would have done for the dance," she muttered, straining at the second, more stubborn boot.

"Not really." His voice was soft as Jake caressed the firmly rounded, silk-clad slope of her hips.

Letting the second boot drop, Lexi turned to him, once again intensely conscious of the moment. His hands cupped her hips while he watched her gaze roam slowly from his face to his chest, then down to where his jeans spread to reveal a wedge of bronzed skin above a pair of low-slung briefs.

She offered no resistance when his hand slid to the back of her calf and he gently lifted her leg until her foot rested on his thigh. The husky rasp of his breath matched her own, each shallow intake coming quicker than the one before as his knuckles brushed the bare flesh of her upper thigh.

With a touch as light as a whisper, he freed the garter and eased the nylon down her leg until it dropped silently to the floor. His movements were tantalizingly slow as he turned to the other leg, repeating his actions until she stood before him clad only in the silky sheerness of bikinis and bra.

Rising to meet her, so close that his chest brushed the tips of her breasts, he took her hands and pressed them down over his hips, peeling away his jeans in the process. As his erection sprang free and brushed against her thigh, Lexi caught her breath in a soft gasp and drew back. His patience at its limit, Jake hurried to rid himself of his jeans. Kicking them aside, he pulled her to him in a fevered kiss that melded them, body and soul. When at length he drew his lips from hers, they both stood panting, still clasped in each other's arms.

"I wish I could have waited," Jake murmured as he slipped his fingertips beneath the lace band of her bikinis. His palms smoothed over the swell of her hips. "Until my ribs were healed, at least. But I think I would have burst from wanting you." He caressed the silken skin of her thighs, sliding the underwear down her legs. "I just hope I don't disappoint you."

"Shh," she whispered, nuzzling his cheek. "The only way you could disappoint me right now is if you stopped."

"There's no danger of my doing that."

With a deft flick of his fingers, he released the fastening on her bra and let it fall atop the panties.

"No matter what happens," Jake said, taking her hand and leading her to the head of the bed. "I promise not to cry out in pain."

Lexi smiled softly as he stripped back the covering and she slipped between the sheets. "And no matter how much I might want to," she swore solemnly, "no bear hugs."

Jake knelt beside her while his eyes raked over her and sighed in wonder. "You take my breath away."

Then he slid in beside her, crushing her breasts against him and covering her glorious body with his as he kissed her with deep and tender reverence. Then he stretched himself out beside her and drew one fingertip down the valley between her breasts and across the hollow of her stomach.

As his finger traced a wandering path into the soft, dark forest of hair just above her thighs, his breath fanned the aching tips of her breasts, his mouth so close she could almost feel its warm succulence. A thousand nerve endings cried out for more.

She twisted toward him, lifting her nipple to brush against his lips as her legs spread in an open invitation to his touch. With a muffled groan, Jake closed his mouth over the turgid peak and suckled her as his fingers parted the moist cleft between her thighs and slipped inside.

CHAPTER TWELVE

HER HEAD RESTING on his good shoulder, Lexi pressed her body against Jake's side. Her leg lay over the top of his. His hand caressed the curve of her thigh.

"How are your ribs?" she asked softly, nuzzling her cheek against the warm, sweat-moist skin just below his shoulder.

He shifted his body against hers, enjoying the lush feel of her breasts and the silky brush of hair against his thigh.

"They may be a little sore tomorrow, but I'll survive," he said with a chuckle at the sheer luxury of holding her in his arms.

He was ready to offer her the world, but he knew better than to put his thoughts into words. In the afterglow of their lovemaking, it would be too easy to make promises he couldn't keep. He was still just a busted-up, nearly broke, over-the-hill cowboy with no future to speak of and nothing to offer a woman who deserved so much.

But still he wanted her. For tonight, for tomorrow, for the day after—he wanted her. For as long as she would have him and for as long as he could take the pain of knowing it could never last, he wanted her.

She raised her leg higher and snuggled closer, and he felt himself stiffen and throb to life. Lexi brushed her thigh over him, stroking her soft, warm skin against his erection. She rolled against him and kissed his shoulder, giggling.

"Vixen."

She giggled again and rubbed herself against his thigh in a sensual invitation. Jake caught his breath in a gasp as every nerve in his body sang in unison and his erection rose into the air, high and hard and aching for attention.

She was sunlight and laughter and dark, dusky desire. She was playful sweetness and passionate abandon. She was everything he had ever wanted in a woman. And she was his.

Taking her hip in his hand, he rolled her onto her back and pulled her under him as he slid between her legs and lifted himself up and into her in one clean thrust. She closed around him like a tight fist, smooth and hot and unbelievably good.

Shuddering with wave after wave of desire, Jake pressed his forehead to hers and whispered her name, his lips brushing hers.

"Lexi."

She drew in her breath in a gasp and rose to meet him, surging with a strength that lifted him beyond passion, beyond pain, through the clouds and spiraling among the stars.

"Jake. Oh, Jake. Oh, Jake." His name was a chant, feathery soft and guttural deep, in rhythm with their thrusts. "Yes, yes, oh, yes."

Hurtling through space in a free-fall, Jake felt his body explode into a thousand pieces. With a single cry, Lexi arched into him and stiffened.

Then slowly she began to move again in tiny circles, clinging to him as she purred softly and floated to earth beneath him. Holding her close until she landed, Jake bit back the words he longed to say, the "I love you" that rushed up from the back of his mind.

The moment would pass. And even if it didn't, he had no right to say those words. Besides, he had already said them with his body, every way he could think of, all night long. Sex was one time, quickly, with a condom . . . *Shit!*

He rocketed bolt upright. *Damn!*

"What's the matter?" Even in the throes of orgasmic afterglow, Lexi could tell something was wrong. When he just stared at her in silent horror, she put her hand on his arm and shook him gently. "Jake? What is it?"

"I'm sorry. I forgot. I meant—"

"What are you babbling about?"

"I didn't—" He gestured to the floor.

Lexi looked down where he had tossed the condoms he had used at the beginning of the night. "Oh my." Well, at least she wouldn't get pregnant. She *did* have that part covered, not that she'd had much need to in recent years.

"I *never* make love without protection," Jake said solemnly. "Never."

"Neither do I," Lexi assured him.

"Then I guess we're both safe that way, which just leaves us with the little problem of what if you get pregnant."

"Oh, you don't have to worry about that."

Jake's eyes narrowed. "Why?"

"Well, because—" She searched for a way to say it delicately. "I, uh, don't leave that up to the man."

"You mean you're on birth control."

"Well, you don't have to say it like it's a dirty word."

"It just hadn't occurred to me that you would need such constant protection."

"Not that it's any of your business, but I just recently started using it again," she snapped, upset that she felt the need to explain herself to him.

The angry gleam in his eye was replaced by a twinkle. "How recently?"

"Recently. That's all you need to know. Recently."

He stretched out on the bed and pulled her down beside him. Draping his leg across her, he turned her face toward his. "You've been planning to go to bed with me since I got here, haven't you?"

"I have not," she denied hotly.

"But you've been thinking about it," he said. "And just in case it happened, you decided to be ready."

"That's no different from a man walking around with a condom in his hip pocket all the time."

"That's true," he said with a grin. "No different at all."

"You needn't look so smug."

His smile softened and he dipped his head to rub the tip of his nose against hers. "You're wonderful."

Lexi slipped her arms around his waist and closed her eyes, surrendering to the happiness that rushed through her. "So are you," she whispered, banishing all thought of what the coming days would bring.

"Maybe we should get some sleep now. It's nearly dawn, and tomorrow could be a busy day."

"I guess so." She didn't want to think about tomorrow. She didn't want to sleep. She wanted to lie awake in his arms and marvel at the wonders the night had brought. "Should we go back now?"

"No." Jake pulled her into the curve of his arm. "Twyla's staying the night with Jamie. I don't think she's expecting us back right away."

"What makes you say that?"

"With all the food she stocked in the kitchen, we could stay holed up here for weeks. Besides, she told me that she and Jamie would be just fine for a day or two, and she thinks you need to get some rest before Frank comes home from the hospital."

Lexi rose up on her elbow and stared down at him. "A day or two? She actually expects me to stay here with you for a day or two?"

Jake smiled. "Yeah. Sounds nice, doesn't it?"

"I couldn't do that." She'd love to, but she couldn't. "What would Jamie think? What would Dad think?"

"Maybe they'd think you were a grown-up woman with a grown-up woman's needs."

She shook her head, wishing it was so but knowing better. "Little boys and fathers don't think that way. Jamie's already showing signs of resenting you."

"I'd hoped I was overcoming that."

"Oh, you are," she assured him. "But as much as Jamie values his friendship with you, he's had me all to himself for a long time now. And he doesn't like the idea of sharing me, not even with you."

"He can learn. In time he'll get used to it."

"In time?"

"Yeah." He pulled her back into his arms. "I've decided I'm going to stick around a little longer. It's been too long since I've had a real home. And your dad's going to need some extra help for a while, especially until we can straighten out the mess McCauley made."

"Is that the only reason?"

"No. It's not even the main reason." He brushed his chin against her hair, nuzzling her as he whispered, "But then you knew that, didn't you?"

She pressed closer to him. "I'd hoped."

"I can't make you any promises, Lexi. I'm too old for you, and I have nothing to give you. The kindest thing I could do is walk away and never see you again."

"Don't talk like that." She brushed her lips against his shoulder, wishing she could find a way to hold him and knowing she couldn't.

He shook his head as if to clear away her words. "It's the truth. There was a time when it might have been different. I was still too old for you, but at least then I had a ranch and the money to operate it."

"You weren't interested in me then," she teased, remembering the confession he'd made in Antonio's over pizza. "I was a sixteen-year-old kid with stars in her eyes, and you were a grown man who needed a real woman."

"I've already told you it wasn't quite like that."

Lexi slid her fingers through the springy curls on his chest, feeling the firm muscles beneath her fingertips. "I know. I just like to hear you say it."

"Okay, here's something I *didn't* tell you. I left that party early for a reason." He touched the tip of her nose with his finger. "You."

"Me?"

"You," he repeated. "After that last slow dance we had, I just couldn't take it anymore. Once you peeled your sexy little sweet-sixteen body off me, I was shocked and mortified to find myself as hard as a piece of petrified wood, if you know what I mean."

"I think I do." Lexi grinned, remembering how she had tried to arouse him and how utterly she had thought she'd failed.

"Don't laugh," he said. "Do you know how depraved I felt?"

"Oh, I wish I'd known," she said in a voice that dripped with regret. "I wanted you so bad that night. It nearly killed me the next morning when Dolores came in bragging about spending the night with you.''

Jake winced, obviously hearing that piece of news for the first time. "I didn't know she'd do that. I'm sorry."

"She knew how I felt about you. She was always good at spotting weaknesses. For a minute, though, I almost thought I had you."

"For a few seconds there, you almost did. Luckily I came to my senses, or you might have gotten a whole lot more than you were bargaining for."

"I don't think so." She shook her head slowly, her eyes never leaving his. "I wanted to go home with you. I wanted you to make love to me. I wanted it all."

"Lexi, for God's sake." Even now he appeared ready to break and run. "You were sixteen. What did you think would happen after that?"

"I was sixteen," she said as if that explained it all. "I thought we'd live happily ever after."

"Life doesn't work that way, sweetheart."

"I know. Instead, I got to be my sister's bridesmaid three months later."

"She told me she was pregnant."

He said it so quietly, Lexi wasn't sure she'd heard him right, and even if she had, she wasn't sure she believed her ears.

She strained toward him. "What?"

"I knew I'd used a condom, but she said it must have broken, because she was pregnant. Hell, she was Frank Conley's daughter. She was your sister. I couldn't just knock her up and abandon her. I offered to pay for an abortion, but she wouldn't go for it."

"Stunned" didn't begin to cover the way Lexi felt at the moment. It was as if she were hearing a nightmare repeated. "What happened to the baby?"

"She wasn't really pregnant. She tried to tell me she'd miscarried, but by that time I knew it was a lie. She was never pregnant. She just wanted to get married." The longer he talked, the more lifeless his voice sounded. "I have no idea why. We were together for three years, and I never understood her."

"Did you love her?"

"No. I tried to. And sometimes she was so sweet I almost thought it might work out after all. Then later there were the other men and the debts she ran up and the bills she hid from me."

He shook his head as if he still couldn't quite believe it. "After it was all over, she ended up with everything that wasn't nailed down, and I ended up with a debt load it took me ten years to pay off. If it hadn't been for your dad, I'd have had to sell my ranch to come up with the cash settlement she demanded. And for all of that, it was worth it just to be rid of her."

"After she left—that night you slept with me—was it like the first night you slept with her?" The question came from out of the blue, and once it was out, Lexi couldn't stop what came after. "Were you just horny, and did I just happen to be handy?"

"Good grief, Lexi," Jake said, obviously torn between shock and disbelief. "Why would you even think something like that?"

"I can't get over the way you left the next morning, Jake, without a word, like I didn't even matter to you."

He was silent for a long time before he finally said, "I had no right to make love to you, Lexi, not then. You were nineteen years old, a virgin. A man doesn't take the gift you were offering when he has nothing to give in return. What I did was unforgivable."

Battling angry frustration, she stiffened and started to twist away, but he stopped her. Wrapping her tighter in his arms, he cradled her against his chest.

"I waited three years for you to be free," Lexi said, only partially mollified by his embrace. "I knew what I was doing, and I wasn't asking for anything in return. I only wanted you."

"Sweetheart, try to understand. By the time my marriage ended, I was no better than a wounded animal. I was in pain, and I was angry. I know I hurt you the way I left, but I'd have hurt you so much worse if I had stayed."

"And what about now? Am I going to wake up some morning soon to find you've done me another favor and left during the night without a word?"

"No. I won't do that again. I can't promise you much right now, but I can promise you that."

Lexi rested her head on his shoulder and listened to the predawn silence. All he had really promised was that he would say goodbye before he left, but even that made her feel better.

"I want more than one night this time," she said softly. "Can you promise me that, too?"

His arm tightened around her, crushing her against him while he buried his face in her hair. "Yes," he whispered against her ear. "I can promise you that, too. I can promise you a whole lot more than one night."

They made love again then, with a passion that only seemed to burn brighter with each attempt to extinguish it.

THE SUN WAS HIGH OVERHEAD, and the closer the pickup got to the hacienda, the more self-conscious Lexi felt in her low-cut, flowered dress and high heels. Her hair hadn't been combed since she'd gotten up, and it looked it. Her makeup had long since worn off. And she was having the damnedest time controlling the grin that kept creeping over her face.

"You look like a very contented cat this morning," Jake said, casting a glance her way as he slowed down for a pothole.

"Yessiree, nobody's going to guess what we've been doing." Her giddy smile robbed her words of any sting they might have had.

"I had planned to get back before everyone got up." He grimaced apologetically. "Now we're going to be lucky to get back before everyone has lunch."

"I hope Twyla isn't upset. Sunday's her day off."

"No problem there. She wasn't expecting us back before Monday, remember? Besides, she told me she wanted to get the house ready for Frank to come home."

"Does she know Dolores may be here sometime this week?"

"Yep. She seemed kind of excited about it. She was a fan of that television series Dolores was in a few years back."

"Well, you certainly seem casual about everything."

"Casual? About what?"

"Well, Dolores for one thing. And last night for another. I still haven't figured out what I'm going to tell Jamie when he asks where we've been."

"Why don't you tell him the truth?"

"Because I don't think I need to discuss my sex life with my ten-year-old son."

Jake laughed at her vehemence, then shook his head. "No, that's not what I meant. Just tell him we went to a dance and we were having so much fun we didn't want to come home."

"I don't know. Kids grow up so fast these days. For all I know, he's already figured out why we didn't come home."

"Well, you've got a lot more experience with kids than I do. I'm sure you'll find the right words when the time comes."

Jake pulled into the wide concrete driveway and parked behind Lexi's car. Twyla's Bronco was parked at the side of the garage. There were no other vehicles in sight.

"It looks quiet," Jake said, helping Lexi from the truck. He held her hand in his all the way to the front door, where he took her by the shoulders and turned her to face him. "Any regrets?"

"Just one. I'm sorry it had to end."

"There's always tonight."

Languid heat flowed through her at the images his suggestion aroused. Lexi closed her eyes and took a deep breath as her body shifted toward his. "Don't tempt me. It wouldn't be fair to ask Twyla to stay another night."

"Maybe we can figure out something else."

"Maybe." Even as she agreed, she was already wishing that night was here and a solution had been found. "You have any ideas?"

"No. I just hate to think of sleeping apart from you."

"Me, too," she said, rising on tiptoe to kiss him gently on the lips. "I guess we'd better go in now. If anyone heard us drive up, they're going to be wondering what's taking us so long."

Reluctantly, he opened the door and ushered her inside. The spicy aroma of cooking drifted from the kitchen and filled the cool, dim foyer.

"Hmm." Jake threw back his head and sniffed deeply. "I guess Jamie couldn't talk Twyla into going out for pizza."

"It smells like she's preparing a feast."

"Well, well, well," came a softly purring voice from the front parlor. "I was beginning to wonder if you two were ever going to show up."

Startled, Lexi whirled and found herself facing an elegant and profoundly overdressed Dolores. In a slim, tailored suit, spike heels and pearls, she looked like Grace Kelly in the 1950s. The two hot pink dots on her cheeks were the only indication of the anger simmering beneath the surface.

"Dolores." Lexi was distressed to hear the word sounding more like the mewl of a weak kitten. She cleared her throat and tried again. "When did you get here?"

"Last night. I went to the dance looking for you, but someone said you'd already gone. Imagine my surprise when you never came home." Dolores smiled and the two dots on her cheeks turned to fuchsia. "Jamie seemed quite upset, and nothing I said appeared to calm him."

"I bet you tried real hard, too," Jake said in a low, menacing growl, his eyes flinty.

Dolores thrust her chin higher. "As a matter of fact, I did. But I'm not a miracle worker. Jamie knew his mother went to the dance with you, and when she didn't come home—well, what could I say?"

"Knowing you, you could have said anything." Jake took a step toward her. "What *did* you say?"

"I think your guilty conscience is showing," Dolores said with a smirk.

"Enough!" Lowering her voice, Lexi pointed her finger at her half sister, who looked back with a startled gaze. "Now you listen to me. My private life is off limits. And any unfinished business you have with Jake, you can just forget about right now. There is going to be *no* tension in this house. Do you understand? None. To-morrow Dad's coming home from the hospital, and there will be no anger, no bitterness and no bickering.''

"I didn't start this!" Dolores cried, moving toward the foyer where Jake and Lexi stood. "I came here to be with my family and to visit the only man who was ever like a real father to me, and what do I find? I find you, my own sister, sleeping with my ex-husband. How do you expect me to react?"

"Well, to begin with, I expect you not to drag Jamie into this," Lexi said in a harsh whisper. At the same time, she put a hand on Jake's arm to stop the fury she felt building in him.

"I didn't," Dolores argued. "You did, by carrying on an affair right under his nose. He's an intelligent, sensitive boy. Did you think he wouldn't notice?"

"I can't take it anymore," Jake growled, breaking free of Lexi's restraining hand.

He charged the short distance into the parlor to tower over Dolores, who did an admirable job of not cringing.

"Nobody's carrying on anything, you ninny," he said in a harsh voice that sizzled with anger. "Last night was the first time we've even been alone together. And what Lexi and I do or do not do is none of your damned business. You gave up any right to an opinion eleven years ago."

"I can't believe you'd say that to me." Dolores's face twisted with the effort to hold back tears.

"Oh, good grief," Jake said with a groan. "Give it up, Dolores. I was married to you for three years. Lexi's known you her whole life. We've seen this act."

Dolores sniffed. "How do you know I'm not sincere?"

"Dolly, hon, the only time you're sincere is when you're admiring yourself in the mirror."

Her eyebrows went up in shock, but a smile touched the corners of her mouth. "Oh, Jake, what a thing to say."

"I don't hear you denying it."

"What's the use?" She lifted her shoulder in a shrug. "You know me too well."

"So," Lexi said, quietly advancing into the room. "Do you think there's a snowball's chance in hell we can all just get along for the next few days?"

"Oh, why not?" Dolores answered. "I'll give it a try. You have been wanting me to come for a visit, haven't you?"

Jake turned and stared at Lexi in surprise. She glanced at him and then looked away. He would never understand unless she told him everything, and she didn't think she was ready to do that yet.

"Yes. Yes, I have," Lexi admitted, turning her attention to her sister. "Of course, that was several months ago, and things were a little simpler then."

"Hey!" Jamie's voice rang out from the top of the staircase, followed by the thud of his boots. "Where have you guys been?" At the foot of the staircase, he rounded the newel post and stood at the end of the hall with his hands planted on his hips. "I've been worried about you."

"I'm sorry, sweetheart. There wasn't a phone or I'd have called. But you didn't have to worry. Jake wouldn't have let anything happen to me."

Jamie emitted a snort of disgust and stomped down the hall. When he reached Jake, he looked up at him through narrowed eyes. "I thought you were my friend," he said. His jaw set in anger, he broke into a run, disappearing through the dining room and into the kitchen before anyone could react.

Twyla's shocked cry of "Jamie!" coincided with the slamming of the back door.

"Oh my goodness," Lexi said in a devastated whisper.

Dolores nodded smugly. "I told you so."

Lexi and Jake both rounded on her at once. "Shut up!"

Their united shout still ringing in the air, Jake turned to Lexi. "Should I go after him? I'm not even sure what he's upset about."

"Neither am I." With a thoughtful frown, Lexi gazed in the direction of the kitchen. "But I think I'd better talk to him first. Like you said, I've got more experience with this."

"Is there anything I can do?" Dolores asked as Lexi started into the dining room.

"Yeah," Jake snarled. "Change into some decent clothes. You're making me nervous in that getup. You're not dining with royalty here."

Dolores's indignant huff was the last thing Lexi heard before she entered the kitchen and encountered Twyla's sympathetic gaze.

"Dinner will be ready soon," the older woman said quietly. "That is, if anyone has any appetite left."

"Thank you." At the door, Lexi paused. "And thank you for last night."

"Oh, it was nothing." Twyla set aside the wooden spoon she was using to stir a pot of stew and gave her full attention to Lexi. "You deserve some happiness, dear. You've had little enough of it lately."

"Now I know why." With a halfhearted attempt at a smile, Lexi said, "The cost can be pretty steep."

"Are you sorry?" Twyla asked, looking as if she already knew the answer.

"Oh, no." The smile on Lexi's face became genuine at the memory of the night just past. She gave her head a gentle shake. "Not even for a minute."

"Well then, go find your son, dear." Twyla lifted her spoon again. "And don't worry. He'll understand."

"I hope so," Lexi called over her shoulder as she left through the back door.

Outside, the sun was brilliant, the day bright and crisp. A perfect autumn afternoon. She cast about the yard quickly and saw no sign of Jamie, but then she'd known she wouldn't. He would be halfway up the hill by now, on his way to the old pine that had been the favored refuge of generations of Conleys. It was there that she had spent some of the best and worst moments of her life, and it was there that she would find Jamie waiting for her.

CHAPTER THIRTEEN

LEXI WAS BREATHLESS as she approached the crest of the hill. Behind her was the ranch house. In front of her was the Sangre de Cristo—blood of Christ—mountain range, named for its distinctive red hue. The mountains were a beautiful sight, and one that never failed to calm her.

At the top of the hill she found Jamie where she knew he would be, sitting on a cushion of pine needles and staring at the mountains in the distance.

Softly, as if she were talking to herself, Lexi said, "I was five years old the first time I came here. My father brought me. We sat right there under that pine, looking at the mountains, and he explained to me what a divorce was and why my mother was leaving. I cried when he said she was taking me with her. I didn't want to leave here."

Jamie shifted, digging his rump deeper into the thick bed of pine needles. He hunched forward, propping his elbows on his knees, moving further into his own world.

Lexi suppressed a sigh and took a step toward him. "A year later, he brought me here again. He had to tell me that my mother was sending me back to live with him, and she was going to keep Dolores in California with her. I didn't cry that time. It hurt too much to cry."

Sitting on the edge of a flat rock a few feet from the sullen lump that was her son, Lexi asked, "Are you mad at me?"

"Yes."

"Why?" She kept her voice soft, aware that this was the place where the toughest questions were answered with love and honesty.

"We don't *need* him."

"You mean Jake?"

"Yeah!" Jamie flashed a glare in her direction, then turned his hunched back to her once again.

"I thought you liked Jake."

"I don't anymore. Grandpa'll be home in a few days, and then everything will be like it was before. You always said Jake would leave then."

She couldn't tell if his voice was hopeful or sad, or a confused mixture of both. "Is that what you want?"

"Yes," Jamie snapped.

"Then why are you so angry?" Lexi prodded gently.

"'Cause you don't *want* him to leave."

"Well, you're right about that," she said with a shrug. "I don't want him to leave. I like Jake. I wish you did."

"Well, I don't!" Jamie cried, clenching his hands into fists. When he turned toward her, his face was twisted with rage. "I hate him! I wish he'd never come here!"

More than anything, Lexi wanted to take her baby into her arms and hold him until all the anger and fear were gone. But he wasn't a baby anymore. He was too old for hugs and kisses to heal his wounds. Her little boy was teetering at the edge of manhood.

Maybe she should have let Jake talk to Jamie first. Maybe a man would have instinctively known the right things to say. As it was, she would just have to make do with the truth, told straight from the heart.

"Jamie," she said softly, "I love you very much. I'll never love anyone else more. You are the single most important person in my life, and you always will be."

"What about *him?*"

"I do love Jake. I wasn't much older than you when I decided I wanted to marry him." She shook her head, wondering if Jamie could understand what she was trying to say. "It never happened. It probably never will, but I'm not going to lie to you. If Jake asked me, I'd say yes."

"He won't." Jamie's voice was more sullen than angry, and tears shimmered in the corners of his eyes. "He's gonna leave. You said so."

"And he may, Jamie, but we can't help that. You don't turn your back on love just because you're afraid it might not last. When love is offered, you take it. Because it's a very precious thing, even when it's just for a while."

"I don't care!" Curling into a tight ball, Jamie drew his knees to his chin and wrapped his arms around his legs. With his head buried between his kneecaps, his muffled voice lost some of its vehemence. "Why'd he ever come here if he was just going to leave again? I *hate* him."

Lexi's resolve crumbled. She just couldn't take Jamie's sadness any longer. There were times when everybody, even little boys with too many people coming and going in their lives, needed a hug. She dropped onto her knees beside him and drew her unprotesting son into her arms.

"Shh, sweetheart," she murmured. "Everything's going to be okay. Your grandpa's going to be home soon, and he's going to be with us for a long, long time. And I'm always going to be here with you, no matter what."

"You didn't come home." He wrapped his arms around her waist and buried his face against her.

"I'm sorry, honey. I didn't mean to stay out so late. I really didn't." Contrite beyond words, Lexi found herself battling back tears. "But Twyla was with you just so you wouldn't be alone. Didn't she tell you?"

"Yeah." He raised his head and sniffed. "But then Aunt Dolores got here, and she was so upset because you didn't come home and she couldn't find you. And then I got scared."

Lexi sighed and brushed her thumb over the single tear that dribbled from the corner of his eye. "Leave it to your Aunt Dolores to get everything in an uproar. I didn't know she would be here so soon. And I'm so sorry. I wouldn't have worried you like that for anything in the world."

"It's okay." With an embarrassed shrug, he began to disentangle himself from her embrace.

Realizing the moment was over, Lexi released him and sat back on her heels. "But you know, I've gone out at night before and you didn't worry like this."

"Jake's different."

"What'd you think he was going to do?" she teased. "Leave and take me with him?"

A frown clouded Jamie's face instead of the smile she'd expected, and Lexi realized she'd accidentally hit a nerve.

"He could have," Jamie said with a defensive jut of his jaw.

"Not without you," Lexi answered firmly. "I will never leave you, and I will never let you go. Do you believe me?"

He nodded and buried his face against her again while his arms tightened in a hold that threatened to cut her in two. She held him in turn until his frantic hug loosened and she could take a deep breath once more.

"So," she asked softly, "are we square now? Is there anything else you're upset about or want to talk about?"

He lifted his head and made a face. "Why is *she* here?"

"Your aunt Dolores?"

Jamie nodded and the resentful expression on his face deepened.

Knowing she was about to fight a whole new battle, Lexi said, "I thought you liked your aunt Dolores."

"We don't need her here right now."

Lexi found it hard to disagree. Dolores's timing was terrible, and she'd always managed to create havoc wherever she went. But still—

"I'd like you to get to know her better, Jamie. After all, she's the only aunt you've got, and I think it's important for you two to spend some time together."

"Why? She doesn't care anything about us. If she did, she'd come see us more often."

"She's here now."

"That's just because of Jake. Soon as she got here last night, she started asking me about him. She wanted to know everything we'd done together, everything he'd said to me. I wish she'd go away."

Lexi's smile thinned dangerously, and she stared at the mountains, trying to regain her composure. "Don't worry, sweetheart. She won't do that again. Are you ready to go back now?"

"Yeah." Jamie straightened himself and rose to his knees. "And, Mom?"

"Yes, sweetheart?"

"I'm glad you're back home now."

She took his hand and squeezed it gently as they turned toward the ranch house. "Me, too, Jamie hon. Me, too."

With a heavy heart, she picked her way down the hillside. The chances of another night with Jake anytime soon had just dropped out of sight. With Dolores in residence and Jamie on guard, there wouldn't be much opportunity for privacy in the coming days.

But then, this wasn't the time for Lexi to concentrate on her own life anyway. In another day, her father would be home from the hospital and in need of attention. And in the midst of that, she had to find a way to get Dolores and Jamie together.

At the back door, Jamie asked permission to ride his bike for a few minutes before coming in for supper. Lexi agreed and went into the kitchen, where she found a note from Twyla saying that everything was ready except for the casserole in the oven, which would be done when the timer went off, and that she would be back in the morning.

Lexi checked the timer and saw that the casserole still had fifteen minutes to cook. She left the kitchen, where there was nothing to be done, and found Jake seated at the desk in the front parlor.

Looking up eagerly when he heard her enter, he put aside his paperwork. "Did you find Jamie? Is he okay?"

"Yes." She dropped into the Victorian lady's chair next to the sofa. "He was more scared than mad."

"He's not still upset with me?"

"Jamie cares about you a lot, Jake. I think that's part of the problem. He's scared he's going to care too much, and you're going to leave."

Jake left the desk and came to sit on the end of the sofa, an easy arm's length away. "And you? Is that what you're afraid of, too?"

The air of honesty of the hillside was still with her, and Lexi found herself admitting what she might otherwise have denied. "At times."

He took her hand between his and looked into her eyes. "What if I said I don't think that's going to happen?"

"I'd say 'thinking' it won't happen isn't much reassurance."

He smiled, a gently teasing smile. "You're not still worried about Dolores, are you? Not after everything I've told you."

Lexi let out a deep breath that stopped just short of a sigh. "I'm worried about so many things right now, I can't keep track of them all. Dad's coming home. Dolores is causing trouble. And I'm still not sure Jamie's told me everything that's bothering him."

Jake turned her hand over and traced the lines of her palm with his fingertips. "It doesn't sound as if there's much room in your life for me," he said without taking his gaze from her hand.

"I'll make room." Impulsively, she reached out and caressed the line of his jaw, coaxing his head up until their eyes met. "It just may take me a little while to do it."

"What about tonight?"

She could hear the disappointment already in his voice and knew that he had guessed what her answer would be. Hating to confirm his suspicion, Lexi shook her head. "I don't dare leave here tonight."

"That doesn't mean I can't see you. Can you at least meet me outside after everyone's gone to sleep? Even if all we do is talk, I want some time alone with you."

She caught her lower lip between her teeth and found herself lost in the seductive green of his eyes. "I'd like that very much."

Wishing the night was here already and they were alone with only the moon and the stars and the rustling of the wind for company, she reluctantly withdrew her hand from his. "I guess I'd better go find Dolores now. I have a few things I need to say to her. Do you know where she went?"

"Up to her room, I think."

Something in his voice caught Lexi's attention. "Did you two fight?"

"No. We just discovered that we didn't have much to say to each other anymore."

Still not convinced, she let the matter drop, knowing she would get no more of an answer from him. "Well, I won't be long." She stood. "Would you turn off the oven in a few minutes? And if Jamie comes back, would you tell him it's almost time to eat?"

"Are you sure you'll have an appetite after you talk to Dolores?"

Lexi smiled. "Well, if we're not down in a reasonable length of time, you and Jamie go on without us. It probably wouldn't hurt for you to have a little time alone together, anyway."

She had reached the doorway when Jake cleared his throat and turned her around with his question. "Uh, just in case it comes up, exactly how much does he know about last night?"

"Jake," she said in a slightly incredulous tone, "he's ten years old. He knows that his mother left with you to go to a dance and didn't come home until the next day. Whatever happened in between is, I hope, still a mystery to him."

"He may know more than you think. I don't suppose you've discussed the facts of life with him yet?"

"Jake!"

"I'll take that as a no."

"On second thought, maybe the two of you *shouldn't* be alone together."

"Relax. Go on. I'll challenge him to a game of checkers if he starts quizzing me about last night."

"Promise?"

"I'll set up the board now, just in case."

"Okay," Lexi said with a smile. "I'll be down as soon as I can."

Upstairs, she found Dolores in what used to be the master bedroom before Frank's heart problems had forced him to move downstairs. Standing in the doorway, Lexi surveyed her half sister, who stood facing the window, staring out at a view overlooking the courtyard. Always slender, Dolores seemed even thinner than usual, yet her figure was more voluptuous than ever. Her naturally blond hair was now white blond and brittle-looking. There was an air of tension about her that showed in the stiffness of her body and the way her hand clutched at the window curtain next to her.

The lecture Lexi had planned was put aside for the moment. Instead she called her sister's name softly, not wanting to startle her. "Are you all right?"

Dolores turned, releasing the drapery she had crumpled in her hand. "I was just watching Jamie. He's riding the bike I gave him for Christmas two years ago. I had been wondering if he really liked it."

"He was thrilled with it. He rides it all the time." Lexi refrained from adding that Dolores could have simply asked him. "Jamie tried to call right after Christmas that year to thank you, but you were on location somewhere."

Dolores shrugged. "Probably Italy or Australia. Those are the only two places I seem to work with any regularity." She smiled, and enthusiasm momentarily bubbled to the surface. "I'm going to have a six-week guest shot on a daytime soap after the first of the year. I'll be playing a twenty-five-year-old stripper, if you can believe it. Before I auditioned, I had a little taken off up here—" she tapped her fingertip just below the corner of her eye, where the beginning of crow's-feet might have once been

"—and a little added up here." She waved her hand across the front of her impressive bustline.

Incredulous, Lexi asked, "You had surgery to get a part?"

"That's show biz. Besides, it worked, and now I'll be playing a character five years younger than I am."

"Five? Dolores, I'm thirty." Lexi touched her own chest with her fingertips, then pointed a finger in her sister's direction. "*You're* thirty-six."

"Hush your mouth!" Dolores glanced around as if someone could have overheard. "Even Harvey thinks I'm only thirty-one."

"Dolores, you're lying to your husband about how old you are?"

"Well, of course. Why shouldn't I? Mother's always lied to her husbands about her age. She's even lied to them about *my* age. And there were a couple who didn't even know that *you* existed."

"What?" Lexi asked blankly, having no idea what Dolores was talking about.

"Oh, you know, after she sent you back here to live. You *do* know why she did that, don't you?"

"No, actually, I don't." Standing behind what had been her grandmother's old rocking chair, Lexi gripped the back of it for support. "Mother never bothered to explain to Dad or to me. She just sent me back."

Dolores laughed, oblivious to the edge of pain in Lexi's voice. "So she wouldn't have to explain who you were, you silly goose. As soon as you were gone, she knocked ten years off her age, added three years to mine, and started telling everyone I was her little sister. Can you believe it?"

Dolores laughed again, a light trilling sound that should have been charming but instead seemed slightly hysterical. "Mother's next two husbands after Frank thought I was her sister and she was my guardian because our parents were dead."

Lexi clung harder to the chair while her mind reeled. Even after everything her mother had done through the years, there had still been some faint, lingering hope that Cordelia wasn't really as unrepentantly self-serving as she seemed.

"How can you laugh?" Lexi looked into her sister's vividly blue eyes, which used to be a pale blue gray before the probable addition of contact lenses. "You were twelve, and she made you pretend to be fifteen? She robbed you of years of your life."

"I got them back again," Dolores said with a negligent shrug. "I married Jake when I was twenty-two, and once I divorced him, I got to go back and be twenty-two all over again. And once I got back up to twenty-five, I stayed there for the next five years."

"So now you're around my age."

"Yes." Dolores smiled as if terribly pleased with herself. "In another few years I'll probably have to become your younger sister."

Seeing no humor in the situation, Lexi asked, "So how old is Mother supposed to be?"

"Oh, she had us when she was *very* young. She was almost still a child."

"Good grief." Lexi rested her head in her hand a moment, waiting for the roaring inside to subside.

More than ever, she realized the debt of gratitude she owed her father. He had given her a life of sanity and normalcy. He had given her security and love. And he had welcomed Jamie without question when Lexi had returned from a seven-month visit to California with Dolores's baby in her arms.

Without her father's steadying influence, she might have accepted deception as a normal part of life the way her mother and sister did.

Shaking off the reverie, Lexi said, "Dolores, we have to talk."

"I thought we had been."

"We have to talk about Jamie."

"Why?"

Lexi left the chair and went to the settee at the foot of the high, four-poster bed. She sank onto the uncushioned wood of the seat, grateful for the relief to her trembling legs.

"Jamie's starting to ask questions about his real mother," she explained. "Well, not actually questions yet. Just hints that he'd like to know. But the questions will come. It's only normal. Almost all adopted children eventually want to know who their real parents are."

"Why did you have to tell him he was adopted?" Dolores asked with unbecoming petulance. "You were supposed to pretend he was yours."

"Who was I supposed to pretend was his father?"

"Anybody you wanted. Who cares?" Agitated, Dolores began to pace.

"*Jamie* will care," Lexi said patiently.

"He's just a child. He'll believe anything you tell him."

"Honesty, decency, fairness. Do those words mean nothing to you?"

"Oh, really, Lexi, you can be such a bore sometimes." In front of the window, Dolores stopped pacing and whirled on her half sister. "If you don't stop this, you're going to ruin everything."

"Dolores, he's your *son*. Don't you feel anything?"

"Sure I do. Of course I do. What do you think I am? You think I haven't wanted to tell him?" She flailed her hands dramatically and began pacing once again. "You think I haven't dreamed about what it would be like? You think I haven't wished it was *me* he was calling 'Mama'?"

Watching Dolores flit around the room was positively unnerving. Listening to her wax poetic about motherhood was even worse. "Then why don't you want me to tell him?" Lexi asked, refusing to be distracted.

"I'm scared, okay? I'm just plain scared. I'm not ready."

"What are you afraid of?"

"What if he doesn't like me? What if he blames me for giving him up? You know—" Dolores's voice suddenly became very soft "—I've been trying to get pregnant. But it's not working. Sometimes I wonder if God's punishing me."

"Oh, Dolores, I don't think He works that way." In spite of herself, Lexi felt a sharp tug of sympathy.

"Still, I've been wondering about a lot of things lately. My marriage isn't what it used to be. Harvey really wants a son. I think sometimes that I may lose him if I can't give him one soon."

"You could always adopt," Lexi suggested, not letting sincerity blind her to the irony of the suggestion.

"No." Dolores shook her head furiously, as if the idea frightened her. Then the look in her eyes softened to one of speculation. "But I think he likes Jamie. Harvey's the one who picked out the bike. He really enjoyed the few times Jamie came for a visit."

"Well, you see," Lexi said, growing excited. "That's exactly the kind of bond I'd like for you and Jamie to form. So when he finds out that you're really his birth mother, it'll be as if he has a second family. After all, you're already his aunt. Nothing really has to change, except that he'll know the truth."

"I'm going to have to get used to this idea." Dolores began to pace again. "It's just so different. After he finds out who his mother really is, what happens if he wants to know more?"

"Like what?"

"Like his father," Dolores whispered, glancing toward the closed door. "What if he wants to know about him?"

"We all want to know about him, Dolores. And it's definitely something that Jamie will need to know."

"No! No way!"

"Was it Jake?" Lexi asked, going back once again to the notion that her sister was perpetuating a mystery and Jake was the only answer that made sense.

"I told you it wasn't!" Dolores backed toward the window with a look approaching horror on her face.

"But at first you told me Jake *was* the father."

"I did not!" Dolores said hotly.

"Yes, you did," Lexi said calmly. "When Jamie was first born and I told you I was too young to take a baby and raise him by myself. You told me the baby was Jake's, and that if I didn't take him, you'd put him up for adoption and Jake's baby would be raised by strangers."

Dolores frowned and a faraway look came into her eyes. "Oh, yeah. I guess I did, didn't I?"

Lexi felt a momentary rush of triumph to finally get something resembling a straight answer from her sister.

"Then when you realized I planned to find Jake and tell him, you changed your story," Lexi went on, remembering it all as if it were yesterday. "You said you'd been with too many men to be sure who the father was, but that you knew it couldn't be Jake. You said you hadn't been sleeping together at the time you got pregnant.''

"That's right," Dolores said, seizing the fact eagerly. "We hadn't slept together in months."

"The only thing is, the more I watch Jake and Jamie together, the more similarities I see," Lexi insisted. "So I have to wonder if you weren't telling me the truth the first time. I have to wonder if Jake isn't really Jamie's father after all."

"That's ridiculous." Dolores went rigid with anger. "And if you ever dare say that to him, I'll make you sorry you ever lived."

"But why, Dolores? Why, after all these years, does it matter who the father really is?"

"Because if Jake thinks he's the father, then he's going to know that I must be the mother."

Her heart hammering at the base of her throat, Lexi tilted her chin defiantly upward. "Not necessarily," she said quietly.

"What do you mean, not necessarily? Who else could it have been? I may have been dating other men, but Jake was totally faithful to me, and I know it."

"You went off with Bobby Hooper for a two-week stay in Maui. And when that was over you moved in with Mom in Marina del Rey and filed for divorce," Lexi said indignantly. "I think by then Jake considered himself a free man!" Her voice dropped sharply. "And so did I."

A nerve twitched at the corner of Dolores's eye and her nostrils flared in a perfect portrait of repressed rage. "*What* are you trying to say, Alexandra? Are you trying to tell me that I was barely out of his bed before you fulfilled your adolescent dreams and seduced my husband?"

"Ex-husband," Lexi corrected.

"The divorce wasn't final."

"It was filed."

"It *wasn't* final!"

Incredulous, Lexi said, "You'd sold all the furniture, emptied the bank account and were going after the only thing he had left—his ranch! It seemed pretty final to *him!*"

"My own sister." Dolores covered her face with her hands and turned away. "How could you do that to me? How could you betray me that way?"

"For heaven's sake, Dolores, you were divorcing him. Call me dense, but I thought that meant you had relinquished your claim."

Dolores bristled with righteous indignation. "And I suppose the whole time we were married, you were just sitting there like a vulture waiting for him to be free again."

"Not the whole time," Lexi said with a shake of her head, unable to believe that she was actually starting to feel guilty. "But after that first year, you told me yourself you were getting restless. I loved you, Dolores, but I loved Jake, too. And you knew it. You knew it when you married him."

Dolores huffed. "You were sixteen."

"I still had feelings. And if I betrayed you, then you betrayed me, too. And you betrayed me first."

"I'm sorry." Dolores sounded genuinely chastened. "I never realized you were serious. I thought it was just, you know, a crush. Something you would grow out of."

"And it never occurred to me that you would care one way or another what Jake did after you left him."

"I guess maybe I shouldn't care." Dolores shrugged and put on a brave face. "It just shocked me. Probably more so because it was you."

"So where do we go from here?" Lexi asked, her mind already moving on to more important issues. "We can't undo what's already been done, but we *can* make sure Jamie doesn't suffer for it."

"I don't know." Dolores frowned, showing signs of relenting. "What exactly is it you want me to do?"

"Spend time with him. Talk to him. Get to know him," Lexi said, leaning forward eagerly.

"So you can tell him that I'm really his mother?" Dolores gave a nervous laugh. "That wasn't our original deal, Lexi."

"You and Mother never consulted me when you made that deal, Dolores. The only choice I ever had was to take Jamie or to watch you give him away to a stranger."

"It was your name on the birth certificate. All you had to do was to tell him you were his mother. We fixed everything so it would look that way."

"And then what was I supposed to do, Dolores?" Lexi asked far too loudly as she felt her temper slipping. "Spend the rest of my life lying to Jamie and to Dad? Who was I supposed to say the father was?"

"Well, who are you going to say it is now?"

"I'm still hoping you will eventually tell me the truth."

Dolores rubbed her hand across her brow. "I don't know. You have me so confused."

"Is the truth really that hard for you?"

"How would you know what it was like? You were raised here with your dad." Flinging out her arm, she turned away. With her back to Lexi, Dolores continued, "You got to keep your childhood."

"At least you had a mother," Lexi shot back.

"Oh, no I didn't." Dolores turned back around, her eyes flashing. "After she sent you back here, I had an older sister, remember? We both lost our mother at the same time, Lexi.''

Belatedly, Lexi remembered the story her sister had told her earlier. "I'm sorry, Dolores. I never knew about that before today."

"It wasn't something I liked to talk about."

Knowing she was walking on eggshells, Lexi took Dolores's hand and looked into her eyes, trying to reach her. "Then can't you understand why it's so important to me that Jamie knows both of his mothers? I never want him to feel cheated the way we did. Please, Dolores, help me."

"Give me some time, little sis. Okay?" Blinking back tears, Dolores withdrew her hand. "I'll spend some time with Jamie. I'll do all I can. And I'll think about the rest of it."

Knowing that would have to be enough, Lexi agreed and left.

CHAPTER FOURTEEN

FLAMES LICKED at the wood logs in the fireplace, the only illumination other than a desk lamp across the room. In the background, the sad sound of Mexican love songs played softly on the stereo.

"Dolores seemed a little subdued tonight." Jake's voice was barely above a whisper. Seated next to Lexi on the sofa, he slipped his arm around her shoulder. "You two must have had quite a talk."

"Did you know that Mother used to tell people Dolores was her sister instead of her daughter?"

"Yeah, she told me all about her blighted childhood." His hand stroked Lexi's arm absently, and he leaned closer.

"You don't sound very sympathetic."

"Just because I understand why she's so screwed up doesn't mean I can overlook the things she does."

"I guess that's reasonable." Lexi rested her head against his shoulder, deeply content just to be alone with him. "Jamie seemed to be in a pretty good mood this evening. I suppose everything went smoothly with you two?"

"Oh, sure. Once I promised that if you and I eloped, we'd take him with us, he seemed perfectly content."

"Oh, Jake." With a perplexed laugh, she turned slightly and looked up into his eyes. "You didn't."

"Yes, I did. That's what he was worried about, so I set his mind at ease."

"He didn't ask you anything about last night?"

"Mercifully, no. I guess you put his mind at ease about that." He nuzzled her hair aside and ran his tongue lightly over the rim of her ear.

His breath was a low roar, fluttering hot against her skin. Shivers of excitement ran down her spine, and Lexi twisted against him, finding it impossible to sit still.

A deep laugh rumbled in Jake's throat. "You like that?" He repeated the action, moving slower, pressing harder.

The shivers began to pervade her entire body, turning first to ripples, then to waves. "A little too much," Lexi gasped as she pulled away in self-defense.

"Have you given any more thought to our dilemma?" he whispered, still close enough that she could feel the heat of his breath on her cheek.

"Oh, Jake, I'm sorry, but I just don't see how we could get away for another night without causing more of an uproar. Even if Jamie is okay now, Dolores is still a little tender on the subject."

"I'm supposed to arrange my love life to accommodate Dolores?" Jake asked, incredulous at the idea. "What do I care what she thinks?"

"But *I* care," Lexi said, looking pleadingly into his eyes. "I need her help with something right now."

"Something that's more important than us?" he challenged.

"Something pretty important."

Realizing she was serious, Jake frowned but softened his tone. "I don't suppose you'd care to discuss it?"

"Not at the moment." She winced in apology, but there was nothing else she could say. Maybe soon she'd be able to tell Jake everything, but right now the secret had to remain exactly that.

"I'm not sure I like the sound of that."

"I'm sorry. It's just something personal that I'm not at liberty to talk about right now."

"If it were any woman but you, Lexi, I don't think I'd accept an answer like that. But for you, I'll let the matter drop. For the moment."

She breathed a sigh of relief and snuggled into the comfort of his embrace.

"Whatever this thing is," Jake grumbled softly in her ear, "it had better be pretty important."

"It is," she assured him. Turning toward him, she pressed her lips against the soft skin of his neck. "Believe me, I don't like this any more than you do."

"I wish this room had a door that locked." He tilted her head, and his mouth sought hers almost frantically. At the end of a long and breathless kiss, he stood and pulled her to her feet beside him. "Let's go for a walk before I explode."

Leaving the house by way of the kitchen, they skirted Twyla's precious herb garden, went past the vegetable patch and through the gate at the back of the yard. Hand in hand in the moonlight, they started up the long, sloping hill that led eventually to the old piñon at the crest.

Jake found a seat on the cushion of pine needles and pulled Lexi down beside him. "Man, look at that view," he said, pointing to the mountains to the east. "You used to come up here a lot when you were a kid, didn't you?"

"Yeah. Sometimes I'd bring a book, stretch out and spend the whole afternoon reading. This is where I came the day I found out you and Dolores were getting married. I spent a long time up here that day."

"I keep feeling as if I should apologize, but you were just sixteen, Lexi. Can you imagine what your father would have done if I had even tried to date you?"

The image readily came to mind, and Lexi laughed. "Okay, you're right. But it seemed like a tragedy to me at the time." She snuggled closer and gazed longingly into his eyes. "You *really* never loved her?"

"No, I really never did. But I was fond of her for a while. She's not all bad, and she wasn't too hard on the eyes. And she did try very hard at first."

Lexi sighed, remembering the effort Dolores had originally put into being a housewife—vacuuming, dusting and rearranging furniture until it had made her crazy.

Jake shook his head. "She was the worst cook I've ever known. The only decent thing she could make was macaroni and cheese from a box. We must have had that for supper four nights out of seven. Poor Dolly. I don't think marriage was at all what she expected it to be."

"How about you? I know why you married her, but I don't know why you stayed with her. If any man ever had cause for divorce, you did."

"That's a tough question."

"Surely you've figured it out by now."

"No," he said, giving her a squeeze. "I *know* why I stayed. It's a tough question because I don't like to admit the truth." He took Lexi by both shoulders and twisted her around to face him. "Oh hell, Lexi, it was you!"

"Me?" Lexi repeated blankly. "What—"

Jake released her shoulders and got to his feet. Moving a few yards away, he leaned against a low boulder. "Sometimes when we made love," he began haltingly, "I'd see your face instead of hers. It wasn't anything I could control. It just happened."

Lexi stayed where she was. She could see the tension in Jake. She could feel the guilt in him and knew the effort this confession was costing him, though for her part she was having trouble feeling anything but pleased.

After taking a deep breath, he went on. "Then one night, while we were making love, I called her by your name instead of hers. It might not have been so bad, except that I did it at a climactic moment, so to speak."

"Oh, Jake." It was all she could think to say. It must have been a horrible moment. Thinking aloud, Lexi said quietly, "No wonder she got so upset today when she found out you and I slept together after she left you."

"She didn't know? You mean she just found out about it today?"

Lexi nodded. "And she was very agitated. It really surprised me. Now I know why."

"You don't know the half of it. It got worse. Every time we'd fight, she'd throw you in my face, saying maybe I'd married the wrong sister."

"And what did you say?" Lexi asked, almost in a whisper.

"What *could* I say? I'd been thinking the same thing for a long time."

"Did this all happen before she started seeing other men?"

"Yeah," Jake said with a jerky nod.

Lexi closed her eyes and let her breath out in a long sigh. She found it hard to believe there was so much she'd never known, never even guessed at. "Damn."

Jake left the boulder and came back to her. Tossing his sling aside, he took her in his arms and kissed her fervently.

"I'm tired of talking," he said when he paused for breath.

"Me, too." She stretched out on the pine needles, and Jake leaned over her, seeking her lips with his. She moved against him, urging him on.

"Ah, Lexi. Here? Now?" He gestured to the dark sky above them and damp ground where they lay.

She pulled him closer. "Yes. None of that matters, and this may be our last chance for a while."

He smoothed her hair away from her face and smiled down at her. "My beautiful pagan. Are you really mine, Lexi? Am I really holding you like this?"

"For today. For tomorrow. For as long as you stay, I'm yours."

JAKE PARKED HIS TRUCK in front of his ranch house and got out, savoring his newfound freedom. This morning the doctor had removed the bandages for good—no more wrapped ribs, no more sling. Twisting at the waist, Jake slowly stretched from side to side and was gratified to feel nothing more than a few twinges and a mild, pervasive soreness.

He reached overhead with his right arm and winced at the sharp pain that stopped his movement halfway up. The stiffness would last awhile, the doctor had said, but the arm could bear weight within reason. Horseback riding should be okay in another week.

Since Frank's return from the hospital three days earlier, Lexi had been busy playing nursemaid to her father while Jake had taken over the duties of foreman for the Lazy C. Evenings were devoted to getting settled into his own house, arranging the few secondhand pieces of furniture that were slowly turning the place into a home once again.

The less he saw of Lexi the easier it was to keep his hands off her until they could have some time alone. That was why he had taken to having lunch by himself at his house since the first of the week.

Unlocking the front door, he went inside and tossed his hat and keys onto the small, scarred desk beside the door. Next he went into the kitchen and put a can of soup on to heat. Taking a loaf of bread, a jar of sandwich spread and a slab of unsliced bologna from the refrigerator, he set them on the counter and began to put together a sandwich.

"Got enough for two?" a soft voice asked from behind him.

Startled, Jake whirled and found Dolores standing in the dining room doorway. She was dressed in a V-necked sweater and lacy leggings. The neck of the sweater plunged low enough to make it obvious she wasn't wearing a bra. He couldn't believe she'd left the house dressed like that. If Frank saw her, he'd have a fit.

Keeping his thoughts to himself, Jake said, "I didn't hear you drive up."

"Oh, I've been here awhile. I parked out back so I could surprise you." She spread her arms in welcome and smiled. "Surprise!"

"You've just been sitting out there waiting?"

"Oh, no." She shook her head, still smiling. "I've been waiting in here."

"Where?"

"In your bedroom."

"How did you get in?"

She giggled, looking very proud of herself. "You never changed the lock."

"You *kept* the key? All these years?"

Dolores crossed her arms beneath her breasts and hugged herself, an act that shoved the majority of her cleavage into eye-popping prominence. "I guess I'm just sentimental."

Impressed by the sheer magnitude of the sight before him, Jake was more incredulous than tempted. He didn't know if she was trying to seduce him or just make him sorry he no longer had husbandly rights.

More to clear his thoughts than for any other reason, he turned and continued making his sandwich. Noticing that the soup had begun to boil, he went to the stove and turned off the burner.

"You didn't really come here for a bologna sandwich, did you, Dolores?"

"Isn't it obvious what I came here for?"

Jake slowly turned back to face her. "Several possibilities come to mind. But I think I'd rather you just told me."

Still hugging her arms in front of her, Dolores presented her profile to him and rested her back against the door frame. "I wish you had come into the bedroom when you got home. This would have been so much easier there."

"Dolores, are you coming on to me?"

She turned to look at him, and her eyes blazed with fierce determination. "I want you to make love to me, Jake." The back of her head rested against the door. Her arms continued to shove the bare mountains of her breasts into view. "I *need* you to make love to me."

"Dolores," Jake said firmly, "what we had was over a long time ago. You're married to someone else now, and quite frankly—"

"Please, Jake." She closed her eyes and begged. "*Please.*"

Her tone was one of supplication, not seduction. Torn between confusion and anger, Jake frowned. "Is this for old times' sake? Or is there some special reason why you're doing this?''

Without warning, Dolores caught the hem of her sweater in both hands and pulled it over her head. With it dangling from her limp fingers, she stood there, bare from the waist up, in high-heeled sandals and white lace leggings that clearly revealed the absence of any underwear.

"Why don't you stop arguing and come a little closer?" she asked in a husky voice.

"Dolores, you are a beautiful woman." Jake ran his hand through his hair. "And I don't know why you're doing this, but I would really appreciate it if you would just put your clothes back on."

"It's because of Lexi, isn't it?" She dropped the sweater at her feet and walked slowly toward him, her hips swaying with each step, her breasts thrust out seductively. "Don't worry about Lexi. This has nothing to do with her. She'll never know. Don't tell me a man like you has never had sex just for the sake of sex?"

"Of course I have."

"Well then?" She stopped right in front of him and took a deep breath. "Come on, Jake. No one will ever know. It'll just be you and me, like we were before. Like the last time." So close she was brushing against him now, she said, "You do remember that last time, don't you, Jake?"

He remembered the last time, though he hadn't known then that it would be. The two of them hadn't done anything but argue for months. Even the sex that had once kept them going had dried up to nothing. The end was near and they both knew it.

Then, without warning, Dolores had come to him with a request for a truce, for one quiet night with just the two of them, like the old days when they were first married. To commemorate the night, she opened a bottle of champagne, put another one on ice and slipped into something comfortable.

When he woke up the next morning, she was gone. When he got home from work that night, so was the furniture.

"I sure do remember the last time," he said as he firmly pushed her away. "And you will *never* get me drunk enough to do that again."

Dolores's seductive pose fell away, and he found himself facing a desperately unhappy woman.

"Jake, please. Please, you don't understand." Her hands clutched at his arms, shaking him.

Disentangling himself, he said, "Put on your clothes." Then he brushed past her into the dining room and on into the living room.

Hurrying behind him, Dolores scooped up her sweater and pulled it over her head. When she caught up to him in the living room, she grabbed his arm and pulled him around to face her.

"Listen, you've got to do this. Please, you're the only one who can, and my marriage depends on it!"

"What the hell are you talking about?"

"I've been trying and trying to have a baby, and it's not working. And if I can't get pregnant soon, I'm afraid Harvey may find somebody else. He wants a son so bad. It's all he talks about anymore."

"What's that got to do with me?"

"I want *you* to get me pregnant, Jake. I know you can do it, and nobody ever has to know it was yours and not Harvey's."

"What makes you think I can get you pregnant if this Harvey guy can't?"

"I know you can. I *know* it."

She said it with such intensity it was almost scary, and Jake found himself backing away from her. Dolores had never been the most stable woman in the world.

"Well, thank you for the vote of confidence," he said as politely as possible. "but I'm afraid I just won't be able to help you with this."

"You're turning me down because of some misbegotten loyalty to Lexi, aren't you?" Clenching and unclenching her fists at her sides, Dolores followed him, advancing for each step he retreated. "Well, let me tell you something about your precious Lexi, okay? She's just as capable of lying as the rest of us. She's done it to me, and she's done it to you."

At that Jake drew up short and glared down at the frantic woman in front of him. "What do you mean by that?"

"Oh, I know all about how she went after you as soon as I was out of the picture. And it only took her eleven years to finally tell me. Don't you wonder what kind of secrets she's been keeping from you, Jake?"

He breathed a sigh of relief, realizing that Dolores was only trying to bait him.

"You don't believe me, do you?" she asked quietly. "You don't think there is a secret. Well, let me tell you, Jake—" her voice dropped to a whisper "—you asked how I knew you could get me pregnant? Because you've done it, Jake. You've *done* it."

For a stunned second, Jake forgot to breathe. Then anger that burned like phosphorus exploded inside him.

"Explain yourself!" He grabbed her by one arm and pulled her against him. "What the *hell* do you mean?"

"That last time we slept together, the time you'd had just a little too much champagne, you forgot something very important. You forgot to use protection. Who would have guessed that once would have been enough?''

"You're lying.''

As she shook her head, her cool blue eyes never left his face. "I had a baby. And you were the father.''

"I don't believe you! And even if you did, how would you know it was mine, anyway? I wasn't exactly your only lover at the time.''

Again she shook her head. "With the others, I made sure. You were the only one it could have been. Besides, he looks just like you. Ask Lexi if you don't believe me. She knows. She's known all along.''

"Lexi?'' He could barely think over the roaring in his head. Dolores began to smile, and seeing her pleasure only doubled his anger. "I'm not going to play guessing games with you. If you're trying to tell me something, then tell me, damn it. What's Lexi got to do with this?''

"Is that all you care about? Lexi? Don't you want to know who your son is? Can't you guess?''

"I said I wasn't—'' Midshout he froze as realization broke over him with icy clarity. *Jamie. My God, it was Jamie.*

"Ah,'' Dolores said with obvious satisfaction. "I see you've figured it out.''

With blood pounding in his temples, angrier than he could ever remember being, Jake managed to pull his mind back from the black abyss of his fury and focus on the woman before him. "You bitch! What did I ever do to you to make you hate me that much?''

"You never loved me.'' She stiffened her spine, and fury to match his own flashed in her eyes. "Why should I give you a son?''

He struggled to form a reply, then realized that she was nothing. It wasn't Dolores's betrayal that twisted like a knife in his chest. Lexi was the one who had raised his son. Lexi was the one who had kept the secret for ten years. She was the one who continued to lie with her silence even as she made love to him with her body. And it was from Lexi that he would get his answers.

Without another word, he whirled and started toward the door. Dolores grabbed his shirtsleeve and he shook her off without slowing.

"Come back here!" she demanded. "I'm not through with you."

He stopped, pivoted and fixed her with a gaze that sizzled with silent warning. "I'll deal with *you* later."

She retreated a step and stared back at him with wide, frightened eyes. "What are you going to do?"

Uncertain himself, Jake turned and left without answering. He only knew that he had to get to Lexi. He had to know why she had done this.

LEXI SAT ON THE SOFA in the front parlor darning one of Jamie's socks. Her father was in his chair in front of the window, sipping at the cocoa that was his favorite afternoon snack. They had spent the last half hour in companionable silence, enjoying the quiet day.

Dolores had gone into town to shop, Jamie would be home from school soon and Twyla would be back before bedtime to help Lexi with her father. Sometime before the day was out, Lexi was hoping Jake would drop by. He hadn't been around much since the first of the week, when her father returned from the hospital. She knew he wanted to allow the family to be alone with Frank, but she missed Jake terribly. As did Jamie and Frank.

It was hard to believe that in one short month Jake had invaded her life so completely that a day without him seemed empty.

"What the devil?" Frank said from his seat by the window. "Who'd drive a—" He stopped, frowning.

"What?" Lexi looked up from her darning to find her father peering intently out the window. "What are you looking at?"

"I'm waiting to see— Why, it's Jake. Probably busted a shock driving that truck like that over these roads. Hmm." Her father drew back from the window and turned to Lexi. "Looks mad as a hornet, too. You two have a spat?"

"Dad!" Lexi frowned and carefully laid the sock and needle in her sewing basket. "You're entirely too perceptive. And no, we haven't had a spat."

Frank grinned. "Don't have to be perceptive. The whole ranch is talking about it. Twyla says you two are practically engaged."

"Don't get your hopes up, Dad. The only thing Jake has said is that—"

At that moment the front door swung open and Jake entered, looking as dark as a thundercloud. His eyes were the deep, shadowy green of a forest floor, and the line of his mouth was tight, hard and angry.

Lexi's carefully controlled eagerness disappeared in an instant. Something was wrong. *Very* wrong. Anxiety replaced the happiness that had accelerated her heartbeat.

"Jake?" She took a hesitant step forward.

His gaze fixed on her. "I want to talk to you." He motioned her closer. "Come on. We're going outside."

"What is it?" She took another step toward him, surprised that her trembling legs would hold her weight. She was scared, just plain scared. This was no small anger, and whatever had caused it would not be easily dismissed.

"See here, what is this?" Frank said, rising slowly from his chair.

Jake motioned for him to stop. "It's okay, Frank. I just want to talk to her." Jake's gaze returned to Lexi. "But what I have to say is between the two of us. Nobody else needs to hear it."

"Don't you touch her," Frank warned.

"I'd cut off my arm first," Jake said, then held out his hand for Lexi. "Come on."

Lexi complied, slipping her hand into his. She didn't like being ordered around, but somehow she knew this wasn't a good time to argue the point. She'd make her stand when Jake stopped trembling with suppressed rage. For the moment, she just wanted to find out what he was so upset about and get the problem straightened out. Whatever it was, it had to be a simple misunderstanding. It just *had* to be.

Leaving the house behind them, Jake pulled her in his wake through the backyard to the base of the hill. He began to climb with her beside him, his furious strides chewing up the ground at a dizzying speed until they were both so out of breath he was forced to slow his pace.

"Thank you," Lexi gasped.

When he glanced at her over his shoulder, the expression on his face was unrelenting. But for the first time, amid the anger, Lexi saw pain. Something was hurting him deeply.

At the top of the hill, Jake stopped abruptly and turned around to face her. "Okay, now why don't you start at the beginning and tell me everything you haven't been telling me about Jamie."

"Jamie?" Lexi stared back at him, nonplussed. She couldn't understand why Jake would be this angry about Jamie.

"Yes, Jamie," Jake snapped. Green fire burned in his eyes. "My son!"

"Your—" Too stunned to think clearly, Lexi took a step backward.

Jake caught her by both arms and pulled her against him. "Talk to me, Lexi," he demanded. "Explain to me why you did it."

"Did—" Her eyes wide, she looked at him, unable to believe this was happening. "What? What are you talking about?"

"You never told me I had a son." His hands tightened on her arms and he pulled her so close he was staring straight down into her eyes. "Even when I asked you about him, you lied to me. You never told me he was mine."

"He isn't. I told you, Jamie isn't mine. I—"

"Stop it, Lexi!" Jake shook her. "Stop it, do you hear me?" He pushed her away from him in disgust. "Dolores told me everything!"

CHAPTER FIFTEEN

CAUGHT OFF BALANCE when Jake released her so unexpectedly, Lexi staggered back a step before she righted herself.

"She told me *everything*," Jake said again in a voice crackling with bitterness.

"Dolores." Lexi nodded. She was stunned, but somehow calmer just knowing what had brought about the sudden tirade. "Dolores told you that you were the father? Who did she say was the mother?"

"Don't play games with me, Lexi." Jake was ramrod stiff. His eyes flashed with silent fury.

"I'm not." She looked him straight in the eye, almost relieved that now she could finally tell him the truth. "Believe me, I'm not. Did she tell you she was Jamie's mother?"

"Yes."

"And you were his father." She said the words softly, almost with wonder. If only it were true.

"Don't act as if you didn't know."

"Oh, Jake." Lexi hung her head and pressed her fingertips to her temples. So much was happening so fast. "I don't know what to think anymore. Every time she opens her mouth a different story comes out."

"What do you mean?" The anger in his voice sounded less certain.

"I spent half an hour on Sunday trying to get her to admit you were Jamie's father because he reminds me so much of you. Instead, she swore you couldn't be." Lexi dropped her hands and faced him again. "She said the two of you hadn't made love for months before she left, so you couldn't possibly have been Jamie's father."

"Then she lied."

"You mean you were sleeping with her? Right up to the end?" The idea hurt, and Lexi couldn't pretend that it didn't.

Jake shook his head impatiently. "No. It had been months since the last time. Then one night I came home to find her waiting for me with candles burning and a bottle of champagne chilled and opened. I was tired, I drank too much and nature took its course."

"You didn't, uh, use anything?" Lexi asked, wondering if he would even be able to remember.

He shrugged. "I'd used my last condom months before. We were so close to divorce I wasn't planning to need one again, at least not with her."

"And that was it? Just that one night?"

"Just the one night. She left the next morning."

"That still doesn't prove he's yours," Lexi said with a frown, wishing something could tell them for certain. "She's lied so many times about this."

Clinging to a slender thread of hope, Jake narrowed his eyes. "You *really* didn't know about this?"

Lexi shook her head, weary just thinking about all the doubts and confusion that had littered the ten years since Jamie's birth.

"We'd better sit down if I'm going to tell you my side of the story. And it may be a little hard for you to believe anyone could be as gullible as I was back then."

He took her hand and led her a few feet away to a comfortable resting place. Looking at the churned-up clumps of pine needles, Lexi had a sudden and embarrassingly vivid recollection of their lovemaking Sunday night.

"Probably right about here," Jake said in her ear as she dropped to the carpet of needles beside him.

When she lifted her surprised gaze to his, he smiled.

"That *is* what you were thinking about, isn't it?" he asked, slipping his fingers through hers.

"Well, yes." She returned his smile and looked away before her blush betrayed her further. "Now, do you want to hear how I ended up with Jamie?"

"He's named James, isn't he? Is he named for me?"

"Yes. For you and for Dad. James Franklin Conley."

"Who did that, you or Dolores?"

"It was the name I'd picked for the son I wanted someday. Dolores used it on the birth certificate."

His hand tightened on Lexi's, but he didn't say anything and she went on with her story.

"It all started about three months after you left," she said. "That would have been about five months after Dolores left. Anyway, I hadn't heard from you, and I was beginning to believe that Dad was right, that you wouldn't be coming back."

Jake took her chin in his hand and turned her face toward him. "I *am* sorry," he said softly. Then he kissed her with a light, sweet, infinitely tender touch of his lips to hers.

"I'm glad you're not mad at me anymore."

He brushed his thumb across her lips before he took his hand away. "I was misinformed. Go on with your story."

"Anyway, Mother called and convinced me that Dolores was desperately lonely and needed my company and that it would be good for all of us to spend some time together again. So she said to pack a bag and come out to California and plan to stay for at least six months. So I did.''

Here Lexi paused for breath and to clear her thinking. It was at this point that the story began to get confusing. What happened next wouldn't have been so bad if only she hadn't been touched that her mother had wanted her, even if it had taken her nineteen years to say so.

''Well, almost as soon as I got there, I realized Dolores was pregnant,'' Lexi continued. ''By this time, of course, your divorce was final. She wasn't dating anyone at the time. In fact, as far as I could tell, she seemed to be hiding. She hardly ever left the apartment, and the only thing she seemed to need me for was to wait on her.''

''Where was your mother?''

''She was married to the husband before Lloyd and lived in another part of town. The only time Mother came around was to take Dolores to the doctor. They never let me go with them. Even when Dolores finally went to the hospital to have the baby, they wouldn't let me go. For four months, I hardly ever left that apartment.''

''Why didn't you go home?''

She smiled, remembering the times when she would lay her hand on Dolores's swollen stomach and feel the baby kick. The hours of shopping and planning, when Dolores gave no hint that she wasn't going to keep the baby.

''You don't know how women are about babies, do you?'' Lexi asked with the dreamy smile still on her face. ''We get very personally involved. I couldn't wait for that baby to be born so I could hold it and feed it and powder it.''

''Didn't you talk about who the father was?''

"No. Dolores wouldn't discuss it. She was very moody, so when she didn't want to talk about something, we didn't talk about it."

"Poor little Lexi." Jake massaged her shoulder with his hand. He'd experienced Dolores's moods firsthand. "That must have been hell for you. What happened after she had the baby?"

Lexi took another deep breath, knowing she was about to plunge into the worst part of the story. She hated even to think about it, but Jake deserved to know the truth. If he really was the father, he needed to know how the deception had come about and why Lexi had stuck with it to this day.

"Once Dolores came home from the hospital, Mom was around a lot more. But I was the only one who seemed to pay any attention to poor little Jamie. They waited until I'd fallen head over heels in love with him, then they told me that Dolores couldn't keep him. It wouldn't be good for her image, and Mother had no intention of being thought of as a grandmother."

"So you offered to adopt him."

Lexi shook her head. "I was still just nineteen. I was single. How could I take on the responsibility of a baby? I didn't even have a decent job." With each reason she listed, she became more upset. "I lived on a ranch with my father, for goodness' sake. What would he say? By this time, I'd been gone so long, he'd probably think the baby was mine."

"You mean you didn't want to adopt him?"

"Of course I wanted to. I just didn't see any way that I could. So they gave me a choice. Either I could adopt him, or Dolores would give him up to an adoption agency. Then Dolores told me the baby was yours."

Jake stiffened and said with deadly calm, "Then you *did* know."

"Let me finish," Lexi said, holding up a restraining hand. "After Dolores threatened to give your baby away to strangers, I started crying and begged her not to. I said I'd take him. I didn't care what it would do to my life, I couldn't stand to let him go. Giving him up was breaking my heart already, but once I thought he was yours, I just couldn't stand it."

"So you knew he was mine," Jake said again.

"I *thought* he was yours," she corrected. "Then, after I'd already begun to think of Jamie as my baby, they told me the real reason they had brought me out to California."

"So you could adopt him."

Lexi shook her head. "No. They thought of that later. They brought me out to stay because my mother had given Dolores my identity to cover her pregnancy. The apartment, the doctor's records, the hospital's records, the birth records, everything you could think of—they were all in my name. Alexandra Lorraine Conley gave birth to James Franklin Conley. That's why they wouldn't let me meet the doctor or go to the hospital. Everybody thought Dolores was me."

"Why in God's name would they do that?"

"So that when Dolores was famous, her younger sister, Alexandra, would be the one who had had the illegitimate baby in a Los Angeles hospital, not Dolores."

"But she was married to me when she got pregnant. That wouldn't make the baby illegitimate."

"No, but that would have made her a heartless bitch who gave up her baby for adoption just so she wouldn't have to drag him around with her. She didn't want a baby, and she didn't want anyone to know she'd ever had a baby. And they did a pretty damned good job of covering it up.''

Stunned, Jake stared at the ground, unseeing. "Holy shit!" he said to himself, shaking his head. Then he looked up again. "What happened then?''

"You mean after I realized that my mother was willing to use my birth certificate to protect Dolores without any regard to what it might do to my life?" Lexi asked bitterly. Even after so many years, the memory didn't fade. "And after they explained to me that I wouldn't have to adopt Jamie because every legal document they could think of already listed me as his mother? Why," Lexi went on with biting sarcasm, "I simply thanked them for the lovely vacation and got ready to take my baby and go home.''

"At this point, I'm still his father?" Jake asked hesitantly.

"Up until this point, yes. Then Dolores realized I might go home and tell Dad the truth, and that we might find you and tell you the truth. So then, once they knew I would take Jamie no matter what, Dolores told me that she lied before because she knew I would never let your baby go. She told me that she had had too many lovers to know exactly who Jamie's father was, but that she was sure it wasn't you because she hadn't had sex with you for months before Jamie was conceived.''

"And you believed her?''

"By that time I didn't know what to believe. And that was exactly what she wanted. After that she said that I was never to tell Jamie or anyone else the truth, that as far as the world was concerned, I was Jamie's mother. She also said that you were never to have any contact with Jamie, and that if you did, I would lose him. Dolores said that she and Mother would be able to take me to court and prove that Jamie wasn't mine.''

''Could they really do that?''

''Probably. They took pictures at the hospital, and Dolores and I look nothing alike. I'm sure tests could prove she was the birth mother. But she'll never do that. She went to too much trouble to get rid of him. I was worried about it when you first came here, but I'm not worried about it anymore.''

''So *am* I his father?'' By this time Jake was as confused as Lexi had been.

''I think so. There's definitely a resemblance. And it's not just the way he looks, it's his expressions, the way he moves.''

''So what happens now?''

Lexi leaned back her head and shook out her hair. The soft strands brushed against the backs of her arms. She felt free for the first time in ten years.

''I don't know,'' she said, gazing at the wisps of cloud overhead. Feathery strokes of white blended into the powder blue sky. ''Dolores is such a loose cannon. Every time I think I have a plan worked out, she goes and does something like this. What was she after, anyway?''

''Let's talk about your plan first. What were you hoping to do?''

''What I would like is for her to spend more time with Jamie. I want the two of them to be friends before I tell him the truth.''

''So you *are* going to tell him?''

''Definitely. He's been hinting that he'd like to know for the past year or so. Any day now he's going to come right out and ask me.''

''You've done a fine job with him, Lexi. Any man would be proud to have Jamie as a son.''

"Including you?"

"Including me."

Lexi turned her gaze toward the mountain and steeled herself for what was to come. "Funny, but that wasn't the impression I got the first time you asked me if Jamie was yours."

"That was when I thought I'd got you pregnant and then gone off and left you to raise our child alone. That was guilt, pure and simple." He took her chin in his hand and gently tugged her face toward him until her eyes met his. "But underneath that guilt, I was almost hoping it was true. Because I'd like nothing better than to have a baby with you—a dozen babies—a lifetime of babies."

"When did this happen?"

"It's always been there. I just finally had the good sense to stop fighting it. I think I love you, Alexandra Conley, and I think I'd like it very much if—"

"Señor Jake!" a voice called from the other side of the hill. "Miss Alexandra, it's me, Manuel. Señor Frank, he says I should come get you. He says you got to come quick."

"What the devil?" Jake said, rising to his feet.

Lexi was already up and across the crest of the hill. Halfway down, Manuel stood waving his hat. Her heart was racing as she started down the hillside to meet him. "What is it, Manuel? Has something happened to Dad?"

"No, he is fine, but he says you got to come quick." Manuel replaced his hat and motioned with his hand for her to hurry. "Señor Jake, too."

Pausing in her flight, Lexi turned and saw Jake hurrying to catch up. Her eyes met his, and she saw in his gaze the same mingling of anxiety and regret that churned through her.

Another few seconds and he might have said something that could have changed both their lives. She only hoped the moment wasn't gone forever. The thought was enough to hold her for the precious seconds it took for Jake to reach her.

He caught her hand in his and they hurried on together, following in the wake of Manuel, who ran ahead. Without slowing, Jake leaned his head toward hers.

"I want you to marry me," he said, breathless from their downhill sprint.

Lexi turned to look at him in surprise. She wanted to stop, to ask if he was serious, to throw her arms around him and cry out with joy. Instead, she sidestepped a sizable rock that was in her path and asked, "Is that a comment or a question?"

At the gate, he stopped and pulled her to a halt with him while they gasped to catch their breath. "A question. Will you marry me?"

At the back door of the house, Manuel called out in exasperation, "Hurry!"

"Yes." Lexi's deeply dimpled smile said more than words. "Yes."

"Good." A lazy grin spread over Jake's face, and his hand tightened possessively on hers. "Now I guess we'd better go inside and find out what this emergency is all about."

"Why do I get the feeling Dolores has something to do with it?"

"Because she probably has." He leaned closer and kissed Lexi firmly on the mouth before they followed Manuel into the house.

"Señor Frank!" Manuel called, preceding them through the kitchen. "I've brought them pronto."

Jake and Lexi entered the foyer on Manuel's heels.
Frank was seated in his chair by the window. He seemed
calm enough, but the steel in his eyes told Lexi that he
was more upset than he appeared.

"Thank you, Manuel. Now, would you go back down
to the highway and watch for Jamie? If he comes home,
bring him straight here."

With a nod, Manuel whirled and was out the door and
across the courtyard with a speed that was astonishing for
a man of his years.

Going into the parlor, Lexi asked, "What's wrong,
Dad?" For her father's sake, she tried to conceal her
mounting anxiety.

"Nothing, I hope."

"You didn't send Manuel after us for nothing," Jake
said. "Something's happened."

"Well, not necessarily." Frank shifted in his chair. "Sit
down, both of you. You're making me nervous hovering
around me."

Lexi went to the armchair that was opposite her father. Jake retrieved a straight chair from the corner and
pulled it beside Lexi's. When they were seated, he took
her hand in his and turned his attention to the older man.

"Okay, exactly what has happened?"

"Well, like I said, it's probably nothing. But when
Jamie didn't show up after school, I called one of his
friends to see if he was over there and had forgotten to
leave word."

"He wouldn't do that," Lexi said. "Not with you just
out of the hospital. He's still too worried about you."

Frank turned his head to hide the smile that threatened, then faced them again. "Yes, well, anyway—" he
cleared his throat "—this friend of his said that Jamie's

aunt came and got him out of class about midafternoon."

Lexi stiffened, torn between shock and outrage. "What?"

"That's what I said," Frank agreed. "But this kid said that someone from the principal's office was with her and that Jamie's aunt had a note from Jamie's mom saying it was okay for him to leave school early with his aunt."

"I asked her to spend more time with Jamie," Lexi fumed. "I didn't give her a note saying she could take him out of school."

"You know, in grade school she used to be able to forge her mother's handwriting," Frank said, shaking his head. "It's a miracle that girl didn't grow up to be a juvenile delinquent. And it's no thanks to her mother that she didn't. I was never so glad in my life as when Cordelia sent you back here to stay with me. I died a thousand deaths the year you were out there alone with that woman."

"So," Jake said, getting the conversation back on track. "We know that Dolores picked up Jamie at school this afternoon and hasn't brought him home yet. Other than the fact that she didn't have Lexi's permission, is there any reason to be worried about that?"

"I don't know." Lexi shrugged. "Maybe helping him skip school is her idea of a bonding experience."

"Would you do me a favor, Lexi?" Frank asked quietly. "Would you go up to Dolores's room and see if all of her suitcases are still there?"

"Why?" The cold chill that raced down Lexi's spine made it difficult for her to control the tremor in her voice. "What haven't you told us?"

"Like I said, it may be nothing." Frank shook his head and refused to meet her gaze. "Just satisfy an old man's curiosity and go look, okay?"

"I'll go with you," Jake said.

Rising from his chair, he kept Lexi's hand tightly gripped in his own. In the hallway, she whispered in a voice tight with fear, "She couldn't have taken him. What would she have to gain? Where would she have gone?"

Jake shook his head and stayed silent as they hurried up the stairs. In Dolores's room, he asked, "Can you tell if there's anything missing?"

"I helped her unpack after we got here." Lexi opened the closet door and saw immediately that the hanging bag was gone, along with the more expensive clothes, including a fur coat. "Would you look under the bed and see if that big suitcase is still there?"

Leaving Jake to do that, she went to the dresser and opened the first two drawers. They were empty. Nothing was left.

"Nothing under here," Jake said. "What's missing?"

"Everything that's not expendable." Closing her eyes, Lexi drew in a deep breath, but it did nothing to slow her racing heartbeat.

Fear pumped adrenaline through her veins until she felt she would explode with the need to do something, but there was nothing to do, no one to shout at and nowhere to run. Knowing what she would find, she went down the hall to Jamie's room and opened the dresser drawers to discover a portion of each stack of clothing gone. She went to the closet and saw empty hangers in the center where clothes should have been.

Collapsing onto the foot of Jamie's bed, Lexi held her head in her hands and wished she could cry or scream or do something that would release the torrent of agony that was rising inside of her. But she was frozen.

"Why?" she said finally. "Why would she do this? She didn't even want me to tell him the truth. Why would she do this?"

"I don't know." Jake sat beside her and gathered her to him. "But I know this. We'll get him back."

"But why would she even want him, Jake? Is she doing this just to hurt me?"

"No, sweetheart." He rocked her in his arms. "I don't think this has anything to do with you. You know Dolores. She doesn't think before she does things. She wants a baby, and I wouldn't help her, so she took Jamie. I think it's as simple as that."

"I don't understand any of this." Lexi straightened and pulled far enough away to look into Jake's eyes. "I know she wanted to get pregnant, but what do you have to do with it?"

"She was waiting at my house today when I came home from the doctor. She was practically hysterical, Lexi, saying things like I got her pregnant once and she knew I could do it again. She wanted me to sleep with her to save her marriage. It was crazy. I got mad and came looking for you."

"What did she do then?"

"I don't know. I left her there. How was I supposed to know she was planning something like this?"

"Oh, Jake, what am I going to do? She's his mother. What if she goes to court to try to keep him?"

"It'll never happen."

"It *could*. Tests would prove she's his mother. What if a judge decided Jamie should be with her?"

"Tests would also prove I'm his father, and I have rights, too." Jake shook his head. "She'll never risk it, Lexi. She's not that crazy. And after you and I are married, no court in the land would give Jamie to anyone but us, even if Dolores was willing to take it that far."

"Oh, Jake, I want him back. I want him back now, tonight. I don't know what I'll do if she's really taken him."

"She'll bring him back. Dolores is confused and overly dramatic, but she's not a monster. Jamie's too smart to be tricked and too big to be forced. He'd never leave the state with her willingly, and she'd never threaten or hurt him. You know that. She's selfish and conniving, but she's not deliberately mean."

"You're right." Lexi rested her head on his shoulder and fought back the tears that finally threatened to flow. "I know you're right." She stood and wiped away the streak of moisture that had escaped the corner of her eye. "We'd better go down to Dad now. I know he's worried, too."

In the parlor, Frank was sitting where they had left him. When he heard them return, he straightened as if he might stand. Then he saw their faces and sank back into his chair, looking suddenly old and tired.

"I was right, wasn't I?" he asked, turning his face to the window.

"Yes, you were right." Lexi sat in the chair opposite him and put her hand on his knee. "How did you know?"

"Her husband called this afternoon. Harvey, isn't it? He said to tell Dolores he'd meet her at the airport tonight." Frank abandoned his intent study of the view outside the window. "He said he was glad to hear I was doing so much better."

"So what do we do now?" Jake asked from the doorway. "If we called the highway patrol, they could probably stop her before she got to the airport with him."

"Oh, no." Lexi stood and turned to face him, horrified at the idea of calling the police on her own sister. "What would we say? That she kidnapped him?"

"Well, she did, didn't she?"

Frank pushed himself to his feet behind Lexi. "Jake's right. We can't just sit here. I'll call the airport in Albuquerque and see if I can find what flight she's taking."

"Maybe we're jumping to conclusions," Lexi offered lamely. "Maybe she's just spending some time with him before she leaves."

Jake took Lexi by the shoulders and looked at her with sympathy. "She packed clothes for Jamie, sweetheart. She must have had it in the back of her mind all along that if things didn't go the way she wanted today, she was taking Jamie with her when she left."

"But what's Jamie going to think if the police stop them and take her away in handcuffs?" Lexi argued.

"What's Jamie going to think if she forcibly removes him across state lines?" Jake asked. "That's a federal offense."

"Hmm, that's funny."

At the sound of Frank's voice, Jake and Lexi both looked in his direction in time to see him hang up the telephone. He stood there, shaking his head as he absentmindedly rubbed his fingers over his chin.

"What?" Lexi prodded.

He glanced toward her as if he were startled to find he wasn't alone. "Uh? Oh, she had reservations, but she canceled them. What do you suppose that means?"

"See? She changed her mind," Lexi said. "They'll probably be back any minute."

"Or else she's decided to drive to California," Jake offered. "That'd be a lot easier than taking a resisting child by air."

"Maybe we *should* phone the police, Lexi, just to be on the safe side." Frank lifted the receiver, waiting for her answer.

"Oh, all right. I hate that it's come to this, but if anything happened to Jamie, I don't know what I'd do. Just tell them that we're worried, okay, Dad? Tell them we're afraid something may have happened. But don't mention kidnapping, all right? Not yet."

Going to the window, she saw dusk settling in and knew that once darkness came it would be harder to stave off panic, harder to reassure herself that Jamie would be home soon and the nightmare would be over.

"I'm going to the kitchen to make hot chocolate," Lexi said with the sudden realization that she had to do something or go crazy.

"I'll go with you," Jake said.

"No." Knowing that she sounded abrupt, she managed a thin smile. "I'm sorry. I just need to be alone for a minute. Would you try to get Dad to sit down and relax when he gets off the phone?"

She cast a worried glance in her father's direction. "What could Dolores be thinking of to do something like this now, of all times, when she knows Dad shouldn't be upset?" Angry and very near tears, Lexi shook her head and hurried out of the room and through the house to the kitchen.

Once there, she stayed busy making cocoa and straightening up until the sound of a car arriving sent her flying back through the house. In the foyer, she stopped Jake at the front door.

"No. If it's them, I want to handle this myself." She placed the flat of her palm against Jake's chest and gazed into his eyes. "Please. The cocoa's poured and sitting on a tray on the kitchen table. Could you bring it in? And whatever happens—" she turned with a look of caution to her father, then back to Jake "—if Jamie doesn't seem upset, don't let him know how worried we've been. This whole thing may have just been in our imaginations."

"I doubt that," Jake said roughly. "But I'll play it any way you want. Go see who it is, and I'll bring in the cocoa."

"Thank you."

With that, she whirled and was out the door and into the courtyard like a flash. When she saw that the car was indeed Dolores's rental vehicle, Lexi slowed her pace and waved a greeting to cover her headlong rush from the house.

Jamie slammed the passenger door and came running toward her, his arms laden with boxes and bags. "Hey, Mom," he yelled. "Look what I got."

"What is all that?"

"Booty, man!" he exclaimed, skidding to a stop in front of her. "Well, some of it's clothes. But some of it's really radical stuff."

"That's good, right?"

He made the face he reserved for some of her less informed comments. "Right."

"So that's what you've been doing all this time? Shopping?"

"Well, for a while we just drove, and then we stopped and talked. But then we went shopping." He grinned. Then he leaned nearer and said in an undertone, "I think Aunt Dolores is kind of upset about something, but she wouldn't talk about it to me. Maybe you can get her to cheer up.''

"I don't know what I can do about that, sweetheart, but I'll certainly have a talk with her.'' Lexi gave him a shadow of the desperate, strangulating hug she longed to give him and then stepped back. "Why don't you run upstairs and hang up your new clothes? I'll be along in a few minutes, and you can show me some of the stuff you got today.''

"Okay."

With a surge of youthful energy, he was off. Lexi watched the front door close behind him before she walked to the car, where her sister waited.

"Hi," Dolores said, nervously hugging the side of the car.

"Do you want to tell me what happened today?'' Lexi asked with a calm that took all of her strength to maintain.

"You mean with Jake?''

"No, I mean with Jamie.''

"You told me to spend more time with him.''

"Harvey called this afternoon, Dolores. He left a message for you with Dad.''

"What kind of message?'' More nervous than ever, Dolores edged away.

Lexi followed her, step for step. "Harvey said to tell you that he'd pick you up at the airport tonight.''

"He must have his days confused.''

"I don't think so. As a matter of fact, if you opened the trunk of this car, I bet it would be full of suitcases. Packed suitcases. I bet there are even some clothes for Jamie in there.''

"Oh my God." Dolores's knees seemed in danger of buckling. She leaned against the back fender of the car to help hold herself up. "I never thought you'd find out."

"Well, I did. And now I want to know why. Why would you do that? Do you think that kidnapping him is the way to establish a relationship with Jamie? Do you think that all you have to do is wave a magic wand and ten years of neglect are just going to disappear?"

Lexi was shouting now, but she couldn't seem to stop. Rage, only slightly dampened by relief, fueled the fire inside her. "That is *my* child," she cried, pointing a shaking finger at the house. "Jamie is *mine*. Do you hear me? Mine. And you will never take him from me."

Dolores cowered as Lexi moved closer and dropped her voice to a menacing hiss. "I offered to *share* him with you. On a limited basis, nothing more—just share. Or is sharing a concept you can't comprehend? How dare you try to steal my son from me."

"I'm sorry," Dolores said with tears streaming down her face. "I was wrong, and I'm so sorry. I realized that when I tried to tell him."

"Tell him what?" Lexi demanded. "Stop blubbering and talk to me."

Dolores drew in a shaky breath and brushed at the tears on her cheeks. "I was going to tell him who I was." She shook her head and gulped back more tears. "I would never have taken him with me if he hadn't wanted to go. I was going to tell him first, and then I thought he would go with me because I was his mother."

Lexi stared at her through flashing, narrowed eyes and bit back the words of recrimination she ached to voice. "What happened to stop you?"

"I pulled into a roadside park somewhere between Santa Fe and Albuquerque, and we talked." She flailed her hand helplessly and let out a laugh that sounded slightly hysterical. "I was going to work up to it slowly. Then I realized that Jamie was looking at me like I was a stranger, a very strange stranger. Oh, Lexi, I think he was scared of me."

Dolores dissolved into tears again. Reluctant to trust her instincts when it came to her sister, Lexi couldn't help but feel that the sobs were genuine. Hesitantly, she reached out and laid a consoling hand on Dolores's shoulder.

"He's just a little boy, Dolores. It wouldn't be hard to confuse him."

"I know." Dolores pulled a tissue from her pocket and blew her nose. Then she sniffed. "I'm going to look a fright. Is my makeup smearing?"

"Not terribly. So what happened then?"

"Well, I realized I was just making a mess of things. I looked into Jamie's eyes, and I knew I couldn't do it. I would have hurt him if I'd told him then. He'd have thought I was a crazy lady, and who wants a crazy lady for a mother?"

Laughing, Lexi put her arm around Dolores's shoulder and gave her a quick squeeze. "Well, crazy lady, I think you've just taken a giant stride forward."

"What do you mean?"

"I think you just did something that was very unselfish. You put Jamie's needs before yours."

Dolores brushed her nose with the tissue. "Is that good?"

"It's the kind of thing a mother would do."

"Really?" Dolores's expression was a mixture of pleasure and surprise.

"Really." With an arm still around her sister's shoulder, Lexi turned them both toward the house. "I assume you'll be staying another few days?"

"If you don't mind. I'd like to give this unselfish thing a little more practice. It's kind of new to me."

"Sure. Maybe I can give you a few pointers."

"I hope you're not joking, because I'd really like it if you would. I've watched you, you know. You really are a good mother. I want to be a good mother, Lexi." Dolores rubbed a hand longingly over her flat stomach. "Not just to Jamie. I want to have a baby, too. And I want to be the kind of mother you are, not the kind ours was. Oh!"

Dolores broke away from Lexi and began to hurry toward the house. "I need to call Harvey before he leaves for the airport."

"Why don't you go on upstairs and use the phone there?"

"Okay."

From several yards behind her, Lexi watched as Dolores opened the front door and entered the foyer, all smiles and blown kisses, her crimes forgiven and her tears forgotten. Jake stood furious and mute, glaring in disbelief as Dolores hurried gracefully past on her way up the stairs.

"Now see here," Frank called out, rising to his feet as Dolores disappeared and Lexi entered.

"It's okay," Lexi said. She caught Jake by the arm and pulled him with her toward her father. "I'll tell you everything I know, and then I want to talk to Jamie."

When her story was done, Frank shook his head and sagged against the back of his chair. "I don't know what to do with that girl. Her little pea brain must rattle around like a marble in that empty head of hers. Of all the tomfool notions."

"Now, Dad," Lexi said, more than happy to be charitable now that her son was safe in his room upstairs. "She *did* bring him back, and that's what counts."

He grunted an answer that didn't sound like an agreement and pushed himself painfully to his feet. "Guess I'd better call off the cops."

"I'm going up to check on Jamie." Lexi stood and turned toward the doorway, only to find her path blocked by Jake.

His arms crossed, his face sober, he might as well have been made of granite. "Not so fast. What about me?"

CHAPTER SIXTEEN

"YOU?" LEXI ASKED, hoping she didn't look as befuddled as she felt. Was it possible that Jake had asked her to marry him only a few hours ago? It seemed like a dream. Maybe it was.

"Yeah." His expression softened, and his fingers trailed gently down her cheek. "Me. You haven't forgotten so soon, have you?"

With a laugh, she let out the breath she'd been holding. "I was afraid I just imagined it. I didn't, did I?"

"No, you didn't imagine it."

"Well, that's done," Frank announced from across the room.

Without taking his eyes from Lexi's face, Jake asked, "What's done?"

"The police." Frank paused between two sturdy chairs, placing a hand on the back of each to steady himself. "They were glad to hear everyone's home safe and sound."

"You're looking tired, Dad," Lexi said, worried suddenly that the day had been too much of a strain.

"I am, sugar," her father said, moving slowly toward them. "I think I'll go lie down awhile. You two will call me, won't you, if any more excitement breaks out?"

Jake laughed. "Don't worry, Frank. We won't let you miss anything."

"Good," Frank answered in the same gruff tone he used whether he was happy or sad. "And by the way, darlin'—" He leaned to kiss Lexi on the cheek as he passed her. "Congratulations."

"Congratulations?" Lexi looked from her father, who smiled and continued on his way, to Jake. "For what?"

Jake cleared his throat. "I, uh, took the liberty of telling him our news."

"Really?" Lexi peered around the arched doorway for a glimpse of her father's retreating figure. "What did he say?" she asked Jake in a whisper.

"I said it was about damned time," Frank answered for himself without pausing in his slow, steady trudge down the hall.

Lexi laughed and turned back to Jake. "When did you have time to talk to him?"

Jake pulled her into his arms. "While you were outside with Dolores." He kissed her tenderly and then sighed deep in his throat. "Man, I hope you're not planning on a long engagement."

Careful of his healing ribs, she snuggled against him. "Just long enough for Jamie to adjust to the idea."

"Oh, I don't think that'll be a problem. He seems to be adjusting pretty well."

Lexi drew back and pinned him with a suspicious stare. "What do you mean by that?"

"Jamie was here when I talked to your dad."

"You *told* him?"

"Yes," Jake said, only slightly defensive. "I hope you don't mind. It was one of those man-to-man things I just thought I should do."

Lexi rolled her eyes heavenward and sighed. A few weeks ago her son had belonged to her alone. Now it seemed she would have to get used to sharing him.

"Well, you *are* his father," she conceded. "What did he say?"

Jake paused in thought, then answered carefully, "Wow. Cool. And I think maybe the word *bitchin'* was used. I didn't understand it all, but he seemed okay with the idea."

Laughing, Lexi relaxed against him. "Oh, Jake, do you realize what we're getting ourselves into?" The enormity of what lay ahead was only beginning to dawn on her.

"We'll just have to be patient, sweetheart." Jake brushed his cheek against her hair and held her closer. "With ourselves and with each other. I can't learn to be a dad overnight, or a husband, either, for that matter. But I'm going to give it all I've got."

"Oh, I'm not worried about that. You'll be terrific." She drew back reluctantly. "I guess I should go talk to Jamie now. I'm sure he's waiting for me."

"Want me to go with you?"

"Not yet. But you might stay close."

"Okay. In the meantime, I think I'll go fire up the grill. How do hamburgers sound for supper?"

"Like heaven. I'm starving." She stood on tiptoe and kissed him lightly in parting.

Jake's arms slipped around her again and pulled her closer, deepening the kiss to a long, passionate promise for the hours to come when they were alone.

When at length he released her, Lexi made her way up the stairs on legs that were loath to move. Fuzzy-headed from the stirring of desire, she tried to remember exactly why she was leaving Jake to go to Jamie. At the door of Jamie's room, her wits still weren't sufficiently collected to recall her original purpose.

Knocking lightly, she pushed the door open a crack. "Hi, hon. Am I interrupting anything?"

"No. Come on in."

Lexi opened the door the rest of the way and saw her son across the room, feet up on his desk, staring at the ceiling. After such a momentous day, she didn't know what she had imagined he would be doing, but this wasn't it.

She looked at the ceiling, hoping for a bug or a spot, anything but the smooth white expanse that was there. "What are you looking at?"

"Nothing." He rolled his head from side to side while his gaze remained fixed above him.

"Oh." She pushed his schoolbooks aside and sat on the end of his bed, facing him. "Pretty strange day, huh?"

Jamie slowly moved his head until his eyes met hers. He nodded.

"Jake said he talked to you." Lexi almost gasped when she heard her own words. She hadn't meant to bring up the subject so soon. She had planned to wait until Jamie opened up to her and mentioned it himself.

He flashed her a crooked grin and shrugged. "Yeah."

"What do you think?"

"Where are we going to live?"

The question took her by surprise. "I don't know. We haven't talked about it." She frowned, thinking of the little house on his own ranch that Jake had begun fixing up. "Jake might want us to live on the Circle T."

Jamie wrinkled his nose. "I don't know. I kind of hate to leave Grandpa."

"Well, you could still spend the night here sometimes. After all, the ranches are adjoining, and they've been run as one for years now. I'm sure with Jake as foreman, they'll stay that way.'' She had the fleeting realization that she and Jake hadn't discussed the future much at all. For all she knew, he might be planning to return to the rodeo circuit eventually. The idea was disquieting.

"Is he going to be my dad now?"

"Jake?" Lexi brought her wandering thoughts back to the present. "Yes. You'll like that, won't you?"

Jamie nodded. "I like Jake. A lot. I didn't want him to leave." Then, frowning with a new thought, Jamie asked, "Does this mean he's gonna get to boss me around now?"

Lexi couldn't help smiling. "Well, theoretically, yes. But I don't think that's what he has in mind. I think Jake just wants us to be a family. You know, spend time together. Do things together. He's downstairs right now cooking hamburgers for supper. That sounds like a pretty good beginning, doesn't it?"

Jamie laughed. "Yeah. I was just thinking about the way he used to yell when he first got here. I sure don't want him getting mad at *me.*"

"Well, he was in a lot of pain then, sweetheart. And then again, I sort of kidnapped him. So he was a little mad at me. But he had reason to be."

"You mean the way Aunt Dolores almost kidnapped me today?"

Lexi gasped audibly and then stared at her son in shock.

Jamie looked uncertain. "Gee, I thought you knew about that."

"Knew about?" she echoed. "Well, yes, I did know about it. But I didn't think you did."

"Mom! I'm not stupid," he cried, looking insulted. "She took me out of school and drove me halfway to Albuquerque. And she kept saying stuff like 'Don't worry' and 'It'll be okay' and 'I'd never hurt you.' She was spooky."

Lexi was aghast. She'd had no idea that Dolores had been so blatant. "What did you do?" she asked, trying to sound much calmer than she felt.

Jamie grinned, obviously pleased with himself. "I was so cool, Mom. I just said, real casual like, how I hoped we wouldn't stay gone too long because I sure wouldn't want Grandpa to get worried or upset or anything with him just being out of the hospital and all."

If Lexi hadn't already been seated, she might have collapsed. "Oh, Jamie, I had no idea."

Revved up and into his story, Jamie continued as if she hadn't spoken. "So then we stopped at this rest area and sat for hours, it seemed like. And she kept telling me what a nice little boy I was, and how she sure wished she had a little boy like me, and then she started telling me about how big her house was in California and how much money her husband has. And—oh, hey, Mom, did you know they've got a pool now? They didn't used to, did they?"

"I don't think so," Lexi answered vaguely, finding the whole conversation a little unreal. "I think Harvey's making more money now than he used to."

"Yeah, well, maybe it wouldn't be so bad then, you know, just to go for a visit sometime. She seemed to like that idea. After that we left and went back to Santa Fe, and she went and bought me all that stuff."

"Oh, Jamie." Lexi couldn't stand it anymore. Her urge to hug him was overwhelming. Gathering her son into her arms, she pulled him onto her lap. "Sweetheart, I'm so glad I have you back with me," she said, ignoring the pointed elbows that gouged her ribs and the bony knees that jutted at awkward angles.

"Mom." Jamie's voice was muffled against her shoulder. "Is Aunt Dolores sick?"

"Sick?" Lexi loosened her embrace and drew back to look at him.

Jamie tapped his head with his index finger. "You know, up here."

"No," she protested when she realized he was questioning Dolores's mental state. "She's just—well, she's just what people call 'high-strung.' And she has a tendency to act first and think later."

"But why was she going to take me back to California with her?"

Lexi took a deep breath for courage. It was too soon to tell him everything, but maybe she could begin to lay the groundwork. Speaking slowly and praying that she could find the right words, she began to answer his question.

"Well, your Aunt Dolores has been wanting a child for a while now, and it isn't happening for her. That makes her very sad because a long time ago she had the chance to have a little boy of her own, and she gave up that chance."

"What did she do?"

"She had a baby, and she gave him up for adoption."

"Why?"

"She was young. She thought what she was doing was for the best. Now she isn't so sure."

Sliding off Lexi's lap, Jamie went to the window and stood facing out, staring at the night with his fingers jammed into his back pockets. His face was reflected against the windowpane, his brows knit in thought, his jaw set.

Even before he spoke, she knew that the moment had arrived, and that she wasn't ready.

"Was that me?" he asked quietly. "Was I the baby?"

Fear more terrible than she had ever imagined clutched at Lexi's heart. She didn't want him to be hurt. She didn't want to lose him. But she knew that in the next few minutes, both of those things could happen.

"How would you feel if I said yes?" she asked, hardly daring to breathe.

"Weird, I guess." His shoulders twitched in a shrug that could have meant anything. "Scared, maybe." He turned just enough to peer over his shoulder. "She couldn't make me go back with her, could she?"

"Oh, no." Lexi shook her head emphatically, almost limp with relief. "That would never happen. If you ever went with Dolores, it would be because you wanted to— just for a visit. You're mine, and you will always be mine."

Jamie's smile was a shaky attempt at humor. "Promise?"

Lexi made the sign of a cross on her breast. "With all my heart. I would never give you up, Jamie. I love you too much."

She looked at him standing there, pressed against the window, so small, so vulnerable, trying to be brave while his world turned upside down. She wished she could find the magic words to make everything all right, but she knew there were none.

For ten years she had waited for this day to come, rehearsing what she would say and dreading the moment. Now that the time had come, nothing seemed adequate.

"Are you okay?" she asked, not knowing what else to say.

"You're still my real mom, right?"

"You better believe it. Nothing in our lives is going to change, except that we'll have Jake now, and we'll be even more of a family than we were before."

"Well, then I guess it'll be okay. She'll still just be my aunt, right?"

"It's all up to you, sweetheart. Whatever you feel like. You don't have to think or act any differently toward your Aunt Dolores than you ever did, if that's the way you feel."

"Okay." He sighed, and some of the stiffness went out of his stance. "As long as I don't have to call her Mom or anything like that."

"Well, I'll tell you, that's a big relief to me." Lexi held out her arms. "Can I have a real big hug now? I think I need it."

He started toward her a little shyly at first. Then, after a few steps, he broke into a run and threw himself into her outstretched arms, burying his face against her neck.

"Mmm, that feels good." She squeezed him as tightly as she dared while tears burned in her throat. "This has been a long, hard day, hasn't it?" she asked in a voice thick with unshed tears.

He nodded and snuggled closer. Then, seeming to remember that he was too old for such things, Jamie eased himself out of her arms again and settled beside her on the bed.

"Well, so, Mom—" He paused and furrowed his brow as he swung his gaze up to hers. "Well, so, if Aunt Dolores was my mother—" He stopped again, then plunged ahead. "So how come you don't know who my dad was?"

Lexi's heart leapt and began to pound harder once again. "Well, because—" Her voice broke. She cleared her throat, swallowed hard and started again. "Because Dolores would never say. Except—"

When she stopped the second time, Jamie leaned closer. His hazel eyes were riveted on her as he nodded his encouragement. "Except," he repeated. "Except what?"

"Except that today..." Lexi stopped, wondering if this would be too much. How much could one little boy stand to learn about his family in one day?

"Today," he prodded eagerly.

Feeling as if each word were forced from her soul, she continued, "Today...Dolores...told...Jake..."

Jamie leapt to his feet and thrust an arm triumphantly into the air. "Yes!" He brought the arm back down and pumped it several more times while doing something that resembled a war dance. "Yes! Yes! Yes!"

"So," Lexi asked tentatively, "you would like it if Jake turned out to be your father?"

The arm went into the air again. "Yes!"

Lexi laughed. "Well, that's great."

"Yes! Is he?"

"I think so."

Jamie let out a whoop, and Lexi's smile spread to the breaking point even as tears filled her eyes. She knew how he felt. She'd been that happy when Jake had asked her to marry him, but with all the commotion, she had never had a chance to celebrate.

Coming back down to earth, Jamie planted his fists on his hips and thrust out his chest proudly. "Boy, is Grandpa going to be happy."

"Maybe it's time we went downstairs and shared some of this celebration with Jake." Lexi stood and held out her hand. "He's been a little worried about how you'd take the news."

Jamie slipped his hand into hers and started toward the door, chanting, "I've got a dad, man. I've got a dad."

THE LIGHTS WERE OUT. The fire was flickering. The house was silent.

On the sofa with his arm around Lexi, Jake said for the dozenth time, "He did seem to take it rather well, didn't he?"

"Don't be modest. Jamie was ecstatic, and you know it."

"Yeah."

Lexi could hear the smile in Jake's voice, and she snuggled closer. "It's hard to believe all the things that have happened today. Was it just five weeks ago I kidnapped you and brought you here?"

"I've never thanked you for that, have I?"

She laughed. "Not in so many words."

"I wasn't really mad, you know."

"You weren't? You sure had me fooled."

His chin brushed her hair as he shook his head. "I was scared. Or maybe *terrified* is a better word."

"Why?" Lexi drew back to look into his eyes.

"Because as soon as I saw you again, I knew I'd just been kidding myself. One look, and I wanted you as bad as ever." His fingertip traced the curve of her lower lip. His green gaze pierced her soul. "If I hadn't been hurt in the arena that night, and if you'd hung around until I was free, I'd probably have done my damnedest to get you into the sack right then and there."

Trying mightily to ignore the distractions of his touch, Lexi arched a questioning eyebrow. "I thought you had to leave as soon as the rodeo was over."

"I lied."

"Jake!"

"Honey, I'm no angel. I never have been." His fingers slid over her cheek with exquisite tenderness. "You must know that by now."

She covered his hand with hers, relishing the warmth of his palm against her skin. "You're too hard on yourself. I've always thought you were pretty fantastic."

"I want to be. For you. From now on."

"Jake, do you think you'll get bored here after a while and want to go back to the rodeo?" she asked, remembering Jamie's questions and how little she really knew about their future.

"The rodeo?" He sounded totally surprised. "I don't think so. I believe I've had about all the misery I really want."

"I thought you liked rodeoing."

"Well, in a way I do. But I'm just too old to be taking that kind of pounding every night. The only reason I went back to it in the first place was that I'd leased my ranch away for ten years and I didn't think I wanted to become a used-car salesman."

"A used-car salesman?" she echoed, trying but not succeeding to keep the laughter from her voice.

"What were my options?" he asked. "Ranching and rodeoing are all I've ever known, Lexi."

Happiness bubbled inside her as she ran her hand over his chest, across to his shoulder and then slowly back again, loving the solid feel of him. "So you think you'll be happy here?"

His lips crooked in a half smile, and he took his time as he answered, "Let me see, now. I get to watch my son grow up, help him become a man and hear him call me Dad." Jake lifted the hand she rested on his chest and, one by one, kissed each fingertip. "I get to be partners with and work beside Frank Conley, a man I have loved and admired my whole life."

Drawing her arm across his shoulder, Jake pulled her closer to him while his voice dropped to the husky rasp that never failed to ignite a flame inside her. "I get to go to bed with you every night for the rest of my life. And wake up in the morning to see your smiling face next to me." She snuggled against him, almost purring in response, and he nodded slowly. "Yeah, I think I'll be happy." His lips brushed her brow and he whispered, "What do you think?"

"I think it sounds like a wonderful life," Lexi answered. "Even better than wonderful." It was all she'd ever wanted, and more than she'd ever dreamed she would have.

Jake's arms tightened around her and drew her into his lap. "The best."

THE CHILDREN'S HOUR

Favorite Mystery Stories

A BOOK TO GROW ON

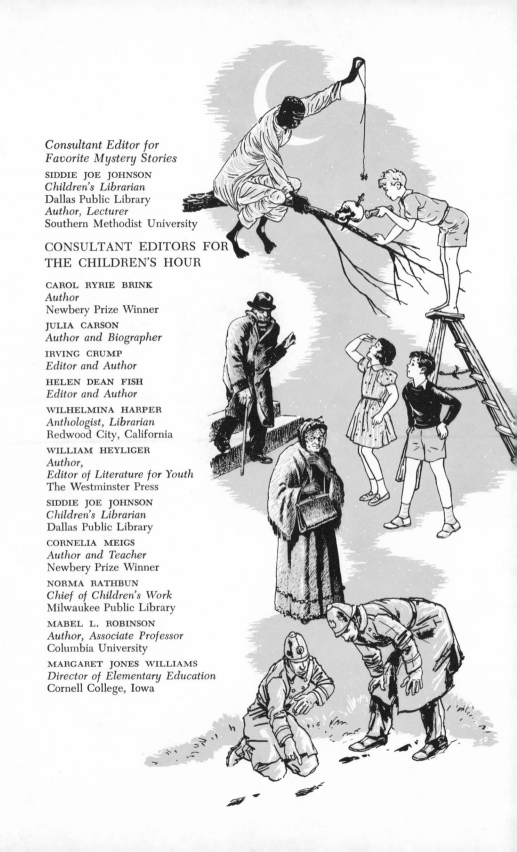

Consultant Editor for
Favorite Mystery Stories

SIDDIE JOE JOHNSON
Children's Librarian
Dallas Public Library
Author, Lecturer
Southern Methodist University

CONSULTANT EDITORS FOR THE CHILDREN'S HOUR

CAROL RYRIE BRINK
Author
Newbery Prize Winner

JULIA CARSON
Author and Biographer

IRVING CRUMP
Editor and Author

HELEN DEAN FISH
Editor and Author

WILHELMINA HARPER
Anthologist, Librarian
Redwood City, California

WILLIAM HEYLIGER
Author,
Editor of Literature for Youth
The Westminster Press

SIDDIE JOE JOHNSON
Children's Librarian
Dallas Public Library

CORNELIA MEIGS
Author and Teacher
Newbery Prize Winner

NORMA RATHBUN
Chief of Children's Work
Milwaukee Public Library

MABEL L. ROBINSON
Author, Associate Professor
Columbia University

MARGARET JONES WILLIAMS
Director of Elementary Education
Cornell College, Iowa

THE CHILDREN'S HOUR

MARJORIE BARROWS, *Editor*

Favorite
Mystery Stories

MATHILDA SCHIRMER
Associate Editor

DOROTHY SHORT
Art Editor

GROLIER INCORPORATED · *New York*

Acknowledgments

The editor and publishers wish to thank the following publishers, agents, authors, and artists for permission to reprint stories and illustrations included in this book:

JAMES BROWN ASSOCIATES for "The Adventure of the Blue Carbuncle" and "The Red-Headed League" by A. Conan Doyle.

CONSOLIDATED BOOK PUBLISHERS for illustrations by Stan Lilstrom for O. Henry's "Calloway's Code."

THOMAS Y. CROWELL COMPANY for "Hunter's Moon" from *Norman Bones, Detective*, by Anthony C. Wilson, copyright, 1949, 1951, by Anthony C. Wilson.

DOUBLEDAY & COMPANY, INC., for "Calloway's Code" from *Whirligigs* by O. Henry, copyright, 1905, by Doubleday & Company, Inc.; "The Adventure at the Toll Bridge" from *Night Boat and other Tod Moran Mysteries* by Howard Pease, copyright, 1942, 1943, by Howard Pease; and "The Strange Pettingill Puzzle" from *The Strange Pettingill Puzzle* by Augusta Huiell Seaman, copyright, 1935, 1936, by Augusta Huiell Seaman.

NORVELL HARRISON for "Miss Hinch" by Henry Sydnor Harrison.

LITTLE, BROWN & COMPANY for "One Alaska Night" from *Alaska Holiday* by Barrett Willoughby, copyright, 1936, 1937, 1939, 1940, by Barrett Willoughby.

METHUEN & CO., LTD., for Canadian permission for "Hunter's Moon" from *Norman Bones, Detective*, by Anthony C. Wilson.

L. C. PAGE & COMPANY, INC., for "Old Houses" from *Beacon Hill Children* by Elizabeth Rhodes Jackson.

STORY PARADE, INC., for "The Secret of Rainbow Ridge" by Audrey Baxendale, copyright, 1950, by Story Parade, Inc.; and "Forgotten Island" by Elizabeth Coatsworth, copyright, 1942, by Story Parade, Inc.

THE VIKING PRESS, INC., for story and illustrations for "The Case of the Sensational Scent" from *Homer Price* by Robert McCloskey, copyright, 1943, by Robert McCloskey.

L. R. DAVIS for "Stalactite Surprise," first printed in *Child Life Magazine*.

MARGARET C. LEIGHTON for "The Legacy of Canyon John" first printed in *American Girl*.

CONSTANCE SAVERY for "The Wastwych Secret."

L. M. SWENSON for "The Mystery of Number 30."

MARGUERITE DE ANGELI for the illustrations for Constance Savery's "The Wastwych Secret."

GENEVIEVE FOSTER for illustrations for Augusta Huiell Seaman's "The Strange Pettingill Puzzle."

MARGARET and FLORENCE HOOPES for illustrations for Elizabeth Rhodes Jackson's "Old Houses."

KEITH WARD for illustrations for L. M. Swenson's "The Mystery of Number 30."

Contents

Elizabeth Coatsworth

FORGOTTEN ISLAND

ILLUSTRATED BY *Corinne Malvern*

THE fortuneteller told them both the same fortune. Jane went into the tent first and sat there with her hand held out across a table covered with an Oriental cloth. She felt a little scared as the woman in the bright-colored skirt and white waist, earrings, and a handkerchief about her head, looked at her palm for a while. Then the fortuneteller said, "There is adventure ahead of you. I see it soon, and yet the adventure is connected with something from far away and long ago."

The fortuneteller said some other things, too, unimportant things that didn't stick in Jane's mind after the sound had left her ears. She paid her quarter and slipped out. John was waiting for her.

"Any good?" he asked.

"I'm not sure," said Jane. "I don't suppose she's a real gypsy."

"The money goes to charity anyhow. I'd better see what she tells me," John said, and he went in.

"What did she tell you?" Jane asked as he came out a few minutes later.

"Oh, a lot of stuff about school, and being on the football team if I only believed I could make it. A lot of stuff like that. And then she said I was to have an adventure, soon, and that it was connected with a faraway place and things that had happened a long time ago."

Jane's gray eyes flashed indignantly.

"I bet she says that to everyone! That's just what she told me. I feel like going in and asking for my quarter back."

1

"Hold on." John was more logical than Jane. "Maybe we might be going to have it together."

They stuck around the tent. It was part of a church affair on Mrs. Sumner's lawn, and it was made up mostly of flower and needlework booths and things like that, with a pony they felt they were too big to ride, and a grab-bag filled mostly with rubber dolls and rubber balls. After getting themselves another bag of brownies, they had plenty of time to question some of their friends who had had their fortunes told.

"Hi, there! Bill, what did she tell you?"

They must have asked five or six children, but to none of them had there been promised an adventure of any kind. It kept them making guesses.

"I bet she means our going up to the cabin. That's an adventure, right on Green Pond, in the woods and everything," Jane said. But John, who was two years older, twelve going on thirteen, shook his head.

"It couldn't be that, Jane," he argued. "The cabin's new. Dad just had it built last winter. And it's on land where nothing has ever been before. That couldn't be it. We'll have to wait."

"I can't bear to wait!" Jane cried.

John grinned at her.

"Don't know what you'll do about it," he said. "Come on, I've got five cents left. That'll get us a piece of fudge, anyhow."

Two weeks later the Lane family were climbing out of their car at the end of a rough Maine wood-road. For a moment they all four stood still, feeling happy. Then Mr. Lane unlocked the back of the car, and they began to carry suitcases and blankets into the new log cabin which stood a little back from the edge of the water. They were as busy as four chipmunks during acorn season.

No one but Mr. Lane had ever seen the place. It was his surprise. He had been traveling up to Maine every week or two since last fall, superintending the building of the cabin. It was made of peeled logs, oiled to make them stay clean and shining. It had a big living room with a boulder fireplace with

2

a fire already laid, which Mother immediately lighted as a house warming. There was a small kitchen, too, with a sink and a new pump painted red under the window, and three bedrooms in a row opening from the big room. Out of John's room went a stair leading up into the loft where cots could be placed when the Lanes had friends.

"James," exclaimed Mrs. Lane. "You've thought of *everything*."

"You're pleased, Janet?" he asked anxiously, "it's the way you thought it would be?"

"Only much nicer!" said Mother.

The Lanes were a family that had very good times together. They loved to go camping together and they could all paddle and fish and swim and build a fire outdoors and flap pancakes on a skillet. So it had seemed perfect when Father found this land on a secluded cove on Green Pond and began having a cabin built. Now that he was a senior member in his law firm, he seemed able to get away from his offices a good deal in summer.

"People don't feel so quarrelsome in warm weather," he used to say—though that was probably a joke. "They get crotchety in the fall and begin to go to law about things after the first hard frosts."

Anyhow, whether he was joking or not as to the reason, Father managed to get away a good deal in the summer. Now they had a place of their own, and he and Mother were happy all day long working on the finishing touches. John and Jane tried to help, and did, too, but there were times when there was no need for them. Then they were likely to get into their bathing suits, pack a light lunch, and take to the canoe to go exploring.

They had named the canoe *The Adventure* because of the church-fair prophecies, but for a long time their excursions were of a quiet character. Green Pond was about ten miles long, but its shoreline was very uneven. Now the pond was a mile or two wide, now it narrowed to a few hundred feet, only to widen once more. Long coves indented its wooded shores,

and here and there an island lay like a frigate becalmed. There were farms along the slopes in many places, but only occasionally did their hayfields stretch down to the water. More often there lay a fringe of woods or rough pastures along the lake. Sometimes, these woods were very thick, extending into the wilderness which covers Maine, the great central wilderness on which the farmlands lie like scattered patches, hardly noticeable to the eagle flying high overhead against the whiteness of the summer clouds.

There were no towns on Green Pond, no summer cottages except their own, no camps. Paddling along with silent paddles the children came upon many things, a deer drinking, or a fox slipping off into the underbrush, or a fish hawk rising, its prey catching the sunlight as it dangled in those fierce claws.

They heard voices calling at the farms, usually hidden from sight, and sometimes came upon a farmer fishing toward evening after the milking was done. But the sounds which they heard most constantly were the clank-clank of cowbells and the slow notes of the thrushes. Less often, they heard sheepbells. And of course there were other birds, too, the warblers and white-throated sparrows and, above all, the big loons which seemed to like them and often appeared floating near them, uttering their lonely cries. But when the children paddled too close, the loons would dive and when they reappeared, it would be a long way off, to teach the young humans that they must keep their distance.

One day as they were eating their lunch on a flat rock under a pine at the opening of a small bay, a curious sound began vibrating through the air. It was hard to tell where it came from. It filled the bay and echoed back from the slopes above the trees, all the time growing louder and more and more insistent.

Jane stopped eating her sandwich.

"What's that?" she asked in a low voice. "It sort of scares me."

John squinted his eyes across the glint of water.

"It must be an outboard motor," he said. "It sounds near. We ought to see it."

But they saw nothing that day.

In the weeks which followed, however, they became acquainted with that sound. Sometimes they heard it at night, waking up to raise their heads from their pillows to listen to its passing; it sounded then as though it circled in front of their cabin, like an animal circling a fire. Sometimes they heard it by day, in the distance, and once, in a thick fog which had come in from the sea, it passed very close to them. They saw the outlines of a boat and of a figure in an old slouch hat at the stern. They waved but there was no gesture from the boat, and in a moment it was gone again. Only the coughing of the engine and the rank smell of gasoline fumes were left to stain the ghostly silver of the day.

"There's something queer about that man," said Jane. "Why don't we ever see him? And why didn't he wave to us?"

John sent the canoe ahead with a powerful stroke of his paddle.

"He probably didn't see us," he said. "I suppose he goes fishing. We just don't happen to come across him."

Jane still had her paddle trailing.

5

"No," she said, "it's a feeling. It's as though he were always sneaking around the lake. Whenever I hear him it scares me, but when the engine stops, it's worse. Then you don't know *where* he is or *what* he's doing. But I know he's up to no good."

"That's just because his outboard motor's old and has that stumbling sound," insisted John. "He's probably a farmer at one of the farms trying to get some bass for supper."

"He chooses very queer hours to go fishing then," Jane said, unconvinced. "And I don't know when he gets his farm work done, either. You know as well as I do that there's something queer about him, John, so don't pretend there isn't."

"Have it your own way, Jen," John said, not admitting anything, but a queer little cold feeling came over him, too, whenever he heard that choking splutter across the water. He, too, felt relieved when several days would go by and no sound of the outboard motor would come.

Often the children would explore the woods along the shore, following little paths or wood-roads when they saw them. One afternoon toward dusk they were going single file along a trail so faint that they were not sure it was a trail at all. Perhaps the deer used it, or a cow coming down to the pondside to drink. And, yet, here and there a twig seemed to have been broken off as though by a human hand.

It was hot in the woods and the mosquitoes bothered them. Jane picked a couple of big fern leaves, and they wore them upside down over their heads like caps, the green fringes protecting their necks, but even so they had to keep slapping.

"I vote we go back," said Jane at last, stopping. But John peered over her shoulder.

"There's a little cliff ahead," he said. "Let's just go that far, and then we'll go back." It seemed wrong to turn around until they'd reached some sort of landmark.

So Jane brandished her pine twigs over her shoulders, slapped a mosquito on her bare knee, and started ahead.

The cliff was very pretty, its seams filled with ferns, while funguses which they called "elephants' ears" seemed to be peeling in great green-and-gray scales from the granite surfaces.

Then the fortuneteller said, "There is adventure ahead of you."

If the channel had actually been cleared, it must have been done a long time ago, for here and there it was completely grown over, and once more the reeds would close about *The Adventure,* scraping its sides with their rubbery touch. Yet by standing upright for a moment in the bow, Jane was always able to see clear water ahead, and they would push forward into a new opening.

The cove was much longer and wider than they had dreamed. They seemed to be moving in a small separate pond surrounded by maple-covered shores; all view of Green Pond was lost now, with its slopes of farmlands and woodlands and the Canton hills along the west. The breeze was lost, too. It was very hot among the reeds, and still. There was a secret feeling, moving slowly along these hidden channels, while the dragonflies darted silently in and out among the leaves.

Deeper and deeper they went into this mysterious place, and as they went they grew more and more quiet. A voice sounded out of place in this silence. First, they spoke in whispers and then scarcely spoke at all, and Jane, balancing herself at the bow when the passage was blocked, merely pointed to the clear water ahead, shading her eyes against the sun.

9

It seemed only natural that they should come upon something wonderful, so that they were excited but not surprised when they saw an island ahead of them. It, too, was larger than one would have expected, and rockier. There were pines on it and tumbled ledges ten or fifteen feet high. The channel led to a cove where a small beach lay between low horns of rock. At a distance it would have seemed merely another knoll in the swamplands, but it was a real island, with the water lying all about it, and the shore of the mainland still some distance away.

It seemed only part of the enchantment of the place that a house should stand above the beach, an old-fashioned house with fretwork scrolls ornamenting its eaves, and an elaborate veranda. Time had been at work here, and it was hard to say whether the walls had been brown or red. One or two of the windows had been broken by falling branches or blundering birds, and the door stood open into the darkness of a hall.

The children exchanged one glance of awed agreement, and in a moment the bow of *The Adventure* grated on the sand. Jane jumped to the shore and turned to pull the canoe further up the beach.

Still in silence they ran up the rotting steps, and with a last glance backward into the sunlight, stepped through the gaping door into the house.

"You never saw anything like it in your life. It was all dusty and spooky with cobwebs over everything!" said Jane.

"And the swallows flew out and nearly scared us to death. They had their nests on the top bookcase shelves—" added John.

"One of them flew straight at my head! I thought it was a bat and would get into my hair."

"And there were footstools made of elephants' feet stuffed with straw, but the rats had got at them, and—"

"You've forgotten about the chairs and table made of horns, John—"

"You mean I haven't had a chance to tell about them! And there was a crocodile made of ebony inlaid with ivory—"

10

"Hold on! Hold on, children! Is this a dream or a new game, or what?" Father demanded.

"It's all real as real as real!" the children cried. "It's the island we discovered."

"They couldn't make up a house like that," Mother said. "You know they couldn't, Jim. What else was there, children?"

"Well," began John, "there had been lion skins and zebra skins on the floor, but they were pretty well eaten up, and on each end of the mantel there was a big bronze head—"

"Of a Negro girl," interrupted Jane. "John thinks they might have been boys because their hair was short, but they looked like girls, and they had necklaces around their neck, and their heads were held high—"

"And there were ivory tusks coming out of their heads. They were holders for the tusks. You'd like them, Mother. And there was another statue standing in an opening in the bookcase, about three feet high, a chief or a god or something with eyes made of sea shells, and hollow."

"Yes, and tell what was written over the mantel in queer letters—you remember we learned it—'Oh, the Bight of' what was it, John?"

> "Oh, the Bight of Benin,
> The Bight of Benin,
> One comes out
> Where three goes in."

"That settles it," said Father. "You two haven't gone mad or been hypnotized or had a dream. Your evidence is too cir-

11

cumstantial. That's the beginning of an old sea-chanty of the African Gold Coast. What else was there in this house?"

The children stared at him, their eloquence brought to a sudden stop.

"That's about all, Dad," John said, wrinkling his forehead, trying to bring back that strange interior with its smell of dust and mice and the stirrings overhead of loose boards. How could he describe how he and Jane had clung together, their hearts hammering, tiptoeing from room to room, ready to run at a moment's notice?

They hadn't gone upstairs. Upstairs had seemed too far from the open door. No one knew where they were. There might be some mysterious person living in this house, after all. They might come face to face with him at any moment. There were ashes in the fireplace. How long would ashes last? And in the dark kitchen into which they had peered for a breathless moment, John had seen fish bones on the sink-drain and an old knife. How long would fish bones last? Who had been using that knife and how long ago?

A sudden squawk from a heron outside had raised the hair on their heads. They had catapulted toward the door and then tiptoed back into what had been the living room.

"Do you think we might take the crocodile?" Jane asked wistfully. "The rats will eat it if we leave it here."

But John had a very strong sense of law.

"We don't know who owns the house," he said. "It would just be stealing. And if the rats haven't eaten it by now, they won't eat it before we can get back." For hours the Lanes sat before their own fireplace, talking over the mysterious house and making guesses about it.

It grew darker and darker outside, but Mother forgot to start supper on the stove and everyone forgot to be hungry. Over and over the children described just where they had found the house in its own lost and secluded cove. Then they went over what they had found inside. Now and then Mother asked a question, but Father hardly said anything but sat looking into the fire, smoking his pipe. It kept going out, and had to be refilled and relighted every few minutes, so the children knew he must be very interested.

"Far away and long ago," said Jane suddenly. "This is our adventure, John."

John was about to answer when the old droning squeal of the outboard motor sounded from the darkness of the lake. Once again it moved nearer and nearer them, and once more it seemed to pass the lights of their windows only to turn and pass them again.

"There's that same fisherman," Mother said, a little uneasily.

Father went to the door.

"Ahoy, friend!" he called into the darkness. "Ahoy! Won't you come ashore and have a visit?"

The engine seemed to check for a minute as though someone were listening. Then it began to sputter and drone again with its sawmill-wheel violence and, after apparently circling them once or twice more, whined off down the pond and at last merged into silence.

"I guess he couldn't hear me, that old outboard of his makes such a racket," Father said as he came back from the open doorway. "Anyway, it's of no importance. It's your island that interests me. Now all I can say is that there are several little ports of the Maine coast which once carried on a regular trade with the Gold Coast in the sailing-ship days. Take Round Pond—that's only about twenty miles from here. Fifty years ago, they say it used to be full of monkeys and parrots and African gimcracks brought back by the sailors. But your house has things too fine for any ordinary sailor to bring home. And why should he build a house on an island in a pond, and then desert it, with everything in it? If he was a captain, why didn't he build a house in a seaport, the way most of them did?"

"Maybe he didn't want people to know where he had gone," Jane suggested.

"Maybe that's it," agreed Father. "But don't you think that's a little too blood-and-thundery? He probably was just a nice old gentleman whose nephew had been on a hunting trip to Africa and brought back a few trophies for his eccentric old

13

uncle. He kept them round for a few years, and then got tired of the place, and went out to California to visit his married sister. He liked it so well that he decided to buy a house, and never bothered to send for the African stuff, which he was tired of anyhow."

John looked at his Father indignantly.

"That might be it, Dad," he exclaimed. "But how about his writing 'Oh, the Bight of Benin, the Bight of Benin'?"

" 'One comes out where three goes in,' " Jane finished the quotation softly.

Father looked thoughtfully into the fire.

"Yes," he agreed, "that has the voice of adventure in it. Maybe it wasn't anyone's eccentric old uncle after all. We'll find out soon enough."

"How?" the children cried, all awake and excited once more.

"We'll go to the town clerk and see who owns the house."

"Tomorrow?" begged the children.

"Tomorrow, rain or shine," said Father.

"And now," said Mother, "what about some scrambled eggs and stewed tomatoes? It's after nine o'clock."

It took old Mr. Tobin over an hour and two pairs of glasses before he found the record of the ownership of the island.

"Here it is," he said at last in some triumph. "A man named E. R. Johnson bought it from old man Deering—the Deerings still own the farm back there on the east shore—paid two hundred dollars for it. That was on April 7, 1867. I remember there was talk about him when I was a boy. But he didn't stay more than two or three years, and I thought the place had burned down or fell down long ago."

He licked his thumb and turned over more pages.

"Let's see, here's the assessment for 1877, thirty dollars—that must have been after the house was built, of course. Paid. Here's 1878, paid too, and 1879. After that it's all unpaid. In 1883 they dropped the assessment to five dollars—guess they thought the house weren't worth much by then."

He went on turning pages with interest, while the Lanes sat about him on kitchen chairs watching his every motion.

14

"Here's 1890. I can't find any record of an assessment at all. I guess they thought a swamp island which didn't belong to anyone weren't worth carrying in the books. Kind of forgot about her. Yes, here's 1891. No sign of her in this, either. Well, let's figure her up. Three years at thirty dollars is ninety. And seven years at first is thirty-five, add ninety, and it makes one hundred and twenty-five dollars back taxes.

"Anyone wanted to pay one hundred and twenty-five dollars would own the island."

Father rose and shook hands with Mr. Tobin and thanked him for his trouble.

"We'll talk it over," he said mildly. "Nice weather we're having, but we need rain."

"My peas aren't filling out," said Mr. Tobin, "just yellowing on the vine. If we don't get a thundershower soon all the gardens in Maine won't be worth cussing at."

Mother couldn't stand it.

"Aren't we going to buy the island, Jim?" she asked.

But Father only looked absent-minded.

"Have to talk it over," he repeated vaguely. "Come, children, in we get. We ought to drive to town and get provisions. Thank you, Mr. Tobin. See you later—maybe."

In the car all the Lanes began chattering at once.

"*Can* we have it?"

"*Are* you going to buy it?"

"Oh, Father, how wonderful!"

"Look here," said Father severely. "You people don't know how to act about forgotten islands. You want to keep them forgotten. Raise as little talk as you can, slip in quietly, buy them quietly, don't start a ripple on the water. You'll spoil it all if you get the whole countryside sight-seeing and carrying off souvenirs. So long as Mr. Tobin just thinks you kids have run across an old ruined cottage on an island, which you'd like as a camping place, he'll hardly give it a thought, but you musn't start his curiosity working."

"But you *will* buy it?" Jane begged.

"Of course, I will. What's more I'll buy it for you and John.

15

You found it and it's going to be yours. What'll you name it? Adventure Island?"

"No," said John, "I like Forgotten Island better. It seems more like the Bight of Benin."

"What *is* a bight?" Jane asked. "I like Forgotten Island, too. Forgotten Island, Forgotten Island. It makes me feel sad and wonderful."

"A bight," said her Father patiently, "is a very large bay. Benin was a great city up the river from the Gold Coast. Those bronzes must have come from there, for the Negroes of Benin were famous for their bronze work. They used to trade in slaves and were very cruel. It was an unhealthy coast for whites. They died from fever and all sorts of tropic diseases."

It was not until late afternoon that the children paddled their parents over to see Forgotten Island. All was as it had been the day before, except that the thunderheads were crowding along the sky to the northwest and there was a little breeze, even across the acres of the water garden. They were lucky in finding the channel again and in managing to keep to it, with Jane as lookout. Once *The Adventure* rasped over a flat stone, and for a second they all thought they might be stuck there, but after a moment or two, they pushed the canoe sideways and were able to go on.

But today there was a different feeling in the air. There was a continual rustling among the maples as though they were preparing for a storm. A big turtle slid off a rock at the edge of the shore and raised its head to stare at them as they went by. It thought itself hidden among the reeds, but they could see its horny nose and the two small beadlike eyes which watched them as intruders from its hiding-place. Even the house had a more secret air about it. The door still stood open, but Jane suddenly thought of a trap, and even with her father and mother there, hung back a little before going in.

However, this curious antagonism, which all felt but no one mentioned, was not strong enough to drown their interest, once the Lanes had stepped across the threshold. All that the children had remembered was true and more still. There were carvings in wood, which they had forgotten, split and stained with age. They found chief's stools upheld by grinning squat figures shaped from solid logs, and hangings of curious woven cloths on the walls. Father and Mother were as excited as the children.

"I can't believe my own eyes," Mother kept exclaiming.

Father said more than once, "Now who the dickens was this man Johnson, and where did he come from, and where did he go to?"

This day they went upstairs, testing each step carefully to make sure that it would hold. There were three bedrooms on the second floor, only one fully furnished, and it did not seem to go with the rest of the house. It had a set of heavy walnut furniture and a photograph of a mountain in a gold frame. The matting on the floor smelled of mold and damp, and a hornet's nest hung papery and lovely from one corner of the ceiling. Not a thing in the room suggested Africa.

The rats and squirrels had wrecked the old mattress for a hundred nests of their own.

"It's as though Mr. Johnson hadn't wanted to think of Africa when he went to bed," Mother said, quietly, as she looked about. "Perhaps the Bight of Benin was something he preferred to think about by daylight."

Jane was standing near the window, and happened to look out. She had a distinct feeling of seeing something move behind the bushes along the shore. But though she thought "It's a man," she really wasn't sure. Things move sometimes in the corner of your glance, half out of sight. This glimpse she had was at the very edge of her vision.

Lightning flashed in the sky, silent, without thunder, and the trees shook their leaves and shivered down all their branches. She could see nothing now but the whitening leaves. Their motion must have been what had caught her attention. She said nothing, but she was ready to go back to the new cabin, which they had built themselves, about which there was no mystery.

The lightning flashed again, brighter this time.

17

"Goodness!" exclaimed Mother. "I suppose we'd better be getting back before it rains. But I feel as though we were leaving a foreign land. I expect to see giraffes staring at us when we push off."

Halfway out of the cove a sound began at some distance.

"Thunder?" Father asked, cocking his head, but the children knew, without waiting to hear it again, that it was the sound of an old outboard motor going about its secret business.

The next day Father bought the island for back taxes and had the deed made out to John Lane and Jane Lane. The children signed it with a sense of awe.

"Now you'll have a place you can call your own," Father said, for Mr. Tobin's benefit. "You can camp there, if you're able to find a spot where the roof doesn't leak."

"Yes, Dad," the children exclaimed dutifully, but their eyes were wild with excitement. Forgotten Island was theirs; they owned its remoteness and its mystery, or it owned them. Anyway, they were bound together for all time.

For two days the words had been going through Jane's head, day and night:

> "Oh, the Bight of Benin,
> The Bight of Benin,
> One comes out
> Where three goes in!"

She woke up with the verse ringing through her mind like the echoes of a gong. It had rained during the night and the air was bright and clear this morning. She was ashamed of the oppression which had overtaken her the afternoon before on the island. The coming storm had set her to shivering like the trees, she thought, and with no more reason. Why had she imagined they were being spied on? If anyone else knew about the island, wouldn't he have taken away the things long ago?

Mr. Tobin saw them to his door.

"Jo Taylor, down the pond Canton way, has lost another heifer. He went out to the pasture lot to give them their salt, and he says only four came for it. He had a look around but

18

couldn't find a sign of her. He's going to report it. There's a man calls himself Trip Anderson came in here last March and built himself a shack on the lake. Jo's suspicious of him, but it's pretty hard to get proof."

"Has Trip Anderson got an outboard motor?" John asked, thinking of the stranger.

"Yes," said Mr. Tobin, "so they say. They don't know where it came from, either. He's taken the old boat Eb Carson used to have before he died and patched it up. Mrs. Carson says she don't grudge him the boat; it was just rotting down by the willows. No one's missed an outboard round here."

"We've been all round the lake," said Jane, "and we've never seen his shack."

"I haven't either," Mr. Tobin agreed. "Don't get down to the pond much these days, though when I was a boy I was

19

there most of my spare time. I'm not sure as anyone's seen his place, but they know it must be there, probably back a piece from the water. He's worked some for people. Told them he was planning to bring his wife and little girl when he got settled. A lot of people think he's all right, and that if anyone's stealing stock, it's likely to be that second Grimes boy who's always been wild, or there's old Nat Graham. He'd as soon take a thing as look at it—vegetables, anyhow."

That afternoon the children spent a rapturous two or three hours on Forgotten Island. Once more the place had its quiet, enchanted air. Even the house seemed to welcome them in as its owners. The swallows had left their nests and with their young were flying about outside.

Jane had brought a broom and begun the task of sweeping the living room, tying her hair up in her sweater when she saw what clouds of dust she raised. John carried out the more torn and bedraggled skins. One of the hangings on the wall was in shreds, but another had held. A zebra skin, too, was in fairly good condition. They put it in front of the hearth, and John gathered enough dead wood outdoors to lay a new fire.

"I'll bring an ax next time," he said, "and we must have matches in a tin box. Jen, have you noticed? This room seems as though it belonged to an older building. It's built stronger for one thing, and the floor boards are nearly two feet wide and the ceiling is lower. I think Mr. Johnson added on the rest of the house to something which was already here."

They went about examining the place and decided that John's guess was right. The windows in the living room had many panes, and in the other rooms they were only divided down the middle in a bleak way, and the thin boarded floors swayed under the children's weight.

"Perhaps we might get the rest torn down some day and have this for the house, with a low shingled roof. We could cook over the open fire."

"And we could have a long window seat built along one wall which we could use for cots—"

"And we'd keep the African things—"

20

They got very excited making their plans. All the time they were talking they worked, and by mid-afternoon the room looked very thrilling. They had rifled the other rooms for anything sound and strong, and now the old part of the house had the aspect of the sitting room of some African trader.

It was John who found the old well, while gathering deadwood for a fire. "We'll bring over a new pail and a rope," he planned. "I think the water looks perfectly good."

They had never been so excited or so happy in their lives. They could not bear to go away from their new possession and kept returning to put a last touch here or there. At last the sun had gone down, and they knew they must go home. But just then Jane discovered a mass of old rubbish behind the bronze figure standing in a sort of niche in the bookcase. It was about three feet high and not as heavy as she had supposed. She dragged at it, but she put too much strength into the effort, and the thing toppled over and fell with a terrifying clang.

"Oh, dear!" cried Jane. "I hope it hasn't been dented! But wait, John, till I sweep up behind him. Then you can help me get him back in place."

The statue lay on its side where it had fallen, and they could see that it was hollow. It had one hand raised above its head. Perhaps it was from inside this hand, or from some corner of the inside of the head, that the things had been jarred which they found on the floor when they started to pick it up.

Gold is gold, and does not rust, no matter how long it may lay hidden. The ring, the crude little crocodile, the bird, the thing that looked like a dwarf—all were of soft virgin gold, almost warm to the children's stroking fingers.

"Look," murmured Jane, "there's gold dust on the floor, too."

The pale light faintly glittered on a haze of gold. Looking at the feet of the statue they could see now that once they must have been sealed over with metal. Someone had pried them open a long time ago, and found the statue filled with gold dust and, perhaps, other treasures like these small ones which had lain concealed.

The children looked and handled and exclaimed, scarcely able to believe their own good fortune. This was "far away and long ago" with a vengeance.

"It's getting late," John's conscience reminded him. "Mother and Dad will be sending out a search party for us soon. Let's put the treasure back where we found it and bring them over tomorrow and surprise them."

"Oh, let's take it back with us!" protested Jane. "You know, John, I've had the queerest feeling twice that we were being watched? Yesterday, when we were all here, and today after the statue fell. Something seemed to be at that window, over there behind me."

"What sort of thing, Jen?"

"I couldn't see. When I turned it was gone. I went over to the window and I couldn't see anything, either."

"Why didn't you tell me?"

"I didn't want you to call me a silly."

John went out quickly and looked under the window which Jane had pointed to. There was a rank growth of nettles there, and not one had been broken.

"You've been seeing things, Jen," he declared cheerfully as he came back. "No one could have been at the window. Now be a good girl and give me the things. Good, those ought to stay put. I've used my handkerchief to help stuff them back in place. Now give me a hand at setting Mumbo Jumbo on his feet again."

All the time she was helping, Jane was protesting and arguing under her breath, but John was the leader and what he said usually went. She felt rather silly, anyway, about the things which she kept imagining that she saw.

"If they've been here safe since 1879, they can stay here a day or two longer," John declared. "Wait till you see Father's face! We'll invite them here for a picnic tomorrow and end up with the treasure."

Next day, however, it rained hard, and the children had to swallow their impatience. They wanted their party to be perfect in every way. In the late afternoon the rain changed into a fog with a little sunlight coming through.

"Can't we go over to the island?" Jane asked.

Father went out and looked at the sky.

"The fog banks are still blowing in," he said. "Smell that sea smell that comes with them! It's likely to rain again in an hour or two."

"Well, can't John and I take a picnic lunch now and just go to Oak Point around the corner?"

"We'd better let them," said Mother. "I've never known you children to be so restless. Perhaps a little paddling and picnicking will help you."

They had almost reached the point, moving through the fog so silently that they startled their friends the loons by coming upon them before they could dive; they had almost reached the point—when they found the man with the outboard motor. Everything about the picture was gray, a shabby gray coat, and a wiry shabby figure working over the motor at the stern, with the fog dripping from the broken rim of an old hat.

"Good evening," John hailed. "Can we help you?"

The man straightened and stared at them.

"No, thanks," he said then, "I'll be all right," and he bent again to his work. The children paddled on and reached the point. They had already on another day built a fireplace of big stones there, and John had brought kindling in his knapsack, so that soon the fire was crackling and the smell of frying bacon filled the air.

Jane felt uncomfortable. "He looks so kind of hungry," she whispered to John. "Go on, ask him if he won't come and eat with us."

"But—" began John.

"I don't care!" Jane broke in. "I don't care what people say. Ask him or I will."

The man who called himself Trip Anderson hesitated and then finally paddled his boat into shore with a crudely whittled-down board which seemed to be his only oar. He ate at the children's fire hungrily, but remembering his manners. He seemed like anyone who was rather down on his luck, except for the way in which he met a person's glance, staring back hard, showing a thin rim of white all around the bright blue iris of his eyes. They all talked a little about the pond and the weather. The man knew a lot about fish. It was interesting, but the children were glad when supper was over and the rain began again.

24

"Guess we've got to go," they said, and he stared at them with his fixed eyes which he never allowed to shift the least bit.

"Much obliged, kids," he said. "I'll do something for you some day."

They told their father and mother that evening who had been their guest, and their elders approved, within reason.

During the night the wind shifted to the northwest and the day came bright and perfect. The greatest excitement reigned in the cabin until 10:30 when *The Adventure*, laden with passengers, baskets, and extra supplies for Forgotten Island, put out into a pond that rippled delightfully.

Father and Mother were much impressed by the changes one afternoon's hard work had made in the living room. John showed Father what the original house must have been like, and he caught their enthusiasm immediately.

"It wouldn't be much of a job tearing off the 1870 part," he said. "We might be able to sell it for old wood, or if we can't, it could be burned on the rocks. Then this would be a wonderful little place. Nothing like it anywhere in the country."

The picnic was eaten in state around the table whose legs were made of horns, while a small unneeded fire crackled in the fireplace to give an added welcome. After the baskets were packed again and the room in order, Father brought out his pipe, while Mother began to knit.

This was the moment for which the children had been waiting for nearly two days.

"Want to see something else we found?" John asked with elaborate carelessness.

Jane bounded forward to help him.

They tugged out the statue and laid it on its back, and John reached far up its depths into the hollow arm, while everyone waited breathlessly.

Jane saw the look of shock and surprise come to his face and knew what had happened before he spoke.

"Why," he said rather blankly. "They're gone, the gold things are gone. There isn't even my handkerchief there.

25

"Sorry, Jane," he muttered to her when she ran forward to help search the crevices of the statue, and she squeezed his hand hard.

"It doesn't matter a bit," she cried, bravely blinking the tears out of her eyes. "Think of all we have left."

They didn't talk any more about the treasure. John felt too badly about it to bear any mention of it. Jane felt badly, too, of course, but it wasn't half so hard for her as for John, who had left the things just where they had found them.

They all paddled home to the cabin, making occasional conversation about nothing much, and that evening Father brought out *Huckleberry Finn* and read for hours, not saying once that his voice was getting tired.

Mother had glanced once or twice at the clock, when they heard a car come down their road and a moment later a knock sounded at the door.

It was late for visiting in the country, and everyone looked at each other in surprise as Father went to the door. Two men stood there whom they didn't know, one of them in uniform.

"Come in," said Father. "I'm James Lane. Did you want to see me?"

The older man shook hands first. "I'm Will Deering, Mr. Lane," he explained, "from over across the pond, and this is Mr. Dexter, of the State Police."

Mr. Lane shook hands with Mr. Dexter and introduced them both to the family.

"Mr. Dexter has come up here on business," Mr. Deering explained. "There've been complaints about a man who calls himself Trip Anderson. One man's lost two heifers and another man, who has a camp over on Muscongus Pond, missed an outboard motor from his boat. They brought Mr. Dexter to me because I know the lake pretty well and had an idea of where his shanty was. I took Mr. Dexter there while he was away, and we searched it and found proof he'd been doing a lot of petty thieving hereabouts. Proof wasn't needed, because when this Anderson came back, Mr. Dexter recognized him as a fellow who'd broken jail at Thomaston a year or so ago."

26

"His real name is Tom Jennings," the other man broke in. "He was serving a term for armed robbery. No, he ain't got a wife nor kids. That was just cover. He's been in and out of jail since he was sixteen."

Mother looked worried, thinking that the children had been having a picnic with such a man only the evening before. But Father knew that, somehow or other, the business must concern them, or these two men wouldn't have knocked at their door at ten o'clock at night.

"Did you wish me to identify him?" he asked, but Mr. Dexter shook his head.

"He don't need identifying," he remarked, pulling out his watch and looking at it. "By now, he's at Thomaston. But just before we took him away he said he had some things he wanted to return. He had them hidden in the flour tin. Said he'd been using the island you've bought, but never took any of the big things because they could be spotted too easy. When you kids began to go there, he kept an eye on you. He's good at that, moves like an Indian. One day when he was hanging round he heard a crash and looked in and saw you find the gold stuff. That was more up his alley. He could melt it down, and no one could ever prove anything against him."

The State Policeman fished again in his vest pocket and brought out first the dwarf, and then the bird, and then the crocodile. The ring came last. He poured them all into Jane's hand, and she quickly brought them to John.

"Think of his giving them back!" she exclaimed. "Oh, thank you for bringing them! We were *so* bothered when we found they were gone."

"Jennings said you were good kids and had asked him to eat with you."

"Do you want to see the things?" John asked eagerly. He took them about so that everyone might examine the little objects close at hand.

Mr. Deering held up the crocodile.

"We have one at home like this," he said, "in the old teapot, I think it is. My grandfather used to say Johnson gave it to him for boarding his horse, after he'd run out of the gold-dust quills he used to get his money from. The day he gave grandfather the crocodile and drove off was the last time he was ever seen around here. 'I took one image from that African temple that was chuck full of gold,' he told Grandfather. 'It stands to reason the other images have gold in them. Anyway, I aim to go and see.'

"But he never came back," continued Mr. Deering. "I figure he could play a trick on the temple priests once, maybe, but next time they'd get him. We never knew where he came from, nor what vessel he took for Africa, but it wouldn't be hard to find one in those days, when there was still a good trade there. Grandfather said he had the bearing of a captain. Probably no one else ever knew that the idol he'd stolen had gold in it, and he came away here, on the quiet, where no one ever *would* know it. But he was a reckless spender, Grandfather said. Money just poured out of his hands while he had it, and then he started back to get more. Anyhow, he never came back."

Everyone had been listening with breathless interest.

"Why didn't your grandfather use the house on the island, or sell it?" Mr. Lane asked.

"It wasn't his," the farmer replied. "Johnson had bought the island out and out. And Grandma didn't want any of that African stuff around the place. She called it outlandish, and my mother didn't like it either. We just minded our own business, and no one else but us had had direct dealings with him

28

or knew much about the place. Every year the cove filled up more and more with pickerel weed and, pretty soon, the island and Johnson were kind of forgotten—"

"That's what we call it—Forgotten Island!" the children cried.

Mr. Deering looked at them and smiled.

"Well, it's yours now," he said. "It's nice to have neighbors on it again. Glad we found you all at home."

Everyone got up to see their visitors to the door. Mr. Deering stepped out first and, as Mr. Dexter turned to say good-bye, Jane asked, "Is there anything we can do for Trip Anderson?"

The officer shook his head.

"He's all right," he said. "Don't worry about him. I guess he was getting pretty tired of his freedom. He said he'd be glad to be back where he'd be taken care of. I'll tell him you inquired."

Then the door closed behind the strangers and, a moment later, there came the roar of a self-starter. Little by little the sound receded up the road and silence settled again in the woods, and, after a while, even the Lanes' cabin was dark and still, and the Lanes, too, were asleep. But on the mantel, in the silence broken only by the occasional calling of the loons, watched the four talismans of gold, keeping guard—the treasure of Forgotten Island, made by dark hands far away and long ago.

Robert McCloskey

THE CASE OF THE SENSATIONAL SCENT

ILLUSTRATED BY THE AUTHOR

ABOUT two miles outside of Centerburg where route 56 meets route 56A there lives a boy named Homer. Homer's father owns a tourist camp. Homer's mother cooks fried chicken and hamburgers in the lunchroom and takes care of the tourist cabins while his father takes care of the filling station. Homer does odd jobs about the place. Sometimes he washes windshields of cars to help his father, and sometimes he sweeps out cabins or takes care of the lunchroom to help his mother.

When Homer isn't going to school, or doing odd jobs, or playing with other boys, he works on his hobby which is building radios. He has a workshop in one corner of his room where he works in the evenings.

Before going to bed at night, he usually goes down to the kitchen to have a glass of milk and cookies because working on radios makes him hungry. Tabby, the family cat, usually comes around for something to eat too.

One night Homer came down and opened the icebox door and poured a saucer of milk for Tabby and a glass of milk for himself. He put the bottle back and looked to see if there was anything interesting on the other shelves. He heard footsteps and felt something soft brush his leg, so he reached down to pet Tabby. When he looked down the animal drinking the milk certainly wasn't a cat! It was a skunk! Homer was startled just a little, but he didn't make any sudden motions, because he remembered what he had read about skunks. They can make a very strong smell that people and other animals don't like. But the smell is only for protection, and if you don't frighten them or hurt them, they are very friendly.

While the skunk finished drinking the saucer of milk, Homer decided to keep it for a pet because he had read somewhere that skunks become excellent pets if you treat them kindly. He decided to name the skunk Aroma. Then he poured out some more milk for Aroma and had some more himself. Aroma finished the second saucer of milk, licked his mouth, and calmly started to walk away. Homer followed and found that Aroma's home was under the house right beneath his window.

During the next few days Homer did a lot of thinking about what would be the best way to tame Aroma. He didn't know what his mother would think of a pet skunk around the house, but he said to himself Aroma has been living under the house all this time and nobody knew about it, so I guess it will be all right for it to keep on being a secret.

He took a saucer of milk out to Aroma every evening when nobody was looking, and in a few weeks Aroma was just as tame as a puppy.

Homer thought it would be nice if he could bring Aroma up to his room because it would be good to have company while he worked building radios. So he got an old basket and tied a rope to the handle to make an elevator. He let the basket down from his window and trained Aroma to climb in when he gave a low whistle. Then he would pull the rope and up came the basket and up came Aroma to pay a social call. Aroma spent most of his visit sleeping, while Homer worked on a new radio. Aroma's favorite place to sleep was in Homer's suitcase.

One evening Homer said, "There, that's the last wire soldered, and my new radio is finished. I'll put the new tubes in it, then we can try it out!" Aroma opened one eye and didn't look interested, even when the radio worked perfectly and an announcer's voice said, "N. W. Blott of Centerburg won the grand prize of two thousand dollars for writing the best slogan about 'Dreggs After Shaving Lotion.' "

"Why I know him, and he's from my town!" said Homer.

Aroma still looked uninterested while the announcer said that next week they would broadcast the Dreggs program from Centerburg and that Mr. Dreggs himself would give Mr. N. W. Blott the two thousand dollars cash and one dozen bottles of Dreggs Lotion for thinking up the best advertising slogan. "Just think, Aroma, a real radio broadcast from Centerburg! I'll have to see that!"

The day of the broadcast arrived, and Homer rode to Centerburg on his bicycle to watch. He was there early and he got a good place right next to the man who worked the controls so he could see everything that happened.

Mr. Dreggs made a speech about the wonderful thing Mr. N. W. Blott had contributed to the future of American shaving with his winning slogan: "The after-shave lotion with the distinctive invigorating smell that keeps you on your toes." Then he gave N. W. the two thousand and one dozen bottles of lotion in a suitcase just like the one that Homer had at home. After N. W. made a short speech the program was over. Just then four men said, "Put 'em up," and then one of them said to N. W., "If you please," and grabbed the suitcase with all of the money and lotion inside it. Everyone was surprised: Mr. Dreggs was surprised, N. W. Blott was surprised, the announcer was surprised, the radio control man was surprised, and everybody was frightened too. The robbers were gone before anybody knew what happened. They jumped into a car and were out of sight down route 56A before the sheriff shouted, "Wait till I send out an alarm, men, then we'll chase them. No robio raiders, I mean radio robbers can do that in this town and get away again!" The sheriff sent out an alarm to the State Police, and then some of the men took their shotguns and went off down 56A in the sheriff's car.

Homer waited around until the sheriff and the men came back and the sheriff said, "They got clean away. There's not hide or hare of 'em the whole length of 56 or 56A."

While they were eating dinner that evening, Homer told the family about what had happened in town. After helping with the dishes he went up to his room, and after he had pulled Aroma up in the basket, he listened to the news report of the robbery on his new radio. "The police are baffled," the news commentator said, "Mr. N. W. Blott is offering half of the prize money and six bottles of the lotion to anyone who helps him get his prize back."

"Aroma, if we could just catch those robbers we would have enough money to build lots of radios and even a television receiver!" said Homer.

He decided that he had better go to bed instead of trying to think of a way to catch robbers, because he was going to get up very early the next morning and go fishing.

He woke up before it was light, slipped on his pants, and ate a bowl of cereal. Then he found his fishing pole and gave a low whistle for Aroma (the whistle wasn't necessary because Aroma was waiting in the basket). Homer put the basket on his bike, and they rode off down 56A.

They turned into the woods where the bridge crossed the brook. And Homer parked the bike and started to walk along the brook with Aroma following right along.

They fished all morning but didn't catch anything because the fish just weren't biting. They tried all of the best places in the brook and when they were ready to go home they decided to go straight through the woods instead of following the brook because the woods path was much shorter.

The path through the woods was an old wood-road that was not used any more. It had not been used for years, and almost everybody had forgotten that it was ever built. Before they had gone very far Homer thought he heard voices, then he smelled bacon cooking. He thought it was strange because nobody ever came up on this mountain to camp, so he decided to sneak up and investigate.

When Homer and Aroma looked around a large rock they saw four men! "THE ROBBERS!" whispered Homer, and indeed they were the robbers. There was the suitcase with the two thousand dollars and the one dozen bottles of after shaving lotion lying open on the ground. The robbers had evidently just gotten up because they were cooking breakfast over an open fire, and their faces were covered with soapy lather, for they were shaving.

Homer was so interested in what the robbers were doing that he forgot to keep an eye on Aroma. The next thing he knew, Aroma had left the hiding-place and was walking straight toward the suitcase! He climbed inside and curled up on the packages of money and went right to sleep. The robbers were busy shaving and having a difficult time of it too, because they

had only one little mirror and they were all stooped over trying
to look in it.

"I can hardly wait to finish shaving and try some of that
fragrant after shaving lotion," said the first robber.

Then the second robber (who had a cramp in his back from
stooping over and from sleeping in the woods) straightened up
and turned around. He noticed Aroma and said, "Look at that
thing in our money!" The other robbers turned around and
looked surprised.

"That, my dear friend, is *not* a thing. It is a Musteline
Mammal (*Genus Mephitis*) commonly known as a *skunk*!" said
the third robber who had evidently gone to college and studied
zoology.

"Well I don't care if it's a thing or a mammal or a skunk, he
can't sleep on our money. I'll cook that mammal's goose!" Then
he picked up a big gun and pointed it at Aroma.

35

"I wouldn't do that if I were you," said the third robber with the college education. "It might attract the sheriff, and besides it isn't the accepted thing to do to Musteline Mammals."

So the robbers put a piece of bacon on the end of a stick and tried to coax Aroma out of the suitcase, but Aroma just sniffed at the bacon, yawned, and went back to sleep.

Now the fourth robber picked up a rock and said, "This will scare it away!" The rock went sailing through the air and landed with an alarming crash! It missed Aroma, but it broke a half dozen bottles of Mr. Dreggs' lotion. The air was filled with "that distinctive invigorating smell that keeps you on your toes," but mostly, the air was filled with Aroma!

Everybody ran, because the smell was so strong it made you want to close your eyes.

Homer waited by the old oak tree for Aroma to catch up, but not for Aroma to catch up all the way.

They came to the bike and rode off at full speed. Except to stop once to put Aroma and the basket on the rear mudguard, they made the trip home in record time.

Homer was very thoughtful while he did the odd jobs that afternoon. He thought he had better tell his mother what had happened up on the mountain. (His father had gone into the city to buy some things that were needed around the place, and he would not be back until late that night.) At dinnertime he was just about to tell her when she said, "I think I smell a skunk around here. I'll tell your father when he gets home. We will have to get rid of that animal right away because people will not want to spend the night at our tourist camp if we have that smell around." Then Homer decided not to say anything about it, because he didn't want his father to get rid of Aroma, and because the robbers would no doubt get caught by the State police anyway.

That evening Homer was taking care of the gas station and helping his mother while his father was in the city. In between cooking hamburgers and putting gas in cars, he read the radio builders' magazine and looked at the pictures in the mail-order

36

catalogue. About eight o'clock four men got out of a car and said, "We would like to rent a tourist cabin for the night."

Homer said, "All right, follow me," and he led the way to one of the largest cabins.

"I think you will be comfortable here," he said, "and that will be four dollars in advance, please."

"Here's a five-dollar bill, Buddy, you can keep the change," said one of the men.

"Thanks," said Homer as he stuffed the bill in his pocket and hurried out the door because there was a car outside honking for gas.

He was just about to put the five-dollar bill in the cash register when he smelled that strange mixture, partly "the distinctive invigorating smell that keeps you on your toes," and partly Aroma. He sniffed the bill and sure enough, that was what he had smelled!

"The robbers! Those four men are the robbers!" said Homer to himself.

He decided that he had better call up the sheriff and tell him everything. He knew that the sheriff would be down at the barber-shop in Centerburg playing checkers and talking politics with his friends, this being Saturday night. He waited until his mother was busy getting an extra blanket for someone because he did not think it was necessary to frighten her. Then he called the barber-shop and asked to talk to the sheriff.

"Hello," said Homer to the sheriff, "those four robbers are spending the night out here at our tourist camp. Why don't you come out and arrest them?"

"Well, I'll be switched," said the sheriff. "Have they got the money and the lotion with them?"

"Yes, they brought it," said Homer.

"Well, have they got their guns along too?" asked the sheriff.

"I don't know, but if you hold the line a minute I'll slip out and look," said Homer.

He slipped out and peeped through the window of the robbers' cabin. They were getting undressed, and their guns were lying on the table and on the chairs and under the bed

and on the dresser—there were lots of guns. Homer slipped back and told the sheriff, "They must have a dozen or two."

The sheriff said, "They have, huh? Well, I tell you, sonny, I'm just about to get my hair cut, so you jest sortta keep your eye on 'em, and I'll be out there in about an hour or so. That'll give them time to get to sleep; then some of the boys and me can walk right in and snap the bracelets on 'em."

"O.K. See you later, sheriff," said Homer.

Later when his mother came in, Homer said, "Mother, I have some very important business, do you think that you could take care of things for a while?"

"Well, I think so, Homer," said his mother, "but don't stay away too long."

Homer slipped up to a window in the robbers' cabin and started keeping an eye on them.

They were just getting into bed, and they were not in a very good humor because they had been arguing about how to divide the money and the six bottles of lotion that were left.

They were afraid, too, that one of the four might get up in the night and run away with the suitcase, with the money, and the lotion in it. They finally decided to sleep all four in one bed, because if one of them got out of bed it would surely wake the others up. It was a tight fit, but they all managed to get into bed and get themselves covered up. They put the suitcase with

38

the money and the lotion inside right in the middle of the bed. After they had turned out the light it was very quiet for a long while, then the first robber said, "You know, this ain't so comfortable, sleeping four in a bed."

"I know," the second robber said, "but it's better than sleeping in the woods where there are mosquitoes."

"And funny little animals that don't smell so nice," added the third robber.

"You must admit, though, that our present condition could be described as being a trifle overcrowded," said the one with the college education.

"Them's my feelings exactly," said the first robber. "We might as well start driving to Mexico, because we can't sleep like this. We might as well ride toward the border."

"No, driving at night makes me nervous," said the other.

"Me too," said the third. Then there followed a long argument, with the first and third robbers trying to convince the second and fourth robbers that they should go to Mexico right away. While they were arguing Homer thought very hard. He guessed that something had better be done pretty quick or the robbers might decide to go before the sheriff got his hair cut. He thought of a plan, and without making a sound he slipped away from the window and hurried to Aroma's hole under the house. He whistled softly, and Aroma came out and climbed into the basket. Aroma had calmed down considerably but she still smelled pretty strong. Homer quietly carried the basket to the spot under the robbers' window and listened. They were still arguing about the trip to Mexico. They didn't notice Homer as he put the basket through the window onto the chair beside the bed. Of course, Aroma immediately crawled out on the bed and took her place on the suitcase.

"Stop tickling," said the tall robber because his feet stuck out and Aroma's tail was resting on his toes.

"I'm not tickling you," said the second robber, "but say, I think I still smell that animal!"

"Now that you mention it, I seem to smell it too," said the third robber.

The fourth robber reached for the light button saying, "That settles it! Let's get dressed and go to Mexico, because *I think I smell that animal too!*"

Then as the robber turned on the light Homer shouted, "You *do* smell that animal, and please don't make any sudden movements because he excites easily." The robbers took one look and pulled the covers over their heads.

"The sheriff will be here in a few minutes," said Homer, bravely.

But five minutes later the sheriff had not shown up. The robbers were getting restless, and Aroma was tapping her foot and getting excited.

Homer began to be disturbed about what his mother would say if Aroma smelled up one of her largest and best tourist cabins, so he quickly thought of a plan. He climbed through the window. He gathered up all of the guns and put them in the basket. Then he gathered up the robbers' clothes and tossed them out of the window. After picking out one of the larger guns Homer waved it in the direction of the robbers and said, "You may come out from under the covers now, and hold up your hands."

The robbers gingerly lifted the covers and peeked out, then they carefully climbed out of bed, so as not to disturb Aroma, and put up their hands.

"We didn't *mean* to do it," mumbled the first robber.

"And we'll give the money back," said the second robber.

"Our early environment is responsible for our actions," said the educated robber.

"I'm sorry," Homer said, "but I'll have to take you to the sheriff." He motioned with the gun and demanded that the fourth robber pick up the suitcase with the prize money and lotion inside. Then he said, "Forward march!"

"Must we go in our pajamas?" cried one.

"And without our shoes?" wailed another.

"Aroma is getting excited," Homer reminded them, and the robbers started marching without any more arguing, but they did grumble and groan about walking on gravel with bare feet (robbers aren't accustomed to going without shoes, and they couldn't have run away, even if Homer and Aroma hadn't been there to guard them).

First came the first robber with his hands up, then the second robber with his hands up, then the third robber with his hands up, and then the fourth robber with his right hand up and his left hand down, carrying the suitcase (of course, Aroma followed the suitcase) and last of all came Homer, carrying the basket with a dozen or two guns in it. He marched them straight down route 56A and up the main street of Centerburg. They turned into the barber-shop where the sheriff was getting his hair cut and the boys were sitting around playing checkers.

When the sheriff saw them come in the door he stopped talking about the World Series and said, "Well, I'll be switched if it ain't the robio raiders, I mean radio robbers!" The sheriff got out of the barber chair with his hair cut up one side and not cut up the other and put handcuffs on the men and led them off to the jail.

Well, there isn't much more to tell. The newspapers told the story and had headlines saying BOY AND PET SKUNK TRAP SHAVING LOTION ROBBERS BY SMELL, and the news commentators on the radio told about it too. Homer's father and mother said that Homer could keep Aroma for a pet because instead of hurting business Aroma has doubled business. People for miles around are coming to the crossroads where 56 meets 56A just to buy gasoline and to eat a hamburger or a home-cooked dinner and to see Aroma.

The next time Homer went into Centerburg to get a haircut, he talked the whole thing over again with the sheriff.

"Yep!" said the sheriff, "that was sure one smell job of swelling, I mean one swell job of smelling!"

L. M. Swenson

THE MYSTERY OF NO. 30

ILLUSTRATED BY *Keith Ward*

JOHN stood looking up and down the street with a frown on his face. His chum Billie had gone downtown to the dentist's with his mother, and John couldn't think of anything interesting to do just by himself. Across the street, Jerome and Frank were busy making a train out of their sleds, but, pshaw, he didn't want to play with babies all the time, and neither of them was over five!

John pulled down the zipper fastener of his jacket. As he did so, his fingers touched a round metal disc pinned to the jacket lining, and his face brightened. It was a metal badge, and it said, "Detective No. 30." It had been one of his Christmas presents. He would practice shadowing! He could do that by himself. But who was there to shadow?

As he looked about, John's eyes again fell on the children across the street. Well, it might not be a bad idea to shadow them.

John sauntered up the street. Of course, Frank and Jerome mustn't suspect that they were being shadowed. At the end of the block he crossed the street and hid behind a tree. Cautiously he looked out. No, they hadn't noticed him. Darting from tree to tree, he approached close to them. Now he could hear what they were saying, and, if they were up to any mischief, they'd better look out! To his great disgust, Jerome, without turning his head, said, "Hello, John. We're making a sled train, an' you can be the engine if you want to. Come on!"

42

John snorted in disgust. Those kids weren't big enough to know a detective if they saw one. Just then he saw old Miss Partridge going down the street. He'd shadow her! She was one of Mother's friends, and she was always calling him her dear little man and wanting to kiss him!

It wouldn't be hard to shadow her, she was so fat. He crept along on tiptoe behind her. It took her so long to turn around that he wasn't afraid of her seeing him. But this time Miss Partridge turned a corner more quickly than usual, and that brought John into view. She stopped and smiled a buttery smile. "Why, if it isn't darling little Jacky! Were you trying to catch up with me, dearie?" She fumbled in her bag. "Here's a penny to buy some nice pink peppermints."

John wanted to say something rude, but he knew that Mother wouldn't like that. Then he felt happier. Miss Partridge didn't realize that she was being shadowed. He *was* a real detective! He would keep up his disguise, and she would think he was just a polite little boy; so he said, "No thank you, Miss Partridge. I don't care for peppermints." As she moved on, John muttered, "It's lucky for you I didn't put handcuffs on you."

Just then he noticed a car parking at the curb, and a man, whom he didn't know, getting out of it. Now this was something like! He'd bet that man was up to something. Well, just let him beware of Detective No. 30, that's all!

The man hesitated, then started up the street toward the drugstore. John followed, pausing to throw a snowball or two, so that no one would know he was on the trail. Nevertheless, when the man entered the drugstore, John was close at his heels, and he followed him back to the telephone booth. There the man shut the door, and John rummaged in his pockets till he found a nickel. Shoving it across the counter, he said, "Gimme a chocolate bar." If the man noticed him at all, he saw only a boy munching candy, and he didn't know that that same boy was following him down the street.

He went to his parked car, and John thought that shadowing job was finished, but now the man did something queer. He got in, started his engine, then pulled up the hand brake

43

and got out, leaving his engine running. Looking about, he hastily walked up the path to the Stone's big house and went around to the rear.

John was all eyes. He didn't dare to follow into the yard, but he must see. On the boulevard stood some empty crates in which goods had been delivered, waiting for a truck to take them away. John crept into one of them, the open side of which was toward the street. Through the cracks he could see both the house and the car. The license tag had been bumped into, apparently, for it was bent up so he could hardly read it at first, but he had plenty of time to make it out. Wasn't that man ever coming out?

Suddenly the front door began to open slowly, and John glued his eyes to the crack. But it wasn't the man he was trailing after all. That man had a smooth face with a big nose, and he wore a hat. The man coming out had fuzzy gray whiskers and wore a gray cap, and was carrying a suitcase.

John wondered whether to wait any longer, but just then the man with gray whiskers passed close to his hiding-place, and John gave such a loud gasp of surprise that the man would have heard him if he hadn't been in such a hurry. He rushed to the parked car, jumped in, released the hand brake, threw in his gears, and was off, lickety-split.

John came out of his crate and looked after the car, eyes and mouth wide open. Just then there came a call, "Hi, J!" Bill always called him J. John started toward him. "Say, Bill, I've—" but Bill gave him no chance to finish. "Say, J, I had ice cream, and then I went to see the Four Marx Brothers, and were they keen? Oh, boy! That's the fourth time I've seen 'em." The two boys became so interested in what Bill had to tell that John forgot his own story.

The next morning at breakfast John sat eating his cereal in an unusual silence. He was trying to think of some way of persuading Daddy to advance his allowance. It wasn't due until Sunday, and the Four Marxes would only be in town until Saturday.

Daddy, who was reading the paper as he ate his breakfast,

44

looked across at Mother. "This lawlessness is getting pretty bad. The Stone house over here in the next block was entered yesterday while the family were all away, and a lot of silver and jewelry were taken. They seem to have carried the loot away in a suitcase they stole. Mr. Stone is offering a reward, but there don't seem to be any clues. Organized gang work, I suppose."

John laid down his spoon. "Would the reward be big enough so I could go to see the Marx Brothers? Would it, Daddy?"

"Don't be silly, Son," answered Daddy. "You don't understand. Mr. Stone is offering a reward to anyone who can help him find the gang that stole his property."

"Yes, I know," persisted John, "but it wasn't a gang, and he

45

had a big nose and a hat when he went in, and when he came out he had gray whiskers and a cap."

"See here, Son," said Daddy earnestly. "If you really know anything about this, tell me." So John told him about Detective No. 30 shadowing the man and hiding in the box and everything.

"Well," said Daddy, "I think I'd better call the police and let you tell them what you saw."

"Will I get the reward, Daddy?" repeated John, but his father was already at the telephone.

In a very short time a car stopped in front of the house, and two big policemen in blue uniforms came into the house. John felt a little afraid of them at first, but one of them looked so jolly and smiled such a broad smile that John couldn't help smiling back.

"So you're the young man who is going to help us catch this thief, are you?" said the jolly one. "Suppose you tell us everything you saw." So John told his story again.

"Now you wouldn't have noticed what kind of a car it was, would you?"

"Yes," said John, "it was a dark green coupé, and it was awful muddy."

"Now that's just fine," said the jolly one. "That helps a lot. Now if we only knew the license number, but of course you didn't notice that."

"Well, the tag was all bent up so it was hard to read, but I had to wait so long I copied it down. I thought a real detective would. I think I've still got it," and John fished a crumpled piece of paper from his pocket. Sure enough, there was the number, B131-466.

"Well, my boy, you've done real detective work," exclaimed his new friend, busily writing in his notebook what John had told him. "You'll be on the Force in no time at all. It oughtn't to be hard for us to pick up that car now, if only it wasn't stolen. If we find it, we shall want you to come down to the station to see if you can identify the man."

The policeman hurried away, and John, seeing Billie across

the street, called, "Say, Bill, want to go down to the police station with me? Maybe I'll get enough reward so I can go to the Four Marxes."

The two boys stayed near the house all day so as not to miss a call, but it was late in the afternoon when Daddy drove up and called for them. "They've got a man down there they think may be the big-nosed man. Now be careful and don't tell anything you aren't very sure of."

The boys were a little awed when they entered the police station and saw a man in uniform sitting behind a desk. There were half a dozen officers in uniform, and at one side stood a group of other men. As the boys looked at these men, they nudged each other.

"Which one of you boys is the private detective?" asked Sergeant Martin, the man behind the desk.

"We both are," answered Bill, "that is, not real ones, of course, but play ones. John is No. 30, and I'm No. 18, but it was John yesterday."

"Well, John," said the sergeant, "the officers have told me what you did yesterday. Now look at those men and see if the man you shadowed yesterday is there."

"Sure, he is," answered John. "It's that fellow with the big nose."

"So that's the one you followed, is it? But you said the man who came out of the house had gray whiskers and a gray cap."

"Yes, he did, but they were the same man," said John.

"Now how are you going to prove it? This man says his car was stolen yesterday from where he'd left it parked, and he found it later downtown."

John grew suddenly shy. "You tell 'em, Bill."

Bill pulled his hand from his pocket and showed some small blue stickers. "You see, it's this way. We try to see how many people we can shadow, and the one who shadows the most in a certain time beats. But we didn't think it was fair just to follow someone a little way and call that shadowing, so I have these blue stickers, and John has red ones. Before we can finish shadowing anyone, we have to get near enough

47

to stick one of these seals on him. That's what John did yesterday when he crowded up against the man in the drugstore."

The officers roared with laughter. "There's a new stunt in shadowing for you," said one of them, but the big-nosed man looked as if he would like to get away.

"What happened then?" asked the sergeant.

John took up the story. "I thought it was a different man, too, coming out of the front door, but when he passed by me, I saw that red seal just back of his overcoat pocket where I'd stuck it. Maybe it's still there," and the two boys ran over behind the big-nosed man. "Yep, there it is," cried Billie, and the officers went up and looked, too.

"The kids seem to have pinned it on you, all right. You might as well own up and tell us where the stuff is. It may help you some," said the sergeant.

"Sure, they have caught me," growled big nose, "but you cops'd never have got me without the kids. They've got brains."

"Well, come on, boys, let's go," said Daddy, anxious to get them away, but John held back. "Do I get the reward, Daddy, and will I get it in time to see the Marx Brothers?"

"You surely do get it," said a gray-haired gentleman, who had been listening but saying nothing. It was Mr. Stone, and he took out his checkbook and filled in the check: "Pay to the order of John Tate, Fifty and no one-hundredths Dollars," and signed his name. "I'm proud that I have such fine young neighbors to help guard my property," he said, shaking hands with the boys.

As they drove home, John said, "Will you lend me some money, Daddy, till I can get some. Tomorrow's the last day."

"Yes, I think this time you deserve it," said Daddy, who was feeling very proud of John.

The following mystery story for
younger children is about some little
English children of long ago.

Constance Savery

THE WASTWYCH SECRET

ILLUSTRATED BY *Marguerite De Angeli*

WHEN we were children we lived with
Grandmamma and Grandpapa Wastwych in their house on the
borders of the gray-green marshes. Our parents were in Africa;
and we had lived at Marigolds for so long that we had lost all
memory of our former life, and Mamma and Papa were only
pleasant dreamland names.

We were happy children, living quiet, sunny lives without
shadow or event. If we were a little afraid of stern Grandpapa
Wastwych, in his white ruffled shirts and brown velvet clothes
and gold repeater, we ardently admired our gay and gracious
grandmamma with the blue eyes and silvery hair. To our
childish minds, she seemed the soul of goodness and dignity
and charm; in all the countryside there was no old lady who
could compare with her. To rebel against Grandmamma's decisions, to question her wishes, to doubt her wisdom and
righteousness—these were crimes beyond the range of our
wildest thoughts.

So, on the day when Jessica Fairlie came to drink tea with
us, we naturally spoke much of Grandmamma in our efforts to
entertain our guest. Jessica was neat and ladylike, with small

49

features and pale gold ringlets. We feared her at first sight; and before tea was over, we knew that she was indeed a person to be respected. She attended a school for young ladies, she was fond of needlework; she thought most games rough and all boys objectionable; she was trusted to pay long visits to her relations all by herself, without a nurse. In fact, our possession of a wonderfully clever and interesting grandmamma was the only point in our favor; in all else we were hopelessly inferior to our visitor.

After tea, therefore, we tried to show her how marvelous a grandmamma we had. We escorted her to a corner of the drawing room and showed her Grandmamma's first sampler.

"Look," we said. "Grandmamma did that when she was six."

We were justly proud of the sampler, for in each corner stood a red flowerpot containing a small orange tree with green leaves and golden fruit. In the middle were the words:

Worked by me, Jane Caroline,
In the year eighteen hundred and nine.

Grandmamma had composed the poetry herself, which shows how very clever she was, even at six years old.

Jessica blinked her pale eyes and said that the sampler was beautiful. Then we took her to see a model under a glass shade—a basket filled with pears and plums and grapes made in wax. Jessica admired it very much and would hardly believe that Grandmamma had really made it.

Next we took her to show her Grandmamma's dried herbs and her pickles and ointments and spices and preserves; and we begged Margery, the still-room maid, to give us a little parsley jelly in a saucer for Jessica, who had never tasted it. Grandmamma's parsley jelly had a surprising and disagreeable taste, but the color was charming—it was a delicate pale green. Jessica shuddered at the first mouthful and put down the spoon in haste.

After that we showed her some white skeleton leaves and our doll's feather furniture, all of which Grandmamma's clever fingers had made for us. Jessica's eyes became as round as sea-pebbles. She said, "I would like to see your grandmamma."

We took her to the window, for we had heard Grandmamma's voice in the drive below. There stood Grandmamma, broom in hand, helping the garden boy to clear away the leaves. She was wearing a great dark blue cloak with a peaked hood; and in spite of her odd attire she looked as dignified as possible.

Jessica studied her hard for a full minute. Then she said, "I'm going home now."

"Why, you have not played with us yet," we protested.

"I'm going home now," replied Jessica.

And she went. The next day we met her taking a walk with her aunt's maid. Nurse Grimmitt and the maid were friendly, so Jessica was told to walk on ahead with Nonie, Tawny, and me.

"Why did you go home so early yesterday?" asked Tawny.

Jessica looked around to make sure that Nurse Grimmitt and the maid could not hear.

"I will tell you if you like," she said mysteriously. "It was because of your grandmamma."

"Because of Grandmamma?" we echoed in confusion and amazement.

"Yes," said Jessica, speaking very calmly. "Your grandmamma is a witch, and I do not like witches."

I cannot well describe the effect her words had upon us; but I know that the sun began to jump here and there in the sky and that cold shuddering thrills ran through our little bodies.

"Grandmamma is not a witch!" gasped Nonie.

"Oh yes, she is," Jessica assured us. "I am quite sure of it. When I heard her name, I thought that it was a witch's name; for of course a witch would be called 'Was-a-witch.' "

"It's 'Wastwych,' " we remonstrated timidly.

"Then that is even worse," returned Jessica, "because 'Wastwych' must mean 'Was-a-witch,' as if she were a particularly dreadful one who was more important than the rest. And I have other proofs. First of all, there is the sampler. No one who was not a witch could possibly have done such a clever piece of work as that. Then there was her horrible jelly, which was just the kind of thing a witch would make. And you yourselves said that she made preserves from sloes and elderberries and crabapples--and of course they are all witchy jams, every one of them. And then nobody but a witch could make leaves turn into skeletons and feathers into dolls' furniture."

"Nonsense!" said Tawny.

Jessica looked at him coldly.

"Listen to me, little boy," she said. "I know all about witches, because there used to be one in our village, and because my papa has a large book on witchcraft in his study. I should not say that your grandmamma was a witch unless I had very good reasons for saying it. Here is another reason—your grandmamma dresses like a witch. I have never seen an ordinary old lady in a blue cloak with a peaked hood!"

We were dumb. Jessica went on impressively, "I still have one more proof; and when you have heard it, I think you will be obliged to confess that what I say is true. Your grandmamma rides on her broomstick to visit the Will-o'-the-Wisp."

"She doesn't!" we cried, midway between terror and belief.

"There is a Will-o'-the-Wisp on the marshes—you can't deny it," replied Jessica with finality.

"Grandpapa says that it is only the light from a little hut where poachers sometimes lurk," said Nonie.

"Aunt's maid says it is a Will-o'-the-Wisp," Jessica said firmly. "We can see it from our house. And every evening just after six o'clock an old woman in a blue cloak goes gliding along the marshes to the light. The first time I saw her she was carrying a broom! I see her every night while I am being put to bed. It is your grandmamma. She walks very fast, in spite of the pools and the quagmires, and on dark nights she carries a horn lantern. She comes home at seven o'clock, gliding over the ground. If you don't believe me, just you watch what she does between six and seven tonight."

We looked at one another in dismay; for strangely enough Grandmamma had lately developed a curious habit of vanishing from the house just at that time. Jessica saw her advantage.

"It is a great disgrace to have a witch in one's family," she said. "Of course, she may be a harmless white witch, but there is never any knowing. I wonder what your friends would think if they could know that your grandmamma was a witch. I am afraid that they would never speak to you again, or to her, either."

"Oh, don't tell anyone, Jessica!" we implored.

"I don't know whether it would be right to keep such a dreadful secret," said Jessica. "Suppose she cast a spell over my Aunt Matilda or blighted the gooseberry bushes in the garden?"

In a moment of time Nonie and I saw ourselves outcasts, witch-children to whom nobody would speak.

"Oh, Jessica, don't tell!" I pleaded. "Here is my little mother-of-pearl penknife—you may have it if you care to take it."

"And here is my mole and blue satin bag," said Nonie, hurriedly thrusting it into Jessica's willing hand. "Dear Jessica, you will not tell?"

"I will think it over," said Jessica. "I will keep the matter a secret for at least one day."

Then the maid summoned her; and we went home with Nurse Grimmitt, our steps dragging as if our shoes were weighted with lead. It seemed unutterably wicked to suspect our dear, beautiful grandmamma of witchcraft; and yet Jessica had produced such an appalling array of proofs that our hearts sank when we remembered them. Our only comfort was in Tawny, who stoutly declared that he did not believe a word of Jessica's crazy talk. His courage went far to revive our flagging spirits; and when we saw Grandmamma sewing peacefully in the drawing-room at home, we actually ventured to laugh at Jessica's story.

Nevertheless, Nonie and I felt restless and uneasy when the hour of six drew nigh.

"Estelle," said Nonie, "do you think it would be very wrong for us to slip into the garden to see where Grannie walks at night? For if she does not go over the marshes, we may feel quite, quite certain that she is not a—you know what. I shall not believe any of those other proofs if only we can be sure that Jessica was mistaken about the marshes."

"Perhaps it is best to make sure," I agreed, though my heart beat fast at the thought of such an adventure. I wished that Tawny could have come with us, but he always spent the hour between six and seven over a Latin lesson with our austere grandpapa. We must fare forth unaided and alone.

Soon we were waiting in the dark shadow of some bushes close by a gate that opened on the marshes, lying all silvery green in the moonlight, with here and there dusky patches of water ringed with treacherous sucking moss. Very cruel and

54

dangerous were the marshes, smile as they might beneath their summer carpet of kingcups and cuckoo-flowers, and peaceful as they looked under the winter moon and stars. Far off we could see the dim blue glimmer from Will-o'-the-Wisp's house; and we shivered as we lingered in the cold, waiting to see what would happen.

Then a door opened softly, stealthily, and a tall figure in a peaked blue hood came down the path. We needed not to be told whose figure it was; for no one save Grandmamma walked with that firm, swift tread. In fear-filled silence we watched her open the gate and step out onto the marshes, walking with such sure, rapid steps that she seemed almost to fly over the ground. Nonie and I needed no further proof. We clasped each other's hands and went back in misery to the house.

I am glad to remember that never for an instant did we fear any personal harm from Grandmamma's witcheries. We were too fond of her to dream that she might hurt us—all that we dreaded was the disgrace that would fall on a family known to have a witch in it. Of that shame and horror we could not bear to think.

Apart from Tawny's sturdy faith in Grandmamma, we had nothing to comfort us in our distress. We dared not confide in Nurse, and Jessica was most unkind. When we next met her, she questioned us strictly; and after she had made us own that we had seen Grandmamma on the marshes, she nodded her head in satisfaction.

"But you won't tell?" we pleaded.

"I think that people ought to know," said Jessica. It was not easy to persuade her to keep our secret a little longer. In the end we gained a week's grace, but in order to obtain it we were obliged to offer her one of our best dolls, a needlecase with a green satin cover, and three cedarwood pencils. As soon as the week was over she met us again, determined to reveal all she knew. Once more we bribed her, this time with my red necklace of coral flowers.

After that, we had to make her a present every day. One by one our dearest treasures disappeared from our three toy-cupboards, for Jessica would never take anything less than the best. In spite of her fear of witches, she became bold enough to invite herself to play with us so that she might choose her presents more conveniently.

We did not enjoy Jessica's visits. When she came, we sat in silent grief, knowing that our hearts would soon be wrung with sorrow. When she went, we hid in our toy-cupboards, crying. But we never thought of resisting. She had all she wanted.

Little by little the toy-cupboards were emptied until there came a dreadful day when Jessica turned away with the disdainful words, "There is nothing worth taking. You have very few toys."

"We used to have plenty," said Tawny.

"I am going to drink tea with the Miss Forrests tomorrow," said Jessica. "They have a much larger playroom than yours, and your baby house is nothing in comparison with theirs. I have told them that there is a secret about your grandmamma, and they are very curious to hear it."

"But you won't tell, Jessica?" we entreated for the hundredth time. "Think of all the things we have given you—all the gilt

tables and chairs from our baby house and Tawny's whip and
his ninepins and his Chinese doll and the jumping frog and the
book of fairy tales and the tea-set and—"

Jessica looked at us with a cold eye.

"I am afraid that I cannot keep such a wicked secret any
longer," she answered. "I have always known that it was wrong
to keep secrets about witches; but in order to oblige you I have
kept your secret for three weeks and three days. And Blanche
and Fanny Forrest are anxious to know it."

"They will tell everyone!" we said.

"You should not have a witch for your grandmamma," said
Jessica. "I shall not come to your house again, for I do not care
to 'sociate with the grandchildren of a witch."

Then she went away. Had the sun fallen out of the sky, we
could hardly have been more dismayed. Tawny spoke quickly.

"I do not believe that Grandmamma is a witch," he said. "I
have never believed it. I will follow her over the marshes this
very evening, and I will watch what happens. And then I shall
tell Jessica the truth."

"But we are forbidden to set foot on the marshes!" I protested.

"I know that," said Tawny.

"And Grandpapa will punish you for missing your Latin lesson," said Nonie. "He will be angry, because you'll not be able to tell him why you went to the marshes."

"I know that, too," said Tawny.

"It is dangerous on the marshes," I said feebly. "And—and, Tawny, suppose you find out that Grandmamma really is a—"

Tawny gave me a look of great contempt, rose, and walked to the door.

Nonie and I would not venture to follow him. We knelt on the window seat and watched the dark shadows dancing outside. Presently Grandmamma's tall figure passed by, and a little later a small black object crept out of the bushes and followed her.

After a while we heard Grandpapa's voice calling angrily for Tawny. Shaking in our shoes, we hid behind the curtains, but Grandpapa saw us.

We were dreadfully afraid of Grandpapa in a temper. When he made us stand like culprits before him, we could not think how to evade his first angry question as to Tawny's whereabouts. Nonie wept and said, "He has gone to find out whether Grandmamma is a witch."

"You impudent little girl!" roared Grandpapa. "What do you mean?"

He looked so fierce that we could scarcely bring ourselves to reply. Making a vast effort, we said, "Jessica Fairlie said that Grandmamma was so clever that she must be a witch. Jessica said that only witches make parsley jelly and wild-fruit jam and samplers with poetry and furniture out of feathers and wore peaked hoods."

I think that if Grandpapa had been angrier he would have burst.

"How dare you—how dare you?" he said. "You believed such rubbish as that?"

"Not quite, Grandpapa," we sobbed. "You see, Jessica said

58

that Grandmamma flew over the marshes every night at six o'clock on her broomstick to visit the Will-o'-the-Wisp. And we watched—and Grandmamma did do it. We did not see the broomstick, but we saw Grandmamma. So then we thought that she must be a witch. And Tawny wouldn't believe it, but he has gone to find out why Grandmamma walks over the marshes so that he may tell Jessica that it isn't true."

Grandpapa's purple color faded away.

"Tawny on the marshes at night! He will be sucked under and drowned!"

And forgetting his anger, he dashed down the stairs like a young man and rushed to the marsh-gate, with Nonie and me after him. And there at the gate stood Tawny, dripping from head to foot with the cruel black mud of the quagmires. Grandpapa was so glad to see him safe and sound that anger had no time to return.

"Well, sir, I hope you are satisfied that your grandmamma is not a witch," he said.

Tawny saw that Grandpapa knew.

"It is not the Will-o'-the-Wisp that Grandmamma visits," he said. "It is a man who is ill and who lives in the Will's hut all alone. He has blue eyes like Grandmamma. I saw him through the window. Grandmamma gave him broth to drink. And there was a broomstick in the corner, but she didn't ride on it. I fell in the pools coming home. Grandmamma is coming now on her feet. She is not a witch at all. May I go to Jessica's house to tell her?"

"You may go to bed!" said Grandpapa. "I will tell Miss Jessica myself." His face wore a most peculiar expression.

Then Grandmamma stepped lightly in at the marsh-gate and gave a cry of alarm at the sight of us all standing there. Grandpapa looked at her horn lantern and basket. "It's that rascal Humphrey, I suppose?"

We did not understand, but Grandmamma did.

"He dared not come home, Richard," she said. "He is ill from want and misery—he sought shelter in the hut and sent word by old Nurse to me. Oh, Richard, forgive him!"

Grandpapa made her a courtly bow.

"Jane, God in His Mercy has preserved us from a great sorrow this night. For that reason, if for no other, I cannot refuse forgiveness to my son. If he is able to come with me, I will go now to bring him home."

Then Grandmamma put her horn lantern into his hand, her face alight with happiness. And Grandpapa walked away over the marshes with slow and ponderous tread.

Jessica never told her secret, for she did not drink tea with the Miss Forrests after all. She went home to her papa and mamma instead, and her Aunt Matilda sent our toys back to us in an enormous parcel by the maid. But the secret escaped nonetheless. We did not tell it, Grandpapa did not, and Uncle Humphrey did not, and Nurse Grimmitt never knew it; so we were at a loss to imagine how it leaked out. We did not think Grandmamma could have told it; for not even such a very gay grandmamma as ours would have liked people to know that two out of her three grandchildren had actually suspected her of being a witch! Yet everyone knew, and everyone teased us. Once we had the supreme mortification of hearing the Misses Forrest say to their new governess, "Look, there are the silly children who thought that their Grandmamma Wastwych was a witch."

L. R. Davis

STALACTITE SURPRISE

ILLUSTRATED BY *Carol Stoaks*

JOHN Kimberley Douglas Ross stood on the eighteenth tee and looked across the smooth Bermuda golf course at the small white roof of his father's cottage. In another minute he had lifted his old-fashioned driver and was swinging down at the ball with all his strength. The ball spurted from the tee and then twisted teasingly in the air. It went five times as far sideways as it had lengthwise, and then was lost in the rough somewhere near the ocean.

"Watch it," John called to his sister Betty, but she was already running toward the place where the ball had disappeared. Golf balls, even badly scarred and battered ones, were things that the Ross family couldn't afford to lose.

When they had hunted for fully five minutes, Betty pushed her hat back off her sunburned face and looked back at the tee. "It came this way," she said, retracing its flight, "and then it began to slice and came over here, but where. . ."

"Look!" John's voice sounded like the excited yap of a fox terrier. He had dropped his bag of golf clubs and was digging into the sun-baked soil with flying fingers.

"Did you find it?" Betty wanted to know. In another minute John had flipped the golf ball into her lap, but he kept on digging furiously until he had to stop for breath. "What do you think that is?" he panted, pointing at the hole.

Betty looked over the pile of dirt. In England she would have been sure it was a fox's hole, but in Bermuda . . . ? She put her head into the hole and listened. "I hear something," she told John. "Something kind of rumbling."

61

"Of course you do," John said, and now they were both digging. "It's the ocean and this is the entrance to a cave, and we've found it!"

Using a piece of board and sharp stick and their hands, John and Betty kept on digging. In a half hour they had a hole big enough to crawl into.

For a moment John hesitated. "It must run through our land," he said, "and we've never seen the mouth of it. Where do you think it comes out?"

Betty shook her head. "Don't know," she said, "but if we can hear the ocean, it must come out on the beach. Let me go first."

That was enough for John, and he began wiggling feet first into the hole, with Betty following.

Almost right away the hole spread out enough so that they could stand up. The air was cold and damp and smelled stale. In the pale light the walls about them shone and glittered dully.

"It's like the Crystal Caves that Father took us to," John said, "only better."

"More exciting," Betty said, "because you can't see so well. D'you think there're any bats?"

The same thought had been flickering through John's mind.

He didn't say anything, but kept on walking. Underfoot there was dry, crusty sand that shifted as they walked. Overhead icicle-like stalactites, made by the slow dripping of water through limestone, caught the dim light like old chandeliers.

When their eyes became more used to the darkness, they made out small chinks of light like bright half-moons ahead of them. "What are those?" Betty asked. "Have you any idea?"

"Those cracks of light are the sky," John said, trying to keep all trace of fear out of his voice. Where you could see crevices of light through the top of the cave, he knew it must be dangerously thin.

They walked on a few more steps, and now they could hear the ocean more distinctly. The pointed icicles had gone, and there were more and more chinks of light to follow.

"I wish . . ." Betty began, and almost as she said it the cave grew quite light. There was firm, wet sand under their feet, and in another minute they were blinking in the bright sunshine on a small piece of beach.

"Where are we?" Betty asked.

Rubbing and poking at his eyes, John looked behind him. On the right was the entrance to the cave and on the left, toward their house, was a sheer wall of coral rock. John pointed to it. "That's the answer," he said. "That's the back of Lookout Hill and we've looked over it lots of times, but it was so steep that we couldn't get down. And anyhow, who would think it was worth it to get to this little spit of beach?"

"Maybe nobody's ever found the cave," Betty's voice was excited. "If they haven't, there's probably treasure in it, and we've got the right to it because it runs through our place."

"And besides, finding's keeping," John finished. "You've got the right to any treasure you find."

They would have started to look right then and there, but the sharp sound of a horn came over the cliff. "It's lunchtime," John said. "That's Father blowing for us to come in."

Betty was trying to scale the back of Lookout Hill, but it was too steep, and the sharp striped rock cut her hands like glass. They looked at the water as it boiled and curled past

63

the edge of the cliff. It was no wonder that no swimmer had ever happened on the mouth of the cave.

"We'll have to go back through the cave," John said. "We've got to get our golf sticks anyhow."

They went back, and this time they went much more quickly than the time before. You can go faster in a cave when you know there are no rocks that are likely to fall on you or bats to come swooping out. In less than five minutes they had picked up the golf clubs and were back inside the small white cottage, washing up for lunch.

Even Mr. Ross was excited about their discovery. He actually put down his *Manchester Guardian* before they went into the dining room to hear the news.

"You mean to tell me that you got in at the golf course," Mr. Ross said, "and came out on that beach that's beyond Lookout Hill?"

John nodded. "And it's got what d'you call 'ems—stalactites —in part of it, just like the Crystal Caves."

"And treasure," Betty put in. "At least we're almost sure there's treasure in it if nobody's been there before us."

Mr. Ross ate his fish without speaking. "I wouldn't count on treasure," he said. "But still there's no telling. Pirates did come to Bermuda more than once in its early days."

John and Betty looked at each other and swallowed the last mouthfuls of their cold pudding.

"It would be very interesting," their father went on more to himself than to them, "if you found any Hispanic remains in that cave of yours."

John and Betty had hardly time to listen. They were already tearing through the house collecting things which they thought would be useful in exploring.

"Folks as goes poking about in ole caves is likely to run into ha'nts," Patricia, the colored cook, grumbled as John stuffed a package of cake into his knapsack on top of a flashlight and four candle-ends.

In a few minutes more, John and Betty were back in the cave and John was pulling some small pieces of kindling out of his

64

knapsack. "We're going to do this right," he said. "We're going to dig over every inch of this cave, but we're not going to go back on our own tracks. We're going to mark out where we've been with these stakes."

Betty was already digging into the shifting sand with the garden spade that she had brought along. The sand was so dry and fine that it slipped off her spade almost as fast as she piled it on, but she kept at it. In the back of her mind was Patricia's remark about the haunts. What *did* people do to protect their buried treasure? Hadn't she heard a story about their burying a corpse on top of each chest of gold, so that the poor man's soul would keep people away?

At that moment something hard and cold touched Betty's neck. For a moment she couldn't speak. Her heart seemed to have stopped and her hands and knees were not her own. It was the bony finger of some avenging terror. "John. . ." she got out finally. "John. . ."

John looked up as she plunged toward him. "What's the trouble?" he asked, but Betty was talking in wild, uncontrolled gasps.

"A ghost! I felt its finger. It's after us." She was rushing past him, but John held her and flashed his pocket flash to the spot where she had been working.

"Look," he chuckled. "There's your ghost's finger. It's still there."

Betty looked and her mouth opened very wide. Directly above the place where she had been digging was a silvery gray stalactite that hung down several inches below the others. She had been working backwards with her spade, and the cold wet limestone had touched her neck. "It did feel like a finger," she said, but John was running toward the stalactite with his flashlight in his hand.

"Th-there is something else!" John's voice sounded as though he didn't quite believe it himself.

Betty started for the entrance, but John's scornful voice stopped her. "Not a ghost, you silly. *Treasure!*"

Betty came back and stood very close to John. Half fearfully she looked up at the stalactite which she had felt on her neck. It was the last on that side of the cave, and the longest. The trickling of lime and water must have been in just the right proportions to make it grow to such a size.

"You're not looking in the right place," John pointed to the right with a finger that trembled with excitement.

Betty looked past the stalactite to where the side of the cave began sloping toward the ground. There, with the light of John's flash on its dark sides, she could see a small square box hung with chains from the ceiling of the cave. "Treasure!" she gasped. "Right next to the icicle."

John was beside himself. "Come on," he said. "We can't reach it from here. We've got to get at it from the top."

Once outside in the hot, cedary-smelling grove, Betty stopped short. "Let's get Father," she said. "He'll know just what we ought to do about claiming the treasure."

John saw a mixed foursome playing off the eighteenth tee and agreed that it was a good idea. They ran all the way to the cottage, and when Mr. Ross heard the news he led them on the run back.

When they got to the cave, John went in after the digging tools, and Mr. Ross went in to see the treasure with his own eyes. Betty climbed up to the top of the hill that was the back of the cave to wait for them.

She could hear the mumbling of their voices and leaned down to hear better. With her ear close to the ground, she could hear them quite plainly and knew that she must be just about over the chest. She pulled up a shaggy bit of juniper to mark the spot and waited for them to come back.

In a few minutes they were beside her, and it was impossible to tell which was the more excited of the two. Betty showed them the place she had marked, and John began to fly at it with his shovel.

"Wait a moment. We've got to take care," Mr. Ross warned him. "Whoever hung that box there had a clever idea. They thought that if anyone dug for it, he'd spade up such a big place that the roof of the cave would fall, and he'd get a broken skull for his pains. What they didn't forsee was someone spying it from the inside and knowing exactly where to dig."

Mr. Ross and Betty stood well back while John dug, so that there wouldn't be too much weight in one place. When John was tired, Mr. Ross dug, and then Betty had a turn. It was hard work trying to break through the rocky soil, but she kept at it, chipping and chiseling her way down. Suddenly her spade sank down to the handle, and she almost fell. As she pulled it out she caught a glimpse of some of the rusty chain. "It's here!" she panted. "It's right here!"

67

Mr. Ross and John lay down flat, to distribute their weight, and put their arms into the hole. After what Betty thought was an unnecessarily long time, they slowly and cautiously pulled up the box. It was small and compact and battered and made Betty think of an ordinary old tackle box.

Mr. Ross made them take it away from the hill, where there was no chance of a cave-in. "It's not really old," he told them, "not more than fifty years, and it's certainly not Spanish. Don't be disappointed if there are only a few fishhooks in it."

John and Betty struggled desperately with the lock. Was it possible that their treasure was going to be a failure after all? Treasure was always old and generally Spanish in the books they'd read. They twisted and turned at the small rusted lock and finally it broke.

For a full minute nobody could say anything.

"It *is* gold," Betty got out.

"English gold," John said. "Kind of moldy, but real."

Mr. Ross picked up one of the pieces in his fingers. "A sovereign," he said. "Minted in 1850. How it got here we'll never know."

"Could it be pirates?" John suggested.

Mr. Ross shook his head. "Just a plain thief's more likely. Pirates weren't common in 1850. Whoever it was thought he'd found a safe storage place, and then for some reason couldn't get back to collect it."

Betty looked at the box and picked up some of the heavy coins. "But is it ours," she asked, "or will someone else come along and claim it?"

Mr. Ross's answer was quick and comforting. "Of course it's yours," he said. "Without a reasonable shadow of a doubt."

Betty looked at John, and John looked at Betty. In their eyes were dreams of new golf clubs, new balls, bicycles, books for Father, and a thousand other things that made the best Christmas or birthday fade into nothing.

Audrey Baxendale

THE SECRET OF RAINBOW RIDGE

ILLUSTRATED BY *Helen Prickett*

"RAINBOW RIDGE must be the most beautiful place in the world," said Cherry Greenwood, as she dangled her feet in the cool, muddy water of the lagoon.

Her sister, Linnet, endowed at twelve and a half with common sense and judgment, answered, "I don't suppose it would seem at all beautiful to anyone but us. Lots of people would find little to admire in a hundred miles of Queensland bush. You'd better come off that log, Cherry, before you fall in. Besides, your jodhpurs will be a mess from that duckweed and slime."

"I shall loathe it when my turn comes to go to boarding school," said Cherry, not moving an inch. "I pity poor Ken and Anthea having to spend the best part of the year away from home. Next year you will have to go, Linnet, and the year after, Roger. Thank goodness I had the sense to be born youngest." She tossed her tawny curls, and her blue eyes sparkled.

Linnet, Roger, and Jacky, the black boy, were lying on the ground under the shade of a large paper-barked ti-tree, watching the antics of a colony of ants busily going back and forth among the sticky cream-colored blossoms. Beyond the farther rim of the lagoon stretched miles and miles of scrub, sloping upwards in a gradual rise which ended in a stony ridge of hills. Far away, between clumps of trees, the faint outlines of grazing sheep were visible.

69

"Dad says when his grandfather first came out from England and took over this station there were heavy rains, and a beautiful rainbow came out just above the ridge over there. He said, 'Perhaps this place will prove to be a pot of gold for me.'" She turned to the young black boy, who was Roger's shadow. "There is a legend of our people, Jacky, an old and beautiful legend, that says there is a pot of gold hidden in the earth at the very spot where the rainbow ends. It's just a fairy tale."

Jacky nodded. He knew exactly what she meant. His own people, the dark-skinned natives of Australia, had their folklore, too. He was aware that white people thought most of the stories nonsense, but this did not offend him. He knew that their disbelief was due to their ignorance of the bush and its magic.

"Black fella have plenty story, too," he remarked now. "My daddy tell me bunyip live in this lagoon one time."

"The *bunyip?*" cried the three voices in chorus, and Cherry hastily took her feet out of the water and began the perilous return journey along the slippery log.

"Jacky, what is the bunyip like, really?" she asked. Like most bush children, she had heard of this fabulous monster, but had only a vague idea of what it was. Jacky glanced uneasily at the weedy surface of the lagoon, starred with the pink lotus blossoms of water lilies.

"Bunyip fella like horse, like crocodile. Bunyip very strong magic. You see him, you die."

Cherry shivered and moved a little farther up the bank. Roger laughed and threw a stick into the water.

"Of course there's no such thing," he said. "It's just black-fellow talk."

Linnet thought that the conversation was taking too eerie a turn. She and Roger were older and unlikely to take it to heart, but Cherry was only eight and highly imaginative. It might make her dream. So she said, "Let's get the horses and start for home. It's almost noon."

When they had saddled up, they headed across the paddocks. Behind them, the ridge lay brown against the bright blue Queensland sky.

70

Roger, his skin tanned to bronze, his fair hair bleached to flaxen by the fierce sun, led the cavalcade on his bay mare, Firefly. Cherry trotted Patches, her piebald pony, just behind. His black-and-white coat had been groomed until it shone like satin. He wore a bridle with a fancy new red forehead band, which had been bought with the contents of Cherry's bank.

"It makes him look like a circus pony," Roger had said, scornfully, when he first saw it.

"Yes, doesn't it?" Cherry had agreed, taking this as a tremendous compliment.

Linnet rode a chestnut with a white blaze on his face and four white stockings. His markings had earned him the name of Socks and had also given rise to the legend that he was vicious. "A chestnut with a blaze is always nasty," declared the stockmen. But Socks loved Linnet, and she vowed that he was as gentle as a rocking horse. Perhaps they understood each other, for the girl's hair was as fiery as the horse's coat.

Bringing up the rear came Jacky. Having no horse of his own, he was usually mounted on a youngster that needed handling. Like so many natives, he had a rare knack with horses. Today he rode Graygown, a flighty little filly that had just been broken-in.

71

Shade trees and vine-covered trellises hid the sprawling homestead from view until they were almost there. Swiveling in her saddle, Linnet looked back across the sun-scorched grass paddocks to the dip where the lagoon lay, and beyond that to the ridge.

"It is lovely, Cherry," she said, thinking of her young sister's earlier remark. "Probably not the most beautiful place in the world, but certainly the dearest to us; for it is our home, and we are the fourth generation of Greenwoods to live here. That's a long time in a new country like Australia, almost a hundred years."

The gray filly shied violently, bumping into Socks, who put back his ears and reefed to show his offended dignity. Linnet almost lost her stirrups, for she had not been prepared for his sudden movement.

"What's up, Socks?" she said. "What's up, Graygown?" And then she saw that a stranger, riding a rangy black horse, had appeared from behind the trees that circled the house. He was unshaven and dirty, and his hair needed cutting.

"What a shady-looking character," said Roger, as the man passed them with a curt grunt in answer to their "Hello!"

"After a job, most likely," said Linnet. "I hope Daddy didn't give him one. He looks like the type that would ride into town every Saturday and spend all his wages at the pub. Hello, Daddy," she called, as she saw her father ahead. "You didn't take that strange man on, did you?"

"He didn't ask me to," said her father. "To tell you the truth, he wanted to buy the place."

"Buy Rainbow Ridge! As if you'd ever sell," cried Roger, in derision. "What a joke! Imagine having the nerve to think anyone but a Greenwood could run Rainbow Ridge."

"Look here, kids," said Colin Greenwood, looking very grave, "before we go in to lunch, there's something I'd better tell you. No, of course, I'm not selling to that fellow. He couldn't put up cash or decent security, and I'm glad because I didn't like him. But I'm afraid the time has come when we've got no choice. We must sell Rainbow Ridge."

72

Jacky led the way . . . with his head still swathed in bandages.

"Sell Rainbow Ridge?" gasped Roger, and Cherry sat down on the veranda steps and burst into tears.

Linnet asked, "Daddy, why?"

Colin Greenwood patted Cherry's tawny head, slapped his son affectionately on the shoulder, and pulled Linnet down to sit beside him on the step with Cherry.

"It's a matter of pounds, shillings, and pence," he said. "Ken will have to be kept at school for at least two more years, and Anthea about three. Next year Linnet will be ready to go, and then Roger."

"Not me for ages yet," said Cherry. "I can study with Mother for years."

"Even you will have to go to school in four or five years," her father said, bending to light his pipe so that they should not see the unhappiness in his eyes. "You see, kids, living out here in the bush is wonderful, but if we lived in town you could all go as day students for less than it takes to send *one* of you to boarding school."

"It's all our fault then," said Linnet.

Her father hugged her, and spoke slowly and reasonably, "No, don't run away with that idea. That's only part of it, the part that concerns you. A station this size carrying thousands of sheep needs several men to run it. That means wages, whether the boss makes money or not. Last year and the year before we had bad droughts. Well, what happens when there is no rain?"

Cherry raised her tear-stained face. "There is no grass, and the sheep starve, and you haven't any wool to sell."

"That's about it. And though there is no money coming in, the men's wages have to be paid regularly, and so do the taxes and Ken's and Anthea's school bills. Also the bills for groceries and clothes and saddles and insurance."

He paused and looked up at them, trying to smile. "And Rainbow Ridge doesn't pay its way any longer. It doesn't keep us; we are keeping it. And much as we love it, we can't afford to live this way. When there's a bad year, with no money coming in but lots going out, I have to borrow from the bank. Well, you see how it is."

"Does that mean we'll all have to live in the city?" asked Roger.

"It seems to be the only solution," said his father. "If we buy a house in Brisbane, your mother and you can live there—and Anthea and Ken of course—and I'll hire myself out as manager of some other chap's station and let him pay me wages for a change!"

"What about the horses? How will they like the Brisbane traffic?" Linnet asked.

"The dogs will get run over by the motor cars and trams!" wailed Cherry.

Colin Greenwood bit hard on his pipe stem. "The horses and dogs will have to be left behind," he said.

Cherry howled. Roger walked away before he should disgrace himself by doing likewise.

Only Linnet sat still and silent. Then she said, "We'll miss the blacks, too. Especially Jacky. But it's worse for you, Daddy, because you've had more years than any of us to love Rainbow Ridge." She raised her face with a valiant attempt at her usual grin, but there were tears shining in her deep blue eyes.

When the young Greenwoods met their father by the veranda steps, Jacky led away the horses to be unsaddled. Usually the

74

children attended to this themselves, so when they did not come he guessed that there was something in the wind. Somebody set him to work cleaning harness but, as soon as he could, he sneaked away to the house.

The children were nowhere in sight but he guessed where to find them. Climbing over the side veranda railings, Jacky tapped at the French windows of Roger's room. The two girls were there with Roger and, when they saw Jacky, they all came out on the veranda. They explained the bad news, for their father had said all the station hands would have to know soon.

Jacky's expressive face quivered. The Greenwoods were his whole world.

"Mine thinkit you fella go Brisbane, Jacky go walkabout too."

"The new owner will give you a job," said Linnet, kindly. "You won't have to leave Rainbow Ridge."

"Mine thinkit more better go walkabout," said Jacky, firmly. Then an idea struck him. "You find pot of gold you can stay?"

"Pot of gold?" Linnet looked puzzled.

"Oh, he means the one at the foot of the rainbow," said Roger. "There's no pot of gold, Jacky. That's just a yarn like the bunyip."

"Bunyip not yarn," he said. "Maybe pot of gold not yarn either."

"Well, you go and find it then," said Roger, who knew when it was useless to continue an argument with Jacky.

That evening in the swift dusk that follows sunset in Queensland, Roger walked over to the blacks' camp looking for Jacky. But no one had seen him since teatime. Roger hurried to the harness room. Graygown's bridle and the old saddle that Jacky used were both gone from the wall.

Roger was aghast at this flagrant breaking of rules. To take a half-trained filly out at night into country full of wombat holes was asking for trouble. Graygown was a valuable filly, and Dad would be furious if she came back with a twisted fetlock or broken knees. He was very indulgent about most things, but never about the mishandling of a horse.

Roger slipped Firefly's bridle over his arm and took his

saddle off the rack. Grimly determined, he started for the small paddock where the riding horses were kept. In a few minutes he was cantering towards the lagoon. Jacky might have gone to set snares, although this had also been forbidden, for Colin Greenwood liked to preserve the harmless wildlife of the station. Still there must be some reason for Jacky to disappear with Graygown into the dark, mysterious night.

What was that noise? Roger reined in Firefly and listened. Galloping hoofs. Could it be Jacky? But certainly he knew better than to risk Graygown's legs by galloping her over that treacherous ground.

The hoofbeats came near, there was a jingle of stirrup.irons, and the startled filly came blundering out of the darkness.

"Whoa there, Graygown, whoa, girl!" called Roger.

The filly saw Firefly, stopped, and blew down her nostrils with fright. She stood quivering while Roger took her bridle and fondled her, speaking gentle words of comfort.

"There, girl, you're all right. What did you do with Jacky, eh?"

He led her back to the lagoon. Half in, half out of the water lay Jacky.

A hoarse cry escaped from Roger's throat as he knelt over the small body. Jacky lay face down, his arm dragging in the water. When Roger touched his face, something warm and sticky came off on his fingers.

"Get up, Jacky, wake up!" Roger cried, but the small black body lay quite still. Roger laid his ear against the ragged shirt. Thank goodness Jacky was alive. His heart was beating.

Roger thought furiously. If he could lift Jacky into the saddle, they could manage to get home. But he knew it was dangerous to move an unconscious person in case he was hurt inside. He gently lifted Jacky's legs out of the water, taking care not to jolt him, then took off his own jersey and pushed it under Jacky's head.

The brilliant tropic stars shone overhead by now. The Southern Cross and its neighbors blazed against the moonless sky, turning the muddy lagoon into a pool of shiny ink.

A bird shrieked. It was only a screech owl, but Roger shivered. The bunyip tales did not seem half so silly as they had in the daylight. What if some monster really did inhabit the lagoons and waterholes of the bush? The natives ought to know.

Roger felt the warmth of Firefly's breath against his arm and realized that he still held the bridles of the two horses. A fleeting temptation came to him. He could fetch help in a very little while if he jumped on Firefly's back and let her gallop away from the sinister swamp towards the twinkling lights of the homestead. He knew they were not far away, although hidden from him now by the dark barrier of trees.

If *I* were hurt, his better self argued, Jacky would not leave me alone in the bush with perhaps a bunyip in the water beside me. Perhaps it had been a bunyip that attacked Jacky. There was that gash in his head.

And then Roger knew what he had to do. He had to stay right there beside Jacky and give the call of the bush, a far-carrying cry that can be heard for great distances.

"Coo-ee!" he shouted, making the syllables long and piercing. "Coo-ee!"

Somewhere in the depths of the lagoon was a splashing and a grunting, and a dark shadow heaved itself up on the opposite bank.

Roger felt his heart give a mighty leap as he listened to the sucking sound of something being drawn out of the mud. Then came blessed relief as he saw the unmistakable shape of a horse and its rider against the sky. It was not a bunyip after all. What a silly chump he had been to set store by blackfellow talk, even for a minute.

He shouted again. "Coo-ee!"

The horseman did not answer but plunged noisily into a clump of ti-trees. Roger wondered what sort of person could thus ignore the recognized bush call of necessity.

When there was no further sound from the mysterious horse and rider, Roger stood up and coo-eed again several times. But it seemed an age before an answering coo-ee came faintly through the night. Then he heard the sound of horses, the jingle of bits, and anxious voices calling his name. In a few minutes they arrived, Linnet, and Dad, and Monty, the overseer.

After making sure that there were no broken bones, Monty gathered Jacky into his great, strong arms.

"You hold him while I mount, sir," he said to Colin Greenwood. "Then I'll take him across my saddle." Thus, cradled in Monty's arms, Jacky came home. Mrs. Greenwood was waiting on the steps to meet them. Cherry, who had been told to go to bed, hovered in the doorway in her pajamas.

"Cherry, put on your slippers and robe at once!" said her mother. Cherry darted away, to return almost immediately with her slippers on the wrong feet, and her cotton robe inside out.

"What's happened?" she wanted to know. "Did Jacky see the bunyip?"

No one answered her. They were too busy examining Jacky's head and washing out the wound.

Jacky did not go back to the black-fellow's camp that night. The gash in his head was bathed and bandaged, and he was tucked into a narrow cot in the men's quarters.

Mrs. Greenwood came into the kitchen where Linnet and Roger were having milk and arrowroot biscuits. Cherry was still lurking in the corner.

"How is Jacky, Mother?" asked Linnet, anxiously.

"Still unconscious, but he'll be all right. Monty and Dad have gone over to the blacks' camp to tell his family. Now, what happened, Roger?"

Roger gave a brief but graphic account of the adventure. He explained how he had missed Jacky, noticed that Graygown's bridle was gone from its peg, and followed the riderless horse back to the lagoon. He told of finding Jacky in the water and how the horseman had appeared and disappeared, ignoring the coo-ee for help.

"I bet it was that nasty character we saw today," said Cherry, betraying her presence in the eagerness of the moment.

"Run off to bed at once, Cherry," said her mother, and then to Linnet, "What does she mean?"

"There was a stranger, a horrid one," said Linnet. "Not at all the sort of person who'd buy a place like this, but he had been asking Dad about it. You just couldn't imagine him on a sheep station."

"Nor any other station except a police station!" said Roger.

"I'm afraid you've been reading far too many penny dreadfuls," said Mrs. Greenwood. "Jacky must have been kicked when Graygown threw him."

"Graygown couldn't chuck Jacky off," Roger said. "Besides, what about that horseman? Why didn't he answer?"

"He was probably watering his horse, and completely unaware that your coo-ee was meant for him."

"Mother dearest," said Roger, looking much like his father, "your logic is so feminine. You don't want to think that there's a mystery."

"And yours, darling, is so very boylike. For you do!"

"Tomorrow I shall look for his tracks, anyway," said Roger.

There was a patter of bare feet on the linoleum, and Cherry was back again.

"There's lightning," she said. "It's going to storm."

"No such luck," said Roger. "The sky has forgotten how to rain here."

"There is, I tell you," insisted Cherry, and, as if to support her words, there came a deep rumble. There were several more, followed by a couple of loud claps and great forks of lightning that seemed to split open the sky. On the galvanized iron roof, the welcome rattle of rain was deafening.

It was still pouring when Roger awoke next morning. It was his job to make the early tea for the family, and today he performed his task with more speed than dexterity.

After serving his parents, he took the tray into his sisters' room.

"Wake up, lazybones," he cried, tugging at the mosquito nets that made a little white tent over each bed.

"Poof, I hate nets," said Cherry, struggling to pull hers back. It was a bit of a tussle, for her mother had tucked them in very firmly.

"The rain brought the mossies out in droves. I could hear them buzzing in my dreams," said Linnet. She dragged her net back and took the cup of weak tea from Roger.

Roger gulped his hastily. "Jacky's all right this morning," he said, "and it *was* that horrible man. He whacked Jacky with a shovel."

"What was Jacky doing at the lagoon after dark?" asked Linnet. "Did he explain that?"

"He won't say. But he insists he wasn't setting snares."

"We'd better go and see what traces we can find," said Linnet, knowing that was what Roger wanted to do. "The rain will have washed away nearly all the tracks, but we might get a clue."

"Now, or after breakfast?" demanded Roger, hopefully.

"Now," said Linnet, finishing her tea. "You'd better not come, Cherry. Be a good sport, and keep the family from missing us."

As they galloped through the driving rain, Linnet said, "Poor old Cherry. She didn't like staying behind. She'd never have kept up this pace bareback, though, and there would be a row if we got our saddles soaked."

"There'll be a row, anyway," said Roger, philosophically. A few minutes later he said, "This is where I found Jacky." He rode round the end of the lagoon and pointed. "Look, there's where the strange man's horse must have crossed the shallow part. The hoofprints go in there, and out over there. A bit risky, riding through like that; might have gotten stuck.

"What was he doing here, anyway?" Linnet wondered. She

poked the remnants of a campfire. "Why would he have a shovel?"

"Jacky said he had a pick as well. Maybe he was a prospector, just passing through."

Linnet was grubbing round in the muddy ashes. "Look," she exclaimed, holding something up. "He must have dropped this." It was a tobacco pouch, muddy and stained. She held it out for Roger to see.

"Do you think we ought to open it? There's certainly more than tobacco in it," she said. She was reluctant to open someone else's property.

"We'll have to," said Roger. "It might contain a clue."

Linnet pushed her sopping wet hair out of her eyes and slid the stiff zipper open.

"Roger, look!" she gasped. But before Roger could see what was in the pouch, a nasal voice spoke sharply behind them.

"Drop it, you kids, that's mine!"

In their excitement, Roger and Linnet had failed to observe the approach of the mysterious stranger of the previous day. He stood, holding out his hand for the tobacco pouch, his unshaven face looking even more sinister in the gray morning.

Linnet was mistress of the occasion. "We were looking for a clue to the owner's identity," she said, politely, and smiled weakly as she gave it to him.

He snatched it and slid the zipper shut. "You shouldn't go sticky beaking into other people's belongings," he said disagreeably.

Roger glared. "Don't you talk to my sister like that," he said fiercely. "After all, this is our property, and we have a right to know who is trespassing on it."

"Now then, sonny," said the man, in a conciliatory tone, "where's your bush hospitality? Surely you wouldn't grudge a poor swagman a fire to boil his billy and cook his bit of tucker?"

Roger looked at the horses, tethered in the clump of trees.

"Swaggies don't usually ride and lead a pack horse," he said boldly.

81

"I'm a modern swaggie," said the stranger, with a nasty leer.

The thud of cantering hoofs on wet ground made them all look up. There on Patches was Cherry.

"Mother says you're to come home at once!" she shouted, importantly.

Never had they been so glad to see their young sister. The stranger stood there, sucking an evil-smelling pipe, not saying a word.

Roger and Linnet lost no time in making good their retreat. Socks was nearly sixteen hands, so Linnet needed a leg up to mount without a stirrup.

"Hurry," whispered Roger, making a pack for her. She set her small canvas-shod foot between his shoulder blades and clambered up somehow though her heart was going bumpety-bump. With a sigh of thankfulness, she tightened her knees against the chestnut's warm, wet sides.

Firefly was smaller than Socks, and Roger was a very agile boy, so he twisted his fingers in her long mane and vaulted on to her back. The very second that she saw Roger was safely up, Linnet gave Socks his head, and side by side the two horses thundered over the ground. They quickly caught up with Cherry.

"Come on, make that circus pony of yours travel," shouted Roger, but Patches needed no urging. If the others were going to race, so would he. His little legs could hardly be expected to match those of Firefly and Socks, but the rain made him feel capable of anything, and he snorted and stretched out like a racehorse.

Colin Greenwood was waiting for them in the yard. "Be sure you rub those horses down well," he said sternly. "You two should have more sense than to go galloping around in this deluge."

"But, Daddy," gasped Linnet, "wait till you hear what happened."

"You can save it till breakfast," said her father, grimly, "and that will be in exactly ten minutes."

Still rather damp, but washed and dressed in dry clothes, the

Helen
Prickett

trio slid into their places at the breakfast table while their father was finishing his porridge.

"Excuse us for being late, please," murmured Linnet, bending over her plate of oatmeal, but watching her parents out of the corner of her eye. By this time they would have questioned Jacky and would know that the stranger was not as innocent as they had thought.

Roger burst impetuously into an account of their adventure. "We knew he wasn't an honest prospector," he concluded, "because he lied and pretended to be a swaggie. I bet Jacky caught him up to no good last night, and that was why he hit him."

"Perhaps Jacky saw what he had in his tobacco pouch," said Linnet.

"Did *you* see?" asked Colin Greenwood sharply.

Linnet smiled triumphantly. "Yes, opals. Live ones, the kind that Mother has in her ring, and you called 'orange pinfire.'"

Her father whistled a long, low whistle of surprise. "Are you positive?"

"Absolutely, Daddy. You yourself taught me how to recognize the different kinds of opal when we visited the mines at Kangaroo Flats last year. You showed us the lifeless potch, and the common blue ones, and the fairly good greens and reds, and the best-of-all orange pinfire that looks as though it had a flame imprisoned in its heart."

"Of course this man may have come over from the diggings at Kangaroo Flats," said Colin Greenwood. "We've no proof that he's been prospecting on our property."

"Well, why would he want to buy the place?" said Roger.

Mrs. Greenwood served the bacon and eggs. "You'd better eat up," she said. "I can see we are going to have no peace until you've solved the mystery."

Colin Greenwood, with Monty and one of the blacks who was noted for his skill as a tracker, rode out to investigate the mysterious stranger. Roger and the girls were highly indignant because they were told to stay near the house.

Jacky, on being questioned further, admitted he had gone

to the lagoon to make magic. He had wanted to find the "pot of gold" for the Greenwoods.

"Make spell to catch plenty rain," he said. "Bimeby rainbow come and show where pot of gold hiding. Then you fellas not go walkabout. Can stay here."

"Did you finish making your spell?" asked Linnet anxiously, hoping that he had not. If Jacky got it into his head that the sudden storm was due to his magic, there would be no end to his superstitious ideas.

"No," admitted Jacky, crestfallen, "White fella crack head belong me too quick."

The riders were back in an hour with encouraging news. Black Billy had traced the stranger's tracks beyond the boundary fence to the road that led into the township. If they took the car, they could catch him easily.

"Now that you know that man is not on the station, may we go out?" asked Linnet.

"All right, go out for a ride," said her father, "but try not to have any more adventures. I prefer a quiet life."

The car had hardly whirled through the gates when an excited cry from Jacky brought the young Greenwoods to his side. He was pointing toward the Ridge with a trembling finger.

A perfect rainbow curved across the horizon beyond the paddocks and the scrub. One end was lost in the clouds, the other dipped to earth in the very center of the Ridge.

"You come," pleaded Jacky. "We find pot of gold."

"There's no pot of gold, but we'll come anyway," said Roger.

It was beginning to clear up into a glorious day, and the whole bush seemed to be rejoicing after the rain. The birds were having a picnic with the worms that had been disturbed by the deluge, kangaroos and wallabies scurried away as the riders approached, and up in the branches of a big blue gum a kookaburra laughed his mirthless cackle. A flock of gold-crested cockatoos rose from the trees and went screaming into the bush, and a few brilliantly plumed parrots flashed amongst the green of the dripping foliage.

The bridle path led the riders through the scrub into a gully and across a creek which had been almost dry the day before. Now, it was "running a banker" as its too hurriedly replenished waters foamed along the hard clay bed.

Jacky led the way. He looked like a pirate with his head still swathed in bandages. A white boy would have needed to stay in bed for a week after such a blow, but the natives of Australia are a hardy race. His forefathers had fought with their wounds unbandaged, but Jacky felt sissy enough to have been pampered with sulfa ointment and sterile gauze.

Behind him came the two girls, and Roger brought up in the rear. On Socks' saddle Linnet had bound a pickaxe and a shovel. Roger carried a substantial lunch of sandwiches, rock cakes, and fruit. Jacky had the billycan and the makings for tea. Cherry trotted unhampered by bundles on plucky little Patches.

It was a long ride to the Ridge by the regular route, but

Jacky had a black-fellow's uncanny knack of short-cutting through the bush. He led through creeks and gullies, in and out of seemingly impenetrable scrub, until in less than two hours the Greenwoods found themselves climbing the steep ironstone sides of the Ridge.

As they reached the crest, Jacky spoke. "Where big fella rainbow gone?"

"It seemed as though it ended right here, didn't it?" agreed Roger. "But it didn't really, Jacky, because it was just the light shining through the moisture in the air, breaking up into prismatic colors." He fumbled for a simpler word and gave it up. Jacky had his own ideas anyway.

"Was just here," he said, and with that he disappeared over the rim beyond.

On the far side of the Ridge was an excavation and near it the signs of a camp. The children followed Jacky, hastily hitching their horses to a lone gum tree that clung to the hillside, fighting for life in the arid soil. Jacky had disappeared into the cave where someone had recently been digging.

Roger grabbed his electric torch from his saddlebag and followed close on the black boy's heels. Hard clay and ironstone had been hewed apart, leaving a deep shaft that ran down into the very heart of the Ridge. By the weak yellow beam of the flashlight Roger revealed a ceiling as sparkling as the rainbow.

"What I tell you?" cried Jacky.

"The rainbow's end!" Cherry said.

"It isn't the rainbow," said Linnet. "It's opal." Like a congealed mass of the rainbow, the shining stuff stretched above their heads.

Roger gouged out a piece carefully with his knife. "Looks like the gem variety, doesn't it, Linnet?"

Linnet studied it, anxiously.

"It is, I'm sure," she said. "It looks just the same as the sort Daddy pointed out when we visited the opal mines. Orange pinfire."

"We'll take some samples home," said Roger. "Now let's eat."

It was a triumphant party that rode home in the crimson sunset. The menfolk were on the veranda, drinking endless cups of tea. They had overtaken the stranger and questioned him, but he had denied all knowledge of Jacky's accident. He swore that he had merely camped overnight by the lagoon, not seeing a soul.

Still, not believing his statements, they had driven into town and waited there till he appeared. They watched him go into the post office and register a small package which might or might not have been opals.

It looked very suspicious to them, but the police sergeant to whom they told their tale, pointed out that he could hardly arrest a man on such slender evidence. So they had waited until the stranger, evidently made uneasy by the sudden interest in his movements, had boarded the Brisbane train.

"I'm afraid we'll never know the truth," concluded Colin Greenwood.

Then Linnet opened her fist and let its contents fall on to the tablecloth. "This is what Jacky found this afternoon," she said, enjoying the expression on her parents' faces.

"Gem opal!" cried her father, picking up the largest piece from the white cloth. "Where did you get this?"

Linnet and Roger kept interrupting each other as they told how Jacky had led them to the "diggings" on Rainbow Ridge. "To think the Ridge kept its treasure a secret all these years," said Linnet when they had finished.

"It was never needed till now," said her father. "If we had found it in our days of plenty, we might have wasted it. Now we shall know how to use it wisely, I trust."

Jacky's face appeared through the railings of the veranda. "No need go walkabout, boss?" he asked, anxiously.

"No need indeed, you rascal!" cried Colin Greenwood. "And, my word, Jacky, a boy smart enough to find a mine like that is smart enough to have a horse of his very own. Graygown is yours, for keeps."

Elizabeth Rhodes Jackson

OLD HOUSES

ILLUSTRATED BY *Margaret and Florence Hoopes*

ALMOST anything mysterious can happen in an old house. That is why I am glad we live in the old part of Boston in a house that was built years and years before Jack and Beany and I were born. So many people have lived in it—perhaps even people so old that they could remember the Boston Tea Party. Our old house seems to be a part of the past, even though it has been made over into apartments. And of course if we had been living in a new house, we never would have known Bobby.

It all began the night when Peter disappeared. No, it really began in the afternoon when we came home from school and found a new game on Beany's bed. It wasn't anybody's birthday, and there wasn't any aunt visiting us, or any special reason for a new game. We ran in and asked Mother, "Where did it come from?" Mother didn't know what we were talking about. She came in and looked at it and said, "I never saw it before. I haven't the faintest idea how it got there."

It was in a box, not quite new but in good condition, and it looked like a very interesting game, to shoot marbles into little pockets around a board. The directions were on the cover

89

of the box. We sat around the dining-room table and played it until the table had to be set for supper. Jack won most of the time, and I was next. Beany only won twice and those times we let him, but he didn't know that, of course. Daddy came home in time to play one game with us, and, of course, he won that.

All through suppertime we kept talking about the game and how it could have come on Beany's bed. Daddy thought Mrs. Lavendar might have brought it down to him. She lives on the floor above and she likes to do kind things; but she would have knocked and given it to Mother. How it could have been put in that room without Mother's knowing it was a mystery.

Jack said perhaps Reginald brought it home in his mouth. Reginald is our dog and he has a great many friends in the neighborhood. He does his own marketing, and the butchers and grocers all know him and give him bones and things to bring home, and he waits for the traffic lights before he crosses the street. And once he did steal a little girl's hat out of a parked automobile. Jack took it away in a hurry and ran down the street and put it back in the automobile. It was only a little bit chewed.

But we all said Reginald couldn't have stolen the game because the box was too big for him to carry. Beany thought it was fairies. Jack said, "We don't know that there are fairies," and Beany said, "But we don't know that there *aren't*." And I said, "Anyway, we can't account for it unless it *was* fairies."

At bedtime Beany always takes his bath first because he's the youngest. Mother had him tucked up, and I was just starting mine when I heard him call out, "Mother, where's Peter?"

Peter is Beany's doll that he takes to bed. We don't play dolls any more, because now that we are older there are so many things to do, but we do like them at night. Beany likes Peter best, though he sometimes takes his rabbit. I take turns with all my dolls because that is only fair to them. Jack sleeps with his Teddy, who is nine years old, older than Beany.

Well, when Beany called out for Peter, who ought to have been in the corner back of his pillow, Mother started to look

for him. But she didn't find him. Then Jack came in and looked
under the bed and under all the chairs, but he didn't find him.

When I was ready for bed, I looked all around my room,
but I didn't find him. By that time Daddy had joined in, and
he looked in all the places where everyone else had looked;
so of course he didn't find him. Poor old Beany was quite
worried, but finally he took his rabbit and dropped off to sleep.

We didn't find Peter in the morning, and we didn't ever find
him until—but I'll tell that when I come to it.

The next mysterious thing happened to me. But it was in
the same room, the boys' room. I was sleeping there because
I fell into the Frog Pond on the Common. The Common is a
very interesting place. It doesn't belong to the city of Boston;
it belongs to the people of Boston. It has belonged to them
for three hundred years. Anyone can walk or sit or even sleep
there and can play ball there, and children can go swimming
in the Frog Pond. Daddy says people used to keep their cows
on the Common, and he thinks we ought to have a cow and
put her out to pasture there because Beany drinks so much
milk.

We were crossing the Common coming home from the movies. It was the first time we had ever gone alone to the movies, but Mother let us go because it was *Little Women*. When we came to the Frog Pond, there was a boy there sailing a boat. We stood in a row along the stone edge of the Pond and watched him. Beany got so excited he lost his balance, and he fell against me so suddenly that I went in. They pulled me right out. It isn't very deep. But it was cold. My teeth chattered all the way home. Mother gave me a hot bath and hot milk to drink and put me to bed in Beany's bed. That was because she wanted to sleep in the room with me that night, and there is only my bed in my own room. Jack was to sleep in my room, and Beany went in with Daddy.

I lay there alone, all warm and comfortable in bed after the cold shivers. I almost went to sleep. Presently I knew someone was looking at me. I didn't bother to open my eyes. I just said, "Is that you, Jack?" No one answered, but there was a little scurry. I said again, "What are you doing, Jack?" and then I opened my eyes—and there was no one there!

Sometimes at camp in the early morning I have waked up and seen a squirrel watching me from the nearest tree. He stays perfectly still till I move or speak. Then like a flash he whisks out of sight. In my half-asleepness I thought at first this was a squirrel. I called out, "How did the squirrel get in?"

Mother heard me speak and came to the door. "What do you want, dear?" she said.

"Who came in?" I asked her.

"No one," she said. "You must have been dreaming."

Then she leaned over and picked up something from the floor.

"Why, where did this come from?" she said.

It was a little red box with a crank. Mother put it into my hands. We had never seen it before. I turned the crank and the sweetest tinkly tune came out of the little box. Jack and Beany heard it and came running in to see what was making the music.

We couldn't explain it at all. Mother said, "I found it right here on the floor."

I said, "I dreamed a squirrel brought it."

Beany said, "It must be fairies again."

We were all excited about it. When Daddy came home, we had a lot to tell him—all about *Little Women* and the Frog Pond and the music box. It was a very exciting time.

Mother gave me supper on a tray in bed, for a treat, and when the others were going to supper, I asked her to put on the light and let me read my fairy book. I told her it was on Beany's bookshelf.

"I don't see it," she said. "I'll ask Beany."

"It's right here on the shelf," said Beany when he came running in.

But it wasn't. It was gone. Just like Peter.

"Perhaps a trader rat took it," said Jack. (He had been reading an animal book.) "Perhaps a trader rat traded the game for Peter and traded the music box for the new book."

"I wish he had waited till we had finished my fairy book," said Beany. "And I wish he would bring back Peter."

"Here," I said. "You take the music box and play it." So Beany played it all through supper. I could hear its little tinkle all the way into the bedroom, and pretty soon it tinkled me to sleep.

Next morning Mother didn't let me go to school. She said I'd better stay in bed in the morning and then if I felt quite well I could get up after lunch. Very soon after breakfast Mrs. Lavendar came downstairs to bring me some lovely flowers, and she stayed and talked. After a while we got to talking about our street, that Mother likes to call the "Street of Memories."

Mrs. Lavendar said that when she was a young lady, she had come to a grand ball in our house, in that very room that we were in. The whole floor that is now our apartment was two big drawing rooms with a wide door between, and to make a bigger dancing floor, a door was cut into the house next door. Two brothers owned the two houses, and the ball was for their two daughters, who were almost the same age and did everything together, more like sisters than cousins. There were shining chandeliers in the ceiling, with little crystal danglers that reflected the lights and twinkled; and the ladies had big puffed sleeves and silk petticoats that rustled; and there were tables filled with favors—those were presents that the gentlemen gave to the ladies when they danced together.

I asked, "What became of the two young ladies?" and Mrs. Lavendar said they both died a good many years ago, and the two houses became the property of some distant relatives. They sold the one we live in to a man who made it over into apartments. The other one, I knew, was still one big house. A very quiet maiden lady lived there. She didn't seem to like children very much. Once she scolded Beany because Reginald left a bone in her vestibule.

After Mrs. Lavendar left, I lay there very still and almost asleep. Suddenly I had that queer feeling again that someone was watching me. I opened my eyes.

There was no one in the room, but the closet door was half open, and it was slowly, slowly closing, as if someone inside were pulling it.

I jumped out of bed. I did remember to put on my warm

94

red bathrobe and my slippers, and then I ran across the room and opened the closet door.

And opposite the door was an open space in the wall; and it looked right through into the next house. I shut the closet door and stepped through.

It was almost like stepping back into Mrs. Lavendar's story of the ball. For the room was a drawing room with white-paneled walls and glittery chandeliers, and between the windows was a long mirror that had once reflected ladies in big sleeves and gentlemen who gave them favors. But the room was empty and silent and lonely, and all I saw in the mirror was a little girl named Dee in a red bathrobe, who looked as if she didn't belong there.

Then a door opened and there was the maiden lady who didn't like children. She looked at me severely through her eyeglasses.

"What are you doing here?" she said, and her voice was not at all friendly. "Who let you in?"

"I came in there," I said. "I live next door."

The space I had come through was still there, where a wooden panel had swung open into the drawing room. The lady walked over and peeked in and saw Beany's and Jack's clothes hanging up and their shoes in a shoebag and some of Mother's dresses, because we haven't much closet room. She gave a very unpleasant sniff.

"Then you can go right back in there," she said. "I had no idea this house was open to the whole neighborhood. I shall have it securely fastened."

"If you please," I said, "I should like to have Peter and my fairy book."

"What?" she said.

I was very polite, but very firm.

"Someone has been coming into our house," I said, "and taking our things, and we should like to have them back. We will give back the game and the music box because Beany would rather have Peter."

She stood a minute looking at me. Then she said, "I'll look into this," and she went into the hall, to the foot of the stairs and called, "Bobby, come down here at once."

I heard very slow feet dragging down the stairs, and then there came into the room a little boy about Beany's age. He had Peter in one hand and the fairy book in the other, and you could see that he was frightened almost to death.

"Is this true, Bobby?" said the lady sorrowfully. "Have you been taking this little girl's toys?"

He sort of gulped and nodded and held them out to me. I couldn't stand it. I had to explain for him, just as if it had been Beany in trouble.

"He didn't really take them," I said. "He just traded. He brought us a beautiful game and a music box instead. He just wanted to be friends and share things."

"Why, Bobby," said the lady. "Aren't you happy here?"

He shook his head slowly.

"But your toys, Bobby! Don't you like them?" she said. "I bought everything I thought a little boy would like."

He nodded but he didn't speak.

"What is it then?" she said. "I don't understand."

Bobby gulped again. "I found the wall would open," he said. "And they have so much fun in there—and there's a boy just my age—" His voice trailed off.

The lady took off her eyeglasses and polished them with her handkerchief.

96

Just then we heard a great commotion on the other side of our closet. Mother was calling, "Dee, where are you?" She had come in to speak to me—and I wasn't there. I guess she was afraid the fairies had taken me away to be with Peter.

She pulled open the closet door and through the open space she saw us, the severe lady polishing her eyeglasses, and Bobby holding Peter, and me in my red bathrobe, and she ran to me and caught me up in her arms.

"What are you doing here?" she said—just what the lady had said—only she made it sound quite different, all glad and loving.

The lady looked at Mother very hard. Then she said, "You are this little girl's mother? My nephew—he is my little boy now, since his parents—" she stopped suddenly as if she didn't want to remind Bobby that his father and mother were dead— "I want him to be happy—would you let him come in to play with your children?"

And then there was a shout, "Oh, Peter!" It was Beany at the panel door.

Bobby ran to him and shoved Peter into Beany's arms, and Beany took Bobby's hand and pulled him through the door into our house.

And that was the beginning of our knowing Bobby, and that is why I'm glad we live in an old house. Bobby is one of our best friends now. And even if his aunt isn't used to children, she does her best, and yesterday she even gave Reginald a bone.

Margaret Leighton

THE LEGACY OF CANYON JOHN

ILLUSTRATED BY *Robert Sinnott*

"SAY!" Angry blood rose under Jerry's tan as he wrenched the steering wheel sharply to avoid a collision with a car which careened madly around the turn. "Who does he think he is, driving like that along this road?"

Linda frowned. "I've seen that man before, but I can't think where," she said.

"Well, he's on his way to your place or mine—there's nowhere else to go up this canyon," Jerry told her. "Except to Old John's, and he's not there," he added, his face clouding.

Linda saw the look and understood. They were fond of Canyon John, the old Indian who had lived in his solitary cabin on the mountain since long before either of them was born. Last of his tribe, he had clung stubbornly to his small corner of the earth until a few months before, when a fall had crippled him so that he had had to be moved down to the Mission Hospital in the valley. Linda and Jerry had taken him some snapshots of his cabin when they had visited him only the week before.

"If the lens has come, maybe we can get some extra-super snaps to take down to Old John next week," Linda suggested.

Photography was the all-absorbing hobby of these two, who had been born on adjoining ranches, had squabbled intermittently from babyhood, but had been inseparable companions nevertheless. Since they had begun to save for college expenses, they had been lured by the sizable award offered for the best picture each year by the State Wild Life Conservation Society.

98

They had thought at first that they would have every advantage in this field, living as they did in remote ranch country, with a vast wilderness of mountain and desert all about them. But without a telescopic lens they had been sadly handicapped in wild-animal photography. Now Linda's uncle, also a camera enthusiast, had written that he was sending them a lens, and they were on their way to the post office to see if it had come.

The mail was in when they arrived, and Ed Travis, the postmaster, waved a package.

"Reckon this is what you've been waiting for," he said. "And there's a letter for Jerry, too."

They sat down on the edge of the porch while Jerry opened the package. There it lay—a slender tube with the shining lens ready to screw into its end!

"Gosh! What do you know!" Jerry's voice was shaking a little. "Here are the instructions, too. No alibis if we don't win the grand prize now, Linda."

"It's strictly up to us," she agreed. "Here, don't forget your letter."

"What is it? Not bad news, Jerry?" she asked a moment later startled by his sober face.

He looked up. "It's from Pia Marquez, the nurse at the Mission Hospital. Old Canyon John died last Sunday."

"Oh!" A lump rose in Linda's throat.

Jerry gave a startled exclamation. "Listen—no, let's read this together!"

She bent over the typed pages. "It was nice of you and Linda Webb to visit the old man here," the nurse had written, "and especially for you to bring those pictures of his home. He kept them under his pillow and was always looking at them. Then, the other day, he asked me to write a letter to you for him. 'Write it just like I say it to you,' he told me. So I took it down and here it is:

"I am a very sick old man, and if I die I like to do something nice for Linda and Jerry. I like to give them a present. But I have only my cabin and my cornfield, and even those are not mine to give away because they must go to the U.S. Government.

99

"I have thought about this a long time, and now I remember that I have something I can give them, and so this letter is to be my will. If I had a son or a grandson I could not give this away, because it belongs to my people, and to my family only among my people—a secret we have kept for many, many years.

"Tell Jerry that he must go up the mountain past my cabin, to the head of my canyon; then across the ridge, and down into the small canyon on the desert side which is called the Canyon del Muerto. There is a trail he can follow. Up on the wall of rock he will see a place where water falls down the cliff, and underneath there is sometimes a little pool. Just beyond this there is a tall rock like a pillar, close up to the canyon wall.

"Tell Jerry to go to the pool, then turn and walk about ten steps toward the pillar. Then he must look carefully. He has good eyes, and he must use them to find this secret. It is too precious to write down on paper. No one else must know about it."

"That was all he would say," Pia Marquez added in conclusion. "But I'm sure he was entirely clear in his mind. I hope you can find whatever it was that he meant, and that it is something you have use for!"

"For goodness sake!" Linda cried, letting out her breath. "What do you suppose it can be?"

Jerry shook his head. "So far as I know, he was as poor as Job's turkey!"

"Do you know that place he described?"

"Yes. I've been in the Canyon del Muerto. There are some

100

interesting looking cliffs there, I remember. Some may have caves in them."

Linda's heart began to beat faster. "Jerry, do you remember those stories about the bandit, Joaquin Murietta? They say he was befriended by the Indians who lived around here. Maybe he gave them some of his treasure. Maybe that's it."

Jerry grinned. "Or maybe it's a clue to the Lost Dutchman Mine, or old Pegleg's cache of nuggets. No, it's probably something that'd be a lot more valuable to Old Canyon John than to us. Maybe a group of pictographs on a rock, or a cave with an olla in it, full of fishing and hunting charms."

Linda's face fell, then brightened again. "Well, that would be exciting to find, too. Maybe we could take some really good pictures, and write it up for one of the magazines."

"Now you're talking!" Jerry got to his feet. "Let's not waste any more time. We can do it today if we get started pronto. We'll stop and tell your folks where we're going, then go on to my place for horses."

The horses started briskly up the winding, rutted road. At sight of Canyon John's withered corn patch, the cabin so deserted and forlorn, Linda felt her eyes sting. How often they had stopped here to talk with the lonely old man.

When she turned forward again something in Jerry's suddenly tense back startled her. He had stopped his horse, and was looking at a car in the brush where the road ended.

"Why, it's the one that passed us on our way to the post office," she exclaimed.

The car was empty, and there was no one in sight. Jerry touched the hood.

"It's cold," he said. "I wonder what that fellow's up to?"

A light broke suddenly in Linda's mind. "Jerry!" she cried. "Now I remember where I saw that man before. He's Dawson, the orderly down at the Mission Hospital."

They looked into each other's startled faces, the same disquieting thought in both their minds.

"He must have heard what Old John told Pia Marquez, or read the letter, or something!" Linda declared. She remembered the malicious glance the man had given them as he passed that morning. "Maybe if he's up there we'd better not go."

Jerry's face darkened. "Canyon John wanted us to have whatever it is, nobody else. Maybe you'd better go back, Linda, but I'm riding up there," he said.

"Go back?" Linda echoed. "And let you go alone? What do you think I'm made of!"

The sun was high by the time they reached the top of the saddle which separated the two canyons. At the crest of the ridge the brush ceased abruptly, and rocks had a burned-out look, as though enormous fires had scorched them in some remote age.

The trail wound down among huge, tumbled boulders. In the burning, cloudless blue of the sky a great bird circled on widespread dark wings.

"If that's a buzzard, it's a big one." Jerry's eyes narrowed against the glare.

"What else could it be?" Linda wondered. "Unless—" She caught her breath and stared upward.

But the bird was too high, the sun too dazzling, for her to see anything but the silhouette of black wings. Nevertheless a little shiver of excitement played along her spine. Somewhere in these mountains a pair of the fast dwindling, all-but-extinct California condors were rumored to have their nest. So rare had these majestic birds become that killing or molesting one was punished by the heaviest fines. Even photographs of them in the wild state were practically nonexistent.

"If it should be a condor, and if we could get a good shot of it with our new lens, we'd have the grand prize picture for sure," she told Jerry.

"Your *ifs* cover a lot of territory," he answered. "Come on. When we get past that last outcrop of black rock we'll be in sight of the place."

But suppose Dawson had already discovered Canyon John's treasure, Linda wondered. Or suppose he was still there? Even with the Indian's letter to show as proof, he wouldn't be likely to hand over anything. What if he should be ugly? In this

102

remote spot anything might happen. The Indians called it
Canyon del Muerto because a murder had been committed here
years ago. Her throat felt dry, and she shivered.

Jerry had pulled in his horse and was holding up his hand.
"Listen!" he commanded.

Linda heard it, too, a metallic, chopping sound, echoing
from the rocky walls. It halted, then began again.

"Someone's digging with a pickax," Jerry said.

When they rounded the last black shoulder of the canyon
they saw him, a tiny figure, toiling away in that immensity
of barren earth and rock. Above him they could see the shine
of the water as it dripped down the cliff to the pool at its

base. The man was digging on the exact spot where the old Indian had told them to look for his secret!

They rode forward. When they were about two hundred yards from him, Dawson looked up and saw them. Quickly he stepped back, laid down his pick, and took something from the ground. When he turned again to confront them, the sun glanced on the barrel of a rifle.

"You two stop right there!" he shouted.

Even to the impetuous Jerry the rifle was a conclusive argument. He pulled his horse to a halt. "What's the matter with you?" he called out. "It's none of your business where we ride."

"I'm making it my business, buddy," the man answered. "I know why you've come here. I read the Injun's letter, and I'm goin' to cash in on it. So you two kids ride right back to your mammas."

The back of Jerry's neck was suddenly flushed with anger. "Why, you—" he began.

But whatever he was going to say was stopped by the sharp click of the rifle bolt sliding into place.

"Start travelin'," Dawson called harshly. "I don't want to hurt you or your horses, but I wouldn't *mind*."

For a terrified instant Linda thought Jerry was going to try to ride the man down. Then he spoke to her over his shoulder. "All right, Linda, let's get going."

Behind the shelter of the first jutting rock they stopped. "I hate worse than poison to let him get away with this." Jerry's voice was unsteady. Linda had never seen him so angry. "But what else can we do?"

"I guess there isn't anything," she agreed. "But I feel just as you do. Can't we get help, the Ranger or someone? It must be against the law to shoot at people."

"Maybe if we told the Ranger that Dawson took something which belonged to John and which he left to us in his will—but how could we prove that? We don't even know what it is," Jerry said. "Besides, it would be just our word against his. If there were another witness—"

. . . they saw him . . . toiling away in that immensity of barren earth and rock.

Linda caught her breath. "A witness! How about the camera? We could take a picture of him, to show that he was digging in the place Canyon John told us to look."

"You're right! With the new lens we could get a picture of him from around the edge of this rock without his knowing it."

Hastily they swung to the ground, and while Jerry set up the tripod and camera, Linda fitted on the lens.

Through the finder Dawson was only a matchstick figure working against the immense backdrop of barren, burning wilderness. Behind him loomed the tall pillar of rock, and far above, the dark-winged bird sailed in its slow, ominous circles.

"It'll make a swell picture, anyway," Jerry said.

They took several shots, to make sure of getting a good one. So intent were they that they did not notice when Dawson stopped his work to peer up at them, until suddenly he reached again for the rifle.

"Look out!" Linda cried.

They jumped back just in time, for the rifle cracked sharply, and a shower of pebbles and sand came sliding down from the cliff above them.

"Say, that hombre's not too careful where he shoots!" Jerry exclaimed. "I wonder if I got a snap of that?"

Peering cautiously around the rock, they saw that Dawson was still holding the rifle ready, and that above his head dark wings were beating the air. A second immense black bird, disturbed by the shots, had risen from somewhere, and, joining the other, was circling higher and higher.

Linda and Jerry rode back over the saddle and down into the other canyon.

"If that picture was as good as it looked, it'll be all we need to set the Rangers on him," Jerry said. "After all, the Government has a lot to say about Indian property."

"And we've got the letter!" Linda added.

Suddenly Jerry gave an exclamation. "Oh, boy! I've just remembered he left his car parked back here. After I get through with that machine Mr. Dawson won't be riding back to town in a hurry!"

But just as they reached the car, an official green truck drove up and Les Burnett, the Ranger, stepped out.

"What's going on back there?" he demanded. "The Fire Warden on Craddock's Peak just phoned me that he'd heard shooting down in Canyon del Muerto."

His brows drew together as they told their story. "Sounds like an unpleasant character," he said. "I'll give him a warning.

He's no business shooting anywhere near you. But as for this treasure business, I'm afraid that's a case of finders-keepers, unless you can prove that it actually did belong to Canyon John. Then, of course, you could take it up with the Indian Agent."

"At least I'd have liked to let the air out of his tires," Jerry grumbled, as they started home.

"Well, cheer up. We got some pictures, anyway. Let's develop and print them right away," Linda said.

Paradoxically, it was in the darkroom that light burst at last on Canyon John's secret. Bending over the trays, they watched the prints come slowly into view. The pictures were turning out better than they had dared to hope. The composition was unexpectedly and superbly dramatic: Like a giant exclamation point the great rock pillar loomed above the toiling human shape, and in many of the shots the dark-winged bird slanted across the sky for an added accent.

The last picture, in which Dawson was pointing his rifle at the camera, came out best of all. They could even see the contortion of anger in his face.

Then something else caught Linda's eyes. "Jerry!" she cried. "Look! In this picture the buzzard's wing is tilted up. Look at it—at the underside!"

Jerry peered. Then—"A patch of white feathers!" he said, almost in a whisper. "Linda, that's not a buzzard! It's a condor!"

But that wasn't all. On a cavelike ledge near the top of the pillar something else was taking shape. It was the bare, snake-like head and half-spread plumage of the other bird *rising from the nest!*

Jerry whistled. "So that was it!" he said. "Of course, that was what Canyon John meant. Don't you remember, Linda? He told us once, long ago, how the Indians prized condors. They used them in their religion, their ceremonial dances. He said they were messengers between the living and the dead. The knowledge of the location of a nest was the most valuable possession anyone could own. It was kept secret, handed down from father to son. That's the secret he left to us!"

Linda nodded. "And Old John knew how much we'd value a chance to get a photograph of a condor. Why, Jerry, now that we know where the nest is we can take dozens of pictures! We'll surely get a prize—maybe the grand prize—with one of them, and we might sell them to natural-history museums, nature magazines, ornithologists. College, here we come!"

Suddenly Jerry began to laugh. "I was just thinking. Poor old Dawson can dig the whole canyon up, for all he'll find there!" he chuckled. "I'm almost sorry for him!"

Augusta Huiell Seaman

THE STRANGE
PETTINGILL PUZZLE

ILLUSTRATED BY *Genevieve Foster*

PETER and Christine never dreamed, when they started on their crabbing expedition that sunny afternoon, of the adventure into which it was going to lead them!

The rowboat was old and leaky, but their mother had made them promise that they would keep near the shore all the time. And as the wide bay was shallow quite far out, Mrs. Cameron felt certain they could get into no danger. Peter at twelve and Christine at ten were good swimmers. So she let them go, equipped with crab nets and fish heads tied to stout string as bait. There was also a market basket in the boat for the captured crabs.

"If you get enough," she called to them from the veranda of the cottage they had taken for the summer, "I'll boil them, and tomorrow you can pick out the meat, and we'll have a fine crab salad!" They shouted to her that they'd try hard and clambered into the boat, Peter grasping the oars.

"I'll row," he announced, "and you watch out at the stern, Chris. If you see any crabs, try to scoop them up with the net. When we get to a really good spot where there are lots of them, we'll drop the anchor and throw out our lines and fish heads. Crabs'll just gobble *them* up and we can scoop in dozens!"

Thus they set out in high hopes, and ten-year-old Chris, gazing down over the stern of the boat at the bright sand under the clear, shallow water, saw an occasional crab scuttling away at the approach of the boat. None, however, remained long enough within her reach to be netted, and none seemed quite large enough to bother about.

"Tell you what," she suggested at last, "let's row around that point of land and into the next cove. Perhaps it's quieter there,

108

with no houses or people, and there'll be more crabs. Mother won't mind as long as we keep close to the shore. It's awfully shallow, 'way out—and I do want to see what's around that point! Just think, Pete! We've only been here one day, and we've got this whole bay to explore!"

Peter agreed that the experiment was worth trying, especially as they had not succeeded in capturing a single crab, so he pulled stoutly for the wooded point of land not a quarter of a mile away.

Overhead the white gulls swooped and curved. The sandy shore was backed by a heavy growth of cedars, and who could tell what surprises and delights awaited them around that intriguing point of land!

Rounding it, they beheld another cove, deeper than their own in its curve. And unlike theirs, which was dotted on the shore by a few scattered summer cottages, it seemed almost uninhabited, except for one curious-looking structure on the bank, not quite halfway around the cove, and very near to the water.

"What's that?" demanded Chris, pointing to it. "Funny looking thing! It seems like a house and yet it's like a boat!"

"Well, I guess you're about right at that," said her brother. "It's a houseboat. I've seen that kind of thing before, only they've always been floating out in the water, and this is pulled up on land. And look at the steps leading up to the deck from the ground, will you! And the stovepipe coming out of the roof! Looks as if somebody really lived there all the time, same as they would in a regular house. That's kind of queer! I thought people only had houseboats floating about in summer and then tied them up to docks in winter and left them. Let's go look at it closer."

"Look!" cried Chris. "There's a boy! He just came out on deck. He's watching something out on the bay, but I don't see anything except gulls flying around. Let's hurry over there and talk to him."

Peter rowed frantically, till they were within a few feet of the strange building on the shore. Then the boy saw them and

waved in a friendly manner. He was just about to go in again, when Peter called out, "Hello!" The boy came to the side of the deck and sat down on it, swinging his bare legs over the edge. He had a tousled mop of hair, a pair of snapping brown eyes, and a wide friendly grin. Peter thought he was about twelve, his own age.

"Where'd *you* come from?" demanded the boy.

"We've taken Mr. Wainwright's cottage for the summer," Peter told him. "He rented it to us 'cause he's a friend of Dad's and he isn't going to use it this summer. We just got here last night. My name's Peter Cameron, and this is my sister Christine."

"Mine's Alan Pettingill," the boy returned. "Do you like birds?" This sudden query rather took Peter's breath away.

"Why—I don't know! I guess so," he answered. "You see, I live in the city, and we don't see many birds there except sparrows, and when we go away in the summer to the country, I'm so busy doing other things, I never think much about 'em."

Alan let that pass, but went on, "So Mr. Wainwright isn't going to be here this summer. I'm sorry, 'cause I'll miss him a lot. He's the one who taught me to like birds and study all about them. I didn't know he wasn't going to be here." His tone sounded rather disappointed.

110

"Well, *we're* here," put in Chris. "We don't know much about birds, but you could tell us. And we'd like to play with you. If you want to. Is this your summer home?" She indicated the houseboat, and Alan grinned.

"It's my summer home and my winter one, too. We live here all the year round—Mother and I!" This completely stunned the two newcomers. To think of living in a houseboat on the shore of this beautiful, wild bay—and probably no school to go to! Could anything be more like paradise? They said as much, and Alan grinned again.

"But don't you believe I don't have to go to school!" he retorted. "There's a good school up in town, and Mother drives me up every day—or I walk there—and I'm going to graduate next year."

"But—but how do you keep *warm*?" demanded Chris. "What's it like in that—that little boat, when it snows—and freezes?"

"We're as cozy as anything," replied the boy, defending the comfort of his strange home. "Come in and see. Mother isn't home just now. She's gone uptown for the mail and groceries. But she won't mind if you come in."

Full of curiosity, they beached their rowboat, forgot all about the crabs, and scuttled up the steps at one end of the houseboat to join Alan on the deck. This they found to be a wider space than they imagined. It was at the rear end of the boat, like a platform, and was neatly railed around with a canvas awning over it for shade. There were two steamer chairs where one could sit as comfortably as on the wide-screened veranda at the cottage. In fact, to the newcomers, it was infinitely preferable to their own, with all the elaborate willow furniture, couch-hammocks, and grass-rugs that theirs boasted. The deck also ran around both sides of the boat in a narrow walk, to join another smaller extension in the front. On this they saw a line with some dish towels hanging out in the sun, and Alan told them it opened out from their small kitchen. Then he led them inside, into a tiny room just off the deck, which reminded them of a ship's stateroom.

111

On one side, raised two feet from the deck, was a berth, neatly made up. And over it was a small shelf of books. On the other side was a comfortable willow chair and a small table. There was a hooked rug on the floor, and two windows, hung with cretonne curtains, gave light from both sides.

"And this is *my* room!" His two visitors uttered cries of delight. "You go through it to get to the living room," went on Alan, "but of course we don't mind that! We haven't many visitors. Look out for these steps now!"

The door at the other side of his room opened on two steep steps, down which they scrambled and stood, almost speechless with wonder at the larger and quite charming room that was the main part of the boat. It had rows of windows all along both sides, nicely curtained with material somewhat similar to that in Alan's room. On the side was a wide, comfortable couch strewn with cushions. Alan said his mother slept there at night. Several willow chairs were scattered about and a little table at one end near the kitchen, set with quaint blue china, was evidently where they had their meals. In another corner was a writing desk with a big, old-fashioned student lamp on it. Part of the wall space was lined with bookshelves, and on top of these stood a few small well-done water-color pictures, which Alan said his mother had painted.

Chris squealed with delight over the odd and pretty room. And Peter heaved a great sigh and exploded, "Golly! I'd give *anything* if we could live in a home like this!"

"You haven't seen it all yet!" cried Alan, plainly very much pleased with his appreciative visitors. "Come and see the kitchen. You have to go up these steps at the other end of the living room."

The kitchen was a tiny compartment at the front end of the boat, elevated above the main room. In it was a small oil stove, shelves all about for china and kitchenware, and a clever arrangement of all sorts of gadgets for making work easy. It also was lighted by two windows and draped with gay curtains.

When this had also been enthusiastically admired, Peter demanded, "And what's the stovepipe for, that I saw sticking

out of the roof? I don't see any stove except this in the kitchen that doesn't need one. How do you keep warm in winter?"

"Oh, we have a big Franklin stove for that!" Alan said. "It's one of those made like an open fireplace, you know, with andirons. It stands in the living room and connects with that pipe. We burn logs in it, and wood that we pick up on the beach. It keeps us nice and warm. Now it's taken down for the summer and is stored in the bottom part of the boat, to give us more room."

"I think you have the *grandest* home!" sighed Chris. "I don't see why we couldn't have one like this, instead of a stupid apartment in a horrid, noisy, dirty city!" But Peter was thinking of something else.

"Tell me something, if you don't mind," he asked Alan. "How is it you live in a terrific place like this, when most people have to live in regular houses? Did you always live in this boat?"

The boy's face clouded, as he stood thinking for a moment how to answer this question. At last he replied, "No, we didn't always live here. We came to it about four years ago. Mother and I used to live in a little house up in town. Mother had more money then, and she painted pictures and things like that, and I'd begun to go to school. But the bank failed where she had all her money and times got awfully hard and she couldn't even afford to rent a house then. She didn't know what to do, but she saw this old houseboat here. It belonged to Mr. Wainwright, who owns your cottage. And he sold it to her cheap, because the bottom of it was going to pieces, and anyway, he didn't want it any more after he built the cottage. Mother fixed it all up the way it is now and moved some of our furniture down into it and sold the rest, and we've lived here ever since. I like it a lot better, too. Mother does some sewing and a little art work, and we'll get along that way till I'm old enough to go to work and can support *her*!"

To the other children this seemed a fascinating misfortune. They began to wish that some such thing might happen to *their* parents, so that they too might be compelled to live in a houseboat! But Alan was going on to tell about something else.

"Have you been around this place much?" he asked. The children told him they hadn't, as they'd only come to the Wainwright cottage the evening before.

"Well, it's kind of pretty in the woods all around here," said Alan. "Lots of birds, too. How'd you like it if I'd show you around a bit?" And, of course, Peter and Chris were enchanted with the idea and said so.

"Come on, then!" said Alan. "Mother won't mind if I leave the place for a while. Nobody ever comes around here. I'll take you through the woods and show you a few things you might not see for yourselves."

They all scrambled out of the houseboat, Alan leading the way, and proceeded through the woods by a lane that led directly back from the boat. The woods of cedar, holly, and pine were very dense on both sides, swarming with bird life, and frequently Alan stopped to point out a thrush or chewink or catbird, or to show them a nest in some hidden nook.

114

"You're crazy about birds, aren't you?" said Chris. "I like them, too, only I don't know any of the birds I see by their names, the way you do."

"Yes, I do love them, and I'm trying to make a study of them, just as Mr. Wainwright does. He has books and books about them, and he's given me a few, too, with beautiful pictures. I'll show them to you sometime."

"What's that?" demanded Peter suddenly, pointing at something just visible through an opening in the woods. "It looks like a great big house!"

"It is," said Alan, his eyes sparkling. "That's the old Pettingill mansion. It's all shut up. No one lives there now."

But—*Pettingill!*" cried Chris. "Why, that's your name, isn't it? Does the mansion belong to you? Why don't you live in it?"

Alan smiled.

"That's our 'family nightmare,' as Mother calls it!" he said. "It belonged to my grandfather—my father's father—and he intended to leave it to *my* father. But he died and didn't leave any will, and a brother of his claimed it, and there was so much law trouble about it that it's been shut up ever since and no one can claim it till the thing's settled. A lot of this land around it belongs to it, too; almost all the land in this cove. Nobody can buy it or build on it, till they can find out who really owns it. But it's a grand house inside. It's all locked up, but I know a way to get into it. I often go in and wander around. After all, it was my grandfather's and really ought to be ours—so why shouldn't I?"

Suddenly Peter had an idea.

"Could you get in *now*—and take us?" he asked. "I'm just crazy to get in and see it—like an adventure you read about—wandering around an old, deserted house!"

Alan looked thoughtful for a moment. "Why, yes, I suppose I could get you both in—and I don't think anyone would mind. I'm sure Mother wouldn't, and there isn't anyone else around here to care. There are lots of queer things about that old house. You'll be surprised!"

"Oh, come *on!*" cried Chris. "I can't wait! How do you get there?"

"I'll show you a secret path to it," said Alan. "The trees and underbrush have grown up so quickly around it all these years that the roads are all grown over. But I know a way!"

Alan led them a bit farther along the little road to a certain clump of thick bushes, which he parted, bidding them go through ahead of him.

"This is my secret path," he told them. "No one knows it's here because I began it purposely behind those bushes where it seems too thick to break through. I always come this way by myself."

There was, indeed, a narrow, trodden path through the undergrowth behind the bushes, winding away out of sight around curves made by larger trees and growths that stood in the way. Leading them, Alan went forward, with the two other children on his trail, thrilled by this secret adventure. Sometimes they almost had to crawl under the tangles of vines and thorny cat brier that closed over the path, but Alan always beckoned them on. Suddenly, before they were aware that they were so near, the old house loomed up before them.

"My, I never saw an old house with so much growing close up around it!" cried Peter. "It's almost hidden by all this stuff." And in truth, the wild growths had so closed the old house in, that bushes and trees were growing up to the very windows themselves.

"No one's done a thing with it for twenty years or more," said Alan, "so it's no wonder. Things grow fast around here. Now just follow me, and I'll show you the way in."

The path led around the house to the rear and stopped by an old rickety cellar door, which slanted toward the foundation of the house. The door was fastened by a rusty padlock, but Alan pulled at it by getting his hand under it at the bottom, and it opened, all but one board that was still held by the padlock.

"I discovered a long while ago that these boards were pretty old and rotten," he told the other children, "and when I pulled hard on them, they came loose by themselves and just left the one with the padlock on it. We have to go in by the cellar way and we can get upstairs inside."

He led the way down the moldy steps, the children tumbling after him, and they found themselves in a big, dim old cellar whose only light came from the entrance through which they had come. At some distance from it they saw a flight of wooden steps leading up to the main floor. To this Alan led them, and they presently found themselves in what was evidently a rear hallway of the old house.

"Follow me!" said Alan. "It'll be lighter in a minute, when we get to the front part." They clung closely to him, needing no command to do so, for once inside, and away from the bright sunshine, the semidarkness and moldy, dusty odor of the deserted old place rather dampened their adventurous spirits.

Presently they stood in a long high-ceilinged room, faintly lighted by the sunlight that slipped in around the corners of the heavy dark shades that were drawn to the bottom of all the windows. Every article of furniture was shrouded in dusty coverings—even the pictures on the walls were tightly draped in dust-covers, and a great chandelier that hung from the ceiling was also swaddled tightly with a huge covering that made it look like a fair-sized balloon hung upside down. Cobwebs were festooned in all the corners, and a general air of desertion hung over the forsaken room. But even so the newcomers could see that it must have been a very grand place in its day.

"My!" exclaimed Chris, under her breath. "It must have been a fine room when all these old rags and things weren't all over the furniture!"

Her comment evidently pleased Alan, who replied enthusiastically, "Yes, this is the drawing-room, as Mother says they used to call it. But you haven't seen anything yet! Come along through the others."

He led them across the hall into a stately dining room, similarly shrouded, through all the pantries and the kitchen, dust-covered and equally forlorn, and into a library crowded with bookshelves and moldy books all leaning wearily against one another. Upstairs they wandered through furnished, deserted bedrooms, and on up to a third floor, where smaller, simpler bedrooms indicated the servants' quarters.

"But you haven't seen the best yet!" Alan informed them. I'm going to show you my special den where I often come to sit and look around and watch the birds. Just follow me up these stairs here."

He led them to a narrow, steep little set of steps in the top hall, clambered up them like a monkey, and the others followed at his heels. When they reached the top, both Peter and Chris gave a long "Oh!" of amazement and delight. For the ladder-like steps ended in the midst of a tiny room, not more than seven feet square, which was in reality a cupola on the very roof of the house. Its four sides were lined with windows, draped in dusty orange curtains, and underneath them were four benches covered with old, orange cushions, where one could sit and look out in every direction over the landscape. To the east was the rolling ocean, out beyond a barrier of sandy dunes. To the west were the blue stretches of the bay, and almost underneath them it seemed as if they could see their own cottage and the tiny houseboat nearer by. To the north and south were great stretches of woods and beach heather, and even the town, more than two miles away, was perfectly visible.

The little nook was very cozy, in the bright sunshine, and the children were fascinated by its delightful possibilities.

"What's this?" cried Chris, suddenly pouncing on an old pair of field glasses, lying on one of the benches.

"Oh, those are my binoculars," Alan informed her. "I watch the birds through them. You can see everything so clearly. Mr. Wainwright gave them to me last year. They're an old pair he had, and he got new ones and said I could have these. Let me fix them for you, and you can see how plain everything is when you look through them." He adjusted them and handed them to Chris, who stared at the landscape through them.

"Oh!" she cried. "Why, everything is so close I can even see Mother out on our porch! She seems to be looking up and down

119

the bay. I guess she must be looking for us and wondering where we've gone!"

"Let me try!" exclaimed Peter, taking them from her and staring through them in his turn. "I can even see a big ship out at sea that you could hardly notice without them!"

"I can see even stranger things than *that*!" Alan said. "Just let me have them for a moment, and I'll show you something you'd never guess." He took the glasses, adjusting them to his own eyes, searched the treetops through one window a moment, then handed them to Chris.

"Do you see that tall old dead pine tree over there—with a bunch of something in the top that looks like a big bundle of sticks?" he said. "Well, look through these glasses at it—and then tell us what you see." Chris took the binoculars and stared through them at the point indicated. Then she began, still staring, to hop up and down.

"Oh, it's a *nest*—and it's full of young birds. I can see their heads and bills sticking out! Oh, and here comes a big, big bird with something in its mouth like a fish—or an eel, and they're all opening their mouths—and the big bird's tearing the fish up and feeding it to them!"

"That's a fish hawk, or osprey," said Alan, laughing. "And it's a good way off, too. You couldn't see all that's going on from here without these glasses."

"Are there any other birds' nests around here that I can see?" asked Chris.

"Not right this minute," said Alan, "but I think there's going to be one soon. There's a queer sort of bird called the great crested flycatcher. I'll show you a picture of him in my books on the boat when we go back. And I've always wanted to see the nest of one. Lately I've noticed one flying around here a lot and snooping around a hollow pretty well up in that big Spanish oak tree over there—that one, right near the house. If he builds a nest there we can see him plainly, for it faces right this way—that hollow does."

"Why do you specially want to see his nest?" demanded Chris.

"Because he does a queer thing with it. They say a crested flycatcher always uses, in lining his nest, some part of a discarded snake's skin. Nobody knows quite what for, unless it's to scare other birds and animals away. If he can't get a snake's skin he uses onion-peel or waxed-paper that looks like it. I've always wanted to see one of those nests—and never have. But maybe we'll have a chance, if this one starts building."

"Say! What a lot you know about birds!" exclaimed Peter in an awed voice. "And I never thought they could be so interesting. I like ships better, but we'll sure have to keep a watch for this flycatcher fellow! But look here! Do you mind if I ask you something else, Alan? I can't understand yet why this fine, big old house is left like this—nobody living in it and all deserted—when it really belongs to your family and—and you have to live in a little houseboat instead. What happened, anyway? Why can't you and your mother live here? Do you mind telling us?"

121

"Well, I don't understand all about it myself," answered Alan thoughtfully. "Mother's told me a little about it and it's something like this: My grandfather, who built this house and owned all this land, had two sons. One was my father—he was the younger one—and the other was much older. Mother says the older one—he's my Uncle Ethan—and my grandfather never did get along well. My Uncle Ethan never did care much about this place or staying here. He wanted to be an explorer or traveler. He loved to spend his time roaming around all sorts of odd places on the other side of the world. But my father loved this place and always wanted to be here—just as his father did. So Grandfather gave his older son a lot of money and told him that that was *his* part of what the two would get after he died, and that he should take it then and go about his affairs. They'd quarreled some about it, Mother says.

"But Grandfather said he was going to leave this house to my father, in his will, and Uncle Ethan needn't come around here claiming it after he was dead. You see, my father was killed in an accident, just a short time after I was born. My grandfather did make a will, too, because my father remembered when he did it. But the queer thing is that after Grandfather died they couldn't find the will anywhere! It had simply disappeared. They knew it ought to be in this house, among his papers, but it wasn't! They searched everywhere but never came across it. Uncle Ethan was off in Australia somewhere when Grandfather died, but after he'd heard the news, he wrote back and said if no will had been found, he claimed this house and land. There were a lot of other puzzling things about it that neither Mother nor I understand. Anyhow it made it all so difficult without any will that the thing has never been settled, and nobody's allowed to use the house till it is. I guess it never will be settled now— the thing's gone so long."

"But if they found the will now, it would be all right, wouldn't it?" cried Peter, excited over the story. "Maybe it *is* hidden around this house somewhere! Why couldn't we look for it?" Alan shook his head.

"No use in that! I thought of it too. But Mother says my

122

father told her that he thought Grandfather had destroyed that will, possibly intending to write another and make it even safer for Father. He mentioned to Father once that he might, only he died very suddenly of a stroke, and they think he may have torn up the old will and didn't have time to make a new one before he died. So there isn't any use hunting for it any more."

"What *I* want to know," interrupted Chris, who had been following this account as intelligently as she could, "is what became of your Uncle Ethan? Is he alive now? Is he still traveling around the other side of the world?"

"Yes, as far as we know," said Alan. "He's a rather old man now. Last we heard of him, he was in India, and he said he was never coming back till this thing was settled. Mother hasn't heard of him for years. He wrote her that he never wanted to see the place again, anyway. If he got it at last, he'd simply sell it and stay where he was. Said he hated America and liked to live in foreign countries. So that's all we know about him!"

Just at this moment a bird flashed by the windows, and Alan forgot his story, seized the glasses, and stared through them eagerly at the olive-winged, yellow-breasted creature.

"*There he is!*" he exclaimed excitedly. "There's the crested flycatcher! See him, Chris? Look at his queer, humpy-looking head!" He handed the glasses to Christine, who was just in time to see the bird swoop through the air, and snap something in its bill that was probably an unwary insect. Then it darted off toward the big Spanish oak tree where Alan had thought it was beginning to build a nest. The three stared at it a while in turn, through the glasses. A little later, they saw the bird dart off again and return to the tree with a piece of straw in its mouth.

"It's building a nest!" cried Alan. "I knew it—I knew it! Now I can see sometime what that nest is like. Maybe I'll see the snakeskin!"

"Look, look, Chris!" suddenly interrupted Peter, gazing through the glasses, but not at the bird. "There's Mother walking along the shore, looking all around on the water. I know she's looking for us. We'd better hurry down and let her see

we're all right, or she won't let us go out by ourselves again!"
All three scurried down to the lower floor, then to the cellar
and out into the bright sunshine of the afternoon. For a moment
Alan stood staring down at the cellar steps before he closed
the door.

"That's *queer!*" he muttered softly to himself, but neither of
the children heard him, for they were intent on getting home.

"Can we come again, Alan?" called back Chris. "Can we
come tomorrow?"

"Sure thing!" shouted Alan. "I'll be looking for you. But don't
wait for me now. You know the way and you'd better not keep
your mother waiting. I want to look at something. Good-bye!"

And he turned back, continuing to stare thoughtfully at
something at the bottom of the cellar steps.

The next two days passed oddly for Peter and Christine and
were among the most thrilling they had ever known. When
they met their mother on the shore, that first afternoon of their
introduction to the Pettingill mansion, they found her very
upset. She had been watching for them ever since their disappearance around the point of the cove. And finally, becoming
disturbed at their long absence, she had come searching for
them along the shore. At first she was annoyed at them for
causing her so much worry. But both the children began to
explain at once. They told of a strange boy who loved birds
and knew all about them, a houseboat in which he lived, and
an old deserted house back in the woods which he had led them
to explore.

"Goodness me!" she cried. "I can't understand half you're
saying! Suppose we get back to the house and do the explaining
there. I'll get into the boat with you and help row back. Daddy
is to be here any minute, and you haven't caught a single crab!"

But once at home, the story finally was put together so that
their parents could understand it. It was a curious tale.

"And can we go to see him again tomorrow, Mother? He's
so nice—and he lives in the best houseboat—and that old mansion is wonderful—and we want to see the crested flycatcher
build his nest."

Mrs. Cameron looked doubtfully at her husband. "Do you think it's all right?" she asked. "It might annoy his mother to have the children around so much."

"The boy must be all right if Jim Wainwright likes him," Mr. Cameron answered, much to the children's joy. "He must be an unusual boy, for Wainwright isn't often attracted to children —old bachelor that he is! As for the old house—if the boy's mother allows him to go in there, I guess there's no reason why our children can't go too. Rather strange situation. If Wainwright weren't away in Alaska just now, I'd ask him about it. I'd like to call at that houseboat sometime, too, and see if it's as attractive as the children say. Suppose we stroll by there while I'm here and see the lay of the land."

"I rather admire the boy's mother, too, for putting up such a brave fight to make a living," added Mrs. Cameron. "She must be rather pleasant, and I'd like to meet her. We'll do that very soon—and meanwhile you children can play with Alan all you wish, provided you don't get into mischief. If I miss you too long again, I will know where you are and not worry!" So it was decided, and the children went to bed that night almost too excited to sleep.

They woke next morning, eager to have breakfast and be off, but to their dismay found the rain pouring down in torrents. And their mother flatly refused to allow them out of the house in such a storm. All morning they watched at the windows forlornly and asked her a thousand times whether *now* it hadn't let up sufficiently for them to go out. Even Mr. Cameron was somewhat disgruntled, as he had planned to spend most of the day on a golf course on the other side of the town. So Mrs. Cameron uttered a sigh of relief when, early in the afternoon, the weather cleared, and all three of them left the house.

"But I can't allow you to use the boat," she warned the children, "because the bay is too rough, and it might rain again before you start back."

"That's all right!" said Peter. "We can walk along the shore just as well—and a lot quicker, I think. And there are no marshes or streams between here and there; I looked yesterday when we rowed back. We'll take our raincoats in case we get caught in a shower, and we'll be back by dinnertime. Alan has a clock in the houseboat." And they were off, flying along the narrow strip of yellow sand along the beach, until Mrs. Cameron lost sight of them around the end of the point.

When they reached the houseboat they found no one about, and the cabin closed; but they clambered up the little side steps and knocked. A very sweet-faced, slender woman came to the door. So great was their surprise at seeing her, when they had expected Alan, that they were speechless for a moment. She greeted them.

"Good afternoon! You must be Peter and Christine Cameron. Alan told me all about you last night. I'm so glad to meet you. I'm Alan's mother. I'm glad to know you. Your father is a friend of Mr. Wainwright, and he is a friend of ours too. Tell your mother I hope to come and call on her soon."

Her smile was kindly, and the children liked her at once. She went on:

"Alan isn't here right now, but he left word that you can find him at the old house back in the woods. He was there all morning and went back right after lunch. I can't imagine why he wants to be there on this stormy day. What a dreary old place on a stormy day!"

"Oh, *I* know!" cried Chris. "He's watching a crested flycatcher build its nest."

"Well, he can't be seeing much of it today—at least not this morning. It was pouring—and birds don't fly about much in weather like that!" replied Mrs. Pettingill. "It must have been something else. But hurry along now and you'll catch him there. You know the way?"

"Yes, we know it!" they cried, as they scurried off through the woods. Before entering the secret path, Peter and Chris put on their raincoats, as the overhanging leaves drenched them at the slightest touch. But they scrambled along, giggling at each shower of raindrops, and presently came to the cellar door, which stood open. Here they stopped and wondered if they had better try to get in by themselves and make their way upstairs or call to Alan that they were there and have him guide them. While they were debating, Alan himself came from the cellar and greeted them, saying he was sure that they would come, so had been waiting around for them down below.

"Shall we go right up to the tower?" demanded Chris impatiently. "I want to see how the flycatcher is getting along. Did you see him this morning, Alan?"

"No, I didn't see him—it was raining too hard," said Alan rather soberly. "I hardly think he'll be about today. It seems to rain a bit every little while. I—I've been doing some things down here that—that interested me. Tell you what! Let's not go up to the tower today. It's no good watching anything from there a day like this. And the house is awfully chilly and damp, all shut up this way. S'pose instead, we go for a walk along the dunes by the ocean and look at the sea gulls and birds there —and the ships too, you like them. After that, we'll go back to the houseboat and look at my bird books, and Mother will give us some lemonade and currant buns that she baked today. She promised she would if I brought you back. How about it?"

For a moment the two children were bitterly disappointed. They had counted so much on the new and wonderful experience of prowling about the queer old mansion again and watching the maneuver of the fascinating flycatcher from the tower that this program of Alan's seemed rather tame in comparison. But as there was obviously nothing else to suggest, and as they were both too polite to express their disappointment, they agreed, and Alan shut the cellar door and proceeded to lead them back through the secret path to the road, and then on over toward the green-capped dunes that flanked the ocean. At the top of the dunes Alan stopped for a moment and gazed back long and earnestly in the direction of the old house.

"What are you staring at, Alan? What do you see?" demanded Peter curiously.

"Oh, nothing—that is—nothing!" answered Alan, a bit confused by the question. "Let's go over to the ocean and walk along on the beach. There's a whole flock of sea gulls gathered farther down, and I'd like to see what they've got there. Sometimes such queer fish and other things come up on the beach in a storm." So he turned and led them down to the beach, but his hesitation in answering the question seemed strange to Peter, and he remembered the incident afterward.

Alan raced down to the edge where the pounding breakers were surging in, rolling back after a wide sweep up the beach, and he pointed out to the others the fearless little snipe or sandpipers that were chasing each wave as it receded, pattering along on their tiny feet, trying to pick up some stray fish or crab in the wake of the breaker. When the next wave rolled in, they scurried back out of range.

"Do you know," he said, "those fellows fly here all the way from Argentina in South America and back each year? Seems as if they'd hardly have time to get here before they'd have to turn around and go back—it's so far away!" The children marveled at this, and then wandered on down the beach to where a flock of dazzlingly white gulls were squabbling and screaming over a dead fish.

"Those are Bonaparte gulls," said Alan. "See their black faces? Sometimes they're called 'black-faced gulls.' They're much prettier than the ordinary brown gulls, I think."

But at this moment a hard shower came down and threatened to last so long that the children agreed to make a beeline for the houseboat and finish the afternoon there. They hurried through the downpour and arrived breathless and dripping, to be dried off and enjoy the buns offered by Mrs. Pettingill. The houseboat seemed very cozy with the rain drumming down on its low roof. Alan's mother talked to them in her quiet, pleasant way. Alan himself was rather silent and said little till later when he showed them some of his beautifully illustrated bird books and explained the pictures. At five o'clock Peter suggested that they had better leave for home, as their mother might begin to worry. They promised to join Alan next morning and then left.

When they were well away from the houseboat, trudging along the shore, Peter suddenly asked his sister, "Chris, did it seem to you as if Alan acted sort of strange—and—and quiet, this afternoon? Not a bit the way he was yesterday?"

"Yes, I thought so too," she agreed. "It seemed to me as though he was worrying about something. I noticed he looked back at the old house a long time when we stood on the dune, and I heard you ask him what was the matter, or what he was looking at, and he said, 'Oh, nothing!' But I'm sure there was something!"

"Yes, he was looking over toward the old house all the time," cried Peter excitedly. "And I'm certain he either saw something or was looking for something. But I didn't like to ask him any more about it, if he didn't want to say. But it seems sort of funny, doesn't it?"

"I didn't like this day so much," complained Chris. "It wasn't nearly as nice as yesterday. I wish Alan wouldn't be worried about things, or else that he'd tell us about them. I hope tomorrow's going to be nicer. I want to go and watch the crested flycatcher build his nest and put snakeskins in it—and I want to explore the old house again!"

They met next morning at the houseboat, and Alan immediately agreed to lead them to the old house to watch the crested flycatcher. The weather was clear again, dry and warm and beautiful, and they planned to spend the morning in the tower. Alan also suggested that possibly they might go down later and make their way to the foot of the tree where the bird was building and find out what was to be seen from there. He might even try to climb the tree and discover, if he could, how the nest looked at that particular period. As they came to the cellar door, and Alan opened it, he stopped and warned them to be careful where they stepped.

"What do you mean?" asked Peter. "Look out how we step *where?*"

"I mean, as you go through the cellar, especially right near the steps, don't walk over the little pile of sand that has drifted in under the door and down the steps. There's something there that I don't want disturbed," Alan answered.

"Look here, Alan, do you mind telling us something?" said Chris. "Is there anything the matter? You aren't at all the way you were the day we first met you. We've noticed you watching the house all day yesterday, even when we went over to the ocean."

Alan looked a bit taken aback for a moment and stood digging his foot into the weeds, apparently thinking the matter over. Finally he said, "I didn't know you'd noticed anything, so I wasn't going to say a word about this. But since you have

130

I might as well tell you. It's a secret, so please don't say anything about it to *anyone*—'specially Mother. And don't tell your own folks, for I wouldn't want to worry them either. Will you promise?"

Peter and Chris nodded, wondering greatly what he was about to disclose. Then he went on. "You know, nobody comes to this old place *ever*—except me—nowadays. There used to be a side road leading to it from the main road, but years ago, after all the trouble about it started, there was a fence put up across that road, and dirt and sand thrown around it, so no one could come through. And after a while bushes and trees grew up around it so thick that no one would even know a road had ever been there. Really there isn't *any* way to it now directly, except that little secret path I made; so no one ever comes to it anymore. But the other day—that first day you came here—when we were going out by this cellar door, I noticed a very queer thing—"

"Oh! What was it? Tell us—*quick!*" Chris interrupted him.

"Wait and don't bother him!" said Peter. "Let him tell it in his own way, Chris."

"Why, it was just this," explained Alan. "You know, I wear sneakers all summer. You two wore them that day, too. Yet when we were coming out of the cellar, I suddenly noticed a footprint, there in that sand at the bottom of the steps—and *it was made by a regular shoe!*" Both of his listeners uttered a gasp of surprise.

"Then—then—" stuttered Peter, "someone—besides ourselves —must have been here!" Immediately Chris was all excited.

"Oh, *show* it to us—quick!" she demanded. Alan led them down the steps and pointed to a flat surface of sand that had evidently blown in or sifted in under the door during some past storm. It was slightly off to one side, so that in their previous entrance they had not stepped directly through the middle of it, though there were the faint prints of their sneakers at the nearer end. But in the middle, well away from their own sneaker-marks, there was the distinct imprint of the sole of a shoe—that is, the front part of one, only. For the back of it,

131

where the heelprint would have been, was on the hard surface of the floor, off the edge of the sand, and so had not made any impression. They all gazed at it in silent surprise for a moment.

"Then someone must have been in here—besides ourselves!" said Peter in a hushed voice. "Who do you think it could have been, Alan?"

"I haven't the slightest idea," said Alan. "You see, the very first time I saw it was that day you first came in here, and then it wasn't till we were coming out that I noticed it. Whether it was here before we came in, I can't say. It might have been, for I was so busy showing you around that I didn't notice. But I think it must have been here before, because if anyone had tried to get in while we were there, we'd have seen him coming through toward the house, from where we were in the tower."

"But we weren't in the tower *all* the time," said Peter. "We spent quite a lot of time exploring around first. He might have got in then."

Alan agreed that this was possible. He said further that he had not been to the old house the day before, as he and his mother had taken a long drive into the country on some business of hers. So the mark might have been made then. If it had been before that, he thought he would have noticed it.

"But who do you think it could be?" insisted Chris. "A man or a woman or a child?" Alan pointed to the shape of the footprint.

"It's hard to tell—from just what's there," he answered. "It's round at the toe and fairly wide. It could hardly be a child's, not a very little one, anyway. If only the heelprint were there, we could tell a lot more about it. But as it is, it might be a man's or a woman's, or a large boy's or girl's. I don't know why, but I somehow think it must be a man's."

Suddenly Peter broke in with another question. "But, Alan, is this the *only* footprint? Have you looked through the rest of the house? Mightn't there be some more somewhere—on a dusty floor—or something like that?"

"I went straight through the house the first day," said Alan promptly, "and I hunted in every nook and corner of it with a flashlight. And there wasn't a *thing*—not another trace of any-

thing disturbed, or any more footprints or fingerprints in the dust, except what we'd made ourselves. I could tell that. No, the person, whoever it was, had certainly gone no farther than the cellar."

"But did you see any footprints outside the cellar door?" asked Chris. "I should think there would be some."

"I hunted around—quite a way—but you see, the ground is all grown over by weeds and grass right around here—no free sand —so you couldn't tell. I don't like the idea of anyone getting in here. It sort of looks queer!"

"Was that why you were watching the place all the time yesterday?" asked Chris. "We saw you staring at it several times."

"Yes, it was," he admitted. "I thought maybe if we weren't around that afternoon, someone would come along—the person who has evidently been here before—and perhaps try it again, and then I could see who it was. I'd been in the house all morning myself, with the cellar door shut, keeping watch, though I hardly expected anyone to try it on such a rainy day. They might have, though, thinking it the best time, with no one around. But no one did."

"Why don't you want your mother to know about it?" asked Peter.

Because it would worry her," Alan replied. "She has always

been afraid some tramps might get in and steal something—or set fire to the place. But these last few years, since it's grown up so much around here and it's so hidden, she has stopped thinking about it."

"Well then, what are you going to do about it?" demanded Peter. "Suppose someone *is* trying to get in—who hasn't any business to?"

"I'm going to really watch the place!" said Alan. "And if anyone tries it again and I see who it is, I'm going to report it to the police in town and have something done about it. But I don't want Mother to be worried about it before there's any need."

Peter walked over and stood looking intently at the footprint in the sandpile. Suddenly he said, "There's one thing I'm certain of it—it wasn't any *tramp* that wore that shoe!"

"How do you know?" said Chris, curiously.

"It's a nice new shoe," he replied thoughtfully. "You can tell by the way it's made such a clear print. Tramps usually wear old, worn-out shoes—don't they?" The two others agreed with him.

Alan grinned. "You'd make a good detective, Pete! You notice things quite a lot!"

Immensely pleased with this praise, Peter cried, "Say—that's an idea! Let's make believe we're all detectives, and see if we can't solve this puzzle! You notice more things than I do, Alan, 'cause you've sort of trained yourself by watching the birds. But we could all try." The two others liked the plan.

"My idea is," Alan added excitedly, "that someone came here the other day and got in this far, through the cellar door, but something scared him off—or he was afraid to go any farther, and he went away. But he may come back and try it again, and then we'll catch him at it. I wish we could come here at night, but I'm certain your folks wouldn't allow it, and I'm pretty sure my mother wouldn't let me either. But anyway I don't think it likely anyone would try it at night, unless they were awfully sure how to get to it. The woods are so dark and tangled. I don't think whoever it is knows about our path—

134

and, anyway, I examined it thoroughly and I didn't see any strange footprints. Whoever it was that came here must have forced his way in through the woods and briars. We'll just have to wait and see. Tell you what—let's go up in the tower now, and we can keep a lookout from there at the same time we're watching the birds." They all agreed, but before they went upstairs Alan closed the cellar door, explaining that if anyone came along, he'd think no one was in the house if it were closed. Otherwise he might go away. Alan took a flashlight from his pocket to light their way in the darkness.

"But we don't want to be shut in here if some stranger is

going to get in!" cried Chris, frightened at such a dangerous possibility. "What would we do?"

"Don't worry!" Alan grinned. "I've plenty of secret places to hide in this house, where no stranger could ever find us. We'd be perfectly safe, though we might have to wait till he got out." Reassured, they all made their way up to the tower.

It wasn't long after they got there that Alan spotted the fly-catcher going toward its nest, with a small twig in its mouth. From that moment all three forgot their excitement over the unknown footprint. They watched the bird fly back and forth, sometimes returning with a wisp of straw, sometimes a twig, once even with a small feather. But Alan was most interested in whether it would bring anything that looked like a snakeskin. He hadn't seen anything like that yet. At last the bird flew away for a long time. And when he finally returned, Alan exclaimed in great excitement, after viewing him through the glasses,—

"Hey—what did I tell you? He has something in his bill that looks white—or sort of shiny! It's just a little piece—whatever it is, but it looks like the real thing! Here, Chris, you take the glasses and look!"

"Yes—oh, boy! I see it, too!" she shouted. "He's just going down into that hole with it!"

"I want to see it, too!" exclaimed Peter, seizing the glasses. "Oh, it's too late. He's gone in with it now!"

"Tell you what!" cried Alan. "Let's run outside, and I'll try to shinny up the tree before it flies back with another bit, and have a look at it. I want to see if it's a real bit of snakeskin. Hurry up, so it won't find us there. It might desert the nest if it thought we were meddling. They often do."

They left the glasses on the seat of the tower and scurried down, the echo of their thudding footsteps resounding through the big, empty house. Suddenly at the top of the stairs going down into the main hall they were halted, frozen into instant terror, by the sound of a terrible "*Crash!*" echoing from somewhere in the house!

Chris grabbed Peter's arm in sheer panic, but Alan halted

them both at the top of the stairs, with outstretched arm.

"Quick! There's someone down there!" he whispered. "Follow me—and I'll show you a good place to hide!" Without a word they crept after him, tiptoeing noiselessly through the long hall and into one of the bedrooms. Alan led them to a door in this room, which he opened, disclosing an empty clothes closet. On the outside of its door was a key, and this Alan took out, inserting it on the inside of the lock.

"Get in here!" he whispered. And without an instant's delay the three huddled inside, and then Alan locked the door after them. Fortunately it was a fairly roomy closet, where they could move about a little and have enough air.

"We're perfectly safe in here," he assured them in a low voice. "Anyone exploring around here couldn't open this door, and we can wait here till we're sure they've gone away. So don't worry, but listen hard to see if we can hear any footsteps coming upstairs."

There was no need to warn the other two children to be quiet. They were still so helpless with terror that their knees were quaking and their throats dry. It was very dark in the closet, but Alan had his flashlight with him, and he put it on from time to time, lighting up their frightened faces and tensely clenched hands. He did not like to keep it on, for the light might

137

shine out through the space under the closet door and reveal their presence to the unknown intruder.

For several moments they kept perfectly silent, listening for the slightest sound. But, much to their astonishment, there was none. They had thought at least to hear footsteps ascending the stairs.

"Do you s'pose he's come in?" whispered Peter at last.

"Can't tell! He may be walking very softly," replied Alan. "He probably doesn't want to make a sound."

"Then why did he make that awful crash in the beginning?" moaned Chris.

"That may have been an accident," explained Alan. "Something fell unexpectedly, I guess." They waited for another silent interval. Presently the tension became too much for Alan.

"I'm going out of here and explore around a bit," he warned them. "You two stay in here and lock the door after me. You can keep the flashlight with you. But I've just *got* to see what's going on. I may not go any farther than the door of this room. Depends on what I see or hear. If you hear me tap three times on this door, let me in as quick as you can. It'll mean I've seen someone. But if not I'll come back and call to you to come out."

"Oh, *don't* go!" wailed Chris. "We'll be just scared to death without you!"

"No, we won't!" whispered Peter indignantly. "At least *I* won't, and you needn't be either, Chris. Alan's right. We can't stay here forever listening for something. Go ahead, Alan!"

Alan turned the rusty key as softly as he could, opened the door, and closed it after him. Peter turned the key on the inside, and the two children were left in darkness for what seemed an eternity. So they listened breathlessly for Alan's three taps, or for cries for help or shouts and groans. But there were none of these. Suddenly there came the sound of feet leaping up the stairs. Again they turned cold with terror, not knowing what to expect next.

"Unlock the door—quick!" cried Chris. "It may be Alan running away from someone!" Peter turned the key with trembling fingers. Then Alan, running along the hall, burst into the room.

138

"Come on out!" shouted Alan, to their enormous relief. "It's all right. Nobody's here now! And with knees still shaking the two emerged from the closet.

"What did you see? What did you hear?" they demanded in a breath. "How do you know he's gone?"

"Come downstairs with me and I'll show you," answered Alan, and more he would not say till he had led them to the cellar door which now stood open. Gratefully they crept out into the welcome sunshine.

"I went all through the house," Alan informed them, "from the tower clear down to here. I examined every nook and corner, and there wasn't a sign of anyone—or even a trace of his having been in here. When I got to the cellar, this door was shut, and I pushed it open and went outside. There was still no sign of anyone—not even a footprint. And nobody was around outside. I was just going to come back, and started to pull down the cellar door after me—when I discovered *this!*" He indicated the cellar door and pointed out to them a spot on the under side where a long splinter of the wood had chipped away from a plank and lay at the foot of the steps.

"And that told me the story," he went on, picking up the splinter and examining it.

"Told you—what?" gasped Chris. "I don't understand what this thin little bit of wood could tell you!"

"Neither do I," confessed Peter.

"Easy—if you just think a minute." Alan grinned. "We heard a big crash—didn't we? It was something heavy falling—and nothing of that sort has happened inside the house. Then I find this cellar door splintered. So it didn't take me long to guess how it was done. Someone came here and tried to get in, as he must have the other day. He'd probably just raised the door when he heard us inside the house. It must have startled him so that he let go the door, and it dropped with a bang—and the wood's so rotten now that it splintered off a bit here at the edge. After that, he must have hustled away into the woods. Scared him, I guess, to find someone in the house when he had thought it was empty!"

139

Peter was intrigued at the simple explanation, but Chris declared, "Well, I know one thing! I'm not going back into that house again—ever! I never was so frightened in my life. And he might try it again—any time."

"Not likely—after he found people were in it," said Alan. "But I don't think myself that it would be a good thing to go back to it again right away. At least not for a while. I have another plan. I've brought my field glasses down out of the tower, so there is nothing in there that we have to go back for. Suppose we stay around here—outside somewhere, but hidden by the bushes. We can find a place where we can watch the flycatcher in his tree—or other birds—and at the same time we can keep watch on the house, too. If anyone comes along we can see him, even better than we could from the tower. And we won't miss out on our bird either."

"But suppose someone *should* come along through the woods," quavered Chris. "What'd we do?"

"We'd stay put, hidden right where we were, and watch what his game was—and get a good look at him," Alan said promptly. "Then we'd know what to do later. But you needn't worry about today. There isn't a chance of his coming back now, after he's been scared off by hearing people in the house. So we're perfectly safe. But we might as well keep right on watching the flycatcher—and the house at the same time. Don't you think so?"

Peter agreed with him thoroughly, even if Chris still remained a bit doubtful and alarmed. Then Alan was suddenly inspired with another idea.

"Look here! It's nearly lunchtime. Your watch, Chris, says quarter of twelve. I suppose we ought to be getting back to our homes for a while, but I don't like to leave this place alone just now. Whoever it was might be hiding out somewhere and watching till we went away, to get another chance to get in the house. Suppose you go on back to your house and eat your lunch, and I'll stay here and watch the place. Then, on your way back, you might stop at the houseboat and ask my mother to fix me two or three sandwiches and some milk, and you could bring them back, and I'd eat here. Then we could stay the rest of the

140

afternoon. You could tell my mother that I didn't want to leave because I'm watching the flycatcher. And that's quite true, for I shall be watching it. Will you do this?"

"But aren't you afraid to stay here all alone?" demanded Chris wonderingly.

"Heck—no!" laughed Alan. "I'm around here all the time—off and on. Always have been. Why should I be scared off by anything now?"

"I wouldn't be either!" said Peter stoutly. "I'll stay here instead of you—if you think it a good idea."

"No, it would be better for me to stay," said Alan. "I know all the hiding-places around here—and you don't, Peter. And, besides, your mother might worry. You both go ahead now, and get back as soon as you can—and don't forget my sandwiches."

When Peter and Chris returned about half-past one that afternoon, they found Alan sitting on the grass by the cellar door, thoughtfully chewing on a twig of sassafras.

"Here are your sandwiches and milk!" cried Peter, producing a small thermos bottle and a package wrapped in waxed paper.

"And here are some pears I took from lunch," added Chris, handing him a couple. "I thought you might like them for dessert. Has anything happened?"

"Thanks for everything!" said Alan accepting the food and beginning at once on his sandwiches. "I sure am hungry! Now for your question, Chris. I'm answering it in a funny way—yes —and no!"

"What do you mean?" she queried. "How could something happen—and *not* happen?"

"Well," explained Alan, "something did happen about *one* thing we were looking for—and nothing did about the other!"

"Oh, for crying out loud!" exclaimed Peter. "Do tell us what you mean and don't tease so much."

"I'm not teasing," went on Alan, drinking some milk from the top of the thermos bottle. "I mean exactly what I said. Nothing happened about the flycatcher—but something did about—the other!"

Immediately they both asked questions at the same time. But

142

Alan only smiled provokingly and took a bite of his pear.

"If I'd said it right at once, you wouldn't have let me finish my lunch—and I was awfully hungry! So I sort of held back on it till I got the sandwiches down at least. Now I'll tell you—and it's a pretty curious thing at that!

"After you'd gone, I sat watching for our bird a while. I figured that whoever had tried to get in here wasn't very likely to come back so soon, and I might as well keep an eye on the flycatcher. But I watched a long while near the tree and never got a single glimpse of him. Maybe I was too near and scared him off—or he may have gone for his own lunch! Anyhow, I gave it up after a while and started to snoop around through the bushes and woods here a bit, trying to find out, if I could, how that person had gotten in here this morning. I figured it wasn't likely he'd come by our path, for that's pretty well hidden and ends over at the other side of the house. He must have pushed his way through the woods from the road, somehow, and I thought I might find some broken branches or trace of some kind that he'd made—maybe another footprint.

"I poked around—in every direction, but mostly toward the road. No good. Nothing at all. Then off toward the south side of the house I found a more open space after you get through the bushes close to the house, and this space—it's hardly more than a narrow path—led off in a roundabout way toward the bay. It's shut off again by a lot of thick-growing cedar trees before you get to the bay. And it was right there that I found where our friend had tried to push through these cedars. He left something behind him, on a spiky sort of branch, for us to remember him by!"

"What was it? What was it?" clamored Chris and Peter in chorus.

Alan thrust his hand in his pocket, pulled something out, and held it before the children's eyes.

"It was *this!*" he said.

It was only a short bit of knitting yarn, about five inches long, and very much kinked, as if it had been unraveled from something a light, gray-blue color.

"What do you make of it?" asked Alan.

"I know!" cried Chris. "He caught his sweater on a tree or branch. He was in such a hurry he just pulled it away and it tore, and this piece got caught there."

"And he probably was in such a hurry that he never even stopped to look behind and see what he'd left!" added Peter.

"Just about what I thought," said Alan. "But we've got a nice clue here to help us find that person. Do you realize that?"

"Look for a man with a blue sweater that color!" said Chris delightedly.

"But lots of men wear sweaters like that!" objected Peter. "How are you going to tell which it is? And where would we look for him, anyway?"

His sister's face fell at having her grand detective scheme sat upon in this ruthless fashion, but Alan came to her rescue.

"Chris is right," he said. "We've got to look for a man in a sweater this color. Peter's right, too, in saying that a good many men wear sweaters this color—but here's the catch. This man tore his sweater pretty badly. I think it must have been up near the shoulder, for it was on a twig about that distance from the ground. So we've got to look for a sweater like this—

144

only a *mended* one, if he had it mended, or a torn one if he didn't. Either way, I think you could notice it if you were near enough."

"But where must we hunt?" insisted Peter. "There are only a few cottages down this way, and no houses at all after you pass this one—not for miles. And the village is quite a long way off from here, and we children don't go there very often."

"Well, I go there fairly often with Mother, when she drives up," retorted Alan, "and I intend to look around a bit when I do. And when you happen to go up—as I suppose you do sometimes—you look, too. But, to tell the truth, I don't think we'll get much out of *that*. As Peter says, lots of men wear sweaters like this. It would be hard to tell. What I'm planning on is something different. I have a notion we're more likely to find what we're looking for down this way. That person must come down the main road to get to this house. There isn't any other road. I've planned that tomorrow we'll go out to the main road and sit hidden in the bushes along this way and just watch who goes by and what colored sweaters they wear."

"Why not do it this very afternoon?" demanded Peter.

"Not a bit of use," Alan declared. "You know what a scare he got this morning, so he wouldn't be likely to try it again *this* day, anyhow. But he might tomorrow. We might as well spend the rest of the day watching the fly—and there he is now!" Alan interrupted himself excitedly, as a bird flew by overhead with a small twig in its bill. At once all three forgot the mystery and turned their attention to the bird and its affairs.

"How are we going to watch what he does?" asked Peter. "We're a good ways off from that tree. I can't even see it from here."

"We must be very quiet and careful about this," Alan cautioned them in an undertone. "He's easily scared off, and we don't want that to happen. Wait till he flies off again—I'm pretty sure he'll go over in this direction—and then we'll creep through the bushes as close as we can to that big oak tree. We'll keep covered by bushes, for he's sharp-eyed enough to see us from above if we don't. Then we'll watch him do his stuff!"

They watched in silence till they saw the bird again flying off over their heads. Then, led by Alan, they crept through the undergrowth to a spot very near the old tree, hid themselves under some thick bayberry bushes, and settled down to their vigil. From where they sat, the old tree was in plain sight, especially the crotch of the branches, in a hole in which the nest was being built. And here they waited during what seemed a very long time for the return of the flycatcher.

"Why don't you climb that tree now, Alan?" suggested Peter. "Maybe you can see what's in that nest while he's away?"

"I've figured I can't shinny up that tree, as I thought I could at first," returned Alan. "It's too big around—not like a small, younger tree. I'll have to get some kind of ladder. We have one at the houseboat that would reach it, I think. Maybe we can get it and bring it here after awhile, but I'd like to watch him a bit first. A ladder here might scare him off before he's finished with the nest. Then we couldn't find out much about it."

"What *I'd* like to know," said Chris, "is where he gets the pieces of snakeskin to put in it. He can't get it off a *live* snake, surely, and where does he find a dead one?"

Alan laughed. "You evidently don't know much about snakes! Don't you know that a snake sheds his skin once a year anyway? He just crawls right out of it where it loosens, around his mouth, and wriggles out with a brand new skin underneath. He often leaves the old one perfectly whole just where he got out of it. I once found one all curled up under the bushes—the empty skin, I mean—and it looked exactly like a real, live snake till I touched it and found it was only an empty shell. I saved it and brought it home in a box, and I've got it yet. I'll show it to you sometime. But I think the flycatcher finds a snakeskin like that and takes pieces of it to put in his nest. If he can't find one, he tries to get something that looks as nearly like it as possible. Here he comes back! Watch and see what he's got this time."

With a whirring of wings, the flycatcher swooped down out of the sky and landed on the edge of the hole in the tree. But

he was only carrying a long straw, and he darted in out of sight with it. The three watchers gave a disgusted sigh.

"Oh, when is he ever coming back with a piece of that stuff we saw him with the other day?" mourned Chris. "Do you suppose he found all he wanted of it then, and isn't going to get any more?"

"Can't tell a thing about it," said Alan. "We'll just have to watch here and see what he does."

They settled down to watching again. Presently the flycatcher emerged from the hole and flew off once more, this time in the opposite direction from which he had come, directly over the roof of the old house.

"If he comes back this time with anything worth-while," remarked Alan, "I think it might be a good idea if we went back and got that ladder. We can easily carry it here between us. It isn't so far. Then I'll go up and look the nest over while he's away." Another long interval followed, during which they were very quiet, watching for the return of the bird.

"There he is!" cried Alan at last. "Coming over the roof of the house. Do you see him? Give me those glasses! He has something different this time!" He adjusted the glasses and looked excitedly.

"It's something white—or shiny!" whispered Chris, almost bursting with curiosity. "I can see if from here!"

147

The bird approached the tree and darted into his hole, but not before all of them had seen that he had something in his bill that glistened in the sunlight—a small straight strip about two inches long. But so rapid was his disappearance that even Alan, who had the glasses, could not determine just what it was.

"Do you think it was snakeskin?" demanded Peter.

"I don't know. Somehow it looked too—too straight for that," explained Alan. "But it might have been. He was too far away—and too quick. He just went in like a flash. Tell you what—now we'll get that ladder! Wait till he comes out and goes off again. Then we'll scoot out of here and get it. I can't wait any longer to see what he has there!"

The bird flew off again soon, and the children scrambled out of their hiding-place, round the house, and were off through the secret path to the houseboat. Within twenty minutes they were back, having had none too easy a time steering the unwieldy stepladder through the woods.

"We'll hide it back of the bushes for awhile," said Alan, "So we won't scare him off by the sight of it. Flycatchers are very quick to see anything unusual lying around. Then we'll watch to see whether he's in or out of his nest now. And the next time he flies off, I'll rush it to the tree and climb up and peek before he gets back."

Not knowing whether, during their absence, the bird was in or out of his nest, they shoved the ladder behind some bushes, hid themselves in their former hiding-place, and resumed their watch. Nothing happened for awhile. Then suddenly the flycatcher appeared, flying from the direction of the dunes by the ocean, with a wisp of dry sea-grass in his mouth, and darted into his hole.

"Now for it!" whispered Alan. "The minute he's off again and out of sight, we'll rush this ladder to the tree, and I'll climb up. But I want to warn you both—don't watch me while I'm up there, but keep looking around to see if you can spot him coming back. I don't want him to find me there and be scared off for good. Keep looking all round, and the minute you see him coming, call to me, and I'll pull the ladder down and at

148

least get away from the tree. Now mind! You'll want to watch
me—but don't!"

They hastily promised, and all three scrambled out to get
the ladder and set it in place. When Alan had planted it firmly,
he scurried up the steps, and the two other children began
searching the sky in every direction for the return of the flycatcher. Once Chris stole a furtive glance at Alan and saw him
examining the interior of the nest with his flashlight, but instantly turned her gaze toward the sky again.

And suddenly, even before the bird's return, Alan was scrambling down the ladder.

"Quick! Help me get this down!" he called. "I've seen all
that's necessary—and got something, too!" No sooner had he
landed on the ground than they all seized the ladder and

rushed it back into the bushes. And they were not a moment too soon, for they had only a moment to snuggle down themselves in their own hiding-place before the flycatcher returned with more beach-grass to add to his nest.

"Whew! That was a fast one!" chuckled Alan. "He never even saw me, I reckon. And I've found something pretty queer!"

"Oh, what is it?" cried Chris. "Where have you got it? Is it the snakeskin?"

"Something stranger than *that!*" chuckled Alan. "I turned the light into the nest, and it's all sort of mixed up in there. It hasn't got things straightened out yet—just collecting 'em, I think. But right on top, where he'd just laid it, I found this." He put his hand in his pocket and brought out something which he held in his palm for the others to stare at, which they did with round wondering eyes.

"It isn't snakeskin," Alan said. "You can feel it if you like, and then tell me if you can guess what it is." Peter and Chris took turns in fingering it gingerly. It was only about two inches long—a straight strip of something that looked a little like paper of a light grayish color, spotted profusely with little brownish dots. One side of it was dull, the other rather shiny. In width, it was only about half an inch or less.

"I can't think what it can be!" declared Chris.

"Nor can I," admitted Peter. "What is it, Alan? Have *you* an idea what it is?"

"I am pretty sure what it is now," said Alan, wetting his forefinger with his lips and placing that finger on the shiny side of the find. "Yes, now I'm certain. It's sticky there. It's the kind of mending-tape that comes in strips, rolled up on a spool."

"Yes, I have seen it," said Peter. "But what I saw didn't have these funny little dots or spots in it. You can't see much through this piece—they're so thick."

"I think I know the reason for that," Alan informed them. "This is a very old piece that's been lying around somewhere, and these spots are sort of rust—or mildew. Everything gets spotty with mildew down this way, after awhile, if it isn't protected or kept dry. It's the salt, damp air does it. But here's the

150

big question we've got to answer. Where in the world did that bird get hold of this queer thing? I can't think where anything of that kind would be lying around loose in these woods. I took this piece out of the nest for two reasons. I wanted to look at it carefully, for one thing. And then, I thought if he missed it, he'd probably go and get some more, and then we could watch where he went. The only place I can think of would be over on the beach, where you can find all sorts of queer rubbish cast up. Only it is quite a long way off, and this bird doesn't go over on the shore much. It prefers to keep to the meadows and woods. So somehow I think it must have been nearer here than the beach."

He sat looking at the scrap of mending-tape thoughtfully, and the other two, rather disappointed that it had not been the snakeskin, let their gaze ramble off toward the nest again. And while they looked, the bird returned with something like a fuzzy bit of feather or down and disappeared into the nest.

Suddenly Alan, who had also seen him, announced, "I have an idea! We must follow this up right away. He's missing this right now, I figure, and will probably go right back for more. Now's the time to catch him! Before he comes out, let's all go around to the other side of the house, and watch where he goes if he flies over the roof, as he did before!"

They wasted not a moment, but scrambled around the house, as inconspicuously as possible, and settled down to wait for his appearance on the same side of the house as the cellar door.

The interval they waited this time seemed to last forever. Even Alan could not account for it, except that the bird might be flying in another direction, or had been scared off completely by their interference, and gone away, never to return. Chris's watch pointed to five-thirty, and they knew they ought to return home shortly.

Suddenly Alan seized an arm of each and whispered, "Hush! Look! I think that's it—perched there on the peak of the tower. I just saw him light. Watch now!"

They watched, scarcely breathing, while the flycatcher sat twisting his head this way and that, peering about with his

151

sharp, bright eyes. Suddenly he made a swooping dive, and landed on the edge of the sloping roof that came down to the second story. There again he sat peering about, as if he sensed that he was being watched. Alan was fairly quivering with excitement. But their amazement was enormous when they saw the flycatcher dive off into the air, hover poised for a moment, and then dart in through the shutters of a tiny window almost directly under the eaves. Some of the slats in this shutter had long since rotted and fallen away, leaving an ample space for him to get through.

"Jeepers!" said Alan. "He's gotten in the house somewhere! There must be a pane of glass broken behind that shutter. It looks that way. Watch now and see him come out!"

Three minutes afterward, the flycatcher emerged, another strand of the same curious adhesive paper in his bill. "That settles it!" Alan cried. "Now we know where he got it." To-morrow we'll explore and find what room that window belongs to. It's too late now. But the queer thing is, I've been all over that house, hundreds of times, and certain that I never saw any such stuff as that paper lying around. What's funnier still, I don't remember a single room that had a window like that."

With eager expectations Peter and Chris hurried off next morning to meet Alan. From the veranda of their house, their mother watched them racing along the beach in the direction of the houseboat and wondered at their deep interest in their new friend and his affairs. They had told her, the night before, of their queer discovery of the flycatcher's nest, but had said nothing about the more disturbing matter of the intruder.

"I'll go with them sometime," she thought, "and see this strange old house. It must be rather interesting. I'd like to meet Alan's mother, too! Well, I'm too busy today. I'll try to plan it tomorrow."

Meanwhile the two children, running along the shore, had spied Alan out in front of the houseboat, digging industriously in the shallow water of the bay.

"Hi! What you doing, Alan?" called Peter, when they were near enough to be heard.

"Digging clams for Mother! There are lots of them here—
soft ones. I've been at it for an hour while I waited for you.
Got a whole basket full, so I guess I'll stop now," he ended,
throwing a shovel on the shore and rinsing off his muddy hands.
"Just wait till I put this basket in the kitchen, and we'll be off."

At this moment, Mrs. Pettingill appeared at the door, with a
package of freshly baked ginger cookies, and offered it to the
children for a snack to cheer them during the morning. And
five minutes later they were hurrying off through the woods.

"What are we going to do first today, Alan?" demanded
Peter. "Find out about that room and the paper—or go over to
the road and see if we can discover the man with the blue
sweater?"

"I think we'll let that fellow rest for a bit," decided Alan.
"He may have been so scared off yesterday that he won't come
back for a long time—perhaps never. But there's something

153

mighty queer about that little window, and where in the house the flycatcher could have found that pasting-strip. We'll do our work there first."

"Oh, we've got something to tell you!" cried Chris. "Last evening after dinner, Daddy decided to take his casting-rod and go over to the beach to do some fishing—surf-casting, you know. We went with him, and what do you think? While we were walking along the beach, there was another man standing down near the edge of the surf, fishing, and Peter and I both noticed that he was wearing a blue sweater that looked a lot like that piece you have!"

"We got so excited—and we didn't want Dad to know just yet—but we had to see whether it was torn or mended near the shoulders. Daddy wanted to go along farther, so we couldn't wait very long, but got as close up to him as we could. And just when we were getting near enough to see, he went and put on a leather jacket, because it was getting sort of chilly! Imagine! But he was sort of a nice-looking man—not the sort you'd think would break into houses."

"What kind of shoes was he wearing?" demanded Alan eagerly. "You noticed that, didn't you?"

"We thought of that specially," answered Peter, "and looked to see. But he was wearing great high rubber hip-boots for fishing, so it was no good."

"It's a new idea, though," Alan consoled them. "I hadn't thought of it. Quite a lot of men come down on this beach to fish, and it might easily be one of them who rambled over here and tried to snoop around. We'll have to look them over. Now let's get right down to brass tacks and look up this business about the window. We won't bother with the flycatcher this morning. He's told us enough! Let's take a good look at that window first."

They walked around to the side where the little window was, under the eaves, and all stood in a row and stared at it intently. It was a very small window, and not especially notice-able in any way. Tucked up close to the overhanging eaves, it appeared to be no more than two feet long and about a foot high. It was closed in by two tiny shutters with slats. In one of these, a few of the slats had evidently fallen away, leaving a gaping space, through which they were near enough to see that there must also be a broken windowpane directly behind it.

"Now, let's see," said Alan. "What room can that little window be in? I told you yesterday that I couldn't remember any window like it from the inside, but it might be in some nook or corner that I never happened to notice. Anyhow, we know it must be on the south side of the house, and I think I know the windows of the rooms that are nearest to it. Let's go right in and upstairs."

"Couldn't we get up to it by your ladder?" suggested Peter. "We could lean it against the house and look in through the window."

"The ladder isn't long enough," Alan said. "Even a tall man standing on top of it couldn't see in that window—much less any of us! You see, that window's a lot higher than the flycatcher's nest, and I had all I could do to see into *that*."

This argument being conclusive, they all ran to the cellar door, where Alan first looked about carefully for any fresh sign of unlawful entry. But there was, apparently, none. The cellar door was in place, and no new footprints appeared, either outside or inside.

"Guess it's O.K.!" Alan grinned. "Here we go!" And turning on his flashlight, disappeared into the cellar.

Up through the old, echoing house they scurried, scampering noisily up the cellar stairs to the main hall and on to the second story, reaching it breathless and laughing.

"This is the side," announced Alan, turning to his left at the top of the stairs. "The little window is somewhere in one of these rooms."

There were three closed doors facing them on that side of the hall. They made their way to the farther one, at the rear of the house, opened it, and entered a comparatively small bedroom that had two windows facing the same direction as the mysterious small one, and another at the end, looking out over the back of the house. There was no sign of the tiny win-

155

dow of their search, not even in the one clothes closet.

"It wouldn't be as far over as this, anyway," announced Alan. "Let's try the middle room." They entered this room next, but with no better result. It had three large windows all in a row, and the closet was on the opposite side of the room.

"Must be in the next then!" cried Peter. "That's the only one left."

They all made a rush for the last door on that side of the hall and entered a very large bedroom, facing both the side and the front of the house. It contained a great, canopied four-poster bed, whose musty draperies were coated with dust. A large bay window faced toward the Bay and must have had a fine view of it before the heavy growth of foliage had cut it off. This the children could see by peeping around the edges of the drawn shades.

In the wall to the left of that was another bay window the same as the front one, but facing toward the south. To the left of this window, three or four feet away, was still another window of the ordinary type. There was no other window in the room. In that same corner a door opened into a clothes closet, but on investigating it, the children found it was dark, with no window in it, as they had hoped. The back wall of the room was blank, being the one which separated it from the middle bedroom. In the corner at this end was a tall set of bookshelves, built into the wall, and crammed with musty old books from ceiling to floor. And that was simply all there was to discover.

"Well, can you beat it!" exclaimed Alan disgustedly. "Here we've searched the whole side of the house, and there isn't a *sign* of that funny little window! What can it all *mean*, I wonder?" The others could not help him out with even so much as a guess. For a moment they all stared about them in deep thought. Suddenly Peter had an idea and popped out into the hall for a moment. But he came back with the same disappointed expression on his face.

"I just thought maybe there might be a closet or something between these two rooms, opening into the hall—and that might have a window in it. But there isn't even a door there."

"I could have told you that!" grumbled Alan. Suddenly he too straightened up.

"I've thought of something!" he cried, and ran over and raised the shade on the smaller window toward the corner of the room. "You, Chris and Peter, stand here at this window, while I run down and outside, over on this side. Then I can tell by where you stand, just how far you are from that little window!"

The other children agreed enthusiastically and took their places at the window, though they were scarcely able to see out of the grimy, dusty panes. Alan left the room. They heard him clattering down the stairs, and then they heard no other sound for a time.

"It's spooky here, Peter, isn't it?" whispered Chris with a slight shiver. "We've never been all alone in this house before."

"Well, Alan's right near. I'm not afraid!" declared Peter stoutly. "We'll see him in a minute."

At that instant, Alan came hurrying into sight from around the corner of the house. He waved to them reassuringly and then proceeded to walk about, staring up at the windows. Presently, they heard him call. He was pointing to the left of their window. Then he waved again, disappeared from view, and in two minutes more was tearing up the stairs towards their room.

"Can you beat it?" he cried excitedly. "There's that little window, right around the corner from this one where the two of you are standing!"

"Then why can't we *find* it?" asked Chris, excitedly.

"I don't know!" declared Alan. "But we'll never stop trying till we *do!*"

"There's something queer about that little window," Alan went on. "You see, it's around the corner of the house from this window where we're standing. That's why you can't see it from here. This whole room stands out more from the side of the house than all the others on this side. I suppose when they built it, they wanted to make it a bigger, wider room. I think this must be the room my grandfather had. It's the biggest bedroom in the house. From the outside you can see that this part of it

157

forms a sort of corner—or *ell,* as I think they call it—and that little window is around in the other part of it. Here! I'll show you what I mean." He dug in his pocket and produced a stub of a lead pencil and a creased and grubby bit of blank paper.

"I carry this around to make sketches of strange birds I see sometimes," he told them. "Helps me to find out what they are from my bird books when I get home. Now here's a rough sketch of this room. It'll show you what I mean better than I can tell you." And he drew a plan of the room and that corner of the house.

"You see," he pointed out, "we're standing right here by the window alongside this big bay one on the south, where I've put the little dot. Then, to the left of it, is the corner which you can't see around from this window. Then here's the other corner of the room where the bookcase is. And here I've made a black space on this plan for that queer little window. You can see it plainly from outside! Then the house has another corner and goes in again before you come to the three windows in the middle room. But here's the puzzle! That little window isn't behind the bookcase—you can see that right away. Yet it *ought* to be there, according to this plan. So where *is* it?"

"I've thought of something!" cried Peter. "Why don't we go down and do a little measuring around that part? My father's an architect, and he's always measuring when he plans new houses or fusses around old ones."

"That's a good idea!" cried Alan. "You hit it right on the nail, Pete! We might get a line on something that way. Tell you what. We haven't anything to measure with here, and it's nearly lunchtime anyhow. Suppose we go on back home for lunch, and when we come back, I'll bring my mother's tape measure and we'll start to do some figuring. Let's not say anything about it yet. I haven't even told Mother a thing about this little window, because I wanted to surprise her by knowing something more about it before I did."

"We told our mother a little about it last night," said Peter, "but it was mostly about the flycatcher and the way he got that paper from a little window. I don't think that will matter much."

"No, it's all right," said Alan, "but I'd rather we would find this thing out ourselves without anybody's help."

Mrs. Cameron noticed that the children were rather excited and absent-minded and ate less than usual at lunch. She questioned them about how they had spent their morning, and they told her that they had been playing around the old Pettingill house.

"I'd like to go back with you this afternoon and see it myself," she remarked much to their consternation, "but I've promised to drop in for tea at our next-door neighbor's. I'll come another day." Both children breathed an inward sigh of relief.

When they met Alan at the houseboat, he had a long tape measure in his hand, and they hurried through the woods back to the old house.

"Funny! We've been so busy with other things, we've never even thought of the man who was trying to get in here!" said Peter, as Alan opened the cellar door.

"Oh, he's kind of discouraged, I guess!" answered Alan. "He must know now that somebody's around this place a good deal of the time, and he's waiting till it's empty. We can forget him for a while! Now, before we go in here, let's go round to that corner and do a little measuring. I want to see how many feet

159

that side on the left of the little window is, before it joins the corner of the middle room."

They scurried through the bushes, around to the spot in question, and began to measure the corner of the house in which the mysterious window was located. Chris held the end of the tape measure, while Peter stretched it, and Alan stood by, jotting down the lengths in feet and inches, on the rough little sketch he had made during the morning.

"Just six feet from the corner here by the little window to the edge of the house next to the window we stood in," said Peter, and Alan marked it down.

"Now for the distance from that corner across under the window to the edge of the next corner!" said Alan. And Peter, with his sister's help, found it to be exactly six feet and six inches. There was one more measurement Alan wanted to make —from that edge back to the next corner where it joined the wall of the middle room. And this again they found to be exactly six feet and six inches.

"That's all that's necessary, I think. Now let's go upstairs and do some measuring in the big room. We may get something by comparing them," remarked Alan. And they all hurried to the cellar stairs and up to the second floor.

"First thing we do," said Alan, "is to measure the width of the bookcase here in the corner. Stretch it out!" The children found this to be about six feet, and Alan jotted it down, comparing it with the same location on the outside—the strip under the little window. "That's about right," he commented. "It's less, of course, but you have to allow a few inches for the thickness of the walls. That fits it. Now try it from the right hand end of the bookcase back along the wall to the corner by that window where you looked out." The others did so and reported a distance of almost twelve feet, lacking only an inch. Alan put it down on his paper.

"That'll do," he said. "Now let's just compare these inside measurements with the outside ones—and see what we get." They all stood studying the paper for several moments. It was Peter who first caught on to something that seemed strange.

160

"Say—what does this mean?" he cried, looking at the paper plan. "Do you see what we found on the *outside*, on that wall to the right of the little window? From the corner there to the point near this window, it was only six feet. And yet when we measured that same side inside the room, from the end of the bookcase to this corner, it was nearly twelve! Why? We couldn't have measured it wrong!"

To the astonishment of the other two children, Alan gave a loud whoop of joy, threw down his paper, and made a dash for the bookcase.

"Peter, you're a whiz!" he chuckled. "You've hit the nail square on the head! Can't you see what it all means? There's something *in* here—*back of this bookcase*—some space that has never been accounted for! Perhaps nobody knows about it. Maybe it's a secret closet or something. Anyway, we're going to find out. Help me get these old books out of here and pile them up on the floor. I'll find out about this if I have to rip the whole bookcase down."

The three children fell eagerly to their task, gathering whole armfuls of the dusty old books at a time and dropping them carelessly on the floor. In five minutes they had the whole space cleared except two shelves near the top. These Alan reached by wheeling a chair before the bookcase and handed the remaining books to Chris and Peter below. Then the whole set of shelves stood bare, revealing only the dusty, dark-stained woodwork behind them. Two shelves near the bottom were wider apart than the others. These must have been intended for the bigger, taller books. At the top of the second shelf, which was about waist high, they noticed that the wood at the edge projected a little beyond the other shelves, and it caught Alan's attention at once.

"Why was this, I wonder?" he asked, giving it a strong jerk as he spoke. To their surprise, it came forward in his hands as he pulled at it, till it projected nearly a foot into the room.

"What's that?" demanded the wide-eyed Chris.

"Oh, I know!" cried Peter. "It's like a little desk—to write on. Dad has one that pulls out like that in his big desk at the office."

161

"That's the idea, I guess," agreed Alan. "Grandfather didn't have any separate writing desk in this room—you can see by the furniture. Maybe he used this. It's just about the right height for a desk. Yes, and here's an old ink stain on it! I just noticed it, here in the corner. That proves it. I wonder whether you can pull it out entirely. I'm going to try!"

He took hold of it by the corners and gave it a tremendous jerk. And what happened next almost sent him reeling over backward. For the shelf gave way, not at both ends, but only at the left-hand one, and swung outward, as if on a pivot at the right. And there was revealed a space at least an inch and a quarter in width, running across the entire shelf. Alan knelt down and applied his eye to the crack—and leaped to his feet instantly, with a shout of triumph.

"We're right—we're *right!* Both of you look through there! Don't you see a little light 'way back? That must be the tiny window we couldn't find that lets it in!" And while the other two were looking at the discovery, he added:

"But how we're going to get in there beats me! There must be *some* way, though—short of chopping down the whole set of shelves!"

"Why do you suppose this writing-shelf was made just this way?" asked Chris, when she had taken a long look through the slit. Does Daddy's work this way, too, Peter—loose at one corner so you can swing it around?"

"No, *sir*—it doesn't!" cried Peter. "It's caught tight all along the back."

"Then there must be some reason for this working the way it does," said Alan. "Just let me run my hand in through this slit and see if I can feel anything behind it." Chris moved away, and Alan knelt down, inserted his hand through the narrow opening, and ran it along from one corner to the other end. And at the left-hand end, they suddenly saw him push his hand in farther and fumble at something hidden. In another instant there was a decided clicking sound, and with his free arm, Alan tugged at one of the lower shelves.

And then, to their utmost amazement, the whole lower part

162

of the bookcase under the writing-shelf moved out into the room like a little door, revealing a space large enough to crawl through or scramble through by ducking the head very low.

And behind that space there stood revealed a very small room, scarcely bigger than a fair-sized closet. It was lighted dimly by a low window with a broken pane and closed shutters through which the daylight filtered into the chinks made by the broken slats!

The children stood fairly speechless at their discovery. It seemed stranger than a fairy tale. And with Alan leading the way, they all scrambled through the newly-found opening into the room of mystery.

It contained only a small table set under the window, holding some writing paper, soiled and weather-stained now and yellowed with age; an empty inkwell and some rusty pens, and one other article which Chris seized upon with a shout.

"Here's our flycatcher's find!" she cried, and held up a little roll of pasting- or mending-paper on a spool, one long end dragged out and torn, where the bird had evidently wrenched it loose.

"He must have flown in the window where it was broken and spied it here on the table. Then he thought he had just what he was looking for!" explained Alan.

For the rest, the room was furnished only with one simple wooden chair and an oil lamp in a brass bracket above the table. The little wallspace that there was was crowded with shelves of tall books in worn leather bindings, all very much alike. These the children scanned hurriedly, discovering that many of them bore only the one word in gilt letters on a black ground—the word "Blackstone."

"That's the name of a famous man who wrote a lot about laws," Alan informed the others, pointing to it. "Mother told me my grandfather had been a very successful lawyer."

The words were scarcely out of his mouth, when they were all startled by a sound, coming from the lower part of the house.

"Oh, *listen!*" cried Chris, seizing Alan's arm. "*Someone is coming up the stairs!*"

A moment of sheer terror followed, while the steps on the stairs came nearer. "What shall we do?" whispered Peter.

"Stay right where we are!" insisted Alan in a low voice. "It's too late to hide—even in here. We'll face whoever it is—and ask him what right he has in here!"

Another moment of listening to the oncoming steps.

"*Alan—where are you?*" came a clear voice from the hall, and the three children breathed a sigh of relief.

"In here, Mother!" called Alan, rushing to the doorway to meet Mrs. Pettingill.

"Mercy!" cried Mrs. Pettingill. "I've had a long hunt for you children. I need you at home, Alan, for a few minutes, to help me with—"

At this instant her eye caught sight of the interior of the room and its chaotic state, with books strewn all over the floor, the bookshelves empty and the lower part all out of kilter.

"What *have* you done here, Alan?" she asked sharply. "You've made a dreadful mess of this room! You know, I told you many times that you mustn't touch anything here. This place is not our property, legally and—"

"Oh, *wait* a minute, Mother!" cried Alan, imploringly. "Wait till you've heard the wonderful story of how we discovered this—it's a secret room! You never knew there was such a thing. And we haven't done any damage—really! Everything can be put right back where it belongs. Just sit down here a minute on this chair, and let me tell you how we came to discover it, and then I'll show it to you."

"I think," said Mrs. Pettingill, distinctly interested, "that I'd rather see it *first*—and have you tell me about it afterward!"

"Oh, *please* let me explain about it first!" begged her son. "You'll understand about it so much better if I tell you how we came to discover it."

So, to please him, Mrs. Pettingill settled down to listen to Alan's account. He told her about the crested flycatcher and how they discovered the room, but said nothing about the intruder. And when he had finished his mother was excited too.

"I must see it!" she cried. "I never heard anything more remarkable. Let's go right in!"

Alan led the way, crawling under the upper half of the bookshelves, and his mother followed him. But as the secret enclosure was so small, the other two children contented themselves with merely crouching at the opening and watching and listening to what went on from there. It was a close fit, even for Mrs. Pettingill and Alan, in that tiny, crowded space.

"I cannot understand it!" exclaimed Mrs. Pettingill. "Yet it *does* explain something I remember your father telling me about once, Alan. I'd almost forgotten. He said Grandfather Pettingill was a very strange man in some ways. He had been a very successful lawyer in his younger years, and made so much money that he could retire from active business in middle life. But even after that, other lawyers used to come to consult him frequently about knotty problems in their cases, and he used to spend long hours in his room working over them. But your father said he had frequently gone to his father's room to find him, when he was supposed to be shut up there, and strangely enough, the room would be empty. Then sometime later the old man would be found in his room again, though how he had gotten back there, he never explained. Your father used to think Grandfather Pettingill had gone out to walk in the woods or on the beach, but undoubtedly this explains it. He must have had this secret room to retire to."

"Mother," began Alan, "is it possible—"

But this was as far as he got. For Chris suddenly broke in, "*Alan—quick!* Come out here a minute."

"What is it?" demanded Alan, crawling out of the low opening.

"I hear footsteps somewhere overhead! Just soft ones, but it seems as if someone were moving around upstairs!"

Quick as a flash, Alan was at the door, followed by the two

166

children and, an instant later, by Mrs. Pettingill. As they glanced out into the hall, a figure was huddled at the top of the stairs leading to the floor above!

"Why—it's a *girl!*" stuttered Chris. "And—and—we thought it was a man, all the time."

The huddled figure at the top of the stairs straightened up. It was indeed a young girl, of about fourteen or fifteen, tall and rather athletic in build, with fluffy light hair on which was perched a gray-blue worsted cap. They noticed that her gray-blue sweater was considerably torn and raveled on one shoulder! The stranger surveyed the group below with smouldering brown eyes and a belligerent expression.

"What business have you got in this house?" she demanded.

"That's just what we were going to ask *you!*" answered Alan indignantly. "You have been trying for several days to get in here. We knew that. We thought it was a man—from the traces you left—but now that we've caught you, you'd better do the explaining yourself!"

"You haven't any right in here—and I have!"

"*Well,* of all the nerve!" began Alan, but his mother laid a restraining hand on his arm.

"I think you'd better explain about this to me, my dear! I don't understand all these allusions of Alan's to an 'intruder,' but if you think you have any right to come into this house, you'd better tell me about it. I'm Mrs. Pettingill, whose husband's father owned this house, and this is my son."

At the mention of the name Pettingill, the stranger's eyes flashed wide open.

"*Pettingill?*" she stammered. "Why that's *my* name, too— Estelle Pettingill!"

"You say your name is Pettingill?" asked Alan's mother. "Suppose you come down and join us here. We are not going to harm you—but I must have an explanation of this."

The girl slowly descended the stairs and joined the group in the hall below. And Mrs. Pettingill led them all into a bedroom across the hall from the one which contained the secret room, raised the dusty shades to admit more light, and introduced

167

Peter and Chris to the newcomer as friends of her son.

"Now, my dear," she began, addressing Estelle, who sat uneasily on the edge of the bed, "you say your last name is Pettingill? Are you, by chance, some distant relative of the man who once owned this house?"

"*Distant?*" cried the girl scornfully. "I'm his *granddaughter!*"
This announcement caused a new wave of astonishment.

"Then you must be the daughter of his son Ethan?"

"That's just who I am," announced the girl. "You must know the family history pretty well, I should say, as Dad hasn't been in this country for over twenty years!"

"I have good reason to know it," said Mrs. Pettingill quietly, "as I married Ethan's only brother Frederick, who is dead now. This is our son—and your Cousin Alan!"

The girl stared at her almost incredulously. "So *that's* who you are!" she said at last. "You know, I never even dreamed that you were anywhere in this region."

"But I don't understand," went on Mrs. Pettingill. "I never heard that your father was married—or had a daughter!"

"He never told anyone over here, I guess," said the girl. "In fact, I think he never wrote to anyone except his lawyers, in this country, and he hasn't written to them for years. He was so disgusted with them because they couldn't seem to settle Grandfather Pettingill's estate."

"Is your father here now?" questioned Mrs. Pettingill.

"No, he's still in India. But Mother and I came over here a few months ago."

"Why don't you begin at the beginning," said Mrs. Pettingill, "and tell us the whole story. When did your father marry?"

"He met my mother in India," began Estelle, "about seventeen years ago. She was an American girl, the daughter of a minister. They were married and lived there for awhile. But he always wanted to travel and explore; so he wasn't home a great deal. Mother and I had to stay alone a lot, but we lived with my other grandfather there; so we weren't very lonely. Grandfather just died about a year ago, and Mother felt very sad about it. She isn't very well, either. The climate affected her

168

health after awhile, and that's why she came away. We visited
in England, but she didn't get any better, so finally we came to
America because she thought it would help her. We were in
New York for three months; then she thought she'd like to try it
down this way, because the doctors said the sea air would be
good for her. We've been staying at the hotel uptown."

"Did you know that it was very near where your grandfather's old place was?" asked Mrs. Pettingill. The girl hesitated
a moment before answering.

"Yes," she acknowledged at last. "We knew it—that's why
we chose this place." There was a moment's silence and Estelle
went on, "Oh, it's such a long, queer story! I might as well
tell you all about it, now. Dad isn't very well any more, either.
He injured his leg a few years ago, while he was hunting in

Indo-China, and it's beginning to bother him so he can't travel any more. And he hasn't much money left either. He used to have a lot that he said his father gave him—but now he only has a small amount left, enough for us to live on simply somewhere. But no more traveling and exploring and things like that!"

"He told me, before we came away, all about his father and this property and his brother—and how things had never been settled up because they couldn't find any will. He said he had been very angry about it once—because he always knew his brother was his father's favorite, and it had hurt him. But now he didn't care any more. He knew his brother was dead and he didn't know what had become of his brother's family—if he had any. He told me he was getting old and tired—and he'd like to come back home and settle down sometime—if only they could get this matter of the property fixed up."

Here the girl's voice broke a bit, for it was evident that her father's condition worried her. But she went on again:

"He said that if Mother and I should get down this way during our stay, that—that I might just try to hunt up the location of the old house and—and look it over quietly if I could, without letting anyone know what I was doing. He said he had always felt certain that grandfather had really left a will—somewhere—though none had ever been found. He thought perhaps if I could be alone in the house, I might find it in some hidden nook or corner. Even if it left the house to his brother, my father thought it might be fixed somehow with his brother's family, if he'd left any—and—and Dad might be able to buy it back—or some such arrangement. Anything, he said, so long as it was settled! If I ever did find anything, I was to write him at once.

"Well, we came down here. I had a bicycle with me, so I could get around quite a bit. After a while I asked in town about the old Pettingill place, and a woman in the drugstore told me where it was, but that I couldn't get to it because it was so overgrown now. I rode down here one day and saw the tower of it from the road and I spent several days trying to poke my way through the woods. But I only tore my clothes and got nowhere;

so I gave that up. One day I hired a rowboat at the public dock in town and *rowed* down here and saw it was much nearer the Bay than the road.

"I poked and fussed around till finally I managed to squirm my way right up to it. I tried all the doors and windows within reach, but I couldn't budge one of them. Then, as I passed the cellar door, I gave it a good pull, just as an experiment, and it came open! Then I knew I could get in. I went down into the cellar and a little way in toward the stairs, but it was all so dark that I decided I'd better come another day and bring my flashlight with me. So I went out and back to the boat again."

"That must have been when you left that footprint in the sand!" exclaimed Alan.

"Did I leave a footprint?" Estelle asked. "I never thought about it."

"That's the first we knew someone had been in there," he explained. "You left a print right at the foot of the cellar steps. But it was only half a print—and we thought it was a man's!"

"I know I have a pretty big foot," smiled Estelle, looking down ruefully, "and these brogues I wear don't make them look any smaller. Well, a couple of mornings later, I took the boat again and rowed to a place near here on the shore and came through the woods. I got to the cellar door, raised it and went in, turned my flashlight on and got as far as the kitchen steps, when I heard voices and footsteps come running down from somewhere upstairs. I was so scared, I just turned and ran to the cellar door and up the steps. And when I went to close the cellar door, I let it fall with a crash. That scared me worse than ever, and I ran off through the woods, as fast as I could go, thinking someone was after me all the time!"

At this point, Alan chuckled and said: "And all *that* time we were hiding in a closet upstairs, thinking there was some terrible man in the house!"

"Alan Pettingill!" exclaimed his mother. "Do you mean to tell me all these strange things were going on—and you never told me a word about it?"

"I didn't want to scare you, Mother!" laughed Alan. "We

were all set to find out first who the intruder was—and we got sidetracked by the crested flycatcher!"

Estelle stared at him, at this remark, as if she thought he had suddenly gone crazy. But after a moment she went on with her story, "I'd torn my sweater on a tree and got pretty well mussed up, so I decided to go on back to town, after I found no one was following me."

"Yes, we have a sample of your sweater right here!" interrupted Alan, pulling the blue-gray wisp of wool out of his pocket. "We've been looking ever since for a *man* with a sweater like that! We found it hanging on a twig over in the woods!"

And at this, Estelle herself laughed. But she continued, "Thinking it over, last night, I decided that it must have been only some children playing in here, because the voices sort of sounded like it. And I made up my mind that I'd try it again today. I was not going to be afraid of any children, and I had decided to shoo them out of here if I found them again. I couldn't get here this morning, but after Mother could spare me, I got away early in the boat and came to the house and found the cellar door shut and no one about. So I got in at last and found my way upstairs with my flashlight. I was just looking around in these rooms on this floor, when I heard voices again—and someone coming up the cellar stairs.

"I wasn't taking any chances till I'd seen who it was, and I didn't know which way to go. But I thought I'd go up to the next floor and try to hide in some closet—or get out of sight somewhere. And I ran to the floor above.

"I was scared stiff till I realized that it *was* some children again and that they didn't seem to be coming up any farther than here, but were all busy doing something or other in that big room across the hall. I had half a mind to go right down and shoo them out, but I thought first I'd listen and see what they were about and why they were in here. I couldn't hear much—and they kept running in and out and then I heard thumping on the floor, like books or something being thrown down. And then all was very quiet. I'd just made up my mind

172

to go down, when I heard someone else coming into the house and a woman's voice calling, 'Alan!'

"Then I felt I was surely caught. I didn't mind some children, but I didn't want to meet any older person. So, while you were all in that room, I decided to slip downstairs and out without being seen, if I could. Unfortunately one of those steps was old and creaky and made a loud sound as I was coming down."

"That's what I heard first!" declared Chris, proud to have done something of interest.

"Well—that's all. I've told you everything—and you've certainly given me the surprise of my life!" ended Estelle.

"No more than you gave us!" said Alan.

During the latter part of Estelle's story, Mrs. Pettingill had been very quiet, evidently sunk in deep thought. But when Estelle had finished, she turned to the children.

"We're going back," she announced, "into that little room we've just discovered. If I'm not mistaken, *that* holds one further secret! I'm going to look for that will. It must be hidden somewhere in that secret room!"

"What in the world are you talking about?" asked the newcomer. "*What* secret room? Was that what you've been so busy about?"

"Right!" cried Alan. "And you'd never guess how we found it! It was a bird that showed us the way!" Estelle gave him a doubtful look, but he only grinned and added, "We'll tell you the whole story later."

When they had entered the big room, Estelle looked about her at the wild confusion of books piled in heaps all about the floor, and the bookcase opened like a door at the bottom.

"So *this* is what you were doing when I heard that thumping and banging! It sounded as if you were wrecking the place. What did you find?"

"They found *this*," said Mrs. Pettingill, a little breathlessly, pointing to the entrance to the secret room. "Never mind how —we'll clear all that up later. The main thing is to get in there, Estelle, you and Alan and myself. Peter and Chris can watch through the opening. I'm sorry there isn't room for us all to get

173

in at once. But it's very fortunate you are here, Estelle, to help us hunt for this document, for you and your parents are concerned in it just as much as we are." The three crawled through the low, narrow opening into the crowded room, and Peter and Chris remained outside. Estelle's eyes were wide with wonder at the strange place and its contents.

"Now, let's see!" said Mrs. Pettingill. "Where shall we begin?"

"How about this table drawer?" asked Alan, pointing to a drawer in the table in front of the window. "That's the likeliest place, isn't it?" He pulled it open with some difficulty, for after years of disuse it stuck obstinately. But to their immense disappointment, it contained only some odd pieces of blank legal paper and a very rusty pair of scissors.

"Might be some secret place in this table—over or under the drawer," he suggested. And pulling the drawer out completely, he examined it with his flashlight, omitting no hidden nook or cranny. But the table had no secret hiding-places, so far as he could tell.

"If it isn't there, I can't think of another place in this room where it might be," said Mrs. Pettingill, surveying the tiny space disconsolately, "except in among all these old law books on the shelves. Come to think of it, it wouldn't be at all unlikely that Grandfather Pettingill might have left it in one of those. Anyway, it's the only place left to look, so we'll have to get at it. Where shall we begin? There must be a hundred or more of these dusty old volumes in here!"

"Wait a minute!" Alan said. "Why couldn't we do it this way? Do you think it would have been likely that Grandfather Pettingill really tried to *hide* that will? I think he may have come in here to look it over—or something like that—and not be disturbed. Wasn't that what we thought he had this room for? So it wouldn't be much good to start hunting among all those old books way at the top and out of reach. If he put it in any one, wouldn't it be likely to be one down here near the table where he was sitting—sort of within reach of his hand? I think we might begin there. Then, if we don't find it, we can go on to the rest."

"Good boy!" his mother smiled. "You do have some worthwhile ideas—at times! Now, let's look along the shelves right here at the right-hand side of the table."

She took out the nearest dusty volume and rifled through its pages without coming upon anything of interest. Alan took the next one, but Estelle decided to begin on the other side of the table and took down a large volume, opening it gingerly.

"This is called *Testamentary Jurisprudence,* she remarked, looking idly at the title. "I wonder what that means?"

Mrs. Pettingill answered, looking up from her own book, "I think that means the laws about making wills. Look through that carefully, Estelle. It sounds hopeful!"

"Oh, *look!* Here *is* something!" cried the girl. "It lay right about in the middle. Can this be it?" And she picked up a folded packet of paper and held it out to Mrs. Pettingill.

"Oh, Estelle, you've *found* it at last!" cried Alan's mother, turning the document on the other side. "See! Here it is printed: *'Last Will and Testament of William Osborne Pettingill'!* Oh, my dears! let's get out of this stuffy place! Come out into the other room and we'll look this over!"

They all scrambled through the opening into the larger room, Mrs. Pettingill bearing the precious document. Peter and Christine, their eyes almost popping out of their heads with excitement, clustered about her to get a view of the amazing find.

"Let's go downstairs and out into the air," suggested Alan.

She agreed promptly, and they were presently outside in the afternoon sunshine, where Mrs. Pettingill sat down on the grass and drew in long breaths of the clear, pine-scented air.

"I'm better now," she said at last. "We'll look over the will and see what it says." And she opened the document carefully. It consisted of four sheets of legal paper, bound with an outer sheet of plain, light blue, fastened with clips at the top and folded twice. The will itself was typewritten, and she looked through it rapidly.

"Oh, *read* it to us, Mother!" cried Alan impatiently. But his mother shook her head, and reaching the last page said,—

"No, I won't read it all—it's rather long and complicated and uses so many legal terms that I don't think you'd understand it. I scarcely do myself—all of it—but this much will interest you:

" 'I do give and bequeath to my younger son, Frederick William, my house and land on the bay shore, free and clear, to have for himself and his heirs, and to do with as he shall see fit.'

So that's that!" She sighed and sat back against the tree.

"Hey!" cried Alan jubilantly. "It's all settled, isn't it! That solves the riddle at last!" He took the document and began looking it over.

"Well," remarked Estelle solemnly, getting to her feet as if she were about to leave, "that about finishes us up, I guess! You have the place now—without any question. So, as that's about all, I think I'll be getting back to Mother. I've left her a long time!"

"Oh, wait a moment, Estelle!" implored Mrs. Pettingill, putting out a protesting hand. "Sit down here beside me again.

176

I—I just want to think clearly for a moment—I'm so confused and upset!" She was silent for a moment. While Estelle sat down beside her, the three other children sat waiting. Mrs. Pettingill spoke presently.

"You must forgive me for this hesitation. I feel so confused that I hardly know what to say. But of one thing I'm certain. We do not want this—shall I call it 'family feud'?—to continue any longer. Two of those most intimately concerned in it are dead and gone now. And your father is the only one left. My husband more than once said to me before he died that he would have been only too glad to share this property with your father, Estelle, if he would only agree to come home and make peace, instead of fighting what he knew to be his own father's wishes. But Ethan never would. Now, I think, he must feel differently.

"But here is my plan, so far as I can make any. After we have taken this will to the lawyers and have the affair settled, I want to make this arrangement. You and your father and mother shall come here, if you all wish, take this old house, with as much ground around it as you care to have, for your own home. I shall deed it over to you for your own. As for the rest, I shall keep an ample piece of land on the edge of the Bay and build a little house there for Alan and myself to live in comfortably. The rest we may sell, from time to time, for land in this region is becoming quite valuable for summer homes. When you go to town, Estelle, Alan, and I will go with you, and meet your mother, and tell her the surprising news. Does that make it all right?"

For an instant the girl looked at her, too astounded to speak. At length she managed to stammer:

"Oh—oh!—you don't know—what this will—mean to us!" And then she flung her arms about Mrs. Pettingill. Suddenly Alan created a diversion by shouting:

"Hey—everybody! I've discovered something! Look at this will! Do you notice that every single page has a bit of that mending-tape on it, just about the middle near the left-hand edge? I bet I know how that happened! Mother, didn't you say

177

that they thought Grandfather had torn up this will? Well, I believe he started to—and then changed his mind and pasted it up again—with that same mending-tape we saw on the desk. Now we know the reason for it!"

This discovery was hailed with wild appreciation by all but Estelle, who had by now regained her poise, and to whom the episode of the bird and the mending-tape was still a puzzle.

"He may have done it the very day before he had that stroke," commented Mrs. Pettingill. "And I think he must have left the will in the secret room accidentally, intending to bring it out and file it with his other papers later—and he never lived to do so or tell where it was!"

"Look! Oh, look, Mrs. Pettingill!" suddenly interrupted Chris, pointing at the roof of the house. "There's the crested flycatcher now! Maybe he's going back in there for more paper!" The olive-tinted bird sat poised for a moment on the roof, his crest glistening in the afternoon sunlight—and then darted out of sight. And at the same moment Alan scrambled to his feet, calling back, "Wait a minute! I'll be back right away!" And he disappeared down the cellar steps.

He was back very shortly with something in his hand, which they instantly saw was the spool of mending-tape. And, unrolling it and tearing it off in short lengths, he ran over to the tree where the flycatcher was building its nest and dropped the whole thing at the foot of it.

"Why did you do that, Alan?" demanded Peter when he had returned to them.

"Because, if it hadn't been for that flycatcher, we'd have never discovered the will," Alan laughed. "It's shown us the way, and now we're going to make things easier for *it*. Instead of trying to get in that broken shutter, it can pick the whole thing up at the foot of the tree. It—well—it's just a kind of *thank-offering!*"

Henry Sydnor Harrison

MISS HINCH

ILLUSTRATED BY *Walter R. Sabel*

IN GOING from a given point on 126th Street to the subway station at 125th, it is not usual to begin by circling the block to 127th Street, especially in sleet, darkness, and deadly cold. When two people pursue so unusual a course at the same time, moving unobtrusively on opposite sides of the street, in the nature of things the coincidence is likely to attract the attention of one or the other of them.

In the bright light of the entrance to the tube they came almost face to face, and the clergyman took a good look at her. Certainly she was a decent-looking old body, if any woman was: white-haired, wrinkled, spectacled, and stooped. A thoroughly respectable domestic servant of the upper class she looked, in her old black hat, wispy veil, and blue shawl. Nevertheless, the reverend gentleman, going more slowly down the drafty steps, continued to study her from behind with a singular intentness.

An express train was just thundering in, which the clergyman, handicapped as he was by his clubfoot and stout cane, was barely in time to catch. He entered the same car with the

179

woman and chanced to take a seat directly across from her. It must have been then after half-past eleven o'clock, and the wildness of the weather was discouraging to travel. The car was almost deserted. Even in this underground retreat the bitter breath of the night blew and bit, and the old woman shivered under her shawl. At last, her teeth chattering, she got up in an apologetic sort of way and moved toward the better protected rear of the car, feeling the empty seats as she went, in a palpable search for hot pipes. The clergyman's eyes followed her candidly, and he watched her sink down, presently, into a seat on his own side of the car. A young couple sat between them now; he could no longer see the woman, beyond occasional glimpses of her black knees and her ancient bonnet, skewered on with a long steel hatpin.

Nothing could have seemed more trivial than this change of seats on the part of a thin-blooded and half-frozen passenger. But it happened to be a time of mutual doubt and mistrust in the metropolis, of alert suspicions and hair-trigger watchfulness, when men looked askance into every strange face and the most infinitesimal incidents were likely to take on a hysterical importance. Through days of fruitless searching for a fugitive outlaw of extraordinary gifts, the nerve of the city had been slowly strained to the breaking point. All jumped, now, when anybody cried "Boo!" and the hue and cry went up falsely twenty times a day.

The clergyman pondered; mechanically he turned up his coat collar and fell to stamping his icy feet. He was an Episcopal clergyman, by his garb—rather short, very full-bodied, not to say fat, bearded, and somewhat puffy-faced, with heavy cheeks cut by deep creases. Well-lined against the cold though he was, he, too, began to suffer visibly, and presently was forced to retreat in his turn, seeking out a new place where the heating apparatus gave a better account of itself. He found one only two seats beyond the old serving woman, limped into it, and soon relapsed into his own thoughts.

The young couple, now half the car-length away, were very thoroughly absorbed in each other's society. The fifth traveler,

181

a withered old gentleman sitting across the aisle, napped fitfully upon his cane. The woman in the hat and shawl sat in a sad kind of silence; and the train hurled itself roaringly through the tube. After a time, she glanced timidly at the meditating clergyman, and her look fell swiftly from his face to the discarded "ten-o'clock extra" lying by his side. She removed her dim gaze and let it travel casually about the car; but before long it returned again, pointedly, to the newspaper. Then, with some obvious hesitation, she bent forward and said,—

"Excuse me, Father, but would you please let me look at your paper a minute, sir?"

The clergyman came out of his reverie instantly and looked up with almost an eager smile.

"Certainly. Keep it if you like; I am quite through with it. But," he said, in a pleasant deep voice, "I am an Episcopal minister, not a priest."

"Oh, sir—I beg your pardon; I thought—"

He dismissed the apology with a smile and a good-natured wave of the hand.

The woman opened the paper with decent cotton-gloved fingers. The garish headlines told the story at a glance: "Earth Opened and Swallowed Miss Hinch—Headquarters Virtually Abandons Case—Even Jessie Dark"—so the black capitals ran on—"Seems Stumped." Below the spread was a luridly written but flimsy narrative, marked "By Jessie Dark," which at once confirmed the odd implication of the caption. Jessie Dark, it was manifest, was one of those most extraordinary of the products of yellow journalism, a woman "crime expert," now in action. More than this, she was a crime expert to be taken seriously, it seemed—no mere office-desk sleuth, but an actual performer with, unexpectedly enough, a somewhat formidable list of notches on her gun. So much, at least, was to be gathered from her own newspaper's loud display of "Jessie Dark's Triumphs":

March 2, 1901. Caught Julia Victorian, alias Gregory, the brains of the "Healey Ring" kidnapers.

October 7-29, 1903. Found Mrs. Trotwood and secured the letter that convicted her of the murder of her lover, Ellis E. Swan.

December 17, 1903. Ran down Charles Bartsch in a Newark laundry and trapped a confession from him.

July 4, 1904. Caught Mary Calloran and recovered the Stratford jewels.

And so on—nine "triumphs" in all; and nearly every one of hem, as even the least observant reader could hardly fail to 10tice, involved the capture of a woman.

Nevertheless, it could not be pretended that the "snappy" paragraphs in this evening's extra seemed to foreshadow a new or tenth triumph on the part of Jessie Dark at an early date; and the old serving-woman in the car presently laid down the newspaper with an irrepressible sigh.

The clergyman glanced toward her kindly. The sigh was so audible that it seemed to be almost an invitation; besides, public interest in the great case was so tense that conversation between total strangers was the rule wherever two or three were gathered together.

"You were reading about this strange mystery, perhaps?"

The woman, with a sharp intake of breath, answered: "Yes, sir. Oh, sir, it seems as if I couldn't think of anything else."

"Ah?" he said, without surprise. "It certainly appears to be a remarkable affair."

Remarkable indeed the affair seemed. In a tiny little room within ten steps of Broadway, at half-past nine o'clock on a fine evening, Miss Hinch had killed John Catherwood with the light sword she used in her well-known representation of the Father of his Country. Catherwood, it was known, had come to tell her of his approaching marriage; and ten thousand amateur detectives, athirst for rewards, had required no further "motive" of a creature so notorious for fierce jealousy. So far the tragedy was commonplace enough. What had given it extraordinary interest was the amazing faculty of the woman, which had made her famous while she was still in her teens. Coarse, violent, utterly unmoral she might be; but she happened also to be the most astonishing impersonator of her time. Her brilliant "act" consisted of a series of character changes, many of them done in full sight of the audience with the assistance only of a small table of properties half concealed under a net. Some of these transformations were so amazing as to be beyond belief, even after one had sat and watched them. Not her appearance only, but voice, speech, manner, carriage, all shifted incredibly to fit the new part; so that the woman appeared to have no permanent form or fashion of her own, but to be only so much plastic human material out of which her cunning could mold at will man, woman, or child.

With this strange skill, hitherto used only to enthrall huge audiences, the woman known as Miss Hinch—she appeared to be without a first name—was now fighting for her life somewhere against the police of the world. Without artifice, she was a tall, thin young woman with strongly marked features and considerable beauty of a bold sort. What she would look like at the present moment nobody could even venture a guess. Having stabbed John Catherwood in her dressing-room at the theater, she had put on her hat and coat, dropped two wigs and her make-up kit into a handbag, said good night to the doorman, and walked out into Broadway. Within ten minutes the dead body of Catherwood was found and the chase begun. That had been two weeks ago. Since then, no one had seen her. The earth, indeed, seemed to have opened and swallowed her. Yet her features were almost as well known as a president's.

"A very remarkable case," repeated the clergyman, rather absently; and his neighbor, the old woman, respectfully agreed that it was. After that she hesitated a moment, and then added, with sudden bitterness:

"Oh, they'll never catch her, sir—never! She's too smart for 'em all, Miss Hinch is."

Attracted by her tone, the divine inquired if she was particularly interested in the case.

"Yes, sir—I got reason to be. Jack Catherwood's mother and me was at school together, and great friends all our life long.

184

Oh, sir," she went on, as if in answer to his look of faint surprise, "Jack was a fine gentleman, with manners and looks and all beyond his people. But he never grew away from his old mother, sir—no, sir, never! And I don't believe ever a Sunday passed that he didn't go up and set the afternoon away with her, talking and laughing just like he was a little boy again. Maybe he done things he hadn't ought, as high-spirited lads will, but he was a good boy in his heart. And it does seem hard for him to die like that—and that hussy free to go her way, ruinin' and killin'."

"My good woman," said the clergyman presently, "compose yourself. No matter how diabolical this woman's skill is, her sin will assuredly find her out."

The woman dutifully lowered her handkerchief and tried to compose herself, as bidden.

"But oh, sir, she's that clever—diabolical, just as ye say, sir. Through poor Jack we of course heard much gossip about her, and they do say that her best tricks was not done on the stage at all. They say, sir, that, sittin' around a table with her friends, she could begin and twist her face so strange and terrible that they would beg her to stop, and jump up and run from the table—frightened out of their lives, sir, grown-up people. And let her only step behind her screen for a minute—for she kept her secrets well, Miss Hinch did—and she'd come walking out to you, and you could go right up to her in the full light and take her hand, and still you couldn't make yourself believe that it was her."

"Yes," said the clergyman, "I have heard that she is remarkably clever—though, as a stranger in this part of the world, I never saw her act. It is all very interesting and strange."

He turned his head and stared through the rear door at the dark, flying walls. At the same moment the woman turned her head and stared full at the clergyman. When he turned back, her gaze had gone off toward the front of the car, and he picked up the paper thoughtfully.

"I'm a visitor in the city, from Denver, Colorado," he said presently, "and knew little or nothing about the case until an

185

evening or two ago, when I attended a meeting of gentlemen here. The men's club of St. Matthias' Church—perhaps you know the place? Upon my word, they talked of nothing else. I confess they got me quite interested in their gossip. So tonight I bought this paper to see what this extraordinary woman detective it employs had to say about it. We don't have such things in the West, you know. But I must say I was disappointed, after all the talk about her."

"Yes, sir, indeed, and no wonder, for she's told Mrs. Catherwood herself that she's never made such a failure as this, so far. It seemed like she could always catch women, sir, up to this. It seemed like she knew in her own mind just what a woman would do, where she'd try to hide and all; and so she could find them time and time when the men detectives didn't know where to look. But oh, sir, she's never had to hunt for such a woman as Miss Hinch before!"

"No? I suppose not," said the clergyman. "Her story here in the paper certainly seems to me very poor."

"*Story*, sir! Bless my soul!" suddenly exploded the old gentleman across the aisle, to the surprise of both. "You don't suppose the clever little woman is going to show her hand in those stories, with Miss Hinch in the city and reading every line."

The approach to his station, it seemed, had roused him from his nap just in time to overhear the clergyman's criticism. Now he answered the looks of the old woman and the divine with an elderly cackle.

"Excuse my intrusion! I can't sit silent and hear anybody run down Jessie Dark. No, sir! Why there's a man at my boarding-place—astonishing young fellow named Hardy, Tom Hardy—who's known her for *years!* As to those stories, sir, I can assure you that she puts in them *exactly the opposite of what she really thinks!*"

"You don't tell me!" said the clergyman encouragingly.

"Yes, sir! Oh, she plays the game—yes, yes! She has her private ideas, her clues, her schemes. The woman doesn't live who is clever enough to hoodwink Jessie Dark. I look for developments any day—any day, sir!"

186

A new voice joined in. The young couple down the car had been frankly listening; and it was illustrative of the public mind at the moment that, as they now rose for their station, the young fellow felt perfectly free to offer his contribution:

"Tremendously dramatic situation, isn't it? Those two clever women pitted against each other in a life-and-death struggle, fighting it out silently in the underground somewhere—keen professional pride on one side and the fear of the electric chair on the other."

"Oh, yes! Oh, yes!" exclaimed the old gentleman rather testily. "But, my dear sir, it's not *professional pride* that makes Jessie Dark so resolute to win. It's feminine jealousy, if you follow me—no offense, madam. Yes, sir! Women never have the slightest respect for each other's abilities—not the slightest. No mercy for each other, either! I tell you, Jessie Dark'd be ashamed to be beaten by another woman. Read her stories between the lines, sir—as I do. Invincible determination—no weakening—no mercy! You catch my point, sir?"

"It sounds reasonable," answered the Colorado clergyman, with his courteous smile. "All women, we are told, are natural rivals at heart."

"Oh, I'm for Jessie Dark every time!" the young fellow broke in eagerly—"especially since the police have practically laid down. But—"

"Why, she's told my young friend Hardy," the old gentleman rode him down, "that she'll find Hinch if it takes her a lifetime! Knows a thing or two about actresses, she says. Says the world isn't big enough for the creature to hide from her. Well! What do you think of that?"

"Tell them what we were just talking about, George," said the young wife, looking at her husband with admiring eyes.

"But oh, sir," began the old woman timidly, "Jack Catherwood's been dead two weeks now, and—and——"

"Two weeks, madam! And what is that, pray?" exploded the old gentleman, rising triumphantly. "A lifetime, if necessary! Oh, never fear! Miss Victorian was considered pretty clever, wasn't she? Remember what Jessie Dark did for her? Nan

Parmalee, too—though the police did their best to steal Miss Dark's credit. She'll do just as much for Miss Hinch—you may take it from me!"

"But how's she going to make the capture, gentlemen?" cried the young fellow, getting his chance at last. "That's the point my wife and I've been discussing. Assuming that she succeeds in spotting this woman-devil, what will she *do?* Now——"

"Do, sir! Yell for the police!" burst from the old gentleman at the door.

"And have Miss Hinch shoot her—and then herself, too?"

"Grand Central!" cried the guard; and the young fellow broke off reluctantly to find his pretty wife towing him strongly toward the door.

"Hope she nabs her soon, anyway," he called back to the clergyman over his shoulder. "The thing's getting on my nerves."

The door rolled shut behind him, and the train flung itself on its way. Within the car, a lengthy silence ensued. The clergyman stared thoughtfully at the floor, and the old woman fell back upon her borrowed paper. She appeared to be rereading the observations of Jessie Dark with considerable care. Presently she lowered the paper and began a quiet search for something under the folds of her shawl; at length, her hands emerging empty, she broke the silence with a timid request:

"Oh, sir—have you a pencil you could lend me, please? I'd like to mark something in the piece to send to Mrs. Catherwood. It's what she says here about the disguises, sir."

The kindly divine felt in his pockets, and after some hunting produced a pencil—a fat white one with blue lead. She thanked him gratefully.

"How is Mrs. Catherwood bearing all this strain and anxiety?" he asked suddenly. "Have you seen her today?"

"Oh, yes, sir. I've been spending the evening with her since seven o'clock and am just back from there now. Oh, she's very much broke up, sir."

She looked at him hesitatingly. He stared straight in front of him, saying nothing, though he knew, in common with the rest of the reading world, that Jack Catherwood's mother lived, not on 126th Street, but on East Tenth. Presently he wondered if his silence had not been an error of judgment. Perhaps that misstatement had not been a slip, but something cleverer.

The woman went on with a certain eagerness: "Oh, sir, I only hope and pray those gentlemen may be right; but it does look to Mrs. Catherwood, and me too, that if Jessie Dark was going to catch her at all, she'd have done it before now. Look at those big, bold blue eyes Miss Hinch had, sir, with lashes an inch long, they say, and that terrible long chin. They do say she can change the color of her eyes, not forever of course, but put a few of her drops into them and make them look entirely different for a time. But that chin, sir, ye'd say——"

She broke off; for the clergyman had suddenly picked up his heavy stick and risen.

"Here we are at Fourteenth Street," he said, nodding pleasantly. "I must change here. Good night. Success to Jessie Dark, I say!"

He was watching the woman's faded face intently, and he saw just that look of respectful surprise break into it that he had expected.

189

"Fourteenth Street, sir! I'd no notion at all we'd come so far. It's where I get out too, sir, the expresses not stopping at my station."

"Ah?" said the clergyman, with the utmost dryness.

He led the way, limping and leaning on his stick. They emerged upon the chill and cheerless platform. The clergyman, after stumping along a few steps, stopped and turned. The woman had halted. Over the intervening space their eyes met.

"Come," said the man gently. "Come, let us walk about a little to keep warm."

"Oh, sir—it's too kind of you, sir," said the woman, coming forward.

From other cars two or three blue-nosed people had got off to make the change; one or two more came straggling in from the street; but, scattered over the bleak concrete expanse, they detracted little from the isolation that seemed to surround the woman and the clergyman. Step for step, the odd pair made their way to the extreme northern end of the platform.

"By the way," said the clergyman, halting abruptly, "may I see that paper again for a moment?"

"Oh, yes, sir—of course," said the woman, producing it from beneath her shawl. "If you want it back, sir——"

He said that he wanted only to glance at it for a moment; but he fell to looking through it page by page, with considerable care. The woman glanced at him several times with timid respect. Finally she said hesitatingly:

"I think, sir, I'll ask the ticketchopper how long before the next train. I'm very late as it is, sir; and I still must stop to get something to eat before I go to bed."

"An excellent idea," said the clergyman.

He explained that he, too, was already an hour behind time, and was spending the night with cousins in Newark, to boot. Side by side, they retraced their steps down the platform, ascertained the schedule from the sleepy chopper, and, as by some tacit consent, started slowly back again. But, before they had gone very far, the woman all at once stopped short and, with a white face, leaned against the wall.

190

"Oh, sir, I'm afraid I'll just have to stop and get a bite somewhere before I go on. You'll think me foolish, sir; but I missed my supper entirely tonight, and there is quite a faint feeling coming over me."

The clergyman looked at her with apparent concern. "Do you know, my friend, you seem to anticipate all my own wants? Your mentioning something to eat just now reminded me that I myself was all but famishing." He glanced at his watch, appearing to deliberate. "Yes, there is still time before my train. Come, we will find a modest eating-place together."

"Oh, sir," she stammered, "but—you wouldn't want to eat with a poor old woman like me, sir."

"And why not? Are we not all equal in the sight of God?"

They ascended the stairs together, like any prosperous parson and his poor parishioner, and, coming out into Fourteenth Street, started west. In the first block they came to a restaurant, a brilliantly lighted, tiled, and polished place of the quick-lunch variety. But the woman timidly preferred not to stop here, saying that the glare of such places was very bad for her old eyes. The kindly divine accepted the objection without argument. Two blocks farther on they found on a corner a quieter eating-place, an unpretentious little restaurant which boasted a "Ladies' Entrance" down the side street.

They entered by the front door, and sat down at a table, facing each other. The woman read the menu through, and finally, after much embarrassed uncertainty, ordered poached eggs on toast. The clergyman ordered the same. The simple meal was soon dispatched. Just as they were finishing it, the woman said apologetically:

"If you'll excuse me, sir—could I see the bill of fare a minute? I think I'd best take a little pot of tea to warm me up, if they do not charge too high."

"I haven't the bill of fare," said the clergyman.

They looked diligently for the cardboard strip, but it was nowhere to be seen. The waiter drew near.

"Yes, ma'am! I certainly left it there on the table when I took the order."

191

"I'm sure I can't imagine what's become of it," repeated the clergyman, rather insistently.

He looked hard at the woman and found that she was looking hard at him. Both pairs of eyes fell instantly.

The waiter brought another bill of fare; the woman ordered tea; the waiter came back with it. The clergyman paid for both orders with a dollar bill that looked hard-earned.

The tea proved to be very hot: it could not be drunk down at a gulp. The clergyman, watching the woman intently as she sipped, seemed to grow more and more restless. His fingers drummed the tablecloth; he could hardly sit still. All at once he said: "What is that calling in the street? It sounds like newsboys."

The woman put her old head on one side and listened. "Yes, sir. There seems to be an extra out."

"Upon my word," he said, after a pause, "I believe I'll go get one. Good gracious! Crime is a very interesting thing, to be sure!"

He rose slowly, took down his hat from the hanger near him, and grasping his heavy stick, limped to the door. Leaving it open behind him, much to the annoyance of the proprietor in the cashier's cage, he stood a moment in the little vestibule, looking up and down the street. Then he took a few slow steps eastward, beckoning with his hand as he went, and so passed out of sight of the woman at the table.

The eating-place was on the corner, and outside the clergyman paused for half a breath. North, east, south, and west he looked, and nowhere found what his flying glance sought. He turned the corner into the darker cross street, and began to walk, continually looking about him. Presently his pace quickened, quickened so that he no longer even stayed to use his stout cane. A newsboy thrust an extra under his very nose, and he did not even see it.

Far down the street, nearly two blocks away, a tall figure in a blue coat stood under a street light, stamping his feet in the freezing sleet; and the hurrying divine sped straight toward him. But he did not get very far. As he passed the side entrance

192

at the extreme rear of the restaurant, a departing guest dashed out so recklessly as to run full into him, stopping him dead.

Without looking, he knew who it was. In fact, he did not look at her at all, but turned his head hurriedly east and west, sweeping the cross street with a swift eye. But the old woman, having drawn back with a sharp exclamation as they collided, rushed breathlessly into apologies:

"Oh, sir—excuse me, sir! A newsboy popped his head into the side door just after you went out, sir; and I ran to him to get you the paper. But he got away too quick for me, sir; and so I——"

"Exactly," said the clergyman in his quiet, deep voice. "That must have been the very boy I myself was after."

On the other side, two men had just turned into the street, well muffled against the night, talking cheerfully as they trudged along. Now the clergyman looked full at the woman, and she saw that there was a smile on his face.

"As he seems to have eluded us both, suppose we return to the subway?"

"Yes, sir; it's full time I——"

"The sidewalk is so slippery," he went on gently, "perhaps you had better take my arm."

The woman did as she was bidden.

Behind the pair in the restaurant, the waiter came forward to shut the door, and lingered to discuss with the proprietor the sudden departure of his two patrons. However, the bill had been paid in full, with a liberal tip for service; and so there was no especial complaint to make. After listening to some markedly unfavorable comments on the ways of the clergy, the waiter returned to his table to set it in order for the next customer.

On the floor in the carpeted aisle between tables lay a white rectangle of cardboard, which he readily recognized as one of their bills of fare, face downward. He stooped and picked it up. On the back of it was some scribbling, made with a blue lead pencil. The handwriting was very loose and irregular, as if the writer had had his eyes elsewhere while he wrote; and

193

it was with some difficulty that the waiter deciphered this message:

Miss Hinch 14th St. subway. Get police quick.

The waiter carried this curious document to the proprietor, who read it over a number of times. He was a dull man, and had a dull man's suspiciousness of a practical joke. However, after a good deal of irresolute discussion, he put on his overcoat and went out for a policeman. He turned west, and halfway up the block met an elderly bluecoat sauntering east. The policeman looked at the scribbling, and dismissed it profanely as a wag's foolishness of the sort that was bothering the life out of him a dozen times a day. He walked along with the proprietor; and as they drew near to the latter's place of business, both became aware at the same moment of footsteps thudding nearer up the cross street from the south. As they looked up, two young policemen, accompanied by a man in a uniform like a streetcar conductor's, swept around the corner and dashed straight into the restaurant.

The first policeman and the proprietor ran in after them, and found them staring about rather vacantly. One of the breathless arms of the law demanded if any suspicious characters had been seen about the place, and the dull proprietor said no. The officers, looking rather flat, explained their errand. It seemed that a few moments before, the third man, who was a ticket-chopper at the subway station, had found a mysterious message lying on the floor by his box. Whence it had come, how long it had lain there, he had not the slightest idea. However, there it was. The policeman exhibited a crumpled white scrap torn from a newspaper, on which was scrawled in blue pencil:

Miss Hinch Miller's Restaurant. Get police quick.

The first policeman, who was both the oldest and the fattest of the three, produced the message on the bill of fare, so utterly at odds with this. The dull proprietor, now bethinking himself, mentioned the clergyman and the old woman who had taken poached eggs and tea together, called for a second bill of fare, and departed so unexpectedly by different doors. The ticket

194

chopper recalled that he had seen the same pair at his station; they had come up, he remembered, and questioned him closely about trains. The three policemen were momentarily puzzled by this testimony. But it was soon plain to them that if either the woman or the clergyman really had any information about Miss Hinch—a highly improbable supposition in itself—they would never have stopped with peppering the neighborhood with silly little contradictory messages.

"They're a pair of old fools tryin' to have sport with the police, and I'd like to run them in for it," growled the fattest of the officers; and this was the general verdict.

The little conference broke up. The dull proprietor returned to his cage, the waiter to his table; the subway man departed on the run for his choppingbox; the three policemen passed out into the bitter night. They walked together, grumbling, and their feet, perhaps by some subconscious impulse, turned eastward toward the subway. And in the middle of the next block a man came running up to them.

"Officer, look what I found on the sidewalk a minute ago. Read that scribble!"

He held up a white slab which proved to be a bill of fare from Miller's restaurant. On the back of it the three peering officers saw, almost illegibly scrawled in blue pencil:

Police! Miss Hinch 14th St. subw—

The hand trailed off on the *w* as though the writer had been suddenly interrupted.

The fat policeman swore and threatened arrests. But the second policeman, who was dark and wiry, raised his head from the bill of fare and said suddenly: "Tim, I believe there's something in this."

"There'd ought to be ten days on the Island in it for them," growled fat Tim.

"Suppose, now," said the other policeman, staring intently at nothing, "the old woman was Miss Hinch herself, f'r instance, and the parson was shadowing her while pretendin' he never suspicioned her, and Miss Hinch not darin' to cut and run for it till she was sure she had a clean getaway. Well now, Tim, what better could he do——"

"That's right!" exclaimed the third policeman. "Specially when ye think that Hinch carries a gun, an'll use it, too! Why not have a look in at the subway station anyway, the three of us?"

This proposal carried the day. The three officers started for the subway, the citizen following. They walked at a good pace and without more talk. As the minds of the four men turned inward upon the odd behavior of the pair in Miller's Restaurant, the conviction that, after all, something important might be afoot grew and strengthened within each one of them. Unconsciously their pace quickened. It was the dark, wiry policeman who first broke into an open run, but the three other men had been for twenty paces on the verge of it.

However, these consultations and waverings had taken time. The stout clergyman and the poor old woman had five minutes' start on the officers of the law; and that, as it happened, was all that the occasion required. On Fourteenth Street, as they made their way arm in arm to the station, they were seen, and remembered, by a number of pedestrians. It was observed by more than one that the old woman lagged as if she were tired, while the club-footed divine, supporting her on his arm, steadily kept her up to his own brisk gait.

So walking, the pair descended the subway steps, came out

upon the bare platform again, and presently stood once more at the extreme uptown end of it, just where they had waited half an hour before. Near by a careless porter had overturned a bucket of water, and a splotch of thin ice ran out and over the edge of the concrete. Two young men who were taking lively turns up and down distinctly heard the clergyman warn the woman to look out for this ice. Far away to the north was to be heard the faint roar of an approaching train.

The woman stood nearest the track, and the clergyman stood in front of her. In the vague light their looks met, and each was struck by the pallor of the other's face. In addition the woman was breathing hard, and her hands and feet betrayed some nervousness. It was difficult now to ignore the too patent fact that for an hour they had been clinging desperately to each other, at all costs; but the clergyman made a creditable effort to do so. He talked ramblingly, in a kind voice, for the most part of the deplorable weather and his train to Newark, for which he was now so late. And all the time both of them were incessantly turning their heads toward the station entrance, as if expecting some arrival.

As he talked, the clergyman kept his hands unobtrusively busy. From the bottom edge of his black coat he drew a pin and stuck it deep into the ball of his middle finger. He took out his handkerchief to dust the hard sleet from his broad hat, and under his overcoat he pressed the handkerchief against his bleeding finger. While making these small arrangements, he held the woman's eyes with his own, chatting kindly; and, still holding them, he suddenly broke off his random talk and peered at her cheek with concern.

"My good woman, you've scratched your cheek somehow! Why, bless me, it's bleeding quite badly."

"Never mind," said the woman, and looked hurriedly toward the entrance.

"But, good gracious, I must mind! The blood will fall on your shawl. If you will permit me—ah!"

Too quick for her, he leaned forward and, through the thin veil, swept her cheek hard with his handkerchief; and, removing

197

it, held it up so that she might see the blood for herself. But she did not glance at the handkerchief, and neither did he. His gaze was riveted upon her cheek, which looked smooth and clear where he had smudged the clever wrinkles away.

Down the steps and upon the platform pounded the feet of three flying policemen. But it was quite evident now that the express would thunder in just ahead of them. The clergyman, standing close in front of the woman, took a firmer grip on his heavy stick and smiled full into her face.

"Miss Hinch, you are not so terribly clever, after all!"

The woman sprang back from him with an irrepressible exclamation, and in that moment her eye fell upon the police. Unluckily, her foot slipped upon the treacherous ice—or it may have tripped on the stout cane when the clergyman suddenly shifted its position. And in the next breath the express train roared past.

By one of those curious circumstances that sometimes refute all experience, the body of the woman was not mangled or mutilated in the least. There was a deep blue bruise on the left temple, and apparently that was all; even the ancient hat remained on her head, skewered fast by the long pin. It was the clergyman who found the body, huddled at the side of the track where the train had flung it—he who covered the still face and superintended the removal to the platform. Two eyewitnesses of the tragedy pointed out the ice on which the unfortunate woman had slipped, and described their horror as they saw her companion spring forward just too late to save her.

Not wishing to bring on a delirium of excitement among the half-dozen chance bystanders, two policemen drew the clergyman quietly aside and showed him the three mysterious messages. Apparently much affected by the woman's shocking end, he readily owned to having written them. He briefly recounted how the woman's strange movements on 126th Street had arrested his attention, and how, watching her closely on the car, he had finally detected that she wore a wig. Unfortunately, however, her suspicions appeared to have been aroused by his interest in her; and thereafter a long battle of wits had ensued between them—he trying to call the police without her knowledge, she dogging him close to prevent that, and at the same time watching her chance to give him the slip. He rehearsed how, in the restaurant, when he had invented an excuse to leave her for an instant, she had made a bolt and narrowly missed getting away; and finally how, having brought her back to the subway and seeing the police at last near, he had exposed her make-up and had spoken her name, with unexpectedly shocking results.

"And now," he concluded in a shaken voice, "I am naturally most anxious to know whether I am right—or have made some terrible mistake. Will you look at her, officer, and tell me if it is—she?"

But the fat policeman shook his head over the well-known ability of Miss Hinch to look like everybody else in the world but herself.

"It'll take God Almighty to tell ye that, sir—saving your presence. I'll leave it f'r headquarters," he continued as if that were the same thing. "But, if it is her, she's gone to her reward, sir."

199

"God pity her!" said the clergyman.

"Amen! Give me your name, sir. They may want ye in the morning."

The clergyman gave it: Rev. Theodore Shaler, of Denver; city address, 245 East 126th Street. Having thus discharged his duty in the affair, he started sadly to go away; but, passing by the silent figure stretched on a bench under the ticket-chopper's overcoat, he bared his head and stopped for one last look at it.

The parson's gentleness and efficiency had already won favorable comments from the bystanders, and of the first quality he now gave a final proof. The dead woman's wadded-up handkerchief, which somebody had recovered from the track and laid upon her breast, had slipped to the floor; and the clergyman, observing it, stooped silently to restore it again. This last small service chanced to bring his head close to the head of the dead woman; and, as he straightened up again, her projecting hatpin struck his cheek and ripped a straight line down it. This in itself would have been a trifle, since scratches soon heal. But it happened that the point of the hatpin caught under the lining of the clergyman's perfect beard and ripped it clean from him; so that, as he rose with a sudden shrill cry, he turned upon the astonished onlookers the bare, smooth chin of a woman, curiously long and pointed.

There was only one such chin in the world, and the very urchins in the street would have known it at a glance. Amid a sudden uproar which ill became the presence of the dead, the police closed in on Miss Hinch and handcuffed her with violence, fearing suicide, if not some new witchery; and at the stationhouse an unemotional matron divested the famous impersonator of the last and best of all her many disguises. This much the police did. But it was quite distinctly understood that it was Jessie Dark who had really made the capture, and the papers next morning printed pictures of the unconquerable little woman and of the hatpin with which she had reached back from another world to bring her greatest adversary to justice.

Edgar Allan Poe

THE GOLD BUG

ILLUSTRATED BY *Robert Sinnott*

MANY years ago, I contracted an intimacy with a Mr. William Legrand. He was of an ancient Huguenot family and had once been wealthy; but a series of misfortunes had reduced him to want. To avoid the mortification consequent upon his disasters, he left New Orleans, the city of his forefathers, and took up his residence at Sullivan's Island, near Charleston, South Carolina.

This island is a very singular one. It consists of little else than the sea sand, and is about three miles long. Its breadth at no point exceeds a quarter of a mile. It is separated from the mainland by a scarcely perceptible creek, oozing its way through a wilderness of reeds and slime, a favorite resort of the marshhen. The vegetation, as might be supposed, is scant, or at least dwarfish. No trees of any magnitude are to be seen. Near the western extremity, where Fort Moultrie stands, and where are some miserable frame buildings, tenanted during summer by the fugitives from Charleston dust and fever, may be found, indeed, the bristly palmetto; but the whole island, with the exception of this western point, and a line of hard white beach on the seacoast, is covered with a dense undergrowth of the sweet myrtle, so much prized by the horticulturists of England. The shrub here often attains the height of fifteen or twenty feet, and forms an almost impenetrable coppice, burdening the air with its fragrance.

In the utmost recesses of this coppice, not far from the eastern or more remote end of the island, Legrand had built himself a small hut, which he occupied when I first, by mere accident, made his acquaintance. This soon ripened into friendship—for there was much in the recluse to excite interest and esteem. I found him well educated, with unusual powers of mind, but infected with misanthropy, and subject to perverse moods of alternate enthusiasm and melancholy. He had with him many books but rarely employed them. His chief amusements were gunning and fishing, or sauntering along the beach and through the myrtles in quest of shells or entomological specimens—his collection of the latter might have been envied by a Swammerdamm. In these excursions he was usually accompanied by an old negro, called Jupiter, who had been manumitted before the reverses of the family, but who could be induced, neither by threats, nor by promises, to abandon what he considered his right of attendance upon the footsteps of his young "Massa Will." It is not improbable that the relatives of Legrand, conceiving him to be somewhat unsettled in intellect, had contrived to instill this obstinacy into Jupiter, with a view to the supervision and guardianship of the wanderer.

The winters in the latitude of Sullivan's Island are seldom very severe, and in the fall of the year it is a rare event indeed when a fire is considered necessary. About the middle of October, 18—, there occurred, however, a day of remarkable chilliness. Just before sunset I scrambled my way through the evergreens to the hut of my friend, whom I had not visited for several weeks—my residence being at that time in Charleston, a distance of nine miles from the island, where the facilities of passage and repassage were very far behind those of the present day. Upon reaching the hut I rapped, as was my custom, and, getting no reply, sought for the key where I knew it was secreted, unlocked the door, and went in. A fine fire was blazing upon the hearth. It was a novelty, and by no means an ungrateful one. I threw off an overcoat, took an armchair by the crackling logs, and awaited patiently the arrival of my hosts.

Soon after dark they arrived and gave me a most cordial welcome. Jupiter, grinning from ear to ear, bustled about to prepare some marsh hens for supper. Legrand was in one of his fits—how else shall I term them?—of enthusiasm. He had found an unknown bivalve, forming a new genus, and, more

than this, he had hunted down and secured, with Jupiter's assistance, a *scarabaeus* which he believed to be totally new, but
in respect to which he wished to have my opinion on the
morrow.

"And why not tonight?" I asked, rubbing my hands over the
blaze, and wishing the whole tribe of *scarabaei* at the devil.

"Ah, if I had only known you were here!" said Legrand, "but
it's so long since I saw you; and how could I foresee that you
would pay me a visit this very night of all others? As I was
coming home I met Lieutenant G——, from the fort, and, very
foolishly, I lent him the bug; so it will be impossible for you to
see it until the morning. Stay here tonight, and I will send Jup
down for it at sunrise. It is the loveliest thing in creation!"

"What?—sunrise?"

"Nonsense! no!—the bug. It is of a brilliant gold color—about the size of a large hickory-nut—with two jet black spots near one extremity of the back, and another, somewhat longer, at the other. The *antennae* are—"

"Dey ain't *no* tin in him, Massa Will, I keep a tellin' on you," here interrupted Jupiter; "de bug is a goole-bug, solid, ebery bit of him, inside and all, sep him wing—neber feel half so hebby a bug in my life."

"Well, suppose it is, Jup," replied Legrand, somewhat more earnestly, it seemed to me, than the case demanded, "is that any reason for your letting the birds burn? The color"—here he turned to me—"is really almost enough to warrant Jupiter's idea. You never saw a more brilliant metallic luster than the scales emit—but of this you cannot judge till tomorrow. In the meantime, I can give you some idea of the shape." Saying this, he seated himself at a small table, on which were a pen and ink, but no paper. He looked for some in a drawer, but found none.

"Never mind," said he at length, "this will answer"; and he drew from his waistcoat pocket a scrap of what I took to be very dirty foolscap and made upon it a rough drawing with the pen. While he did this, I retained my seat by the fire, for I was still chilly. When the design was complete, he handed it to me without rising. As I received it, a low growl was heard, succeeded by a scratching at the door. Jupiter opened it, and a large Newfoundland belonging to Legrand rushed in, leaped upon my shoulders, and loaded me with caresses; for I had shown him much attention during previous visits. When his gambols were over, I looked at the paper and, to speak the truth, found myself not a little puzzled at what my friend had depicted.

"Well!" I said, after contemplating it for some minutes, "this *is* a strange *scarabaeus*, I must confess; new to me; never saw anything like it before—unless it was a skull, or a death's-head, which it more nearly resembles than anything else that has come under *my* observation."

"A death's-head!" echoed Legrand—"Oh—yes—well, it has something of that appearance upon paper, no doubt. The two upper black spots look like eyes, eh? and the longer one at the bottom like a mouth—and then the shape of the whole is oval."

"Perhaps so," said I; "but, Legrand, I fear you are no artist. I must wait until I see the beetle itself, if I am to form any idea of its personal appearance."

"Well, I don't know," said he, a little nettled, "I draw tolerably—*should* do it at least—have had good masters and flatter myself that I am not quite a blockhead."

"But, my dear fellow, you are joking then," said I; "this is a very passable *skull*,—indeed, I may say that it is a very *excellent* skull, according to the vulgar notions about such specimens of physiology—and your *scarabaeus* must be the queerest *scarabaeus* in the world if it resembles it. Why, we may get up a very thrilling bit of superstition upon this hint. I presume you will call the bug *scarabaeus caput hominis,* or something of that kind—there are many similar titles in the Natural Histories. But where are the *antennae* you spoke of?"

"The *antennae!*" said Legrand, who seemed to be getting unaccountably warm upon the subject; "I am sure you must see the *antennae.* I made them as distinct as they are in the original insect, and I presume that is sufficient."

"Well, well," I said, "perhaps you have—still I don't see them"; and I handed him the paper without additional remark, not wishing to ruffle his temper; but I was much surprised at the turn affairs had taken; his ill humor puzzled me—and, as for the drawing of the beetle, there were positively *no antennae* visible, and the whole *did* bear a very close resemblance to the ordinary cuts of a death's-head.

He received the paper very peevishly and was about to crumple it, apparently to throw it in the fire, when a casual glance at the design seemed suddenly to rivet his attention. In an instant his face grew violently red—in another as excessively pale. For some minutes he continued to scrutinize the drawing minutely where he sat. At length he arose, took a candle from the table, and proceeded to seat himself upon a sea-chest in the farthest corner of the room. Here again he made an anxious examination of the paper, turning it in all directions. He said nothing, however, and his conduct greatly astonished me; yet I thought it prudent not to exacerbate the growing moodiness of his temper by any comment. Presently he took from his coat a wallet, placed the paper carefully in it, and deposited both in a writing desk, which he locked. He now grew more composed in his demeanor; but his original air of enthusiasm had quite disappeared. Yet he seemed not so much sulky as abstracted. As the evening wore away he became more and more absorbed in revery, from which no sallies of mine could arouse him. It had been my intention to pass the night at the hut, as I had frequently done before, but, seeing my host in this mood, I deemed it proper to take leave. He did not press me to remain, but, as I departed, he shook my hand with even more than his usual cordiality.

It was about a month after this (and during the interval I had seen nothing of Legrand) when I received a visit, at Charleston, from his man, Jupiter. I had never seen the good old Negro look so dispirited, and I feared that some serious disaster had befallen my friend.

"Well, Jup," said I, "what is the matter now?—how is your master?"

"Why, to speak de troof, massa, him not so berry well as mought be."

"Not well! I am truly sorry to hear it. What does he complain of?"

"Dar! dat's it!—him neber 'plain of notin'—but him berry sick for all dat."

"*Very* sick, Jupiter!—why didn't you say so at once? Is he confined to bed?"

"No, dat he ain't!—he ain't find nowhar—dat's just whar de shoe pinch—my mind is got to be berry hebby bout poor Massa Will."

"Jupiter, I should like to understand what it is you are talking about. You say your master is sick. Hasn't he told you what ails him?"

"Why, massa, tain't worf while for to git mad bout de matter —Massa Will say noffin at all ain't de matter wid him—but den what make him go about looking dis here way, wid he head

206

down and he soldiers up, and as white as a gose? And den he keep a syphon all de time—"

"Keeps a what, Jupiter?"

"Keeps a syphon wid de figgurs on de slate—de queerest figgurs I ebber did see. Ise gittin to be skeered, I tell you. Hab for to keep mighty tight eye pon him noovers. Todder day he gib me slip fore de sun up and was gone de whole ob de blessed day. I had a big stick ready cut for to gib him good beating when he did come—but Ise sich a fool dat I hadn't de heart arter all—he look so berry poorly."

"Eh!—what?—ah yes!—upon the whole I think you had better not be too severe with the poor fellow—don't flog him, Jupiter— he can't very well stand it—but can you form no idea of what has occasioned this illness, or rather this change of conduct? Has anything unpleasant happened since I saw you?"

"No, massa, dey ain't been noffin onpleasant *since* den—'twas *fore* den I'm feared—'twas de berry day you was dare."

"How? What do you mean?"

"Why, massa, I mean de bug—dare now."

"The what?"

"De bug—I'm berry sartain dat Massa Will bin bit some-where bout de head by dat goole-bug."

"And what cause have you, Jupiter, for such a supposition?"

"Claws enuff, massa, and mouff too. I nebber did see sich a bug—he kick and he bite ebery ting what cum near him. Massa Will cotch him fuss but had for to let him go gin mighty quick, I tell you—den was de time he must ha got de bite. I didn't like de look ob de bug mouff, myself, no how, so I wouldn't take hold ob him wid my finger, but I cotch him wid a piece ob paper dat I found. I rap him up in de paper and stuff piece ob it in he mouff—dat was de way."

"And you think, then, that your master was really bitten by the beetle, and that the bite made him sick?"

"I don't tink noffin about it—I nose it. What make him dream bout de goole so much, if tain't cause he bit by de goole-bug? Ise heerd bout dem goole-bugs fore dis."

"But how do you know he dreams bout gold?"

207

"How I know? Why, cause he talk about it in he sleep—dat's how I nose."

"Well, Jup, perhaps you are right; but to what fortunate circumstance am I to attribute the honor of a visit from you to-day?"

"What de matter, massa?"

"Did you bring any message from Mr. Legrand?"

"No, massa, I bring dis here pissel"; and here Jupiter handed me a note which ran thus:

"My Dear———, Why have I not seen you for so long a time? I hope you have not been so foolish as to take offense at any little *brusquerie* of mine; but no, that is improbable.

"Since I saw you I have had great cause for anxiety. I have something to tell you, yet scarcely know how to tell it, or whether I should tell it at all.

"I have not been quite well for some days past, and poor old Jup annoys me, almost beyond endurance, by his well-meant attentions. Would you believe it?—he had prepared a huge stick, the other day, with which to chastise me for giving him the slip, and spending the day, *solus,* among the hills on the mainland. I verily believe that my ill looks alone saved me a flogging.

"I have made no addition to my cabinet since we met.

"If you can, in any way, make it convenient, come over with Jupiter. *Do* come. I wish to see you *tonight,* upon business of importance. I assure you that it is of the *highest* importance.

"Ever yours,
"WILLIAM LEGRAND."

There was something in the tone of this note which gave me great uneasiness. Its whole style differed materially from that of Legrand. What could he be dreaming of? What new crotchet possessed his excitable brain? What "business of the highest importance" could *he* possibly have to transact? Jupiter's account of him boded no good. I dreaded lest the continued pressure of misfortune had, at length, fairly unsettled the reason of my friend. Without a moment's hesitation, therefore, I prepared to accompany the negro.

Upon reaching the wharf, I noticed a scythe and three spades,

all apparently new, lying in the bottom of the boat in which we were to embark.

"What is the meaning of all this, Jup?" I inquired.

"Him syfe, massa, and spade."

"Very true; but what are they doing here?"

"Him de syfe and de spade what Massa Will sis pon my buying for him in de town, and de debbil's own lot of money I had to gib for em."

"But what, in the name of all that is mysterious, is your 'Massa Will' going to do with scythes and spades?"

"Dat's more dan I know, and debbil take me if I don't blieve 'tis more dan he know, too. But it's all cum ob de bug."

Finding that no satisfaction was to be obtained of Jupiter, whose whole intellect seemed to be absorbed by "de bug," I now stepped into the boat and made sail. With a fair and strong breeze we soon ran into the little cove to the northward of Fort Moultrie, and a walk of some two miles brought us to the hut. It was about three in the afternoon when we arrived. Legrand had been awaiting us in eager expectation. He grasped my hand with a nervous *empressement*, which alarmed me and strengthened the suspicions already entertained. His countenance was pale even to ghastliness, and his deep-set eyes glared with unnatural luster. After some inquiries respecting his health, I

209

asked him, not knowing what better to say, if he had yet obtained the *scarabaeus* from Lieutenant G‑‑‑‑.

"Oh, yes," he replied, coloring violently; "I got it from him the next morning. Nothing should tempt me to part with that *scarabaeus*. Do you know that Jupiter is quite right about it?"

"In what way?" I asked, with a sad foreboding at heart.

"In supposing it to be a bug of *real gold*." He said this with an air of profound seriousness, and I felt inexpressibly shocked.

"This bug is to make my fortune," he continued, with a triumphant smile, "to reinstate me in my family possessions. Is it any wonder, then, that I prize it? Since Fortune has thought fit to bestow it upon me, I have only to use it properly and I shall arrive at the gold of which it is the index. Jupiter, bring me that *scarabaeus!*"

"What! de bug, massa? I'd rudder not go fer trubble dat bug —you mus git him for your own self." Hereupon Legrand arose, with a grave and stately air, and brought me the beetle from a glass case in which it was enclosed. It was a beautiful *scarabaeus,* and, at that time, unknown to naturalists—of course a great prize in a scientific point of view. There were two round, black spots near one extremity of the back and a long one near the other. The scales were exceedingly hard and glossy, with all the appearance of burnished gold. The weight of the insect was very remarkable, and, taking all things into consideration, I could hardly blame Jupiter for his opinion respecting it; but what to make of Legrand's agreement with that opinion, I could not, for the life of me, tell.

"I sent for you," said he, in a grandiloquent tone, when I had completed my examination of the beetle, "I sent for you, that I might have your counsel and assistance in furthering the views of Fate and of the bug—"

"My dear Legrand," I cried, interrupting him, "you are certainly unwell, and had better use some little precautions. You shall go to bed, and I will remain with you a few days, until you get over this. You are feverish and—"

"Feel my pulse," said he.

I felt it, and, to say the truth, found not the slightest indication of fever.

"But you may be ill, and yet have no fever. Allow me this once to prescribe for you. In the first place, go to bed. In the next—"

"You are mistaken," he interposed, "I am as well as I can expect to be under the excitement which I suffer. If you really wish me well, you will relieve this excitement."

"And how is this to be done?"

"Very easily. Jupiter and myself are going upon an expedition into the hills, upon the mainland, and, in this expedition, we shall need the aid of some person in whom we can confide. You are the only one we can trust. Whether we succeed or fail, the excitement which you now perceive in me will be equally allayed."

"I am anxious to oblige you in any way," I replied; "but do you mean to say that this infernal beetle has any connection with your expedition into the hills?"

"It has."

"Then, Legrand, I can become a party to no such absurd proceeding."

"I am very sorry for we shall have to try it by ourselves."

"Try it by yourselves! The man is surely mad!—but stay!—how long do you propose to be absent?"

"Probably all night. We shall start immediately and be back, at all events, by sunrise."

"And will you promise me, upon your honor, that when this freak of yours is over, and the bug business settled to your satisfaction, you will then return home and follow my advice implicitly, as that of your physician?"

"Yes; I promise; and now let us be off, for we have no time to lose."

With a heavy heart I accompanied my friend. We started about four o'clock—Legrand, Jupiter, the dog, and myself. Jupiter had with him the scythe and spades—the whole of which he insisted upon carrying, more through fear, it seemed to me, of trusting either of the implements within reach of his master, than from any excess of industry or complaisance. His demeanor was dogged in the extreme, and "dat bug" were the sole words which escaped his lips during the journey. For my own part, I had charge of a couple of dark lanterns, while Legrand contented himself with the *scarabaeus*, which he carried attached to the end of a bit of whip-cord; twirling it to and fro, with the air of a conjurer, as he went. When I observed this last, plain evidence of my friend's aberration of mind, I could scarcely refrain from tears. I thought it best, however, to humor his fancy, at least for the present, or until I could adopt some more energetic measures with a chance of success. In the meantime I endeavored, but all in vain, to sound him in regard to the object of the expedition. Having succeeded in inducing me to accompany him, he seemed unwilling to hold conversation upon any topic of minor importance, and to all my questions vouchsafed no other reply than "we shall see!"

We crossed the creek at the head of the island by means of a skiff and, ascending the high grounds on the shore of the mainland, proceeded in a northwesterly direction, through a tract of country excessively wild and desolate, where no trace of a human footstep was to be seen. Legrand led the way with decision; pausing only for an instant, here and there, to consult what appeared to be certain landmarks of his own contrivance upon a former occasion.

In this manner we journeyed for about two hours, and the sun was just setting when we entered a region infinitely more

dreary than any yet seen. It was a species of tableland, near the summit of an almost inaccessible hill, densely wooded from base to pinnacle, and interspersed with huge crags that appeared to lie loosely upon the soil, and in many cases were prevented from precipitating themselves into the valleys below merely by the support of the trees against which they reclined. Deep ravines, invarious directions, gave an air of still sterner solemnity to the scene.

The natural platform to which we had clambered was thickly overgrown with brambles, through which we soon discovered that it would have been impossible to force our way but for the scythe; and Jupiter, by direction of his master, proceeded to clear for us a path to the foot of an enormously tall tulip tree, which stood, with some eight or ten oaks, upon the level, and far surpassed them all, and all other trees which I had then ever seen, in the beauty of its foliage and form, in the wide spread of its branches, and in the general majesty of its appearance. When we reached this tree, Legrand turned to Jupiter, and asked him if he thought he could climb it. The old man seemed a little staggered by the question, and for some moments made no reply. At length he approached the huge trunk, walked slowly around it, and examined it with minute attention. When he had completed his scrutiny, he merely said,—

"Yes, massa, Jup climb any tree he ebber see in he life."

"Then up with you as soon as possible, for it will soon be too dark to see what we are about."

"How far mus go up, massa?" inquired Jupiter.

"Get up the main trunk first, and then I will tell you which way to go—and here—stop! take this beetle with you."

"De bug, Massa Will!—de goole-bug!" cried the negro, drawing back in dismay—"what for mus tote de bug away up de tree?"

"If you are afraid, Jup, a great big negro like you, to take hold of a harmless little dead beetle, why, you can carry it up by this string—but, if you do not take it up with you in some way, I shall be under the necessity of breaking your head with this shovel."

"What de matter now, massa?" said Jup, evidently shamed into compliance; "always want fur to raise fuss wid old nigger. Was only funnin anyhow. *Me* feered de bug! What I keer for de bug?" Here he took cautiously hold of the extreme end of the string and, maintaining the insect as far from his person as circumstances would permit, prepared to ascend the tree.

In youth, the tulip tree, the most magnificent of American foresters, has a trunk peculiarly smooth and often rises to a great height without lateral branches; but, in its riper age, the bark becomes gnarled and uneven, while many short limbs make their appearance on the stem. Thus the difficulty of ascension, in the present case, lay more in semblance than in reality. Embracing the huge cylinder as closely as possible, with his arms and knees, seizing with his hands some projections, and resting his naked toes upon others, Jupiter, after one or two narrow escapes from falling, at length wriggled himself into the first great fork, and seemed to consider the whole business as virtually accomplished. The *risk* of the achievement was, in fact, now over, although the climber was some sixty or seventy feet from the ground.

"Which way mus go now, Massa Will?" he asked.

"Keep up the largest branch—the one on this side," said Legrand. The negro obeyed him promptly, and apparently with

214

but little trouble, ascending higher and higher, until no glimpse of his squat figure could be obtained through the dense foliage which enveloped it. Presently his voice was heard in sort of halloo.

"How much fudder is got for go?"

"How high up are you?" asked Legrand.

"Ebber so fur," replied the negro; "can see de sky fru de top ob de tree."

"Never mind the sky, but attend to what I say. Look down the trunk and count the limbs below you on this side. How many limbs have you passed?"

"One, two, tree, four, fibe—I done pass fibe big limb, massa, pon dis side."

"Then go one limb higher."

In a few minutes the voice was heard again, announcing that the seventh limb was attained.

"Now, Jup," cried Legrand, evidently much excited, "I want you to work your way out upon that limb as far as you can. If you see anything strange, let me know."

By this time what little doubt I might have entertained of my poor friend's insanity was put finally at rest. I had no alternative but to conclude him stricken with lunacy, and I became seriously anxious about getting him home. While I was pondering upon what was best to be done, Jupiter's voice was again heard.

"Mos feered for to ventur pon dis limb berry far—'tis dead limb putty much all de way."

"Did you say it was a *dead* limb, Jupiter?" cried Legrand in a quavering voice.

"Yes, massa, him dead as de door-nail—done up for sartain—done departed dis here life."

"What in the name of heaven shall I do?" asked Legrand, seemingly in the greatest distress.

"Do!" said I, glad of an opportunity to interpose a word, "why, come home and go to bed. Come now!—that's a fine fellow. It's getting late, and, besides, you remember your promise."

"Jupiter," cried he, without heeding me in the least, "do you hear me?"

"Yes, Massa Will, hear you ebber so plain."

"Try the wood well, then, with your knife, and see if you think it *very* rotten."

"Him rotten, massa, sure nuff," replied the negro in a few moments, "but not so berry rotten as mought be. Mought ventur out leetle way pon de limb by myself, dat's true."

"By yourself!—what do you mean?"

"Why, I mean de bug. 'Tis *berry* hebby bug. S'pose I drop him down fuss, and den de limb won't break wid just de weight ob one nigger."

"You infernal scoundrel!" cried Legrand, apparently much relieved, "what do you mean by telling me such nonsense as that? As sure as you let that beetle fall, I'll break your neck. Look here, Jupiter! do you hear me?"

"Yes, massa, needn't hollo at poor nigger dat style."

"Well! now listen!—if you will venture out on the limb as far as you think safe, and not let go the beetle, I'll make you a present of a silver dollar as soon as you get down."

"I'm gwine, Massa Will—deed I is," replied the negro very promptly—"mos out to the eend now."

"*Out to the end!*" here fairly screamed Legrand, "do you say you are out to the end of that limb?"

"Soon be to de eend, massa,—o-o-o-o-oh! Lor-gol-a-marcy! What *is* dis here pon de tree?"

"Well!" cried Legrand, highly delighted, "what is it?"

"Why tain't noffin but a skull—somebody bin lef him head up de tree, and de crows done gobble ebery bit ob de meat off."

"A skull, you say!—very well!—how is it fastened to the limb? —what holds it on?"

"Sure nuff, massa; mus look. Why, dis berry curous sarcumstance, pon my word—dare's a great big nail in de skull, what fastens ob it on to de tree."

"Well, now, Jupiter, do exactly as I tell you—do you hear?"

"Yes, Massa."

"Pay attention, then!—find the left eye of the skull."

216

"Hum! hoo! dat's good! Why, dar aint no eye lef at all."

"Curse your stupidity! Do you know your right hand from your left?"

"Yes, I nose dat—nose all bout dat—'tis my lef hand what I chops de wood wid."

"To be sure! you are left-handed; and your left eye is on the same side as your left hand. Now, I suppose, you can find the left eye of the skull, or the place where the left eye has been. Have you found it?"

Here was a long pause. At length the negro asked,—

"Is de lef eye of de skull pon de same side as de lef hand of de skull, too?—cause de skull ain't got not a bit ob a hand at all— neber mind! I got de lef eye now—here de lef eye! What mus do wid it?"

"Let the beetle drop through it, as far as the string will reach —but be careful and not let go your hold of the string."

"All dat done, Massa Will; mighty easy ting for to put de bug fru de hole—look out for him dar below!"

During this colloquy no portion of Jupiter's person could be seen; but the beetle, which he had suffered to descend, was now visible at the end of the string, and glistened, like a globe of burnished gold, in the last rays of the setting sun, some of which still faintly illumined the eminence upon which we stood. The *scarabaeus* hung quite clear of any branches, and, if allowed to fall, would have fallen at our feet. Legrand immediately took the scythe, and cleared with it a circular space, three or four yards in diameter, just beneath the insect, and, having accomplished this, ordered Jupiter to let go the string and come down from the tree.

Driving a peg, with great nicety, into the ground, at the precise spot where the beetle fell, my friend now produced from his pocket a tape-measure. Fastening one end of this at that point of the trunk of the tree which was nearest the peg, he unrolled it till it reached the peg, and thence farther unrolled it, in the direction already established by the two points of the tree and the peg, for the distance of fifty feet—Jupiter clearing away the brambles with the scythe. At the spot thus attained a

second peg was driven, and about this, as a center, a rude circle, about four feet in diameter, described. Taking now a spade himself, and giving one to Jupiter and one to me, Legrand begged us to set about digging as quickly as possible.

To speak the truth, I had no especial relish for such amusement at any time and, at that particular moment, would most willingly have declined it; for the night was coming on, and I felt much fatigued with the exercise already taken; but I saw no mode of escape and was fearful of disturbing my poor friend's equanimity by a refusal. Could I have depended, indeed, upon Jupiter's aid, I would have had no hesitation in attempting to get the lunatic home by force; but I was too well assured of the old negro's disposition to hope that he would assist me, under any circumstances, in a personal contest with his master. I made no doubt that the latter had been infected with some of the innumerable Southern superstitions about money buried, and that his fantasy had received confirmation by the finding of the *scarabaeus*, or, perhaps, by Jupiter's obstinacy in maintaining it to be "a bug of real gold." A mind disposed to lunacy would readily be led away by such suggestions, especially if chiming in with favorite preconceived ideas; and then I called to mind the poor fellow's speech about the beetle's being "the index of his fortune." Upon the whole, I was sadly vexed and puzzled, but at length I concluded to make a virtue of necessity—to dig with a good will, and thus the sooner to convince the visionary, by ocular demonstration, of the fallacy of the opinions he entertained.

The lanterns having been lit, we all fell to work with a zeal worthy a more rational cause; and, as the glare fell upon our persons and implements, I could not help thinking how picturesque a group we composed, and how strange and suspicious our labors must have appeared to any interloper who, by chance, might have stumbled upon our whereabouts.

We dug very steadily for two hours. Little was said; and our chief embarrassment lay in the yelpings of the dog, who took exceeding interest in our proceedings. He, at length, became so obstreperous that we grew fearful of his giving the alarm to some stragglers in the vicinity; or, rather, this was the apprehension of Legrand; for myself, I should have rejoiced at any interruption which might have enabled me to get the wanderer home. The noise was, at length, very effectually silenced by Jupiter, who, getting out of the hole with a dogged air of deliberation, tied the brute's mouth up with one of his suspenders and then returned, with a grave chuckle, to his task.

When the time mentioned had expired, we had reached a depth of five feet, and yet no signs of any treasure became manifest. A general pause ensued, and I began to hope that the farce was at an end. Legrand, however, although evidently much disconcerted, wiped his brow thoughtfully and recommenced. We had excavated the entire circle of four feet diameter, and now we slightly enlarged the limit and went to the farther depth of two feet. Still nothing appeared. The gold-seeker, whom I sincerely pitied, at length clambered from the pit, with the bitterest disappointment imprinted upon every feature, and proceeded, slowly and reluctantly, to put on his coat, which he had thrown off at the beginning of his labor. In the meantime I made no remark. Jupiter, at a signal from his master, began to gather up his tools. This done, and the dog having been unmuzzled, we turned in silence towards home.

We had taken, perhaps, a dozen steps in this direction, when, with a loud oath, Legrand strode up to Jupiter, and seized him by the collar. The astonished negro opened his eyes and mouth to the fullest extent, let fall the spades, and fell upon his knees.

"You scoundrel," said Legrand, hissing out the syllables from between his clenched teeth—"you infernal black villain!—speak, I tell you!—answer me this instant, without prevarication!—which—which is your left eye?"

"Oh, Massa Will! ain't dis here my lef eye for sartain?" roared the terrified Jupiter, placing his hand upon his *right* organ of vision and holding it there with a desperate pertinacity, as if in immediate dread of his master's attempt at a gouge.

"I thought so!— I knew it! hurrah!" vociferated Legrand, letting the negro go, and executing a series of curvets and caracoles, much to the astonishment of his valet, who, arising from his knees, looked mutely from his master to myself, and then from myself to his master.

"Come! we must go back," said the latter, "the game's not up yet"; and he again led the way to the tulip tree.

"Jupiter," said he, when he reached its foot, "come here! was the skull nailed to the limb with the face outward, or with the face to the limb?"

"De face was out, massa, so dat de crows could get at de eyes good, widout any trouble."

"Well, then, was it this eye or that through which you dropped the beetle?"—here Legrand touched each of Jupiter's eyes.

" 'Twas dis eye, massa—de lef eye—jis as you tell me," and here it was his right eye that the negro indicated.

"That will do—we must try it again."

Here my friend, about whose madness I now saw, or fancied that I saw, certain indications of method, removed the peg which marked the spot where the beetle fell, to a spot about three inches to the westward of its former position. Taking, now, the tape measure from the nearest point of the trunk to the peg, as before, and continuing the extension in a straight line to the distance of fifty feet, a spot was indicated, removed by several yards, from the point at which we had been digging.

Around the new position a circle, somewhat larger than in the former instance, was now described, and we again set to work with the spades. I was dreadfully weary but, scarcely understanding what had occasioned the change in my thoughts, I felt no longer any great aversion from the labor imposed. I had become most unaccountably interested—nay, even excited. Perhaps there was something, amid all the extravagant demeanor of Legrand—some air of forethought, or of deliberation—which impressed me. I dug eagerly, and now and then caught myself actually looking, with something that very much resembled expectation, for the fancied treasure, the vision of which had demented my unfortunate companion. At a period when such vagaries of thought most fully possessed me, and when we had been at work perhaps an hour and a half, we were again interrupted by the violent howlings of the dog. His uneasiness in the first instance had been evidently but the result of playfulness or caprice, but he now assumed a bitter and serious tone. Upon Jupiter's again attempting to muzzle him, he made furious resistance and, leaping into the hole, tore up the mold frantically with his claws. In a few seconds he had uncovered a mass of human bones, forming two complete skeletons, intermingled with several buttons of metal, and what appeared to be the dust of decayed woolen. One or two strokes of a spade upturned the blade of a large Spanish knife, and, as we dug farther, three or four loose pieces of gold and silver coin came to light.

At sight of these the joy of Jupiter could scarcely be restrained, but the countenance of his master wore an air of extreme disappointment. He urged us, however, to continue our exertions, and the words were hardly uttered when I stumbled and fell forward, having caught the toe of my boot in a large ring of iron that lay half buried in the loose earth.

We now worked in earnest, and never did I pass ten minutes of more intense excitement. During this interval we had fairly unearthed an oblong chest of wood, which, from its perfect preservation and wonderful hardness, had plainly been sub-

jected to some mineralizing process—perhaps that of the bi-
chloride of mercury. This box was three feet and a half long, and
quite broad, and two and a half feet deep. It was firmly
secured by bands of wrought iron, riveted, and forming a kind
of trelliswork over the whole. On each side of the chest, near
the top, were three rings of iron—six in all—by means of which
a firm hold could be obtained by six persons. Our utmost united
endeavors served only to disturb the coffer very slightly in its
bed. We at once saw the impossibility of removing so great a
weight. Luckily, the sole fastenings of the lid consisted of two
sliding bolts. These we drew back—trembling and panting with
anxiety. In an instant, a treasure of incalculable value lay
gleaming before us. As the rays of the lanterns fell within the
pit, there flashed upwards, from a confused heap of gold and
of jewels, a glow and a glare that absolutely dazzled our eyes.

I shall not pretend to describe the feelings with which I
gazed. Amazement was, of course, predominant. Legrand ap-

peared exhausted with excitement and spoke very few words. Jupiter's countenance wore, for some minutes, as deadly a pallor as it is possible, in the nature of things, for any negro's visage to assume. He seemed stupefied—thunder-stricken. Presently he fell upon his knees in the pit and, burying his naked arms up to the elbows in the gold, let them there remain, as if enjoying the luxury of a bath. At length, with a deep sigh, he exclaimed, as if in a soliloquy:

"And dis all cum ob de goole-bug! de putty goole-bug! de poor little goole-bug, what I boosed in dat sabage kind ob style! Ain't you shamed ob yourself?—answer me dat!"

It became necessary, at last, that I should arouse both master and valet to the expediency of removing the treasure. It was growing late, and it behooved us to make exertion, that we might get everything housed before daylight. It was difficult to say what should be done, and much time was spent in deliberation—so confused were the ideas of all. We finally lightened the box by removing two-thirds of its contents, when we were enabled, with some trouble, to raise it from the hole. The articles taken out were deposited among the brambles, and the dog left to guard them, with strict orders from Jupiter neither, upon any pretence, to stir from the spot, nor to open his mouth until our return. We then hurriedly made for home with the chest; reaching the hut in safety, but after excessive toil, at one o'clock in the morning. Worn out as we were, it was not in human nature to do more just then. We rested until two and had supper; starting for the hills immediately afterwards, armed with three stout sacks, which by good luck were upon the premises. A little before four we arrived at the pit, divided the remainder of the booty, as equally as might be, among us and, leaving the holes unfilled, again set out for the hut, at which, for the second time, we deposited our golden burdens, just as the first streaks of the dawn gleamed from over the treetops in the East.

We were now thoroughly broken down; but the intense excitement of the time denied us repose. After an unquiet slumber of some three or four hours' duration, we arose, as if by preconcert, to make examination of our treasure.

The chest had been full to the brim, and we spent the whole day, and the greater part of the next night, in a scrutiny of its contents. There had been nothing like order or arrangement. Everything had been heaped in promiscuously. Having assorted all with care, we found ourselves possessed of even vaster wealth than we had at first supposed. In coin there was rather

more than four hundred and fifty thousand dollars; estimating the value of the pieces, as accurately as we could, by the tables of the period. There was not a particle of silver. All was gold of antique date and of great variety; French, Spanish, and German money, with a few English guineas, and some counters, of which we had never seen specimens before. There were several very large and heavy coins, so worn that we could make nothing of their inscriptions. There was no American money. The value of the jewels we found more difficulty in estimating. There were diamonds—some of them exceedingly large and fine —a hundred and ten in all, and not one of them small; eighteen rubies of remarkable brilliancy; three hundred and ten emeralds, all very beautiful; and twenty-one sapphires, with an opal. These stones had all been broken from their settings and thrown loose in the chest. The settings themselves, which we picked out from among the other gold, appeared to have been beaten up with hammers, as if to prevent identification. Besides all this, there was a vast quantity of solid gold ornaments: nearly two hundred massive finger and earrings; rich chains—thirty of these, if I remember;—eighty-three very large and heavy crucifixes; five gold censers of great value; a prodigious golden punch bowl, ornamented with richly chased vine-leaves and Bacchanalian figures; with two sword-handles exquisitely embossed, and many other smaller articles which I cannot recollect. The weight of these valuables exceeded three hundred and fifty pounds avoirdupois; and in this estimate I have not included one hundred and ninety-seven superb gold watches; three of the number being worth each five hundred dollars, if one. Many of them were very old, and as time-keepers valueless, the works having suffered more or less from corrosion; but all were richly jewelled and in cases of great worth. We estimated the entire contents of the chest, that night, at a million and a half of dollars; and, upon the subsequent disposal of the trinkets and jewels (a few being retained for our own use), it was found that we had greatly undervalued the treasure.

When, at length, we had concluded our examination, and the intense excitement of the time had in some measure subsided, Legrand, who saw that I was dying with impatience for a solution of this most extraordinary riddle, entered into a full detail of all the circumstances connected with it.

"You remember," said he, "the night when I handed you the rough sketch I had made of the *scarabaeus*. You recollect also, that I became quite vexed at you for insisting that my drawing resembled a death's-head. When you first made this assertion I thought you were jesting; but afterwards I called to mind the peculiar spots on the back of the insect, and admitted to myself that your remark had some little foundation in fact. Still, the sneer at my graphic powers irritated me—for I am considered a good artist—and, therefore, when you handed me the scrap of parchment, I was about to crumple it up and throw it angrily into the fire."

"The scrap of paper, you mean," said I.

"No: it had much of the appearance of paper, and at first I supposed it to be such, but when I came to draw upon it, I discovered it, at once, to be a piece of very thin parchment. It was quite dirty, you remember. Well, as I was in the very act of crumpling it up, my glance fell upon the sketch at which you had been looking, and you may imagine my astonishment when I perceived, in fact, the figure of a death's-head just where, it seemed to me, I had made the drawing of the beetle. For a moment I was too much amazed to think with accuracy. I knew that my design was very different in detail from this—although there was a certain similarity in general outline. Presently I took a candle and, seating myself at the other end of the room, proceeded to scrutinize the parchment more closely. Upon turning it over, I saw my own sketch upon the reverse, just as I had made it. My first idea, now, was mere surprise at the really remarkable similarity of outline—at the singular coincidence involved in the fact that, unknown to me, there should have been a skull upon the other side of the parchment, immediately beneath my figure of the *scarabaeus,* and that this skull, not only in outline, but in size, should so closely resemble my drawing. I say the singularity of this coincidence absolutely stupefied me for a time. This is the usual effect of such coincidences. The mind struggles to establish a connection—a sequence of cause and effect—and, being unable to do so, suffers a species of temporary paralysis. But, when I recovered from this stupor, there dawned upon me gradually a conviction which startled me even far more than the coincidence. I began distinctly, positively, to remember that there had been *no* drawing on the parchment when I made my sketch of the *scarabaeus.* I became perfectly certain of this; for I recollected turning up first one side and then the other, in search of the cleanest spot. Had the skull been then there, of course I could not have failed to notice it. Here was indeed a mystery which I felt it impossible to explain; but, even at that early moment, there seemed to glimmer, faintly, within the most remote and secret chambers of my intellect, a glowworm-like conception of that truth which last night's adventure brought to so magnificent a demonstration. I arose at once and, putting the parchment securely away, dismissed all further reflection until I should be alone.

"When you had gone, and when Jupiter was fast asleep, I betook myself to a more methodical investigation of the affair. In the first place I considered the manner in which the parchment had come into my possession. The spot where we discovered the *scarabaeus* was on the coast of the mainland, about a mile eastward of the island, and but a short distance above high-water mark. Upon my taking hold of it, it gave me a sharp bite, which caused me to let it drop. Jupiter, with his accustomed caution, before seizing the insect, which had flown towards him, looked about him for a leaf, or something of that nature, by which to take hold of it. It was at this moment that his eyes, and mine also, fell upon the scrap of parchment, which I then supposed to be paper. It was lying half-buried in the sand, a corner sticking up. Near the spot where we found it, I observed the remnants of the hull of what appeared to have been a ship's longboat. The wreck seemed to have been there for a very great while; for the resemblance to boat timbers could scarcely be traced.

"Well, Jupiter picked up the parchment, wrapped the beetle

in it, and gave it to me. Soon afterwards we turned to go home, and on the way met Lieutenant G___. I showed him the insect, and he begged me to let him take it to the fort. On my consenting, he thrust it forthwith into his waistcoat pocket, without the parchment in which it had been wrapped, and which I had continued to hold in my hand during his inspection. Perhaps he dreaded my changing my mind and thought it best to make sure of the prize at once—you know how enthusiastic he is on all subjects connected with Natural History. At the same time, without being conscious of it, I must have deposited the parchment in my own pocket.

"You remember that when I went to the table, for the purpose of making a sketch of the beetle, I found no paper where it was usually kept. I looked in the drawer and found none there. I searched my pockets, hoping to find an old letter, and then my hand fell upon the parchment. I thus detail the precise mode in which it came into my possession; for the circumstances impressed me with peculiar force.

"No doubt you will think me fanciful—but I had already established a kind of *connection*. I had put together two links of a great chain. There was a boat lying on a seacoast, and not far from the boat was a parchment—*not a paper*—with a skull depicted on it. You will, of course, ask 'where is the connection?' I reply that the skull, or death's-head, is the well-known emblem of the pirate. The flag of the death's-head is hoisted in all engagements.

"I have said that the scrap was parchment and not paper. Parchment is durable—almost imperishable. Matters of little moment are rarely consigned to parchment; since, for the mere ordinary purposes of drawing or writing, it is not nearly so well adapted as paper. This reflection suggested some meaning—some relevancy—in the death's-head. I did not fail to observe, also, the *form* of the parchment. Although one of its corners had been, by some accident, destroyed, it could be seen that the original form was oblong. It was just such a slip, indeed, as might have been chosen for a memorandum—for a record of something to be long remembered and carefully preserved."

"But," I interposed, "you say that the skull was *not* upon the parchment when you made the drawing of the beetle. How then do you trace any connection between the boat and the skull—since this latter, according to your own admission, must have been designed (God only knows how or by whom) at some period subsequent to your sketching the *scarabaeus?*"

"Ah, hereupon turns the whole mystery; although the secret, at this point, I had comparatively little difficulty in solving. My steps were sure and could afford but a single result. I reasoned, for example, thus: When I drew the *scarabaeus,* there was no skull apparent on the parchment. When I had completed the drawing I gave it to you and observed you narrowly until you returned it. *You,* therefore, did not design the skull, and no one else was present to do it. Then it was not done by human agency. And nevertheless it was done.

"At this stage of my reflections I endeavored to remember, and *did* remember, with entire distinctness, every incident which occurred about the period in question. The weather was chilly (O rare and happy accident!), and a fire was blazing on the hearth. I was heated with exercise and sat near the table. You, however, had drawn a chair close to the chimney. Just as I placed the parchment in your hand, and as you were in the act of inspecting it, Wolf, the Newfoundland, entered and leaped upon your shoulders. With your left hand you caressed him and kept him off, while your right, holding the parchment, was permitted to fall listlessly between your knees, and in close proximity to the fire. At one moment I thought the blaze had caught it and was about to caution you, but, before I could speak, you had withdrawn it and were engaged in its examination. When I considered all these particulars, I doubted not for a moment that *heat* had been the agent in bringing to light, on the parchment, the skull which I saw designed on it. You are well aware that chemical preparations exist, and have existed time out of mind, by means of which it is possible to write on either paper or vellum, so that the characters shall become visible only when subjected to the action of fire. Zaffer, digested in *aqua regia* and diluted with four times its weight of water, is sometimes employed; a green tint results. The regulus of cobalt, dissolved in spirit of niter, gives a red. These colors disappear at longer or shorter intervals after the material written upon cools, but again become apparent upon the reapplication of heat.

"I now scrutinized the death's-head with care. Its outer edges —the edges of the drawing nearest the edge of the vellum—

were far more *distinct* than the others. It was clear that the action of the caloric had been imperfect or unequal. I immediately kindled a fire and subjected every portion of the parchment to a glowing heat. At first, the only effect was the strengthening of the faint lines in the skull; but, on persevering in the experiment, there became visible at the corner of the slip, diagonally opposite to the spot in which the death's-head was delineated, the figure of what I at first supposed to be a goat. A closer scrutiny, however, satisfied me that it was intended for a kid."

"Ha! ha!" said I, "to be sure I have no right to laugh at you— a million and a half of money is too serious a matter for mirth—

but you are not about to establish a third link in your chain; you will not find any especial connection between your pirates and a goat; pirates, you know, have nothing to do with goats; they appertain to the farming interest."

"But I have just said that the figure was *not* that of a goat."

"Well, a kid, then—pretty much the same thing."

"Pretty much, but not altogether," said Legrand. "You may have heard of one *Captain* Kidd. I at once looked on the figure of the animal as a kind of punning or hieroglyphical signature. I say signature; because its position on the vellum suggested this idea. The death's-head at the corner diagonally opposite had, in the same manner, the air of a stamp, or seal. But I was sorely put out by the absence of all else—of the body to my imagined instrument—of the text for my context."

"I presume you expected to find a letter between the stamp and the signature."

"Something of that kind. The fact is, I felt irresistibly impressed with a presentiment of some vast good fortune impending. I can scarcely say why. Perhaps, after all, it was rather a desire than an actual belief;—but do you know that Jupiter's silly words, about the bug being of solid gold, had a remarkable effect on my fancy? And then the series of accidents and coincidences—these were so *very* extraordinary. Do you observe how mere an accident it was that these events should have occurred on the *sole* day of all the year in which it has been, or may be, sufficiently cool for fire, and that without the fire, or without the intervention of the dog at the precise moment in which he appeared, I should never have become aware of the death's-head, and so never the possessor of the treasure?"

"But proceed—I am all impatience."

"Well; you have heard, of course, the many stories current—the thousand vague rumors afloat about money buried, somewhere on the Atlantic coast, by Kidd and his associates. These rumors must have had some foundation in fact. And that the rumors have existed so long and so continuously, could have resulted, it appeared to me, only from the circumstance of the buried treasure still *remaining* entombed. Had Kidd concealed

Jupiter wriggled himself into the first great fork.

his plunder for a time, and afterwards reclaimed it, the rumors would scarcely have reached us in their present unvarying form. You will observe that the stories told are all about money-seekers, not about money-finders. Had the pirate recovered his money, there the affair would have dropped. It seemed to me that some accident—say the loss of a memorandum indicating its locality—had deprived him of the means of recovering it, and that this accident had become known to his followers, who otherwise might never have heard that treasure had been concealed at all, and who, busying themselves in vain, because unguided, attempts to regain it, had given first birth, and then universal currency, to the reports which are now so common. Have you ever heard of any important treasure being unearthed along the coast?"

"Never."

"But that Kidd's accumulations were immense is well known. I took it for granted, therefore, that the earth still held them; and you will scarcely be surprised when I tell you that I felt a hope, nearly amounting to certainty, that the parchment so very strangely found involved a lost record of the place of deposit."

"But how did you proceed?"

"I held the vellum again to the fire, after increasing the heat; but nothing appeared. I now thought it possible that the coating of dirt might have something to do with the failure; so I carefully rinsed the parchment by pouring warm water over it, and, having done this, I placed it in a tin pan, with the skull downwards, and put the pan upon a furnace of lighted charcoal. In a few minutes, the pan having become thoroughly heated, I removed the slip, and, to my inexpressible joy, found it spotted, in several places, with what appeared to be figures arranged in lines. Again I placed it in the pan and suffered it to remain another minute. Upon taking it off, the whole was just as you see it now."

Here Legrand, having reheated the parchment, submitted it to my inspection. The following characters were rudely traced, in a red tint, between the death's-head and the goat:—

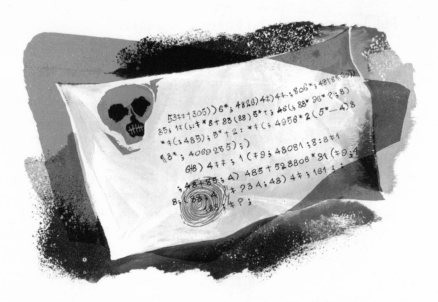

53‡‡†305))6*;4826)4‡.)4‡);806*;48†8¶60))85;;]8*;:‡*8†83(88)5*†;46(;
88*96*?;8)*‡(;485);5*†2:*‡(;4956 *2(5*—4)8¶8*;4069285);)6†8)4‡‡;1(‡9;
48081;8:8‡1;48†85;4)485†528806*81(‡9;48;(88;4(‡?34;48)4‡;161;:188;‡?;

"But," said I, returning him the slip, "I am as much in the
dark as ever. Were all the jewels of Golconda awaiting me
on my solution of this enigma, I am quite sure that I should be
unable to earn them."

"And yet," said Legrand, "the solution is by no means so
difficult as you might be led to imagine from the first hasty
inspection of the characters. These characters, as any one might
readily guess, form a cipher—that is to say, they convey a meaning; but then, from what is known of Kidd, I could not suppose
him capable of constructing any of the more abstruse crypto-
graphs. I made up my mind, at once, that this was of a simple
species—such, however, as would appear, to the crude intellect
of the sailor, absolutely insoluble without the key."

"And you really solved it?"

"Readily; I have solved others of an abstruseness ten thousand times greater, Circumstances, and a certain bias of mind,
have led me to take interest in such riddles, and it may well be
doubted whether human ingenuity can construct an enigma of

the kind which human ingenuity may not, by proper application, resolve. In fact, having once established connected and legible characters, I scarcely gave a thought to the mere difficulty of developing their import.

"In the present case—indeed in all cases of secret writing—the first question regards the *language* of the cipher; for the principles of solution, so far, especially, as the more simple ciphers are concerned, depend on, and are varied by, the genius of the particular idiom. In general, there is no alternative but experiment (directed by probabilities) of every tongue known to him who attempts the solution, until the true one be attained. But, with the cipher now before us, all difficulty is removed by the signature. The pun on the word 'Kidd' is appreciable in no other language than the English. But for this consideration I should have begun my attempts with the Spanish and French, as the tongues in which a secret of this kind would most naturally have been written by a pirate of the Spanish main. As it was, I assumed the cryptograph to be English.

"You observe there are no divisions between the words. Had there been divisions, the task would have been comparatively easy. In such case I should have commenced with a collation and analysis of the shorter words, and, had a word of a single letter occurred, as is most likely (*a* or *I*, for example), I should have considered the solution as assured. But, there being no division, my first step was to ascertain the predominant letters, as well as the least frequent. Counting all, I constructed a table, thus:

Of the character 8 there are 34
;	"	27
4	"	19
)	"	16
‡	"	15
*	"	14
5	"	12
6	"	11
(	"	9
†	"	8

235

1	"	7
0	"	6
9 2	"	5
: 3	"	4
?	"	3
¶	"	2
] — .	"	1

"Now, in English, the letter which most frequently occurs is *e*. Afterward the succession runs thus: *a o i d h n r s t u y c f g l m w b k p q x z*. E, however, predominates so remarkably that an individual sentence of any length is rarely seen, in which it is not the prevailing character.

"Here, then, we have, in the very beginning, the groundwork for something more than a mere guess. The general use which may be made of the table is obvious—but, in this particular cipher, we shall only very partially require its aid. As our predominant character is 8, we will commence by assuming it as the *e* of the natural alphabet. To verify the supposition, let us observe if the 8 be seen often in couples—for *e* is doubled with great frequency in English—in such words, for example, as 'meet,' 'fleet,' 'speed,' 'seen,' 'been,' 'agree,' &c. In the present instance we see it doubled no less than five times, although the cryptograph is brief.

"Let us assume 8, then, as *e*. Now, of all *words* in the language, 'the' is most usual; let us see, therefore, whether there are not repetitions of any three characters, in the same order of collocation, the last of them being 8. If we discover repetitions of such letters, so arranged, they will most probably represent the word 'the.' On inspection, we find no less than seven such arrangements, the characters being ;48. We may, therefore, assume that the semicolon represents *t*, that 4 represents *h*, and that 8 represents *e*—the last being now well confirmed. Thus a great step has been taken.

"But, having established a single word, we are enabled to establish a vastly important point; that is to say, several commencements and terminations of other words. Let us refer, for example, to the last instance but one in which the combination

236

;48 occurs—not far from the end of the cipher. We know that the semicolon immediately ensuing is the commencement of a word, and, of the six characters suceeding this 'the,' we are cognizant of no less than five. Let us set these characters down, thus, by the letters we know them to represent, leaving a space for the unknown—

t eeth.

"Here we are enabled, at once, to discard the '*th*,' as forming no portion of the word commencing with the first *t;* since, by experiment of the entire alphabet for a letter adapted to the vacancy, we perceive that no word can be formed of which this *th* can be a part. We are thus narrowed into

t ee,

and, going through the alphabet, if necessary, as before, we arrive at the word 'tree' as the sole possible reading. We thus gain another letter, *r*, represented by (, with the words 'the tree' in juxtaposition.

"Looking beyond these words, for a short distance, we again see the combination; 48, and employ it by way of *termination* to what immediately precedes. We have thus this arrangement:

the tree ;4(‡?34 the,

or, substituting the natural letters, where known, it reads thus:

the tree thr‡?3h the.

"Now, if, in place of the unknown characters, we leave blank spaces, or substitute dots, we read thus:

the tree thr . . . h the,

when the word '*through*' makes itself evident at once. But this discovery gives us three new letters, *o, u,* and *g*, represented by ‡ ? and 3.

"Looking now, narrowly, through the cipher for combinations of known characters, we find, not very far from the beginning, this arrangement,

83(88, or egree,

which, plainly, is the conclusion of the word 'degree,' and gives us another letter, *d*, represented by †.

"Four letters beyond the word 'degree,' we perceive the combination

;46(;88*.

"Translating the known characters, and representing the unknown by dots as before, we read thus:

th . rtee.

an arrangement immediately suggestive of the word 'thirteen,' and again furnishing us with two new characters, *i*, and *n*, represented by 6 and *.

"Referring, now, to the beginning of the cryptograph, we find the combination,

53‡‡†.

"Translating, as before, we obtain

. good,

which assures us that the first letter is *A*, and that the first two words are 'A good.'

"To avoid confusion, it is now time that we arrange our key, as far as discovered, in a tabular form. It will stand thus:

5	represents	a
†	"	d
8	"	e
3	"	g
4	"	h
6	"	i
*	"	n
‡	"	o
(	"	r
;	"	t

"We have, therefore, no less than ten of the most important letters represented, and it will be unnecessary to proceed with the details of the solution. I have said enough to convince you

238

that ciphers of this nature are readily soluble, and to give you some insight into the *rationale* of their development. But be assured that the specimen before us appertains to the very simplest species of cryptograph. It now only remains to give you the full translation of the characters upon the parchment, as unriddled. Here it is:

"'A good glass in the bishop's hostel in the devil's seat twenty-one degrees and thirteen minutes northeast and by north main branch seventh limb east side shoot from the left eye of the death's-head a beeline from the tree through the shot fifty feet out.'"

"But," said I, "the enigma seems still in as bad a condition as ever. How is it possible to extort a meaning from all this jargon about 'devil's seats,' 'death's-heads,' and 'bishop's hotels'?"

"I confess," replied Legrand, "that the matter still wears a serious aspect, when regarded with a casual glance. My first endeavor was to divide the sentence into the natural division intended by the cryptographist."

"You mean, to punctuate it?"

"Something of that kind."

"But how was it possible to effect this?"

"I reflected that it had been a *point* with the writer to run his words together without division, so as to increase the difficulty of solution. Now, a not over-acute man, in pursuing such an object, would be nearly certain to overdo the matter. When, in the course of his composition, he arrived at a break in his subject which would naturally require a pause, or a point, he would be exceedingly apt to run his characters, at this place, more than usually close together. If you will observe the MS., in the present instance, you will easily detect five such places of unusual crowding. Acting on this hint, I made the division thus:

"'A good glass in the bishop's hostel in the devil's seat—twenty-one degrees and thirteen minutes—northeast and by north—main branch seventh limb east side—shoot from the left eye of the death's-head—a beeline from the tree through the shot fifty feet out.'"

"Even this division," said I, "leaves me still in the dark."

"It left me also in the dark," replied Legrand, "for a few days, during which I made diligent inquiry, in the neighborhood of Sullivan's Island, for any building which went by the name of the 'Bishop's Hotel'; for, of course, I dropped the obsolete word 'hostel.' Gaining no information on the subject, I was on the point of extending my sphere of search, and proceeding in a more systematic manner, when one morning it entered my head, quite suddenly, that this 'Bishop's Hostel' might have some reference to an old family, of the name of Bessop, which, time out of mind, had held possession of an ancient manor-house, about four miles to the northward of the island. I accordingly went over to the plantation and reinstituted my inquiries among the older negroes of the place. At length one of the most aged of the women said that she had heard of such a place as *Bessop's Castle* and thought that she could guide me to it, but that it was not a castle, nor a tavern, but a high rock.

"I offered to pay her well for her trouble, and, after some demur, she consented to accompany me to the spot. We found it without much difficulty, when, dismissing her, I proceeded to examine the place. The 'castle' consisted of an irregular assemblage of cliffs and rocks—one of the latter being quite remarkable for its height as well as for its insulated and artificial appearance. I clambered to its apex, and then felt much at a loss as to what should be next done.

"While I was busied in reflection, my eyes fell on a narrow ledge in the eastern face of the rock, perhaps a yard below the summit upon which I stood. This ledge projected about eighteen inches and was not more than a foot wide, while a niche in the cliff just above it gave it a rude resemblance to one of the hollow-backed chairs used by our ancestors. I made no doubt that here was the 'devil's seat' alluded to in the MS., and now I seemed to grasp the full secret of the riddle.

"The 'good glass,' I knew, could have reference to nothing but a telescope; for the word 'glass' is rarely employed in any other sense by seamen. Now here, I at once saw, was a telescope to be used, and a definite point of view, *admitting no variation,* from which to use it. Nor did I hesitate to believe that the phrases, 'twenty-one degrees and thirteen minutes,' and 'northeast and by north,' were intended as directions for the leveling of the glass. Greatly excited by these discoveries, I hurried home, procured a telescope, and returned to the rock.

"I let myself down to the ledge, and found that it was impossible to retain a seat on it unless in one particular position. This fact confirmed my preconceived idea. I proceeded to use the glass. Of course, the 'twenty-one degrees and thirteen minutes' could allude to nothing but elevation above the visible horizon, since the horizontal direction was clearly indicated by the words, 'northeast and by north.' This latter direction I at once established by means of a pocket-compass; then, pointing the glass as nearly at an angle of twenty-one degrees of elevation as I could do it by guess, I moved it cautiously up or down, until my attention was arrested by a circular rift or opening in the foliage of a large tree that overtopped its fellows

241

in the distance. In the center of this rift I perceived a white spot but could not, at first, distinguish what it was. Adjusting the focus of the telescope, I again looked and now made it out to be a human skull.

"On this discovery I was so sanguine as to consider the enigma solved; for the phrase 'main branch, seventh limb, east side,' could refer only to the position of the skull on the tree, while 'shoot from the left eye of the death's-head' admitted, also, of but one interpretation, in regard to a search for buried treasure. I perceived that the design was to drop a bullet from the left eye of the skull, and that a beeline, or, in other words, a straight line, drawn from the nearest point of the trunk through 'the shot' (or the spot where the bullet fell) and thence extended to a distance of fifty feet, would indicate a definite point—and beneath this point I thought it at least *possible* that a deposit of value lay concealed."

"All this," I said, "is exceedingly clear and, although ingenious, still simple and explicit. When you left the 'Bishop's Hotel,' what then?"

"Why, having carefully taken the bearings of the tree, I turned homewards. The instant that I left 'the devil's seat,' however, the circular rift vanished; nor could I get a glimpse of it afterwards, turn as I would. What seems to me the chief ingenuity in this whole business, is the fact (for repeated experiment has convinced me it *is* a fact) that the circular opening in question is visible from no other attainable point of view than that afforded by the narrow ledge on the face of the rock.

"In this expedition to the 'Bishop's Hotel' I had been attended by Jupiter, who had no doubt observed, for some weeks past, the abstraction of my demeanor, and took especial care not to leave me alone. But, on the next day, getting up very early, I contrived to give him the slip and went into the hills in search of the tree. After much toil I found it. When I came home at night my valet proposed to give me a flogging. With the rest of the adventure I believe you are as well acquainted as myself."

"I suppose," said I, "you missed the spot, in the first attempt at digging, through Jupiter's stupidity in letting the bug fall through the right instead of through the left eye of the skull."

"Precisely. This mistake made a difference of about two inches and a half in the 'shot'—that is to say, in the position of the peg nearest the tree; and had the treasure been *beneath* the 'shot,' the error would have been of little moment; but the 'shot,' together with the nearest point of the tree, were merely two points for the establishment of a line of direction; of course the error, however trivial in the beginning, increased as we proceeded with the line and, by the time we had gone fifty feet, threw us quite off the scent. But for my deep-seated conviction that treasure was here somewhere actually buried, we might have had all our labor in vain."

243

"I presume the fancy of *the skull*—of letting fall a bullet through the skull's eye—was suggested to Kidd by the piratical flag. No doubt he felt a kind of poetical consistency in recovering his money through this ominous insignium."

"Perhaps so; still, I cannot help thinking that common sense had quite as much to do with the matter as poetical consistency. To be visible from the devil's seat, it was necessary that the object, if small, should be *white;* and there is nothing like your human skull for retaining and even increasing its whiteness under exposure to all vicissitudes of weather."

"But your grandiloquence and your conduct in swinging the beetle—how excessively odd! I was sure you were mad. And why did you insist on letting fall the bug, instead of a bullet, from the skull?"

"Why, to be frank, I felt somewhat annoyed by your evident suspicions touching my sanity, and so resolved to punish you quietly, in my own way, by a little bit of sober mystification. For this reason I swung the beetle and for this reason I let it fall from the tree. An observation of yours about its great weight suggested the latter idea."

"Yes, I perceive; and now there is only one point which puzzles me. What are we to make of the skeletons found in the hole?"

"That is a question I am no more able to answer than yourself. There seems, however, only one plausible way of accounting for them—and yet it is dreadful to believe in such atrocity as my suggestion would imply. It is clear that Kidd—if Kidd indeed secreted this treasure, which I doubt not—it is clear that he must have had assistance in the labor. But, the worst of this labor concluded, he may have thought it expedient to remove all participants in his secret. Perhaps a couple of blows with a mattock were sufficient, while his coadjutors were busy in the pit; perhaps it required a dozen—who shall tell?"

O. Henry

CALLOWAY'S CODE

ILLUSTRATED BY *Stan Lilstrom*
and *I. Heilbron*

THE New York *Enterprise* sent H. B. Calloway as special correspondent to the Russo-Japanese-Portsmouth war.

For two months Calloway hung about Yokohama and Tokio, shaking dice with the other correspondents for drinks or 'rickshaws—oh, no, that's something to ride in; anyhow, he wasn't earning the salary that his paper was paying him. But that was not Calloway's fault. The little brown men who held the strings of Fate between their fingers were not ready for the readers of the *Enterprise* to season their breakfast bacon and eggs with the battles of the descendants of the gods.

But soon the column of correspondents that were to go out with the First Army tightened their field-glass belts and went down to the Yalu with Kuroki. Calloway was one of these.

Now, this is no history of the battle of the Yalu River. That has been told in detail by the correspondents who gazed at the shrapnel smoke rings from a distance of three miles. But, for justice's sake, let it be understood that the Japanese commander prohibited a nearer view.

Calloway's feat was accomplished before the battle. What he did was to furnish the *Enterprise* with the biggest beat of the war. That paper published exclusively and in detail the news of the attack on the lines of the Russian General Zassulitch on the same day that it was made. No other paper printed a word about it for two days afterward, except a London paper, whose account was absolutely incorrect and untrue.

Calloway did this in face of the fact that General Kuroki was making his moves and laying his plans with the profoundest secrecy as far as the world outside his camps was concerned. The correspondents were forbidden to send out any news whatever of his plans; and every message that was allowed on the wires was censored with rigid severity.

The correspondent for the London paper handed in a cablegram describing Kuroki's plans, but as it was wrong from beginning to end, the censor grinned and let it go through.

So, there they were—Kuroki on one side of the Yalu with forty-two thousand infantry, five thousand cavalry, and one hundred and twenty-four guns. On the other side, Zassulitch waited for him with only twenty-three thousand men, and with a long stretch of river to guard. And Calloway had got hold of some important inside information that he knew would bring the *Enterprise* staff around a cablegram as thick as flies around a Park Row lemonade stand. If he could only get that message past the censor—the new censor who had arrived and taken his post that day!

Calloway did the obviously proper thing. He lit his pipe and sat down on a gun-carriage to think it over. And there we must leave him; for the rest of the story belongs to Vesey, a sixteen-dollar-a-week reporter on the *Enterprise*.

Calloway's cablegram was handed to the managing editor at four o'clock in the afternoon. He read it three times; and then drew a pocket mirror from a pigeonhole in his desk, and looked at his reflection carefully. Then he went over to the desk of Boyd, his assistant (he usually called Boyd when he wanted him), and laid the cablegram before him.

"It's from Calloway," he said. "See what you make of it."

The message was dated at Wi-ju, and these were the words of it:

Foregone preconcerted rash witching goes muffled rumor mine dark silent unfortunate richmond existing great hotly brute select mooted parlous beggars ye angel incontrovertible.

246

Boyd read it twice.

"It's either a cipher or a sunstroke," said he.

"Ever hear of anything like a code in the office—a secret code?" asked the m.e., who had held his desk for only two years. Managing editors come and go.

"None except the vernacular that the lady specials write in," said Boyd. "Couldn't be an acrostic could it?"

"I thought of that," said the m.e., "but the beginning letters contain only four vowels. It must be a code of some sort."

"Try 'em in groups," suggested Boyd. "Let's see—'Rash witching goes'—not with me it doesn't. 'Muffled rumor mine'— must have an underground wire. 'Dark silent unfortunate rich- mond'—no reason why he should knock that town so hard. 'Existing great hotly'—no, it doesn't pan out. I'll call Scott."

The city editor came in a hurry and tried his luck. A city editor must know something about everything; so Scott knew a little about cipher-writing.

"It may be what is called an inverted alphabet cipher," said he. "I'll try that. 'R' seems to be the oftenest used initial letter, with the exception of 'm'. Assuming 'r' to mean 'e,' the most frequently used vowel, we transpose the letters—so."

Scott worked rapidly with his pencil for two minutes; and then showed the first word according to his reading was the word "Scejtzez."

"Great!" cried Boyd. "It's a charade. My first is a Russian general. Go on, Scott."

"No, that won't work," said the city editor. "It's undoubtedly a code. It's impossible to read it without the key. Has the office ever used a cipher code?"

"Just what I was asking," said the m.e. "Hustle everybody up that ought to know. We must get at it some way. Calloway has evidently got hold of something big, and the censor has put the screws on, or he wouldn't have cabled in a lot of chop suey like this."

Throughout the office of the *Enterprise* a dragnet was sent, hauling in such members of the staff as would be likely to know of a code, past or present, by reason of their wisdom, information, natural intelligence, or length of servitude. They got together in a group in the city-room, with the m.e. in the center. No one had heard of a code. All began to explain to the head investigator that newspapers never used a code, anyhow—that is, a cipher code. Of course the Associated Press stuff is a sort of code—an abbreviation, rather—but—

The m.e. knew all that, and said so. He asked each man how long he had worked on the paper. Not one of them had drawn pay from an *Enterprise* envelope for longer than six years. Calloway had been on the paper twelve years.

"Try old Heffelbauer," said the m.e. "He was here when Park Row was a potato patch."

Heffelbauer was an institution. He was half janitor, half handy man about the office, and half watchman—thus becoming the peer of thirteen and one-half tailors. Sent for, he came, radiating his nationality.

"Heffelbauer," said the m.e., "did you ever hear of a code belonging to the office a long time ago—a private code? You know what a code is, don't you?"

"Yah," said Heffelbauer. "Sure I know vat a code is. Yah, apout dwelf or fifteen year ago der office had a code. Der reborters in der city-room haf it here."

"Ah!" said the m.e. "We're getting on the trail now. Where was it kept, Heffelbauer? What do you know about it?"

"Somedimes," said the retainer, "dey keep it in der little room behind der library room."

"Can you find it?" asked the m.e. eagerly. "Do you know where it is?"

"Mein Gott!" said Heffelbauer. "How long do you dink a code live? Der reborters call him a maskeet. But von day he butt mit his head der editor, und—"

"Oh, he's talking about a goat," said Boyd. "Get out, Heffelbauer."

Again discomfited, the concerted wit and resource of the *Enterprise* huddled around Calloway's puzzle, considering its mysterious words in vain.

Then Vesey came in.

Vesey was the youngest reporter. He had a thirty-two-inch chest and wore a number fourteen collar; but his bright Scotch plaid suit gave him presence and conferred no obscurity upon his whereabouts. He wore his hat in such a position that people followed him about to see him take it off, convinced that it must be hung upon a peg driven into the back of his head. He was never without an immense, knotted, hardwood cane with a German-silver tip on its crooked handle. Vesey was the best photograph hustler in the office. Scott said it was because no living human being could resist the personal triumph it was to hand his picture over to Vesey. Vesey always wrote his own news stories, except the big ones, which were sent to the rewrite men. Add to this fact that among all the inhabitants, temples, and groves of the earth nothing existed that could abash Vesey, and his dim sketch is concluded.

Vesey butted into the circle of cipher readers, very much as Heffelbauer's "code" would have done, and asked what was up. Someone explained, with the touch of half-familiar condescension that they always used toward him. Vesey reached out and took the cablegram from the m.e.'s hand. Under the protection of some special Providence, he was always doing appalling things like that and coming off unscathed.

"It's a code," said Vesey. "Anybody got the key?"

"The office has no code," said Boyd, reaching for the message. Vesey held to it.

"Then old Calloway expects us to read it, anyhow," said he. "He's up a tree, or something, and he's made this up so as to get it by the censor. It's up to us. Gee! I wish they had sent me, too. Say—we can't afford to fall down on our end of it. 'Foregone, preconcerted rash, witching'—h'm."

Vesey sat down on a table corner and began to whistle softly, frowning at the cablegram.

"Let's have it, please," said the m.e. "We've got to get to work on it."

"I believe I've got a line on it," said Vesey. "Give me ten minutes."

He walked to his desk, threw his hat into a wastebasket, spread out flat on his chest like a gorgeous lizard, and started his pencil going. The wit and wisdom of the *Enterprise* remained in a loose group and smiled at one another, nodding their heads toward Vesey. Then they began to exchange their theories about the cipher.

It took Vesey exactly fifteen minutes. He brought to the m.e. a pad with the code-key written on it.

"I felt the swing of it as soon as I saw it," said Vesey. "Hurrah for old Calloway! He's done the Japs and every paper in town that prints literature instead of news. Take a look at that."

Thus had Vesey set forth the reading of the code:

Foregone-conclusion
Preconcerted-arrangement
Rash-act
Witching-hour of midnight
Goes-without saying
Muffled-report
Rumor-hathit
Mine-host
Dark-horse
Silent-majority
Unfortunate-pedestrians
Richmond-in the field
Existing-conditions

Great-White Way
Hotly-contested
Brute-force
Select-few
Mooted-question
Parlous-times
Beggars-description
Ye-correspondent
Angel-unawares
Incontrovertible-fact

"It's simply newspaper English," explained Vesey. "I've been reporting on the *Enterprise* long enough to know it by heart. Old Calloway gives us the cue word, and we use the word that naturally follows it just as we use 'em in the paper. Read it over, and you'll see how pat they drop into their places. Now, here's the message he intended us to get."

Vesey handed out another sheet of paper.

Concluded arrangement to act at hour of midnight without saying. Report hath it that a large body of cavalry and an overwhelming force of infantry will be thrown into the field. Conditions white. Way contested by only a small force. Question the *Times* description. Its correspondent is unaware of the facts.

"Great stuff!" cried Boyd excitedly. "Kuroki crosses the Yalu tonight and attacks. Oh, we won't do a thing to the sheets that make up with Addison's essays, real estate transfers, and bowling scores!"

"Mr. Vesey," said the m.e. with his jollying-which-you-should -regard-as-a-favor manner, "you have cast a serious reflection upon the literary standards of the paper that employs you. You have also assisted materially in giving us the biggest 'beat' of the year. I will let you know in a day or two whether you are to be discharged or retained at a larger salary. Somebody send Ames to me."

Ames was the kingpin, the snowy-petalled marguerite, the star-bright looloo of the rewrite men. He saw attempted murder in the pains of green-apple colic, cyclones in the summer zephyr, lost children in every top-spinning urchin, an uprising of the down-trodden masses in every hurling of a derelict potato at a passing automobile. When not rewriting, Ames sat on the porch of his Brooklyn villa playing checkers with his ten-year-old son.

Ames and the "war editor" shut themselves in a room. There was a map in there stuck full of little pins that represented armies and divisions. Their fingers had been itching for days to move those pins along the crooked line of the Yalu. They did so now; and in words of fire Ames translated Calloway's brief message into a front-page masterpiece that set the world talking. He told of the secret councils of the Japanese officers; gave Kuroki's flaming speeches in full; counted the cavalry and infantry to a man and a horse; described the quick and silent building of the bridge at Suikauchen, across which the Mikado's legions were hurled upon the surprised Zassulitch, whose troops

252

were widely scattered along the river. And the battle!—well, you know what Ames can do with a battle if you give him just one smell of smoke for a foundation. And in the same story, with seemingly supernatural knowledge, he gleefully scored the most profound and ponderous paper in England for the false and misleading account of the intended movements of the Japanese First Army printed in its issue of *the same date.*

Only one error was made, and that was the fault of the cable operator at Wi-ju. Calloway pointed it out after he came back. The word "great" in his code should have been "gage" and its complemental words "of battle." But it went to Ames "conditions white," and of course he took that to mean snow. His description of the Japanese army struggling through the snowstorm, blinded by the whirling flakes, was thrillingly vivid. The artists turned out some effective illustrations that made a hit as pictures of the artillery dragging their guns through the drifts. But, as the attack was made on the first day of May the "conditions white" excited some amusement. But it made no difference to the *Enterprise,* anyway.

It was wonderful. And Calloway was wonderful in having made the new censor believe that his jargon of words meant no more than a complaint of the dearth of news and a petition for more expense money. And Vesey was wonderful. And most wonderful of all are words, and how they make friends one with another, being oft associated, until not even obituary notices them do part.

On the second day following, the city editor halted at Vesey's desk where the reporter was writing the story of a man who had broken his leg by falling into a coalhole—Ames having failed to find a murder motive in it.

"The old man says your salary is to be raised to twenty a week," said Scott.

"All right," said Vesey. "Every little helps. Say—Mr. Scott, which would you say—'We can state without fear of successful contradiction,' or, 'On the whole it can be safely asserted'?"

A. *Conan Doyle*

THE ADVENTURE OF
THE BLUE CARBUNCLE

ILLUSTRATED BY *J. Allen St. John*

I HAD called upon my friend Sherlock Holmes upon the second morning after Christmas, with the intention of wishing him the compliments of the season. He was lounging upon the sofa in a woolen dressing-gown, a pipe-rack within his reach upon the right, and a pile of crumpled morning papers, evidently newly studied, near at hand. Beside the couch was a wooden chair, and on the angle of the back hung a very seedy and disreputable hard-felt hat, much the worse for wear and cracked in several places. A lens and a forceps lying upon the seat of the chair suggested that the hat had been suspended in this manner for the purpose of examination.

"You are engaged," said I; "perhaps I interrupt you."

"Not at all. I am glad to have a friend with whom I can discuss my results. The matter is a perfectly trivial one" (he jerked his thumb in the direction of the old hat), "but there are points in connection with it which are not entirely devoid of interest and even of instruction."

I seated myself in his armchair and warmed my hands before his crackling fire, for a sharp frost had set in, and the windows were thick with the ice crystals. "I suppose," I remarked, "that, homely as it looks, this thing has some deadly story linked on to it—that it is the clew which will guide you in the solution of some mystery and the punishment of some crime."

"No, no. No crime," said Sherlock Holmes, laughing. "Only one of those whimsical little incidents which will happen when you have four million human beings all jostling each other

254

within the space of a few square miles. Amid the action and reaction of so dense a swarm of humanity, every possible combination of events may be expected to take place, and many a little problem will be presented which may be striking and bizarre without being criminal. We have already had experience of such."

"So much so," I remarked, "that of the last six cases which I have added to my notes, three have been entirely free of any legal crime."

"Precisely. You allude to my attempt to recover the Irene Adler papers, to the singular case of Miss Mary Sutherland, and to the adventure of the man with the twisted lip. Well, I have no doubt that this small matter will fall into the same innocent category. You know Peterson, the commissionaire?"

"Yes."

"It is to him that this trophy belongs."

"It is his hat."

"No, no; he found it. Its owner is unknown. I beg that you will look upon it, not as a battered billycock, but as an intellectual problem. And, first, as to how it came here. It arrived upon Christmas morning, in company with a good fat goose, which is, I have no doubt, roasting at this moment in front of Peterson's fire. The facts are these: about four o'clock on Christmas morning, Peterson, who, as you know, is a very honest fellow, was returning from some small jollification and was making his way homeward down Tottenham Court Road. In front of him he saw, in the gaslight, a tallish man, walking with a slight stagger and carrying a white goose slung over his shoulder. As he reached the corner of Goodge Street, a row broke out between this stranger and a little knot of roughs. One of the latter knocked off the man's hat, on which he raised his stick to defend himself, and, swinging it over his head, smashed the shop window behind him. Peterson had rushed forward to protect the stranger from his assailants; but the man, shocked at having broken the window, and seeing an official-looking person in uniform rushing towards him, dropped his goose, took to his heels, and vanished amid the labyrinth of small streets which lie at the back of Tottenham Court Road. The roughs had also fled at the appearance of Peterson, so that he was left in possession of the field of battle, and also of the spoils of victory in the shape of this battered hat and a most unimpeachable Christmas goose."

"Which surely he restored to their owner?"

"My dear fellow, there lies the problem. It is true that 'For Mrs. Henry Baker' was printed upon a small card which was tied to the bird's left leg, and it is also true that the initials 'H. B.' are legible upon the lining of this hat; but as there are some thousands of Bakers, and some hundreds of Henry Bakers in this city of ours, it is not easy to restore lost property to any one of them."

"What, then, did Peterson do?"

"He brought round both hat and goose to me on Christmas morning, knowing that even the smallest problems are of interest to me. The goose we retained until this morning, when there were signs that, in spite of the slight frost, it would be well that it should be eaten without unnecessary delay. Its finder has carried it off, therefore, to fulfill the ultimate destiny of a goose, while I continue to retain the hat of the unknown gentleman who lost his Christmas dinner."

"Did he not advertise?"

"No."

"Then, what clue could you have as to his identity?"

"Only as much as we can deduce."

"From his hat?"

"Precisely."

"But you are joking. What can you gather from this old battered felt?"

"Here is my lens. You know my methods. What can you gather yourself as to the individuality of the man who has worn this article?"

I took the tattered object in my hands and turned it over rather ruefully. It was a very ordinary black hat of the usual round shape, hard, and much the worse for wear. The lining had been of red silk, but was a good deal discolored. There

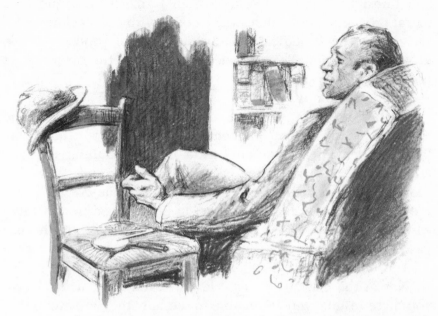

was no maker's name; but, as Holmes had remarked, the initials "H. B." were scrawled upon one side. It was pierced in the brim for a hat-securer, but the elastic was missing. For the rest, it was cracked, exceedingly dusty, and spotted in several places, although there seemed to have been some attempt to hide the discolored patches by smearing them with ink.

"I can see nothing," said I, handing it back to my friend.

"On the contrary, Watson, you can see everything. You fail, however, to reason from what you see. You are too timid in drawing your inferences."

"Then, pray tell me what it is that you can infer from this hat?"

He picked it up and gazed at it in the peculiar introspective fashion which was characteristic of him. "It is perhaps less suggestive than it might have been," he remarked, "and yet there are a few inferences which are very distinct, and a few others which represent at least a strong balance of probability. That the man was highly intellectual is of course obvious upon the face of it, and also that he was fairly well-to-do within the last three years, although he has now fallen upon evil days. He had foresight, but has less now than formerly, pointing to a moral retrogression, which, when taken with the decline of his fortunes, seems to indicate some evil influence, probably drink, at work upon him. This may account also for the obvious fact that his wife has ceased to love him."

"My dear Holmes!"

"He has, however, retained some degree of self-respect," he continued, disregarding my remonstrance. "He is a man who leads a sedentary life, goes out little, is out of training entirely, is middle-aged, has grizzled hair which he has had cut within the last few days, and which he anoints with lime-cream. These are the more patent facts which are to be deduced from his hat. Also, by the way, that it is extremely improbable that he has gas laid on in his house."

"You are certainly joking, Holmes."

"Not in the least. Is it possible that even now, when I give you these results, you are unable to see how they are attained?"

"I have no doubt that I am very stupid; but I must confess that I am unable to follow you. For example, how did you deduce that this man was intellectual?"

For answer Holmes clapped the hat upon his head. It came right over the forehead and settled upon the bridge of his nose. "It is a question of cubic capacity," said he; "a man with so large a brain must have something in it."

"The decline of his fortunes, then?"

"This hat is three years old. These flat brims curled at the edge came in then. It is a hat of the very best quality. Look at the band of ribbed silk and the excellent lining. If this man could afford to buy so expensive a hat three years ago, and has had no hat since, then he has assuredly gone down in the world."

"Well, that is clear enough, certainly. But how about the foresight and the moral retrogression?"

Sherlock Holmes laughed. "Here is the foresight," said he, putting his finger upon the little disk and loop of the hat-securer. "They are never sold upon hats. If this man ordered one, it is a sign of a certain amount of foresight, since he went out of his way to take this precaution against the wind. But since we see that he has broken the elastic, and has not troubled to replace it, it is obvious that he has less foresight now than formerly, which is a distinct proof of a weakening nature. On the other hand, he has endeavored to conceal some of these stains upon the felt by daubing them with ink, which is a sign that he has not entirely lost his self-respect."

"Your reasoning is certainly plausible."

"The further points, that he is middle-aged, that his hair is grizzled, that it has been recently cut, and that he uses lime-cream, are all to be gathered from a close examination of the lower part of the lining. The lens discloses a large number of hair-ends, clean cut by the scissors of the barber. They all appear to be adhesive, and there is a distinct odor of lime-cream. This dust, you will observe, is not the gritty, gray dust of the street, but the fluffy brown dust of the house, showing that it has been hung up indoors most of the time; while the marks of moisture upon the inside are proof positive that the wearer perspired very freely and could, therefore, hardly be in the best of training."

"But his wife—you said that she had ceased to love him."

"This hat has not been brushed for weeks. When I see you, my dear Watson, with a week's accumulation of dust upon your hat, and when your wife allows you to go out in such a state, I shall fear that you also have been unfortunate enough to lose your wife's affection."

"But he might be a bachelor."

"Nay, he was bringing home the goose as a peace-offering to his wife. Remember the card upon the bird's leg."

"You have an answer to everything. But how on earth do you deduce that the gas is not laid on in his house?"

"One tallow stain, or even two, might come by chance; but when I see no less than five, I think that there can be little doubt that the individual must be brought into frequent contact with burning tallow—walks upstairs at night probably with his hat in one hand and a guttering candle in the other. Anyhow, he never got tallow-stains from a gas jet. Are you satisfied?"

"Well, it is very ingenious," said I, laughing; "but since, as you said just now, there has been no crime committed, and no harm done, save the loss of a goose, all this seems to be rather a waste of energy."

Sherlock Holmes had opened his mouth to reply, when the door flew open, and Peterson, the commissionaire, rushed into the apartment with flushed cheeks and the face of a man who is dazed with astonishment.

"The goose, Mr. Holmes! The goose, sir!" he gasped.

"Eh? What of it, then? Has it returned to life and flapped off through the kitchen window?" Holmes twisted himself round upon the sofa to get a fairer view of the man's excited face.

"See here, sir! See what my wife found in its crop!" He held out his hand and displayed upon the center of the palm a brilliantly scintillating blue stone, rather smaller than a bean in size, but of such purity and radiance that it twinkled like an electric point in the dark hollow of his hand.

Sherlock Holmes sat up with a whistle. "By Jove, Peterson!" said he, "this is treasure trove indeed. I suppose you know what you have got?"

"A diamond, sir? A precious stone. It cuts into glass as though it were putty."

"It's more than a precious stone. It is *the* precious stone."

"Not the Countess of Morcar's blue carbuncle!" I ejaculated.

"Precisely so. I ought to know its size and shape, seeing that I have read the advertisement about it in *The Times* every day lately. It is absolutely unique, and its value can only be conjectured, but the reward offered of £1000 is certainly not within a twentieth part of the market price."

"A thousand pounds! Great Lord of mercy!" The commissionaire plumped down into a chair and stared from one to the other of us.

"That is the reward, and I have reason to know that there are sentimental considerations in the background which would induce the countess to part with half her fortune if she could but recover the gem."

"It was lost, if I remember aright, at the 'Hotel Cosmopolitan,' " I remarked.

"Precisely so, on December 22d, just five days ago. John Horner, a plumber, was accused of having abstracted it from the lady's jewel-case. The evidence against him was so strong that the case has been referred to the Assizes. I have some account of the matter here, I believe." He rummaged amid his newspapers, glancing over the dates, until at last he smoothed one out, doubled it over, and read the following paragraph:

" 'Hotel Cosmopolitan Jewel Robbery. John Horner, 26, plumber, was brought up upon the charge of having upon the 22d inst. abstracted from the jewel-case of the Countess of Morcar the valuable gem known as the blue carbuncle. James Ryder, upper-attendant at the hotel, gave his evidence to the effect that he had shown Horner up to the dressing-room of the Countess of Morcar upon the day of the robbery, in order that he might solder the second bar of the grate, which was loose. He had remained with Horner some little time, but had finally been called away. On returning, he found that Horner had disappeared, that the bureau had been forced open, and that the small morocco casket in which, as it afterwards transpired, the countess was accustomed to keep her jewel, was lying empty upon the dressing table. Ryder instantly gave the alarm, and Horner was arrested the same evening; but the stone could not be found either upon his person or in his rooms. Catherine Cusack, maid to the countess, deposed to having heard Ryder's cry of dismay on discovering the robbery and to having rushed into the room, where she found matters as described by the last witness. Inspector Bradstreet, B division, gave evidence as to the arrest of Horner, who struggled frantically and protested his innocence in the strongest terms. Evidence of a previous conviction for robbery having been given against the prisoner, the magistrate refused to deal summarily with the offence, but referred it to the Assizes. Horner, who had shown signs of intense emotion during the proceedings, fainted away at the conclusion and was carried out of court.'

"Hum! So much for the police court," said Holmes, thoughtfully, tossing aside the paper. "The question for us now to solve is the sequence of events leading from a rifled jewel-case at one end to the crop of a goose in Tottenham Court Road at the other. You see, Watson, our little deductions have suddenly assumed a much more important and less innocent aspect. Here is the stone; the stone came from the goose, and the goose came from Mr. Henry Baker, the gentleman with the bad hat and all the other characteristics with which I have bored you. So now we must set ourselves very seriously to finding this gentleman and ascertaining what part he has played in this little mystery. To do this, we must try the simplest means first, and these lie undoubtedly in an advertisement in all the evening papers. If this fail, I shall have recourse to other methods."

"What will you say?"

"Give me a pencil and that slip of paper. Now, then: 'Found at the corner of Goodge Street, a goose and a black felt hat. Mr. Henry Baker can have the same by applying at 6:30 this evening at 22ʙ, Baker Street.' That is clear and concise."

"Very. But will he see it?"

"Well, he is sure to keep an eye on the papers, since, to a poor man, the loss was a heavy one. He was clearly so scared by his mischance in breaking the window and by the approach of Peterson, that he thought of nothing but flight; but since then he must have bitterly regretted the impulse which caused him to drop his bird. Then, again, the introduction of his name will cause him to see it, for everyone who knows him will direct his attention to it. Here you are, Peterson, run down to the advertising agency and have this put in the evening papers."

"In which, sir?"

"Oh, in the *Globe, Star, Pall Mall, St. James's, Evening News, Standard, Echo,* and any others that occur to you."

"Very well, sir. And this stone?"

"Ah, yes, I shall keep the stone. Thank you. And, I say, Peterson, just buy a goose on your way back, and leave it here with me, for we must have one to give to this gentleman in place of the one which your family is now devouring."

When the commissionaire had gone, Holmes took up the stone and held it against the light. "It's a bonny thing," said he. "Just see how it glints and sparkles. Of course it is a nucleus and focus of crime. Every good stone is. They are the devil's pet baits. In the larger and older jewels every facet may stand for a bloody deed. This stone is not yet twenty years old. It was found in the banks of the Amoy River in Southern China and is remarkable in having every characteristic of the carbuncle, save that it is blue in shade, instead of ruby red. In spite of its youth, it has already a sinister history. There have been two murders, a vitriol-throwing, a suicide, and several robberies brought about for the sake of this forty-grain weight of crystallized charcoal. Who would think that so pretty a toy would be a purveyor to the gallows and the prison? I'll lock it up in my strong box now and drop a line to the countess to say that we have it."

"Do you think that this man Horner is innocent?"

"I cannot tell."

"Well, then, do you imagine that this other one, Henry Baker, had anything to do with the matter?"

"It is, I think, much more likely that Henry Baker is an absolutely innocent man, who had no idea that the bird which he was carrying was of considerably more value than if it were made of solid gold. That, however, I shall determine by a very simple test, if we have an answer to our advertisement."

"And you can do nothing until then?"

"Nothing."

"In that case I shall continue my professional round. But I shall come back in the evening at the hour you have mentioned, for I should like to see the solution of so tangled a business."

"Very glad to see you. I dine at seven. There is a woodcock, I believe. By the way, in view of recent occurrences, perhaps I ought to ask Mrs. Hudson to examine its crop."

I had been delayed at a case, and it was a little after half-past six when I found myself in Baker Street once more. As I approached the house I saw a tall man in a Scotch bonnet with a coat which was buttoned up to his chin, waiting outside in the bright semicircle which was thrown from the fanlight. Just as I arrived, the door was opened, and we were shown up together to Holmes's room.

"Mr. Henry Baker, I believe," said he, rising from his armchair and greeting his visitor with the easy air of geniality which he could so readily assume. "Pray take this chair by the fire, Mr. Baker. It is a cold night, and I observe that your circulation is more adapted for summer than for winter. Ah, Watson, you've come at the right time. That your hat, Mr. Baker?"

"Yes, sir, that is undoubtedly my hat."

He was a large man, with rounded shoulders, a massive head, and a broad, intelligent face, sloping down to a pointed beard of grizzled brown. A touch of red in nose and cheeks, with a slight tremor of his extended hand, recalled Holmes's surmise as to his habits. His rusty black frock coat was buttoned right up in front, with the collar turned up, and his lank wrists protruded from his sleeves without a sign of cuff or shirt. He spoke in a slow staccato fashion, choosing his words with care, and gave the impression generally of a man of learning and letters who had had ill-usage at the hands of fortune.

"We have retained these things for some days," said Holmes, "because we expected to see an advertisement from you giving

"Just as I arrived, the door was opened."

your address. I am at a loss to know now why you did not advertise."

Our visitor gave a rather shamefaced laugh. "Shillings have not been so plentiful with me as they once were," he remarked. "I had no doubt that the gang of roughs who assaulted me had carried off both my hat and the bird. I did not care to spend more money in a hopeless attempt at recovering them."

"Very naturally. By the way, about the bird, we were compelled to eat it."

"To eat it!" Our visitor half rose from his chair in his excitement.

"Yes, it would have been of no use to anyone had we not done so. But I presume that this other goose upon the sideboard, which is about the same weight and perfectly fresh, will answer your purpose equally well?"

"Oh, certainly, certainly," answered Mr. Baker, with a sigh of relief.

"Of course, we still have the feathers, legs, crop, and so on of your own bird, so if you wish—"

The man burst into a hearty laugh. "They might be useful to me as relics of my adventure," said he, "but beyond that I can hardly see what use the *disjecta membra* of my late acquaintance are going to be to me. No, sir, I think that, with your permission, I will confine my attentions to the excellent bird which I perceive upon the sideboard."

Sherlock Holmes glanced sharply across at me with a slight shrug of his shoulders.

"There is your hat, then, and there your bird," said he. "By the way, would it bore you to tell me where you got the other one from? I am somewhat of a fowl fancier, and I have seldom seen a better grown goose."

"Certainly, sir," said Baker, who had risen and tucked his newly-gained property under his arm. "There are a few of us who frequent the 'Alpha Inn,' near the Museum—we are to be found in the Museum itself during the day, you understand. This year our good host, Windigate by name, instituted a goose club, by which, on consideration of some few pence every week, we were each to receive a bird at Christmas. My pence were duly paid, and the rest is familiar to you. I am much indebted to you, sir, for a Scotch bonnet is fitted neither to my years nor my gravity." With a comical pomposity of manner he bowed solemnly to both of us and strode off upon his way.

"So much for Mr. Henry Baker," said Holmes, when he had closed the door behind him. "It is quite certain that he knows nothing whatever about the matter. Are you hungry, Watson?"

"Not particularly."

"Then I suggest that we turn our dinner into a supper, and follow up this clew while it is still hot."

"By all means."

It was a bitter night, so we drew on our ulsters and wrapped cravats about our throats. Outside, the stars were shining coldly in a cloudless sky, and the breath of the passers-by blew out into smoke like so many pistol shots. Our footfalls rang out crisply and loudly as we swung through the Doctors' quarter, Wimpole Street, Harley Street, and so through Wigmore Street into Oxford Street. In a quarter of an hour we were in Blooms-bury at the "Alpha Inn," which is a small public-house at the corner of one of the streets which runs down into Holborn. Holmes pushed open the door of the private bar and ordered two glasses of beer from the ruddy-faced, white-aproned land-lord.

"Your beer should be excellent if it is as good as your geese," said he.

"My geese!" The man seemed surprised.

"Yes. I was speaking only half an hour ago to Mr. Henry Baker, who was a member of your goose club."

"Ah! yes, I see. But you see, sir, them's not *our* geese."

"Indeed! Whose, then?"

"Well, I got the two dozen from a salesman in Covent Garden."

"Indeed? I know some of them. Which was it?"

"Breckinridge is his name."

"Ah! I don't know him. Well, here's your good health, land-lord, and prosperity to your house. Good night."

"Now for Mr. Breckinridge," he continued, buttoning up his coat, as we came out into the frosty air. "Remember, Watson, that though we have so homely a thing as a goose at one end of this chain, we have at the other a man who will certainly get seven years' penal servitude unless we can establish his innocence. It is possible that our inquiry may but confirm his guilt; but, in any case, we have a line of investigation which has been missed by the police and which a singular chance has placed in our hands. Let us follow it out to the bitter end. Faces to the south, then, and quick march!"

We passed across Holborn, down Endell Street, and so through a zigzag of slums to Covent Garden Market. One of the largest stalls bore the name of Breckinridge upon it, and the proprietor, a horsey-looking man, with a sharp face and trim side whiskers, was helping a boy to put up the shutters.

"Good evening. It's a cold night," said Holmes.

The salesman nodded and shot a questioning glance at my companion.

"Sold out of geese, I see," continued Holmes, pointing at the bare slabs of marble.

"Let you have 500 tomorrow morning."

"That's no good."

"Well, there are some on the stall with the gas-flare."

"Ah, but I was recommended to you."

"Who by?"

"The landlord of the 'Alpha.' "

"Oh, yes; I sent him a couple of dozen."

"Fine birds they were, too. Now where did you get them from?"

To my surprise the question provoked a burst of anger from the salesman.

"Now, then, mister," said he, with his head cocked and his arms akimbo, "what are you driving at? Let's have it straight, now."

"It is straight enough. I should like to know who sold you the geese which you supplied to the 'Alpha.' "

"Well, then, I sha'n't tell you. So now!"

"Oh, it is a matter of no importance; but I don't know why you should be so warm over such a trifle."

"Warm! You'd be as warm, maybe, if you were as pestered as I am. When I pay good money for a good article there should be an end of the business; but it's 'Where are the geese?' and 'Who did you sell the geese to?' and 'What will you take for the geese?' One would think they were the only geese in the world, to hear the fuss that is made over them."

"Well, I have no connection with any other people who have been making inquiries," said Holmes, carelessly. "If you won't tell us the bet is off, that is all. But I'm always ready to back my opinion on a matter of fowls, and I have a fiver on it that the bird I ate is country bred."

"Well, then, you've lost your fiver, for it's town bred," snapped the salesman.

"It's nothing of the kind."

"I say it is."

"I don't believe it."

"D'you think you know more about fowls than I, who have handled them ever since I was a nipper? I tell you, all those birds that went to the 'Alpha' were town bred."

"You'll never persuade me to believe that."

"Will you bet, then?"

"It's merely taking your money, for I know that I am right. But I'll have a sovereign on with you, just to teach you not to be obstinate."

The salesman chuckled grimly. "Bring me the books, Bill," said he.

The small boy brought round a small thin volume and a great greasy-backed one, laying them out together beneath the hanging lamp.

"Now then, Mr. Cocksure," said the salesman, "I thought that I was out of geese, but before I finish you'll find that there is still one left in my shop. You see this little book?"

"Well?"

"That's the list of the folk from whom I buy. D'you see? Well, then, here on this page are the country folk, and the numbers after their names are where their accounts are in the big ledger. Now, then! You see this other page in red ink? Well, that is a list of my town suppliers. Now, look at that third name. Just read it out to me."

"Mrs. Oakshott, 117, Brixton Road—249," read Holmes.

"Quite so. Now turn that up in the ledger."

Holmes turned to the page indicated. "Here you are, 'Mrs. Oakshott, 117, Brixton Road, egg and poultry supplier.' "

"Now, then, what's the last entry?"

" 'December 22. Twenty-four geese at 7s. 6d.' "

"Quite so. There you are. And underneath?"

" 'Sold to Mr. Windigate of the 'Alpha,' at 12s.' "

"What have you to say now?"

Sherlock Holmes looked deeply chagrined. He drew a sovereign from his pocket and threw it down upon the slab, turning away with the air of a man whose disgust is too deep for words. A few yards off he stopped under a lamp-post and laughed in the noiseless fashion which was peculiar to him.

"When you see a man with whiskers of that cut and the 'pink 'un' protruding out of his pocket, you can always draw him by a bet," said he. "I dare say that if I had put £100 down in front of him, that man would not have given me such complete information as was drawn from him by the idea that he was doing me on a wager. Well, Watson, we are, I fancy, nearing the end of our quest, and the only point which remains to be determined is whether we should go on to this Mrs. Oakshott tonight, or whether we should reserve it for tomorrow. It is clear from what that surly fellow said that there are others besides ourselves who are anxious about the matter, and I should—"

His remarks were suddenly cut short by a loud hubbub which broke out from the stall which we had just left. Turning round we saw a little rat-faced fellow standing in the center of the circle of yellow light which was thrown by the swinging lamp, while Breckinridge the salesman, framed in the door of his stall, was shaking his fists fiercely at the cringing figure.

"I've had enough of you and your geese," he shouted. "I wish you were all at the devil together. If you come pestering me any more with your silly talk I'll set the dog at you. You bring Mrs. Oakshott here and I'll answer her, but what have you to do with it? Did I buy the geese off you?"

"No; but one of them was mine all the same," whined the little man.

"Well, then, ask Mrs. Oakshott for it."

"She told me to ask you."

"Well, you can ask the King of Proosia, for all I care. I've had enough of it. Get out of this!" He rushed fiercely forward, and the inquirer flitted away into the darkness.

"Ha! this may save us a visit to Brixton Road," whispered Holmes. "Come with me, and we will see what is to be made of this fellow." Striding through the scattered knots of people who lounged round the flaring stalls, my companion speedily overtook the little man and touched him upon the shoulder. He sprang round, and I could see in the gaslight that every vestige of color had been driven from his face.

"Who are you, then? What do you want?" he asked, in a quavering voice.

"You will excuse me," said Holmes, blandly, "but I could not help overhearing the questions which you put to the salesman just now. I think that I could be of assistance to you."

"You? Who are you? How could you know anything of the matter?"

"My name is Sherlock Holmes. It is my business to know what other people don't know."

"But you can know nothing of this?"

"Excuse me, I know everything of it. You are endeavoring to trace some geese which were sold by Mrs. Oakshott, of Brixton Road, to a salesman named Breckinridge, by him in turn to Mr. Windigate, of the 'Alpha,' and by him to his club, of which Mr. Henry Baker is a member."

"Oh, sir, you are the very man whom I have longed to meet," cried the little fellow, with outstretched hands and quivering fingers. "I can hardly explain to you how interested I am in this matter."

Sherlock Holmes hailed a four-wheeler which was passing. "In that case we had better discuss it in a cosey room rather than in this windswept market place," said he. "But pray tell me, before we go farther, who it is that I have the pleasure of assisting."

The man hesitated for an instant. "My name is John Robinson," he answered, with a sidelong glance.

"No, no; the real name," said Holmes, sweetly. "It is always awkward doing business with an *alias*."

A flush sprang to the white cheeks of the stranger. "Well, then," said he, "my real name is James Ryder."

"Precisely so. Head-attendant at the 'Hotel Cosmopolitan.' Pray step into the cab, and I shall soon be able to tell you everything which you would wish to know."

The little man stood glancing from one to the other of us with half-frightened, half-hopeful eyes, as one who is not sure whether he is on the verge of a windfall or of a catastrophe. Then he stepped into the cab, and in half an hour we were back in the sitting room at Baker Street. Nothing had been said during our drive, but the high, thin breathing of our new companion, and the claspings and unclaspings of his hands, spoke of the nervous tension within him.

"Here we are!" said Holmes, cheerily, as we filed into the room. "The fire looks very seasonable in this weather. You look very cold, Mr. Ryder. Pray take this chair. I will just put on my slippers before we settle this little matter of yours. Now, then! You want to know what became of those geese?"

"Yes, sir."

"Or rather, I fancy, of that goose. It was one bird, I imagine, in which you were interested—white, with a black bar across the tail."

Ryder quivered with emotion. "Oh, sir," he cried, "can you tell me where it went to?"

"It came here."

"Here?"

"Yes, and a most remarkable bird it proved. I don't wonder that you should take an interest in it. It laid an egg after it was dead—the bonniest, brightest little blue egg that ever was seen. I have it here in my museum."

Our visitor staggered to his feet and clutched the mantelpiece with his right hand. Holmes unlocked his strongbox, and held up the blue carbuncle, which shone out like a star, with a cold, brilliant, many-pointed radiance. Ryder stood glaring with a drawn face, uncertain whether to claim or to disown it.

"The game's up, Ryder," said Holmes, quietly. "Hold up, man, or you'll be into the fire! Give him an arm back into his chair, Watson. He's not got blood enough to go in for felony with impunity. Give him a dash of brandy. So! Now he looks a little more human. What a shrimp it is, to be sure!"

For a moment he had staggered and nearly fallen, but the brandy brought a tinge of color into his cheeks, and he sat staring with frightened eyes at his accuser.

"I have almost every link in my hands, and all the proofs which I could possibly need, so there is little which you need tell me. Still, that little may as well be cleared up to make the case complete. You had heard, Ryder, of this blue stone of the Countess of Morcar's?"

"It was Catherine Cusack who told me of it," said he, in a crackling voice.

"I see—her ladyship's waiting-maid. Well, the temptation of sudden wealth so easily acquired was too much for you, as it has been for better men before you; but you were not very scrupulous in the means you used. It seems to me, Ryder, that there is the making of a very pretty villain in you. You knew that this man Horner, the plumber, had been concerned in some such matter before, and that suspicion would rest the more readily upon him. What did you do, then? You made some small job in my lady's room—you and your confederate Cusack —and you managed that he should be the man sent for. Then, when he had left, you rifled the jewel-case, raised the alarm, and had this unfortunate man arrested. You then—"

Ryder threw himself down suddenly upon the rug and clutched at my companion's knees. "For God's sake, have mercy!" he shrieked. "Think of my father! of my mother! It would break their hearts. I never went wrong before! I never will again. I swear it. I'll swear it on a Bible. Oh, don't bring it into court! For Christ's sake, don't!"

"Get back into your chair!" said Holmes, sternly. "It is very well to cringe and crawl now, but you thought little enough of this poor Horner in the dock for a crime of which he knew nothing."

"I will fly, Mr. Holmes. I will leave the country, sir. Then the charge against him will break down."

"Hum! We will talk about that. And now let us hear a true account of the next act. How came the stone into the goose, and how came the goose into the open market? Tell us the truth, for there lies your only hope of safety."

Ryder passed his tongue over his parched lips. "I will tell you it just as it happened, sir," said he. "When Horner had been arrested, it seemed to me that it would be best for me to get away with the stone at once, for I did not know at what moment the police might not take it into their heads to search me and my room. There was no place about the hotel where it would be safe. I went out, as if on some commission, and I made for my sister's house. She had married a man named Oakshott and lived in Brixton Road, where she fattened fowls for the market. All the way there every man I met seemed to me to be a policeman or a detective; and, for all that it was a cold night, the sweat was pouring down my face before I came to the Brixton Road. My sister asked me what was the matter, and why I was so pale, but I told her that I had been upset by the jewel robbery at the hotel. Then I went into the backyard and smoked a pipe and wondered what it would be best to do.

"I had a friend once called Maudsley, who went to the bad, and has just been serving his time in Pentonville. One day he had met me, and fell into talk about the ways of thieves, and how they could get rid of what they stole. I knew that he would be true to me, for I knew one or two things about him; so I made up my mind to go right on to Kilburn, where he lived, and take him into my confidence. He would show me how to turn the stone into money. But how to get to him in safety? I thought of the agonies I had gone through in coming from the hotel. I might at any moment be seized and searched, and there would be the stone in my waistcoat pocket. I was leaning against the wall at the time, and looking at the geese which were waddling about round my feet, and suddenly an idea came into my head which showed me how I could beat the best detective that ever lived.

"My sister had told me some weeks before that I might have the pick of her geese for a Christmas present, and I knew that she was always as good as her word. I would take my goose now, and in it I would carry my stone to Kilburn. There was a little shed in the yard, and behind this I drove one of the birds—a fine big one, white, with a barred tail. I caught it, and, prying its bill open, I thrust the stone down its throat as far as my finger could reach. The bird gave a gulp, and I felt the stone pass along its gullet and down into its crop. But the creature flapped and struggled, and out came my sister to know what was the matter. As I turned to speak to her the brute broke loose and fluttered off among the others.

" 'Whateve: were you doing with that bird, Jem?' says she.

" 'Well,' said I, 'you said you'd give me one for Christmas, and I was feeling which was the fattest.'

" 'Oh,' says she, 'we've set yours aside for you—Jem's bird, we call it. It's the big white one over yonder. There's twenty-six of them, which makes one for you, and one for us, and two dozen for the market.'

" 'Thank you, Maggie,' says I; 'but if it is all the same to you, I'd rather have that one I was handling just now.'

" 'The other is a good three pound heavier,' said she, 'and we fattened it expressly for you.'

" 'Never mind. I'll have the other, and I'll take it now,' said I.

" 'Oh, just as you like,' said she, a little huffed. 'Which is it you want, then?'

" 'That white one with the barred tail, right in the middle of the flock.'

" 'Oh, very well. Kill it and take it with you.'

"Well, I did what she said, Mr. Holmes, and I carried the bird all the way to Kilburn. I told my pal what I had done, for he was a man that it was easy to tell a thing like that to. He laughed until he choked, and we got a knife and opened the goose. My heart turned to water, for there was no sign of the stone, and I knew that some terrible mistake had occurred. I left the bird, rushed back to my sister's, and hurried into the backyard. There was not a bird to be seen there.

" 'Where are they all, Maggie?' I cried.

" 'Gone to the dealer's, Jem.'

" 'Which dealer's?'

" 'Breckinridge, of Covent Garden.'

J. Allen St. John

" 'But was there another with a barred tail?' I asked, 'the same as the one I chose?'

" 'Yes, Jem; there were two barred-tailed ones, and I could never tell them apart.'

"Well, then, of course I saw it all, and I ran off as hard as my feet would carry me to this man Breckinridge; but he had sold the lot at once, and not one word would he tell me as to where they had gone. You heard him yourselves tonight. Well, he has always answered me like that. My sister thinks that I am going mad. Sometimes I think that I am myself. And now—and now I am myself a branded thief, without ever having touched the wealth for which I sold my character. God help me! God help me!" He burst into convulsive sobbing, with his face buried in his hands.

There was a long silence, broken only by his heavy breathing and by the measured tapping of Sherlock Holmes's fingertips upon the edge of the table. Then my friend rose and threw open the door.

"Get out!" said he.

"What, sir! Oh, heaven bless you!"

"No more words. Get out!"

And no more words were needed. There was a rush, a clatter upon the stairs, the bang of a door, and the crisp rattle of running footfalls from the street.

"After all, Watson," said Holmes, reaching up his hand for his clay pipe, "I am not retained by the police to supply their deficiencies. If Horner were in danger it would be another thing; but this fellow will not appear against him, and the case must collapse. I suppose that I am commuting a felony, but it is just possible that I am saving a soul. This fellow will not go wrong again; he is too terribly frightened. Send him to jail now, and you make him a jailbird for life. Besides, it is the season of forgiveness. Chance has put in our way a most singular and whimsical problem, and its solution is its own reward.

Howard Pease

THE ADVENTURE
AT THE TOLL BRIDGE

ILLUSTRATED BY *Brinton Turkle*

FOG hazed across the low country that night as Tod Moran, with the utmost caution, drove his little car along the levee road. This was not a tule mist, he told himself as he peered past the windshield wiper; this was a real sea fog which sometimes crept upriver from San Francisco Bay. It made driving mighty slow. And at midnight he must be at the tollhouse on Bridge No. 3 to take over the graveyard watch.

When the levee road fell away behind and he glimpsed the white rails curving to the left, he breathed easier. Steadily the old Ford climbed in a sweeping curve until it was high above the river, then the roadway straightened out for its mile-long span across the San Joaquin. From the gloom ahead soon emerged the lights of the little toll office.

Buck Collinson stuck his head out the Dutch door. "About time you're here, young feller," he called. "Two minutes to midnight."

"Well, I made it, didn't I?" Tod retorted. He swung his car out onto the narrow parking space opposite the office. "How's business?"

"Rotten." Buck opened the office door for him to enter. "I guess you'll have plenty of time to get your studies done. What's it tonight? Math again?"

"No such luck. History. Feudal age."

"Huh!" Buck Collinson snorted in disgust as he buttoned his suède jacket across his chest. "I can't see how studyin' about tripe like that'll get you anywhere these days."

279

Tod wholeheartedly agreed. He opened the cash drawer, counted the money with a practiced hand, and signed a paper showing he had received one hundred and forty-odd dollars from the four-to-twelve shift. "What's in these envelopes, Buck? Bills paid?"

"Yep. Some o' the trucks dropped 'em off when they crossed tonight. Three hundred and two dollars in checks and currency. Count it. Better watch that drawer careful too. We don't want to be left without change like we was after that holdup last month."

Tod grinned as he closed the money drawer. "Don't worry. This boy knows how to use a pistol."

"That so?" Buck Collinson's dark face showed concern. "Listen, brother. If any tough birds come along asking you to hand over that cash I'd advise you to do it. I ain't too keen about taking flowers to you in the hospital—or to your funeral either."

"Right you are, Buck. I'll watch my step." Tod nodded slowly, his gray eyes thoughtful. "It's No. 2 those guys have been after lately, isn't it? More money there."

"Yep—but more lonesome here." Buck opened the door with a quick movement. "See you later."

Buck's small red coupé disappeared into the fog toward the mainland. Tod stood at the door until the sound of the motor receded into the distance. For eight hours now he would be alone. Even the cars and trucks that passed during the night would be relatively few, for Toll Bridge No. 3 was no longer on the main artery of travel between Sacramento and the Bay. And on a foggy night there would be even less traffic. Pulling up his coat collar, he listened. No car was coming. Time now to make his rounds.

He plunged into the dripping grayness and turned toward the mainland. A few yards brought him to the safety barrier. He pulled down the long black-and-white arm, noting with satisfaction that its red light instantly went on. He pushed it up again and the light winked out.

Back he went to the tollhouse, crossed the checking bar and the weighing scales, and came to the end of the concrete road-

280

way. Before him lay the steel section which was raised vertically in the manner of a lift whenever a steamer passed through. His shoes rang loudly as he advanced to the middle of the lift and leaned over the rail, facing upriver. The tide was on the ebb. He could hear far below him the current washing softly against the steel and masonry foundations of the towers. Through the fog the colored lights were dimly visible. The gray obscurity closed about the red and the green lamps as if bent upon shutting out all sense of direction for oncoming ships. But Tod was not worried. The telephone always announced the approach of a steamer from No. 2 downstream or from the smaller drawbridge that spanned the San Joaquin several miles up its course. When word reached No. 3 on a thick night, there was plenty of time to switch on the foghorns.

Crossing to the downriver side, he found the lights there even more obscured. No matter. Toll Bridge No. 3 had never yet been the scene of an accident with any seagoing freighter from the Bay.

A heavy truck, roaring up the incline from Marsh Island half a mile away, sent him hurrying on to the other safety barrier beyond the lift. The signal was in perfect working order. He waited for the truck to emerge from the mist and then jumped upon the step and rode back to the office. The truck, carrying a load of asparagus, was on its way to the mainland and the early market in San Francisco. He weighed it quickly, had the driver sign the slip, and then listened to its departing rumble. Silence once more pressed close about him.

Time now for a little real work. Slamming shut the upper half of the door, he turned to the high desk and opened his history. *The feudal system,* he read, *was the direct outgrowth of a need for protection in a world not yet civilized.* He read slowly, intently, just as he always did when alone on the graveyard shift.

Tod Moran worked for three nights every week end on Toll Bridge No. 3. As relief man he allowed the three regular men to get their weekly day off. It was a good job, Tod knew, and

paid his expenses at college. Moreover, he usually had some time for study.

Yet tonight, for some unknown reason, he didn't seem able to concentrate. Maybe it was because Buck Collinson's jibe still echoed in his mind. Buck was right, too, Tod decided. There was no connection between the old feudal age in Europe and this modern machine age in America. Reading this stuff was not only boring; it was useless as well. But an outline had to be ready for his history instructor on Monday. Once the blamed thing was finished he could proceed to forget what it was all about.

Again he turned to his book. *When a runner announced the coming of an enemy to the lord of the castle. . .* Settling himself on the stool, Tod hunched his shoulders. This was better. He read with mounting interest. The only sound in the little office was the soft purr of the electric stove at his feet.

Interrupted only twice during the next hour, he was deep in his outline of the Carolingian age when he abruptly rubbed his eyes. His pencil, poised over the word *vassal*, dropped to the desk. The bridge lights winked once—twice! Darkness surrounded him.

Without misgivings he waited for them to flash on again. He wasn't concerned—not yet. Over at the substation across the delta islands the night engineer always switched the bridge onto another line when anything like this occurred. But always before, he suddenly recalled, the juice had gone off when a storm was raging in the Sierras and sweeping down into the valley. On a still night with only fog hanging over the river country any interruption in the service was unusual.

When he noticed the glowing units of the electric stove gradually grow dim and entirely disappear he became slightly uneasy. Maybe he'd better telephone the substation. Often during the small hours of the morning he had to raise the lift to allow a seagoing cargo-carrier to pass through on its way to the port of Stockton. Before he phoned, however, he'd better see if the line which served the motor was also out of order.

He flung open the office door, and at once the fog swirled in. Diving across in the darkness, he made his way more slowly into the motor shed. He lighted a match and pulled down the big switch. The motor began its shining whir. He was relieved. It was only the lights then.

Back in the office again, he felt for the telephone book. Several matches aided him in finding the number. He lifted the receiver from its hook.

"Hello," he said in a voice that rang loud in the confined space. "Operator!"

No answer. Not even a faint buzz sounded over the wire. He suddenly felt his heart turn cold. The line was dead.

Seated perfectly rigid on his stool, he tried to collect his thoughts. If the electric lights alone had gone off he wouldn't have felt so apprehensive. But the telephone too! It couldn't possibly be a coincidence. Something was up.

On the instant he slid off the stool. He took a step toward the little drawer at one end of the desk. When his fingers came in contact with cold steel and his hand closed round the butt of a pistol he gained new courage. Funny thing though, he hadn't heard any car.

Cautiously he turned to the door, leaned out the upper section, and listened. The fog seemed to blot out any sound. Yet he suspected that from either the island shore or the mainland someone would be coming quickly, intent upon gaining possession of the money in the drawer. The money! He whirled, opened the cash drawer, and felt around in the back until he found a soft cotton bag. This he hurriedly filled. He'd leave only ten or fifteen dollars in the till.

A moment later he was at the door. He had decided where he would hide the money. He ran for a short distance toward the Marsh Island end of the bridge and drew to a stop in the center of the steel roadway. Here on the lift would be a safe place. Feeling his way to the rail, he dropped the bag at his feet. On a thick night like this it would be overlooked here. As he turned away his hand felt for the revolver in his pocket. He drew it out and examined it in the darkness. It was loaded.

To his ears at that moment came the muffled sound of a car approaching from Marsh Island. He could hear the motor as it sped up the incline. Was it a casual fare—or did the car contain an enemy?

An enemy. . . Through his mind flashed a sentence he had read an hour before. *When a runner announced the coming of an enemy to the lord of the castle the first order given was to raise the drawbridge.* As though impelled by an urgent command Tod turned and raced for the motor shed. If he raised the great steel lift between him and the approaching car he could cut off the enemy.

In the shed he struck a match and pulled down the heavy switch. A steady whine came from the motor. At once he took a firm hold on a second switch and pressed it up into place. A loud rumble reached his ears. The steel section of the bridge was slowly lifting.

The next moment a thought struck him like a blow. Suppose it was merely an unsuspecting fare coming across the bridge? While the safety barriers would drop the very instant the lift began rising, there would be no red glow to warn the oncoming car, which might break through the wooden pole and dive off the concrete into the river. In that deep channel, with the

current sweeping down toward the bay, only one end could await the occupants—death. With a hand that trembled he reversed the switch. Slowly the lift descended.

He brought it to a stop, however, before it had settled into place on its foundations; then he rushed out to see how far above the roadway it rested. The night was so black that he had to stretch forth his hands. The lift had stopped nearly three feet above the road.

Taking a deep breath, he waited. The oncoming car, apparently unsuspecting, was still racing toward him from Marsh Island. He could hear its motor clearly now; it was almost up to the lift. An instant later he caught the muffled crash of breaking wood. The car had plunged through the safety barrier.

Tod stood utterly still. He heard the grinding of brakes and a curse that ripped through the fog. The car had come to a halt. Good. Friend or foe, there was now no danger of its catapulting into the river. Yet a man could easily hop up three feet to the lift and run across. A man? . . . He recalled that it had been two men who had held up Buck Mulligan a month before. It had been a black sedan, Buck never tired of telling, that had driven up to the toll office; and, while the driver kept him covered with an automatic, a confederate had rifled the money drawer. Suppose, Tod reflected, the same two men were now across there in the darkness, jumping from their black sedan?

At the thought he made a dive for the shed. It took him only a moment to switch on the power. An instant later the steady grind of the lift sounded deep and prolonged as it rose like an immense elevator into the night. There was no need for him to remain here longer. When the lift reached the top of the towers it would automatically stop.

Outside he could see nothing. The damp fog, pressing about his face, beaded his eyelashes with moisture. High above him the lift was still slowly rising. No sound of any kind came from across the open river. He turned back toward the toll office. What if another car came from the mainland? He couldn't be sure it would mean only another broken safety barrier.

Quickly he felt his way across to the little parking space. He climbed into his Ford, started the motor, switched on the lights, and then drove the car out into the roadway. When the lowered barrier pole hung directly across his headlights he pulled up short and, leaving the lights on, jumped out. Above him he heard the lift stop; only a faint purr came from the shed. Yet in his ears was the steadily growing sound of another motor. He listened. From the mainland a car was coming.

Instinctively his hand went to his pocket. He drew out the revolver and, standing well back in the shadow of his car, faced the safety barrier. Now he was ready. Let them come.

Out of the fog emerged two headlights. The bumper and radiator of a car took form as it slowed down and drew to a stop directly in front of Tod's own lights shining wanly through the mist. The arriving car was new and black in color.

A voice rang out. "Steamer going through?"

"Yes." Tod's voice was firm. "Stay right where you are. I've got you covered."

There came a startled grunt, then the voice went on. "What's the big idea? I'm Dr. Grover—on my way to a patient on Marsh Island."

Tod had never heard of any Dr. Grover. "Where are you from?" he questioned.

"Brentwood. I took over Dr. Taylor's practice six weeks ago. I've got to get through to the island as quickly as possible."

"Serious?"

"I'm not sure. It's old Mrs. Jameson. Taylor told me she's always getting him out in the middle of the night. But she does pay her bills." He paused for a moment. "Anything wrong?"

Tod moved forward a step. "I think so."

The rays of the Ford's lights disclosed the head and shoulders of a middle-aged man leaning out of his car window. "You're not very complimentary, young man. Who do you take me for?"

He listened in silence as Tod briefly told him. Finally he nodded. "So the other car's opposite, eh? Then I can't get across?"

"Not a chance."

There was no hesitation in his reply. "What can I do to help?"

"Turn around and go back to the first house a hundred yards from the bridge. That's the Stevens' place. Ask Mrs. Stevens

287

to phone Buck Collinson and have him get in touch with the sheriff. Tell him to phone the substation and the telephone company too."

"That all?" Dr. Grover was slightly sarcastic. "And how about my patient?"

"The quicker you make it the bigger chance you'll have to save her."

"Oh, I'm not worried." The doctor's head disappeared. His car backed away, turned, and a moment later its red taillight vanished into the fog.

Once more Tod was alone. Somewhat uncertainly he glanced over his shoulder. Not more than twenty feet behind him lay the abyss that dropped away to the river far below. He raised his eyes to the steel tower, and his heart missed a beat at what he saw.

High above on the upraised lift he could faintly make out the beam of a small flashlight against the steel girders. By thunder, he had forgotten something! Ladders led up to the towers on each side of the lift. Someone from that other car had climbed up the ladder on the far tower, made his way across the lift, and was now coming down to the tollhouse. How many were coming? One man—two?

On quick feet Tod went past the motor shed to the base of the steel tower. Putting his ear against the ladder, he listened. Footsteps, clearly audible, were descending in the darkness.

Without hesitation he raised his revolver. Aiming at the sky, he pulled the trigger. A shot cracked out, loud and abrupt.

"Better not come down," he shouted up into the fog.

There was no answer to his challenge. There was nothing he could see as he peered upward. The beam of the flashlight had vanished.

Again he put his ear to the ladder. The footsteps were still descending. So the shot had not been enough of a warning! Maybe he'd better take aim and show that he meant business. He could just hit the steel somewhere, not really plug the fellow. But in this pitch darkness—

At that moment, from upriver and appallingly close, sounded the dull blare of a whistle. His body grew taut. A steamer! All thought of the man on the ladder dropped from his mind. Once more came the muffled blare of the whistle, closer this time.

He knew that sound. This was no river steamer with a rear paddle wheel; this was one of the seagoing cargo carriers that loaded grain at Stockton for the East Coast. Of six or eight thousand tons, it would need every safety device on Bridge No. 3. And the lights were out! Were the foghorns still working?

He rushed into the shed, swung down the proper switch and, hardly daring to breathe, waited for the sound of that first long wail of warning. He was familiar with them—the north horn loud and deep, the south one shrill and more abrupt. But no sound broke the stillness. The foghorns, too, were dead.

In a panic he swung about. That great deep-sea freighter was in danger. Bridge No. 3 was in danger. Outside he flung an agonized glance about him. The headlights of his Ford caught his eye.

Instantly he raced across to the open door of his car. Flinging himself into the seat, he started the motor, swung her into gear, turned, and drove with perilous speed past the dark little office straight for the void where the road dropped away. He put on his brake and stopped the car within two feet of the

edge. Then he switched on his foglights in the desperate hope that their gleam, pouring downward, would be seen by the approaching ship. At the same time his other hand went into action. Under the intermittent pressure of his fingers the horn punctuated the stillness with steady notes of warning.

Would the captain and the river pilot aboard that big freighter realize that something was wrong on No. 3? When they heard the shrill horn sounding would they order full speed astern and stop to investigate? Between sounds he listened. He caught the faint clang of a bell, the steady throb of the steamer's engines. Upstream and almost level with himself he discerned a red light slowly approaching. It was the port light on the ship's navigation bridge shining warmly through the mist. Then, below it, portholes suddenly came into view. But the great ship was losing headway. He breathed easier.

Far below him the lookout on the forecastle head suddenly raised his voice. "Bridge twenty feet off starboard bow!" Almost at once a powerful searchlight on the navigation bridge flung its rays through the fog. The cone of light leaped down to the starboard, then swung back in a wide arc to port.

Abruptly Tod started. Something blunt and hard was pressing against his ribs. He turned his head. The shadowy figure of a man leaned over the car door. His face was muffled, his hat pulled low over his eyes. "Where's the coin, buddy?"

"In the office." In vain Tod tried to keep his voice steady.

"Twelve bucks? Come clean, buddy, if yer don't want to find yourself floating belly up. Where's the rest?"

The money. How unimportant it had suddenly become. The only thing that counted now was to get this steamer through in safety. "I put the money in a bag," Tod said quickly.

"Well, hand it across."

"You'll find it against the rail on the upstream side of the lift. Somewhere near the center of the span."

"Is this straight?"

"Yes. Can't you see all I want is to get this freighter through?"

"Okay. If I don't find it"—the pressure against Tod's side increased for a second—"I'll be back."

He was gone. His husky voice was only a memory that somehow didn't quite seem real.

From the river came the clang of a bell. Tod craned far out, gazing down to one side past his windshield. The blurred outline of the ship's wheelhouse drifted slowly by. Then a lifeboat hanging from its davits swam vaguely past. The low murmur of voices reached his ears. Two portholes of a lighted cabin came into view, drew abreast, and disappeared downstream. The big freighter had passed through Bridge No. 3.

On legs that were strangely weak Tod crawled from his car. Sweat stood out on the palms of his hands. By thunder, that was a close call. The money? It didn't matter.

He looked up in the darkness. Nothing but blackness met his gaze. Crossing to the motor shed, he leaned against the door. A low blare came from downstream. The steamer was reaching the point where the San Joaquin joined the Sacramento.

Suddenly he raised his head. Across the open span a motor was starting. Well, what of it? Let it go. He heard the car turn and speed away toward Marsh Island. The man must have found the bag all right. Oh, why had he told him just where it was? Why hadn't he said the opposite rail? It was too late now. There'd be a nice little report for him to write up in the morning.

Slowly on tired feet he entered the motor shed, pulled down the switch, and heard the low rumble of the lift as it descended. There was nothing he could do but wait for Dr. Grover to return.

The doctor came back fifteen minutes later. "Everything all right? Good. Mrs. Stevens helped me do all the telephoning. Buck Collinson wasn't home yet, but I left word with his landlady. Now may I cross to my patient?"

"Thanks a million, Dr. Grover." Tod's voice was low, tired. "I'll get along okay now."

"How about the car that brought the men? They didn't get the money, did they?"

"Yes."

"Too bad. Well, I'll see you in about an hour."

Soon afterwards the sheriff arrived with a deputy, and almost on his heels followed a telephone lineman and a troubleshooter from the electric-light company. While the deputy went back to town to broadcast the alarm the sheriff plied Tod with questions. "About four hundred and fifty dollars, you say? How much in checks?"

"More than a hundred."

"They won't be cashed. The radio cars will soon be scouring this whole delta country. They'll pick up every black sedan on the roads."

Tod was once more his old self. "But how can we be sure it was a black sedan? I didn't even see it." He paused. "Let me have your flash, Sheriff, will you?"

"Okay."

Tod took it, entered the dark office, sat down upon his stool, and flung open his history text.

Behind him he heard a grunt of amazement. "What in thunder are you doing?" The sheriff stared down at the book. "Say, has this holdup driven you wacky? Or are you just a cool one? What you doing—studying?"

The office was suddenly flooded with light as the electricity came on. The foghorns began sounding, low and mournful.

"Shut off the horns, will you please, Sheriff?"

"I suppose they're bothering your studying, eh?" The sheriff stomped out in disgust.

Swiftly Tod searched in his history for a passage he vaguely remembered. Something was hammering in the back of his mind, something he could not put into words; but he knew that if he could only find the clue this half-formed idea would flash crystal clear. He read a page quickly, then turned to the next. Of a sudden he sat up straight. He had it. *With the drawbridge raised the castle would be safe for weeks, even months. It was only when there lurked an enemy—*

For some time he remained seated at his desk in silence. Finally he looked up to stare unseeingly out a window. At length he jumped from his stool, took the pistol from his rear pocket, and went out.

The sheriff met him by the motor shed. "Well, I turned 'em off. I don't suppose you even noticed."

"No," Tod told him, "I didn't."

The sheriff stared. Tod raised the revolver, pointed it aloft at one of the steel girders mistily visible in the light, took aim, and fired.

"You're a rotten shot, Moran. But what's the big idea?"

"I just wanted to see if my hand still shook."

"Well, it musta shook plenty to make you miss at this distance." The sheriff turned away.

Tod called after him. "Where are you going?"

"I'm going to take your little car if you don't mind and make a beeline for the Sacramento River. I've a hunch those birds might find their way blocked and turn back."

"Don't go yet." Tod spoke in all seriousness. "How long does it take a car to go upstream along the levee road, cross on the little drawbridge up there, and swing back along the mainland?"

"You mean to drive in a circle and come back to this point? About fifty minutes. In this fog, longer."

Tod took out his watch. "Then stay here. In half an hour the car you're hunting will be coming back to this bridge."

"Are you cuckoo?"

"No." Tod threw him a friendly grin. "Like you, I've a hunch; that's all."

"Well, I won't stay—see? If you're scared you can phone my office for another deputy when the line's fixed."

"Wouldn't you rather pick up this car yourself?" Tod urged.

"Baloney!" The sheriff regarded him with a puzzled frown. He moved off toward the parked Ford, hesitated, then sat down on the running board. "I'll stay just thirty minutes." he said.

The half-hour had almost dragged by when Dr. Grover pulled up on his way home from Marsh Island. "She was asleep when I arrived. Everybody sleeps but a doctor."

Three minutes later an empty truck rumbled up from the mainland. When it had disappeared toward the island shore the telephone rang. "Hi, Sheriff," Tod called. "She's working again."

For five minutes the sheriff kept the line hot. At last he swung about to Tod. "They've picked up five black sedans."

"But it isn't a black sedan we want," Tod insisted.

"I suppose," the sheriff remarked with heavy sarcasm, "you lamped a yellow limousine with pink stripes and forgot to mention it to me."

Tod had his head out the Dutch door, listening intently. His eyes flashed with sudden fire. "Get ready, Sheriff. Here comes a car. I think it's the one we want."

From the direction of the mainland an automobile was coming across Toll Bridge No. 3. Soon two headlights broke through the curtain of fog. The car slowed down and drew to a stop at the narrow parking space opposite the office. It was a smart red coupé.

"That's your man, Sheriff." Tod's voice was tense. "Take no chances."

Buck Collinson flung himself out the door. "Say, what's doing?" he called. "My landlady said Dr. Grover left word for me to come."

The Sheriff dropped his automatic to his side. "Rot! It's only Buck."

Tod reached for the sheriff's pistol. "I'll trade with you," he said quickly. He raised the automatic and pointed it directly at the man who worked the four-to-twelve shift. "We've got you, Buck."

294

Buck Collinson's dark face flushed. "What's the idea?"

"Stand right where you are," Tod commanded.

The sheriff looked across at Tod. "Do you mean, Moran," he asked in a low tone, "you recognized the man who held you up tonight? You can swear it was Buck Collinson?"

Tod shook his head. "No, I didn't recognize him—or his voice either. But it was Buck just the same."

"He's gone nuts, Sheriff." Buck's voice broke on laughter that was far from steady.

"Oh no, I haven't, Buck." Tod's hand never wavered as he faced the man in the suede jacket. "You made one mistake, Buck. Remember you told me that reading about the feudal age was just so much tripe? Well, it wasn't. It gave me an idea."

"Yeah?" Buck's low tone was filled with angry insolence. "An' what was this sweet little idea you got?"

Tod spoke with vibrant intensity. "You weren't held up last month, Buck. You took the money yourself and told a tall tale about it. And tonight you cut the wires—and came near wrecking a steamer. Furthermore, you substituted blank cartridges for the ones in the company's pistol."

"Bilge!" The word came forth with an oath, but Tod caught a glimpse of sudden fright in the man's dark eyes.

"We'll prove it. Sheriff, give that revolver of mine the once-over."

The sheriff at length looked up with amazement. "You're right, Moran. These are all blanks."

Turkle

295

"Don't you see," Tod hurriedly explained. "Buck kept coming down that ladder after I fired because he knew there was no real danger from my revolver. He planned to change these blanks again when he came on duty at four this afternoon."

"You lie!" Buck challenged hoarsely.

Tod never took his gaze from the man's face. "Did you have time to hide the money? You needn't answer. Sheriff, maybe you'd better search his car. I wouldn't be surprised if the blamed fool didn't feel so sure of himself that he brought the loot along with him. The bag's got the company's name on it."

Tod heard the sheriff cross to the small red car and throw open the door. After a short while came his comment, "Nothing here." Then the rumble seat was opened. A moment later a grunt of surprise greeted Tod and his prisoner. "Moran, here's the bag—and it's full!"

Even as the sheriff spoke Buck Collinson made a swift dart forward and flung himself at Tod's legs. The youth went down to the pavement. But the sheriff was at his side in an instant, and when Tod finally rose it was to find Buck with handcuffs locked round his wrists.

The sheriff's face was grim. "It's a good thing I stayed with you, Moran. I apologize for saying maybe you were afraid."

"Maybe I was—a little," Tod admitted.

The sheriff grinned. "I thought you'd gone nuts. Honest I did. I thought you were studying that history book." He paused and dropped his voice low. "Just what were you up to?"

"Reading about the feudal age, Sheriff. Look, I'll show you." Tod entered the office and came back with the book. I'll read you the lines. *With the drawbridge raised, the castle would be safe for weeks, even months. It was only when there lurked an enemy within the gates that imminent danger threatened.*" Tod stopped and looked across at the sheriff's prisoner. "You were the enemy within the gates, Buck Collinson."

"Hmm!" The sheriff nodded thoughtfully. "It strikes me, young feller, that the world hasn't changed so much after all. Maybe we can learn a thing or two from reading history."

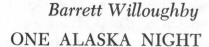

Barrett Willoughby

ONE ALASKA NIGHT

ILLUSTRATED BY *Kay Lovelace*

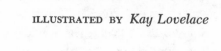

A ROOT tripped me and threw me flat in the trail that led through the blueberry thicket. The thick brush closed over me, shutting out the ranks of Alaska hemlock, already somber in the sundown light. Too tired for a moment to stir, I lay, face on my arms, feeling that I'd been foolhardy to start out alone on a ten-mile hike across an unfamiliar peninsula; yet comforting myself with the thought that it could not be much farther to the coast fox ranch, which was my destination.

For some time I had been breasting through this growth of blueberry brush which met thinly above my trail, but as my mind was intent on a story I was planning, I had failed to take this for what it was—a warning of something wrong. Now, nose to the ground, I became aware of a rank, musky odor that brought my head up with a jerk. Something queerly crawling touched my cheek. I slapped my hand over it and, with a chill premonition, looked at what I'd caught—a long tuft of coarse brown hair dangling from a twig above.

One startled glance, and I knew it had been raked from the side of an Alaskan brown bear—the largest carnivorous animal that walks the world today.

Earlier in the afternoon I had seen an enormous track in a patch of damp clay beside my path and, with a shiver, had placed my own foot inside it. The imprint, from heel to claws, was exactly twice the length of my number two-and-a-half boot.

I would have turned back then, had I not remembered that these beasts commonly avoid trails much traveled by man. Now, with the tuft of hair clutched in my hand and sudden alarm sharpening my perceptions, I scrutinized the path leading forward under the leafy tunnel in which I lay. All along it, evenly spaced in the damp, brown mold, were deep depressions, round and large as dinner plates. The roots across it were plushed with moss and unmarred. Men tread on the roots in their trails; animals step over them. Obviously no human being had passed this way for at least a year.

The truth came with a shock—I had been following a bear trail! It was already getting dark, and I was unarmed.

I had read many articles written by tourist sportsmen setting forth the theory that these fifteen-hundred-pound brutes, literally as big as a horse, will not attack man unless first provoked. But, being an Alaskan, I found this theory of no comfort now. All my life I'd been seeing bear-maimed men brought in from the woods—unarmed men who had been struck down by a single swipe of a brownie's barbed paw. I had seen them with their arms torn from the sockets, their legs raked clean of flesh. Some were dead.

I'm not a hunter. I'm not even a brave woman. And I'd never before been alone in a bear-infested forest with night coming on. In that first chill of apprehension my one absurd desire was to make myself very small, like a wood mouse, and snuggle down under some concealing leaf until the sun came up again. Then I recalled the fact that bears do most of their traveling after dark—and I was lying prone in the middle of one of their thoroughfares.

I leaped to my feet, turned off the trail, and began plowing through the brush, intent only on putting all possible distance between me and that place before dark.

Almost at once the bushes thinned out, and I was able to make

298

good time through stretches of short ferns; but the gray hemlocks linked their boughs above every open space, and the light was fading fast. In the deep gloom there was a curious hush that made me anxious to get out of the timber to the openness of the seacoast. Oddly, it was only now, when I was safely away from the bear trail, that this fact dawned on me—I had no idea which way to go. I was lost.

In that instant of realization all my strength seemed to ooze out of me into the ground. Then panic came upon me. I had a senseless, almost uncontrollable, impulse to dash madly through the trees, regardless of direction, bears, or anything else. But I got hold of myself, decided on a course, and with forced calmness went forward, watching tensely for that breaking away of the timber which foretells an approach to the sea.

Every step took me deeper into the darkening wilderness. There was no wind. Not a thing moved except myself—not a leaf; not a twig. Even the white hanks of deer moss pendent from the hemlock boughs hung still, like the hair of an old woman, long dead.

The very silence began to frighten me. It was a sly, listening stillness as if, among the trees, some form of life had hushed its action just an instant before my coming, to watch me and fall in behind me after I'd passed. I found myself stepping furtively, trying not to make any noise and straining to hear the slightest sound. I kept glancing back over my shoulder; and every few feet I'd stop suddenly, holding my breath while I studied a moss-grown log, or the long arm of a thorny shrub which I was sure had stirred a second before.

I never could surprise any movement or hear any sound; yet slowly terror was growing in me.

Ferns, moss, bushes—all were losing their green now, and the ground was dim with a swimming vagueness which caused me to miscalculate my steps. I stumbled often. I knew I should stop and build a fire for the night while there was yet light enough to gather a pile of wood. But the desperate hope of reaching the open beach drove me on.

I was groping with my feet, my gaze fixed ahead when, out

of the tail of my eye, I saw a blurred stirring in the shadows under the hemlocks. I jerked my head around to look.

Nothing moved.

I went on, tiptoeing now, and presently began to be fearsomely aware of the hemlocks. Hemlocks—somber witch-trees of the North, holding night under their long dark arms. . . . I could have sworn they were moving, slyly closing in around me . . . watching . . . waiting for something unhuman to happen. The mystery and cruelty of the woods seeped into that primeval level of my mind where eerie personalities of childhood tales lie buried. Lesiy, half-human Thing of the forest, with ears like a horse's, and moss-covered legs like a goat's, came alive in the ferny obscurity under the trees. Lesiy, master of bears, who tricks the wayfarer into losing his trail; and then, at dusk, turns him into a laughing maniac by peeping out from behind tree trunks, smiling horribly and beckoning with fingers a foot long. . . . Once I forced myself to go close and touch a yellowish-green fungus fanning out from a hemlock bole—to make sure it was a fungus, and not the face of Lesiy.

I wondered if the "woods-madness" that seizes lost persons was coming upon me so soon.

And then, I paused to stare at a murky clump which I hoped was only bushes looming against the vague knoll ahead. The clump, big as a truck horse, started toward me. It kept coming, slowly, ponderously, swinging a great, low head. Brush rattled under its shambling tread. I smelled the rank, musky odor of bear.

The next instant I had turned from the monster and was running madly through the semidarkness of the forest.

I was nearly exhausted when I burst through the timber and saw the log cabin crouching in the middle of a small, wild meadow of bearweed. Not another thing grew in the clearing except a single towering hemlock tree about fifty feet from the cabin door. I was running toward this refuge with all the speed left in me when, despite the terror I felt to be behind, something in the aspect of the place caused me to slow up. I came to

a stop at the hemlock tree and peered apprehensively through the dusk.

There was something distinctly sinister in the very quality of the silence that hung over the cabin. This wasn't due to the boarded windows, the smokeless stovepipe, and the air of desolation that marks every abandoned dwelling in the wilderness. There was something else—a feeling as if death brooded there. The boarded windows on each side of the closed door stared back at me like eye sockets in a brown and weathered skull.

My recoil from the place was so strong that I turned to go back; but after one glance into the black forest where a live monster lurked, I changed my mind. Slipping my belt ax from its sheath, I grasped it firmly and moved forward through the round, rustling leaves of the bearweed. My senses were nervously alert, but my feet were clogged by a nameless dread.

At the edge of the dooryard I came upon a stump and again hesitated. My fingers, absently exploring the stump's broad top, felt a crosshatch of ax marks. A block for chopping firewood, I thought, glancing at the nearby stack of dead hemlock boughs.

For some reason, this evidence of human workaday activity heartened me. I moved on through the whispering bearweed that grew untrampled to the very walls of the cabin and paused before the closed door. It was a homemade door of heavy, unplaned planks, silvered by the beating of many storms. In place of a knob, it had a rawhide latch thong hanging outside. The thong had curled up into a hard, dry knot.

Obviously, no one had drawn this latchstring for many months; yet, when I gave it a pull, I leaped back, expecting—I don't know what.

The creaking door swung in of its own weight, revealing an interior so dark I could distinguish no detail. I listened. All was silent. I sniffed. The place gave off the faint rancid odor that clings to a cabin in which raw furs have been dried.

Suddenly impatient at my senseless hesitancy, I plunged inside and bumped against a crude table in the middle of the floor. My outflung hand encountered a bottle with dribbles of wax on the side. I struck a match, lighted the candle stub still

remaining in the neck, and, after shutting the door, turned to inspect my shelter.

In one corner of the single room was a rusty sheet-iron stove; in another a stout pole frame laced with strips of cured bearskin to make a bunk. There was a chair made of slabs, and on the floor two mink-stretchers and a steel bear trap with a broken jaw. That was all. Clearly, this was the very ordinary abode of some trapper who had abandoned it for other fields. Nothing here to alarm even the most timorous woman. Yet—I continued to feel uneasy.

The sensible thing to do now was build a fire and then eat a sandwich. Luckily I had a couple remaining from the lunch I had brought from the trolling boat.

Early in the morning I had left town with some fishermen to get first-hand material for a novel I was planning. By the time my notes were complete, the boat had reached the vicinity of a fox ranch where Lonnie, a schoolmate of mine, was spending the summer with her father, who owned the place. I had never been there, and this part of Alaska was strange to me; but the trollers pointed out a trail cutting in from the beach and crossing the peninsula to the ranch. I persuaded them to put me ashore so that I might walk over and make a short visit, while they fished. They were to call for me late in the evening on their way back to town, fifty miles distant. No doubt they were at the ranch at this moment, and everyone was wondering where I was.

I wondered about that myself. A trail, of course, must lead out from here; and I knew I could find it when the sun came up. As I raked the ashes from the stove, I began searching my memory for all I had heard of this region in which I had lost myself.

The first thing that popped into my mind was the story of five prospectors who, a few years before, had vanished on this peninsula without leaving a trace. Rumor had it that they had met foul play at the hands of a crazy trapper—"Cub Bear" Butler. I didn't know whether or not the mystery had ever been solved. But—a crazy trapper. . . I glanced back over my shoulder, wishing I hadn't thought about that.

A moment later, ax in hand, I reluctantly went out-of-doors to the chopping block to cut some wood for the stove.

A large, round, blood-gold moon, just topping the hemlocks, threw long tree-shadows across the meadow. The rounded leaves of the bearweed caught the light, making the clearing look as if it were paved with silver dollars. Each clumsy blow of my ax rang out unnaturally loud, then stopped with a thud against the encircling black wall of timber. My sense of loneliness and isolation deepened.

In nervous haste I chopped an armload of wood, then, stooping, began piling the sticks on my arm. I was reaching for the last stick which had fallen in the bearweed when my groping fingers touched something which made me recoil so violently that all my wood fell to the ground. Hurriedly I struck a match and, leaning forward, lowered it until the tiny light fell on the thing which lay half-concealed under the moonlit leaves.

It was a fleshless, skeleton hand, severed at the wrist.

Transfixed with horror I stared at it while tales of wilderness-crazed men raced through my mind. . . . A hapless wretch, slumped beside this stump, legs bound, arms outstretched across the top, and a hairy, gleaming-eyed maniac whirling an ax——

The match burned my fingers. I dropped it. I was backing away when my eyes, now adjusted to the darkness, fell on another set of bony fingers thrust out from under a round leaf of bearweed. Then, just beyond that, a third skeleton hand took shape in the gloom.

My brain went into a sickening tailspin. I tried to scream, but could make no sound. I tried to run, but my legs seemed turned to water. Then the hope that my eyes had tricked me in the dim light brought back a measure of calmness. I struck another

match and, sweeping aside the weeds with my foot, bent to look.

They were there—all three of them.

I don't know how I nerved myself to make a thorough search of the ground around that ax-marked stump, but I did. And in the dense bearweed I saw twelve skeleton hands, all severed at the wrist. There wasn't a skull or bone of any other kind.

Somehow I got back inside the candle-lit cabin with an armload of wood, and, shoving the door shut, latched it. The fastening was an unusually sturdy bar of wood, one end of which was affixed to the middle of the door by a peg which allowed it to swing up and down. The other end slipped into a stout wooden stirrup on the log wall. The only way to lift and lower the bar from the outside was by means of the latch thong. I pulled this through its small hole, grateful that the door was strong and that no one could enter unless I lifted the bar.

But—I was hollow with dread. My hands trembled so that I could scarcely build the fire. And my mind kept swirling about Cub Bear Butler, the crazy trapper, and the five prospectors who had vanished. The men were last seen on this peninsula when Butler was living in the vicinity running his trap lines. Was it possible that I had stumbled on to Cub Bear's cabin? Could those skeleton hands belong to—

"But there were only *five* prospectors." I was startled to find I had spoken aloud. There were six pairs of fleshless hands out there bleaching under the Northern moon. To whom did the sixth pair belong?

I was so unstrung by these thoughts that, even after the fire was going, I couldn't eat a sandwich. Instead, after making sure that the door was still barred, I snuffed the candle, knowing it must soon burn out anyway. With my wadded jacket for a pillow, I lay down in the bare bunk, my little ax handy by my side.

I didn't intend to go to sleep, but gradually fatigue began to triumph over nerves. I remember thinking, half-coherently, "If Butler chopped the hands from five men and afterward amputated one of his own, how could he sever his other hand?"

306

Then my grisly speculations trailed off into sleep.

I don't know what awakened me; but suddenly I found myself sitting bolt upright, heart pounding, ears straining, eyes
wide open. In the sooty darkness I could see nothing except a
streak of moonlight lancing in through a knothole in one of the
slats over the window. The stillness was intense. Yet, I knew
that some sound, either inside the cabin or out, had penetrated
my sleep.

I was about to get up to light the candle when it came again:
Thump! . . . Thump-thump-thump! Someone was knocking to
get in!

I chilled to the pit of my stomach, for the summons, heavy,
imperative, was curiously muffled as if the visitor were rapping
not with firm knuckles, but with—I shoved the horrible thought
from me.

"Who—who's there?" I called unsteadily.

Silence.

Ax in hand, I eased out of the bunk, lighted the candle, and
turned to inspect the door. It was barred. Everything in the dim

307

room was just as it had been when I had gone to sleep.

"Who is it?" I demanded in a firmer voice.

The stillness tightened around me. My blood thudded in my eardrums. I knew anyone knocking for admittance at this hour of the night would identify himself—unless he were a____

Again I put from me the thought of a dead man, with no hands. I do not believe in ghosts.

I was trying to convince myself that the knocking had been born of my overwrought nerves when—*Thump! . . . Thump-thump-thump! Thump! . . . Thump-thump-thump!* Twice this time, hollow-loud, seeming to fill the room, yet having that sickening softness—like the fleshy stub of an arm hammering on wood.

Leaden with fright, I managed to reach the door and press my ear against it. "Who—what do you want? Answer me!"

I heard a faint rustling, as of a loose garment brushing against the rough log wall outside. After a dozen seconds had elapsed, I had a sudden, desperate impulse to end the suspense. I lifted the bar, flung open the door, and looked out.

Nothing.

The high moon lighted the clearing with a brilliance almost like that of day, but there was neither movement nor sound in the breathless Northern night.

Puzzled as well as frightened, I went back inside.

No sooner had I dropped the bar in place than it came again—*Thump! . . . Thump-thump-thump!* Instantly I jerked open the door.

No one was there. But the slithering sound, plainer than before, seemed to come from the corner to the right, as if someone had knocked, and then run to play a joke on me.

A flash of anger momentarily banished my fear; I darted out and ran all the way round the cabin.

There was no one.

I stood in front of the door scrutinizing the chopping block, the low pile of limbs beside it, every inch of the meadow, bright with moonlight to the very edge of the dense timber. The nearest cover—the tall hemlock—was fully fifty feet away. Nothing human, no matter how fleet, could possibly have traversed that distance in the second between the last knock and my abrupt opening of the door. No creature larger than a rabbit could have concealed itself from my searching gaze anywhere in the meadow surrounding the cabin. Indubitably, the clearing lay untenanted by any living being, other than myself.

Then gooseflesh broke out all over me. With a rush of supernatural terror came the thought that I was gazing on no ordinary wild meadow. Under the bearweed were skeleton hands— so many of them that this was literally a meadow of the dead. Only one thing knocks and remains invisible to mortal eyes!

For an instant I was so scared I thought I was going to faint. A sharp, unmistakably real blow on my instep brought me out of it. I became aware that my nerveless hand had let go my ax, and the blunt end had dropped on the most sensitive part of my foot, causing pain so acute that it restored a fraction of my faculties.

I was trembling, and though it was not from cold, I wanted the comfort of a fire—a great, flaming fire. Accordingly, I dragged the pile of dead limbs over to the hut, averting my eyes from what I knew lay in the weeds about the chopping block, and kindled a roaring blaze just outside the door. The crackling, the warmth of it put new courage into me. I sat on the threshold, my back against the doorjamb, and watched the clearing.

Nothing further disturbed me. After a while I began to nod.

I woke with a start, thinking I heard laughter and someone calling my name. Late morning sun flooded the clearing. A pair of excited squirrels, shrieking as though disturbed, were racing up and down the trunk of the lone hemlock. Then I saw a slim, blonde young woman in breeches and a windbreaker, running across the meadow toward me. Lonnie, my friend of the fox ranch! Behind her strode her father, a lean sourdough Alaskan who had, as I well knew, no very high opinion of a woman's ability to take care of herself in the woods.

My joy at their appearance was such that I could have rushed upon them and fallen to embrace their knees. But pride kept me from betraying myself to the quizzical eyes of Lonnie's father, whom I always called "Dad." I assumed a nonchalant manner and strolled out from the door to greet them.

"There, Dad!" said Lonnie, laughing. "I told you she'd be cool as a cucumber!" She gave me a hug. "I knew you'd be all right, but Dad had a fit when you failed to show up last night. Sent two of the ranch hands to search the woods to the north and east. As soon as it was daylight, he and I started out in this direction."

"A woman," declared Dad, "should never go into the woods alone. Women have no bump of location. They're always getting lost." He readjusted the heavy holster on his hip. "I was afraid you'd run into a bear—there are a lot of brownies around this summer. You can thank your lucky star you stumbled on to Butler's cabin."

Butler's cabin! But even as a shivering thrill ran through me, Dad's I-told-you-so manner nettled me.

"It's not only women who get lost," I retorted. "How about those five prospectors who disappeared in these woods a few years ago?"

"Oh, those chaps!" He waved their vanishment aside with the confident air of a man who has a practical solution for every problem. "It's likely they were drowned in the tide-rips off the Cape."

"No, they weren't, Dad," I said quietly. "They were killed— murdered—right here at Butler's cabin."

He and Lonnie stared at me as if they thought I had gone insane. Then Dad began to laugh. "Now, Sis, don't try to put over any of your writer's imaginings on an old fellow like me."

"It's not imagination. Come. I'll show you."

I led the way to the chopping block, and, brushing aside the bearweed with my foot, one by one revealed the skeleton hands, stark white in the sunlight.

Dad looked grave. "By George," he muttered. "This looks bad. I mind there was some talk about Cub Bear Butler, but——" He stooped and picked up one of the bony things.

After a moment's inspection he deliberately tossed it back into the weeds, and brushed his hands together. "Just like a woman!" he drawled, grinning at me. "Those are not human hands, Sister. They're the skeleton paws of cub bears."

I must have looked uncommonly foolish, for he patted my shoulder consolingly. "Don't let that take the wind out of your sails, my dear. Nine men out of ten would have made the same mistake. You see, the skeleton of a bear's paw, particularly the small bones of a cub's, is almost identical with that of the human hand."

"But—why are there no other bones here?"

"Cub Bear Butler, like all other trappers, skinned his catch at the traps in the woods—all except the feet, which demand a good deal of care. He brought the pelts back here to his cabin to skin the paws at his leisure. He trapped only cubs, yearlings. That's how he got his nickname."

Feeling very much deflated, I followed him into the cabin.

"Poor old Cub Bear," he said. "They finally got him."

"Who got him?" I asked, remembering that Butler had been called "the crazy trapper."

"Bears. The Indians round here swear it was the Great She-Bear, the Spirit Bear, who took revenge on him for killing so many cubs. At any rate he was found crumpled down right there"—Dad pointed to a spot just outside the threshold of the open door—"killed as a bear kills a man. He'd been dead only a couple of days, and the tracks of a big brownie were still visible in the dooryard, which wasn't overgrown with bearweed then."

"But I don't understand why he didn't shoot the beast if it jumped him in his own yard."

"Couldn't reach his gun. When they found him, his rifle, his ax, and a fresh cub pelt were all here in the cabin, and the door was barred, and the latch thong broken off."

"What a strange thing!"

"Nothing strange about it. What happened was plain enough. Cub Bear must have come in from his trap line with the pelt. He dropped it when he put his rifle on the table, and then went out——for water, likely—shutting the door behind him. Possibly

311

the mother of the cub he'd just killed did follow him home, and—well, an angry she-brownie is just about the most terrifying creature a man can run up against anywhere. When she went for him, he ran for his cabin to get his rifle and, in his haste, jerked the latch thong so hard he broke it off. Then he couldn't open the door. And it is so stout he couldn't break it in. So—the beast got him."

"How terrible—and ironic!" I shuddered as my mind involuntarily supplied details.

"Tough luck, all right. Bert Slocum, one of my ranch hands now, spent a couple of months here afterward, trapping mink. He came out with a fine, large tale about Cub Bear's ghost hanging around here, and——"

"Ghost," I started, and turned to stare at the spot outside the open door where Butler must have stood frantically beating on the heavy plank barrier trying to get in.

"Yes, so Bert claims." Dad chuckled as if vastly amused. "But Bert's a case. Biggest liar in Alaska. He'd be a good one to put in some of those books you write. The way Bert tells it, Cub Bear——"

Thump! . . . *Thump-thump-thump!* With the door wide open it came, and before I knew it I had leaped to my feet.

"What in heck's the matter with you, Sis?" inquired Dad. "Bouncing up with your eyes sticking out like a crab's?"

I looked from the empty door to the imperturbable faces of my companions. "Didn't you hear it?" I demanded.

"Hear what?"

"That knocking."

"Oh, those pesky flying squirrels," drawled Dad. "The country's getting overrun with 'em. On a moonlight night a man can't get a wink of sleep, the way they play humpty-dumpty on the roof. They——"

"Flying squirrels," I interrupted, doubtingly. "I'd like to see one—playing."

"No trouble. Just stand there inside the door, sort of hid, and keep your eye on that lone hemlock out in front."

I took up the position he indicated.

After a moment, sure enough, a small, furry form soared out from the top of the tree and, with little legs outspread, came gliding down to land with that soft, solid *thump!* on the roof. Then, quickly, *thump-thump-thump!* it bounded down to the eaves, and off, racing back toward the tree.

"What a cunning little creature," I observed, turning round with what must have been a sickly smile.

As I did so, my attention was caught by the door, swung in so that the outside of it was very close to me. Years of Alaska weather—beating rain and wind and snow, alternating with hot summer sun—had worked the rough grain of the unfinished planks into a coarse, light-gray nap. Visible now on the sun-struck surface, and about even with the top of my head, were curious marks—depressions in the weathernap of the wood, such as might have been made by the edge of heavily pounding fists.

"What are you staring at now, Sis?" Dad broke in on my concentration.

"Those marks on the door."

He laughed. "You must have been pretty excited when you got here last night—knocking that hard. But that's just like a woman—never able to tell whether a cabin's deserted or not." He came to his feet and picking my jacket from the bunk, held it for me. "Come, now. Slip into this. It's time we were toddling. I'm hungry enough to eat boiled owl, and it's eight miles to the ranch."

A few minutes later, as we were walking away across the sunny clearing. I fell a step behind the other two and turned to look back at the cabin in which I had spent the most terrifying night of my life.

I was remembering that two days ago there had been a heavy southeast gale which must have beat directly on that closed door. Yesterday's sun drying out the planks would have raised the woodnap, obliterating any depressions that might have been there before I reached the cabin. Yet—marks were there, as if two fists had pounded on the door. Dad thought I had made them.

I looked down at my hands, and though I don't believe in ghosts, I went a bit queer in the pit of my stomach. The marks were there, plainly visible when the sun struck the door just right. But I knew that my two small fists had never made them.

For I had never knocked, or even thought of knocking, on the door of that grim, deserted cabin in the clearing.

Anthony C. Wilson

HUNTER'S MOON

ILLUSTRATED BY *Henry C. Pitz*

IT WAS a cold, foggy morning in late November. Breakfast had been cleared away, and Henry was busy experimenting with a new type of secret ink when suddenly the door burst open and Norman came in.

"I say, Henry, care to come down to Devonshire with me?"

Henry glanced out of the window. The fog was turning into an unpleasant drizzle, and a sad-looking blackbird sat hunched in the ivy outside. If Norman's manner had been a little less earnest, Henry would have thought he was joking.

"Of course, it's not quite the season to see the West Country in its full glory, I know," added Norman, observing his cousin's trend of thought, "but this is business, Henry. Urgent business, by the sound of it. I've just had a letter." He produced it from his pocket and held it out for his cousin to look at. "Recognize the hand?"

Henry did. It was from Mr. Rogers, a schoolmaster who had been billeted for a while at Norman's home during the war. He was a pleasant, sensible man, with whom they had both done much hiking and exploring. Later he had taken a job as tutor to two boys, Bill and Michael Dawson, at a lonely house on the edge of Dartmoor.

"Well? What's he say?"

"He seems to be in trouble, Henry. I don't know the details, but as far as I can gather he was left in charge of those two boys while Mrs. Dawson went to stay with her husband up in the north of Scotland. Soon after she had gone, Bill—that's the elder—suddenly vanished from his bedroom, fully dressed, in the middle of the night, and hasn't been seen since."

315

"How extraordinary! Didn't anyone hear anything? How about Michael?"

"No. Michael was sleeping in a different room and heard nothing. Of course the police have been informed, and I understand they're working on the theory that Bill ran away to join his parents. The trouble is nobody knows exactly where the parents are. Mrs. Dawson had promised to send their address as soon as possible but hasn't yet written."

Henry considered. The case sounded interesting. But Dartmoor in November! Why couldn't it have been somewhere a little nearer? And what would his parents say? They knew Mr. Rogers well enough and had a great respect and liking for him. But Henry guessed it would take a great deal of persuasion to make them agree to his shooting off to Devonshire at this time of year, and he wondered what his cousin's parents thought of the idea. Well, he would find out about that presently. First, he wanted to know what else Mr. Rogers had said in his letter. "Who else is there in the household besides Mr. Rogers and the two children?" he asked.

Norman scanned the page. "Two others," he replied. "A funny old nurse who has lived in those parts all her life, and a Welsh cook who has been with the family for fifteen years."

"And can't they supply any clues to Bill's disappearance either?"

"I don't know, Henry. Very likely they can. The point is, are you coming down to Dartmoor with me to find out?"

"Is that all Mr. Rogers says?"

"That's all of importance. Here, take a look for yourself." Norman tossed the letter across to his cousin, and Henry read it through carefully. It had obviously been written in some haste, and it was quite clear that the poor tutor was upset.

The blackbird in the ivy hopped rheumatically to another branch, and a shower of spray fell to the damp earth below. Henry handed the letter back again; he had gleaned no more about the case than Norman had told him, and he knew there was only one way of learning further.

"What do Auntie and Uncle say, Norman?"

"About going down to Devonshire?"

"Yes."

"I can't say they were keen about it, but they've agreed all right. They'd promised I should go next summer anyway, so it's just a matter of making the trip about seven months earlier, that's all."

"Then if you want me to come too, perhaps you could get around my parents in the same way. I feel you'd manage it rather better than I would!"

Norman's powers of persuasion were certainly considerable, and both his own and Henry's parents had great trust in him. He had, after all, his full share of common sense and had reached an age of reasonable discretion. His father was sensible enough to realize that responsibility was good for him, and although Mrs. Bones still thought of him as a child, he was one no longer. Mr. Bones held the opinion that the less he was balked and repressed, the sooner he would grow up—and the better. A journey from Norfolk to Dartmoor in November would not be too easy nor very pleasant; but let him find these things out for himself.

So Norman gained his parents' consent without too much difficulty, but Henry's case was different. Henry could be trusted, and he had proved himself capable of looking after himself, but he was two years younger than his cousin. Moreover, his mother, Norman's Aunt Jane, entertained a completely false idea that he was delicate and highly strung, and had it not been for her husband's insistence that the idea was utter nonsense, Henry might have led a very restricted life. As it was, his father, who was a huge, robust man, consistently stamped on any suggestions that his son was not equally hardy, and when Mrs. Bones protested that such a trip down to Devonshire in midwinter would assuredly lead to pneumonia, Mr. Bones immediately took the opposite view on principle and declared that a little Dartmoor air would do the boy good!

Though this was not the end of the battle, everything was ultimately settled, and Henry's mother mournfully packed his winter woolies while the rest of them looked up the next train to Tavistock. They found one arriving at five fifteen. They would then have to take a bus to Torbury and walk across the moor to the Grange, the Dawson's house. If all went well, they should arrive about seven o'clock.

The journey was long and cold and tedious, but they alighted at last on Tavistock platform and made their way to the bus station. As luck would have it, the next bus to Torbury was just about to leave, and they squeezed themselves into it, among a crowd of fully proportioned rustics, plus hampers, parcels, and even a crate of chickens. It was a cheerful, friendly crowd, and soon they were rattling through the town and out into the wild Devonshire countryside.

As the passengers disembarked in twos and threes at the little villages en route, the cold evening air swept in through the open door and struck them with an unpleasant chill. They knew that they must be approaching the moor itself, and a strange feeling of awe and excitement took possession of them. They wiped the moisture from the window and peered out into the gathering darkness. Yes, there it was at last—a dark, sinister outline ahead of them, a black, undulating fringe stretching away into the mist. Dartmoor! There could be no mistaking it. And as the bus jolted on up a winding, stony road, they thought of the final lap in their journey—their walk from Torbury along a lonely moorland track.

It was the Torbury village policeman who set them on the
right road. "It b'ain't the shortest way," he told them, "but if ye
be strangers down these parts, ye'd best keep to the 'igh road.
Then ye can't go wrong. Just keep straight on till ye come to
the crossin', then turn down the lane to the left. Ye'll find the
Grange at the end of it."

They thanked him and set off at a brisk pace in the direction
he had indicated. The policeman's idea of a "high road" was
not theirs, but they had flashlights and found it easy enough to
follow. The ground on either side of them was blanketed now
by night and fog, so they could only guess at what far-reaching
landscape must lie there. That the road ran unattended and

exposed they had proof, however, for a bitter wind blew unchecked across it, stinging their faces, and the rain had swollen the moorland streams so that they spread over its surface and ran in gurgling rivulets among the ruts. How glad they were when at last they came in sight of their destination and saw the Grange looking like some huge monster crouching in the deepening gloom before them! With what relief they shortly found themselves in the warmth of the Dawsons' drawing room, with an appetizing meal spread out on the table, and the merry singing of a copper kettle in the hearth.

Mr. Rogers was delighted to see them again and did his best to revive them after their long journey. But he was worried, terribly worried. There had still been no news of Bill, and disturbing thoughts of what might have happened to him kept forcing their way into his mind.

"I knew you were interested in detective work, Norman," he said anxiously, "and I thought you might be able to help us."

"We'll certainly do what we can," replied Norman. "Won't you tell us some more about it?"

"That's just the trouble," said Mr. Rogers despairingly. "If only we could find a clue of some sort."

"Didn't the police find any footprints?"

"Yes. Under Bill's window. But it was quite impossible to follow them. The lawn comes almost up to the house, and the grass didn't help."

Norman took another piece of hot buttered toast. He was ravenously hungry, and so was Henry, but they were both eager to hear all that the tutor could tell them, and there was no reason why they shouldn't eat and listen at the same time.

"When did you first discover Bill was missing?" Henry asked.

"Three days ago. Last Tuesday morning. I went in to call him as usual at seven fifteen, and bless my soul—nobody there! I thought at first that he must have got up early and gone out for a walk before breakfast, but as time passed on and there was still no sign of him, I realized that—well, that something was wrong."

"How about the old nurse? Hadn't she anything to say?"

"You'd better talk to her yourself, Norman. She's a queer old thing. Believes in lucky charms and pixies and all that sort of stuff. She'll be down in a minute with Michael."

They did not have long to wait. A shuffling of carpet slippers in the passage, followed by a loud knock at the door, announced her arrival. Bent, wrinkled, with untidy gray hair trailing from under an old-fashioned frilled cap, Nurse Crocker seemed herself to be part of the moor she had known from childhood. Her voice was cracked and croaky, like the voices of the frogs that played in the Dartmoor rills, and her manner was distant and defensive. Yet somehow one felt that beneath this hard exterior she had a warm heart, and to young Michael she showed every sign of care and devotion.

Michael was too young to appreciate the anxiety felt for his brother. His conversation was entirely on the subject of a big quarry he and Nurse Crocker had visited that afternoon out on the moor.

"Nurse thought we might see some fairies playing about at the bottom of it," he chimed in excitedly. "It was ever so deep, and we threw bits of rock down and watched them splash in a puddle right down below."

"And how many fairies were there?" asked Norman.

"None at all. Nurse said they'd all gone to bed. Didn't you, Nurse?"

Nurse Crocker nodded. "Yes, that's right, Michael. They'd all gone to bed," she said. "Every one of them."

"And that's where you ought to be too, Michael," added Mr. Rogers, glancing at the clock. "By the way, Nurse, I'm afraid I haven't introduced you. These are two young friends of mine, Norman and Henry Bones. They've come to help us search for Bill."

The old nurse eyed them suspiciously. "I can't answer for what's happened to that boy," she replied. "Now Michael here, he behaves himself properly, but Bill—he'd do anything, would Bill. Always up to mischief of some sort. Now, if he'd carried a rabbit's skull in his pocket, like I've so often told him, no harm would have befallen him. A rabbit's skull will keep away even the worst evil spirits."

"Can't you give us any clues to Bill's disappearance at all?"

The old woman looked suspicious. "What do you mean?" she muttered.

"Well, on the night he left, for instance, did you hear any unusual sounds?"

"I only heard the wind in the chimney. It makes a lot of noise up here, the wind does. When the wind blows over the moor, you can hardly hear anything else at all."

"It was windy on the night Bill vanished, was it?"

"Terrible windy. And raining too, off and on. A nasty sort of night it was."

Norman looked thoughtful. He couldn't feel certain that old Nurse Crocker wasn't trying to hide something from them. Or was it merely her strange, harsh voice that gave him that impression?

"What did Bill do in his spare time?" inquired Henry. "Was he fond of reading, or drawing, or anything like that?"

"Oh dear me, no," the old nurse answered. "Little Michael here, he liked drawing, but not Bill. He was a noisy boy, Bill was. A dreadfully noisy boy. Never still a minute."

"Bill preferred outdoor sports," explained Mr. Rogers. "His greatest ambition was to be a bareback rider at a circus!"

Just then Polly came in to clear away. She was small and trim and spoke with a delightful Welsh accent.

"I hope your guests have enjoyed their tea, Mr. Rogers," she said. "They must have been hungry after their long walk from Torbury."

"We've enjoyed it very much indeed, thank you, Polly," Norman hastened. "I hear you've been cook here for fifteen years."

"Yes indeed, Master Norman. It's a long time, it is, but Mrs. Dawson, she's always been most kind to me, and I've been most contented, I have."

"Without Polly I just don't know what we'd do," said Mr. Rogers. "And Nurse Crocker too, for that matter."

"I'll be taking Michael up to bed now," said the old woman firmly. "He's tired after that long walk we had, aren't you, my dear?" Michael didn't altogether agree with this statement, but he knew it was no use protesting. After saying good night to Mr. Rogers, Polly, and the boys, he allowed himself to be led off without further ado, and they heard Nurse Crocker's carpet slippers flopping away along the passage.

Outside, the rain was lashing against the windowpanes, and the chimney rumbled in the gale that was sweeping over the hills. They drew closer to the fire, and the tutor, glancing from one to the other of the young detectives, wondered how accurately he would be able to describe them if suddenly called upon to do so in their absence. The police had recently asked him for a detailed description of the missing Bill, and he had found it much harder than might have been supposed. He looked at Norman. About five feet six in height. Black hair brushed well back, exposing a wide forehead. Brown eyes. Fresh complexion. Expression—difficult to say, for it changed so quickly, sometimes serious and contemplative, as now, but more often intensely keen and alive. Build, lithe and muscular. Manner, quiet, courteous, unruffled. Clothes, tan sports coat, gray flannels, bluish-green pullover, dark blue tie with red stripes. And Henry? Height, five feet four, perhaps. A mop of fair hair. Gray eyes. Rather a snub nose. Complexion a trifle pale, except when lit up by his very friendly smile. Figure, spruce without being athletic. Dressed in a gray flannel suit, blue pullover, and red-and-brown tie. Not very good descriptions, he felt, even with the boys before him.

For a few minutes nobody spoke. And as the storm beat about the house, Mr. Rogers' thoughts returned to Bill. Was it possible that Bill could be out in all this, a wretched, drenched figure, perhaps, groping about on the moor, and scanning the black horizon for a friendly, welcoming light? It was Polly who broke the silence.

"I've just thought of something that happened about four days ago, Mr. Rogers," she said. "A stranger called here. An old gipsy woman—"

Mr. Rogers turned around sharply. "You never told the police that, Polly."

"No, Mr. Rogers. I should have done. It was stupid of me. I can't think how it slipped my memory."

"What did she want?" asked Norman hopefully.

"She was selling clothespins. It must have been about ten o'clock in the morning. Bill was in the kitchen, watching me make some cakes. Last Monday it was."

"And what happened? How long did she stop?"

"About two minutes, I should say. When I refused to buy

324

any pins she turned quite nasty, she did. Called me names and cursed like anything."

"I hope you sent her packing," said Henry.

"Oh yes, Master Henry. I'm no dragon, look you, but this time I got quite annoyed, I did. 'Get out, you old hag,' I cried, and she vanished through the gate before you could say knife."

On the face of it there seemed little reason to suppose that the visit of this gipsy could have any bearing on Bill's disappearance, yet it was definitely a piece of information that could not be ignored.

"What was this gipsy woman wearing?" Norman asked.

"She was dressed in black," replied Polly, "with an old red knitted shawl over her shoulders, and a dirty, yellow scarf tied around her head. She had golden earrings, and a gold ring on her finger."

Mr. Rogers did not consider the matter worthy of much attention. If anyone had kidnaped Bill, it was hardly likely that an old woman had done so, though, of course, there was just a possibility that she might have come to spy out the land for others. Yet why on earth should anyone wish to kidnap Bill? It wasn't as though his parents were rich or that a large ransom could be expected for his return. And how could a kidnaper have got into Bill's room? It had been a stormy night, and the window had been closed and fastened. To reach his room from outside would have meant passing both Polly's room and Nurse

Crocker's, yet neither of them had been disturbed. It really was a complete mystery.

By the next morning the wind had subsided, and the sun was making a brave attempt to pierce a wintry sky. The police reported that no news had been received during the night, and, much to Mr. Rogers' dismay, the morning post brought no letter to inform him of Colonel and Mrs. Dawson's whereabouts.

As far as Norman and Henry were concerned, their plan of campaign was quite definite. They would start by taking a stroll out on the moor. It was certain that Bill was nowhere in the Grange itself, for the house, though a large one, had been searched from top to bottom many times. The country immediately surrounding, therefore, seemed to offer the best chance of solution. And then there was that quarry that Michael had spoken of. Norman was interested in that quarry. He couldn't help wondering whether old Nurse Crocker had had any special reason for taking a walk to it on the previous day.

It was about nine thirty when the two boys set out. They both wore raincoats, for the weather was uncertain, and Henry had even taken the precaution of bringing a few sandwiches in case they should have difficulty in finding their way back again in time for the next meal. He carried also, in his top pocket, a little red notebook and a pencil. Into this notebook Henry was always entering information that he considered might some time prove vitally important, though in actual fact it was usually scribbled in such haste, and under such adverse conditions, that neither he nor anybody else was able to read a word of it.

Passing through the shrubbery at the back of the house, they came to a small wicket gate. This gate formed the only break in a tall yew hedge that extended the greater way around the grounds, and through the gap the boys had their first real view of the moor by daylight. There it lay, stretching out for miles before them—grim, bare, and unfriendly, yet with a strange, inexplicable grandeur about it that somehow took their minds back through the centuries to prehistoric times, when men lived there in rude stone huts and hunted and died on its bleak, lonely hills.

Leading from the gate was a rough, sandy track, a short cut to Torbury, some two miles away. Mr. Rogers had drawn a map of it for them and had marked with a cross the point on it where they must branch off if they wished to take a look at the quarry. They had no difficulty in discovering this point, for it was at the peak of a hill upon which were piled, like the playthings of a giant, a number of vast, gray boulders. Once off the path, they found it hard going. Numerous jagged rocks lay half concealed in the heather, and near the streams the ground became unexpectedly boggy.

It was some ten minutes later that they came to a halt on the quarry's edge. Below them lay the pool into which Michael had thrown the stones, and near it stood a flock of black-faced sheep gazing up at them with surprised expressions. Away to the west, nestling at the foot of a hill some quarter of a mile off, was a cottage. A thin wisp of blue smoke threaded its way from the chimney, and it was this alone that attracted their attention to it. The building itself was of somber gray stone and toned in so completely with the surrounding countryside that it was almost unnoticeable. Yet, even as they looked, a figure caught their eyes. He was tramping slowly along a footpath that stretched from the cottage garden away over the moor towards the village. At first they were inclined to think him a peat-digger, but Norman rapidly came to the conclusion that he walked too well and was too upright for a man of that trade, and indeed his whole dress and bearing proclaimed him as no Devon son of the soil.

"Who can he be?" said Henry. "How can we find out?"

"Go and ask him!" replied Norman.

"You mean that?"

"Why not? It can't do any harm. No need to tell him who we are, of course. We'll pretend we've lost our way or something. See, he's almost reached his cottage now. He's just approaching that old tree that stands some hundred yards away from it."

"Right. Come on, then," cried Henry. "Ouch! How I hate all these rocks. I shan't have any shins left soon!"

Arriving at the cottage door, Norman knocked boldly, but for some moments there was no response. The garden, they could see, was well cared for and in the summer must have been quite gay, and there was a small pond through which crystal-clear water was flowing. The tree that they had noticed from the top of the quarry seemed to be dead and hollow and was obviously waiting to be chopped down for firewood.

Presently they heard footsteps within, and then a bolt was shot back and the door was opened.

"Good morning."

Before them stood a tall, well-built gentleman of some forty years. He was dressed in tweeds and wore horn-rimmed spectacles.

"Oh, good morning," said Norman. "I'm sorry to bother you, but my cousin and I were walking to Torbury over the moor, and I'm afraid we're lost. We wondered if you could put us right."

"That's easily enough done," replied the gentleman politely. "But first come inside and rest a few minutes, won't you? It's lonely out here, and I'm only too glad to see somebody."

"Well that's very kind of you. We mustn't stay long, Mr.—er—"

"Bryson's the name. James Bryson. Mind your head on the beam. It's a bit low."

The two boys found themselves in a comfortably furnished room, the window of which faced due south and commanded an extensive view across the moor. A peat fire was smouldering in the grate, and to the right of it stood a large case completely filled with books on natural history. On the top of this book-

"I'll wait here by this tree and keep watch till you get back."

case stood a large stuffed owl. There was no glass around the bird, and it was fixed in such a realistic pose that Henry uttered a cry of astonishment when he saw it.

"Phew! I thought for a moment it was alive, Mr. Bryson!" he exclaimed.

"Yes, it is pretty lifelike, isn't it!" said Mr. Bryson, stroking the bird's soft feathers with his finger. "Shot it myself, as a matter of fact. It was sitting on a rock out on the moor in the moonlight. I must show you my collection of butterflies and moths. My fossils too."

"You're something of a naturalist?" asked Norman.

"Yes, well that's my work, you see. That's why I live right out here on Dartmoor. Wonderful place for natural history, Dartmoor."

The walls, too, proclaimed Mr. Bryson a nature-lover, for they were covered with photographs of birds and animals of all kinds. He told them that he had taken many of them himself, and that he was using the best ones in a new book he was writing.

"I hope you haven't got your feet very wet," he said. "There are some treacherous bogs around here. I advise you to be careful."

"We've managed to avoid the worst of them so far," Norman answered. "The biggest bit of water we've seen is a pool at the bottom of that quarry over there." He pointed towards a rugged cliff face just visible from the cottage window.

"Oh, you came by the quarry, did you?" returned Mr. Bryson, and then he was silent for a few seconds, gazing thoughtfully out in the direction Norman was pointing. Presently he turned. "A nasty place, that quarry," he continued. "You've heard about the accident there, I suppose?"

"Accident?" said the boys together.

"I don't mean a recent accident. This happened a long time ago now. About 1890, I believe. Make yourselves comfortable, and I'll tell you about it, if you're interested." He beckoned them into easy chairs placed one on each side of the fire. "There was a huntsman in these parts named Tom Royd, and very

329

frequently he would take his hounds out on the moor. Now on the moor there apparently lived at that time a particularly crafty old fox, and this old fox had a hole which opened onto a narrow ledge about three feet down from the top of the quarry."

"I noticed a ledge when we were up there," said Henry.

"Probably the same one," replied Mr. Bryson. "Anyway, the accident occurred one frosty evening at just about this time of year. Tom Royd had been out with his pack and was returning home after a somewhat unprofitable day. Suddenly a fox appeared, only about fifteen yards in front of them. In a moment the whole pack was in full cry. But the fox ran at high speed straight towards the edge of the quarry. The huntsman realized the danger, of course, and tried to call the hounds off. But the cliff was close by, and it was too late."

"Good heavens!" said Henry. "You mean—"

"Yes. Over the edge, every one of them. They were dashed to pieces on the boulders far down below."

"How dreadful!" The whole scene stood out only too clearly in the boys' minds.

"Some say that Tom Royd himself, in a desperate effort to head off the pack, failed to pull up in time and went over as well. Though whether that part's true or not I can't say. But there's one thing I *do* know."

"What's that?" asked Norman.

"On wintry nights, when the wind blows wild and the moon shines through a ring of haze, you can still hear the hounds as they rush across the moor. And you can still hear the huntsman's horn too, summoning them to stop as it did in that last fateful chase."

Mr. Bryson paused and knocked his pipe out against the grate. Then he continued, "When I first came here I thought this story of the ghostly pack was just a local superstition. The people in these out-of-the-way places are often illiterate and imaginative. I thought it was probably a legend that had been handed down from one generation of yeomen to the next. But I don't think that now. You see, I've heard the hounds myself."

"You've heard them, Mr. Bryson?" exclaimed Norman. It sounded incredible.

"Yes. I've heard them several times. I couldn't believe my ears at first. But Dartmoor's a very queer place, you know. Things happen here that don't happen anywhere else on earth, and I wouldn't go out on the moor at night, not for a hundred pounds."

He got up from the corner of the table upon which he had been sitting and went over to a polished mahogany cabinet which was standing on a sideboard. "Ah well, let's talk about something else, shall we?" he said. "I promised to show you my collection of butterflies and moths, didn't I?"

The collection was certainly a fascinating one. It ranged in size from a death's-head hawk-moth down to specimens so minute that they were scarcely visible to the naked eye. There was an album of moorland flowers to be seen as well, and the fossils all neatly arranged in trays. It was almost half an hour before Norman and Henry were able to tear themselves away, and then it was only their sudden recollection of Bill Dawson that made them go.

It was about a quarter past one when they arrived back at the Grange. The remainder of their exploration had been un-

331

eventful, and they were glad to find lunch awaiting them, for, despite Henry's sandwiches, they were both ravenously hungry. No further news had come in during the morning, and it was not until five o'clock that evening that anything affecting the case really occurred. At about that hour, however, the post arrived, and much to Mr. Rogers' relief it contained a letter from Mrs. Dawson. She and Colonel Dawson had settled at a small hotel in Lochney, about thirty miles north of Aberdeen. They expected to stay there a week.

"I must write to them this evening—now—straight away," declared Mr. Rogers. "Mrs. Dawson hasn't been able to give me an address before because they've been moving about so much. Dear me, it's going to be a terrible shock to her. To both of them." He stretched out his hand for pen and note paper.

"Why not send them a telegram?" suggested Norman.

"What? Tonight?"

"Yes. A letter'll take ages."

"Yes. Of course. You're quite right, Norman. The sooner I can let them know the better. Now, let me see. How shall I word it?"

Outside it was growing dark, and the wind was again rising. Beside the fire sat old Nurse Crocker, the red light reflecting on her wrinkled features. She was knitting, but the operation seemed automatic, and her thoughts were probably with those queer little people she was always telling Michael about who lived on the moor and held nightly revels around the cairns in the moonlight. Michael was lying full length on the floor drawing a picture. It was not a very good picture, but Henry got it right the first time.

"It's Beauty," he said. Beauty was Bill's Dartmoor pony.

"That's right!" shouted the young artist. "I thought you'd guess. Now I'll draw Bill sitting on her back, shall I?"

"Think you can?" said Henry.

" 'Course I can. Bill's easy to draw. I've drawn Bill lots of times." He seized the pencil and returned to his work with renewed vigor.

Norman, who had been listening to this conversation, was

332

thinking hard. Something Mr. Rogers had said the previous evening had just come back to him. "Bill was an outdoor boy. His greatest ambition was to be a bareback rider at a circus." Was it possible that the boy had gone out in the night, harnessed his pony, and ridden off in search of a circus that would train him? But no. Michael's next remark put that theory to an end almost immediately.

"I guess Beauty misses Bill," he mused. "She looked sad this morning, so I gave her an extra lump of sugar. She was standing in her meadow with her head resting on top of the wall, looking out over the moor."

Mr. Rogers got up from the desk at which he had been writing. "There," he said. "I think that makes the situation quite clear."

Nurse Crocker looked around sharply. "Who's going to take the telegram down to Torbury and send it off, that's what I'd like to know?" she croaked. "It'll be dark coming back, and I can't see in the dark."

"Oh, that's all right, Nurse," replied Mr. Rogers confidently. "Polly'll take it for us, won't you, Polly?"

Polly, who was just drawing the library curtains, turned rather pale. "What, *me*, sir? Tonight, sir? Oh well, sir, of course I'll do anything I can to help you. But I was thinking about the supper, sir. I'm just in the middle of cooking, you see."

"Henry and I will take it for you, Mr. Rogers," said Norman. "We'd like to."

"Oh, that's very kind of you, Norman. I'm afraid it's a rotten sort of night—"

"That's all right. We know the way. We went to Torbury this morning."

"Yes. But don't get off the path, will you. You might lose your bearings at night. The post office takes the telegrams. It's the first house you come to as you enter the village. If the shop is shut, go around to the back. Bloggs is the name. Ebenezer Bloggs."

The shop *was* shut. By the time they arrived it had been shut nearly an hour. So they went around to the back as they had

333

been instructed. Mr. Bloggs answered the door himself. He was a pleasant old man, with a red, weather-beaten face and a neatly trimmed beard. As soon as he understood the object of their visit, he asked them to follow him through into the shop. This was typical of thousands of village post offices up and down the country, for, besides working for the government, Mr. Bloggs also carried on a small grocery business of his own, and the shelves were piled high with cans and packages of every description. The ceiling was low, and there was a black patch just over the paraffin stove. And on the window sill stood a row of half-empty candy jars. But it was the telephone that interested the boys the most. What a quaint, old-fashioned instrument it was! They wondered how Mr. Bloggs would ever manage to transmit the telegram by it. This indeed proved no easy task. Mr. Bloggs was rather deaf, and the line was rather faint. It took at least five minutes of turning handles and shouting "Hello, there" before the operator at Tavistock realized anything was happening, and even then the message could hardly have been accurately received. After every few words the old man gave the machine a vicious thump with a can of baked beans, and judging by the state of it, this had been his habit for a good many years. At last, however, he declared the telegram had been sent, and there was a distinct note of triumph in his voice as he told them.

"But it's a bad business about young Bill, that it be," he continued. "Can't make out what can have happened to the lad."

"You knew him pretty well, I suppose?" said Norman.

"Oh, aye. Indeed I did. He used to come down here for his sweets every Saturday mornin'. Chewing gum, that's what he liked best."

"Still, we've got the wire off, so that's something done," added Henry. "And now, Norman, we'd better be getting back to the Grange, hadn't we?"

"Yes, Henry," replied Norman. "I think we had." He did not sound altogether enthusiastic, yet time was getting on and they knew they must not delay.

"It's a bad night for you boys to be about on the moor," commented Mr. Bloggs as the oil lamp flickered in the draught that was blowing through every tiny chink. "I hope ye don't lose your way or nuthun."

"Oh, I think we shall be all right," said Norman. "There's a moon, actually. What you call around here a Hunter's Moon, I believe."

"Aye, that's right," answered the old man thoughtfully. "Hunter's Moon. H'm. Now it's funny ye should happen to mention Hunter's Moon."

"Oh? Why?"

"I hadn't remembered it, not till this minute. It must have been the last time Bill Dawson come down here for his chewing gum. Aye, it were the last time. He asked me to tell him about poor old Tom Royd."

"Tom Royd? Oh yes, of course. The huntsman who fell over the quarry."

"Aye. Told Bill the whole story, I did."

"Did he seem frightened?"

"Frightened! Bless ye no. He said next time there was a Hunter's Moon he'd go out and join in the chase."

"That's interesting," said Norman, pricking up his ears. "But tell me, Mr. Bloggs, do *you* believe in these phantom hounds?"

Mr. Bloggs did not answer at once. It seemed to the boys that he somehow resented being asked. His reply, when it did come, was noncommittal and evasive. "Well, maybe I does and maybe I doesn't. The moor's a very queer place at night, and there's folks around here what say they've actually heard the hounds for themselves."

"Golly! I hope we don't meet the ghostly hunt on our way home to the Grange!" said Henry nervously. Norman was inclined to agree with him.

Out on the moor the wind had now reached almost gale force, and the boys had to shout to make each other hear. A watery moon shone spasmodically through rifts in the black clouds that were chasing across the sky, and when it did so, the vast, desolate landscape was brought into a strange, silvery relief. Before

335

them the sandy path stretched like a silken ribbon, and away to their left they could see the black sentinel of the district that was Lingmere Tor.

"This wind!" cried Henry, clutching onto his cap. "We must be careful not to get off the track."

"I know," shouted Norman. "And it's just starting to rain too."

Conversation was a severe strain on the vocal chords, and it was some while before Henry made a second attempt.

"Funny thing—that story about Tom Royd hunting on the moor," he said.

"Yes. Just a legend, if you ask me. I don't believe anyone has ever heard the ghostly hounds at all. Extraordinary how people can believe these fanciful tales. Anyone would think we were still living in the fifteenth century."

The words were hardly out of Norman's mouth when suddenly, far away in the distance, the two boys heard a sound that froze them to the spot and made them clutch each other's arms in horror. Yes! There was no mistaking it! Through brief lulls in the gale it was borne to them. Away among those rolling hills beyond the quarry—a pack of hounds in full cry!

"It—it—can't be," stammered Henry. A cold shiver ran down his back, and his heart was beating wildly.

"Yes," cried Norman. "Listen! Hear that?"

"The sound of the huntsman's horn!"

"They're coming nearer!"

Their first impulse was to run, but following the path by flashlight was none too easy. Trembling, they remained where they were, and as they hesitated the baying of the hounds grew louder and louder. At any moment they expected to see their ghostly forms approaching through the blackness, but presently the noise began to diminish, and it seemed the pack must have turned off towards the valley. There came a last eerie blast of the hunting horn, and then the noise of the gale swallowed all else, leaving Norman and Henry still rooted to the ground in fear and amazement.

"They've gone," cried Henry. "Quick. Let's go back to Torbury!"

Norman didn't want to. Now that he had recovered from the first shock, his curiosity was getting the better of his fright.

"Wait a bit, Henry," he answered. "Where did you think the sound of that hunt seemed to come from?"

His cousin tugged violently at his sleeve. "For heaven's sake, come on!" he pleaded.

"Don't be in such a hurry, Henry. I've just had an idea."

"Yes. So have I."

"What?"

"Get back as quickly as possible."

"No. Listen to me, Henry. There was something very queer about the cry of those hounds."

"I know," replied Henry desperately. "That's just the trouble!"

Norman was unmoved. "Although the noise appeared to grow louder and then to die away again," he said, "it seemed to me to come from exactly the same place all the time."

"But how *could* it come from the same place, Norman? The hounds must have been moving. I don't see what you mean."

"Follow me, Henry." Norman took Henry's arm and, turning, left the path and struck off at a brisk pace across the moor.

"Hey! Where on earth are you going, Norman?" yelled Henry. "Have you gone mad? This isn't the way to Torbury. And it isn't the way to the Grange, either!"

"No, Henry," replied Norman calmly. "But it's the way to Mr. Bryson's cottage. There is something queer about all this. Come on!"

It was from the leeward of the old, hollow tree that they surveyed the cottage not very long afterwards. Standing there alone in the moonlight it looked deserted, almost unreal. The blinds were drawn, and the only sign of habitation was smoke from the chimney, still curling up as it had been in the morning.

"I wish to goodness you'd explain why you've brought me here," complained Henry. When Norman did things for which he could not understand the reason, it annoyed him intensely, the more so because he knew that his cousin's motives were usually sound ones.

"I *will* explain," replied Norman. "It was no good trying to make myself heard out on that hill, but it's better behind this tree. It does offer us a little protection and—"

His sentence was not completed, for just at that moment there came once again a sound they knew only too well. Faint at first, and then growing in volume, the cries of the ghostly hounds once more fell upon their ears. But this time there was a difference. Yes! It seemed incredible. The sound was coming from above them!

"They're in the sky!" blurted Henry.

Norman was flushed with excitement. "Not the sky, Henry," he declared. "They're in this hollow tree! At least, the loud-speaker is!"

"The loud-speaker?" Henry stared at his cousin in astonishment.

"Yes. I see it all now. Mr. Bryson must have a radio or record-player in his cottage with a cable leading to a loud-speaker in that hollow branch. To give the effect of the hounds approaching, and then dying away again, he simply uses the volume control."

"My hat! But what's the big idea?"

"All this ghostly pack business is obviously a stunt of Mr. Bryson's to keep people from nosing about on the moor at night."

"Yes. I see. But why should he mind people nosing about?"

"I don't know. Listen!"

A new sound was carried to them by the wind that swept over the rocks and heather—the sound of an engine, a truck. It came from the direction of the quarry.

"I wish I knew what was going on here!" said Henry.

"We'll soon find out," replied Norman. "Hello! What's this?" He held up a small piece of paper. Henry turned his flashlight on it. The paper was yellow.

"The wrapper off a pack of chewing gum!"

"Yes. And that's what Mr. Bloggs told us Bill always buys—chewing gum!"

"I know."

338

"You must run back to the post office, Henry, and ring up the police. Ask them to pick you up there, then come on with them and show them the way."

"All right. But what about you, Norman?"

"I'll wait here by this tree and keep watch till you get back."

"Right. I'll have the entire police force here in about fifteen minutes. Trust me!" And with previous fears forgotten in his excitement, Henry disappeared in the direction of Torbury as fast as his swollen shins would allow him.

When Henry eventually arrived back with Inspector Martin, Sergeant Higgs, and four stalwart constables, Norman was still waiting by the tree. But he hadn't been there all the time.

"It's black marketeering, as far as I can gather," he replied in answer to Inspector Martin's query. "There's a truck over there in the quarry with three men loading up boxes from a cave. They won't get away in a hurry, though, because I crept up and let the air out of two of the tires!"

"Splendid. Splendid," said the inspector. "And what about this Mr. Bryson Henry was telling me of?"

"He's in his cottage. He walked over to the quarry about ten minutes ago, gave some directions, then came straight back again. He seems to be the boss."

"Right." The inspector beckoned to Sergeant Higgs. "Sergeant, take your men over to the quarry and surround the truck and the cave."

"Very good, sir."

"I'll keep Armstrong here in case of trouble at the cottage."

"Right, sir."

"Norman and Henry, you can come with me. We'll just see what this Bryson fellow's up to."

Arriving at the cottage, Inspector Martin knocked loudly. A thin, drizzly rain had set in again, and they turned up their collars to try to keep dry. Presently the door was opened, and a tall, dark figure stood silhouetted on the threshold.

"Are you Mr. Bryson?"

"Yes."

"Good. I'm Inspector Martin of—"

It was Henry who first spotted the pistol. Precisely what happened next will always be something of a mystery. The inspector's flashlight was hurled from his hand and fell with a splash in the rock pool. There came a cry of anger from Mr. Bryson as the constable attempted to catch his arm. Then the whole doorway seemed to be filled with struggling men. The pistol dropped to the ground, and Norman managed to grab it. With repeated cries of "Get out of here, I tell you," Mr. Bryson tried to close the door and bolt it, but his efforts were in vain, and he was quickly overwhelmed. There came a metallic click, and the constable announced with satisfaction that the handcuffs were securely fastened. This, however, was by no means an end to the captive's vocal warfare. Shouting and protesting, he was led into the sitting room, and it was some considerable time before they could induce him to listen to reason.

"Get out of here, the lot of you," he cried hoarsely again and again. "You don't know what you're doing."

"We'll all get out of here in a minute, Mr. Bryson," stated the inspector. "But not till you tell us where you've got Bill Dawson, we shan't."

"I don't know what you're talking about. I've never seen Bill Dawson," retorted the enraged prisoner.

"No?"

"No."

"Then search the house, Armstrong. Norman and Henry, you search, too."

They did not have to search long. A muffled cry was heard. It came from a small cupboard near the fireplace. Henry flung

340

open the door. It was dark inside, and the cupboard went back a considerable distance. But Norman shone his flashlight in, and presently he yelled out, "Here he is! Bound and gagged!"

"What!" exclaimed the inspector. "Here. Give me that knife, Henry." Henry handed Mr. Martin a breadknife that was lying on the sideboard. "All right, sonny. I won't be a minute." He began to hack at the ropes. Mr. Bryson, realizing that the game was up, watched him sulkily. Presently the bonds fell apart, and the gag was slipped off. The boy sat up and gazed around him. He was dazzled by the light.

"Thanks," he said. "It's—it's been awful."

"Are you Bill Dawson?" inquired Norman, though he knew from Mr. Rogers' description that it could be no one else.

"Yes. Who are you?"

"My name's Norman Bones. Thank goodness we've found you at last."

The boy took hold of the table and pulled himself up. His pullover was torn, and there was a cut on his face, but otherwise he did not look much the worse for his experiences. All at once he remembered something.

"The quarry, sir!" he cried. "Go down to the quarry. They've got a truck there. They were going to take me away in it."

"That's all right, Bill," said the inspector soothingly. "I've sent some men down to the quarry already. Now take it easy, old chap, and tell us how you came to be tied up in that cupboard."

341

"It was Mr. Bryson there," replied Bill. "He's been keeping me in a cave in the quarry."

"But why did you come out on the moor at night, Bill?"

"I heard some hounds, sir, and I wanted to see what they were like."

"H'm. And did you see these hounds?"

"No, sir. I climbed up a hollow tree just near this cottage so I could get a better view all around, and when I was up there I found a thing like a loud-speaker hidden in one of the branches."

The inspector nodded. "And what then?" he asked.

"Well sir, just as I was examining it with my flashlight, Mr. Bryson came out and saw me, and before I could get away he caught me and tied me up."

"I see."

"He's got a phonograph hidden in a big bird's-egg cabinet through there in the next room."

"Ah! Just as we thought!" exclaimed Henry. And he disappeared into the adjoining room to investigate. At that moment the front door was flung open and Sergeant Higgs entered.

"Good news, sir," he reported. "We've caught the lot. Five of 'em. Black market all right. They've been using the cave as a storehouse."

Inspector Martin was delighted. "Better take them back straight away, Sergeant," he ordered. "And you can take Mr. Bryson along with them."

"Right, sir."

Without saying a word, but looking daggers at Norman, the captured naturalist allowed himself to be taken away. Norman saw him as a gigantic moth that had suddenly found itself enclosed in a net from which it knew there was no escape.

"By the way, Norman," said Inspector Martin. "I understand from your cousin Henry that you've been suspicious of that fellow Bryson."

"Yes, Inspector," Norman replied. "In fact I volunteered to walk to the post office tonight with the special intention of paying him a visit on the way home."

Henry, who had overheard the conversation, returned from the next room. "Good heavens, Norman," he cried. "Do you mean to say you guessed Mr. Bryson was a crook even before we heard the hounds?"

"Yes, Henry."

"But how?"

"It was the stuffed owl that gave him away."

Henry cast an eye towards the bookcase. The bird was still on top of it in the same position as previously, staring down at them with the same fixed expression. "That owl there?" said Henry.

"Yes. Don't you remember? Mr. Bryson told us he shot it himself by moonlight, out on the moor."

"Yes, I know."

"And yet a few minutes later he distinctly told us he was so frightened of the ghostly hounds that he wouldn't go out on the moor at night even for a hundred pounds!"

"Of course! Yes! I never thought of that!" Henry cursed himself for having missed such an obvious slip in the naturalist's story.

"He clearly wanted to scare people off the moor at night, and yet, by telling us he shot the owl, he admitted that he himself wasn't really frightened of the hounds at all. So I guessed he had something to do with them, you see."

Henry did see. Only too plainly. "Yes. Not bad deduction that, Norman," he replied casually. "Wouldn't be surprised if you were to become a detective one of these days!" It looked as though there was going to be quite a rough-and-tumble between the boys, but Inspector Martin interposed.

"Now then, you two—we've had enough trouble for one night," he said. "I can't have you knocking each other out before I've had time to congratulate you! I shall have to make a full report of all this 'phantom hound' affair when I get back. I shall commend both of you most highly."

The two boys thanked the inspector warmly.

"It'll be a great scoop for our local paper. My word it will!" he continued. "I wonder what the headlines will be. 'Mystery of the Moor Solved,' I expect. Or 'Spectral Hunt Enjoys Record Chase'!"

Mr. Martin had hardly finished speaking when far away, as it seemed, and yet growing nearer every second, there came for the third time that night the yelping of hounds from the bleak, windswept hills outside. For a moment they looked at each other in blank amazement. Then there came a burst of laughter from the next room, and young Bill stood in the doorway.

"It's all right," he said. "It's only me! I've found the record, and I just put it on the phonograph. Sounds funny, doesn't it!"

They went in to look at it. The phonograph was concealed in what appeared to be a bird's-egg cabinet. But the drawers of this were dummy ones, and the whole front let down to reveal the turntable and controls. A record with a maroon-colored center was revolving, and they could hear the needle faintly vibrating to the sounds of the huntsman's horn.

The maroon center interested Norman, for he knew that most of the records sold for stage effects have bright red centers.

"Here. Let's take it off a minute and see what it says on the label," he suggested. Bill lifted the pickup and pressed a switch. The record circled to a standstill; then Norman chuckled.

"Ha! Cunning old blighter, that Mr. Bryson!" he commented. "He's even taken the trouble to change the nameplate."

"Why?" asked Henry. "What does it say?"

"It says 'Bird Songs at Eventide,' Henry!"

345

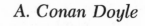

A. *Conan Doyle*

THE RED-HEADED LEAGUE

ILLUSTRATED BY *J. Allen St. John*

I HAD called upon my friend, Mr. Sherlock Holmes, one day in the autumn of last year, and found him in deep conversation with a very stout, florid-faced, elderly gentleman, with fiery red hair. With an apology for my intrusion, I was about to withdraw, when Holmes pulled me abruptly into the room and closed the door behind me.

"You could not possibly have come at a better time, my dear Watson," he said, cordially.

"I was afraid that you were engaged."

"So I am. Very much so."

"Then I can wait in the next room."

"Not at all. This gentleman, Mr. Wilson, has been my partner and helper in many of my most successful cases, and I have no doubt that he will be of the utmost use to me in yours also."

The stout gentleman half-rose from his chair and gave a bob of greeting, with a quick, little, questioning glance from his small, fat-encircled eyes.

"Try the settee," said Holmes, relapsing into his armchair and putting his fingertips together, as was his custom when in judicial moods. "I know, my dear Watson, that you share my love of all that is bizarre and outside the conventions and humdrum routine of everyday life. You have shown your relish for it by the enthusiasm which has prompted you to chronicle and, if you will excuse my saying so, somewhat to embellish so many of my own little adventures."

"Your cases have indeed been of the greatest interest to me," I observed.

"You will remember that I remarked the other day, just before we went into the very simple problem presented by Miss Mary Sutherland, that for strange effects and extraordinary combinations we must go to life itself, which is always far more daring than any effort of the imagination."

"A proposition which I took the liberty of doubting."

"You did, doctor, but nonetheless you must come round to my view, for otherwise I shall keep on piling fact upon fact on you, until your reason breaks down under them and acknowledges me to be right. Now, Mr. Jabez Wilson here has been good enough to call upon me this morning and to begin a narrative which promises to be one of the most singular which I have listened to for some time. You have heard me remark that the strangest and most unique things are very often connected not with the larger but with the smaller crimes, and occasionally, indeed, where there is room for doubt whether any positive crime has been committed. As far as I have heard it is impossible for me to say whether the present case is an instance of crime or not, but the course of events is certainly among the most singular that I have ever listened to. Perhaps, Mr. Wilson, you would have the great kindness to recommence your narrative. I ask you, not merely because my friend Dr. Watson has not heard the opening part, but also because the peculiar nature of the story makes me anxious to have every possible detail from your lips. As a rule, when I have heard some slight indication of the course of events, I am able to guide myself by the thousands of other similar cases which occur to my memory. In the present instance I am forced to admit that the facts are, to the best of my belief, unique."

The portly client puffed out his chest with an appearance of some little pride, and pulled a dirty and wrinkled newspaper from the inside pocket of his greatcoat. As he glanced down the advertisement column, with his head thrust forward, and the paper flattened out upon his knee, I took a good look at the man and endeavored, after the fashion of my companion, to

347

read the indications which might be presented by his dress or appearance.

I did not gain very much, however, by my inspection. Our visitor bore every mark of being an average commonplace British tradesman, obese, pompous, and slow. He wore rather baggy gray shepherd's-check trousers, a not over-clean black

frock coat, unbuttoned in the front, and a drab waistcoat with a heavy brassy Albert chain, and a square pierced bit of metal dangling down as an ornament. A frayed top hat and a faded brown overcoat with a wrinkled velvet collar lay upon a chair beside him. Altogether, look as I would, there was nothing remarkable about the man save his blazing red head and the expression of extreme chagrin and discontent upon his features.

Sherlock Holmes's quick eye took in my occupation, and he shook his head with a smile as he noticed my questioning glances. "Beyond the obvious facts that he has at some time done manual labor, that he takes snuff, that he is a Freemason, that he has been in China, and that he has done a considerable amount of writing lately, I can deduce nothing else."

Mr. Jabez Wilson started up in his chair, with his forefinger upon the paper, but his eyes upon my companion.

"How, in the name of good fortune, did you know all that, Mr. Holmes?" he asked. "How did you know, for example, that I did manual labor. It's as true as gospel, for I began as a ship's carpenter."

"Your hands, my dear sir. Your right hand is quite a size larger than your left. You have worked with it, and the muscles are more developed."

"Well, the snuff, then, and the Freemasonry?"

"I won't insult your intelligence by telling you how I read that, especially as, rather against the strict rules of your order, you use an arc-and-compass breastpin."

"Ah, of course, I forgot that. But the writing?"

"What else can be indicated by that right cuff so very shiny for five inches, and the left one with the smooth patch near the elbow where you rest it upon the desk."

"Well, but China?"

"The fish that you have tattooed immediately above your right wrist could only have been done in China. I have made a small study of tattoo marks and have even contributed to the literature of the subject. That trick of staining the fishes' scales a delicate pink is quite peculiar to China. When, in addition, I see a Chinese coin hanging from your watch-chain, the matter becomes even more simple."

Mr. Jabez Wilson laughed heavily. "Well, I never!" said he. "I thought at first that you had done something clever, but I see that there was nothing in it, after all."

"I begin to think, Watson," said Holmes, "that I make a mistake in explaining. '*Omne ignotum pro magnifico*,' you know, and my poor little reputation, such as it is, will suffer shipwreck if I am so candid. Can you not find the advertisement, Mr. Wilson?"

"Yes, I have got it now," he answered, with his thick, red finger planted half-way down the column. "Here it is. This is what began it all. You just read it for yourself, sir."

I took the paper from him and read as follows:

"To the Red-Headed League: On account of the bequest of the late Ezekiah Hopkins, of Lebanon, Pa., U.S.A., there is now another vacancy open which entitles a member of the League to a salary of £4 a week for purely nominal services. All red-headed men who are sound in body and mind and above the age of twenty-one years, are eligible. Apply in person on Monday, at eleven o'clock, to Duncan Ross, at the offices of the League, 7 Pope's Court, Fleet Street."

"What on earth does this mean?" I ejaculated, after I had twice read over the extraordinary announcement.

Holmes chuckled and wriggled in his chair, as was his habit when in high spirits. "It is a little off the beaten track, isn't it?" said he. "And now, Mr. Wilson, off you go at scratch and tell us all about yourself, your household, and the effect which this advertisement had upon your fortunes. You will first make a note, doctor, of the paper and the date."

"It is *The Morning Chronicle*, of April 27, 1890. Just two months ago."

"Very good. Now, Mr. Wilson?"

"Well, it is just as I have been telling you, Mr. Sherlock Holmes," said Jabez Wilson, mopping his forehead; "I have a small pawnbroker's business at Coburg Square, near the city. It's not a very large affair, and of late years it has not done more than just give me a living. I used to be able to keep two assistants, but now I only keep one; and I would have a job to pay him, but that he is willing to come for half wages, so as to learn the business."

"What is the name of this obliging youth?" asked Sherlock Holmes.

"His name is Vincent Spaulding, and he's not such a youth, either. It's hard to say his age. I should not wish a smarter assistant, Mr. Holmes, and I know very well that he could better himself and earn twice what I am able to give him. But, after all, if he is satisfied, why should I put ideas in his head?"

"Why, indeed? You seem most fortunate in having an *employé* who comes under the full market price. It is not a common experience among employers in this age. I don't know that your assistant is not as remarkable as your advertisement."

"Oh, he has his faults, too," said Mr. Wilson. "Never was such a fellow for photography. Snapping away with a camera when he ought to be improving his mind, and then diving down into the cellar like a rabbit into its hole to develop his pictures. That is his main fault; but, on the whole, he's a good worker. There's no vice in him."

"He is still with you, I presume?"

"Yes, sir. He and a girl of fourteen, who does a bit of simple cooking and keeps the place clean—that's all I have in the house, for I am a widower and never had any family. We live very quietly, sir, the three of us; and we keep a roof over our heads and pay our debts, if we do nothing more.

"The first thing that put us out was that advertisement. Spaulding, he came down into the office just this day eight weeks, with this very paper in his hand, and he says,—

" 'I wish to the Lord, Mr. Wilson, that I was a red-headed man.'

" 'Why that?' I asks.

" 'Why,' says he, 'here's another vacancy on the League of the Red-headed Men. It's worth quite a little fortune to any man who gets it, and I understand that there are more vacancies than there are men, so that the trustees are at their wits' end what to do with the money. If my hair would only change color, here's a nice little crib all ready for me to step into.'

" 'Why, what is it, then?' I asked. You see, Mr. Holmes, I am a very stay-at-home man, and as my business came to me instead of my having to go to it, I was often weeks on end without putting my foot over the doormat. In that way I didn't know much of what was going on outside, and I was always glad of a bit of news.

" 'Have you never heard of the League of the Red-headed Men?' he asked, with his eyes open.

351

" 'Never.'

" 'Why, I wonder at that, for you are eligible yourself for one of the vacancies.'

" 'And what are they worth?' I asked.

" 'Oh, merely a couple of hundred a year, but the work is slight, and it need not interfere very much with one's other occupations.'

"Well, you can easily think that that made me prick up my ears, for the business has not been overgood for some years,

and an extra couple of hundred would have been very handy.

" 'Tell me all about it,' said I.

" 'Well,' said he, showing me the advertisement, 'you can see for yourself that the League has a vacancy, and there is the address where you should apply for particulars. As far as I can make out, the League was founded by an American millionaire, Ezekiah Hopkins, who was very peculiar in his ways. He was himself red-headed, and he had a great sympathy for all red-headed men; so, when he died, it was found that he had left his enormous fortune in the hands of trustees, with instructions to apply the interest to the providing of easy berths to men whose hair is of that color. From all I hear it is splendid pay and very little to do.'

"'But,' said I, 'there would be millions of red-headed men who would apply.'

"'Not so many as you might think,' he answered. 'You see it is really confined to Londoners and to grown men. This American had started from London when he was young, and he wanted to do the old town a good turn. Then, again, I have heard it is no use your applying if your hair is light red, or dark red, or anything but real bright, blazing, fiery red. Now, if you cared to apply, Mr. Wilson, you would just walk in; but perhaps it would hardly be worth your while to put yourself out of the way for the sake of a few hundred pounds.'

"Now, it is a fact, gentlemen, as you may see for yourselves, that my hair is of a very full and rich tint, so that it seemed to me that, if there was to be any competition in the matter, I stood as good a chance as any man that I had ever met. Vincent Spaulding seemed to know so much about it that I thought he might prove useful, so I just ordered him to put up the shutters for the day and to come right away with me. He was very willing to have a holiday, so we shut the business up and started off for the address that was given us in the advertisement.

"I never hope to see such a sight as that again, Mr. Holmes. From north, south, east, and west every man who had a shade of red in his hair had tramped into the city to answer the advertisement. Fleet Street was choked with red-headed folk, and Pope's Court looked like a coster's orange barrow. I should not have thought there were so many in the whole country as were brought together by that single advertisement. Every shade of color they were—straw, lemon, orange, brick, Irish-setter, liver, clay; but, as Spaulding said, there were not many who had the real vivid flame-colored tint. When I saw how many were waiting, I would have given it up in despair; but Spaulding would not hear of it. How he did it I could not imagine, but he pushed and pulled and butted until he got me through the crowd and right up to the steps which led to the office. There was a double stream upon the stair, some going up in hope, and some coming back dejected; but we wedged in as well as we could and soon found ourselves in the office."

"Your experience has been a most entertaining one," remarked Holmes, as his client paused and refreshed his memory with a huge pinch of snuff. "Pray continue your very interesting statement."

"There was nothing in the office but a couple of wooden chairs and a deal table, behind which sat a small man, with a head that was even redder than mine. He said a few words to each candidate as he came up, and then he always managed to find some fault in them which would disqualify them. Getting a vacancy did not seem to be such a very easy matter, after all. However, when our turn came, the little man was much more favorable to me than to any of the others, and he closed the door as we entered, so that he might have a private word with us.

" 'This is Mr. Jabez Wilson,' said my assistant, 'and he is willing to fill a vacancy in the League.'

" 'And he is admirably suited for it,' the other answered. 'He has every requirement. I cannot recall when I have seen anything so fine.' He took a step backward, cocked his head on one side, and gazed at my hair until I felt quite bashful. Then suddenly he plunged forward, wrung my hand, and congratulated me warmly on my success.

" 'It would be injustice to hestitate,' said he. 'You will, however, I am sure, excuse me for taking an obvious precaution.' With that he seized my hair in both his hands and tugged until I yelled with the pain. 'There is water in your eyes,' said he, as he released me .'I perceive that all is as it should be. But we have to be careful, for we have twice been deceived by wigs and once by paint. I could tell you tales of cobbler's wax which would disgust you with human nature.' He stepped over to the window and shouted through it at the top of his voice that the vacancy was filled. A groan of disappointment came up from below, and the folk all trooped away in different directions,

354

until there was not a red head to be seen except my own and that of the manager.

" 'My name,' said he, 'is Mr. Duncan Ross, and I am myself one of the pensioners upon the fund left by our noble benefactor. Are you a married man, Mr. Wilson? Have you a family?'

"I answered that I had not.

"His face fell immediately.

" 'Dear me!' he said, gravely, 'that is very serious indeed! I am sorry to hear you say that. The fund was, of course, for the propagation and spread of the red-heads as well as for their maintenance. It is exceedingly unfortunate that you should be a bachelor.'

"My face lengthened at this, Mr. Holmes, for I thought that I was not to have the vacancy after all; but, after thinking it over for a few minutes, he said that it would be all right.

" 'In the case of another,' said he, 'the objection might be fatal, but we must stretch a point in favor of a man with such a head of hair as yours. When shall you be able to enter upon your new duties?'

" 'Well, it is a little awkward, for I have a business already,' said I.

" 'Oh, never mind about that, Mr. Wilson!' said Vincent Spaulding. 'I shall be able to look after that for you.'

" 'What would be the hours?' I asked.

" 'Ten to two.'

"Now a pawnbroker's business is mostly done of an evening, Mr. Holmes, especially Thursday and Friday evenings, which is just before payday; so it would suit me very well to earn a little in the mornings. Besides, I knew that my assistant was a good man, and that he would see to anything that turned up.

" 'That would suit me very well,' said I. 'And the pay?'

" 'Is £4 a week.'

" 'And the work?'

" 'Is purely nominal.'

" 'What do you call purely nominal?'

" 'Well, you have to be in the office, or at least in the building, the whole time. If you leave, you forfeit your whole position forever. The will is very clear upon that point. You don't comply with the conditions if you budge from the office during that time.'

" 'It's only four hours a day, and I should not think of leaving,' said I.

" 'No excuse will avail,' said Mr. Duncan Ross, 'neither sickness nor business nor anything else. There you must stay, or you lose your billet.'

" 'And the work?'

" 'Is to copy out the "Encyclopaedia Britannica." There is the first volume of it in that press. You must find your own ink, pens, and blotting-paper, but we provide this table and chair. Will you be ready tomorrow?'

" 'Certainly,' I answered.

" 'Then, good-bye, Mr. Jabez Wilson, and let me congratulate you once more on the important position which you have been fortunate enough to gain.' He bowed me out of the room, and I went home with my assistant, hardly knowing what to say or do, I was so pleased at my own good fortune.

"Well, I thought over the matter all day, and by evening I was in low spirits again, for I had quite persuaded myself that the whole affair must be some great hoax or fraud, though what its object might be I could not imagine. It seemed altogether past belief that any one could make such a will, or that they would pay such a sum for doing anything so simple as copying out the 'Encyclopaedia Britannica.' Vincent Spaulding did what he could to cheer me up, but by bedtime I had reasoned myself out of the whole thing. However, in the morning I determined to have a look at it anyhow, so I bought a penny bottle of ink, and with a quill pen, and seven sheets of foolscap paper, I started off for Pope's Court.

"Well, to my surprise and delight, everything was as right as possible. The table was set out ready for me, and Mr. Duncan Ross was there to see that I got fairly to work. He started me off upon the letter A, and then he left me, but he would drop in from time to time to see that all was right with me. At two o'clock he bade me good day, complimented me upon the amount that I had written, and locked the door of the office after me.

"This went on day after day, Mr. Holmes, and on Saturday the manager came in and planked down four golden sovereigns for my week's work. It was the same next week, and the same the week after. Every morning I was there at ten, and every afternoon I left at two. By degrees Mr. Duncan Ross took to coming in only once of a morning, and then, after a time, he did not come in at all. Still, of course, I never dared to leave the room for an instant, for I was not sure when he might come, and the billet was such a good one, and suited me so well, that I would not risk the loss of it.

"Eight weeks passed away like this, and I had written about Abbots and Archery and Armor and Architecture and Attica, and hoped with diligence that I might get on to the B's before very long. It cost me something in foolscap, and I had pretty nearly filled a shelf with my writings. And then suddenly the whole business came to an end."

"To an end?"

"Yes, sir. And no later than this morning. I went to my work as usual at ten o'clock, but the door was shut and locked, with a little square of cardboard hammered onto the middle of the panel with a tack. Here it is, and you can read for yourself."

He held up a piece of white cardboard about the size of a sheet of notepaper. It read in this fashion:

"THE RED-HEADED LEAGUE

IS

DISSOLVED.

October 9, 1890."

Sherlock Holmes and I surveyed this curt announcement and the rueful face behind it, until the comical side of the affair so completely overtopped every other consideration that we both burst out into a roar of laughter.

"I cannot see that there is anything very funny," cried our client, flushing up to the roots of his flaming head. "If you can do nothing better than laugh at me, I can go elsewhere."

"No, no," cried Holmes, shoving him back into the chair from

which he had half risen. "I really wouldn't miss your case for the world. It is most refreshingly unusual. But there is, if you will excuse my saying so, something just a little funny about it. Pray what steps did you take when you found the card upon the door?"

"I was staggered, sir. I did not know what to do. Then I called at the offices round, but none of them seemed to know anything about it. Finally, I went to the landlord, who is an accountant living on the ground floor, and I asked him if he could tell me what had become of the Red-headed League. He said that he had never heard of any such body. Then I asked him who Mr. Duncan Ross was. He answered that the name was new to him.

" 'Well,' said I, 'the gentleman at No. 4.'

" 'What, the red-headed man?'

" 'Yes.'

" 'Oh,' said he, 'his name was William Morris. He was a solicitor and was using my room as a temporary convenience until his new premises were ready. He moved out yesterday.'

" 'Where could I find him?'

" 'Oh, at his new offices. He did tell me the address. Yes, 17 King Edward Street, near St. Paul's.'

"I started off, Mr. Holmes, but when I got to that address it was a manufactory of artificial kneecaps, and no one in it had ever heard of either Mr. William Morris or Mr. Duncan Ross."

"And what did you do then?" asked Holmes.

"I went home to Saxe-Coburg Square, and I took the advice of my assistant. But he could not help me in any way. He could only say that if I waited I should hear by post. But that was not quite good enough, Mr. Holmes. I did not wish to lose such a place without a struggle, so, as I had heard that you were good enough to give advice to poor folk who were in need of it, I came right away to you."

"And you did very wisely," said Holmes. "Your case is an exceedingly remarkable one, and I shall be happy to look into it. From what you have told me I think that it is possible that graver issues hang from it than might at first sight appear."

"Grave enough!" said Mr. Jabez Wilson. "Why, I have lost four pound a week."

"As far as you are personally concerned," remarked Holmes, "I do not see that you have any grievance against this extraordinary league. On the contrary, you are, as I understand, richer by some £30, to say nothing of the minute knowledge which you have gained on every subject which comes under the letter A. You have lost nothing by them."

"No, sir. But I want to find out about them, and who they are, and what their object was in playing this prank—if it was a prank—upon me. It was a pretty expensive joke for them, for it cost them two and thirty pounds."

"We shall endeavor to clear up these points for you. And,

Holmes stopped in front of it and looked it all over.

first, one or two questions, Mr. Wilson. This assistant of yours who first called your attention to the advertisement—how long had he been with you?"

"About a month then."

"How did he come?"

"In answer to an advertisement."

"Was he the only applicant?"

"No, I had a dozen."

"Why did you pick him?"

"Because he was handy and would come cheap."

"At half-wages, in fact."

"Yes."

"What is he like, this Vincent Spaulding?"

"Small, stout-built, very quick in his ways, no hair on his face, though he's not short of thirty. Has a white splash of acid upon his forehead."

Holmes sat up in his chair in considerable excitement. "I thought as much," said he. "Have you ever observed that his ears are pierced for earrings?"

"Yes, sir. He told me that a gypsy had done it for him when he was a lad."

"Hum!" said Holmes, sinking back in deep thought. "He is still with you?"

"Oh yes, sir; I have only just left him."

"And has your business been attended to in your absence?"

"Nothing to complain of, sir. There's never very much to do of a morning."

"That will do, Mr. Wilson. I shall be happy to give you an opinion upon the subject in the course of a day or two. Today is Saturday, and I hope that by Monday we may come to a conclusion."

"Well, Watson," said Holmes, when our visitor had left us, "what do you make of it all?"

"I make nothing of it," I answered, frankly. "It is a most mysterious business."

"As a rule," said Holmes, "the more bizarre a thing is the less mysterious it proves to be. It is your commonplace, featureless

361

crimes which are really puzzling, just as a commonplace face is
the most difficult to identify. But I must be prompt over this
matter."

"What are you going to do, then?" I asked.

"To smoke," he answered. "It is quite a three-pipe problem,
and I beg that you won't speak to me for fifty minutes." He
curled himself up in his chair, with his thin knees drawn up to
his hawklike nose, and there he sat with his eyes closed and his
black clay pipe thrusting out like the bill of some strange bird.
I had come to the conclusion that he had dropped asleep, and
indeed was nodding myself, when he suddenly sprang out of
his chair with the gesture of a man who has made up his mind,
and put his pipe down upon the mantelpiece.

"Sarasate plays at the St. James's Hall this afternoon," he
remarked. "What do you think, Watson? Could your patients
spare you for a few hours?"

"I have nothing to do today. My practice is never very
absorbing."

"Then put on your hat and come. I am going through the
city first, and we can have some lunch on the way. I observe
that there is a good deal of German music on the program,

362

which is rather more to my taste than Italian or French. It is introspective, and I want to introspect. Come along!"

We traveled by the Underground as far as Aldersgate; and a short walk took us to Saxe-Coburg Square, the scene of the singular story which we had listened to in the morning. It was a pokey, little, shabby-genteel place, where four lines of dingy two-storied brick houses looked out into a small railed-in enclosure, where a lawn of weedy grass and a few clumps of faded laurel bushes made a hard fight against a smoke-laden and uncongenial atmosphere. Three gilt balls and a brown board with "JABEZ WILSON" in white letters, upon a corner house, announced the place where our red-headed client carried on his business. Sherlock Holmes stopped in front of it with his head on one side, and looked it all over, with his eyes shining brightly between puckered lids. Then he walked slowly up the street, and then down again to the corner, still looking keenly at the houses. Finally he returned to the pawnbroker's, and, having thumped vigorously upon the pavement with his stick two or three times, he went up to the door and knocked. It was instantly opened by a bright-looking, clean-shaven young fellow, who asked him to step in.

"Thank you," said Holmes, "I only wished to ask you how you would go from here to the Strand."

"Third right, fourth left," answered the assistant, promptly, closing the door.

"Smart fellow, that," observed Holmes, as we walked away. "He is, in my judgment, the fourth smartest man in London, and for daring I am not sure that he has not a claim to be third. I have known something of him before."

"Evidently," said I, "Mr. Wilson's assistant counts for a good deal in this mystery of the Red-headed League. I am sure that you inquired your way merely in order that you might see him."

"Not him."

"What then?"

"The knees of his trousers."

"And what did you see?"

"What I expected to see."

"Why did you beat the pavement?"

"My dear doctor, this is a time for observation, not for talk. We are spies in an enemy's country. We know something of Saxe-Coburg Square. Let us now explore the parts which lie behind it."

The road in which we found ourselves as we turned round the corner from the retired Saxe-Coburg Square presented as great a contrast to it as the front of a picture does to the back. It was one of the main arteries which convey the traffic of the city to the north and west. The roadway was blocked with the immense stream of commerce flowing in a double tide inward and outward, while the footpaths were black with the hurrying swarm of pedestrians. It was difficult to realize as we looked at the line of fine shops and stately business premises that they really abutted on the other side upon the faded and stagnant square which we had just quitted.

"Let me see," said Holmes, standing at the corner, and glancing along the line, "I should like just to remember the order of the houses here. It is a hobby of mine to have an exact knowledge of London. There is Mortimer's, the tobacconist, the little newspaper shop, the Coburg branch of the City and

Suburban Bank, the Vegetarian Restaurant, and McFarlane's carriage-building depot. That carries us right on to the other block. And now, doctor, we've done our work, so it's time we had some play. A sandwich and a cup of coffee, and then off to violin-land, where all is sweetness and delicacy and harmony, and there are no red-headed clients to vex us with their conundrums."

My friend was an enthusiastic musician, being himself not only a very capable performer, but a composer of no ordinary merit. All the afternoon he sat in the stalls wrapped in the most perfect happiness, gently waving his long, thin fingers in time to the music, while his gently smiling face and his languid, dreamy eyes were as unlike those of Holmes, the sleuthhound, Holmes the relentless, keen-witted, ready-handed criminal agent, as it was possible to conceive. In his singular character the dual nature alternately asserted itself, and his extreme exactness and astuteness represented, as I have often thought, the reaction against the poetic and contemplative mood which occasionally predominated in him. The swing of his nature took him from extreme languor to devouring energy; and, as I knew well, he was never so truly formidable as when, for days on end, he had been lounging in his armchair amid his improvisations and his black-letter editions. Then it was that the lust of the chase would suddenly come upon him, and that his brilliant reasoning power would rise to the level of intuition, until those who were unacquainted with his methods would look askance at him as on a man whose knowledge was not that of other mortals. When I saw him that afternoon so enwrapped in the music at St. James's Hall I felt that an evil time might be coming upon those whom he had set himself to hunt down.

"You want to go home, no doubt, doctor," he remarked, as we emerged.

"Yes, it would be as well."

"And I have some business to do which will take some hours. This business at Coburg Square is serious."

"Why serious?"

"A considerable crime is in contemplation. I have every rea-

365

son to believe that we shall be in time to stop it. But today being Saturday rather complicates matters. I shall want your help tonight."

"At what time?"

"Ten will be early enough."

"I shall be at Baker Street at ten."

"Very well. And, I say, doctor, there may be some little danger, so kindly put your army revolver in your pocket." He waved his hand, turned on his heel, and disappeared in an instant among the crowd.

I trust that I am not more dense than my neighbors, but I was always oppressed with a sense of my own stupidity in my dealings with Sherlock Holmes. Here I had heard what he had heard, I had seen what he had seen, and yet from his words it was evident that he saw clearly not only what had happened, but what was about to happen, while to me the whole business was still confused and grotesque. As I drove home to my house in Kensington I thought over it all, from the extraordinary story of the red-headed copier of the "Encyclopaedia" down to the visit to Saxe-Coburg Square, and the ominous words with which he had parted from me. What was this nocturnal expedition, and why should I go armed? Where were we going, and what were we to do? I had the hint from Holmes that this smooth-faced pawnbroker's assistant was a formidable man—a man who might play a deep game. I tried to puzzle it out, but gave it up in despair and set the matter aside until night should bring an explanation.

It was a quarter-past nine when I started from home and made my way across the Park, and so through Oxford Street to Baker Street. Two hansoms were standing at the door, and, as I entered the passage, I heard the sound of voices from above. On entering his room I found Holmes in animated conversation with two men, one of whom I recognized as Peter Jones, the official police agent, while the other was a long, thin, sad-faced man, with a very shiny hat and oppressively respectable frock coat.

"Ha! our party is complete," said Holmes, buttoning up his

pea jacket and taking his heavy hunting crop from the rack. "Watson, I think you know Mr. Jones, of Scotland Yard? Let me introduce you to Mr. Merryweather, who is to be our companion in tonight's adventure."

"We're hunting in couples again, doctor, you see," said Jones, in his consequential way. "Our friend here is a wonderful man for starting a chase. All he wants is an old dog to help him to do the running down."

"I hope a wild goose may not prove to be the end of our chase," observed Mr. Merryweather, gloomily.

"You may place considerable confidence in Mr. Holmes, sir," said the police agent, loftily. "He has his own little methods, which are, if he won't mind my saying so, just a little too theoretical and fantastic, but he has the makings of a detective in him. It is not too much to say that once or twice, as in that business of the Sholto murder and the Agra treasure, he has been more nearly correct than the official force."

"Oh, if you say so, Mr. Jones, it is all right," said the stranger, with deference. "Still, I confess that I miss my rubber. It is the first Saturday night for seven-and-twenty years that I have not had my rubber."

"I think you will find," said Sherlock Holmes, "that you will play for a higher stake tonight than you have ever done yet, and that the play will be more exciting. For you, Mr. Merryweather, the stake will be some £30,000; and for you, Jones, it will be the man upon whom you wish to lay your hands."

"John Clay, the murderer, thief, smasher, and forger. He's a young man, Mr. Merryweather, but he is at the head of his profession, and I would rather have my bracelets on him than on any criminal in London. He's a remarkable man, is young John Clay. His grandfather was a royal duke, and he himself has been to Eton and Oxford. His brain is as cunning as his fingers, and though we meet signs of him at every turn, we never know where to find the man himself. He'll crack a crib in Scotland one week and be raising money to build an orphanage in Cornwall the next. I've been on his track for years and have never set eyes on him yet."

"I hope that I may have the pleasure of introducing you tonight. I've had one or two little turns also with Mr. John Clay, and I agree with you that he is at the head of his profession. It is past ten, however, and quite time that we started. If you two will take the first hansom, Watson and I will follow in the second."

Sherlock Holmes was not very communicative during the long drive and lay back in the cab humming the tunes which he had heard in the afternoon. We rattled through a labyrinth of gas-lit streets until we emerged into Farringdon Street.

"We are close there now," my friend remarked. "This fellow Merryweather is a bank director and personally interested in the matter. I thought it as well to have Jones with us also. He is not a bad fellow, though an absolute imbecile in his profession. He has one positive virtue. He is as brave as a bulldog and as tenacious as a lobster if he gets his claws upon any one. Here we are, and they are waiting for us."

We had reached the same crowded thoroughfare in which we had found ourselves in the morning. Our cabs were dismissed, and, following the guidance of Mr. Merryweather, we passed down a narrow passage and through a side door, which he opened for us. Within there was a small corridor, which ended in a very massive iron gate. This also was opened, and led down a flight of winding stone steps, which terminated at another formidable gate. Mr. Merryweather stopped to light a lantern and then conducted us down a dark, earth-smelling passage, and so, after opening a third door, into a huge vault or cellar, which was piled all round with crates and massive boxes.

"You are not very vulnerable from above," Holmes remarked, as he held up the lantern and gazed about him.

"Nor from below," said Mr. Merryweather, striking his stick upon the flags which lined the floor. "Why, dear me, it sounds quite hollow!" he remarked, looking up in surprise.

"I must really ask you to be a little more quiet," said Holmes, severely. "You have already imperiled the whole success of our expedition. Might I beg that you would have the goodness to sit down upon one of those boxes and not to interfere?"

The solemn Mr. Merryweather perched himself upon a crate, with a very injured expression upon his face, while Holmes fell upon his knees upon the floor, and, with the lantern and a magnifying lens, began to examine minutely the cracks between the stones. A few seconds sufficed to satisfy him, for he sprang to his feet again and put his glass in his pocket.

"We have at least an hour before us," he remarked; "for they can hardly take any steps until the good pawnbroker is safely in bed. Then they will not lose a minute, for the sooner they do their work the longer time they will have for their escape. We are at present, doctor—as no doubt you have divined—in the cellar of the city branch of one of the principal London banks. Mr. Merryweather is the chairman of directors, and he will explain to you that there are reasons why the more daring criminals of London should take a considerable interest in this cellar at present."

"It is our French gold," whispered the director. "We have had several warnings that an attempt might be made upon it."

"Your French gold?"

"Yes. We had occasion some months ago to strengthen our resources, and borrowed, for that purpose, 30,000 napoleons from the Bank of France. It has become known that we have never had occasion to unpack the money, and that it is still lying in our cellar. The crate upon which I sit contains 2000 napoleons packed between layers of lead foil. Our reserve of bullion is much larger at present than is usually kept in a single branch office, and the directors have had misgivings upon the subject."

"Which were very well justified," observed Holmes. "And now it is time that we arranged our little plans. I expect that within an hour matters will come to a head. In the meantime, Mr. Merryweather, we must put the screen over that dark lantern."

"And sit in the dark?"

"I am afraid so. I had brought a pack of cards in my pocket, and I thought that, as we were a *partie carrée,* you might have your rubber after all. But I see that the enemy's preparations

370

have gone so far that we cannot risk the presence of a light. And, first of all, we must choose our positions. These are daring men, and though we shall take them at a disadvantage, they may do us some harm unless we are careful. I shall stand behind this crate, and do you conceal yourselves behind those. Then, when I flash a light upon them, close in swiftly. If they fire, Watson, have no compunction about shooting them down."

I placed my revolver, cocked, upon the top of the wooden case behind which I crouched. Holmes shot the slide across the front of his lantern, and left us in pitch darkness—such an absolute darkness as I have never before experienced. The smell of hot metal remained to assure us that the light was still there, ready to flash out at a moment's notice. To me, with my nerves worked up to a pitch of expectancy, there was something depressing and subduing in the sudden gloom, and in the cold, dank air of the vault.

"They have but one retreat," whispered Holmes. "That is back through the house into Saxe-Coburg Square. I hope that you have done what I asked you, Jones?"

"I have an inspector and two officers waiting at the front door."

"Then we have stopped all the holes. And now we must be silent and wait."

What a time it seemed! From comparing notes afterwards it was but an hour and a quarter, yet it appeared to me that the night must have almost gone, and the dawn be breaking above us. My limbs were weary and stiff, for I feared to change my position; yet my nerves were worked up to the highest pitch of tension, and my hearing was so acute that I could not only hear the gentle breathing of my companions, but I could distinguish the deeper, heavier in-breath of the bulky Jones from the thin, sighing note of the bank director. From my position I could look over the case in the direction of the floor. Suddenly my eyes caught the glint of a light.

At first it was but a lurid spark upon the stone pavement. Then it lengthened out until it became a yellow line, and then, without any warning or sound, a gash seemed to open and a

371

hand appeared, a white, almost womanly hand, which felt about in the center of the little area of light. For a minute or more the hand, with its writhing fingers, protruded out of the floor. Then it was withdrawn as suddenly as it appeared, and all was dark again save the single lurid spark which marked a chink between the stones.

Its disappearance, however, was but momentary. With a rending, tearing sound, one of the broad, white stones turned over upon its side and left a square, gaping hole, through which streamed the light of a lantern. Over the edge there peeped a clean-cut, boyish face, which looked keenly about it, and then, with a hand on either side of the aperture, drew itself shoulder-high and waist-high, until one knee rested upon the edge. In another instant he stood at the side of the hole, and was hauling after him a companion, lithe and small like himself, with a pale face and a shock of very red hair.

"It's all clear," he whispered. "Have you the chisel and the bags. Great Scott! Jump, Archie, jump, and I'll swing for it!"

Sherlock Holmes had sprung out and seized the intruder by the collar. The other dived down the hole, and I heard the sound of rending cloth as Jones clutched at his skirts. The light flashed upon the barrel of a revolver, but Holmes's hunting crop came down on the man's wrist, and the pistol clinked upon the stone floor.

"It's no use, John Clay," said Holmes, blandly. "You have no chance at all."

"So I see," the other answered, with the utmost coolness. "I fancy that my pal is all right, though I see you have got his coat-tails."

"There are three men waiting for him at the door."

"Oh, indeed! You seem to have done the thing very completely. I must compliment you."

"And I you," Holmes answered. "Your red-headed idea was very new and effective."

"You'll see your pal again presently," said Jones. "He's quicker at climbing down holes than I am. Just hold out while I fix the derbies."

"I beg that you will not touch me with your filthy hands," remarked our prisoner, as the handcuffs clattered upon his wrists. "You may not be aware that I have royal blood in my veins. Have the goodness, also, when you address me always to say 'sir' and 'please.'"

"All right," said Jones, with a stare and a snigger. "Well, would you please, sir, march upstairs, where we can get a cab to carry your highness to the police station?"

"That is better," said John Clay, serenely. He made a sweeping bow to the three of us and walked quietly off in the custody of the detective.

"Really, Mr. Holmes," said Mr. Merryweather, as we followed them from the cellar, "I do not know how the bank can thank you or repay you. There is no doubt that you have detected and defeated in the most complete manner one of the most determined attempts at bank robbery that have ever come within my experience."

"I have had one or two little scores of my own to settle with Mr. John Clay," said Holmes. "I have been at some small expense over this matter, which I shall expect the bank to refund, but beyond that I am amply repaid by having had an experience which is in many ways unique, and by hearing the very remarkable narrative of the Red-headed League."

"You see, Watson," he explained, in the early hours of the morning, as we sat over a glass of whiskey-and-soda in Baker Street, "it was perfectly obvious from the first that the only possible object of this rather fantastic business of the advertisement of the League, and the copying of the 'Encyclopaedia,' must be to get this not over-bright pawnbroker out of the way for a number of hours every day. It was a curious way of managing it, but, really, it would be difficult to suggest a better. The method was no doubt suggested to Clay's ingenious mind by the color of his accomplice's hair. The £4 a week was a lure which must draw him, and what was it to them, who were playing for thousands? They put in the advertisement, one rogue has the temporary office, the other rogue incites the man to apply for it, and together they manage to secure his absence every morning in the week. From the time that I heard of the assistant having come for half-wages, it was obvious to me that he had some strong motive for securing the situation."

"But how could you guess what the motive was?"

"Had there been women in the house, I should have suspected a mere vulgar intrigue. That, however, was out of the question. The man's business was a small one, and there was nothing in his house which could account for such elaborate preparations, and such an expenditure as they were at. It must, then, be something out of the house. What could it be? I thought of the assistant's fondness for photography, and his trick of vanishing into the cellar. The cellar! There was the end of this tangled clue. Then I made inquiries as to this mysterious assistant and found that I had to deal with one of the coolest and most daring criminals in London. He was doing something in the cellar—something which took many hours a day for months on end. What could it be, once more? I could think of nothing save that he was running a tunnel to some other building.

"So far I had got when we went to visit the scene of action. I surprised you by beating upon the pavement with my stick.

374

I was ascertaining whether the cellar stretched out in front or behind. It was not in front. Then I rang the bell, and, as I hoped, the assistant answered it. We have had some skirmishes, but we had never set eyes upon each other before. I hardly looked at his face. His knees were what I wished to see. You must yourself have remarked how worn, wrinkled, and stained they were. They spoke of those hours of burrowing. The only remaining point was what they were burrowing for. I walked round the corner, saw that the City and Suburban Bank abutted on our friend's premises, and felt that I had solved my problem. When you drove home after the concert I called upon Scotland Yard and upon the chairman of the bank directors, with the result that you have seen."

"And how could you tell that they would make their attempt tonight?" I asked.

"Well, when they closed their League offices that was a sign that they cared no longer about Mr. Jabez Wilson's presence— in other words, that they had completed their tunnel. But it was essential that they should use it soon, as it might be discovered, or the bullion might be removed. Saturday would suit them better than any other day, as it would give them two days for their escape. For all these reasons I expected them to come tonight."

"You reasoned it out beautifully," I exclaimed, in unfeigned admiration. "It is so long a chain, and yet every link rings true."

"It saved me from ennui," he answered, yawning. "Alas! I already feel it closing in upon me. My life is spent in one long effort to escape from the commonplaces of existence. These little problems help me to do so."

"And you are a benefactor of the race," said I.

He shrugged his shoulders. "Well, perhaps, after all, it is of some little use," he remarked. "'L'homme c'est rien— l'œuvre c'est tout,' as Gustave Flaubert wrote to Georges Sand."

Index

THE CHILDREN'S HOUR

But the children had no eyes for the woods at that moment. Around the faint bend of the trail something was hanging from a high branch. Jane gave a little scream of surprise and then stood staring. For it was the carcass of a sheep, such as she had sometimes seen in a butcher's shop, but strange and terrifying to come upon here in the midst of the woods.

For once the children said nothing. They stared and stared and then turned, and John made room for Jane to pass him and go first, while he brought up the rear with one horrified look over his shoulder. They crashed through the woods like two runaway colts and never stopped until *The Adventure* was well out from shore.

Then Jane heaved a great sigh. "Well!" she said.

"Well!" said John.

Their father was quite matter-of-fact about their tale.

"Probably a farmer has killed one of his sheep and didn't have any way of getting it up to the icehouse just then. So he may have hung it high out of reach of foxes until he can bring down a horse or a wheelbarrow for it."

"Dad, a horse or a wheelbarrow couldn't get to that place, and it wasn't near any sheep pasture, either," John said.

"It's the man with the outboard motor!" cried Jane.

"You're jumping to conclusions, Jen," her father declared.

7

"You haven't an iota of evidence that would stand in court."

But after a day or two of inquiry, they heard from the postmaster at the little postoffice, a mile or two away on the crossroads, that several sheep and heifers had disappeared in the neighborhood during the spring and summer. Some people thought that maybe a bear had come down from the north, or worse still, a lynx. If dogs had been ruining the stock, there would probably have been more noise. People inclined to think that the killer was a bear. There had been one seen for a while four or five years ago.

"A bear doesn't butcher his meat and hang it up in a tree," said Father, and told the postmaster where the children had seen the carcass. They felt very important for a little while and would have gone on discussing the affair, if something had not happened to put it altogether out of their minds.

About three miles from the Lane's cabin, across the pond, there was a cove lying between low marshy banks, where the swamp maples stood thick, with now and then a few pines on a knoll. The cove, too, was very shallow, choked with water plants of all sorts. Water lilies, both yellow and white, lay along the outskirts in archipelagoes of broad leaves and floating flowers. Beyond grew the pickerel weeds with their thin arrow-shaped leaves and their spikes of purple flowerlets, and there were bulrushes and joint-stem grasses through which the big-eyed dragonflies flew, like splinters of sunlight.

Several times John and Jane had forced their way for a few yards into this marine flower garden, but the canoe moved very slowly. John had to use his paddle for poling while Jane peered ahead, alert for the old submerged logs which here and there lay on the shallow bottom, the bark long since peeled away, but the white stubs of branches still thrust out to rake against the bottom of a passing boat.

They had soon turned back, until one day, when pushing in as usual among the reeds, they came upon a sort of channel leading up into the cove.

"It almost looks as though it had been made," said John, "anyhow, let's go up it."

8

Index